Alexandra Jones was b[...] parents in the Colonial S[...] winning short stories, t[...] with her splendid histo[...] and *Fire Pheasant*, all published by Futura. She now lives in Kent, and is married with three sons.

Also by Alexandra Jones from Futura:

ALEXANDRA JONES

Face to the Sun

Futura

A Futura Book

First published in Great Britain in 1990 by
Macdonald & Co (Publishers) Ltd
London & Sydney

This edition published in 1991 by Futura Publications

ISBN 0 7088 4855 9

Printed in Great Britain by
BPCC Hazell Books
Aylesbury, Bucks, England
Member of BPCC Ltd.

Futura Publications
A Division of
Macdonald & Co (Publishers) Ltd
Orbit House
1 New Fetter Lane
London EC4A 1AR

A member of Maxwell Macmillan Pergamon Publishing Corporation

For Toby, Nann and Richard,
with love and gratitude

Division of Spain
July 1936

- ▨ Republicans
- ☐ Nationalists
- ⁖ France/Portugal and other neutrals

THE SPANISH MONARCHY

Spanish Bourbons and Carlist Claimants

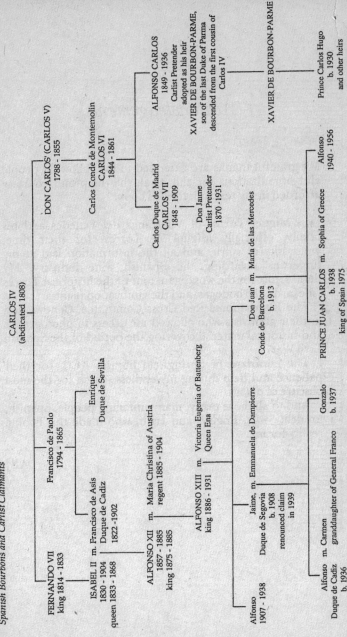

Acknowledgements

My grateful thanks are extended to the following people and organizations for the invaluable help and courtesy afforded in my research for this book:

Don Miguel Torres of Vilafranca del Penedès and his family, especially Miguel A. Torres, for their time, generosity of spirit, and all the information laid at my fingertips regarding the Spanish wine industry. My thanks, too, for the wonderful tour of the historical Torres vineyards, the bodegas, and the vinification plant.

The International Red Cross Committee, Geneva, and to their archivists who allowed me access to photographs and historical material covering the period of the Spanish Civil War.

The librarians of Springfield library, KCC, for their patience and help during my endless search for the most obscure of details.

And to all those many, many unfailing people, Spanish, French, Swiss, English and Irish, who made this book a reality for me.

ABJ

Contents

Preface
Rue du Faubourg St Honoré, Paris, France: 27 December 1938

He tried to contain his astonishment. So! It had been an *affaire de coeur* after all. No other reason could possibly account for such a complete turn-around. It had ended in disaster, obviously: that's why she was here now. What was the famous saying – 'Court a mistress and she'll deny you, but let her alone and she will court you?'

She shifted her position in the leather armchair, and recrossed her long shapely legs. Desperately tired, she longed for a bath.

Still with his back to her, staring down at the traffic in the wide boulevard below his office windows, he was beginning to irritate her. The hum reached up to them like thousands of bumble-bees heady from gasoline, not nectar. Had he been a Noël Coward type, his hands would have been used as the elegant extension of a Kensitas, while he repeated some devastatingly witty remark to put her at ease. Had he been a priest, he would have kept his hands around his rosary beads with serene custody of the senses. Instead, she had to endure the jingling of loose change in his pockets, setting her teeth on edge.

'You must go back,' he said, still addressing the windowpane.

'No! The reason why I am here is to ask for another assignment. It's all there, in that *mochila* on your desk. Names, dates, places, everything you asked for, so there's no reason for me to go back. I'll do anything – go anywhere, even as a nanny to Berghof if that's what you want.'

11

Only then did he turn back to face her. He took his hands from his pockets and, leaning towards her over his desk, said, 'What we want is that you should return to Spain in your previous capacity. The war there is by no means over, while another is brewing on the Hitler horizon. We need to know more about the Fifth Column and their movements, since the front line has shifted from Madrid to Barcelona. Above all, we need more information on SIM. On the Catalonian front, I'm counting on you now, so you *must* return to Spain.'

'And afterwards?' she asked. 'Supposing I don't go the same way as my – as my predecessors?'

'Afterwards,' he turned back to the window, 'we face the rest of Europe.'

The throb in her head was insistent, set to the words of the Nationalist hymn, the 'Cara Al Sol': 'Face to the sun, wearing the tunic, which yesterday you embroidered. Death will find me, if it calls me, and I do not see you again ...'

PART ONE
The Angel's Share

'There's nought the likes of you or I can do, miss, when the seats of heaven are occupied by politicians in London,' said Cassy.

CHAPTER ONE

Dublin: New Year's Eve 1922

The rich might inhabit St Stephen's Green, but to live in elegant Merrion Square, with its rosy brick houses and graceful front doors, was the hallmark of professional respectability.

Ravenna Mealdow Quennell, not far off her tenth birthday, considered herself to be a true professional (RIP in her people-spotting book meaning Respectable Intelligent Person), although Timothy said it certainly wasn't respectable to blackmail people unless one made a good living from it. Raven followed his advice, and espionage took on a whole new meaning.

Progressing from the dumb-waiter and dark recesses of the broom cupboard smelling of feather dusters and lavender polish, Raven found that the wide sill of the nursery bedroom window was another good crow's-nest from which to monitor the world. She was able to keep tabs on who was walking out with whom, and from which rung of the social ladder – basement footman, attic chambermaid, or one of the Lon-Dubbers behaving indiscreetly. She soon discovered that the upper and lower classes had a great deal in common, for they neither cared nor troubled themselves about who saw them behaving outrageously, while those from the middle bracket kept the blinds down and pretended they were not at home.

Blackmail, from a purely financial aspect, however, turned out to be disappointing. But there were compensations. For a start, it beat making samplers for Cassy with texts like 'With thy dear children may she have a part, and write thy name thyself upon her heart'. Her

15

needlework was never much good in any case, and Cassy made her unpick the wretched stitches over and over again. Blackmail was also far more educational than having to memorize tedious columns of spellings, or reciting aloud multiplication tables for the sole benefit of grisly Governess Lockwood, who, in any case, was as deaf as a post.

'I spy with my little eye.' Raven, her eyes tight shut in grim concentration, paused for effect.

Sonny and Roxana waited with bated breath for yet another interesting scandal to break. On this occasion, it was something to do with Mother's close friends, known as the 'Lon-Dub Set' by people who considered Lady Quennell and her entourage to be *fast* rather than professional or respectable. Lon-Dubbers had to be wealthy, titled, good-looking, and usually infamous to qualify for membership into the bosom of Merrion Square life. 'Amery and scarf-woman – I see them now – well, it was last night actually. In the back of the Daimler. It wasn't Lyra, either.' Raven opened her eyes wide, waiting for their reaction.

Timothy called her sleuthing skills tetra perception. Tetra, he explained for the lesser intelligence of the girls and young Sonny, was a foursquare extra-terrestrial word meaning more than just super. So tetra stuck: 'Gosh! just look at Amery's tetra new car! And isn't Lyra's new frock tetra ghastly! Mother's off to New York again on the tetra *Mauretania*!'

'A Blue Riband holder is better than tetra, so there!' was Sonny's candid opinion.

Sonny was the real true professional (a genius Cassy said), for he was so clever he could play solo violin in any major musical composition by Paganini, and Sonny was only seven.

Roxana was eager for more details. 'Were they doing anything?'

'Doing what?'

'You know, Raven, spooning!'

'Who?'

'Amery and his new flame.'

'Oh that! I thought we'd changed the subject.'

'How do you know *who* it was? It was pitch dark when you

16

almost fell over the bedroom window-sill spying on everyone. Besides, Amery's car wasn't parked anywhere near the house. Only La Tart was hanging about under the lamp post.'

'Roxana! Why do you always spoil my fun? I suppose you're keeping a people-spotting book too, just because I have one!' Raven glared at Roxana.

'Come on, Raven who was it?' Tim asked, bored with the whole business of tetra perception, which Raven conducted with the same dedication he gave to train-spotting, only train-spotting was infinitely more interesting than finding out what Amery Noughton Peel was up to.

'A husband *never* kisses his wife with passion on the back seat of a motor car, unless they're on their honeymoon, because they have a bed to go to.'

'What happens if they're tramps?' Sonny wanted to know.

'Shh, Sonny! You're spoiling my concentration! Tramps have park benches. It wasn't Lyra last night, I know. Besides, Amery and Lyra always end up arguing on the back seat of the Daimler because of Amery being squiffy at parties and ogling the girls.' Raven held up a scarf. 'Guess?'

'Couldn't possibly,' replied Tim with an exaggerated yawn. 'Come on, old girl, just spill the beans!'

Like Sybil Thorndike on stage, eyelids aflutter with theatrical passion, chest heaving with exaggerated bursts of ecstasy, Raven wafted the scarf under their noses. 'Mmmm, "Schiaparelli"! Lyra wears Guerlain's "Mitsouko" or "Jicky". The scarf is from Woolworth. Amery's chauffeur put it in the litter bin after Amery's ladyfriend hopped out and disappeared like the White Rabbit. Then Amery sauntered across the road looking as though butter wouldn't melt in his mouth.'

'Poo! It can't altogether smell of "Schiaparelli" then – unless it's Shocking!' Roxanna giggled at her own wit. 'Was it Mama spooning in the Daimler with Amery? She wears "Schiaparelli S".'

'I'm not telling,' said Raven. 'You have to guess. But I'll give you a clue. She looks like a lamp post with glass shades that reflect the light.'

17

'Why wasn't Amery's car parked right outside our front door if he came to play charades last evening?' Sonny persisted.

'Just in case Papa stuck his head out and saw Mama on the back seat of Amery's Daimler, Sonny!'

'Oh. I never thought of that, Roxa. Thanks.'

'Are you going to blackmail Amery with the scarf?' Roxana wanted to know.

'Of course she is!' Tim said. 'Fortunes can be made and reputations ruined by just the kind of book Raven keeps in the broom cupboard.'

Raven rounded on him fiercely. 'Tim! How did you know I keep it in there?'

Tim tapped the side of his fourteen-year-old nose, 'Tetra perception, my dear Watson. I'd hide it in there if I wanted to blackmail the servants. They'd never dream of looking for it in the broom cupboard since cleaning became a thing of the past. And you can hear every word from the kitchen and servants' hall while polishing your own boots. But there's not much point in blackmailing a servant. Their wages aren't worth going to prison for.'

'You didn't read it, did you Tim?'

'Course not! I'm not a sneak.'

'Whose scarf is it, Raven, if it's not Mother's?' Roxana could hardly wait to find out.

'Clare Fenchurch's.' Raven declared with relish.

'Clare Fenchurch's!' the other three echoed. 'From the library?'

Raven nodded in satisfaction.

'But she can't afford Schiaparelli scent,' Tim scoffed. 'Not if she shops at Woolworth. Besides, she's an intellectual. Not Amery's sort at all.'

'Maybe Amery bought her some,' Roxana said. 'You know, for services rendered and all that scarlet harlot stuff Cassy gets so cross about whenever we ask her about La Tart who stands outside the front door every night.'

'What's wrong with Woolworth?' Sonny piped up. 'Cassy always takes me to Woolworth on the way back from confession at Father Donahoe's big church. And she *always* buys me a penny lolly from the sweet counter.'

'But it's Catholic, Sonny, and you oughtn't to let Cassy

blackmail you with lollipops in return for that Catastrophe rubbish she makes you learn.'

'*Catechism*, Roxa! And it's not rubbish. I like it. And I like the singing, even if the rain does come through Father Donahoe's rafters. Anyway, Woolworth isn't only for Catholics to buy their lollipops.'

Roxana bent towards him and emphasised the point she was trying to make, one Sonny never seemed to fully grasp. 'We are *Prot-est-ants*!'

'I know. But I don't know what they *really* are.'

'Oh. Sonny! Protestants are English for what the Irish believe in. Father and Mother are half and half, that's why they're Protestants.'

'Half and half what?'

'Anglo-Irish, silly! That's not the same as being a Cassy or a Cathal Swilly.'

'Father Donahoe's a friend of the Pope. He's the Holy Father. He's like God. Cassy said so. That's why they're praying to the Pope for a new roof.'

'Oh, come on,' Tim said impatiently, 'I've had enough of this stupid game. I'm going riding in the park. Coming Raven?'

She decided she would go with him. Raven put aside Clare Fenchurch's scarf to blackmail her later in the week. Clare was tall and thin and shapeless, with no bosom to speak of, and she wore glasses. So what on earth had made Amery want to pick her up in the first place from the stamp desk in the public library? Amery and Lyra never read a thing except signposts, so what was he doing there in any case? She must look a little deeper into this. As for Clare Fenchurch, next time Raven went to the junior section of the library, she would wave the scarf at her. Clare might not be so eager to palm off the books she thought 'suitable for a little girl who was not yet ten', instead of the books Raven wanted to read; and it wasn't *Black Beauty* for the dozenth time!

After supper at six-thirty, Raven, knees drawn up under her chin, sat on the wide window-sill of the nursery bedroom. Sonny was having his bath so she had at least a quarter of an hour to herself. The night was bitterly cold and the street lamps had been lit for ages. Luminescent haloes of light prodded the icy darkness around the square, and smoke from the chimneys went straight upwards into the still, frosty air, as though all the houses had grey, fluffy tails. Raven hoped it would snow by the morning, although it was a bit too cold for snow. *La Pierreuse* was nowhere to be seen.

Raven wrote in her people-spotting book, *The latest occupants of number one are definitely PQ.*

PQ in her card index of behaviour patterns, found at the back of the people-spotting book, meant Peasant Quality. One didn't necessarily have to be poor to possess it. The young woman who sometimes wandered up and down the street and smoked a cigarette under every lamp post was not PQ but AQ – Artistic Quality. She was also FOHT, meaning Fallen On Hard Times. She had brassy-red hair, not naturally Raphaelesque like Mother's and Roxa's, but out of a henna bottle. Tim had nicknamed her *La Pierreuse*, which meant 'tart'. Not one of the innocent pastry variety either, but, according to Cassy, a scarlet harlot with dyed hair, who was a cuss to decent womanhood'. After that, they, the children, that retarded breed by the look in some of the Lon-Dubbers' eyes, had spent many curious hours spying on the dyed scarlet harlot tart, who, cold and ever hopeful, kept the wrought-iron torch-stands company each evening.

To Raven, however, La Tart's gentlemen friends were of more notable interest, since there was every possibility of uncovering a famous parliamentarian or pious clergyman scandal beneath the lamp posts. Not tonight though; tonight La Tart was probably at home making her New Year resolutions.

Raven scribbled frantically, *I wish Sir William Wilde and his poetess wife, with her* nom de plume *of Speranza, still lived at number one. Even if their blinds were kept lowered in permanent mourning following the rise and fall of their notorious son, Oscar, born first turning right, Westland Row, they would have been far more interesting than the present dull residents. I should have liked to ask Daniel O'Connell (number fifty-eight) about the Black Death, so that I can put Governess Lockwood (a Protestant) in her place. Lockwood's always saying the famine was the fault of the narrow-minded Irish, because they ought to have planted other things besides potatoes. Rice, for example, which needs lots of rain. At times, Lockwood herself's apt to display PQ symptoms. Alas, poor Daniel died in exile following the potato famine; before my time of course.*

More recently, however, and far more interesting because Raven suspected him of being her mother's latest 'flame', William Butler Yeats, following his election as a senator in the new parliament of the Irish Free State, had moved into number eighty-two. William was Grand Master of the White Magic Circle.

Oh, William is tetra! Raven wrote. *Handsome and distinguished, even if he is an older man. His poetry's better than tetra, it's heavenly!* 'Being high and solitary and most stern? Why, what could she have done being what she is? Was there another Troy for her to burn?'

Raven could almost see herself as Helen on the stage of the Abbey Theatre, saying things like that, which William had written especially for her, instead of the famous actress, Maud Gonne.

Alas, poor Maud has indeed gone out of William's life. Many years ago she departed Dublin. Cassy told me Maud married Major MacBride and broke poor William's heart. But William still has Mrs Yeats and Lady Gregory to love him, so I don't know why he should always look so sad, unless it's because the Major was shot in the Easter Uprising almost seven years ago, leaving Maud free again, though now William isn't ...

Raven thoughtfully chewed the end of her pencil. Although William was not strictly a Lon-Dubber but a respectable professional, he did roam between London and Dublin like Mother and Father, Lyra and Amery, and the rest of The Set. Father and William were good friends and had magic séances in the library. Not the public library where Clare Fenchurch checked out the books with a worn-out rubber date stamp that kept having to be dunked firmly onto the ink pad, but the one at home. They also discussed spiritual things like hedonism and horticulture.

She had waited for Father to find out about Mother and William, but was a little disappointed when nothing happened, for scandal lent spice to life; it was sometimes awfully dull at home. From her father's imposing library with its painted ceiling depicting the biblical story of Solomon and Sheba by the famous Faenza artist, Vincent Waldre, Raven had 'borrowed' a work by William entitled 'The Secret Rose'. Cassy had scolded, saying little girls shouldn't steal their father's books, which were far too valuable and probably not suitable at all for a child to read. Raven had hoped to read between the lines and thereby uncover a scandal in William's secret spoken word: but there was no mention of the name Daphne.

Raven's grey eyes gleamed. Mother, a fragrant rose in every way, had invited Mr and Mrs Yeats to her New Year's Eve party. Perhaps she could slip out of the nursery later on tonight, find William, and ask him herself who the Secret Rose really was.

'*Boo*!' Timothy made her jump, creeping up behind her with a scary rubber mask that was supposed to be the Devil with horns. 'Sonny's finished in the bath. It's your turn, and Cassy says be quick.'

'Oh blow! – Tim, do you think Mother is William's Secret Rose?'

'What do you mean?'

'His poem, 'The Secret Rose', do you think it's because he's lovelorn over Mother like he once was over Maud Gonne?'

'Don't be daft. 'The Secret Rose' is about Ireland, not a woman.'

'How do you know?'

'Literature. We're doing Irish writers and poets at the moment.'

Tim went to Harrow with Bennett d'Ildarte. He also went to bed at nine o'clock instead of eight.

'Oh, I see.' Raven, wishing she was as grown up and as brainy as Tim, gathered up her people-spotting book along with her bath things. She had found a jolly good new hiding-place for her secret writings, and didn't want Tim nosing it out. 'Why can't Roxana go to bed before me? I bet she can't be found again, conveniently!'

Sometimes Raven wished she didn't have a sister,

especially a twin-sister. Tim and Sonny were tetra, but Roxana was a brat! Funny how twins could be so different. She and Roxa didn't even look like sisters, let alone twins. Roxa had blue eyes and Raphaelesque-red hair (as *she* described herself!). Roxana wasn't as tall, and was a lot plumper. Cassy said Roxa stuffed herself with too many of their mother's expensive chocolates and Bennett d'Ildarte's liquorice sticks. Raven had asked Cassy if Roxana had been adopted, for then she wouldn't have felt quite so obliged to feel sisterly towards her. But Cassy had said, 'Don't be a goose, miss. I was there to catch you both. You and then Miss Roxana, heads first as you popped into this world eleven minutes apart. And Lord love us, what cry-babies you two were! Never stopped squawking from the moment you was born, and haven't closed your mouths since.'

'But why don't we look like twins? Twins are supposed to look the same.'

'Does scrambled egg resemble poached egg, miss?'

'No. But what's that got to do with it?'

'Same egg prepared differently, miss, that's what!' Cassy had retorted, and Raven had to be satisfied with that description of Roxana and herself as twins.

As usual, Roxana was hiding somewhere in order to delay going to bed. Instead of wasting valuable time, Cassy packed Raven into the bath next, and sent Tim off to find Roxana.

The nursery bathroom at Quennell House was as large as a church, and usually as freezing until bathtime was over. By then the cathedral-like atmosphere had become acceptably warm and steamy, and Tim was the one to benefit most. To Sonny, the only cheery thing about keeping clean was the shiny aluminium hot-water cylinder looking like a German torpedo suspended above the white enamelled bathtub. All bones on the bath mat, thin arms crossed over his chest to keep himself and his goose bumps together, Sonny stuttered through tortured lips, 'Come on Cassy! My fingers are f-f-f-frozen. I shan't be able to practise the violin before bedtime as Papa says I must. It's

23

going to snow shooting stars tonight, and I don't want to miss them.'

As dumpy as an aubergine, cheeks pendulous and purple and streaked with a network of tiny pink hair-veins, Cassy was like a hothouse fruit that only bloomed in the steamy atmosphere of nursery bathrooms. Her red, chapped hands pummelled Sonny dry with a large, white, fluffy towel, not for one moment knowing what Master Sonny meant, only that genius had to be excused.

Raven submerged herself in the warm bathwater with a sigh of contentment. She loved bathtime. It was the one hour of the day to talk about *real* things. Px1 (meaning Father in the people-spotting book) and Px2 (standing for Mother) were usually too vague or not there at all when she wanted, desperately, to talk to them and find out the answers to a great many burning questions stored up in her head. Most of the time, especially in adult company, little children were supposed to be seen and not heard, and family life shrank to the dimension of one of those snow-scenes captured inside a glass waterbubble kept on the nursery shelf.

One had to shake and shake the glass bubble to see the snowflakes fall. They always did, in a veritable snowstorm. Sadly, it had turned out to be unreal. There was no actual snow inside the glass bubble. Timothy had explained it was a catalyst change to do with chemicals reacting with the water inside the glass bubble to produce that pretty effect of falling snow. She wanted to know all about the glass bubble with its sweet little cottage and flower garden beneath a deep blue sky, and why the snow fell in summer. Mother said it was too tiresome to watch children fidgeting in one's presence, or to have to answer tedious questions. One question in Mother's direction and they were shunted back to Cassy's care. Tim, of course, didn't have to put up with the glass-bubble existence of Quennell House, except in the holidays.

The glass bubble confused Raven in the same way that she was confused as to her family's role in Ireland. Quennell House and the lives they led within its affluent and unassailable walls were like living in the glass-bubble

24

effect of snow in summertime. It was unrea̶
when one listened to people like Cathal Sw̶
Agnes, and tried to relate the two contrasting p̶

'Cassy, is it true?'

'Is what true?'

'About them being – you know, horrible things ̶
that gory stuff?'

'Now wherever did you hear that nonsense in this ̶
and age?'

Raven always knew when Cassy wasn't really listening,
because she invariably churned out that silly remark
without knowing what it was she was replying to. Cassy was
too busy huffing and puffing while she got Sonny into his
flannel pyjamas.

'Father and Mother. They were talking while Mother
was on the floor …'

'On the floor, Miss Raven?'

'Yes. Dobson has the day off with septic tonsils. Father
dropped his diamond collar stud on the floor – it was a
birthday present from Mother and he didn't want Dobson
walking off with it to the pawn shop. So Mother went
down on her hands and knees to help look for it. Then she
began to sneeze because of the dust she discovered which
hadn't been cleaned out from under the spare bed in
Father's dressing-room. She rang for Maisie, who started
to cry when Father sentenced her for not doing her job
properly. Maisie promised faithfully to mend her slovenly
ways. She's going to have a baby, you see, but she isn't
married to the father of it. Only Mother and Father don't
know that yet. Chambermaids, you know, Cassy, are
always terrified of getting the sack in case they end up on
the streets like La Tart. The father of her bastard …'

'Miss Raven! Wherever did you hear that kind of
language?'

'Cathal Swilly. Maisie's lover is the lower footman from
Merrion Square, south.'

'Lord above! Whatever next will you be finding out,
miss? And her ladyship never goes down on her knees for
anyone, not even for the Lord on high. If she did, she'd set
a good example to you children who are growing up to be
proper little heathens.'

'Cassy, I'm trying to tell you about the men sentenced to death! They're going to die tomorrow morning — you know!'

'Eavesdroppers and Peeping Toms, Miss Raven, are the thieves of truth, which is the sin of the Divil himself!'

'I heard them talking down in the servants' hall. Kelly had a puncture at the tradesman's entrance and sold Agnes a dozen of his rotten mutton pies while waiting for the patch on his inner tube to dry. Mother thinks Agnes cooks the pies herself and always congratulates her on her light pastry and French *cuisine*'. Raven imitated her mother's perfect French accent pronouncing the word *cuisine*. 'She'd have a fit if she knew Agnes sent out for pies from smelly Kelly, who spits on them before handing them over. That's why I never eat meat pies, just in case they come out of his bicycle box.'

'Miss Raven, have you done yet?'

'Kelly was on his favourite subject again, and we all know what that is! Only this time it wasn't the Germans to blame for the Great War. Ireland's war and the Four Courts going sky high was the fault of the Americans for sending money to supply the IRA with bombs and guns to blow us all up in our beds. That's what Kelly said.'

Kelly said, Swilly said, Agnes said, Eileen Hyde said; Cassy wished they would all be quiet. The children listening to adult conversations not intended for young ears was a bone of bathtime contention with her.

'Eileen is still blaming the explosion for her perforated eardrums,' Raven continued regardless. 'I think she needs the wax syringed properly, instead of poking her ears with a toothpick.'

Cassy sighed indulgently. Eileen Hyde was nowhere near the Four Courts on that day. She turned her own deaf ear to Raven's chatter. 'Master Sonny, come back here at once and clean your teeth!'

Sonny painted the washbasin with pink toothpaste, while Raven added chattily, 'Would you believe! Right in the middle of afternoon tea, wilting Flox arrived with flowers for tonight's party. Full of woe over her bunions and chilblains and the blood splashed all over the demolished columns of the Four Courts, as well as her flower stall, which happened to be planted right next to the bomb, she was her usual cheerful self, ha-ha!'

'Miss Raven, if you've finished soaking yourself, kindly step out of that tub and save us all a lot of earache.'

'Flox said the eyeballs of the Black and Tans rolled around the pavement like lost marbles. That's news! Last time, the Black and Tans had planted the bomb themselves, before melting away like Michael Collins's resistance men so that the IRA got the blame for blowing everyone up. I'm inclined to agree with Agnes, Flox is *terribly* neurotic.' Raven took a deep breath, her smooth forehead creased anew with ponderous thoughts. 'Father is supposed to have said it was a heinous crime when he passed sentence, and now Mother is worried in case he becomes a target for those who hate him. I don't think she's too worried about us.' Raven lowered her voice dramatically, '*Terrorists must suffer the consequences of their heinous crimes*! We've heard it all dozens of times before – politics, politics, politics – haven't we, Cassy?'

'Listen Miss Flap-Ears, politics is not my business and neither is it yours right now. All that IRA bombing business happened six months ago,' said Cassy brusquely, not knowing what heinous meant apart from terrorism having many faces. 'Impartial, miss, there's wisdom! Impartial like your pa to be on the safe side.' Cassy fussed around like a mother hen, fetching dry towels, tossing wet ones into the linen box, wishing all the time she could put her feet up for five minutes. ' 'Tis best to forgive and forget. Not pour more oil on troubled waters. Blessed are the peacemakers, that's what we've forgotten, miss, even after the Great War was supposed to teach us all a mortal lesson about hatred breeding death.'

'Wouldn't you be the same as Mrs Widow Flox if your sons and husband had died while incarcerated inside Dublin Castle prison?' Raven lingered on the word incarcerated, a lovely word she had heard Cathal Swilly use. Lockwood had said wonders would never cease.

'Any son o'mine – which I never had, thank the Lord, for the times we live in are mighty evil – daft enough to starve himself to death, can't blame the English for measuring the coffin after he's laid out. As for Padraich, 'twas nobody's fault him being electified through faulty wiring in his cell, except that of other poddle rats digging a new way out of Bermingham Tower.'

'Elec-*trif*-ied, Cassy, but it's really electrocuted. Supposing the English purposely made it happen to Liam and Padraich like Cathal says?'

'Cathal says! And who is Cathal Swilly but a butler? Is he Lord Lieutenant o' Ireland? Nay lass, leave the Lord himself to judge and mete out retribution to those responsible for terrorizing others.'

'Which lord?' Raven persisted.

Cassy made a 'tching' sound with her loose dentures. 'There's nought the likes of you and I can do, Miss Raven, when the seats of heaven are occupied by politicians in London. So get yourself out of that tub before you turn into a prune – Master Sonny, leave yourself alone and pull up your pyjamas at once! Nice boys know better than to be so rude and extend themselves like barrage balloons in front of ladies.'

'Why's it rude, Cassy?'

' 'Tis a sin of the flesh and the Divil to play around with ourselves.'

'Why hasn't Raven got one the same as me?'

'Because little girls are made with a place for the Immaculate Conception like the Virgin Mary.' Cassy also felt the time had come to to stop overlapping bath times. They were all getting far too old and precocious, and she didn't know how to cope with their questions any more.

'Cassy – they're here! Dozens and dozens of Mama's pretty people.' Lips and cheeks bright scarlet with her mother's rouge, blue chalk from the classroom on her eyelids, Roxana, wearing her teatime frock of blue and white checked flannel with lacy sailor collar, tottered into the bathroom in a pair of her mother's high-heeled shoes. A fashionable ebony and silver cigarette holder was stuck between her cupid-bow lips, while one of her mother's fur tippets graced her shoulders.

Cassy raised despairing eyes to the ceiling. Mercifully, Hon Gal had already smoked the cigarette; at least, Cassy hoped she had. 'In all m'born days! You look like a fallen woman, Miss Roxa.'

Raven giggled, 'Down the stairs or down the street of sin like a scarlet harlot tart, Cassy?'

'And that's enough from you, miss!' Cassy snapped, taking the sponge from between Raven's feet to scrub Roxana's face. 'Cosmetics is the cuss of modern Babylonia. And I *don't* mean the Catholic Church as some puritans like to think. Keep still, Miss Roxa, and stop twisting like an eel.' Cassy wheezed gustily, the effort of scrubbing Roxana's face while Roxana shrieked about soap getting in her eyes made the pain in her chest take over her mind, and she felt dizzy. 'That stuff's coming right off, like it or not! De Valera, with Spanish blood in him mark, might iron the American flag and set fire to Ireland doing it, but I'll not have you young gals aping flappers, not at your age. The War brought it on, a million good men gone, and flappers painting themselves like railway posters to attract those what are left. I've told her ladyship about flighty ways, but she jest laughs and calls Cassy O'Carey old-fashioned. So pardon me for being old-fashioned!'

Roxana, face smarting, cheeks glowing more redly than the rouge Cassy had just scrubbed off, stamped her foot and used her most imperious 'little-madam' voice guaranteed to make Cassy even more determined not to give in to her, 'Cassy, Mother said I may stay up late tonight.'

Cassy got her breath back before scouring out the bathtub with Kleenoff.

'All right then, if you don't want to listen, I'll talk to Raven, instead. Raven, Father still can't find his diamond collar stud and …'

'We've heard the story from your sister, miss!' Cassy snapped again.

'I was talking to Raven – Father accidentally trod on Mother's hand and chipped her nail enamel. Eileen fled in case she got shouted at like Maisie for her dusty floors, and Father wanted to know who the Hades gave Dobson the day off. Mother told him nobody gave the valet the day off except *he* alone. Then Father told Mother her nails reminded him of poppy petals and he didn't care to be reminded of Flanders. But she kissed him, and then he kissed her back very passionately. Grown-ups can be so silly! One minute arguing with each other and the next kissing and cuddling. I was hiding in the big wardrobe.' Roxana giggled at her own daring. 'I saw everything – he had his hands all over her, even her bosom ...'

'Miss Roxana, you're giving me a mortal headache!' Cassy said sharply, reattacking the tide mark left by Raven and Sonny.

'I think Father has a guilty conscience, that's why ...'

'We don't wish to know your opinion, Miss Roxa.'

'There are going to be lots of dead men in the morning. All Father's fault. Cathal Swilly, who reads the newspapers instead of polishing the silver, says they can even be drawn and quartered afterwards, just like a carcass of beef. But I think that would be too gory even for the British.'

'Miss Roxa, please will you get ready for your bath!' Cassy implored.

'What did they expect, those men who blew up half of Dublin last summer? It wasn't Father's fault they didn't go the same way as Michael Collins, who is now a glorious hero for dying like an Irish cowboy in the middle of a Republican ambush. When I grow up, I shall probably be a filmstar like Mary Pickford in *Pollyanna*,' she added blithely.

'You've never seen Mary Pickford in *Pollyanna*!' Raven accused, slipping her white flanellette nightie over her head.

'I know about Mary Pickford, too! *And* she was in *Little Lord Fauntleroy*, which Mother says I may see in London as a special treat for my birthday. Clare Fenchurch let me have *Pollyanna Grows Up*.'

Raven took a deep breath of dismay. It would be *her* birthday, too, and she had no desire to see *Little Lord Fauntleroy*, which was very childish. She would much rather see *Pygmalion* at the Irish Literary Theatre. Mr Shaw had stayed to tea once at Quennell House, and Raven had been most impressed by him, though she still preferred William. 'Clare let you have *Pollyanna Grows Up*? She told me she didn't have it in stock.'

'Well then, she told a lie. It was right there on the shelf in the junior section. Perhaps she was thinking about Amery when she dunked her rubber stamp.' Roxana, starry-eyed, dwelt happily in her fantasy world. 'Lyra and Amery have a new Mercedes Benz. I heard Amery telling Father that it can do sixty miles an hour!'

Cassy grunted something indistinguishable from the gurgling of the hot-water cylinder as it refilled.

'Mama's dress is heavenly! White and tinselly, with a sweeping train, like Salome wearing a tiara in Richard Strauss's opera – the one the Abbey Theatre did of Oscar Wilde's play which Mother took us to see. Lyra's dress isn't as chic as Mother's. It's crimson, crinolinish and terribly old-fashioned. All those multicoloured sequins make her look like Bloody Mary with measles.'

Lyra no longer the object of her schoolgirl crush, Roxana had found a new heroine in the shape of the Countess d'Ildarte with more to offer. But Raven doubted Prince Charming in the gooey shape of Bennett d'Ildarte would be gracing tonight's ball, because Mother had told Roxana that he was far too young to receive an invitation to a grown-up party. Roxana had gone away to pine and sulk in the toy cupboard while dreaming up ways to outwit Mother. Raven didn't know what Roxana saw in Bennett, who was plump, pimply and pathetic.

'Bennett's mother's dress is really tetra,' Roxana continued to gush. 'It's black and gold and sparkly like a midnight sky. The material is metallic, the very latest from the House of Rococo Channel.'

'Coco Chanel – *Sch – anel*. not Channel,' Raven corrected her, determined, at the earliest opportunity, to blackmail Clare Fenchurch with the scarf for having favoured Roxanna by letting her have *Pollyanna Grows Up*.

Roxana then launched another vanguard action upon Cassy. 'Mother *said* I may stay up to hear the bells, because I've been good and not bothered her at all. I stayed quietly in the schoolroom crayoning my pictures and practising my handwriting, so you *will* let me go to her party, won't you, Cassy?'

'Miss Roxa, if the Angel Gabriel himself was to appear in Merrion Square this midnight, I'll not give in. A young girl of nine needs her beauty sleep ...'

'I'm nearly ten!'

'Your mother was *never* permitted to stay up till

31

midnight, New Year's night or any other night, until she was a grown woman. Never mind what goes on elsewhere, miss, while you're in the nursery, you'll abide by Cassy O'Carey's rules. So I'll be forgiven for dishing out the orders around here. Now get out of that day-dress and into that tub like your sister, who does as she's told without argument!'

Roxana sneered, stamped her foot again and endangered her mother's high heels. Cassy didn't care for her attitude one bit, the little hussy!

'Not if Sonny's been bathing in it, or Raven. I refuse to bathe in polluted water. I know for a fact Sonny wees in the bath.' This time Roxana's pout was less like Lyra's and more like the Stygian spout on one of the lead-faced rainwater heads adorning the roof of Quennell House.

Cassy ignored the scowl. She was used to these tantrums from the most difficult Quennell of the lot. 'You'll do as you're told, miss. The water's clean and the bath scrubbed to your ladyship's requirements. I can't abide your fuss and nonsense, so you've got your fresh water, though why I give in to your wingeing the good Lord knows. But I'll have a clear conscience in the confessional by knowing I've done my duty where you children are concerned.'

Sonny reappeared on the threshold, a dried circle of pink toothpaste round his grinning mouth. He had put in the required violin practice while the girls took their time, and now he wanted Cassy to tuck him in. 'Cassy, you sound just like Father Donahoe after the bombing took his tiles off and the workmen told him what his leaky church roof would cost to repair.'

'Or John the Baptist when he saw his head on a plate.' Timothy towered behind Sonny. 'Haven't you girls finished yet?'

'No!' Roxana snapped. 'So buzz off while I undress.'

'*Girls*!' Tim snorted derisively. 'Always a pain in the neck. I want to get some sleep before Mama's dashed midnight party wakes me up again.' He made a Stygian face like Roxana, his fingers predatory antennae in her hair. 'Hellfire and damnation! Cassandra O'Carey calls down curses on all you wretched Quennells who wear rouge, play with their willies, don't say their prayers, don't get into the bath at the proper time, don't go to confession or say a dozen Hail Marys before breakfast, lunch, tea, supper, bedtime and in between. What are we if not a confused mixture of Protestpopes and Coffeelicks, so save us all from hell and purgatory, Cassy.'

Roxana squealed in delight and started drenching Timothy with expensive bathwater, having just tipped the last of her mother's Coty's 'Rose Parfum' into the tub. The free-for-all attracted Sonny.

Cassy's chest hurt more than ever and her back was breaking through stooping for so long over the bath. Hands on her ample hips, she glared at the children mocking her and soaking the floor. 'Blaspheme if you must, Master Tim! But I warn you children, God is terrible in battle against the heathen, yet merciful to them who trust and believe in him.'

'Where does it say that, Cassy?'

Cassy pulled out the plug, much to Roxana's consternation.

'Cassy, I *want* my bath! I went to a lot of trouble to get Mama's bath essence without her or Eileen finding out, and now you've wasted it.'

'Too bad, miss. Bed, at once. Out, go on, shoo!'

Raven, stuck in the doorway, said, 'Cassy, Roxa's right. So is Cathal Swilly. He showed me a bit in the newspaper about the old laws which haven't been changed for hundreds of years. Irish terrorists who kill the British can still be hanged, drawn and quartered like Guy Fawkes. Is it true, Cassy?'

'What's truth, Miss Raven? And what's it to any of us who can't prevent such things happening?'

'Now Cassy sounds like Pompous Pilot,' Tim said, adding for argument's sake, 'Guy Fawkes happened to be burnt at the stake.'

'No, he wasn't! He was hanged, then cut up into pieces,' Raven insisted.

'Why must you children always hark on the dark side of life, eh? Forever discussing bombs and hangings and people being electified, cut up, shot, or put on bonfires. Or it's spitting in pies, spying, or picking things out of dustbins that are no concern of ours. I saw you last night,

Miss Raven, taking something from that litter bin by the park gates after Mr Amery's chauffeur got rid of it. What was it? No – don't tell me. Perhaps I don't want to know. Why can't you all talk about *nice* things for a change?'

Still in a wickedly teasing mood, despite the severity of Cassy's lecture, Timothy said, 'Cassy, did you know King David had an airplane?' He gazed innocently into the looking-glass above the blue-and-white-flowered Royal Doulton washbasin streaked with pink toothpaste. Cracked and leaky, the washbasin had a bucket under it to catch the drips.

Cassy, following Raven out of the bathroom, a fresh towel in her hand to dry Raven's long hair, turned on the threshold. She reproached Tim in a tone not quite sure of itself, 'Get along with you, Master Tim!'

He presented her with the face of a choir boy. 'It's true. David took flight into the wilderness of Judah and sat in the shadow of his wings. It says so in Psalms. I found it one day when I was looking for rude biblical things like buggery and the difference between Coffeelicks and Protestpopes. I'll need to shave soon. Do you think Dobson might lend me his razor, Cassy?'

'Get on with you, Master Tim! Your chin is as smooth as a birdie's ...'

'Bum?'

'Beak.' She flicked him with the towel, while wondering to herself what other wicked things his posh English public school was teaching him.

Ushering them all off to bed, Cassy sighed to herself: Solomon the judge and Salome the flapper, God preserve her! What a riotous, as opposed to righteous, brood they had produced between them!

Roxana had hung over the circular stairwell long enough. She was frozen stiff from neglect and disappointment. Her neck felt like stretched elastic, and she hated Cassy! God would punish Cassy for being so mean by not letting her go to the New Year's Eve party when Mama had said she could!

Another Waldre masterpiece depicting a biblical story

adorned the hall ceiling like the one in her father's library. But Samson and Delilah this time, not Solomon and Sheba. Roxana had envisaged herself as Delilah the temptress. Try as she might she could not see Bennett as Samson. Nor could she gain the attention of the circulating guests below, especially that of Countess d'Ildarte, who simply did not know of her existence.

Roxana, a large blue Alice bow tying up her red-gold curls, the colour of Agnes's polished copper saucepans in the kitchen, tossed her head. 'Who cares!' she said to herself. When she grew up, she was going to be one of the Lon-Dub Set, with a chauffeur and a Rolls Royce *and* a Mercedes Benz. She would dance and sing all night, and listen to jazz on the phonograph. She would shop at Harrods, and wear wildly chic and expensive *haute couture* clothes from Bond Street or Schiaparelli, Paris. She would breed horses out at Kildare, race and grace the turf of The Curragh and Longchamps, win the Derby, the Oaks and the St Leger with one of her tetra racehorses, and pout prettily at gentlemen who took her fancy, just like Lyra Noughton Peel. She was getting into practice, rehearsing her future role as Lady Roxana La-di-da, but preferably Roxana, Countess d'Ildarte.

The d'Ildartes were frightfully rich. Bennett's father was an Italian count who had inherited Carrara marble mines in Tuscany, while his mother was equally wealthy in her own right. She was really Irish, but her family had made their fortune in the diamond and gold mines of South Africa, so Bennett, who was an only child, had everything in the world. Roxana knew she was madly in love with Bennett, because her palms went sweaty, her toes curled and she couldn't stop blushing when Bennett came near. She knew he cared for her too, because he always offered her a liquorice stick, which he never did for anyone else, not even Raven who tried to take *everything* away from her by being so goody-goody the whole time. She would really *hate* to be Raven, who was going to be tall and lanky with straight black hair, which Cassy braided into two ugly plaits. Raven would be *really* funny-looking when she grew up! Father, Tim, and Raven were all the same, thinking only of war and duty and all that intellectual stuff, which was so boring! Sonny was different. He played the violin very prettily, so he *could* be forgiven, *and* he had coppery curly hair. But *she* was going to be most like Mama, with her Raphaelesque hair and blue eyes, so there!

One day Bennett would inherit his parents' vast fortune – gold, diamonds, marble, a string of pricelss racehorses, and palatial houses all round the world. Roxana couldn't wait for the day Bennett would propose to her on one knee: she would make him wait. At least five times she would make him beg for her to marry him, and then she would say yes, just as he was fainting from desire at her feet. So blow the grown ups down there! She poked her tongue out at them, but they still didn't see her.

Disgruntled at being thought of as just another silly child and consequently ignored, Roxana crept back to the warmth of the nursery bedroom.

She glanced across the dividing space, the dressing-table separating her bed from Raven's. Raven pretended to be asleep. Oh well, she wouldn't tell Raven about her New Year's resolution, or how babies were made. She had managed to wheedle out some of the details from Tim, and they were unbelievable! She rather thought Tim had made it all up just to be disgusting. Bennett, at least, was a little more cultured. Roxana felt very cheated by Raven's cold-shouldering. Raven always was so superior! A paragon of virtue, just like Cassy's statue of the Virgin Mary; cold, old and good. Raven never wanted to be neighbourly or friendly and discuss sisterly things with her. All she wanted to do was scribble in a stupid exercise book she called her people-spotting book. Yuk!

Roxana pulled the covers over her frozen shoulders and fell asleep, curled into an exhausted sea anemone with tentacles in repose.

Raven was not asleep. Her eyes might have been closed, but she was only waiting for Roxana to start snoring before she crept out of bed to Cassy's room. Hands behind her head, dark hair like an ink stain on the white pillow, she thought about a lot of things.

Cold moonlight silvered the ceiling, and frost was beginning to make patterns on the windowpanes. By morning, thin sheets of ice, transparent and as brittle as a biscuit, would have formed on the marble washstand, and a long stalactite would hang from the cold-water tap on the cracked basin in the bathroom.

Ragtime and jazz music were loud and throbbing from downstairs, the not-so-sober Georgian house tonight shuddering to the strains of the Jog-Trot, Twinkle, Vampire, Shimmy, Missouri Walk, and a dozen other boisterous dances, as the adults greeted the New Year. The Nègro band her mother had hired was the real thing, all the way from the United States of America! America seemed like a dreamland. Mama talked about Gimbels, and Macy's Store, and 'bargain basements', and Bloomingdales, and Fifth Avenue, and Park Avenue and The White House. Mother and Father had even met the President of the United States of America, Mr Woodrow Wilson! But that was four years ago, and WW wasn't President any more. She thought that she might like to go to America one day, like Mother, who was always flitting across the Atlantic. That's how she had known about the Louisiana Tune Coons. Mother and Lyra were jazz-crazy, so was Roxa: so she said! Raven stared at the silvery ceiling.

She would be glad when Christmas and the New Year festivities were out of the way and they could go to County Kildare. Roxana and she usually spent their birthday at Hollyberry House. She wished she could have had a birthday without sharing it with another person. Father had promised her a new pony, and had assured her, in his precise monosyllabic way, it would not be one of Tim's cast-offs, but a brand new one straight from the Noughton Peel stud. Roxa had requested her own grand piano (a white one) and professional singing lessons so that she could entertain Bennett d'Ildarte, although Raven knew Roxa had kept Bennett's name out of it when making her request.

Hollyberry House was the place Raven liked best in the world. Once, at Hollyberry House, Tim had ridden his pony into the huge kitchen, and all the servants had roared with laughter when it did its business on Agnes's freshly washed tiles. Tim was always such good fun when he was home, and Hollyberry House had nice memories; warm, welcoming and safe, as a family house should have. Her mother, the Honourable Daphne Moynahan, before she married Father, had been born and brought up there by Cassy O'Carey, Family Nurse.

In Dublin, Raven always felt as though she were in limbo: perhaps it was something to do with being half-and-half, like Roxana had said, and not belonging to the real Ireland at all. Maybe it was because she preferred classical music to jazz: Paganini, Beethoven, Rachmaninov's Second Concerto in C minor, Opus 18, which made her want to cry. Sonny had said the Third Concerto in D minor, Opus 30 was far more controlled, subtle, and had considerable dimension, which Opus 18 somehow lacked. Sometimes Sonny frightened her with the depth of his genius, his passion for music, all perfectly controlled within his undersized frame and curly russet head. When he played 'Through Tara's Halls' to his own violin interpretation, even gristly old Kelly and Cathal Swilly had tears in their eyes.

Raven wished she could sort everything out like Sonny into neat little compartments so that she knew where she was: Cassy and Cathal Swilly; IRA and the Black and Tans; Protestants and Catholics; William Butler Yeats and Maud Gonne; Mother and her crazy, frivolous lifestyle; Father, who had won the Victoria Cross for bravery at Passchendaele under the motto, *Quis Separabit*, Who Shall Separate? She knew her parents loved her in a strange, disconnected way, and she loved them in return. But she loved Cassy best, because Cassy *cared*, and she had hated Grandmother Moynahan most, who had *never* cared about her grandchildren, only her racehorses.

Grandmother Moynahan-Graeme-Taulor-Bradshaw (listed according to her four husbands) had died two years ago, leaving millions of Irish pounds to her only daughter and son-in-law, even though she had managed to spend quite a few million gracing the turf of The Curragh.

'All this and heaven too,' Cassy had said, possibly exaggerating a great deal, while insinuating that Grandmother Moynahan 'liked having a good time', really meaning that she had had a lot of rich lovers during her eighty-four years, contrary to the law of God and Cassy O'Carey. Raven remembered Grandmother quite well, rather a strange old woman, dressed in regal black, wearing ropes of pearls and huge hats with black embroidered veils. Through her *pince-nez* and veils, Grandmother Moynahan seemed to have spent her days peering at, and dissecting, the outside world. Everyone had been in awe of her, all except Cassy, who referred to her, in rather a derogatory manner, as *the dowager* lady, or her *lady*ship Moynahan. Raven wondered why Cassy had disliked Grandmother so much and yet stayed to work for her at Hollyberry House.

Mother, too, had certainly inherited that Moynahan *joie de vivre*. To sit beside her as she raced her smart little red Austin Seven through the country lanes or city streets, smiling, waving, and noisily tooting the horn to let everyone know she was back in town, was an experience! Many a time they had heard the frosty Protestant vicar admonishing Mother for running him into the ditch when he had been out riding on his bicycle. Lady Quennell would kill someone one day, he had grumbled to Cassy. Yes, Cassy had replied, Hon Gal (Cassy's own special name for her) would kill Cassy O'Carey with purgatorial anxiety, because Hon Gal was a heathen and bringing up her children the same way. Mother had called the vicar a sluggish slowcoach.

But because she was a patron of the Irish White Cross, servants, tenants, and vicars were prepared to forgive her anything, even to running them into the ditch. Pressmen and fashion photographers with popping flash-bulbs were also part of her entourage, eagerly pursuing her when she was engaged on raising money for the Relief of Ireland Fund. She was often being featured in fashionable magazines, especially *The Tatler*, because she was so pretty and so popular.

By that same token, while she hated answering their childish questions, when she did ask for them to be taken back to the nursery, Mother usually tempered her impatience with right royal indulgences like 'Charbonnel et Walker' chocolates: and, in rare flashes of maternalism, once a sapphire brooch to Roxana, a grand silk frock with an *haute couture* label to her, Raven, (it didn't fit, but mother had said save it for when she was grown up), and adult tickets for Tim and Sonny to see a play at the Abbey Theatre. Cassy, of course, utterly disapproved of their mother's extravagant gestures and told her she was 'casting *stimulated* pearls before uncultured piglets!'. Far better Hon Gal read the children a nursery story at bedtime to show that she cared for them, than give away expensive gifts. Mother, who only read menus, transatlantic sailing timetables, signposts, like Amery and Lyra, and the Court circular, continued to ignore the gospel according to St Cassy.

Father, on the other hand, Baronet and Judge of the High Court of Ireland, read everything, including the death sentence. With his cadaverous cheeks, burning dark eyes, and white hair, he had the distinguished aspect of a gowned and bewigged statesman of God. Cassy, who sang their father's praises like no one else, had told them that this tall, stark, and awesome ex-colonel in the Irish Guards had turned white overnight at Passchendaele, and had lost his tongue and his youth somewhere on the Hindenburg Line. Cassy excused his unfatherly behaviour by saying that a man who had fought on the Somme, Canal du Nord and Drocourt-Quéant (Cassy knew all their father's battles), and who had bits of shrapnel in the back of his head (the cause of his severe headaches), and an injured left side (where the Hun had bayoneted him), and who had won the VC for bravery (at the age of thirty-nine) didn't want to listen to children making a noise by sliding and clattering down the stairs on the butler's silver tray.

In her mind's eye, the picture her brave but austere father presented disturbed her very much. She would see him now with a black cap on his distinguished white head saying things like, 'you will be hanged by the neck until you are dead', or, 'you will be blindfold and shot at dawn, may God have mercy on your soul'. That must *surely* take an awful lot of what she could only describe as *an inhuman quality*. And afterwards, the judge, her own father, with the power of life and death in his hands, just like God, to dance the Vampire at midnight and then go to bed and not have nightmares: one couldn't help *but* be in awe of

40

him. No wonder so many people in Ireland were afraid of the power he wielded in the name of the British Empire!

Raven turned over to look at her bedside clock in the shape of a big yellow sunflower with luminous black dots for numbers one to twelve. Five minutes to midnight. Laughter and music were certainly growing louder and more uncontrolled. Soon they would all be singing 'Auld Lang Syne' and popping balloons and champagne corks to greet the New Year. Raven wondered if Amery was reeling by now or had sneaked away to seduce Clare Fenchurch behind her rubber stamp, or if Lyra had found an even more youthful, as well as useful, beau under the mistletoe. What a pity, Raven thought wistfully, she wasn't just a little older herself. Then she might have been allowed to ask William about the young girl who had broken his heart and to whom he had dedicated his poem 'To A Young Girl': could her name possibly be Ravenna Mealdow Quennell?

Along the nursery corridor, the night light from Cassy's open bedroom door at the far end was like a slice of Raven's favourite quince tart baked by Agnes's plump pink hands when autumn touched County Kildare. The rosy glow fell across the polished wooden floor of the bare corridor, and Raven was unable to resist its lure. She wanted to wish Cassy a Happy New Year, as well as ask her an important question.

Cassy would still be awake, reading her Bible and mumbling over her rosary beads. That ritual of rosary beads and making the sign of the cross over her body intrigued Raven. It was like one of the rites performed by the White Magic Circle downstairs in Father's library. She had peeked in on them once, crouched on the dumb-waiter when it was being lowered from top floor nursery dining-room to basement kitchen. The dumb-waiter had to pass down the shaft next to Father's library. She had held onto the ropes, stopping it between floors so that she could find out what Father and Mr Yeats and the others were doing through her own very special peephole – the hollow centre of a stucco rose on the wall beside the great fireplace. She hadn't much cared, though, for the experience of finding herself perched precariously on the food lift stuck between floors.

Raven got out of bed. She wouldn't be able to sleep until

she had the answer to her important question. She peeked into the boys' bedroom. Timothy was not in his bed, he must have gone to the bathroom. Sonny, asleep, looked like an angel, with his halo of tight coppery curls. Sonny's precious violin, not a Stradivari but the next best thing, a rare Gagliano given him by Mother and Father for Christmas, was never very far away from him. It rested in its case against Sonny's bedside table so that he could see it first thing in the morning. Raven drew up in the pool of light from Cassy's half-open door. Her important question went completely out of her head. She knew it was late, the latest she had ever been when visiting Cassy in her bedroom, but tonight was rather special, and she didn't think Cassy would mind.

But Cassy was too engrossed in what she was doing in front of her dressing-table mirror to be aware of another presence in the room.

Raven trembled as much as Cassy's hands tipping the bottle to her lips without the grace of a glass. Cassy hadn't even bothered to disguise the grand brand-name on the bottle. Raven could see only too well that it was her father's best Cognac, which he only brought out after dinner. Cassy just closed her eyes, clenched the neck of the bottle and drank down the liquor in one long, crude gulp, as though she were accustomed to tossing back the drink in this fashion and burping after it.

Raven did not mind Cassy being a 'wine-bibber and tippler of spirits': Cathal Swilly was both down in the pantry. Agnes said drink was only a sin if one became drunk and violent, or kept it a secret. A little tipple now and then hurt no one. It was one way of getting through the hard times, and God knew, Agnes had said, these were hard enough times in Ireland. Raven herself realized that Agnes often liked to 'tipple' on cooking sherry reserved for the trifle. It was because Cassy tippled secretively, and with her bodice undone, that Raven felt cheated. She definitely did not understand the peculiar habits of adults.

She crept a little nearer, but still Cassy didn't see her. Then Cassy began to peel away some strips of soiled and bloodstained linen wrapping her chest. Raven felt faint. She wanted to cry out, say something, but it was as though she were captured in a nightmare in which disjointed and horrifying actions took precedence over speech. Everything was falling apart in a slow-moving, soundless scene, just like the glass bubble shaken to bits, scattering white lies in the form of make-believe snow.

Cassy was ill. Cassy was going to die, but not beautifully like Roxana said: one wasn't prettily laid out in one's wedding-dress, with arum lilies on one's breast, the grieving lover shedding his salty tears over one's bosom smelling of lilies as he kissed one's lips so that death was vanquished for ever in that instant resurrection. Death was horrible and ugly, nasty and messy; the same as living, just like Flox said. Cassy's bosom was rotting away, eaten up by those very worms and maggots of 'corruption and destruction' just like Cassy told her the Bible said, and Cassy wasn't even dead yet!

Raven clamped her hands over her mouth, haunted eyes fixed on Cassy's reflection in the mirror. Raven sensed that Cassy knew the 'end was nigh', proclaimed often enough on the sandwich-boards of old tramps on Dublin's streets, because Cassy's eyes were moist and dark and sad-looking.

Then Cassy's expression changed. From certainty and conviction and total acceptance of the situation, her eyes mirrored uncertainty, accusation, and finally anger as she whirled to meet the luminous eyes of the inquisitive little ghost in white flannel reflected in her looking-glass.

'Cassy, oh Cassy!' Raven breathed, 'I thought you were going to heaven, not hell, which you said is for sinners. Have you done something very wicked, Cassy? Are you a wine-bibber of spirits and things like the Bible and Agnes say and that's why you're being eaten up by maggots and worms?'

Image of accusation, and pain, and a lot more besides, Cassy said bitingly, 'Spying, Miss Raven! You're always sneaking about the place, listening at doors, or asking your stupid questions! One day your snooping is going to get you into mortal trouble.'

'Cassy, I'm not snooping, or spying on you, I promise!'

Raven hurt, as if Cassy had boxed her ears, feeling bruised inside by Cassy's harsh words, wanted only to be loved and approved of by Cassy: and she also wanted to be certain of her facts. 'Cassy, *are* you going to die because you've done something very bad and now your heart's rotting away?'

'We're all going to die, miss. From the cradle to the grave we spend our in-between years slowly dying at other people's hands, party to all kinds of evil deeds rotting us in a million different ways!'

Raven had never heard Cassy so scornful, bitter and *dead*!

Cassy's vicious words ringing in her ears, she turned and fled from the room. Cassy had sounded as if there was nothing left except to be eaten away with holes through her body, like woodworm in the beams of a mouldy old house!

Cassy stared after the girl: Miss Raven with the receptive heart, who was so different to the others. She cared, and she appreciated that other people had feelings too, which ought to be respected. Cassy braced herself against the chest of drawers, the past flooding in on her as never before: the daughter had filled the gaps left by the mother whom she, Cassy, had first nursed when a mere girl herself. At the age of thirteen she had gone into the service of Lord and Lady Moynahan at Hollyberry House, County Kildare. For thirty-seven years she had served the family faithfully. She had loved and cared for Hon Gal as though she were her own child, but Hon Gal never cared about that as she grew older: she had her own golden life to be getting on with. Sometimes Cassy wished she had gone away and lived her own life instead of devoting herself to the Moynahan-Quennell family – but it was too late now to wish anything: half a century had caught up with her.

But she hadn't meant to be quite so rough with Miss Raven, or drive her away in such a cruel fashion: she did not want her to be disillusioned. But neither could Raven, the child, depend upon Cassy, the nurse, for ever. Her little girl had to grow up. She had to realize that life was not just a parlour-game of pretence, or a book in which one scribbled fancy stories; it was a rough-and-tumble road full of false hopes, false dreams, deceit, lies and betrayals; and always death and corruption. It didn't matter how sweet-smelling the life, for pine, oak or yew, when Catholic and Protestant were laid side by side, coffin wood was only ever the prize ...

She must not give in to the Divil! Hastily Cassy crossed herself, '*Hail Mary full of Grace, the Lord is with thee ...*' Cassy returned to a lifelong doctrine, and remembered the sin of faltering footsteps and the betrayal of one's faith: she had to cling to the belief that there was a power beyond. 'Dear Heavenly Father,' she prayed, 'give me the strength to believe in the resurrection of the body and the life everlasting. Lend me an open mind, ready to accept Father Donahoe's comforting words, that death is a place of refuge from life's sordid ills, the brilliant light at the end of the long, dark tunnel of earthly strife and struggle.'

Cassy took a deep breath, and in time the calmness of soul and spirit returned, as in those introspective moments of the past at Hollyberry House, when the routine of her life turned from something trivial and dull, into a drama to be reckoned with. Then, with a soft clean polishing cloth in her hand, the balance had been restored between the things that required to be done and the mind's ability to accept that the mundane was also life's tin of Kleenoff necessary to put one's own scratches into proper perspective.

She had been young, and if not pretty like Maud, then at least passable! She had cherished a wild dream of love with a debonair little man, a copper-haired, freckle-faced schoolmaster. But he had had eyes for no one except her 'ladyship' Maud Moynahan, who was already married. And because she had been only a humble maidservant, he had never known the extent, or the tragedy of her love for him before he had disappeared for ever from Ireland. Cassy remembered those far-off days of unrequited love even while the new day for her was already dawning.

Peace! She stared into the face of the future, mirrored in the New Year of 1923, and the word peace somehow vanquished the shadow that lay over her.

One day Raven would understand: one day Raven would find someone else to whom she could give back the great store of her love, loyalty and affection. But Cassy was

45

too numbed and too tired to go after the little girl to tell her these things. She reached once more for the blessed relief that came from the bottle of her master's brandy.

Raven banged her shin on Sonny's bed and didn't feel the pain. Back through a corridor of tears, down an avenue of new awakenings: Cassy dying, Cassy, mother of the universe, the one figure of stability in a world of changing patterns, riddled with a killing disease and keeping it to herself.

Cassy, who nursed everyone, made them better, sat long hours with people like Flox's old mother, was there no one to help her in her own hour of need? Is that why Cassy pretended there was nothing wrong with her? Was Cassy afraid to tell anyone in case she was shunned, or lost her job and was put out on the street with no money and nowhere to go except the poorhouse? Cassy had a dread of the poorhouse as much as she feared a Catholic purgatory, or a hell of fire and brimstone. But that was silly. Mother and Father wouldn't put Cassy out on the street, not after all the years Cassy had devoted to them. They would look after her now. Cassy would be pensioned off, given a nice little cottage in the grounds of Hollyberry House, and all her medical bills would be paid by Father.

Raven thought about it: yes, of course, Cassy was afraid! *And* she was too proud to beg for anything, including her life. Raven made up her mind there and then to nurse Cassy if no one else was willing. She would also go to Father Donahoe first thing in the morning. The dying had a right to be comforted – it was called absolution, Cassy had said so. Father Donahoe was Cassy's confessor, and if Cassy hadn't told him about her rotten chest, then she would have to tell him. She would also have to tell Mother so that Mother could call the doctor to give Cassy medicines, or to cut out the bad parts with a scalpel, which surgeons did to make people better.

Her tetra perception was letting her down suddenly. Somehow, she did not feel that this was Cassy's punishment for being a sinful drunkard, as the Bible described the likes of Cathal Swilly, whose boy had gone to the side of the Irish Republican Army, and whose death was only a question of time. It had made Cathal silly in the head, all that sorrow and misery, and drinking to help forget his sorrow and misery. And neither could she believe it was Cassy's punishment for having told a bad lie, even though she knew that one simply *did not* buy 'baby-pills' in a little jar over the apothecary's counter to take every day for nine months! Mr McGuire had looked at Roxana and her as though they were both half-wits that time, and then he had offered them a condescending pat on the head, a secret smile and some Dolly Mixtures. Cassy, Agnes and Eileen had all been lying about how babies were made, and yet Cassy had always said telling lies was wicked. Oh dear, it was all far too complicated, this growing older! Perhaps she would be better off staying nine years, eleven months and one week old. But somehow Raven felt that this time the answers were not black and white any more; there were whole areas of grey as well, and questions no one could answer.

Yet she didn't want Cassy to die. Cassy was different. Cassy was personal. Cassy was approachable, Cassy was here all the time and more of a *real* mother than their own mother. If Cassy died, Mother wouldn't be able to cope like Cassy. Then Roxa would really get out of hand and uppity, and Timothy would bully Sonny, and there would be nobody to answer her questions or tell her interesting stories at bathtime.

Raven, rubbing her bruised shin, saw that Timothy was still not in his bed. He had obviously sneaked off to the stables to see Armorial Shanks, his beloved horse, otherwise he'd have been back from the bathroom by now. Raven wondered if she should wake Sonny and get him to pray with her. Two voices were bound to be heard sooner than just one. They simply *had* to get God on their side for Cassy's sake.

But Raven was in a dilemma; she did not know what religion she should choose in order to have her prayers answered. That's what she had intended to ask Cassy tonight: should she be a Catholic or a Protestant, a Communist or a Nazi? Amery had told them all the other night, with the drawing-room doors left wide open, that he was an English Nazi, and after everyone had looked at him in sudden astonishment and silence, they had all started to laugh. Father had even joked, 'Well done, Amery! For a moment you had us all fooled with your Red Diamond, Black Jackboot charade.' Amery had replied seriously, 'No charade, Francis, I'm of the New Party, the new *raison d'etre*: *SA*!' 'Oh, Sex Appeal, darling!' someone called Drusilla Penfold-Smythe had interrupted, and everyone had started to laugh again. Then Amery had become really angry and had shouted at everyone, '*Sturmabteilung*!'

Raven hadn't known what that meant. Later on she had asked Timothy, who was learning German, as well as Latin, Greek and French. Tim knew at once what Amery had meant during charades. 'Oh, *SA*, that's Hitler's Sports' Division, stands for *Sturmabteilung*. It really means storm-trooper. Storm-troopers wear brown shirts and march to stirring music glorifying the Fatherland. Amery told me all about *SA*. He was very excited about it, and is going to join the English Fascist Party because of this thousand years of peace and prosperity which the Nazis have promised everyone.'

It was all most confusing. Which was God's favourite religion and the one he was most likely to listen to first?

'Sonny – wake up! Ought we to become Catholics or Nazis so that God will listen to our prayers about Cassy? What about the Quakers, or even the Salvation Army? Or should we first ask Father which religion is best?' It was a measure of her distress over Cassy's state of mind and body that she even considered going to her father in this matter. Raven shook Sonny's shoulder harder than ever, but he wouldn't open his eyes. 'It's important, Sonny, God mightn't listen if we choose the wrong religion.'

He moaned in his sleep and turned over. Then, finding herself on her knees by Sonny's bed, Raven stayed there.

She began to wonder about many things without actually petitioning God for anything, not just yet anyway. She had to sort things out for herself first. Certain facts were only just beginning to impose themselves upon her young girl's vision: God was deliberately trying to confuse the issue by making people all wrong. There were rich and poor people, sick and healthy people, happy and sad people, hungry people, and satisfied people. Why complicate life even further by having religious and political people, too? Px1 and Px2 didn't appear to believe in anything except having a good time – and they were rich and contented, whereas Cassy was very, very kind and good and believed in God utterly, and was unhappy, poor and painfully ill; it didn't make sense. If there was a God who granted all these things, why couldn't he just make everyone happy, healthy, rich and contented, and when they died, everyone could go to heaven? So much simpler! If she were God, she wouldn't complicate matters by making people different; she would make everyone the same.

Raven thought about it a bit longer and then decided, no, that wouldn't work either. Life would be awfully dull and monotonous and there would be nothing much happening of real interest: just imagine millions and millions of Lyras swanning around the world, or liquorice-licking Bennett d'Ildartes, or Amery Noughton Peels who went to fascist rallys in a Daimler, or Mothers who liked jazz. Raven shuddered and supposed there was no real answer. In the end she decided that, after all, it was better the way God had it, because then everyone could work out life for themselves.

Glass-bubble lies began to make sense at last, as she worked out for herself the disparity between the lives of the ruling class of Ireland and those of Cassy's class. The difference was deep and wide, somehow indecent, rather like the ugly crack in the smooth enamel of the bathroom basin, which leaked when it needn't …

And then, quite suddenly, as though God had heard her and was answering her back while she knelt against the iron legs of darkness, church bells and jazz music were swallowed up in one great roar of compelling sound as all the discordant notes of heaven and earth came together.

Raven felt as though she were falling through space, her mind taken over by the stories and scenes of her childhood. In a spiralling shaft of darkness and débris, she clung to the foot of Sonny's bed as her whole world contracted downwards into a bottomless pit. Rumbling, tumbling masonry and immense beams tossed aside by

Samson's mighty arms and roaring breath; Delilah's red mouth seemed to spit blood and screams. Solomon and Sheba fell into each others arms, before turning to dust as Waldre's magnificent ceilings were blown out into New Year's dawn like an extra special firework display.

In the library, away from their guests dancing the night away in the grand salon, Sir Francis and his wife had been toasting each other with champagne and a private New Year kiss. Timothy Quennell was on the servants' stairs, wending his way secretively back to bed after having spent the last three hours asleep in the warm straw close to his beloved horse. Just a few minutes, in his case, represented the short span of life from the moment when he awoke with a guilty start in Armorial Shanks's box in the mews behind the house, to the moment when the bomb, hidden in the elmwood doughbox in the pantry directly below the library, was timed to go off. Had he stayed those extra few minutes with his horse, Timothy would have been nowhere near the heart of the explosion, and would have lived to claim his inheritance.

CHAPTER TWO

New York City: January 1923

Frozen snow, shovelled off the streets onto the pavements, looked like grimy pavlovas. A few days into the New Year, yet the city was as unnaturally deserted as Ellis Island following the Emergency Quota Act, and as bleak as Prohibition holding the festive season by the throat.

Only those duty bound, or with nowhere else to go, clung to the inhospitable streets.

On West 15th Street, a thin, shabbily-dressed man in his mid-fifties struggled with himself and a two foot plank nailed to his left hand.

He managed, at last, to find City Hospital. The injured hand and its wooden extension had been sloppily wrapped in an old mackintosh. He tried to manoeuvre himself through the doors of the Accident and Emergency department, but wedged himself widthways, and the mackintosh slipped off.

Like New York City, he thought his heart had frozen solid and his blood had stopped circulating. When he saw it all start up again, he cursed with Irish eloquence. Blood poured through the fingers of his right hand supporting the weight of the plank, and he got himself into an even worse coil. He wished his heart really *had* stopped; there wasn't much to live for, after all.

The injured man hoped the night porter wouldn't skid and break his neck outside his own entrance. Shuffling his feet in the sticky red mush under his worn boots, this way, he reasoned in some confusion, the blood would be less noticible. Then he used his heels and shoulders to enter backwards through the offending swing doors.

A young trainee nurse, putting a sling on a boy's broken wrist, gave a suffering sigh. Several patients, steadfastly waiting their turn to see a doctor, looked at this latest casualty as a most unwelcome addition to the emergency list of City Hospital. Others couldn't have cared less and continued screaming blue murder for attention.

'Put a sock in it, Mr Hoppenmier,' growled Head Nurse Winifred Winston, or Winnie as she was called by some of the more irreverent interns. 'It ain't my fault you dropped boiling spaghetti on your bare foot. Sign these forms and you might get some attention. I thought you folks only ate kosher pastrami.'

'It was vermicelli, Nurse. Sign these forms, sign these forms! What's with you medical people? A guy can die signing away his life before he sees a doctor. And I didn't drop nothing. My wife did.'

After Mr Hoppenmier had signed for treatment, Nurse Winston told him to sit down and wait since his scalded foot wasn't a matter of life and death. Then she stuck her head between the green screens of an examination cubicle and wheezed gustily, 'A crucified lush bleeding to death over the floor, or a vacuum-sealed Coca-Cola queen who can't sit down. The choice is yours, Doc.'

'*Jesus!*'

'Sure, if he's walking the streets tonight. Let's all pray the Eighteenth Amendment holds out a bit longer, so's we get even more oddballs in here.'

Nurse Winston was about to walk off, but Intern Keiren Hunter Devlin, desperately trying to locate in his patient a vein that hadn't collapsed, called her back. 'Hey hey, Winnie – wait a minute. Try ringing around again for Zimmerman. He should be helping out here.'

'Listen Doc, who we know should be here ain't here, and by the time it *gets* here, the guy whose crucified himself won't want circumcizing either. The trouble is he's on welfare. He *says* he's the odd job feller at The Leprechaun, so they'll cover his medical expenses since he was working for them when he screwed himself. What do I do with him, chuck him out and hope he don't die on the doorstep?'

'Get him to sign, and then get his blood typed for me, Win.'

'I got a houseful of dumb jiggers out there speaking every goddamn lingo except English. Most ain't never seen an ink pen before, only a pig pen. So now I'm White House Secretary and Interpreter to the whole friggin' American system. So what about my time? I don't get paid doc's wages, feller.'

'I don't get paid them, either.' Keir straightened up to ease his aching back, and took time off to grin at her.

That's what she loved most about Devlin, his baby-blue eyes and touching sense of humour; must be his thick Irish blood. Nor would her nights be the same without the great, ugly, cuddly brute, Winnie thought happily while she pandered to his tongue. 'Have it your way, Doc, but *someone's* going to end up in the cemetery by morning unless you can read your anatomy text right way up first time. Try the ankle if you wanna vein. Frau Gratz sure as hell has thick enough ones.' She withdrew her head from between the green screens.

The amused voice behind them said, 'Hey Winnie, is it old Fogharty from The Leprechaun?'

Nurse Winston stuck her head back in saucily, and reminded Keir of a recurring nightmare. 'How should I know, honeychile? Winnie don't have time to fraternize at The Leprechaun. Not like some. The Paddy ain't saying much. Dense as dottle, if you ask me.'

'That's him. What's his problem – how come the crucifixion, I mean?'

'Now, you're asking! *He* hasn't a problem, I'm the one with the friggin' problems which nobody and nothin' can cure.'

'You ever considered a Dettol mouthwash, Winnie?'

Flashing black eyes, thick purple lips, and big white teeth treated him to a wonderfully engaging smile. 'A real lush, as well as a bum carpenter if you ask me, and we're full of 'em tonight. Fixed his left hand to piece of wood. Lost, I reckon, two pints on the way. Only the weather froze *this* one's ass before he could bleed to death. He needs unfastening by skilled hands; mine ain't.' She waddled back to her nurses' station.

Keir sweated and grunted and probed around behind the patient's left ankle for a blood vessel sufficiently patent in which to insert his needle, and eventually said, 'Frau Gratz, you do this again and I'll be forced to notify Sergeant O'Reilly down at the Precinct. Understood?'

Four times the size of her husband, the woman wasn't so far gone she couldn't understand the warning. Her eyes widened and filled with tears above the hospital blanket.

The husband, a sandy little man with a big belly, bald head, and bushy, tobacco-stained moustache, fussed around the trolley on which his wife lay like a beached whale. 'Sure, Doc, she unnerstan's okay. She vill not do it again or I kill her myself, eh *Schatzchen*?' Tenderly he stroked her pasty forehead while gazing lovingly into her glazed eyes.

Herr Gratz reminded Keir of a ginger walrus hauled unwillingly onto the same stretch of sand as his whale-sized wife. He sighed long-sufferingly, 'Why *does* she do it? I'd like to know.'

The German shrugged. '*Mein Metzgeri*, it makes big loss, Doc. Tammany bosses take too much protection money vant from small butcher business like mine. *Schweinefleisch* and blood sausage the Yids do not like, so I much kosher custom from Five Point district lose.'

'Try fishballs,' Keir murmured.

'New Yorkers, they do not *Boche* salami vant, either. They like *besser* the Irish vhiskey. Prohibition, it stink! Everyone in New York make no money except the rich ones – who do not vant *Boche* salami *never*! Now Helga have baby but no husband first, so Gertrude *der Brot* knife take to cut her own throat instead of throat of *Tochter*, okay?'

'Okay. But next time tell her to sharpen the breadknife better. This is the third time in as many months she's tried to commit suicide.' Keir called for a nurse. 'She's all fixed up. Not too fast with the saline, keep it steady, we don't want to overload her circulation. Operating room is on standby to darn the holes in her gullet. Tell Dr Morton, doing the op, her blood type is already on record. Blood bank will deliver the first bottle in fifteen minutes.' Keir turned back to Herr Gratz. 'Afterwards, if, and I emphasize if, they can patch her up without any more problems, it's the same psychiatric ward, same head nurse.'

'*Mein Gott*! I that Murphy woman with *mein* guts hate!'

'Careful. That Murphy woman happens to be a countrywoman of mine.'

'Then for you, *Herr Dokter*, I am sorry that you must work with a woman like that one, with a *Schnauz* worse than Sergeant Cop O'Reilly.' Herr Gratz brought his finger down through the air in a very precise gesture. 'Nurse Murphy she *hate* the suicide ones, because they do not make good job first time. She make me nervous.' First generation Gratz who had passed through the barriers of Ellis Island in 1919 then looked at Keir curiously, 'But you are *americanisch*, not an Irish man like Sergeant Big Mouth Cop.'

'Right.' Keir got Herr Gratz to sign some papers.

Tongue between his teeth, Herr Gratz laboriously signed the hospital forms in his tiny, cramped signature. 'O'Reilly, *mein Gott*, has one big *Schnauz* and shouts loud ven I to sign American naturalization papers in precinct *gehen*. Now all New York is knowing that Rudolph Gratz in America is here only four years, and must twenny-four vait to become *americanish!*'

'Good night, Herr Gratz. I shouldn't hang around any longer. There's nothing more you can do. Go home and start filling your *Schweinefleisch* sausages.' Keir rescued his pen from the German. 'Your wife won't know anything till tomorrow when she wakes up and discovers she's got a feeding tube from her nose to her stomach to bypass the daylight in her throat.'

After Herr Gratz had left, Keir couldn't believe he had sounded so unfeeling, so unconcerned, and so cynical. He ran a weary hand through his hair and helped himself to more black coffee from the Thermos jug Winnie had thoughtfully provided.

The weather was appalling, adding to the human burden. Overworked and short-staffed, most of the internees were off with flu – and those that weren't swung the lead like Zimmerman, so he'd kill the fellow for not showing some dedication to his chosen profession when he himself was in the pink of health! No doubt he was off somewhere laying some female on hospital time. Why was it bad weather always increased an intern's lot tenfold? It couldn't altogether be blamed on the balmy atmosphere produced by steam-heating and artificial ventilation, could it? Yes it could! These goomers deliberately injured themselves, or took overdoses, so that they could come in here and keep cosy.

Hospital hypochondriacs the worst to contend with, Keir peeled off another layer of sweater and worked in his shirt-sleeves. Dog tired, he just wanted to crawl into bed and sleep for a week. He wondered how his mother was getting along. He hadn't even had time to visit her lately, missing out on Christmas and the New Year, so that he felt doubly guilty.

Before his concentration slipped any further, and he fell asleep where he stood, he stuck his head out of the cubicle, 'Okay, Winnie, the next one.'

Nurse Winston carefully placed paper on the examination couch to protect it from the dirt and gore clinging to the patient's boots. Having settled him, she scuttled off without taking too much notice of the look on Doc's face: poor Dev, Winnie gloated to herself, he always managed to look like an overgrown black-haired, blue-eyed codfish searching for words when he had to treat hobos who deliberately messed with themselves. Well, since he knew this Fogharty guy who didn't want *her* to see his private possessions, let Dev sort him and his welfare card out: bums who couldn't pay for treatment made her sick.

'Christ!' Keir stared in horror at the man he hadn't seen for six years, and didn't want to see now.

'Sorry son, didn't know where else to go. I'm a little skint at the moment, you see, but I knew *you'd* do your poor old pa a favour, like.'

'You could have gone to the Samaritan Hospital.'

'Right you are, son. If you're ashamed of yer old father, I'll not stop, despite the mortal shock of me terrible injury. I shall take myself off to the charity hospital, where a kindly doctor will fix me up since there is no charity to be found here.'

Josslyn Hunter Devlin, picking up the vestiges of his dignity, struggled to get off the examining couch, although his left hand gave him the very devil.

Keir pushed his father down again. Joss, supporting the plank with his good hand yelped, 'Not so rough, son! I'm in

56

mortal agony.'

Keir ignored the cry for sympathy; it had come too late. Knowing Joss, Keir couldn't help feeling that he had very likely pinned himself deliberately to the board to gain attention. 'You allergic to horses, Pa?'

'Now what sort of question is that, son? I've not ridden a horse in a hundred years.'

'Ever had an anti-tetanus injection before?'

'Can't say I have. What's it to do with horses?'

'Serum. Some people have an allergy to horse serum. Could be fatal — never mind!' Keir began to draw up injections of anti-tetanus serum and a local anaesthetic. 'How could you have been so stupid? Were you drunk?' Yes, of course he was drunk. Why ask, thought Keir while struggling to retain his professional image. But compassion *did* interfere deep down inside. He was appalled to see his father so down on his luck and so horribly injured.

'I know you're ashamed of me, son. It has always been *most* obvious. That is why you didn't ask your old father to your graduation, eh, boy?'

'Wasn't my fault.'

'To be sure it wasn't, it was all mine.' Joss rubbed the side of his bristly face on the shoulder of his threadbare jacket. His eyes a bleary, bloodshot blue, tears sidled out of the corners.

If the old fool started to blubber, Keir knew he'd probably throw him out, plank and all. Let him go to the Samaritan! But instead, he ground his teeth, and tried to harness his wayward emotions; emotion was bad for business. In a resigned, more tolerant manner, Keir asked, 'How did you do it, Pa?'

'I was putting up a shelf for dear old Nurse Lilly Wald, when the hammer and the nail I was holding slipped through me fingers.'

'And so you walked from Jefferson nailed to a board. Why?'

'Ouch! Be careful, son, that hurt!'

'It probably did. And you'll probably get lockjaw now that you're free of your shelf.' In disgust Keir tossed the splintered plank into a corner of the cubicle. The nail was old and rusty and at least four inches long. He cleaned up the hand and hoped to goodness blood poisoning wouldn't set in. Alcohol probably had a lot to do with anaesthetizing Joss from the after-effects of self-destruction, and that was why he had managed to walk so far without collapsing. Keir hoped that the whiskey circulating in Joss's veins would also provide an antiseptic cover against wound infection.

Joss whined about how many more needles was his son intending to stick in him, and then gave his feeble explanation: 'I was coming to tell you, dearest son, that your mother hasn't seen you for a whole month and wondered if you were all right?'

'How do you know? Have you been to see her?' Keir was used to his father's tall stories. Alcoholics imagined the truth.

'I saw her this afternoon at Nurse Lilly's when I was putting up her little wooden shelf. I think that is what made me lose my concentration, the sight of your dear, sweet mother after not seeing her for so long. She is as pretty as ever, a real lovely woman to look at still, even though she is well over-the-hill like meself. Oh God, 'tis a long time ago when all was light and sunshine.' Joss sniffed, hawked in his throat, glanced around, and with no sidewalk to spit on, swallowed the phlegm. 'Uncle Brook sends his fondest regards. He and darlin' little Mo keeps me filled with the news of the family in view of the fact they do not wish to see their old father in his feeble old age. I am indeed a cursed and most unfortunate individual to be abandoned by me nearest and dearest.'

Keir ignored Joss's histrionics; they reminded him too much of the old days.

'Little Mo tells me Jenny's courting that nice all-American boy, Nick Barker, with a view to marrying him.'

'His name is Nicoli Barca and he's Sicilian,' Keir said tonelessly. He wasn't sure how much of his father's story was due to shock and loss of blood, how much due to illegal and caustic booze, or downright play-acting to gain sympathy. All he knew was that his father adopted the brogue of the old country whenever he hit the whiskey, despite Joss being three generations removed from his Irish roots, nor had he ever set foot in Ireland.

'Oh, you know about them then?'

'No, I don't know. I've just seen Jenny with him sometimes, that's all.'

'Where?' Joss scrubbed his itchy nose.

'Woolworth.'

'Woolworth?'

'Yeah. I guess he was buying her a Mafia wedding-ring.'

Unshaven and dirty, Joss looked every inch the dosser from Hell's Kitchen, which is what he had become. Keir was more than ever ashamed of him. Uncle Brook had promised he wouldn't supply Joss with any more bootleg hooch, but it looked as though Uncle Brook had reneged on his word.

His father's hand swabbed with antiseptic, Keir hesitated about plugging the nail-hole with *tulle gras* or anything else. Wounds like this one, with a high risk of tetanus infection, had to be left open. Knowing Joss, however, he wouldn't take care of his hand, the dirt would get in, and he'd catch something else equally poisonous.

'Is that it?' Joss asked, gazing at the palm of his left hand, bright red with a liberal painting of *lotio rubeus*. 'Aren't you going to bandage me up? Or am I not worthy of such consideration, darlin' son?'

Keir bandaged the hand. His anger mainly due to insoluble frustration where his father was concerned, Keir tried to keep his conflicting emotions in check; it was too late to start feeling sorry for Joss, the damage had been done a long time ago.

His father winced. 'To be sure, you're an ungentlemanly doctor, son. Can I go now?'

'No. You need a blood count, and to be kept under observation for at least twenty-four hours.'

'Why?'

'Because I say so.'

'You don't love me, do you, son?'

'I love you, Pa, but I don't like you.'

'Now there's a funny ting I don't understand for a moment.'

'You don't understand a lot of things.'

'I understand you don't want your old pa here.'

'Not when he's soused to the gills and a darn nuisance to everyone.'

'Ohhh! I see! But I shan't tell a soul I'm your old papa – not even the black one built like a coal-mine who shoved me in here.' Stiff silvery whiskers on Joss's chin looked like Chinese acupuncture needles. He grinned, pulled a wink, and put a finger against his lips. Then he whispered, 'I shall be the very soul of discretion. I wouldn't want to let down me golden boy whose become a real credit to his ma and Onk Brook. Now, where was I when you graduated from high school? And where was I when you took your place among the toffs at Cornell Medical College, eh boy? Where was your old pa but drunk beneath the Bowery bower, and here's wishin' he'd stayed there, eh-eh? Is that what's contained up here in your *educated* skull, eh boy?' He stretched up his good hand and tapped his son's forehead.

Sitting on the side of the high examination couch with his thin legs dangling in his shabby pants, string wound around his ankles to keep out the draught so that he resembled a baggy sack of horse manure, Joss's broken, dingy smile was idiotic when once, long ago, it had been full of charm and bright with hope. Oh God! Keir thought, in that ghastly moment of once more facing reality, is this really my father? What went wrong?

'I know what you're tinking and I'm not offended, indeed I'm not. I know I've been a failure to you and your ma, and to me darlin' Jenny. So I cannot blame any of you for tinking I'm a chicken's arse.' Joss blinked nervously. 'Never did you and Jenny much good when you were growing up to have a soak like me littering up the sofa in that shitty little apartment house at Jefferson, eh boy? Go on, get it off your chest. Tell me you hate me for ruining your life.'

'You're very drunk still, Pa.'

'That's unkind, son.'

'It happens to be the truth.'

'Then I shall not be taking up any more of your precious time with me drunken ways, *Doctor* Devlin, me darlin' boy. I shall not occupy a bed a more worthy occupant than I could be occupying this wintry night. Neither shall I consent to any more needles being stuck into me frail old body.'

'Then go home. I don't want to be had up for assault. Shall I call a cab?'

'Indeed I shall walk, if only to get the smell of this place out of me nostrils.'

'Please yourself.'

Shakily, Joss edged himself off the side of the couch. Shrugging off Keir's outstretched hand of assistance in a childishly defiant gesture, he said stubbornly, 'Goodnight, son. Remember, I may be *drunk*, but I still have a heart, which, being broken, doesn't alter the pride and the love I feel for me very own flesh and blood.'

That at least was true; Joss had only ever loved himself. Keir asked the trainee nurse to see the patient out.

Joss struggled into his dirty, bloodstained mackintosh, the nurse trying to help him.

Not much to keep out the cold, thought Keir, as he watched his father with his thickly-bandaged hand weave his way between the rows of patients in the reception area. A real hopeless case, and nothing to feel sorry for in the least, for Joss, now that he had two hands free again to hold a bottle, was no doubt heading straight for the nearest speakeasy.

But Keir's heart did give a little lurch of pain and guilt for having dismissed the old man so peremptorily; after all, Joss was still his father.

The next moment, he had shrugged off the feeling. Joss was a real Brodie, no two ways about it. He had had the same opportunities as Uncle Brook, yet Joss had chosen Skid Row instead. Neither would Keir easily forget the beatings and violence at Joss's hands, and the many ways in which he had humiliated Mother and Jenny. Life had been hell while he and Jenny had been growing up. But for the efforts of his mother, Nurse Lillian Wald, Jacob Schiff, and Uncle Brook, he would never have managed to break away, get out of the gutter, and make the grade through medical school.

But that was thankfully all behind him. He was twenty-three this year, an intermediate assistant doctor with only a couple of years more to do before he was fully qualified, no thanks to Joss. So he wasn't going to start feeling sorry for him now.

Intern Zimmerman slapped Keir between the shoulder blades. 'Hi, dreamer!'

Keir reached again for the Thermos and more black coffee. 'Where the hell have you been?'

'Flying ambulance – oh, don't look so dumb! This prize new idea of our little gods to put interns out on the streets like cops and hookers to treat for "shock on the spot" before a time lapse fouls up the chances of a patient's recovery.'

'Sounds like a good idea to me. Saves them all crowding in here at once.'

'And then I attended the *big* meeting.'

'What big meeting?'

'Environmental issues – lecture hall! Don't you ever read the notice board?'

'Never have time. Too busy running this place single-handed.'

Zimmerman grinned. 'Here's what was on the agenda then …'

'Don't bother.' Once he got going, Zimmerman always managed to sound like Cornell University's Medical Encyclopaedia. 'Coffee?' Keir cocked an eyebrow and the Thermos flask at Zimmerman.

Zimmerman shook his head. 'They're planning on *six and a half acres* of hospital complex between 68th and 70th Streets, wow! The new hospital will be affiliated to CUMC. Can you imagine all those miles of corridors to negotiate in an emergency? And supposing the elevators fail?'

Allan Zimmerman had rich and influential parents living in the best part of town – Park Avenue. They also had another magnificent mansion, with swimming pool and tennis court, out at Newport, Rhode Island, to which he, Keir, had been invited last summer. Zimmerman's father was a big noise in City Hall and the Democratic Party, with powerful friends in all walks of life, including the Board of Supervisors of City Hospital. The son knew things about hosptial policy before anyone else, and Keir guessed that if Zimmerman's old man could pull the right strings, the son would probably end up Head of Neurology even before he sat his final examinations.

Keir yawned. 'Or trying to find your way to bed when you're a walking dingbat.'

'My point exactly!'

Zimmerman managed to take the hint at last. He peered into Keir's bloodshot eyes. 'How much sleep have you had in the last two days?'

'None.'

'Then go to bed for a couple of hours. I'll cover for you.'

'Good idea.'

Zimmerman studied the casualty list in his hands. 'Who's this nut, Joe Hunt, who tried to crucify himself?'

'My pa.'

Intern Zimmerman was miles away when he asked, 'Does he need to be followed up in six weeks' time?'

'No. No follow up with us. He's a charity case for the Samaritan. He'll go there for his next booster shot. Goodnight.'

'Good – wait a minute, Devlin! You always made out your old man was dead.'

'So I did. How forgetful of me. But you know me and my big heart, Zim, always trying to pick up anything off the streets and point them towards a soup kitchen. So where's your Yiddish sense of humour?'

Intern Zimmerman grinned. 'Sonofabitch! I never know when you're goofing around, you big boso!' He gave Keir a hearty slap on the back.

Keir left the department. He hadn't been joking; far from it. He had been deadly serious and all screwed up inside because of it. But he had been far too tired and much too ashamed to explain to Zimmerman that just for a moment back there he had wavered, and had wanted to confess to still having that father he had long ago disowned.

Out in the street, the shock of the freezing night air took Keir's breath away. He rearranged his grey woollen scarf over the lower half of his face and thrust his gloved hands into the pockets of his overcoat. He simply had to see Uncle Brook; it was most important, so sleep would have to come later.

Keir decided to walk the six blocks to Gramercy and Lexington, where Uncle Brook Devlin and Marion Loupe, his common-law wife, had inherited a modest little hotel; or rather Marion had inherited it, Uncle Brook merely supervised the inheritance.

Brook's first wife, Agatha, a dull plain woman from Boston, had died childless six years ago. Rather than go through all the legal bother of marrying again, Brook lived with Marion without the blessing of the Roman Catholic Church.

Marion didn't hold much with religious rites, either. Marriage to a Tammany Hall boss, Micky (Chucko) Loupe, had put her off religious ceremonies and wedding-rings, which, once slipped on a woman's finger, couldn't easily be slipped off again, not even when a husband used brute force on his wife. When Chucko Loupe, a *padrone*, or Italian labour boss, was found at the bottom of the East River a year after his marriage, Joss had claimed the Mafia had done it, and serve Chucko right.

Joss had always blamed Chucko for his own downfall, and had shown scant remorse over his death. Uncle Brook, too, was a dark horse. Shortly after Chucko's death, he had moved into the *padrone's* place, bed, breakfast and Buick. Marion could not have raised any great objection to the arrangement because Uncle Brook had been living and loving there on Lexington very comfortably since Chucko's death.

Keir couldn't help reflecting that Uncle Brook had fallen on his feet, whereas Joss had fallen flat on his face and taken his family with him.

Family ties were the worst to contend with, for the simple reason that one could choose one's friends, but never one's relatives. Keir felt that his life would be less of a hassle and a cover-up-job when family skeletons stopped popping out of the closets. But he was too much of a coward to run away from those skeletons; they were *his* skeletons, a fact of life; there was no escape no matter how fast or how far he ran.

The poisoned roots of his family tree went back four generations to County Wexford. His great-grandfather, John Devlin, had left the little farming community of Ballyslaney after his wife and seven children had died of starvation and fever during the dreadful famine of 'forty-seven–'forty-eight. Like thousands of others seeking a new world, Great-Grandfather had left Ireland to start afresh in America. The Irish potato crop might have failed, but injustice, the deliberate political assassination of the Irish population while Irish wheat was still being shipped off to England, had been the real reason why Great-Grandfather Devlin had left Ballyslaney, never to return.

Aboard the *Sir Robert*, a Liverpool steamship carrying emigrants to America, John met an Irish girl from his home county. Connie Murphy and her parents were also escaping the effects of the failed potato harvest that had brought disaster to Ireland. With her parents' blessing and the captain's offices, John and Connie were married aboard ship. Determined to start over, and make a better life together in a new country, they stepped off the *Sir Robert* at Castle Garden, New York, and within a year Great-Grandfather had started a second family on 116th Street.

Grandfather Patrick Devlin was the first generation of Devlins to be born on American soil. Pat, it appeared, had been the handsome, shrewd and charming one, for he eventually married a refined and educated lady named Joyce Hunter Hamilton, the pampered only child of a father who owned a fur import-export business and a boat on the East River. When Joyce's father died without a son and heir, Grandfather Pat inherited his father-in-law's business, and the boat. The year by now was 1879, and he and Joyce had two sons, Josslyn Hunter aged ten and Brooklyn Hunter, eight. The boys were given the very best in life by their proud parents.

When his father died, Joss, in turn, inherited everything. He was now the owner of a profitable little empire based on expensive and exclusive garments for those who had the vanity, as well as the wherewithal, to pay: it couldn't go wrong. Upon this good, firm foundation, Joss had much to give his own family, for by now he had met and married Michelle Deauvier, a pretty Swiss-French girl whose stepfather (himself in the fur trade) had introduced her to young, handsome Joss with so much going for him. Jennifer Ann was born in 1897, and himself, Keiren Hunter, three years later.

65

The wheel of fortune during the first decade of the new century then started to turn drastically against Joss and his brother, Brook. Those were crucial years, too, of Keir and Jenny's childhood. Tammany bosses started interfering and demanding 'protection money', outrageous legislative dues from Hunter-Devlin Bros. Fur Traders of New York City. Now Joss and Brook had for years associated themselves with Irish-American nationalist policies, first belonging to the revolutionary Clan na Gael, and then, in 1903, the Gaelic American. Clan na Gael, through the Gaelic American organization, mounted a campaign against the British Empire, against Home Rule, and against the Irish Parliamentary Party itself. Money contributed from the company for the relief of Irish refugees began to find its way back to Ireland and, unbeknown to Joss and Brook (as they both later pledged in an American court), into the hands of the Irish Republican Army.

Joss took to drinking heavily and left Brook to deal with the threats of corrupt officials, and one boss in particular, Micky Loupe.

One day, the New York Customs and Excise Department made an unscheduled inspection of the Hunter-Devlin warehouse fronting the East River. They examined the Devlin brothers' new boat, *Hunter II*, named after their father as well as the fur trade. The boat was essential to the fur business, because it conveyed the uncured pelts from the north, down the Hudson River to the Devlin factory, where they were cured, cut, and finally contracted out to immigrant sweatshop workers from the Garment District, who made the furs up into luxury items destined for top Fifth Avenue stores. Concealed under all the furs aboard the *Hunter II*, the Customs and Excise officials uncovered a huge cache of arms due to be loaded aboard the *S.S. Connemara* in New York harbour. The *Connemara* was bound for Ireland.

Joss had been sentenced to three years hard labour for the illegal smuggling of arms and, according to City Hall, operating without a current trading licence. Brook had been treated less harshly with a suspended sentence and a severe warning, but the fines imposed on the company had been crippling. The family boat was impounded, and the fur business had to shut down by orders of City Hall. Someone wanted to see the end of Hunter Devlin Bros., Fur Traders of New York City, no reasons given. Perhaps Joss had been setting himself up to be what Tammany Hall didn't want, a threat to their monopolistic control within the city: perhaps Brook had been doing the underhand thing with those guns destined for Ireland – without Joss's knowledge – and Chucko had found out. Keir, from his remote position in time and distance, could only conjecture upon Joss's ultimate downfall.

The family fortune having disappeared almost over-night, they were forced to sell Grandfather Patrick's big house on the corner of Grand Street and East River Park, to move into a cheaper tenement block in the Lower East Side, on Jefferson Street.

Before his imprisonment, Joss's drinking had been bad enough, but after his release in 1916, the year of European turmoil, of Sinn Fein tearing Ireland apart in the Easter Uprising, of the drowning of Lord Kitchener, Secretary of War when the *Hampshire* struck a mine while on its way to Russia, and the dreadful battle of the Somme, Joss's own battle with himself took a turn for the worse. Prison had only served to accelerate his downhill slide.

Had his father been a less sensitive and more resilient man like Brook, Keir couldn't help feeling that Joss would have tried to pick himself up and start afresh. But he did not. Broken, embittered, disillusioned, Joss gave in more and more to the demon drink. Keir's mother had had to take a job to feed the family, and to pay the accumulating bills.

At first, Michelle did a little typewriting for Nurse Lillian Wald, who lived in the same apartment block, at number twenty-seven, Jefferson Street. Miss Wald had trained as a nurse. She had seen the suffering of the immigrants converging upon the Lower East Side after 1914. Overcrowding in cheap shanty-built tenements with-out bathrooms and lavatories, without kitchens, without playgrounds for the children, without the language to communicate – all of them, even the children, working twelve and fifteen hours a day to survive: for America was not such a golden dream after all. But, instead of moving out when less fortunate immigrants were moving into a district, which seventy years before was a prosperous ward owned by the great names of American history, the Rutgers and De Lanceys, where affluent merchants like Patrick Hunter Devlin, and famous sea captains of the day had resided in elegant mansions close to South Street and the East River, Lilly Wald had stayed.

Moreover, she had decided to do something about the new immigrant poverty in her area. She started a welfare nursing agency which went from strength to strength. In a few short years, Nurse Lilly had somewhere in the region of thirty nurses on her books. They provided home care, friendship and comfort for the sick, poor, elderly and dying, and they made arrangements for anyone requiring medical attention in hospital, but who was too poor to afford it, to be admitted into charity hospitals under the Settlement Scheme.

Lilly had next approached the Jewish millionaire philanthropist, Jacob Schiff, for funds to endow medical charities in the Lower East Side. Jacob Schiff surpassed Lilly Wald's wildest dreams by giving vast sums of money to keep the welfare organization going, for it could only function to improve the lot of poor and ignorant immigrants out of private funds. He also bought properties on Henry and Montgomery Streets, which he donated for the use of the Lower East Side Social Settlement Programme.

Michelle helped in the organizatiorn of all this work. She and Lilly Wald were two of a kind, compassionate, hard-working, and indestructible women who only saw the positive side of life. Keir, while idolizing his mother, also retained the deepest respect and regard for the energetic, caring fifty-six-year-old nurse who had done so much to ease the plight of the East European immigrants, yet had still found time to lend a helping hand to his own family.

To supplement the family income when Joss couldn't find employment or was too soused to work, Nurse Wald had found Keir a portering job during weekend and school vacations at the Medical Centre on Henry and Montgomery Streets. She knew how badly he wanted to be a doctor, but that his family background and lack of funds (never mind their past glory, it was the *present* that mattered) remained the drawback. Boys from working-class and trading-class families, no matter how bright or industrious they might be, were excluded by the 'elitists' who ran the American medical profession. Nevertheless, she told Keir not to give up hope, she would speak to Jacob Schiff on his behalf.

The next thing he knew was that he had been selected as 'a special scholar' to benefit from further education under the Jacob Schiff Educational Alliance. Although the Educational Alliance had been set up primarily to help non-English speaking immigrant communities, especially Jews, Keir discovered that it was *who* you knew in the end, not *what* you knew that mattered most in life. He, a white American Gentile, a Catholic, was being helped along by Lilly's patron, a Jew. How and why, he never questioned. He was only grateful for people like Lilly Wald and Jacob Schiff, who did not let social, religious or class barriers prejudice them from humanitarian acts to all concerned.

A special scholar was required to attend high school for four years, followed by a two-year course at college. As he wanted to go in for medicine, he would receive instruction in biology, chemistry and physics. If he acquitted himself well and passed the necessary examinations laid down by the American General Education Board, in the year 1920 he would be eligible to enter Cornell University Medical School, another foundation endowed by a capitalist philanthropist, Ezra Cornell, a friend of Jacob.

Keir managed to acquit himself admirably and not let the side down – his mother, Uncle Brook, Lilly Wald, and above all Jacob Schiff, who had made it all possible in the first place. But the irony of it all was that in 1920, just as he was taking his place in the medical profession by scholarship and not through money, name or fame, a battle sprang up between the corporate philanthropy of Rockefeller, John Hopkins, and Carnegie, and the general public, who wanted to see such charitable foundations, and the necessary evils that went with private selection and class distinction, abolished. One more year, and he might not have needed Jacob Schiff or anyone else!

Yet, having scraped in by the skin of his teeth, the shattering costs of his medical training at Cornell to be met by the generosity of Jacob Schiff's scholarship programme, Keir was still indebted to Jacob and Lilly even while training to be a doctor became a heavy burden. Had he not mortgaged his soul to Jacob Schiff and Lilly Wald? And had he not had to work twice as hard as anyone else in order to prove himself in everyone's eyes?

He was the proverbial poor boy who had made good, but while he didn't care two hoots about that, what he did care about was having a father like Joss lurking in the background. Keir felt restricted, suffocated and at times demoralized when he thought about his weak, gutless father and what he had done to them as a family. The last thing on earth Keir wanted was that he, Mother, and Jenny should be looked down on as being 'shanty Irish' by fellows like Zimmerman who had reached Cornell via birthright, not brains. So he had kept the seamier side of his life to himself, and had survived on a lot of little white lies about his father, former Company Director of the well-established and well-respected firm of Hunter-Devlin Bros. Fur Traders of New York City, having passed on. And even though Joss was no criminal, merely the 'fall guy' whose love for his native land and the desire to see the Irish people set free from the yoke of British Imperialism had been his undoing, the fact remained, under the 1920 Firearms Act, which stipulated that 'No firearms or ammunition may be possessed by anybody unless he holds a certificate granted by the chief police officer of the police district where he resides', the Hunter-Devlin brothers did not hold such a certificate. Further disregard of the Firearms Act had provoked Joss's prison sentence on the whim of a corrupt city official because, 'such a certificate will only be granted when the applicant satisfies the police that he has a good reason for wanting a firearm and that no danger to the public safety or the public peace is apprehended'. Arms for Ireland had been interpreted as being in breech of public peace. And that terrible fear about the truth being one day disclosed, as well as fear of upper-class condescension or, even worse, their pity, or that he might, after all, be thrown out of Cornell because of his unsavoury background, had made Keir very tight-lipped, solitary and cynical: Joss, because of his prison record, had taken the gilt off the gingerbread.

Those then were the skeletons in his closet. They had shaped his life and his character and his personal relationships, the lush of a father, the shady uncle living with an ex-gangster's moll, a mother and sister keeping a low profile for his sake down in the Lower East Side, and oh, how are the mighty fallen! And if it wasn't so goddamn tragic, it would have been funny.

Keir was so tired, so deep in introspective thought as he spanned the lost years of his youth, that when he stepped off the sidewalk to cross Fifth Avenue, the sudden noisy braking of motor cars, honking of klaxons, and the hubbub of shouting voices made him leap back in alarm. But he wasn't the one responsible for bringing Fifth Avenue traffic to an abrupt halt.

Keir looked up in time to see the sodden grey hump of a man's body being tossed into the air as lightly as a paper bag caught on a puff of breeze. It had bounced off the bonnet of a car, only to be flung down twenty feet further along the street. After the impact, the car swerved, accelerated, and had sped off up Fifth Avenue.

The body of the victim was curled into a foetal position, as though comfortably asleep in the gutter. Keir recognized the dazzlingly-white bandaged hand like a gentle paw in front of the man's face, and the blow to his senses was so great, he suddenly felt as though he, too, had been struck from life to become as amorphous as that thing that had once been human. The violent contraction of his stomach muscles made him turn aside quickly.

A brewer's cart hauled by huge dray horses, since Prohibition conveying sacks of coal, came from the direction of Union Square and turned out of East 17th Street. Sergeant O'Reilly, on a late street beat, paused long enough from his whistle-blowing to frighten to death the driver of the draycart by telling him to back off, otherwise he'd book him for obstructing the public highway with an illegal beer-wagon.

'Hoy there – hoy *you*! Yes, you, Intern Devlin! Don't make out you don't see me, or what's going on. Get your medical ass over here and see what you can do for this guy. Does he need the hospital or the morgue – looks like the guy's already been in the hospital, eh, Doc, and was figuring on another free meal ticket at the morgue?' O'Reilly's jaw chomped gum between whistle-blowing and wisecracks.

Blood, black and sticky as treacle, oozed slowly from Joss's left ear. Keir asked someone, he didn't know who, to find something to cover the body. A woman handed over a brown knitted shawl and Keir covered his father with it. 'He's dead, Sergeant.'

'Okay, thanks Doc.' O'Reilly gave another shrill blast on his whistle and almost swallowed his chewing gum. 'You there, Pellati, get this stiff to the morgue, and get some details on him. I also want details on the car and the driver who did this hit and run. No ruddy traffic moves till we get some witnesses to the accident. Anyone see what happened? How about you, Doc?'

'No. Can't say I did – bit too far away.' Keir, on his haunches beside Joss's dead body, felt sick.

O'Reilly bent over and peered at Keir under the peak of his black police cap. 'You all right, Doc? You look a bit green around the gills. I know the feeling. Too much work and not enough shuteye, so, even when a guy's used to the sight of bloody stiffs, the last one always gets him right in the gut.'

'Yeah – you're right, Sergeant.' Keir got to his feet.

He wanted to run as fast as he could. Instead, he walked away.

The clientele of The Leprechaun Hotel were usually commercial travellers and insurance salesmen whose expense accounts were picked up by their respective firms. On most nights, Marion Loupe, a tiny bleached blonde with a tender heart, would be at the hotel bar as agony aunt to men from places like Detroit, Buffalo, Chicago and Pittsburg. All of them were trying desperately to drum up business, but finding New York a very tough nut to crack.

On the lookout for pretty and entertaining girls, preferably both, to take away the rough edges of the competitive rat race or the tedious monotony of their dull lives, an introduction to the bright city lights was what these travelling men required during their brief stopover: never mind the little lady back home. Marion understood this need in a lonely man far away from Head Office: it was natural. A thoroughly nice and uncomplicated person herself, she was in the business to offer what hospitality she could. She ran an agency, though not one on the same lines as Nurse Wald's wholesome establishment. She did, however, make a stipulation. No hanky-panky inside her hotel. Her's was a strict, legit escort agency and nothing more. What anyone did outside her hotel was their business, she wanted no trouble from the police department for running a house of ill repute. Marion had her code of ethics, too.

She had just provided a traveller in bakelite wares with an escort for the evening, and she watched the couple, arm in arm, smilingly depart the hotel. Perhaps now, thought Marion happily as she patted her trim blonde shingle, she could go to bed with a cup of hot chocolate and a romantic novel, which was what she really enjoyed last thing at night. Brook and his pals would be playing poker in the back room, so he wouldn't come to bed until the early hours, that was for sure.

She had just put the green night shades over the desk lamps and placed the notice on the reception desk, 'Ring Bell For Attention', hoping that old Fogarty, the night porter who pretended to be as deaf as a Mormon at an anti-polygamy rally so that he could sleep all night, would answer the bell, when a young man burst into the lobby. The revolving doors behind him continued to whiz round at the dizzy speed of a carousel.

'Keir!' Marion slid out like a dainty silver fish from behind the mahogany reception desk. Looking like a child up against him, she took Keir's arm, her smooth, bland face suddenly changing to frightened little puckers. 'What's wrong, feller?'

'Brook – I must speak to him.'

Marion did some quick thinking. Brook wouldn't like to be disturbed by Keir, not without warning, and Keir was obviously in a bad way. 'Come in here,' she pulled him by the sleeve into her private parlour behind the reception desk. 'Sit down ...'

Marion was flabbergasted when Keir, whom she had come to regard as a great, hulking, self-assured lady-killer, sat down and burst into tears. Elbows on his knees, gloved hands covering his stricken face, Keir didn't just weep, he practically suffocated in an orgy of emotion. The tears poured through his fingers and huge sobs wracked him. He gulped between his sobs, 'I – I left him, I couldn't help it. I just didn't want to be associated with him, so I cut and run, leaving him dead in the gutter – oh, Jesus!'

'I'll fetch Brook – look here, honey – don't tell a soul, but it'll do you the world of good.' Marion bent down and drew back the edge of the carpet. From under a loose floorboard, she lifted a bottle. She splashed some whiskey into a glass and thrust it between Keir's damp, woolly fingers. Then she shoved the bottle back into its hiding-place and left the room.

She knew Keir would feel awful for having broken down in front of her. She couldn't tell Brook his nephew was crying like a baby, that would be too humiliating for Keir. She felt like crying herself when she had seen him just now with all his defences down. She had wanted to gather him into her arms, smooth his hair, croon, 'there-there honey, it's going to be all right, Auntie Mo's here', but she knew he would simply hate that. So she had left him alone to get over the reason for such grief: and he would probably never shed another tear in his life.

There was always something so infinitely touching about a big man weeping his heart out, thought Marion. It was worse than watching a child cry. And that had been no Irish weep either, Keir had acted as though his heart was broken. 'Come quick,' was all she said to Brook when she interrupted his poker game. 'Keir wants you.'

'*Shite*! What does he want at this time of night, Mo?'

She shrugged. 'Ask him yourself. I'm off to bed.'

Keir drank the whiskey in one gulp: Irish whiskey of the very best water. He wondered how his uncle managed to get his hands on it when the Eighteenth Amendment was so stringent. Uncle Brook had obviously been supplying Joss with some of the stuff. Keir marvelled at his uncle's acquisitive powers: expensive furs, arms for Ireland, Tammany hotels, the newest motor car, other men's wives, Prohibition booze, and always on the right side of the law. He wondered how Uncle Brook managed to get away with it. Poor old Joss had always been the miserable scapegoat, while Brook was a real Alibi Ike.

Keir took out his handkerchief and blew his nose loudly. What an idiot Marion must think him!

He looked around her little 'parlour' and shuddered as he always did when he saw the flocked fleur-de-lys paper, the New Orleans bordello decor, and the cheap imitation Art Nouveau lamps. All genuine bakelite, as opposed to genuine opaline. Tiffany, Lalique, or the dime-and-nickel store, it was all the same to Marion. A terrific little person who could be relied on never to ask questions or give away any secrets, Mo had the most abysmal taste. Culture didn't enter into it, only bizarre visual effects. You only had to step into her hotel lobby to feel yourself being welcomed by the red plush throat of an obliging rhinoceros. No, he much preferred his mother's unpretentious apartment on Jefferson Street, for the bare bones of an honest poverty somehow had its dignity.

Keir put his hand to his head, the nausea he had experienced when squatting beside Joss returning.

He got up, opened the door, and on the threshold bumped into his uncle smoking a Havana.

'What the …' Brook, pushed rudely out of the way, watched his nephew fleeing across the lobby in the direction of the lavatories.

Brook shrugged, went inside the parlour, shut the door and helped himself to a large glass of whiskey from Marion's secret store. He added a dash of soda to his glass and then sat down on the plush sofa.

Nothing at all like his brother, Brook was a big, hearty, handsome man of fifty-two, with a head of hair that was smooth, dark and glossy. Joss, shrivelled and stooped for years, as though he bore all the troubles of the world upon his shoulders, had hair as grey and sparse as his pockets. The shining glow that Brook always managed to reflect, even in his big, broad smile, appeared to have a lot to do with a liberal amount of brilliantine. Brook and his haircream positively *oozed* that easy-going though somewhat slippery hold he retained on life. His sartorial tastes, too, were very much on the lines of Marion's questionable interior decor. The check of his broad-lapelled suit was loud. His socks and tie matched perfectly his silk shirt in a curious shade of magenta. The handkerchief folded in a neat pyramid peeping from his breast pocket was a fresh summer-green. Brook's large feet were encased in blinding two-tone, tan and white patent leather. The gold identity bracelet on his wrist was heavy and ostentatious, as was the ring in the design of a skull and crossbones on the little finger of his left hand. The same ugly motif was on his tiepin and cuff-links, while the expensively elegant Rolex he proudly sported on his right wrist only accentuated the confusion in his dress.

Brook impatiently puffed his Havana. He wanted to get back to his poker game: he was on a winning streak tonight. He wondered why Keir wanted to see him. His nephew *never* graced The Leprechaun lest he could help it.

When Keir opened the door and sheepishly entered, Brook could tell from his pale, tight face something was very wrong indeed. 'What's up son?'

'Pa's dead.'

Brook held still, his knuckles wrapped around his glass tensing. 'How?'

'Automobile accident.'

'Where?'

'Fifth Avenue.'

'When?'

'Half an hour ago. It was a hit and run.'

Brook motioned to a chair, his heavy black brows drawn together in a frown. 'Sit down son, you want a drink?'

'No thanks, I've had one.' Keir didn't mention that he'd just thrown up on the whiskey Marion had given him, black coffee being his limit of intoxication.

He sat down opposite his uncle who asked, 'Deliberate?'

'Any reason to think so?' Keir parried.

Brook shrugged indifferently. 'No reason. Why should

anyone want to do in a lush like Joss with nothing to offer? Someone panicked when they saw the body lying in the street and decided to beat it fast. People do funny things under pressure.'

'Yeah – I was on my way here to ask you if you were supplying Pa with booze to keep him happy, and if you were, then not to. Now it's too late.'

'Me? Now would I be so stupid as to let him get his hands on whiskey when the stuff's been his ruination and our damnation? I might like an occasional drink myself, as you well know, but there's moderation in everything. Something your pa never learnt. I certainly wouldn't let him get his hands on the stuff at my expense. Or you and your ma's, come to that.'

Keir wanted to believe his uncle. 'Joss said he was here. That you and Mo told him everything about Ma, Jenny, and me.'

'Joss always was a cool liar and a short-sighted stymie. You oughtta know that by now, son. I promise you, I haven't had dealings with him for years, not officially that is. I've seen him wandering around all over town, sure; who hasn't? But he never came here, and never interfered with Mo and me. Ever since his release from prison, Joss has pretended I don't exist. He sure hated me, your poor old pa, and for what reason, I'll never know. Anyhow, when did he spin you this yarn about coming here?'

'Tonight. He said he'd been putting up a shelf for Nurse Lilly, when he knocked the nail through his hand. I was on duty when he walked in drunk as a skunk.'

'He was never anywhere near Lilly's place this afternoon. I know, because I was there myself.' Brook took the green silk handkerchief from his breast pocket and blew his nose like a foghorn. 'He always was a cool liar, but I don't like to hear he's dead.' He shoved the handkerchief back untidily.

Keir's face felt bristly, unclean, his eyelids like sticky fly-papers with the flies still stuck to them. Sick and guilty in the knowledge that he was partially responsible for his father's untimely death, he knew he could have prevented it had he insisted that Joss remain at the hospital under observation. Joss had been too weak, feeble, and too damn

pie-eyed to go wandering alone on the streets after he'd
lost so much blood.

Keir realized the truth too late. He knew of some of his
father's activities, because Jenny, from time to time, got to
hear things about Joss through her welfare work. Joss had
been evicted from his one room in Bowery the last time
he'd heard anything about him from Jenny. Since then,
Joss had taken to living in a dirty little basement between
35th and 42nd Streets, near the pushcart market known
as Paddy's Market. It was an area designated Hell's Kitchen
because of the gangster element found on that side west of
Ninth Avenue. Joss, frozen stiff, hungry, friendless and
mindless, had, no doubt, deliberately nailed his own hand,
or got one of his dosser friends to do the job for him, so
that he had an excuse to go to the hospital, where he knew
his son would be on duty. It had been a cry for help, that
was all, a cry which he, the son, had deliberately ignored.

Keir put his head in his hands: as if such a negligent act
as dismissing into the freezing cold night a sick old man,
who had bled so much, was not in itself bad enough, he
had compounded his culpability by turning his back and
walking away from the dead body of that sick old man, his
own father. It was hard, too, to reconcile that pathetic
creature in the accident department of City Hospital just
now, to the violent and despicable father who had so often
beaten him, first with his fists and then, when he had
grown bigger and heftier than Joss, with an iron poker:
hard to believe that the man who had so often abused and
humiliated Mother and Jenny was the sad, dead sack lying
in the roadway …

Keir could remember even now the horror, the
humiliation, the fear that Jenny and he had experienced
whenever Joss staggered in after one of his abandoned
drinking bouts. Or the days between, with Joss sleeping off
the effects. Or Joss making amends by promising never to
touch the stuff again in his fawning, cringing, sickening
bid for forgiveness and affection. Jenny and he had been
too afraid and too disgusted with Joss to grant him
anything. Keir, even to this day, remembered the time he
had lain on his bed, staring up at the ceiling, praying that
his parents would get a divorce or Joss would fall down the

stairs and break his neck, just so that they could get some peace around the place. Keir did not know which had been worse, those nerve-wracking truces with Joss shaking with delirium tremens and lying around the living-room in a docile stupor, wondering when he would be sober enough to be able to walk to the nearest bar again without falling down four flights of stairs, or Joss at the height of one of his blind drunk, violent turns.

Nurse Lilly had seen, heard, and knew everything. She had been perturbed, as well as understanding. Then Joss, in one of his violent moods one day, went too far. He struck Michelle so hard she fell and banged her head on a piece of furniture. Lilly had thought his mother had a fractured skull and had called the police. It had all been so shameful, so sordid, and so unnecessary. Awful! Keir even now shuddered at those soul-destroying memories of his unsettled and unhappy boyhood.

Joss had been charged with assaulting his family while under the influence of drink, and ordered to appear before the City Magistrate. Michelle had mercifully recovered, having sustained nothing more than severe concussion. Joss, of course, hadn't been aware of what he was doing, or the extent of his problem. He had been ordered to receive treatment at a rehabilitation clinic for alcoholics. Joss had attended six sessions and then hadn't bothered to turn up for any more.

It was very, *very* hard, even now, to relate that terrifying and uncaring father to the one tonight, unable to ask for help other than by nailing himself to a board: and even in that last measure Joss had resorted to violence, the easy way out.

'Hey, son!' Uncle Brook's voice sounded concerned. 'You okay?'

Keir, carried away by the force of his feelings, looked up then. 'Sorry – I was thinking. What were you saying?'

'It'll keep – why don't you go upstairs and get some kip. There's always the boxroom if all the hotel rooms are full. You look dead beat, son.'

'No. I've got to see Ma.'

'I can tell her about Joss.'

'I'd rather tell her myself. Thanks all the same, Brook.'

Keir got up, and went out into the lobby. He took his coat and scarf from the coatstand where he had left them when he came out of the washroom. While he was putting on his coat, the revolving doors started whirling, and Sergeant O'Reilly stepped into the lobby.

'Thought I'd find you here. What the merry shit are you playing at, *Intern* Devlin?'

For no apparent reason, Sergeant O'Reilly was habitually aggressive towards everyone.

'Look Jim, fight with me tonight, okay?' Brook put a placating hand on Sergeant O'Reilly's shoulder, but O'Reilly shrugged it off.

'Swell! But first I want to know what wise guy's little game is.'

'Give him a break, Jim, and come back tomorrow. Can't you see he's out on his feet?'

'All I can see is a stiff on a slab identified by his welfare card, issued in the 20th Precinct district, as being a certain Joe Hunt, unemployed! Name ring a bell? Okay, since you both look as guilty as a couple of Maggie Rabs when the cat's got her tongue, I'll fill in the rest of the picture. Joe Hunt turns out to be one Josslyn Hunter Devlin, when the records are properly checked, capeesh? And this ...' Sergeant O'Reilly slapped a photograph down on the reception desk, 'Funny coincidence, huh? Now we all know how many friggin' Devlins live in New York City, don't we? And without putting too fine a point on it, seems to me this one fits the picture nicely.' He jabbed a finger into Keir's chest.

Keir and Brook stared at the faded sepia picture, cracked and dog-eared. It had obviously been looked at many, many times. Keir couldn't say anything. It was a picture of him taken on the day of his high school graduation.

'Recognize yourself, Devlin? Course you do! That's you, your ma, your sister, Nurse Lilly Wald, and guess who else? Yeah, Jacob Schiff! Millionaire Yid wonderboy gazing in awe at his blue-eyed sockdollager. Proud of yourself, huh, Doc? Wonder where your pa was on that day? A stiff like you'd hoped? Nope, I don't reckon so any more. Guess where we found the picture? In the morgue, taken from the pocket of the old dosser knocked down in Fifth Avenue, the drunk you were so running shit-scared of, you couldn't even own up to him being your poor old pa, huh, college boy?'

Sergeant O'Reilly chomped gum and when Keir still didn't say a word, said, 'Chrissakes Devlin! That was your old man ten-pinned in front of your nose by another goddamn lush driving at some crackpot speed. Why the hell we passed the Eighteenth Amendement when there are more drunks now on the streets of New York than ever there was before Prohibition, beats me!'

'Listen Jim, let me explain …'

'Shove it, Brook! I don't want any of your big-uncle excuses. Not this time. College boy here is educated and ugly enough to speak for himself. Come on, Devlin, give. What's your reason for denying your old man? Ashamed of him, huh? Didn't want anyone to find out about him? Kept it all to yourself all through your fancy medical school in case you'd be called shanty Irish? Afraid of what little rich boy Zimmerman might think of poor boy Devlin with a pa whose nothing but a gimp from Hell's Kitchen, not to mention a lug from the slammer? So what? But Sergeant Jim O'Reilly ain't so dumb, even though he might look it. I've done a lotta living on the streets, boy, and I know a thing or two about pride. *Pride!* The making and the breaking of a man. So I know why you kept your mouth shut just now. Yeah, I think I do.' Sergeant O'Reilly waited for Keir to defend himself.

'Cut it out, Jim. Can't we go some place else and talk quietly?'

'Brook, I thought I told you to can it? We'll be talking later. You never told me you had a brother called Joe Hunt, a bum pushcart fink from Paddy's Market, not to mention an ex-con. I only ever got to hear about *Josslyn Hunter Devlin*, big boss of a grand fur house bought out after the big boss died.'

Incensed by O'Reilly's bogside tongue, Brook turned on his heel and disappeared into Marion's parlour, making sure he slammed the door in O'Reilly's face: and when *Sergeant* Jim O'Reilly next came to him for any special favours, he'd trap him in the revolving doors of his own mouth!

'Let me tell you something, son.' Sergeant O'Reilly turned his attention back to Keir and continued pedantically, 'Nobody's going to blame you for not wanting to own up to having a lush for a father. But I'm sure as hell going to book you for holding out on me when you were a witness to the accident. I *want* that guy in his fancy automobile who knocked down your old pop, and I'm going to book him for manslaughter so's he don't kill no one else on *my* beat, capeesh?' Sergeant O'Reilly smacked the palm of his hand down flat on the polished surface of the reception desk and made Fogarty in the corner leap up in fright. 'You gotta good look at things. I want you to tell me what you saw.'

'You and Pellati were there, Sergeant,' Keir said calmly. Listening to O'Reilly rabbiting away had left him totally unmoved. O'Reilly tried it on. He delighted in imposing on everyone, scared-stiff immigrants especially, his tough Brooklyn fly-cop image by bullying them, making them feel that the only righteous law-abiding citizen in town was Sergeant Jim O'Reilly, recently promoted to clean up the streets around 14th Precinct. 'You must have seen as much as I.'

'Don't give me any of your clever lip, Devlin, otherwise I'll take you apart right now. Pellati and me were busy evicting a couple of hookers from one of the big stores and so we weren't there to get the number of the car involved in the accident.'

'On what charge are you going to book me?'

'Obstructing the law.'

'Not a chance. Just because I didn't tell you Joss was my father?'

'Right!'

'Won't hold up in a court of law. But you're quite right, I was ashamed to admit it, and that's why I backed off, chicken-shit-scared. So okay, it was a blue Rolls Royce.'

Sergeant O'Reilly's eyes narrowed to mere slits of malice. 'A blue Rolls Royce? You pulling my tit?'

'Now why should I want to do that? A blue Rolls Royce, even without a number plate, should be easy to find. I hope you also find the chauffeur. Then you can book *him* on a homicide charge, too. Joss might not have amounted to much when he was alive, but at least he died right royally. I'm sure he'll be tickled pink to know he was killed by a shiny blue Rolls Royce, and not a common black Ford. Joss, by the way, deliberately stepped out in front of the Rolls. It wasn't the chauffeur's fault, he couldn't avoid hitting him.' Keir flung his scarf around his neck. 'Now if you'll excuse me, I've got to tell my mother her husband's dead, and then I've got to get back on duty.'

'I want you down at the morgue to identify the body.'

'I thought you'd already done that.'

'Listen good, *Intern* Devlin, I need to establish certain facts from the next-of-kin. Personal identification.'

'Uncle Brook is Joss's brother. I'm sure he qualifies as next-of-kin.'

'Nerks Devlin! You're a real asshole yourself.'

'Like father, like son, eh, O'Reilly?'

Sergeant O'Reilly, his elbows leaning on the reception desk behind him, his jaw moving like a robot's, watched Keir cross the lobby towards the revolving doors. A slow calculating grin spread across his broad flat features. 'How's that sweetie pie sister of yours, Doc?'

'Fine.'

'Married yet?'

'No.'

'Shame! Say, all-American college boy,' he came up off the reception desk, and readjusted his police cap smartly, 'if you want a lift in a common black two-sixty-dollar Ford, Pellati and me'll drive you to your ma's.'

'Thanks, but I'll take the subway.'

'Aw shit, listen here, Devlin. I know your momma and sister live with the Wops and Yids down in the Lower East Side. But I'm no nobby. It's not where a guy's come from, but where he's going to that's important. I'm real sorry it had to be your pa on Fifth Avenue. It kindda fouls up the clean-cut Cornell image you and Onk Brook have been fostering all these years, telling everyone your rich old man, heir to an empire, Hunter-Devlin Bros., Fur Traders of New York City, with a boat on the East River, was dead and buried at sea, or some such crap. But if you still want it kept that way, Joe Hunt is fine by me, and Josslyn Hunter Devlin stays dead and buried in the East River.'

'Joss *was* dead and buried till tonight. Ask Brook for the lulus you cop off him for any special favours. And thanks for nothing, Sarge.'

His mother had the chain on the door.

'Ma, it's me.'

'Keir, goodness – at this time of night!' She struggled with the latch-chain and opened the door.

His sister, Jenny, tying the sash of her dressing-gown, appeared behind her mother. 'Who is it? Oh, it's him. It's lovely to see you, Doc, but what a time to make a house call!'

'*Chéri*, is something wrong?' His mother stood on tiptoe to kiss his cold, bristly cheek. 'You look and smell awful. Did you come on the subway, darling?' She led the way into the cramped kitchen.

Jenny began making coffee, yawning sleepily while it percolated.

Keir took his place at the table, but waited until Jenny had set down three steaming mugs of coffee on the table before saying, 'I came to tell you Pa's dead. It was a traffic accident. He stepped off the sidewalk without paying attention to where he was going.'

'Oh no!' His mother stared at him with wide, disbelieving eyes.

Jenny flicked back her braid of dark hair over her shoulder and said defiantly, 'I can't say I'm sorry. In fact, all I feel is a great sense of relief.'

Presently, as though she hadn't heard Jenny's remark, his mother said, 'You know, Keir, New York is a great city if one makes the grade. *Success* is what America is all about. If you don't succeed first time round, nobody gives you a second chance. So you've just got to give it all you've got in round one, *chéri*. Your father couldn't. Even though he had such a wonderful start, Joss went under because he was too afraid to pitch out with the big guys. Don't *ever* be afraid of the big guys, Keir. You're as good as any of them, and better! Get in there and show Cornell what you're made of, son.'

'Don't upset yourself, Ma.'

84

'I always knew Joss would get himself run over one day, if his liver didn't rot first. I used to see him weaving in and out of the traffic on the main streets as though he didn't care one way or another about getting knocked down.'

Michelle Deauvier Devlin picked up the mug of hot coffee, the expression in her blue eyes far away as she stared over the rim. 'It's funny, you know, but suddenly I can only remember the good times – he was handsome, your pa, and always neat, always very jolly, always wanting to do what was right and best for the family as well as the business, not to mention anyone remotely connected with Ireland. The trouble was he couldn't handle the aggravation from Tammany Hall. Life has to be tackled head on when the going gets rough, and Joss couldn't do that.' Michelle was not condemning, merely trying to fathom how it had all gone so badly wrong – but now, what did it matter any more about the hard times? Only the good times and their outcome were important. She had Joss to thank for her two precious children. Michelle set down the coffee mug and went into her bedroom and closed the door.

Keir said to Jenny, 'I hear you're getting married to Nick Barco.'

She scoffed at that. 'Who told you such rubbish?'

'News has a habit of getting around.'

'Then you heard wrong. Nicky is just a good friend. He buys me beefsteak and potato chips in a restaurant sure, but only when he or I feel the need to talk. I nursed his mother when she was dying and so he thinks he owes me, that's all. But listen good, Brother Doc, I'm *never* getting married. I couldn't bear it: not after what *she's* been through.' Jenny jerked her head, indicating their mother's bedroom. 'Marriage is only for those who wish to do themselves mortal harm.'

'Perhaps you're right.' Keir drank his coffee. 'I've got to go. I'm supposed to be on duty. See you sometime, Jenny Wren.'

She nodded distantly. He stood up and kissed the top of her head before tapping on his mother's door to say goodnight, or rather, good morning, as it then was.

'Come in, Keir,' she said, 'I'm not asleep or doing anything silly like weeping crocodile tears.'

Before sitting on the edge of the bed, he moved aside the pretty patchwork quilt his mother had spent long, painstaking hours making. 'I'm sorry I didn't get to see you for Christmas or the New Year. I couldn't get any time off.'

'You don't have to make excuses to me, *chéri*. I'm so proud of you. Every time I think of you and what you've achieved all by yourself, the tears come into my eyes. Dope that I am!' She mopped her eyes, smiled and pinched his cheek. 'Jacob Schiff has bought me a new typewriter. It's a Remington. He says I'll be able to churn out twice the number of letters I already type in a day. The Settlement Scheme is attracting so much attention, I think Lilly and I will soon have to move into larger premises.'

'That's great, Ma.'

'And you? You're not burning the candle at both ends, are you?'

He smiled. 'No. I've got a whole eight hours off tomorrow night to catch up with my housework and washing.' He looked at his watch with a rueful grin. 'Tonight's night. How time flies!'

She cherished his flippancy, whilst noticing, with a mother's love, the tell-tale shadows of strain under his eyes. She squeezed his hand, 'Keir – I loved him very much despite everything. He was such a lovely man before the drink turned his mind. He had to move out, for all our sakes. I could have coped with the rough times, but not with seeing him wilfully destroying himself – I wish it could have been different, for you and for Jenny ...'

'I know.' He held the hand that had been the life-line of his earlier existence. 'Don't talk about it any more. Jenny and I understand.'

'I admit he was never much of a father to you both, but he was still your father, so you must try to forgive and forget. He's gone now, out of our lives for ever, and the past cannot be altered. But don't let that experience sour you for the rest of your life. Love and marriage *do* go together, and it is still the best institution in the world. Especially when there are people like you and Jenny at the end of it to make everything worthwhile. Now then, no more preaching. Ask Brook to see to the funeral arrangements, please *chéri*. And would you, for my sake, try and be there yourself?'

'I'll try.' He kissed her, and left.

By the time Keir returned to the Accident and Emergency unit, it was half-past three in the morning, and Nurse Winston was tearing out her tight, crinkly roots. Her night shift only halfway through, Winnie didn't see why interns, who were only medical assistants, should go wandering off like lemmings, when she hadn't even time to get her bum down on a lavatory seat: and she told him of it in no uncertain terms, adding, 'Jeeze, Dev, where the hell have you been?'

'Miami.'

'I hope you scorched your ass off. It's been like a madhouse.'

'Still is by the sound of things. What's Zimmerman doing, murdering somebody?'

'*Somebody* ought to murder the stupid broad. She's hollering her head off like a hysterical hooker about some guy roughing her up a little. She won't let Zimmerman near her with the needle. I'd slap her hysterical face myself, only I don't like the idea of O'Reilly pinning an assault charge on me. An' do I know jest what them quarrelsome Wops can do to a face they don't like!'

'What Winnie?'

'*Cee-ment*! East River's become a cement-ery lately for people wearing Wop overcoats. Two of ma nurses are holding her down on the couch right now.'

'Lucky her.'

'Says she's a Broadway star and we've no right to treat her like a hooker. Why I do this job at all, the Lord knows. Ain't no different to being a shit-shoveller. Wops are the worst goddamn *shticks* of all.'

He mentally digested the patient's notes and previous case history, and then went to see what the row was about with the Italian lady to whom Winnie had taken such an aversion.

What he couldn't help seeing was a mass of honey blonde waves, a pair of shapely legs in a pair of pink silk

87

camiknickers doing the cancan from a very awkward supine position, two strapping nurses pinning the arms of the victim to the sides of the couch, and Zimmerman trying to inject himself with Paraldehyde. 'Hey, you guys will be had up for assault and battery. You can't use a hypnotic drug like that on her.' He tossed the broken glass evidence into the waste bin.

Zimmerman grit his teeth and snarled, 'I said a couple of hours, not the whole damn night! Miss Bolli is refusing to cooperate. She's causing grievous bodily harm to everyone trying to help her.'

'You should know better, Zim, than to try to help Miss Bolli cause grievous bodily harm to *anyone*.'

'You know what I mean, dammit. Neither is this the time for your puerile wisecracks – Miss Bolli, please let go!'

Scarlet talons had grabbed Intern Zimmerman's tie and he was halfway to being throttled by one slim, strong hand that had escaped custody.

Across Intern Zimmerman's back, Keir peered into Miss Bolli's vandalized face, wiggled his fingers and smiled. 'Hi, Miss Bolli, remember me?'

'Who's this nut?' Miss Bolli demanded, momentarily keeping still as she regarded him with suspicion.

'It's the inherited Celtic charm, you folks,' said Nurse Winnie, creeping up on everyone. She winked at Zimmerman meaningfully. 'Works wonders when all else fails. I bin here time out of mind, but there ain't *no* intern who can charm the pants off anyone like big-boy Dev, here. All pozzy to you, Doc.' She waddled away, chuckling to herself.

'Saturday matinée,' said Kerr ignorning Winnie, 'third row from the front, ten seats along. I'm Keir Devlin. You gave me two tickets for your Broadway performance. It was a jazz musical called *Lover Boy*.'

'Let me *outta* here!' The leg kicked again, almost knocking Intern Zimmerman's front teeth out.

He flung down the unused glass syringe of Paraldehyde, jerked his tie and white coat into order, and left the cubicle in a rage. '*You* deal with her, Devlin, I've had enough for one night. This isn't medicine, it's an outrage!'

'Okay, lady, enough's enough. Just cut it out. If you

don't want medical attention, don't waste our time. You can go. She can go,' Keir repeated for the benefit of Miss Bolli's two guardian angels. 'But make sure you write in her notes, "self discharge" and get her to sign it. We don't want to get the blame when she ends up back in here with blood poisoning and tetanus.'

One of the nurses seemed doubtful about releasing the patient, and hesitated. The Broadway star promptly spat in her eye. 'Gee, she's all yours, Doc,' said the nurse, and she and her colleague gladly left the cubicle.

Miss Bolli, her green cat's eyes narrowed, demanded, 'What's that?'

'What's what, Miss Bolli?'

'Tet whatever you said.'

'Oh, nothing much to worry about when you're dead.'

'That bad, huh?'

'Depends on your point of view of life.'

She dived for her high-heel shoes, ready, Keir felt sure, to gouge out his eyes.

Instead, she found herself imprisoned in two strong arms, pinning *her* arms by her sides. Her back pressed up against the front of his white coat, she stopped struggling. Smoothly, Keir said in her ear, 'If you want to go around for the rest of your life looking like a razor-slashed hooker, then you're very welcome, Miss Bolli. But go quietly. There are sleeping children out there who aren't half the pain in the butt you are. I know you're all blewed thinking you'll never get a job on Broadway again with a face about as pretty as Quasimodo's right now, but …'

'You can talk!' she spat like a green-eyed cat.

'I can stitch that cut and you'd never know the difference. Once the stitches come out, you'll be as pretty as a picture all over again. All you'll ever see for that big bloody – meaning blood-encrusted – gap right now, in future days will be a real true laughter-line. And, if I'm on duty, you can always come back for more tucks when you're a grandmother. My ma taught me to sew when I was three, and I can do needlepoint as neat as any great aunt's pin cushion.'

Her throaty chuckle was deep, full of untapped possibilities, and Keir liked the sound of it.

'You won't feel a thing, I promise.'

'Promise?'

'Sure.'

'You're some kind of doc, Doc.'

Whether she spoke out of genuine admiration, or the lowest form of wit, he was none too sure, but he thought he'd better clarify his position. '*Intern* Devlin. Strictly speaking, I'm not a proper doctor as yet. I'm only graded as an assistant doctor, as I haven't taken my final exams ...' He knew his mistake the moment she opened her mouth to yell for help. He clamped his hand over it. 'Shut up or I throw you out right now.' Carefully he removed his hand. 'Please behave yourself like a responsible adult, Miss Bolli, and not a complete idiot.'

'Do you bully all your patients like this?'

'Only the ones I care about. Now get on the couch or get out. Here's the pen to sign your discharge papers if you'd rather leave without treatment.' He took the pen from the pocket of his white coat and offered it to her.

She didn't take it, but instead climbed back on the couch and spread her skirts decoratively over her legs.

She had very nice legs. Green eyes looked at him from under thick honey-blonde lashes. He suddenly felt at a disadvantage. 'Did I really give you two tickets for *Lover Boy?*' she asked.

'Indirectly. Your agent, Harry Vincenti ...'

She shrieked, '*Never* mention the name of that scumbug to me again!'

He thought she was going to throw a scalpel at him, blade first, and hastily moved the dressing trolley to one side with his foot. 'Sorry.' He began to swab the matted and bloody cut on her face, a nasty razor slash, deep and long, from under her right eye into the scalp. Keir cleaned up the side of Miss Bolli's head and face, then drew up some local anaesthetic into a syringe.

'Hey, you're not going to stick a needle in me?'

'Fraid so.'

'I'd rather you stuck something else my way.'

He steadied his hands on the glass syringe.

'Pass over my smokes. If you're going to operate, I don't want to know. My purse is over there – *there*! Draped around that funny gadget.'

The funny gadget happened to be the oxygen cylinder. 'No smoking,' he said feebly, but she ignored the warning, dug down in her purse, found what she was looking for and lit her cigarette.

Unwilling to antagonize her again, or jeopardize the future of City Hospital, Keir hastily removed the cylinder to a safe distance and tried to do his best through the thick fog that suddenly enveloped him.

'Go on then.'

'Go on what?'

'You were telling me how you got tickets for *Lover Boy*.'

'A guy, who shall remain nameless between us, gave them to my uncle, Brooklyn Hunter Devlin, who had asked for them to treat his ladyfriend, my Auntie Mo, to a performance of *Lover Boy* for the fifth anniversary of their unblessed union. This nameless individual was, I emphasize *was*, a pal of my Onks, because they play poker together at The Leprechaun Hotel, Gramercy and Lexington. Since Auntie Mo and Uncle Brook didn't use the tickets after all, they passed them over to me.'

'Both tickets?'

'Yep.'

'You and who else saw *Lover Boy*?'

'Just me. I still have the other one in my billfold.'

'You married?'

'Not yet.'

'Aim to be?'

'Perhaps.'

'Got someone?'

'Only my ma. But she's always too busy – like me. Otherwise I'd have dragged her along to see *Lover Boy*.'

'Are you a ma's boy?'

'Sure I am. My ma's always nice to me.'

'And females ain't? Gee, I can believe that after the way you treat 'em. Say feller, don't you really like females?'

'Love them – when I have time.'

'But you got time off to see *Lover Boy*?'

'I didn't actually *see* it. I hate to say this, Miss Bolli, but I fell asleep during the matinée – oh, nothing at all personal, you were great. It was just that I'd been working rather a lot, and was a little way worn.'

'Do you always work a lot?'

'Yup.'

'Why?'

'I like what I do. You want me to make out a police report about the knifing?'

'Hell, no! That'll ruin my reputation. Forget him. You wanna be my agent instead?'

'Instead of what?'

'Harry Asshole Vincenti, that's what! You're real cute, you know that intern-man? You want any more tickets for *Lover Boy*, let me know. How's the needlepoint coming along, Doc?'

'Nearly finished.'

'And I didn't feel a thing. I hope that doesn't mean I won't feel something some other time?'

'Some other time, sure. Right now my reputation is at stake.'

She gave him a big, beautiful smile, and he couldn't help noticing what beautiful teeth she had, and how beautiful her smiling mouth was, and her slanting green eyes with their honey-blonde lashes, and how beautiful she was with catgut on her face, and how fantastic her legs were in their pink camiknicks. She had beautiful hair, too: he could just imagine himself drifting around in all that beige silk …

No: he couldn't possibly imagine, he *mustn't* imagine! He must stop himself from imagining such things. He'd only get himself struck off for getting himself struck on a lady patient, so what was he dreaming of!

She prodded him in the ribs with a red talon. 'Stop staring at me like you wanna gobble me up. Gee, I like you, I sure do. There's something about you that's mighty appealing, and it sure ain't your bedside manner, Doc. You're not a bad looking guy either, for those who like virgin apemen. You wanna stop by for breakfast when you're done here?'

'I'm not doing anything in between needlepointing.'

She seemed pleased about that, and again dug down deep in her purse.

She handed him a neat little card which he read out loud, 'Miss Francesca Bolli. Actress and dancer. Greenwich Village, south – is that right!'

Her smiling eyes and lips were full of promise. She lit another cigarette and puffed smoke in his face. 'See you in Sloane Court for breakfast, Doc – you'll find it between Bleecker and Houston.'

After she'd gone and the place had quietened down, Keir looked again at that little card of hers before tucking it safely into the pocket of his doctor's white coat. On Broadway, off Broadway, whatever next? he asked himself: and then he remembered he had the whole of tonight's night off.

'Winnie!' He whispered hoarsely through the green screens, because there were sleeping patients making a night of it in the reception area. 'Find me another victim for my needle, and some more coffee – hot, black, and sweet, just like y'darlin' self.'

CHAPTER THREE

Catalonia, Spain: Autumn 1924

The Hispano Suiza looked like a dark shuttle threading the verticle warp of the Monterey pines until it reached the main road, turned left, and disappeared from view.

The avenue of pines had been planted at the turn of the century to provide shade in summer and to act as a windbreak during autumnal storms. Vineyards stretched into the distance, row after row covering the Penedès hillsides like a marching army. This was the Parque Vinarosa, the land in the possession of the de Luchar family for over four hundred years. *El Grandee* also had a castle on the hill of Montjuic overlooking Barcelona Harbour, a textile factory employing three hundred workers at Llobregat on the outskirts of Barcelona, and bodegas in Vilafranca.

The Mas Luchar was a typical Catalonian farmhouse of sprawling stone beneath a terracotta roof. Small shuttered windows were designed to keep out the sun, leaving the large interior rooms cool and dark. Hand-carved sombre furniture made by craftsmen on the estate, and icons and images of the Virgin Mary filled every gloomy niche. Intriguing barns and outhouses and cellars containing old-fashioned wine presses resembling prehistoric monsters, bodegas and caves filled with casks of maturing brandy and liquors and racks of wines laid down in the previous century, all were just waiting for an inquisitive child to explore: a new people-spotting book was commenced without delay.

By a 'most unexpected quirk of Purnell genealogy' Raven's life had been changed for ever. She still could not believe it, and sometimes she had to pinch herself to make sure she hadn't died and gone to heaven after the bombing of Quennell House, Dublin.

She, Roxana and Sonny, when they had first arrived in Spain, had stayed at the castle – not the farmhouse near Vilafranca, for the two dwellings were as separate as chalk from cheese and not dissimilar from the standpoint of Quennell House in the city to Hollyberry House in the country.

At the Castillo de Luchar in Barcelona, Raven remembered the thrill of taking breakfast outdoors on a terrace with views over the Mediterranean Sea. She was reminded of Dublin Bay.

'Peedee, who lives in that other castle along the bay?' Sonny had asked.

'Montjuic fortress, dear boy, is a prison. It has a bloodthirsty history I cannot go into now, so eat up, please. We have lots to do today.'

Roxana, for once, had remained utterly tongue-tied with excitement. Only her blue eyes, as sparkling as the sea, had given away her true feelings regarding knights in shining armour riding white horses across the drawbridge of her dreams.

But dreams, they had all discovered, even the foolish ones, *did* come true.

To be brought all the way from Ireland to a Spanish nobleman's castle where bona fide Spanish grandees rode in black Spanish Hispanos (which beat white horses for comfort any day) was truly incredible! And when Roxana had found out that Don Ruiz and Doña Jacqueline had four handsome sons all older than she, her schoolgirl crush on Bennett d'Ildarte had faded into a childish thing of the past.

Grandfather Percival Dunbar Purnell had turned out to be the catalyst agent who had facilitated such an extraordinary change in their lives, an amazing little man who had picked up the pieces of their shattered souls and stuck them back again, just like a jigsaw puzzle.

It had been amazing to discover that they had a grandfather at all, as, in the past, Cassy had told them that all their grandfathers were dead and buried. There had been four husbands belonging to Grandmother Moynahan of Kildare, and one to Grandmother Quennell of Dublin, Wexford and Louth. Yet, ten days after the bombing of Quennell House, and close on the heels of one of Lyra Noughton Peel's flying and crying visits (bearing chocolates which she promptly devoured herself), a dapper little sandy man, wearing a russet velvet bow tie, had turned up in the children's ward of the Rotunda Hospital. He brought with him an unusual assortment of gifts, unusual in so far as they were not the obligatory chocolates, fruit, or flowers, and not frankincense, gold, or myrrh, but a mandolin with garish transfers of Spanish dancers waving fans and castanets, a print of a *toreador* sticking *espinars* into a snorting blood-spattered bull, and a golliwog wearing a red bow tie.

He had thrust the golliwog at Roxa, the mandolin at Sonny, and the picture of the bullfight at Raven. 'Before you all swallow your tonsils wondering who I am, I am your grandfather,' he had blithely announced. 'You may call me Peedee: P.D. stands for Percy Dunbar. Percival makes me squirm, and Grandfather sounds like an antiquity. I am not ready to grow old despite the fact of having three grandchildren. I am Peedee to my Spanish employers, and it will do for you to address me in the same way. I am only fussy where it concerns my palate.'

Raven remembered their reaction to this quite clearly; they were left without words.

There had been far too much to take in after the bombing of Quennell House, too much horror attached to that unforgettable night to adjust easily to anything. Suddenly to find that they had a grandparent, after all, had been most disconcerting. It would take considerable time to get used to this new development. She had rather liked the idea of being an orphan. It was somehow romantically tragic, and might have made William B.Y. sit up and take notice of her plight by dedicating a poem to her.

Roxana, trust her, had been left virtually unscathed by the blast, suffering only minor concussion, bruising and scratches. Sonny and she had not been so lucky. Sonny had been terribly injured, and had not been expected to live.

His right arm and left foot had been so badly crushed under falling masonry, they had to be amputated. She herself had remained unconscious for two days with a fractured skull, a deep gash across the top of her head and forehead requiring sixty stitches. Sister Anne, a Roman Catholic nursing sister, had said it was a miracle the two of them were alive.

It was only because she had managed, in the end, to crawl under Sonny's iron cot, dragging him with her as the house disintegrated and caught fire, that their lives had been saved. Mother, Father, Tim, Agnes, Cassy and two tweenies, had perished. Tim had been creeping up the back stairs at the time, they thought, while the two housemaids, who had shared a basement bedroom, had gone to bed as they had to get up very early to black lead the grates and rake out the dead ashes from the fireplaces, and so they were practically next-door to the elmwood doughbox when the explosion occured. Agnes had been found in the pantry.

Raven was not sorry that Cassy had died in the destruction of Quennell House, for she was now spared a long drawn-out, painful death from her illness, whether or not it was due to cancer or some other wasting disease. And it was a sheer fluke that Cassy had died in the bombing, for only those near the kitchen quarters and Waldre's library had taken the brunt of the explosion. Had Cassy remained on the nursery floor at the top of the house her life would have been spared, but for some reason she had gone downstairs after Raven's untimely intrusion into her bedroom.

Raven marvelled that God had actually spared time to take notice of her, and, what was more, had replied so promptly concerning Cassy going to heaven. Now she knew Cassy had been right about God hearing the smallest prayer and answering it, if and when He thought fit. She was just upset that Tim hadn't been able to take Armorial Shanks with him as he would miss A.S. very much: on the other hand, maybe God did provide stables in heaven, for Cassy had said God had chariots of fire.

Although it was stated in the papers that her father had been the main target for IRA aggression, it had been pure chance, too, that he had happened to be in his library when the bomb planted directly underneath, in the pantry doughbox, had blown up the back of the house. He could very well have chosen to remain in the grand salon at midnight along with his guests. But he and Mama had sneaked away for a few minutes on their own, the less delicate newspapers had stated, in order to toast one another over champagne and a private New Year's kiss. Raven had taken a very philosophical and romantic view of her parents' death: they had died for love in each other's arms. She hoped that she could go to heaven like that when it was her turn.

When Cathal Swilly and Eileen Hyde had visited, they had been full of the horrors of that night, what with clanging ambulances and fire engines and water and death everywhere. Even Clare Fenchurch (not at the New Year's party) without her rubber stamp but with plenty of children's books, was good enough to call upon them. Poor old Clare had wept buckets, just like Lyra. She didn't know why such dreadful things had to happen to innocent children. She had even offered to adopt them had she been married. Raven was infinitely glad that Clare wasn't. Amery had a broken arm due to the explosion which had blown out all the windows. Lyra herself had two very black eyes and had come to the Rotunda wearing dark glasses. Amery was at home in St Stephen's Green, with his arm in plaster and a bottle of whiskey by his side, recuperating from the shock-blast, according to Lyra. So, when Peedee, like a well rehearsed imposter, had appeared on the scene, they were all very wary of him. They had just been settling down into the routine of the Rotunda, and now, here was something else to think about.

Peedee had not let their blasé reception of him deter him in any way from gaining their attention; he had done that very nicely. He was used to young people and their recurring mental blockages when confronted by the adult of the species. These little people were gulping down the fact that they were not unclaimed orphans any more, and that perhaps they did not care to be reclaimed like three pieces of lost baggage at Paddington station.

He came back the following afternoon, this time without

presents, but with the prime intention of making them realize that he, too, had had his world turned upside down overnight, and that the role of grandfather, father and Holy Ghost into which he had been forced, was one he did not relish.

Peedee had a very *precise*, gravelly English voice with not a trace of an Irish accent, so they were more than ever disconcerted by him. 'I've come from Spain – that's a part of Africa that got pushed aside by the British at Gibraltar,' he said, regardless of their continuing dazed expressions. 'Now I know you've all been through purgatory, but so have I. I've been Tutor to a very nice Spanish family for the past thirty-two years. Not to the same sons, of course, they change places every two decades or so. I like Spain, I like the climate, I like my dear little house. I'm very fond of my Spanish employers. I hate blockheads, spoilsports and anyone without a grain of imagination. I detest noise, disruption and disorganization. I cherish Garcia Lorca, he's a poet, playwright and friend, and I adore *gambas* in garlic. A *gamba*, by the way, is a prawn as well as a monetary unit of one hundred pesetas. Garcia and I love to mull over our *gambas* along with those two other seductresses of the night, *vino tinto* and moonlight. Any questions so far?'

All three of them lay mute in their beds. For the second day running Raven couldn't think of a single question.

'Then, if none of you has any questions, I shall continue. By a most unexpected quirk of Purnell genealogy I happen to be your grandfather. Thirty-seven years ago I was a very young man with no sense or sensibility. I was your Grandmother Moynahan's errant lover ...'

'What's errant?' Sonny, still battle-scarred and bruised, had been the first to break the ice.

'Errant in my case, dear boy, means wandering minstrel. An adventurer.' Peedee had put his finger into the deep dimple like a well in the middle of Sonny's chin, and had rotated his finger as though he were winding up a clockwork toy. Peedee reminded Raven of a mischievous Peter Pan with all sorts of naughty jokes stored up behind his sparkling blue eyes.

'Maud and I produced between us, nine months later, a

daughter, according to Nurse Cassy for whom I have ...'
He cleared his throat and lowered his freckled sun-brown
forehead. He examined the backs of his freckled hands
with an intensity that denoted he was deeply moved by the
mere mention of Nurse Cassy's name. 'For whom I had a
deep regard. I also loved her, briefly, oh, ever so briefly,
for extricating me from a sticky wicket. It was a very sticky
wicket, I might add. The story, dear children, gets a little
out of hand here, so I'll stick to the facts.' He had looked at
them then with almost a scowl of anguish. Two piercing
blue eyes with a frieze of spiky sun-bleached lashes
subjected them to even closer scrutiny as his sandy head
jerked forward with the question, 'Did you two girls lose
your tongues in the bombing of Quennell House?'

'No Grandfather,' they had chorused.

'Then that's a blessing! I don't want to start learning the
deaf-and-dumb alphabet at my age. I'm suffering from
shock as it is. To find oneself a grandfather of three,
without ever having married a woman in one's entire life,
isn't conducive to a feeling that all is well with the world. It
makes me feel that my life is at last catching up with me.'

'How old are you Grandfather?'

'Twenty plus five plus thirty-two makes what, Sonny
boy?'

'Fifty-seven, Grandfather.'

'Then I am, God forbid, fifty-seven.'

Raven's curiosity had by now managed to reassert itself.
'Does that mean you are *our* mother's *real* father, and *not*
Grandfather Moynahan?'

'That is correct, dear girl.'

'What about Grandfather Moynahan? Didn't he know
about you?'

'Oh cripes, he knew, and how! But it was all hushed up
to preserve face – Gladdy's face. You see, Gladstone could
not have been Daphne's father, because, firstly, he was
impotent and, secondly, he was away in Italy for two years.
That's when I stepped into the breach, or out of them, if
you'll pardon the pun.'

'Are you as impotent as Grandfather Moynahan and a
Peer of the Realm?' Roxana had asked outright.

Peedee sounded as if he had a frog in his throat when he

had answered. 'Im-*por*-tant is the word you seek in this instance, dear girl, although Peers of the Realm can also be er – impotent: that, dear children, has a different meaning altogether. Impotence is the inability to reproduce, while im-*por*-tance is the ability to produce too much of oneself. A Peer of the Realm might be deemed im-*por*-tant on account of his noble feathers, though fine feathers do not a – yes, well, never mind. And no, I am not of such a breed, I am merely a humble schoolmaster.'

'Then how …?'

Peedee had anticipated Roxana's next question and said quickly, 'I taught your grandmother music and drawing. Her watercolours were superb. She had a wonderful eye for tone and form. As far as her music was concerned, she played the piano like a carthorse with all four shoes in urgent need of a blacksmith. Neither had she a semiquaver in her entire auricular factory. Never mind, she made up for it in other ways during the long hours we spent alone together. Any more questions?'

'Yes please, Peedee.' Given such an opening, Raven had jumped in with both feet. 'Wasn't Grandfather Moynahan very angry with you for giving his wife a baby while he was away?'

'Very angry! In fact, he was so angry, he had an apoplectic seizure, although the dear old – so'dier had difficulty in functioning properly even when he was normal.' Peedee scratched his ear and gave a sickly little smile. 'That's why he and Maud had no children. He was *very* much older than your grandmother. In his dotage in fact, which is how Maud liked her husbands. The fault, therefore, reproductively speaking, lay with Gladdy, although he refused to admit it. Only Nurse Cassy and I knew the truth. Gladstone, you see, wanted everyone to think that he had fathered Daphne. We all carried it off rather well in the end. Gladdy, however, never spoke to Maud again, or to his daughter, she being far too young in any case. He bundled himself off to the South of France soon after he found out about my fatherhood, and died of a stroke a few months later, no doubt precipitated by too much port wine and his feelings of inadequacy.'

Raven could not help thinking that Grandfather Peedee

was gloating over Grandfather Moynahan's downfall.

'By then,' Peedee continued, 'I had been nicely pensioned off by old Gladdy who was very generous despite being cuckolded by me. After he told me to make myself scarce and never show my face around Hollyberry House again, and never to admit to anyone that I was Daphne's real father otherwise he would shotgun me like a jack rabbit, I took him at his word and travelled the world on the five hundred pounds he gave me to facilitate my speedy departure from Ireland. I went to India and lived like a maharajah. From India I went to Siam where I learned to ride elephants and paint watercolours along with certain ladies of the Siamese Court, after which I returned to Europe. By the time I reached the Iberian Peninsular ...'

'Where's that?'

'Dear boy, the Romans called the Spanish mainland Iberia. Have you received no education whatsoever these past seven years?'

'Yes sir. But my tutor, Mr Hulke, doesn't know very much about geography because he's a Quaker. And I have to spend a lot of time practising my music too.' Sonny chewed his lip and fell silent.

A question had occurred to Raven. 'If Grandfather Moynahan was dead, why didn't *you* marry Grandmother Maud?'

Peedee had looked at her as though it was a good time to take his leave. 'Because, dear girl, I was probably on the North West Frontier and so nobody could be bothered to come and look for me. Besides, Maud would never have married me. I was only half her age, and far too poor in any case. She only wanted husbands who were rich, famous, titled, and about to kick the bucket. I, therefore, did not qualify. After Gladstone Moynahan's death, she married one of her other loves, Lord Graeme of Tyrone. He was immensely rich, infamous, and titled. He managed to survive the marriage for twelve years, I believe, before kicking the bucket like old Gladdy, whereupon, Maud had two more husbands, though not both at the same time.'

'Poor Mother, to have all those dying stepfathers,' Raven murmured.

'Yes indeed, dear girl. Now may I continue? I have much I want to say to you children so that you know what you are doing should you say yes to accompanying me back to Spain. Neither have I any wish to be late for my dinner, which, my landlady assures me, will be boiled beef and horseradish sauce. A misnomer if ever there was one, for I think it will be more like boiled riding boots and horsemanure sauce.'

'Are you staying in a hotel, Grandfather?'

'A Dublin hotel, Sonny, dear boy, is a luxury I cannot afford. I am presently dwelling in a boarding house.'

'Like kennels?'

'God help me, yes, since Quenell House was unfortunately blown up. So please, dear children hurry and make yourselves well enough to leave this hospital. I have no desire to remain in Dublin lodgings for longer than is absolutely necessary. Now where was I?'

'Iberia,' Sonny had prompted.

'Thank you, dear boy. By the time I reached Spain, Gladdy's money had given out, and I was once again singing for my supper. One day, in the Rambla in Barcelona, where I was painting pictures of nothing in particular, Don Ruiz de Luchar's father, the old grandee, over my shoulder asked me what else could I do besides draw. Upon learning that I was an impoverished English gentleman recently back from the Far East, he promptly hired me as Tutor to his only son and heir, Ruiz. There were, and still are, several females in the family, Ruiz's sisters, but they were not considered im-*por*-tant enough to be educated alongside their brother, and continued to receive their women's education in the kitchen. I am now Tutor to Don Ruiz's four sons, and no one can accuse me of not being consistent. I have become a family industry. That, my dear little people, is the story in a nutshell.'

Roxana, who had listened to Peedee with haughty disdain, had turned aside and said to Raven, 'You know what this means? Our mother is illegitimate!'

'Was,' Peedee had murmured undiplomatically.

'Which means she wasn't a hundred per cent Hon Gal as Cassy said, and that Cassy herself was an old liar, something I always suspected.'

'Cassy was *not* a liar!' Raven stuck up for Cassy. 'She was protecting Mother's reputation, and Father's.'

'And mine,' Peedee chipped in.

'What about ours?' Roxana had glared at Peedee. 'This means I shall never marry into the d'Ildarte family now. I have a shameful past they're bound to find out about. I know that when noble blood is diluted by a commoner, it becomes – it becomes ...'

'Rosewater?' Peedee didn't seem at all perturbed about his past as he supplied Roxana with the missing noun and a handkerchief. 'Dear girl, I'm awfully sorry about the illegitimate side of things, and that's why I'm here. To make amends. I must say, that I, too, was deeply upset when I heard that an Irish bomb had killed my only daughter, her husband, and my eldest grandson, not to mention dear sweet Cassy. I never met my son-in-law: I would have liked to. I knew all about the hero of Hazebrouck and the Hindenburg Line, about Tim and the rest of you, through Nurse Cassy, who couldn't spell to save her life, poor darling. However, nobody else knows about Daphne's rosewater blood, except perhaps Garcia and Antonio. The three of us would have some wonderful little chuckles over the *gambas* on how I managed to cuckold a lord! I had to repeat the story over and over again for their benefit. They think I'm a bit of a card, as well as a cad.' He chuckled to himself.

Roxana subjected Peedee to a baleful glare from her round blue eyes. '*You* told them, about *us*?' She seemed about to burst into tears.

'They are my best friends,' Peedee had reassured her. 'My secrets are their secrets.

'Who is Antonio?' Sonny asked.

'Another poet, my boy. "*Y si la vida es corta, Y no llega la mar a tu galira, aquarda su partir ye siempre espera, que el arte as largo y, además, no importa*".'

'What does that mean?' Raven had asked. She had loved the musical lisping of Peedee's recitation.

'And if life is short and the sea does not reach your boat, wait still without departing and be patient, for art is large and that is all that matters.'

'What does it mean?'

'*No importa?* A marvellous philosophy. Even better than *mañana*. It means, dear child, that nothing in this life is that important, not even missing the boat, when *tapas* awaits one alongside a bottle of *vino tinto*, moonlight, and one's true friends. Machada is a wise man.'

'I thought you said his name was Antonio?'

'So it is, dear boy. The Spanish, like us, also have surnames: An-ton-i-o Ma-cha-da,' Peedee repeated in elongated emphasis upon the vowels, like a master of ceremonies announcing the guests at a reception at Quennell House.

'How did you know about the bombing and us?'

'From Father Donahoe's telegram. Sonny, you must learn to be more grammatical. If I meet Mr Hulke, I will tell him what I think of his teaching methods. He wasn't by any chance a disciple of Montessori, was he? If so, he may be forgiven.'

'Who is Monty Sorry?'

'Not a Spaniard, that's for sure. Italian chappie – never mind, it is only of interest to we who teach others the joy of free expression. Anyway, Father Donahoe's telegram arrived before the newspapers, hence my presence at the Rotunda.'

Raven had done some quick thinking. Father Donahoe had been Cassy's priest and confessor. Cassy could easily have confessed to him the truth about Grandmother, Peedee and their illegitimate baby – their very own mother! After all, truth was what confessions were about. Why had Father Donahoe contacted Peedee, if not because he, too, knew that Peedee was their next-of-kin, and would have to take the responsibility for their future? Father and Mother had been only children, all legitimate grandparents were dead, and nobody else had stepped forward to claim three Quennell orphans. It appeared, therefore, that Father Donahoe had been the invisible orchestrator of their illegitimate grandfather's hasty removal from Spain. It also occured to Raven that for the last thirty-seven years a great deal of activity had gone on behind the scenes where grown-ups, priests and shady secrets were concerned. Perhaps that was what Cassy had meant about being 'party to all kinds of evil deeds rotting us in a million different ways!'

Peedee continued, 'When I got that telegram apprising

me of the bombing of Quennell House and the terrible loss of life, and that I should come soon, I was in a dilemma. You see, dear children, I did not know where to begin, and yet I had to face the truth: I was the one responsible for your being on this earth in the first place. Immortality, on that scale, I was quite unprepared for. Nor did I wish to resign from my post as Tutor to Don Ruiz's sons. It took me ten long days to make up my mind not to hide behind my anonimity any longer, and to face up to facts. You know, I almost didn't come to claim you. One day, you'll all probably wish the same.'

'Are you thinking of taking us back to Spain with you?' Roxana had asked with renewed horror.

'Dear girl, I thought I'd made that perfectly clear by now.' Here, Peedee, had seemed to lose a little of his confidence. 'There is no alternative. I would be most unhappy living in a bombed city, as Dublin has become. I would die of morbid starvation without *churros* dunked in hot chocolate for my breakfast, and *gambas* and *vino tinto* for *tapas*. *Tapas* by the way, since you are all going to learn Spanish, means a snack: and I would most certainly become a living corpse with rheumatism if I got no sunshine into my fragile old bones.'

A grave silence had met such dire predictions.

Peedee had taken advantage. 'Don Ruiz and Doña Jacqueline themselves were simply mortified by my tentative resignation. At such short notice, they would have been quite unable to find a replacement of my calibre. Even though my salary leaves much to be desired, I do have some wonderful perquisites, which compensates for the sterile hours spent trying to drum into Spanish heads that schoolhouses are the Republican line of fortifications. Do you know who said that, Sonny boy?'

'No, sir.'

'Horace Mann, my son. American Senator in the House of Representatives sometime during the last century. Therefore, I preferred not to resign my teaching post. I mentioned to my employers the delicate subject of extended leave due to mitigating circumstances. I had to sort out what to do with you three. Then Doña Jacqueline was struck by divine inspiration; why did I not have my three grandchildren to live with me at Cabo Alondra? In that way, I could keep my job, her sons would finish their gentleman's education, you three would have a home, and everyone would be happy and provided for. Brilliant! I accepted the offer, *lo más pronto posible*.'

'Cabo Alondra?'

'Yes, that is the name of my little house on the hillside. It looks like a dolphin – or a lighthouse with a tail: it's as the eye perceives. The sea is my front garden, and vineyards the back.'

'What does Cabo Alondra mean?' Raven asked.

'Cape Skylark.'

They had all chewed over this new development. Cape Skylark sounded a nice place.

'Does the sun shine every day in Spain?' Sonny wanted to know.

'I advise you to read *Don Quixote*, dear boy. It gets very cold in the mountains in winter. Spain is extremely mountainous, you know, Sonny. But because I live on the coast, it doesn't get that cold. We do, however, get the wretched Tramontana or the Levanter blowing down on us at times, and hot winds from Africa which cause great thunderstorms. Thunderstorms and hailstones are fun indeed, and I like to go fishing then.'

'I *hate* thunderstorms,' Roxana had declared fiercely. 'I want to stay here with Bennet's family. I shall write to Countess d'Ildarte today.'

'You must do as you think fit, my dear,' Peedee had replied with great tact. 'I cannot force you to do anything against your will.'

They realized, of course, that he could. He was their grandfather and had travelled all the way from Spain to assume responsibility for their welfare, which meant that they would have to obey him. Roxana, however, had refused to be beaten. She had written to Countess d'Ildarte in her neat script and the Countess had replied at once: *My dear Roxana, thank you so much for your sweet letter. It would have been perfectly delightful to have you stay with us for a little while, but, unfortunately, I am off to Venezuela shortly, and the house will be quite shut up. So sorry, my dear, to have to disappoint you in this way. But have a lovely time in Spain with*

your grandfather. Bennett sends his love. Yours truly, Hermione,
Countess d'Ildarte.

So that was that, and Roxana had had to admit defeat, though she had done it with very bad grace lasting for several months. When the stitches in Raven's scalp were removed, she and Roxana had been transferred to a private clinic run by Catholic nursing sisters, close to the Rotunda Hospital, where Sonny had to remain in order to undergo further surgery.

Peedee spent the following months sorting out the chaos and confusion that had resulted in the family's affairs through the deaths of their parents. He was in daily consultation with lawyers, accountants, bank managers, business managers, estate managers, doctors, surgeons, Father Donahoe, Miss Lockwood, and numerous other old retainers. From all walks of life, the people who had been in their parents' service were legion.

When everything had been finally settled, Peedee informed them that as soon as Sonny was fit and well, and able to travel long distances, they would go to Belfast, where Sonny would get a new arm and foot made to measure at one of the leading institutes in the world for such things, The Kirk and Pringle Artificial Limb Company.

'But can you afford it on your poor tutor's salary?' Raven had asked, as Peedee never appeared reluctant to bemoan his pecuniary circumstances when the occasion suited.

'No, my dear, but your brother can. Sir Robert Summerson Quennell, Baronet, aged eight, had become a rich man, a very rich man indeed.'

So, nine months after the bombing of Quennell House, Sonny had been fitted with his new limbs. From Belfast, they had crossed the Irish Sea to Holyhead. From Holyhead to London, and from London they had taken the boat-train to Paris. From Paris (always travelling first class since Sonny could afford it) the train to Perpignon, thence to Barcelona and the Spanish castle belonging to the de Luchar family. From that moment on, Roxana's sulkiness disappeared, and she began to smile at Doña Jacqueline as she had once smiled at Lyra Noughton Peel and Hermione, Countess d'Ildarte.

Raven noticed too, sadly, that since the fitting of his

artificial limbs, Sonny seemed to have withdrawn further into himself, and had lost all interest in music. He never once picked up the mandolin Peedee had presented him with, or asked where his precious Gagliano had got to.

Far away in thoughts centred upon Cassy's Dublin, Raven, standing between the vine rows, consumed more grapes than went into her basket. The hot, harsh glare was something she still hadn't got used to, even though she had been in Spain for a whole year. The light hurt her eyes. It gave her a dull headache, despite the shady hat. Sometimes, she longed for the soft diffused light of Ireland. Headaches and eye strain and the permanent scars to her head and forehead, the Irish doctors had told her, were things she was going to have to learn to live with.

Together with the de Luchar girls, Marta and Nina, Raven assisted with the grape harvest. Only the boys, Sonny included, were exempt. During the week they did their lessons with Peedee at the Mas Luchar. Roxana was supposed to be helping, all spare hands to the vine in this busy month of October, but *she* had found a shady little arbour beneath one of the vine-goblets (so called because of the shape in which Juan pruned them) and was reading *Little Woman*. Marta and Nina were not much company either, for they chattered away to each other in Spanish at a speed that defied the ear.

Raven tried her best to be friends with them, but Roxana made no bones about the fact that she utterly loathed the two *vacas Espaniolas*, and much preferred to identify herself with Miss Alcott's Amy waiting for her high-spirited Laurie beneath the goblet-shaped vine, than try to communicate with the 'two dull Spanish cows!'.

Raven wished morning lessons were over so that they could all go back to Cabo Alondra for lunch and siesta – something she thought she would hate. It seemed a total waste of time to sleep away the afternoons of one's life. But during the hottest hours of the day (winter was different), it was a sensible arrangement which Raven couldn't fail to recognize for its 'perks', for Peedee allowed them to stay up until eleven or twelve o'clock at night, which would surely

109

make Cassy turn in her grave.

Poor Cassy, Raven reflected, then, just in time, stopped herself from dwelling on the past, Cassy had Agnes to talk to up in heaven, and life in Spain had many more advantages than living in Ireland. She should be grateful to have a grandfather like Peedee who had been willing to share his life and his home with them. At least, she, Sonny, and Roxa had not been abandoned to their fate in some miserable orphanage. Nor did she have to learn her multiplication tables, columns of tedious spellings, know where Lake Titicaca was, or make old-fashioned samplers to keep her quiet and occupied in the glass-bubble existence of Quennell House. It looked as though she and Roxana were to go the same way as most Spanish women, into the paella dish of unstimulated, non-mental domesticity.

While she wasn't altogether dismayed at not having to do lessons in some stuffy classroom, Raven wasn't too sure whether or not she'd like to make paella her long-term career.

For the moment, though, she was enjoying her freedom and making the most of this unsupervised and idyllic interlude to think about her future: it was Peedee's problem since he had assumed responsibility for her welfare.

During the past year she had managed to pick up quite a lot of French as well as Spanish. Lockwood had taught them French with an English accent, and, giggling behind their hands, they had never learned a thing. Left to their own devices, they suddenly found that learning a language was much more fun by living it every day, rather than by conjugating dreary verbs by the hour. Social studies came under the heading of reading the newspapers, something that had been frowned upon at Quennell or Hollyberry House. She had had to win Cathal Swilly to her side in order to get a sneaky look at the newspapers, sent down via the dumb-waiter each evening from the morning-room and Waldre's library after her father had finished with them. Newspapers gave her a great insight into current affairs, scandal, trades unions and political parties such as the Anarchist Doctrinal Vanguard, or the Revolutionary (anti-Stalinist) Communists. She did not know if they were important; they sounded tedious and very much like some of Amery's *Sturmabteilung* friends. She much preferred to know about the Municipal Water Authority with whom Don Ruiz was always battling it out, as they turned off his water just when his vineyards most needed it.

Raven found her new life infinitely interesting, and the people-spotting book was highlighted with bright new characters and their secrets. Yesterday, there had been a peasant revolt in the vineyards. It had been great fun to listen to the Spaniards arguing with each other. Hands and tongues and tempers flying in all directions as they nit-picked over what was fair and what was not, Peedee had been brought in to sort everyone out.

Don Ruiz's own estate workers, as well as the hired hands taken on as casual labour for the harvest months, had threatened a walkout. That would have meant acres of unpicked grapes left to the ravages of the Tramontana and autumn hailstones, no wine to fill his vats in Vilafranca, and no wine to export to Cuba or Morocco, so no additional income to pay the workers what they demanded. In this respect, she was also learning economic issues Vinarosa-style. Vineyards had been at a standstill for the whole day, and the situation had only been resolved when Peedee stepped in as arbiter.

He managed, in the end, to soothe everyone down, told the old and faithful estate hands not to be influenced by anarchist agitators from Barcelona, that Don Ruiz worked twice as hard as anyone else to provide them with jobs, food, a roof over their head, and that he desired, above all, their happiness and welfare. As a gesture of goodwill, Don Ruiz was giving everyone as much wine as could be drunk at the *Fiesta Vendimia* being organized on their behalf when the grapes had been harvested. Doña Jacqueline had said that the wives could have bread, oranges, lemons and olive oil to stock their larders. There would be singing, dancing and music, and gifts for the children. They would be unable to find a better cooperative (the word used loosely in this instance by Peedee, since cooperatives was what the dispute was all about) than at Vinarosa. Therefore, if they did not like it, they had best buzz off and go work elsewhere, and they'd be lucky to find any! Otherwise, they should all shut up and get back to work, *lo más pronto posible*.

Afterwards, Peedee, in his crumpled linen suit, had stepped off his orangebox, taken off his straw hat, wiped his sweaty freckled forehead with a red polka-dot handkerchief, and beamed upon the workers, who dutifully went back to picking grapes.

Raven couldn't help feeling that they had all behaved rather like recalcitrant schoolchildren who needed a good firm hand to show them the error of their ways. Peedee had been the perfect arbiter. The vineyard hands themselves had seemed happy enough to cooperate with someone 'neutral' whom they had come to admire and respect during the past thirty-odd years, even if those years had done little to change her eccentric Anglo-Saxon grandfather from just being himself!

Peedee had explained that this had all come about because the dictator, General Primo de Rivera, had become more powerful than King Alfonso. He had changed the laws governing the distribution of land, and now any *labrador* who had worked his smallholding for fifty years or longer was entitled to a share of the ground he had cultivated. Spain was going through what France had been through one hundred and fifty years ago, but one hoped it wouldn't lead to revolution as it had done in France. Raven herself thought it would be a great shame if the de Luchar family ended up on the steps of the guillotine. She had become fond of Don Ruiz and Doña Jacqueline, although she did not mind too much about Marta, Nina or Ramiro. And *labradors*, Peedee had gone on to explain, were not the doggy variety in case they were wondering, but in Spanish meant labourers.

After that, the three of them went around crying woof-woof every time they saw a Spanish *labrador*, before collapsing with laughter at their own wit. Marta and Nina became prime targets for this display of simple Quennell humour, and would rotate their fingers to their heads in sympathy: poor peculiar English children, they couldn't help being mentally affected by a bomb which had turned their reasoning.

When she had seen the Hispano Suiza leave the Mas just

before lunch, an event which, in itself, predisposed one to imagine the very worst, Raven wondered whether Don Ruiz had not been summoned urgently back to Barcelona. The Fabrica de Luchar was under the management of Don Ruiz's brother-in-law, Señor Salas Rivales. He was having trouble with the textile workers who were again on strike for better wages and conditions. The newspapers reported the violence on the streets of Barcelona when anarchist workers and trade unionists were unable to get their way. Raven was relieved that Peedee had managed to quell the vineyard workers' tempers before the voluble dispute had flared into physical violence. Then she forgot about Spanish problems, which reminded her all too disconcertingly of the Ireland she had thought she had left behind, when she saw Sonny limping awkwardly in his leather limbs, all straps and springs and levers, even though they were supposed to be the best artificial limbs in the world, evolved out of the horrors of the Great War.

Raven's heart went out to poor little Sonny. Arm and foot chafed and perspired and made Sonny's amputated stumps red-raw in the heat, so that, in desperation, he would ask for his false limbs to be unstrapped. Whenever she could, Raven relieved Sonny of his burdens, and mothered him to a degree that was becoming bad for his own independence. Peedee himself had noticed over the past year how much Sonny was relying on Raven for the smallest thing.

'Raven, Raven! Are you there? Peedee's waiting for you and Roxa.'

His heavy schoolbooks under his left arm, even on a hot day like today, Sonny wore a long-sleeved flannelette shirt, the cuff of which fell over the prosthesis that replaced his right arm from the elbow. Poor Sonny, with no flesh-and-blood hand left to hold the bow that had made the divine music from his precious violin, Raven knew that he would never pick up the instrument again.

'I'm coming.' She thrust a few more grapes into her mouth, hoped she had room for Carina's huge lunch, and rushed to her brother's rescue.

Unfortunately, they met the vineyard overseer. Juan was not pleased with her share of grapes in the basket.

113

'Señorita,' he grumbled, 'if you are to pick grapes with us, you must make certain they are without leaves and stalks. The bunches must not be separated into lots of little branches which will clog up the wine presses. You are wounding the grapes, and that is not good for wine. Now someone must come along and sort out the good clusters from the bad. Please stay out of my vineyards if you do not know what you are doing.'

Marta and Nina giggled together, loving it when Juan grumbled at the English girls.

'I'm sorry, Juan. I didn't know I was wounding anyone, least of all a grapehead. Come along Sonny, let's go. Roxa, if you're coming, come, otherwise stay there and get bitten by a woof-woof. I wish I hadn't bothered.' She tossed her two long dark pigtails, disdainfully subjected Juan, Nina, and Marta to a frosty look from her grey eyes, and departed with Sonny.

'Honestly,' she continued later, 'Juan needs to take a good look in the bottom of *their* baskets sometime. He'll find other things besides leaves and stalks, and by that I mean great lumps of mud and rock to make out they've picked more than they have. Juan thinks they're such good, quick workers, but they're nothing but little cheats. And that's not the only thing, I'd *never* drink de Luchar wine, not after I saw what Ramiro did.'

'What did he do, dear girl?' Peedee was curious.

'He put a live toad into one of the vats because José dared him. It was all mashed up with the black grapes. Juan will never know the difference between toad's blood and *Ull de Llebre*. One day I'll tell Don Ruiz his children are responsible for his red wine tasting like liquid mud or toad's blood.'

'What's biting you?' Peedee asked, hoisting Sonny onto the bicycle saddle.

'Juan, Ramiro, Nina and Marta. They don't like us Peedee.'

'Nonsense. You've got a persecution complex, dear girl. The Spanish are terribly friendly. Ask Sonny.'

Sonny nodded.

'That's because he's a poor little afflicted boy as far as they're concerned. The Spanish love that.'

'Marta and Nina don't mean to be spiteful, they just don't

understand you and Roxa, I expect.'

Sonny rode home seated on Peedee's bicycle. Peedee, stronger than he appeared from his wiry, less-than-average-sized frame, pushed and steered energetically like a man ten years younger. The cool shade along the avenue of Montery pines was wonderful after the prickly heat of the vineyards.

Roxana trailed in the rear, bemoaning the fact that Cabo Alondra was a mile and a half away from the Mas Luchar, and why couldn't they have their lunch with everyone else in the farmhouse kitchen. Peedee patiently explained, (as he had told Roxa many times before) that he preferred Carina's cooking to that of Isaba's, but, if she wanted to remain behind and give them all some peace while they lunched without her at Cabo Alondra, then by all means stay at the Mas Luchar.

This technique of Peedee's with Roxana never failed. If he said she could do something, she invariably did the opposite.

When they got to the main road junction, they did not take the left hand turning Pedro, Don Ruiz's chauffeur, had taken for Vilafranca and Barcelona, but turned right towards the sleepy little orange-roofed town of Toril. The unmade road began to climb steeply towards the headland, and Peedee started to puff and perspire – Sonny and the bicycle together no light weight. 'Raven, I've been thinking.'

For Peedee to make that remark was alarming. Whenever Peedee said he was thinking, it usually meant something afoot which affected them personally. 'How would you and Roxa like to go to school in Switzerland?'

Raven did not answer immediately. She turned around and saw Roxana trailing far behind. School in Switzerland would have been a wonderful idea without Roxana who was such a fly in the ointment. Raven felt she would spend as much time in Switzerland looking after only Roxana, as she spent in Spain looking after Sonny and herself; and she much preferred to be with uncomplaining, stoic little Sonny.

'Well?' Peedee, standing still, wiped his brow with his handkerchief, his other hand keeping hold of the handlebars. He let the bicycle, with Sonny's weight on it, lean slightly against him to keep it steady, and took second wind now that they had came out on top of the flat headland.

The dazzling white double-storeyed villa with its orange roof had an unusual shape. The front was rounded, like a lighthouse, and the view from the rondel was spectacular. To the rear of the villa, an extension had been built, sloping away like a tail. Cabo Alondra reminded Raven of a small white dolphin left high and dry and looking longingly out to sea with big blue eyes. It was a fascinating home, something 'different' from the traditional casas of the region, and that's why she imagined it had appealed to Peedee. High-arched windows of a Moorish influence had blue shutters hooked back like tinted eyelashes. Windows on the ground floor had filigree wrought-iron grills to stop intruders getting in when they were left wide-open during the hot summer months. It was strange, too, to see a huge chimney built onto the 'tail' part of such an obvious summer villa. Really, whoever had been responsible for designing Cabo Alondra, must have had a wonderful time at his architectural drawing-board, Raven couldn't help thinking, yet, Cabo Alondra had turned out to be just perfect in every way.

Alone and unmolested, without other buildings encroaching upon this wild, rocky coastline, many varieties of brilliant flowers and cacti could be found among the stump-grasses and boulders surrounding the villa. There were no boundaries. The untamed headland was their garden, the tang of the sea and the scent of oranges, lemons, walnuts, olives and vines, the essence of Cabo Alondra.

Further along the coast, the land fell away into a little depression. Visible through the noonday heat-haze, the orange-tiled roofs of Toril trembled like water. The one-horse town, Peedee called it, although he went there quite regularly on his bicycle to the bullfights in Toril's ancient Roman amphitheatre. Majolica blue domed roofs of the Basilica and the Convent of the Franciscan Order of Santa Camillus of Lellis and the Blessed Charity rose into the fevered air above the cheek-by-jowl houses clinging to steep picturesque streets.

The convent bell could be clearly heard, summoning the Camillus Dames, with their unusual winged head-dresses, to the office of Nones. Raven was reminded in that moment of the sounds of Ireland. She had always taken for granted Cassy's religion, Cassy's Dublin, Cassy's fight for all four of their souls, Tim's, hers, Roxa's and Sonny's, and now, fifteen hundred miles away from Cassy's burial ground, the world had shrunk to the haunting echo of a convent bell. Raven was disturbed by it: it seemed as though that bell was trying to tell her something.

'I think that the trouble with you and Roxa,' Peedee continued when no answer seemed forthcoming from Raven, 'is that you two are bored with nothing to do but argue and fight all day long. It's different for Sonny and the de Luchar boys whose minds and time are occupied with study. Spanish women aren't usually considered in the same light as the men. A Spanish woman's career is thought to be marriage and children. If I were to allow you and Roxa into my classes, as I had considered, four young chauvanistic Spaniards would down tools immediately and walk out of the classroom.'

'I would simply *hate* to sit beside Ramiro in any classroom,' Raven said so fiercely that Peedee was taken aback.

'So I think it would be a very good idea if you and Roxana received a decent education in Switzerland,' he got in while the going was good.

'But they will come home in the holidays, won't they, Peedee?'

'Of course, dear boy. Now, if that's all settled, I will make enquiries to Doña Jacqueline, who herself was educated in Switzerland.' Then Peedee thoughtfully added a postscript. 'Your father left you all well-endowed. A trust fund has been set up on your behalf, so there is no question about a Swiss education. The very best for our Quennell women, eh, Sonny boy? After all, I think we can afford it.'

By now Roxa had caught up with them. 'Afford what?' She asked, bright red and breathless, hoping Peedee meant new dresses.

'Boarding school in Switzerland,' Sonny supplied. He

was not keen to lose Raven, but didn't mind if Roxa went. Raven and Peedee he would miss most in the world should another bomb spoil things for everyone. Peedee was super, better even than Father Donahoe, who had brought him a toffee apple whenever he had come to visit Cassy: and even when Cassy had taken him and Raven to Father Donahoe's Roman Catholic church, where they had had to bend their knees and cross themselves so many times with holy water they had been wet all over, Father Donahoe had managed to produce a toffee apple from a plate of communion wafers so that he had considered the priest to be a very clever magician indeed. Peedee didn't have toffee apples, but he had promised to take them to see the bullfight in Toril.

Roxana's reaction was most agreeable, and therefore unexpected. 'I should love to go to Switzerland and get away from those two fat cows ...'

'Dear girl, you mustn't address other women as cows. It isn't nice,' Peedee said, as he absent-mindedly dusted the knees of Sonny's worn dungarees.

'Then they are toads. Nina and Marta are very spiteful, Peedee. Yesterday they put three kittens in a sack, weighted it with bricks, and tossed the sack into the sea. They're perfectly horrid little toads and I hope one day someone will do the same to them.'

'Now now, my dear, temper won't resolve the state of war that exists between you four women. By the by, how old are you gals?'

'Eleven years, nine months,' said Roxana without hesitation.

'Then that is certainly a good age to begin a lady's education.' Peedee grinned, immensely relieved that the problem of what to do with the two girls for the next few years until they were married off had been so easily resolved. The optimum way to handle pretty young ladies approaching puberty was something he was not able to include in his curriculum vitae, and while he was prepared to cope with Robert Summerson, the two girls flustered him.

More so when two dear little kittens were produced by Roxana at the end of the day. Cat fur always made him

118

sneeze and wheeze, but he hadn't the heart to do anything about it.

'I thought you said they had been drowned?' he accused Roxana.

'Three were. But Raven and I rescued these two before they could be popped into a sack.' Roxana handed one of the tiny black kittens to Sonny, who held it carefully in his lap, while she nosed the other, kissing and caressing it and almost flattening it in her loving enthusiasm. Both kittens, with white socks, as though they had been dipping daintily into white paint, were so sweet, Peedee decided to forget his allergy and find some milk. 'That one, the one Sonny's holding, is called Morgan, and this one is Le Fay. Aren't they just tetra?'

'Please don't use that word, Roxana.'

Roxana looked up, the distinctly chilly tone Raven had adopted when all of them had been ooh-ing and ahh-ing over the kittens, suddenly putting a damper on the proceedings. 'Why not?'

'Because it was Tim's word.' Raven got up and ran out of the room, leaving behind her a great depression.

On the Saturday following the *Fiesta Vendimia*, the celebration of the harvesting of the grapes, the trio Quennell once again accompanied Peedee to dinner at the Mas Luchar. He added his own distinctive touch to the occasion by sporting a jaunty, jade-green velvet bow tie with orange spots, which was strangely at variance with his surroundings. Huge, gloomy rooms, masses of dark, heavy Castillan furniture, and hand-carved wooden effigies of the Virgin Mary lent a sombre atmosphere to any meal. But the most uncomfortable thing whilst eating dinner was to be looked upon by a sad-eyed Jesus and his long-faced disciples at the Last Supper. This enormous mural occupied one whole wall of the dining-room and never ceased to depress Raven. She felt that every mouthful she took was being weighed and judged by a discerning Lord who remembered all the times she had forgotten to say grace before her meals. The mural disturbed her like Toril's convent bell.

119

The place-settings were always the same, Raven seated between José de Luchar and Ramiro, as though Doña Jacqueline was already envisaging an arranged marriage. José, sixteen, was Don Ruiz's eldest son. Ramiro, next, was fifteen. Ram was easily the best looking of the four Spanish boys. Black hair, golden complexion, intense light grey eyes and curvaceous (though, in Raven's candid opinion, somewhat cruel) lips gave him an arresting and decidedly sensual appearance. Something about Ramiro's character frightened Raven. She had seen him take a tiny fieldmouse and spike it on a sharp cactus plant. Ramiro had appeared to enjoy every moment of its wriggling, squeaking, helpless contortions, until Raven herself had managed to put the fieldmouse out of its misery. Afterwards, in tears, she had struck Ramiro on his shoulder with her fist, and he had caught hold of her with such ferocity, she thought she was the next one to be nailed to the cactus. Then Ram, just as suddenly, pushed her away with a mocking laugh so that she had bumped down on her back. Anything helpless, toads, fieldmice, butterflies and little girls, seemed to be a target for Ramiro's warped sense of humour. No, she didn't like Ramiro's tactics in the least.

Roxana sat between Ram and Jaime. Jaime was the nicest of them all. Gentle, kind, respectful, and always desiring to please, even helping Isaba to pass round the dishes. Jaime was fourteen, while brother Carlos, thirteen, sat next to his grandmother.

Carlos sent a paper aeroplane to dive-bomb Doña Maria's soup. No one except his grandmother noticed its untimely descent as conversation buzzed around the table. 'Papa, when can I be a pilot?'

'Soon, one hopes.' Doña Maria fished the paper plane out of her soup and tossed it damply away over her shoulder with a hiss of disgust. She *detested* Saturday evenings in the company of her uncouth grandsons. Señor Peedee had a lot to answer for as their tutor, thought Doña Maria, though, in in all fairness to him, she also made allowances for the boys' Latin high spirits.

Don Ruiz's mother lived in a pretty, bougainvillaea-covered house in the Parque Vinarosa with her spinster daughter, Leah. Tía Leah, seated at the right hand of her brother, was a heavy woman with a dark little moustache, a big wart on her chin, and manly black brows in a continuous line above her Spanish eyes. Tía Leah sounded very much like tingalinga, and so Tía Leah became Tingalinga and was added to their woof-woof repertoire: 'Look, there's Tingalinga taking her favourite woof-woof for a walk among the wounded grapeheads' became a joke guaranteed to give them hysterics.

Sonny, as always, found himself squashed between twelve-year-old Marta and eleven-year-old Nina. Every Saturday evening Sonny had to endure the de Luchar girls' heavy-handed and fussy ministrations, hacking his food into bite-sized chunks, using their own cutlery to scoop up the mashed mess, shovelling it down his throat, afraid he might otherwise starve to death.

Sonny, who was very fastidious in all his habits, was once again becoming agitated at being treated like a baby. Raven knew that Sonny also dreaded Saturday evenings at the Mas Luchar, but was unable to do a thing about it. He could not bring himself to hiss rude remarks at the girls, as she and Roxa would have done, so he stoicly yet miserably continued to endure their well-meaning but overbearing attentions, while wishing they would allow him to use his own artificial fingers.

Raven tried kicking Marta's shins under the table, but she couldn't quite reach. She would have a word with Roxa afterwards, so that next Saturday Roxa, who might be able to reach them better, could do the shin-scraping on Sonny's behalf. Otherwise, if they did not leave poor Sonny alone, Marta and Nina might just find a bevy of baby crabs with pincer-sharp claws in bed with them!

But Doña Jacqueline, unlike her two ugly daughters, was a real lady left over from the *belle époque* era. Raven, who still religiously jotted down all her personal observations in her new people-spotting book after she had said her prayers each night, had discovered that Doña Jacqueline had been a great friend of the Empress Eugénie Marie de Montijo de Guzman, the wife of Napoleon III. To be seated at the same table with anyone even *remotely* connected with the great name of Napoleon made Raven hold her breath in awe every time Doña Jacqueline spoke to her. Although she had teenage sons, D.J.'s classical features and flawless complexion were still breathtaking enough to warrant a second glance: she must have been a truly stunning woman in her day, because she wasn't bad in her middle age, thought Raven while picking at her food: and that was another thing, one always seemed to be eating in Spain. She was still full from Carina's enormous lunch completed at three o'clock this afternoon. No wonder Spanish women were so fat! All except Doña Jacqueline …

Raven glanced up and caught José's and Ramiro's eyes upon her and knew they were talking about her; she ignored them, they were tiresome!

Along with the *ensalada de Otoño*, which Raven disliked because of the flavour of the sweet anise, Doña Jacqueline mentioned some suitable educational establishments in Switzerland. They came under the headings of Basel, Bern, Fribourg, Geneva, Lausanne, Lugano and Zurich.

'You see, Peedee, I have already done my homework, just as you asked me. I have a girlfriend in the Swiss Embassy in Madrid who was with me at my finishing school in Lausanne. She has prepared a list of the very best schools in Switzerland for your granddaughters. Tomorrow I will let you have it, but not tonight, because I forget where I put it after my glass of wine.'

Raven thought about toad's blood and mud.

'Afterwards, they too, might like to go to Madame Baillière's finishing school in Lausanne, which is the very best in Switzerland. I will put in a good word for the twins. But I must tell them now, smoking is not permitted, not even in the bathrooms.'

Aware that *any* school rule would be no deterrent as far as Roxana was concerned, Peedee reserved opinion, while hoping to find an establishment that incorporated a 'finishing' term into the final year's curriculum.

Don Ruiz changed the subject of women's education, and congratulated Peedee on the way he had handled the *rabassaires* dispute the previous week.

'It was nothing,' Peedee replied nonchalantly. 'They were merely trying to make a point about the vines being twenty-five years old.'

'They are always trying to make a point,' Don Ruiz said, while taking nothing to heart. Raven couldn't help reflecting that life to Don Ruiz was just a big bowl of grapes. A burly, broad man, strong, square features and receding hairline of crinkly black hair, he looked more like an Andalusian *caballero*, not a Catalonian 'capitalist', as Raven had heard mentioned on occasions.

When Raven had asked Peedee what all the fuss was about between vineyard workers and landowners like Don Ruiz, Peedee had explained that the vine cultivators, who had previously owned their tenancy for half a century or more, were now finding that their tenancy was in dispute after only twenty-five years. In Spanish law, when the vine died, the tenant farmer had no more legal right to land rented from large estates. It had all come about because, at the turn of the century, disease had wiped out the old vines, and the new stock lasted only twenty-five years, not fifty as before. The *rabassaires'* union was now fighting for security of tenure for their members. Not only that, but due to the heavy taxes imposed by France on the importation of all Spanish wines, the vine cultivators were having a hard time all round.

Don Ruiz raised his very large, long-stemmed wine glass to Peedee. 'What do you think of this one, Señor Peedee?'

'Hmm — not bad, I suppose.' Peedee squinted at the colour of his own glass of wine by the light thrown upon the table by two chandeliers.

Raven knew Peedee was being polite rather than honest.

'Not bad! You *suppose!* Is that all you can say about my wine?' Don Ruiz chuckled. 'Then you think I should mix my Tempranillo with French grapes?'

'It wouldn't hurt to try.'

'I know what you are thinking, Señor Peedee.'

'What am I thinking, Don Ruiz?' Peedee was also smiling.

'You are thinking that I am wasting my time trying to compete with France in this business of wine production. You think that Spain is a big joke where her wines and spirits are concerned, eh, my *rabassaires'* friend?'

'On the contrary. I think that once the Catalan vine

growers get themselves better organized, there will be a great future for Spanish wines. Not this one, though.' Peedee pulled a face. 'If you wish me to be perfectly honest, Don Ruiz, it tastes like, um, let me see – toad's blood, I think.'

Peedee wasn't looking at her when he said it, but Raven quickly bent her head so that Don Ruiz couldn't see her smile.

'It was a bad year for reds. The white Parellada is better,' Don Ruiz said thoughtfully. 'So, you do not think we Spaniards take our wines seriously enough, and we must become more like the French if we are to succeed in gaining world recognition. Where do you stand in all this, Señor Peedee? With the Unio de Rabassaires who believe the land belongs to the people, or with the Regionalist League of the Catalan Right?'

'I am an Englishman, Don Ruiz, a neutral in all this.'

'Pull the other leg, Señor Peedee. Isn't that what you often used to say to me in the classroom? However, I will not compromise your loyalties. Let's talk instead about my brandies and liquors.'

'Ah! Now there you have potential. But Catalonia must produce its own distinctive brandies and not try to compete with French Cognac.'

'You are a great connoisseur of French wine and brandy, eh Señor Peedee?'

'I am a great connoisseur of what constitutes good art. Cognac, like poetry, the ultimate freedom of expression, is one of the great art forms in life. I should one day like to see de Luchar *eau-de-vie* win an award for its meritorious art form, or, failing that, captured on canvas and immortalized by Señor Picasso in one of his abstract designs.'

Don Ruiz burst out laughing, a lovely barrel-resonance of sound. 'Señor Peedee, there is nobody in the world like you! I am still not sure who you are secretly laughing at, myself, yourself, or Pablo the degenerate genius.'

'Far be it from me to scoff at anyone's genius, especially Picasso's. Degenerates are usually the most genuine geniuses of all,' Peedee said breezily, deliberately keeping the mood light. 'I am merely expressing an opinion.'

'A very definite opinion, I think, eh, Señor Peedee? However, I am indeed glad to have you to show me the error of my ways every Saturday night.'

'She was a nyphomaniac,' piped up the querulous voice of Doña Maria.

'Who was, Mother?' Don Ruiz, thrown off balance by his mother's untimely remark, frowned at her.

'Why, Queen Isabella, of course, Ruiz! They sacked her and Father Claret, her confessor, and the whole Court-caboodle of Miracles. Then they brought in that bourgeois duke, Amadeo, and made him king. It won't do! The people will resort to violence.'

'Yes, Mother dear,' Don Ruiz said patronizingly, for his mother's calendar was sixty years out of date, 'but now we are talking about King Alfonso.'

'Never heard of him.'

'King Alfonso XIII, Mother dear! The King of Spain.'

'*Querida Madre*, eat up your *pichon*,' Tía Leah whispered across the table and José and Ramiro exchanged grins.

'I do not like squabs vinaigrette,' replied Doña Maria, for, by now, the main course had been served. 'Isaba makes it far too acid for my stomach. I shall be up all night with indigestion. Jacqueline, you should sack Isaba and have Carina back.'

'Good lord, no,' said Peedee in alarm. 'Doña Maria, have you tried a little camomile in milk last thing at night? It's a wonderful aid in relieving nocturnal indigestion.'

'I have tried everything, Señor Peedee. But I am always so filled up with the wind, I become like the nocturnal Tramontana blowing down the pines.'

The boys choked to death on this. Doña Jacqueline hastily asked for the dessert to be brought in. 'Mama,' she turned to Doña Maria with a smile, 'if you don't want the main course, then you must try the dessert. It's an English 'pudding'. I asked Carina for the recipe to give to Isaba who has specially prepared it for you and Señor Peedee, because I know how much you both like chocolate.'

Again, the boys dissolved into relentless mirth. Raven didn't know what they found so amusing, and neither did their grandmother. Doña Maria's walking stick hung on the back of her chair. She reached round, took up the stick, and stretching across the table, gave José a hefty clout on the shoulder. 'Stop laughing at me you horrible boy! I shan't leave you anything in my will.'

Behind Raven's back, José hissed something to his brother, and the two boys turned purple with suppressed laughter.

Don Ruiz had to bring his sons to heel, '*Basta*! Enough.'

They carried on eating in utter silence, until a little sound from Doña Maria's direction and a nervous giggle from Roxana, set them off again.

'I said, enough!' roared Don Ruiz at José and Ramiro, and the two boys then decided to pull themselves together because Peedee frowned at them.

When the pudding was brought to the table, Peedee tucked into the chocolate and cream mousse, thinking to himself that Isaba had indeed excelled herself this time. Doña Jacqueline watched him with amusement as he scraped the last morsel from his dish. Peedee caught her eye and cocked a sandy eyebrow, 'Any more mousse? It's delicious.'

Peedee's innocent remark set everyone off again, so that even Tía Leah had to wipe her eyes with a corner of her table napkin.

'Why are they laughing, Raven?' Sonny, always very serious, whispered across the table. 'Have I missed the joke again?'

'I think it's because they thought Peedee asked for more mouse — they don't really have a word for mousse in Spanish, you see Sonny, although the word *maus* means the same as it does in English.'

Sonny grinned. 'What do they call mousse, then?'

Raven shrugged. '*Pastel*, I think.'

When the laughter had settled down into sporadic bursts, Peedee said slyly, 'After twenty-five years the old vine stock has shrivelled up and died, so I think, Don Ruiz, it's about time you gave your tenants a fair deal and planted new vines. Forget about mixing with French varieties for the time being. Be more imaginative with your vineyards. Go wholeheartedly for traditional Penedès stock, the Garnacha, Cariñena and Tempranillo. Be selective in your choice of customer, too, and go for a market where people want quality every time rather than how many pesetas de Luchar wine costs per bottle. The rich are always with us, just like the poor, but we can discount the latter since they don't drink wine – unless of course it's Communion wine or a miracle made from water. But Don Ruiz de Luchar's wines and spirits *must* be the *very* best on the Catalonian market, and in order to achieve that status you must employ experts who know the business thoroughly.'

'You just told me to be imaginative, not reckless.'

'Take the bull by the horns. Send José to Dijon as soon as they will have him, so that he can learn the ins and outs of the business from *the experts*.' Peedee, smug in his retort, elicited a glowering response from José.

'But I require José here at Vinarosa, Señor Peedee, to take my place and speak up for the family when I am elsewhere on business. We have men laying down tools on the slightest pretext, militant *rabassaires* and *labradors* who ...'

'Woof-woof,' said Sonny and this time it was Raven and Roxana who fell off their seats laughing.

It was hopeless to try and hold a sensible conversation in the face of such juvenile behaviour. Don Ruiz stood up and said with good grace, 'Come, Señor Peedee, let us leave this stupid family of ours and go and enjoy our cigars while we drink some of my grandfather's not bad brandy. I want to hear more about your ideas on how I can improve my vineyards to make them a long-term investment. Perhaps, right into the nineteen-nineties, eh?'

The following afternoon, Peedee insisted on taking them all to the bullfight in Toril. Sonny was sick, Roxana felt faint and Raven wanted to go back to Cabo Alondra without waiting to see the grand finale of the *corrida*.

Outside the bullring, while order was being restored with flapping handkerchiefs and paper bags, Peedee turned to Raven and said quite innocently, 'Did you not like the picture of the bullfight I gave you as a present?'

'I hate it!' Raven cried. 'I only keep it on the wall so as not to hurt your grandfatherly feelings!'

'What a darling child!' He leapt up at once from where he had been hunkering on his heels while blowing cold air into Roxana's face. Peedee clapped his hands together. 'Dear girl, I can't *tell* you how that statement fills me with joy. You have my full permission to throw it away. I myself am anti-blood sports – oh, listen to me first! Today is the first day I have watched a bullfight for many, many years: since 'ninety-one in fact, the year I got here. When I say I'm going to the bullfight, I normally stand outside the bullring with my placards.'

'What placards?'

'Presently, dear girl, don't rush me.' He cleared his throat. 'This outing was an exercise. I brought you all to see a bullfight in order to test your individual strength and sensitivity. I am glad to say none of you have let me down. I am proud of you all. I wanted you to make up your own minds concerning the cruelty and barbarism surrounding such a sport. One can never be the judge of anything, or pass an opinion, unless one knows what one is talking about. The Spanish love it of course. It's their national pastime. Bullfighting is a sacred ritual to them, part of their Mithras heritage.'

Before the bullfight, Peedee had left his bicycle propped against the old stone walls of the bullring, and now he removed from the copious canvas bag attached to the handlebars, a placard in Spanish, *PROHIBIR EL USO DE TOREAR*.

The placard, on its length of string, Peedee put around his neck so that it hung down his back. He took out a bottle of lemonade from the bicycle bag, some straws, and a newspaper. 'Here, take these.' He thrust them at Raven. Then he used two hands to haul Roxana up off the cobblestones where she had been moaning with her back to the old Roman wall, and assisted her over to a shady seat in the plaza by the bullring.

It was crowded with Spanish out for the afternoon. Raven began to feel self-conscious from all the funny little stares, odd smirks and shaking heads, the Spaniards not knowing quite what to make of Grandfather and trio Quennell.

'Don't worry,' said Peedee, his placard in bold red print

dotted with realistic droplets of blood visible to anyone seated a hundred yards away. 'Torilians all know my views on the subject. They think I'm a harmless old English eccentric. I do wish they took me more seriously.' Peedee parked himself on a bench and unfolded his newspaper.

Presently a woman came up to him. Having watched Sonny's awkwardness, and his foot swinging in its leather boot as he sat sipping lemonade beside his grandfather, she caught hold of Sonny, pushed up his shirtsleeve, pulled up the left leg of his dungarees, patted him on his burnished angel curls, and then glared at Peedee while subjecting him to a stream of Spanish abuse, most of which escaped Raven. Then she flung a handful of pesetas in Peedee's astonished face.

'What did she say?' Sonny asked when the robust Spanish lady, still shaking her fist, had to be dragged away by her husband before she could lay Peedee out cold on the plaza stones.

Peedee shrugged indifferently and picked up the coins, which he dropped into Sonny's pocket. 'Oh, she was merely abusing me for letting someone as young and as angelic as you take part in bullfighting. She thought I was against it only because you'd been injured in the bullring. I now see what she was driving at.'

Sonny grinned.

Peedee, too, patted his angelic head. 'I've never had that sort of reaction from anyone before. But then, I've never had Robert Summerson with me before. A strange unpredictable race, the Spanish. She thought I'd sold you to the *toreadors*, and now, because you're injured, I am playing on public sympathy by using you for monetary gain in my campaign against bullfighting. Dear boy, my first thought is that you might do my anti-blood sports campaign a monumental favour were I to bring you here every day, and my second thought is, unless we get out of here fast, I shall have the Civil Guard after me for turning you into the youngest bullfighter in Spain.'

Chuckling to himself, Peedee went back to his bicycle with his tattered newspaper. He lifted Sonny onto the saddle, the placard left trailing down his back while they walked home to Cabo Alondra with Roxana behaving like the dying maiden.

Doña Jacqueline had left the list of Swiss schools she had promised to give to Peedee. Carina picked it up off the kitchen table and handed it to him.

There were at least twenty boarding schools listed, and Peedee, not the only one wilting like a plucked lily after the long walk home, groaned in anguish. 'How about Lausanne?' He hoped they would not argue.

Roxana, all at once recovering her strength, made the excuse that Lausanne was bound to be filled with provincial-minded little zits and she would rather go to Geneva or Zurich.

'Please qualify the word zit, dear girl.'

'Pus spot.'

'I wish I hadn't asked. How about sticking pins in and taking pot luck?'

Sonny thought that a marvellous idea and wanted to be chief pin-sticker.

'First second and third choices so that each of you gets a democratic say in the matter, and then I shan't be accused of pulling rank if it turns out you girls hate your school. I shall write to the headmistresses concerned, asking them to forward all the usual bumf high-class educational institutes delight in churning out in order to justify their scandalous fees. Besides, we might not be able to have our first choice if all the places are filled. It is rather late in the autumn term, dear girls.'

Sonny's pin stuck between Basel and Bern so they chose Bern. L'Académie Française de Madame Claude Armand. 'With emphasis upon the Arts for our Young Ladies, i.e. pastel drawing, flower pressing and decorative arrangement.'

'Oh, that sounds awfully fusty, Raven,' Sonny declared. 'Who wants to draw bowls of chocolate mousse all day long?'

Roxana stuck her pin in Zurich, The Lady Elizabeth School, principal, Miss D.K. Fairfax-Honeyboem. 'That's more like it,' Roxana said happily. 'Zurich is right at the heart of things!'

Raven suspected Roxana had her eyes half open when sticking her pin into the list. She herself came up with

Geneva: L'École Internationale. It sounded suitably anonymous and uninspiring, and she would have plumped for L'École Internationale as first choice. However, it ranked third, so it looked as though it would have to be either Bern or Zurich.

It did not turn out to be so, and for once in her life Raven found things swinging in her favour rather than Roxana's. Madame Claude Armand had no vacancies, and neither had Miss D.K. Fairfax-Honeyboem.

'Oh well,' were Peedee's words of wisdom and solace, 'Madame Armand did sound as though she ran an uppercrust bordello.'

'What's a bordello?' Sonny asked.

'Er – an establishment, dear boy, where young women conjugate rather than assonate: and before you ask me, assonance is the resemblance of sound between two syllables.'

'Gosh, Peedee, Roxa would find all that French terribly boring.'

'Yes indeed,' Peedee murmured.

Roxana scowled at him. 'You didn't tell them, did you, Peedee?'

'Tell who, what, dear girl?'

'Miss Fairfax-Honeyboem and Madam Armand about our illegitimate background?'

'Good heavens, would I be such a cad? Well now, let's just wait and see what Madame Roget at L'École Internationale has to say before starting all over again with the pin sticking. What about Lugano?'

'That's in the Italian part, Peedee! How could you even *consider* Italian as an education. All we could ever hope for from the dining-room would be pasta and pizza to make us fat.' Roxana said peevishly.

'Perhaps you're right. But then Zurich is in the German part, and you didn't seem to mind sauerkraut and sausages to make you fat.'

Madame Eugénie Roget turned out to be the answer to a prayer.

She was a widow who ran a little school for a hundred and sixty girls, right in the heart of Geneva, in the Rue de Lausanne. Although the school was of a Calvinist foundation, all denominations were catered for, and Protestant English girls made up a large proportion of her pupils. She sent a photograph of the school, which reminded Raven of the sober façade of Quennell House before it had been bombed.

Wonderful! thought Peedee. Just the kind of modest bourgeois establishment he had hoped for. Even the fees were reasonable, nothing like the extortionate rates charged by the other two.

There were many parks close-by, including La Perle du Lac and the Parc Mon Repos. English, French, German, Spanish and Italian were compulsory languages; hockey and lacrosse were optional extras: the girls played in the park since the school *jardin* was unable to accommodate team games. The school, however, did boast of three tennis courts in its own grounds. Visits to the theatre, art galleries and the Conservatoire were encouraged. Gentlemen visitors (unless a close relative) were not encouraged beyond the front entrance, and until the age of discretion, not encouraged at all.

'Sounds boring,' was Roxana's opinion.

Madame Roget went on to add that she had just two places left starting in the January term. If Mr Purnell could let her know within the next three weeks, as the requests for places were simply pouring in, she would reserve places for his granddaughters at L'École Internationale from January 1925 until June 1931, when they would be eligible for matriculation as well as entering the finishing sector of her school which 'lent the final polish to a young lady's education'.

'Doubly boring,' said Roxana.

Peedee replied to Madame Eugénie Roget that very same evening, accepting two places for his granddaughters, at L'École Internationale, Maison Roget, Rue de Lausanne, Geneva.

Once they knew for certain that Raven and Roxana had been accepted into Madame Roget's little school, Sonny reassured them, 'Don't worry. I'll take care of Morgan and Le Fay. And you mustn't be homesick. Peedee has promised to take me to the Reichenbach Falls, so we'll visit you on our way to Belfast the next time I have to go there to be fitted with my artificial contraptions.'

'What's so special about the Reichenbach Falls, Sonny?'

'I want to take a good look around at the bottom of the mountain in case Sherlock Holmes is alive and hiding in a cave after Moriarty pushed him to his death. If Mr Holmes *is* still alive, he could help Raven with her people-spotting book, and if he's in need of a new part of himself, I can be Dr Watson and tell him where to go to get the very best arms and legs in the world, Kirk and Pringle, Belfast.'

Raven, a lump in her throat, hugged Sonny tightly. 'Oh, Sonny, you *are* a funny little brother!'

She would miss him dreadfully, as she still missed Tim.

CHAPTER FOUR

New York City:
December 1926 – April 1927

Bentine DaWinter, Orthopaedic Chief, had arranged a party on Christmas Eve for his 'noble little team'. Hand-picked and sifted, they were the *crème-de-la-crème* of City Hospital.

Keir's reply was tentative, and not the steadfast affirmative he knew DaWinter expected, 'I'm not sure if I can make it, sir. Christmas Eve is Jodi's birthday. I'll try and be there after I've helped blow out the candles. Momma Bolli has made his birthday cake, you see, and she'll be offended if I don't show up, even for half an hour.'

'Attaboy!' The great man, who always maintained that ash was perfectly sterile, rested his Chesterfield carefully on the edge of the surgical sink, before scrubbing up for his next operation. 'There's nothing I like better in my men than loyalty to the family. Remember, Dr Devlin, wife, ma-in-law, and children, in that order. All else second, including career, if you wish to maintain a happy matrimonial atmosphere.'

'Yes, sir.' Keir, who could not believe he had already completed two years of post-graduate general surgery, did not know how to interpret that advice from he who had dedicated his life to his profession.

Brilliant, suave and handsome, even though he was as bald as an egg, DaWinter was the very quintessence of the Boston Brahmin. Condescendingly courteous at all times,

134

with an aura about him that only status could buy, his impeccable medical credentials came from Heidelburg and Harvard. He did not suffer fools gladly, and an invitation to anything from the Chief was obligatory. Therefore, a Christmas party organized by he and Mrs DaWinter was not a social occasion to mark up on one's Advent calendar as just another jolly good excuse to get Prohibition drunk on lemonade, it was *the* party of the season. It was also an asterisk in the favour of Dr Keiren Hunter Devlin who had received personal recognition from the Chief. Keir felt that registrarship slipping through his surgical fingers lest he come up with a way to attend one goddamn Orthopaedic Christmas party, which happened to coincide with his son's third birthday!

Vetting for senior citizenship within the hospital hierarchy had already begun. A bright young man with a great future ahead of him would be required to take on, in ten months' time, the duties of Orthopaedic Officer. All those invited to the Christmas party were, undoubtedly, on the short list for such a coveted post-graduate position. Keir was only thankful that Zimmerman had transferred to Neurology, otherwise there would have been no hope for him. It also meant a substantial rise in salary, and nothing but mercenary gain would have induced him to crawl a little longer at the feet of the man who could make or break him in his future career. Francesca, Keir thought ruefully, had turned out to be an expensive wife unable to manage on his humble three and a half thousand dollars a year.

Under running water, DaWinter carefully scraped beneath his manicured nails with a metal bone-file. He shut off the long-levered surgical spigots with his elbows so as not to waste more water than was absolutely necessary. Then he flicked his hands to rid them of excess moisture before taking the fresh towel the nurse had ready for him. He never forgot a name or a face or a subtitle, and his manners (to high and lowly alike) were always impeccable. 'Thank you, Nurse O'Neill. Now then, Dr Devlin, what is your answer? The ayes have it or the nays, who don't?' He dried his hands, picked up his cigarette and took another puff, then began scrubbing up all over again. The routine

135

was always the same, DaWinter managing to get through some four or five towels from the expensive central autoclave supply. When he had smoked the entire length of his cigarette he would get the nurse to take away the stub in a sterile receiver. Theatre farces often having repeat performances, it became a standing joke when one theatre nurse doing her duty of butt removal during the scrubbing-up and smoking ritual (which could take anything up to half an hour) described her role very aptly as that of 'midwife to the great white Chief's aborted foetus'.

Keir, assisting at this operation to remove osteosarcoma in the hip of an eight-year-old boy, with the hope that the child might live another year at least, dried his hands on the sterile green towel the theatre nurse was now patiently holding out for him. The used towel was discarded into the appropriate surgical bin. He chose his words carefully. 'Of course I'd love to come to your Christmas party, sir, but we must first see if we can get Fran's mother or one of her sisters to babysit.'

The nurse turned back to the trolley, picked up a sterile surgical gown, unfolded it, held it out to him by its tapes, and Keir, fists clenched, slipped it on. She tied the tapes at the back. Mask and cap donned, he waited for the nurse to hand him the sterile rubber gloves, powdered inside to make them easier to draw on.

Keir would not entrust his son to the safekeeping of anyone other than the Bolli family or Jenny, who still lived in the same tenement block as Nurse Lilly Wald, even though their mother had left Jefferson Street two years ago.

It had come as a blow to both Jenny and him when, after Joss's funeral, Michelle had announced her intention of returning to Switzerland, her home country. She wanted to see her sister again. Eugénie, also a widow, had been asking her for years to come to Geneva, and had even offered her a temporary job as School Secretary until she found her feet. Michelle had gone on to add that she had a little money saved for the purpose, having taken Uncle Brook's expert advice over the years to invest with the Chase National Bank, who had paid out dividends of twenty per cent on invested capital. Swiss francs seeming a good stable currency, she wanted to use her savings to start a new life away from New York. Only then Keir realized what a shrewd businesswoman his mother had been all these years on the small salary she had earned as a secretary-stenographer. Keir had remembered his mother saying, somewhat indignantly, when he had asked if she intended living in Europe permanently, 'Why not? I'm not *that* old to start again!'

Two years later, and in the light of his own parenthood, was he able to smile about it. One could never be certain of anything in life, not even one's own mother.

While knowing that they did have Swiss connections, and an aunt who ran an exclusive boarding school for girls in Geneva, when Joss had been alive Michelle had never talked about her private desires, or her own family background: and, as far as Keir was concerned, he and Jenny would never be anything *but* New Yorkers!

'What about your job with Nurse Lilly Wald?' Keir had also asked at the time, trying everything to keep his mother where she belonged.

'Lilly doesn't need me any longer. She can get all the secretaries and stenographers she wants now that the Settlement Scheme is attracting so much attention. We'll miss each other, naturally. We were both in on the Settlement Scheme programme from its inception. But I am a free person at last, my darlings, so don't prevent me from doing what I want now that I no longer have you both, or Joss, to think about. I feel I must do something for myself. I have a yen to travel, a longing to see the world and my sister again before I die. The world is *not* New York despite what you two might think or feel. Don't worry about me, I was on this earth long before you two and know how to fend for myself.'

'I wish you all the luck in the world, Ma,' he had told her sadly, knowing that he could never be the one to stand in her way. She had a right to live her life as she chose: and, God knew, she had given up enough to see him through medical school.

Keir had then made it his business to find out everything about his mother's family, and what Michelle was letting

137

herself in for by heading back to Europe.

Michelle's father had been Swiss, her mother American. The Crowborrows, a wealthy Pennsylvanian family, were on a three month vacation in Switzerland in the summer of 'seventy-eight when their daughter, Nancy, (his maternal grandmother) had met and fallen in love wth Daniel Deauvier. In Nancy's parents' opinion, Daniel was nothing but a poor peasant, a mountain guide unfortunately following the same path to the Junge Frau as their daughter. Nancy was headstrong, seventeen and American; she was also of an independent spirit. In due course, Nancy informed her parents that Daniel and she had become lovers and that she thought she might be expecting his child. It turned out to be true. Crowborrow parents, a very zealous couple whose religious principles centered upon keeping their faith intact rather than human relationships, had no choice but to marry their unrepentent daughter off to her seducer as soon as a Swiss wedding could be decently arranged. Afterwards they told Nancy they never wanted to see her again, and returned to Pennsylvania.

Four years later Daniel Deauvier died in an avalanche accident, and Nancy had become a widow with two daughters, Michelle, three, and Eugénie, one. Daniel's ageing parents were less than well-off and could not accommodate all three of them, while the Crowborrows of Pennsylvania wanted nothing to do with their disgraceful and wilful daughter or her children, especially Michelle who had been conceived out of wedlock: bad blood would only taint the rest of the family. Nancy, in quandary, made her decision, she would leave Eugénie in Switzerland with Daniel's parents when she returned to America, where fortunes were more readily made than in the old world. She would take Michelle with her, one child easier to raise than two. A bargain was struck. In return for Eugénie being raised by her ageing grandparents, she was, when the time came, expected to look after them; they also wanted Nancy to remit money from America for Eugénie's upkeep.

Nancy had nothing to do with her Pennsylvanian family once she found herself back on American soil. She never attended either parent's funeral, and Crowborrow money was left to a nephew. Nancy took a job as Chambermaid at the Barclay Hotel, New York, and very soon found another husband, a prosperous widower whom she met through turning down his bed one night. Oakley Harman recognized the lady in Nancy despite her lowly capacity of chambermaid, and, because he was lonely and Nancy attractive, willing, and twenty-five years younger than he, by mutual consent they tied the nuptial knot. Nancy was able to give up her poorly-paid chambermaid's job to bring up Michelle properly. With her new husband's blessing Nancy was also able to send money to Daniel's parents for Eugénie, now the child of her Calvinist grandparents. Little Michelle grew up adoring, and was adored in return by her elderly stepfather, a hard-working New York furrier. Years later Michelle's stepfather was the one to introduce her to a smart and good-looking, blue-eyed, all-American boy, Josslyn Hunter Devlin, himself in the fur trade.

His mother had gone full circle and Keir couldn't blame her. She still had many years of her life left. He would be the last one to say, no, don't go back to Europe Ma, stay in America and see your grandchildren grow up: Jenny, Francesca, Jodi, and I need you. It would have been untrue in any case. Francesca, he, and the baby could manage perfectly well without Michelle Deauvier Devlin, and Jenny didn't need anyone, for she was a very determined, down-to-earth, tough New York lady.

Even so, he and Jenny were bereft when their mother sailed away for Europe, and out of their lives.

Michelle, however, had stayed on long enough to see the son she had struggled half her life to educate as a gentleman become a fully qualified doctor, and her first grandchild arrive in the world, before leaving America.

Thinking about Jodi always filled Keir with tender feelings. Jodi would be three years old next week, Christmas week; unbelievable! Where had the time gone? Keir's heart swelled with pride concerning his son, Francesca's Christmas present to him to complete that incredible year of 1923.

And, thinking about Christmas presents, he'd better start buying some. He'd stop at one of the big stores and buy Jodi, Francesca, and Jenny something, in case he didn't get around to it next week. He wondered what he could get them; he wasn't terribly good with presents, sentimental words, or remembering everyone's birthday and anniversary. Neither did he relish the idea of having to buy Christmas presents for the battalion of Italian in-laws he had gained along with Francesca. He might just leave that side of the bargain to his terribly efficient sister, as he always did.

He stood like a priest, fully accoutred, his hands clasped together as if in prayer to keep them from touching anything except the sterile area surrounding the patient who, anaesthetized, was being wheeled into the operating theatre. Quite suddenly, remembering that he hadn't posted his Christmas letter to his mother in Geneva, Keir clapped an anxious gloved hand to his forehead, and received a dirty look and a frosty reprimand from the dour theatre sister.

'Fresh gloves for Dr Devlin, Nurse O'Neill,' she snapped. 'Be quick about it. Mr DaWinter will be here any minute. Size ten and a half.'

Mr DaWinter hated to have to wait on his housemen. It was always a black mark to be unready at the operating table when he arrived. Keir was only thankful that DaWinter always managed to take longer than anyone else to get himself organized and to the operating table, on account of his fetish for washing his hands between nervously puffing his 'intersurge' cigarette, as his housemen irreverently called it. He almost ripped the new pair of sterile gloves the nurse handed him with a resigned air: 'So, what the hell does it matter if he finds me without my gloves on?' he asked himself, and answered himself on that same wavelength of anxiety. 'It matters, hell, it matters to me – I *want* that registrarship.'

Keir managed to get the second pair of difficult rubber gloves on just as Mr DaWinter appeared from the scrubbing-up room, capped, gowned, masked, gloved, and wearing a pair of outsize, sterile rubber boots, as though he anticipated paddling in rivers of blood.

'Right, my good people,' Mr DaWinter said cheerfully, slapping his rubber hands together with hearty team spirit, 'let us begin.' He took his place at the table, and the first antiseptic swab from Theatre Sister. 'These thy gifts for our use, and us for thy service, uh-huh, Sister?' He said the same thing every time, without requiring an answer, and neither would Thoresen have supplied one.

Bentine DaWinter methodically worked over the area, cleansing the operation site visible within the square area of sterile green hospital towels. The swab nurse standing on the perimeter of the operating area with blackboard and chalk, began her swab count.

'The sooner we get into our new hospital, the better.' Mr DaWinter began conversationally, while all Keir wished to do was get this last operation of the day over and done with so that he could dash home to see Francesca and Jodi, whom he hadn't seen for nigh on a week.

'These lights are atrocious! But, soon, I emphasize *soon*, we shall be able to operate under shadowless conditions when the new Medical Centre is completed. The operating rooms have been designed to perfection, and will be equipped with every modern piece of scientific apparatus so far invented to make the lot of the surgeon and the physician a happy one.'

Chief DaWinter reminded Keir very much of Zimmerman during those long nights they had spent together as lowly interns on Accident and Emergency.

'Operating in here certainly *feels* as though City Hospital is the oldest hospital in New York. Do you know the history of your hospital, Nurse O'Neill?' Mr DaWinter paused for a second, hazel eyes above his surgical mask honing in on Nurse O'Neill, still in training and helping to count swabs.

'O' yuss, sir. 'Twas the first hospital to be built in Noo York City, and they put the army in here at the revolution, which was granted a royal charter by no less a person than His Majesty, King George the Tird of England, himself!'

There were smiles behind the masks at young Nurse O'Neill's broad, breathless Irish brogue. Mr DaWinter, however, did not share in the murky smirks going on around the table. His approval of Nurse O'Neill was absolute. 'Well done, Nurse O'Neill! Every intern I've put that question to has remained abysmally ignorant of the history of the place in which he lives, breathes, and works. Remember, all you noble people gathered here, that this part of the world was a British Colony until the British lost the war: hence the presence of wounded British and Hessian soldiers lying, perhaps, on this very floor upon which you now stand.'

Here goes the Boston Brahmin again, thought Keir, he and the anaesthetist at the head of the table exchanging mutually resigned looks; his next statement will be, not, remember the Alamo, but, remember the Boston Tea Party! Why didn't he just get on with things instead of all the chit-chat – and why did his nose always start to itch at the wrong moment?

'How soon will that be, sir, the – ah?' Keir's voice was muffled behind the stuffy, damp mask.

'Don't sneeze now, Dr Devlin. Try biting your lip. How soon will the new hospital open? That, Dr Devlin, is the holy-dollar question. Next year, one hopes, if all goes according to plan. How much hexamethonium has this lad been given? Good, good, we don't want a bloody battlefield when we open him up, do we? All right, left hip – are we sure this is his left hip? We don't want to operate on the wrong one, do we? Thank you, Sister Thoresen, at least someone knows what she is doing. Carry on, Dr Devlin, all is yours. I'm taking a back seat at this one.'

'Scalpel, Sister!' Keir called out loudly, and Thoresen slapped it down into the palm of his gloved hand so that he winced. Theatre Sister Thoresen always made sure one got the feel of things right from the start.

While his concentration was absolute, and he knew exactly what he was doing, there were moments when his thoughts strayed to his home life, which, Keir couldn't help feeling, had always been a battlefield like this operating area in which he stood, performed, and afterwards left with blood on his hands. He had become a programmed robot, nothing more. No private life, no home life, no enjoyment of fatherhood, nothing outside of germ warfare in an antiseptic environment.

Home was an attic in Greenwich Village, south, amongst the arty people, Italians, and out-of-work actors. That might not have been so bad had it not been for Francesca's monumental laziness and inefficiency when it came to housekeeping. God knew, the top-floor apartment in Sloane Court was small enough, but with his wife's clutter, it was like living in an overspill trash can. The bathroom was a cupboard in which he couldn't even take a bath or shower properly because of being six-three, while the sitz tub had been designed for a two-foot-one midget. Jodi's wet diapers, Francesca's lingerie and silk stockings, like irritating lianas, were always in evidence, either strangling or suffocating him as he shaved, while their one cramped bedroom contained a sagging double bed and Jodi's second-hand cot, the rest of the floor-space devoted to cases of cosmetics, racks of shoes and clothes. Everything had to be negotiated like the Catskill mountains in order to reach Jodi to say goodnight, or hi fella, are you still there amongst the garbage!

Lust had gone to his head. It had all happened so quickly, three years, eleven months later, he was still reeling from the impact of that first encounter with the female of the species: his mother had never prepared him for the Francescas of the world!

It had been a mad, passionate, heady, sexual affair right from the word go. He and Francesca had been married as soon as they knew she was expecting his child. What he hadn't known then was that Francesca was a totally selfish and pleasure-loving person, notoriously absent-minded and hopelessly untidy. It was only through Momma Bolli's regular efforts to clean up the apartment they were able to get through the lobby door at all. He was only thankful he hadn't got to live there the whole week. Francesca had refused to move from *The Village* after they were married, because it was close to Broadway.

'*West* Broadway!' he had maintained with a certain amount of scepticism.

She had told him quite firmly, 'I'm not moving! I've managed to better myself by my own efforts on the stage. Remember *Lover Boy*?' (the production had failed dismally after six performances, but Francesca still rested on her laurels). 'And you're not my bread and butter even if you are my husband. I don't want to go back to living in any spaghetti ghetto like Momma and Poppa on Mulberry

Street. It's nice here.'

His argument had been, 'It would be nice if we could see out of the windows or get through the door occasionally!' The bread and butter bit had really hurt. He had tried anaesthetizing the pain with tact. 'We don't *have* to live in any spaghetti ghetto, we can get comfortable medical quarters.'

'Medical quarters? Are you mad? I *hate* the smell you bring home with you on the rare occasions I do see you. I'd suffocate to death with all that carbolic under my nose. Decomposing zuccini smells better than you on a bad day, Doc.'

He had never pursued the subject since he spent most of his time in medical quarters, anyway. Home to him was, and ever would be, New York City Hospital. After all, home was where the heart was, and his heart was firmly entrenched in gore, guts, and germ warfare.

So, his marriage to Francesca had continued to be stormy, in bed and out of it, and, while there was no one on earth who could make love like Francesca, there was no one else in the world either, who could chuck Bolognese sauce about like Fran in a red-hot temper. In two such flaming episodes her passion had been so great, each time she had miscarried the child she had been expecting, and Jodi so far remained their only offspring. He hoped for a daughter some day, in the same way he always half hoped Momma Bolli or one of the Bolli sisters were there to stand between him and Francesca when she got really mad. Five feet eleven in her stockinged feet, she was his green-eyed, honey-blonde Valkyrie loaded with Italian tempestuousness, still hoping to make it on Broadway as opposed to off it. Totally incompatible as a couple, they both knew it. Francesca had also turned out to be his soul's torment. Winnie Winston had been right. She had told him Francesca only ever thought about two things, Francesca and Bolli.

Francesca hadn't changed one iota in three years of marriage and motherhood; he was the one who had changed.

Macy's Store fronting Broadway sold everything from

eighteen-carat gold toothpicks to wheelbarrows. Fortunately, it was late night shopping, what with Christmas week approaching, so he was able to get his presents just before the store closed. Wandering up and down miles of aisles, Keir never ceased to be amazed at the amount of merchandise available to those with hard cash – no credit allowed here.

He had bought Francesca a crocodile-leather handbag, Jenny a matching set of fur gloves and muffler, and for Jodi, a Jack-in-the-box with a yellow and white polka-dot bow tie. Although his bank balance was sadly depleted, his spirit was buoyant. He even remembered to post his letter to his mother. It would not reach her until well into the new year, but at least his conscience was clear. Pleased with his purchases, he was looking forward to sharing the conjugal bed, all night, with Francesca.

He turned his key in the yale lock, expecting to find the chain on the door. He usually yelled at Francesca or one of her numerous relatives invariably occupying the sofa to come and take the chain off the door, but tonight he was able to let himself in. 'Hi, it's only me, anyone home?' He entered the narrow hall and closed the lobby door behind him.

Keir took advantage of the moment to stuff the chic, gift-wrapped Christmas parcels from Macy's behind the clobber in the lobby cupboard. Clothes, shoes, piles of old newspapers, and glossy fashion magazines were all thrown in haphazardly. He made sure no tinsel wrappings showed, and closed the door, bursting on its hinges. He picked up off the floor an issue of *Bona Dia*, a magazine for women, left out in his haste to put everything back into the junk cupboard before Francesca caught him hiding things, and took the magazine with him into the living-room.

Every light in the place was on. He dropped the tattered magazine on the coffee-table covered in ring-marks from hot, sticky cups, and unwound his thick woollen scarf. He left his scarf and overcoat on the back of the sofa. 'Fran, I'm home. Didn't I tell you always to keep the chain on the door? You never know who's about, especially at night.'

Keir went into the kitchen. One couldn't turn around without knocking something over, and he sniffed in disgust. The air was blue with smoke. A meal was halfway to being prepared. Water had run dry in a saucepan, and what had been cooking was now unidentifiable charcoal. Wrinkling his nose, he turned off the electric plate and doused the saucepan under cold water. Burnt offerings hissed and fizzed like active squibs. One more skillet for the trashcan, he thought in resignation. He left the saucepan in the stone sink.

He wondered where Francesca had got to. Nor did he want to think about the next quarter's electricity bill. Francesca was so careless, and so extravagant! He sighed: and so much for a welcome homecoming! But, in all fairness to Francesca, she didn't know he was coming home tonight. Keir appreciated it was his fault really for not letting Francesca know that he had time off. Mrs. Guggenheim, in the apartment on the next mezzanine floor below, had a telephone. She would have been willing to take a message for Francesca had he telephoned his intention of spending his night-off at home instead of in his tiny, cramped 'bachelor' room in medical quarters shared with a friendly skeleton called Wendover, his silent revisionary colleague and aid to surgical anatomy.

Keir found a bottle of beer in the refrigerator. Retrieving a glass from the dish-drainer, he went back into the living-room.

He put a gramophone record on the turntable, Gershwin's 'Rhapsody in Blue', a favourite of his. The stylus was scratchy and he inserted a new one. Then he went into the bedroom. Lights were on in there as well, and as he tugged at his tie to remove it, Jodi struggled to stand up in his cot, rubbing his sleepy eyes. 'Dada – drinky.' He put out his chubby arms and grinned at Keir, before shoving his fist coyly into his mouth and sucking his dimpled knuckles.

He was such a happy child. Contented by himself, or in company, it made no difference to his smiling, beguiling nature. Waking or sleeping, sick or well, Jodi never cried or complained.

'Hi fella, where's Momma?' Keir lifted him over the sides of the wooden cot and kissed him. His son didn't smell very nice. A kind of stale, sickly odour clung to his clothes, and his nose was horribly runny. Keir wiped it with his own handkerchief.

'Gone,' Jodi said, bouncing in Keir's arms.

'Gone? Gone where? To the bathroom?' Keir banged on the door. 'Fran, have you fallen alseep in the tub?'

No reply, and so he slid back the door that was on runners because the bathroom wasn't big enough for a door to open inwards. It was very obvious Francesca was not taking a bath or a leak.

'Gone,' Jodi repeated, grinning more broadly than ever while he fisted Keir's cheeks to make them pop. He liked it when his father played with him and made funny faces. 'Me not cry,' he reassured Keir.

Fear paramount, Keir took Jodi down one flight to the mezzanine landing and banged on Mrs Guggenheim's door. One neighbour at least would be sure to know of Francesca's whereabouts. Mrs Guggenheim knew everyone's business in the house, not only because she was General Telephone Company for most of the residents, but also because she spent more time in other apartments rather than her own.

'Do you know where Fran is, Mrs Gee?' Keir asked when she came to the door. 'Did she say where she was going?'

Metal hair-curlers, shabby grey dressing-gown, and carpet slippers with the toes through, Mrs Guggenheim had guessed who the caller might be. She had seen the wife dashing down the stairs a little while ago. With a Virginia stuck to her lower lip, spilling ash as she spoke, Mrs Guggenheim, whose late husband had been a theatrical agent, shrugged her skinny shoulders. 'She never tells me where she's going, Keir, not any more. We don't speak since our bad row, over a month ago. She complained about Tiptop keeping her awake when she was trying to get in some sleep, and I told her she shouldn't be sleeping at twenty after one in the afternoon when she's gotta kid to care for.'

Tiptop was Mrs Guggenheim's whippet, and he couldn't blame Francesca for getting mad at it, it never stopped yapping day or night. He could hear it now, doing its bit somewhere in the background.

Mrs Guggenheim smiled and touched Jodi's hand gently. 'Hi, Jodi, you wan' a fortune cookie?'

'Yup.'

She went away and fetched him two. Jodi tried to fill his mouth with both at the same time.

'She didn't leave him again on his own, did she? I'm always telling her she shouldn't, but she never listens.'

'I thought you said you weren't on speaking terms?'

'Speaking terms, peaking terms, you know how it is. But we don't speak like we used. Now we only seem to yell insults at one another. I've stopped interfering, Keir. It's none of my business. But you oughtta tell her she's taking a risk leaving Jodi on his own like that, even for a couple of minutes to go to the grocery or drugstore. You never know who's about these days or if the house will catch fire.'

'Thanks, Mrs Gee.'

He went back into his own apartment, shut the outer lobby door and sat down on the sofa with Jodi on his lap.

'Drink!' Jodi insisted, crumbs all round his gooey pink mouth.

'Oh sure, sorry!' He fetched Jodi a cup of milk, and afterwards sat him on his tin pot because Jodi asked for it, thanks again to Momma Bolli's careful training ever since he was ten months old, because Francesca wouldn't have had the patience to potty-train Jodi in between dashing off to her rehearsals: and that was another thing; Francesca had refused to give up work after Jodi was born. She had been in one or two minor productions off Broadway, nothing brilliant, but he felt he couldn't stand in the way of her career; she had every right to it, as he had to his. He was only grateful for people like his sister and in-laws, as well as Mrs Guggenheim, who came to the rescue whenever a babysitter was required for Jodi. What he would not forgive Francesca was her reason for leaving Jodi alone tonight. If she had gone to the grocery store, even for a few minutes, then she should have taken Jodi with her if she had been unable to get a last-minute minder.

Keir resettled himself on the sagging sofa, Jodi at his feet, taking his time on the tin pot brought into the living-room. 'Rhapsody in Blue' had finished, but Keir couldn't be bothered to take off the gramaphone arm which was making an aggravating 'sishing' noise on the turntable.

Keir started to time Francesca's absence to the last second.

In front of him on the coffee table was the women's fashion magazine from the junk cupboard. It was hopelessly out of date – January 1923. He had still been an intern. Ye gods, didn't Francesca chuck anything away!

An irresistible face stared back at him: exquisite features, and soft blue-grey eyes beneath eyebrows only spoiled by the dictates of fashion in that they were pencilled in. Delectable mouth, lower lip full and red and packed with promise; a pointed chin, a long smooth, white neck adorned with a pearl necklace, no doubt genuine and not a cheap imitation. The colour of the hair was not apparent, covered as it was by a fashionable jade-green hat worn low and close to the head.

He spent a long time analyzing that beautiful face, wondering who the mysterious and compelling woman was with her fine aristocratic haughtiness, coupled with the 'catch-me-quick' sparkle in her eyes. The more he gazed in abstraction at the glossy image of the unknown woman, the more she seemed to take on substance, reaching out to him in a strange, disconcerting way. And because he had nothing to do in that off-guard moment except stargaze upon a face that had drawn his attention so compellingly, he began to flick over the pages to the feature article under its glamorous heading, 'The Angel's Share'.

It was all about an Anglo-Irish society lady, patron of the Irish White Cross, married to one of Ireland's most distinguished judges, Sir Francis Quennell, Baronet. Before her marriage, Lady Quennell had been the Honourable Daphne Moynahan, one of the *La Maison Moderne* of her generation. There were glossy pictures of Lady Quennell's racehorses and cars, Lady Quennell at The Curragh, Longchamps, and Epsom's Derby Day, and at the wheel of her smart little red Austin Seven, Lady Quennell at a society wedding in London, and with her husband as part of Eamon de Valera's entourage at the Waldorf-Astoria Hotel on 23 June, 1919, when de Valera had made his first public appearance in America. The President of the new Irish Free State had been hoping to raise from the American people a five million dollar loan to 'secure the recognition of the Irish Republic'. The magazine article disclosed a picture taken of Sir Francis and Lady Quennell at The White House, shaking hands with President Woodrow Wilson. Another picture showed her opening an Irish knitware store on Fifth Avenue on St Patrick's Day, 1921, during a fund-raising campaign on behalf of the Irish White Cross. There was also a family group taken at the country mansion, Hollyberry House, County Kildare, Lady Quennell, in hunting dress, smiling somewhat glassily at her four good-looking children astride their ponies.

Lucky for some, thought Keir wryly, at least they had something in common, Ireland! Then he read the obituary by the female writer of that sycophantic women's interest article: Lady Quennell, her husband, and their eldest son, Timothy Quennell, had been killed by an IRA bomb at their home in Merrion Square, Dublin, on New Year's Day, 1923. The other three children had been badly injured. *Bona Dia* in its quarterly issue, was paying its own tribute to a lady who had done so much to awaken the American conscience in raising money on behalf of charitable and welfare organizations concerned in the Relief of Ireland Fund. Lady Quennell's memory would live on through the Irish White Cross, still in urgent need of support; all donations to be sent to the address at the foot of the page:

And angels are summoned back to heaven, Keir couldn't help reflecting as he tossed the magazine aside. The lady was a ghost. The article and the captivating woman had somehow lost their appeal.

'Hi, Jodi, what've you found there?' Keir took away the stale crust of bread Jodi had ferreted out from under the sofa cushion, and replaced it with a biscuit from the tin in the kitchen. He emptied Jodi's pot, and then washed Jodi's face and hands, and tidied him up a little. By the time Francesca arrived back, he had been sitting on the sofa with Jodi on his lap for fully twenty-seven minutes.

She carried a bag of groceries, and over the top of the brown paper carrier, she greeted him without a care in the world. 'Hi, Doc, what a surprise! I thought I wouldn't see you till next year. Hi fella, kiss Momma. You been a good boy? I told you I wouldn't be long, so not to cry, didn't I? He wasn't bawling when you arrived, was he, Keir?'

'Would it have made any difference?' By now he was so worked up, he was shaking. Taking Jodi, he went in to the bedroom, placed him back in his cot, told him to go back to sleep like a good boy, shut the bedroom door, and then faced Francesca with such pent-up fury, he thought he might throttle her if she said the wrong thing. 'Where were you?' He followed her into the filthy kitchen where she set down her grocery package on the table before tossing her smart coat onto the back of a chair.

If the apartment was a pigsty, his son in need of a bath, and his clothes to be washed, she herself was impeccable. She wore a beautifully tailored dress in a heather wool mixture that fitted her Junoesque figure like a glove. The dress was obviously brand-new. Her costume jewellery, the genuine article being unaffordable, had been carefully and tastefully selected. Her nails were manicured and painted, not a long fingernail broken or snagged, and she smelled divine against the stale kitchen odours. Francesca tossed her head, crimps and bangs restyled only that afternoon at the hairdressers, and her green eyes flashed defiantly. She riled him more than ever, because she knew she was cornered, so tried backchatting him. 'What do you mean where was I? I was at Sam's grocery store doing the shopping, that's where!'

'How many times have you left Jodi on his own like this?'

'Not a lot.'

'That's not what Mrs Guggenheim told me.'

'That old cat ought to have her tongue spayed.'

She started to put away the stores in the cupboard, but he grabbed her arm and whirled her round to face him. 'I've been here for half an hour, so how long were you gone before I arrived?'

She pulled her arm away. 'How should I know! Jesus! What is this, some kind of inquisition?'

'Damn right! I could kill you, Francesca. Don't you *ever* leave Jodi alone again. Anything could have happened to him while you were gone. The place could have burned down. I walked in here and found every goddamn light on, the stove on, spaghetti burnt away to nothing. You might at least have taken him across to Mrs Gee while you went shopping.'

'I'm not speaking to her.'

'I don't care whether you're speaking to her or not, *don't leave Jodi!*'

'Stop yelling at me like that! And look who's talking! You don't exactly lend much of a helping hand yourself, do you Doc? So let me tell you something. Yasmin downstairs was keeping an eye on Jodi while I was fetching the groceries, that's why the lobby door was left open – aw shucks! Now look what you've made me do!' In her confusion at being caught out by him, she had cut her finger, sliced deeply by the jagged tin lid, and she dashed her hand under the cold water tap before the blood stained her new dress. 'Anti-tet, Doc?' She turned, and eyed him warily, her finger in her mouth.

'Why don't you try buying some fresh food for a change, instead of tins and cartons the whole time?' He accused, while rummaging in a drawer for the first-aid-box.

'Sure, buster! Just *you* try buying fresh New York tomatoes in December on the pittance you bring home!'

'Don't start that again, Francesca.'

'This is welfare week, remember?' Her green eyes glinting, her mouth bunched into an expression of put-upon resentment, surprisingly she didn't lose her temper and scream and shout and fling things around as she usually did when he spoke his mind.

Everything was in such a mess, he couldn't even find an adhesive plaster. Keir, calming down because she had hurt herself, said less harshly, 'Come on, let's see what you've done.' Guilt was beginning to creep up on him, and he did not like the feeling one bit. Fran was right. He didn't do enough of his fair share around the house, especially when it came to caring for Jodi, so he had no right to accuse *her* of neglect. He just wished there were sixty-four hours in a day, and then perhaps he might find the time to be a proper husband and father.

Francesca held out her finger. 'I'll take a rain check if you're nice to me.' Thrusting her finger in his mouth, she smiled seductively. 'Since you're out for blood, Doc.'

He suddenly forgot her injury, and pulled her to him in a fierce embrace, heedless of her bleeding finger messing up his white shirt. 'What am I going to do with you, Fran?

152

You're a hopeless case, you know that?' He was willing to forgive her: but only this one last time concerning Jodi being left alone. Keir cupped her face in his hands, his thumb caressing the thin white razor line he had mended so perfectly. 'I could always earn a better living as a cosmetic surgeon, I suppose,' he said thoughtfully, adding the plea, 'Please don't leave Jodi alone again. Why didn't you get Momma over?'

'She's got the sniffles and I didn't want her to give anything to Jodi. I got enough problems taking care of him without him being sick as well.'

'Then why didn't you get Sylvie or Stella?'

'They've gone to the movies with their boyfriends.'

'Then starve to death, Fran,' he said, releasing her. 'But don't leave Jodi ever again, you hear?'

'Yeah, I hear, big daddy, and I'm tellin' you something, no more kids, Doc, not till I'm eighty. Now, you want some pasta, or not?'

'Christ! Don't mention the stuff. Is that all you know how to cook, Fran?'

'Yep. So what do you want to eat?'

'Nothing. Leave it.' He attended to her finger, having at last found some tacky dressing tape. 'Let's go to bed.'

'Not yet, I'm starving. I haven't eaten all day.' She sat down at the table and dug into a carton of yoghurt. She didn't look at him. 'You go to bed if you want, I'll come in a minute. Only don't wake Jodi again.'

He stood in the kitchen doorway watching her for a few seconds. 'What's up? Afraid I've forgotten what a French letter is?'

'Nothing. It just takes time getting used to a part-time husband.'

'Sorry! What do you want me to do, give up my job to be a full-time bum on welfare?' He went into the bedroom, undressed, and lay down on the unmade bed. His arms behind his head, he stared up at the ceiling, a simmering anger and frustration still with him. After a while, listening to Jodi's sweet baby snores, he relaxed and counted his blessings. At least there was Jodi to make it all worthwhile.

The doorbell buzzed and Francesca's voice from the

kitchen yelled, 'I'll get it.' He had no intention of getting up and answering it himself.

Ten minutes later she came into the bedroom, undressed, and hung up her new dress on the back of the door.

'Who was it?' he asked, hardly caring as he opened one eye to look at her. She had forgotten to switch off the living-room light and remained silhouetted like a magnificent naked Amazon between the two rooms.

'Mrs Guggenheim asking if I'd got back yet. Nosey bitch! I swear one of these days I'll poison that bandy-legged pile of old soup bones.'

'Poor Mrs Guggenheim.'

'Haven't you noticed how people and their pets resemble each other?'

'Do they?'

'Sure. You in the mood, Doc?'

A little while ago he had been so angry with her, he just wanted to get shot of the sight of her. Now he wasn't so sure. The extreme weariness he had experienced all evening evaporated. He regarded her steadily, and knew that he'd like to do all those things he'd missed out on for a long time. Superb breasts and legs, she straddled the threshold of the two rooms as well as his lust, Francesca enticing him as always. 'I guess I am,' he said, reaching for her. But he took her down in the other room for fear of waking Jodi, and because the bed was always so darned uncomfortable and noisy.

It was as though they both had to make up for lost time, the ferocity of their mating the only thing that mattered. Astride him like some golden Valkyrie, her lustrous beige hair and breasts and belly twice that of any other woman, she was like some glorious goddess of the universe screwing it for her own gratification: and again there was no gentleness, no tenderness, no real love involved, only Francesca riding to war. Her voracious appetite and passionate nature never let him down, he could guarantee it, for it was never an act of love, nor even of sex really: to be fucked was what she wanted, every time and any how, punctuated with the kind of whore talk she thought would turn him on. In the end he was always left with a feeling of distaste and disgust and demoralization, even when she had given him all the pleasure and satisfaction a man could want, for Keir got the feeling that Francesca would do this with anyone.

But he only thought about that afterwards, when the excitement and the sensation wore off and the suspicion, accusation and wondering where she had learned to say and do all those things, took over his mind. Right now he wanted satisfaction and be damned to the agonized groaning of squeaky floorboards, or of falling through the living-room floor into the apartment below. In the end, exhausted and empty, he flung himself away from her, and on the saggy sofa slept the sleep of the dead.

On the mezzanine landing, Mrs Guggenheim peered out. She was thankful to see that the two men, one black, one white, who had rung the Devlin doorbell a little while ago, were nowhere to be seen. She had noticed them hanging around Doc's place before, and she didn't trust them. She shut the door again. 'Movie directors!' she snorted contemptuously as she lovingly cradled her little bandy-legged whippet in her arms to stop Tiptop's noisy excited yapping. 'They've gone now, Tiptop. Nasty foul-mouthed men! I was only doing my duty like a good neighbour by telling them Doc was home tonight, so that kind of language to a lady ain't nice. I don't know what the world is coming to!' Mrs Guggenheim went inside her lobby and locked and chained her door.

A few afternoons later, Keir decided to drop in unexpectedly at the apartment while another surgeon covered his duties. He felt guilty about trying to catch Francesca out, but he simply didn't trust her not to slip off to a matinée performance or rehearsal, leaving Jodi alone again. He made the pledge to himself that if Francesca was home, he would lend a domestic hand this afternoon by doing the grocery shopping and keeping Jodi amused for her. Had it been warmer, he would have taken Jodi to Washington Square Park. He consoled himself with promises that as soon as the first day of spring arrived, he and his son would do just that. A regular fatherly routine *had* to be established, he *must* spend more time with his family, and allow Francesca free time to herself. It wasn't fair that she had to be the one to make all the baby-minding arrangements, marriage was a partnership, after all. Immediately Keir felt better for having decided to do something about his erratic married life, even while wondering how he was supposed to juggle Chief DaWinter's operating lists, plus post graduate studies, in order to keep everyone happy.

To his relief, big Momma Bolli was taking care of Jodi, and so his time and conscience was salvaged. He wouldn't need to do the shopping as Momma always brought bags of food with her.

He had great affection for both his in-laws. Momma was a hearty, robust woman built like a docker and blessed with the health and energy of an Olympian athlete. Poppa, with magnificent grey whiskers, but a streaky rasher of bacon beside his meaty wife, was a porter at Penn Street station. He and Momma had been married for forty-two years, and had eleven children (seven still living at home in the cramped confines of a Mulberry Street apartment). Keir felt that if Francesca grew in character and nature as gracefully as Momma, he would have nothing to complain about; he lived in hope. Momma took in other people's washing, baked pizzas, pies and pâtes for a local Italian delicatessen, sat with the sick, delivered the maternity cases, and laid out the dead. Yet she still found time to mind Jodi, who appeared to have inherited his grandmother's sunny disposition.

Momma Bolli left the linen she had been ironing on the kitchen table, thumped down the flat iron onto the electric plate, before smacking half a dozen kisses all over his face. 'Good to see you, Doc.' Her large, round, pudding face and raisin-dark eyes crinkled into a happy smile of welcome as she held his cold face in her large, hot hands. Her treble chins trembled with pride. She had been thrilled to bits when her lovely Francesca married Kier, *dottore primo primo!* Such a lovely man was Doc, she always knew her Francesca would go far in the world. 'What brings you home today, Doc?'

'Love of you, Ma,' He smiled, tossing his damp coat and

156

scarf onto the back of a kitchen chair.

'Tch-tch! Now I know why this place it looks like Paddy's Market!' Momma Bolli eyed him reprovingly as she tucked straying wisps of grey hair back into her bun held in a hairnet. Then she took up his coat and scarf to hang in the lobby cupboard. 'You are a big, untidy man, just like my Francesca. Many things on your mind, uh, Doc?'

'Where's Jodi?' He followed his mother-in-law out of the steamy kitchen.

'Shhh! He's asleeping, Keir.'

He went into the bedroom to take a peek at his son. Keir could tell at once Momma had bathed and fed him and changed his clothes. Jodi looked like a freshly-laundered cherub, thumb in his mouth, sweet baby smile on his face. Keir left Jodi to his afternoon nap and quietly shut the door.

'Don't mess up with the sheets, Keir, an' Momma will make one best cup of Italian coffee only for you.' Momma Bolli fussed around the clean clothes as he took his place at the kitchen table. Then she busied herself with making coffee and setting plates on the table. 'I bring you *dolci* I make myself. You wanna *tarta di pasta frolla*, or *pesche ripiene*?'

'Both, Ma, never ask.'

Her pleasure was doubled. She positively beamed with housewifely pride. 'You have one big appetite, Doc. I like to see this thing in my men. I getta the Marsala from your Uncle Brooklyn. Mr Cini at the delli, he make me a rise this week. Two cents more for one hour. Wow! Momma is big millionaire now.'

'So what're you going to do with this big raise of yours?'

'I bring you one big heart full of *pesche ripiene*.'

'Something money can't buy, eh, Momma?'

'Francesca, she oughtta know with one big momma like me, the way to a man's heart is in his belly, no?'

'Close,' he said, cutting through mouthwatering short-crust pastry, and, on the same plate, sponge as only Momma could make with the thickest, sweetest peaches and almonds. 'So where's Francesca this afternoon?'

'You mean you donna know?' She stopped wielding the iron over one of his shirts and started at him. 'She donna tell you nuttin'?'

'Nothing.'

'She's makin' a movie.'

He stopped eating. His mouth full, he stared at Momma Bolli in astonishment. 'Making a movie?'

'Yup! My Francesca, she is goin' to be a big movie star like Mary Pickaford. I like to see this movie again, *Daddy On A Leg*.'

'*Daddy Longlegs*, Momma.'

'Maybe my Francesca make a *big* movie with Douglas Fairbanks, eh, Doc? Just like this Mary Pickaford.' Momma Bolli smartly folded the clean sheet and slapped it down on the pile of ironed clothes. She opened one half of the kitchen window, and leaned out, her huge, rounded bottom dangerously poised over the windowsill as she pulled in the washing-line on which more linen was drying on the sooty face of the building. She tossed the damp, smoke-begrimed clothes on the table and almost into his plate, slammed shut the window and turned to beam upon him over the household linen and the *pesche ripiene*. 'Your wife, Doc, she is goin' to be famous one day.'

'Where?' He resumed his eating thoughtfully.

'Hollywood, where else?'

'I mean where in New York is she making this movie?'

'Mr Al's Studio, West Broadway, 42nd Street.'

'Thanks for the tart, Ma. I've got to get back on duty.'

'Never you finish your food proper, Doc! Always you goin' someplace. You mind you donna getta the ulcer yourself.'

He grinned, 'I'll mind.' He kissed her goodbye, and taking his coat and scarf from the lobby cupboard, which he was glad to see had been tidied, he banged the door behind him so that Mrs Guggenheim would be aware that he was taking his leave.

It took him an hour to find the studios Momma Bolli had mentioned.

At least they existed, manifest in the large sign above the door: Mr AL, STAR-WAY TO THE MOVIES. For a while he had been sceptical of any Mr Al Moviemaker, unless it was Mr Al Jolson himself. In this sleazy area off Times Square, Keir very much doubted the great man with the golden voice would be engaged in making low-budget silent movies. Relying on a gut feeling, he knew he was right when two men, one black, one white, tried pushing him back onto the street after he'd hammered on the studio door for fully ten minutes.

'We're busy this afternoon, man.' Keir received a shove in the stomach from the flat pink palm of the fat little black man.

Mr Al's second bodyguard, in contrast pale, thin, and seedy, blew cheroot smoke in Keir's face from under the brim of his fedora. 'Get lost, mister!' He wore white braces, a white tie, baggy black trousers, and a black shirt, no jacket. He chewed his cheroot and swaggered again, 'We're heavily booked.'

'If you don't let me talk to my wife, I'll fetch the cops,' Keir said, keeping his fists firmly in his pockets: remember, that registrarship, he warned himself.

'Your wife, suck?'

'Yeah, *Mrs* Francesca Devlin. I want to know just what kind of movie she's making.'

'None of your business. She's under contract.'

Behind the two men was a flight of basement stairs. Without arguing further, Keir pushed Mr Al's guardian angels aside, and before they could stop him, loped down the stairs two at a time. Several doors led off from a central dark passageway, but one of the doors had a flashy red light above it, obviously the one he was looking for. Keir banged on the door and then rattled the handle. 'Francesca, if you're in there, I want to know what you're doing!'

The black man came panting up behind him, the white one following. 'Hey, you can't go in there, they're busy.'

'I bet!' Keir shoved hard with his shoulder. The flimsy sliding bolt on the inside of the studio door snapped. Bright studio lights dazzled him, and instinctively he put up a hand in front of his face.

When his eyes adjusted to the scene Keir saw the pictures. Nude females right through the skin spectrum, black, brown, coffee, yellow, cream, and white, in a variety of erotic poses, covered the walls. Keir felt sick.

Francesca was very swift in reaching for her robe while

the photographer, another black man, but bigger, broader, and far more handsome than the bodyguard, temperamentally flung his expensive Eastman camera on the floor. 'Ain't you assholes aware I am trying to take pictures of this accommodating female here? Now you gone and ruined my best art work!'

His suspicions well-founded, Keir asked, 'Why, Fran?'

'Why don't you get off my back for once, Keir!' Francesca, who never called him Keir except when she was livid, furiously tied the sash of her robe before she went behind some very-thoughtfully-provided screens, which Keir knew didn't mean a thing. She was abusive as never before, 'Why do you think I take my clothes off? For money, you *schtoonk*!'

'Listen mister white guy, get oughtta here,' said Mr Al, picking up his camera and examining it. 'This is a private *art* studio with a legit licence to sell *art* photography to the general public, and you are upsetting my best model. Francesca generates a lotta bucks, so you back off, or I call the cops.'

'No! *You* back off, or *I* call the cops!' Keir went up to the smart Negro and prodded a finger at one of his broad lapels. 'Francesca is my wife, sucks! And I've come to take her home.'

'Aw shit!' Mr Al, over the top of the screen, said, 'You never told me you was a married lady, honeychile. Mr Al don't employ married ladies, only the *un*-complicated single ones. It was in the contract! Can't you read? There's too much shit involved when husbands turn up, *demanding* their conjooglar rights. You're fired, honeychile.' He turned back to Keir, 'Now listen, dude, compensation for your little lady, or rather, I should say correctly, *big* lady, revealing herself to other assholes without *your* permission, because I don't want no trouble from you.' He opened his fancy snakeskin billfold, took out a wad of dollar bills, and slapped them on the leopard skins on which Francesca had been baring all.

Keir took up the money, which he then thrust down the front of Mr Al's smart blue vest. 'I don't deal in mean greens, *Mister* Al. And any more porno-pictures, I tell the cops where they can get their money's worth.'

160

On the balls of his feet, the suave Negro rocked towards Keir, gave a little gurgle of mirth, and then took out an English pinchbeck calling-card case from his inside breast pocket. He drew out a thin brown cheroot, lit it, and blew smoke in Keir's face, just as his stooge had done. 'They already know it, wise guy. Mr Al, you see, pays *City Hall's* gilt-edged lulus, capeesh?'

The Negro's cool-cut insolence made Keir clench his hands even more tightly by his sides. Cracked knuckles wouldn't get him that orthopaedic officership, he warned himself.

'And, strictly for the record, wise guy, I'm not Mr Al. *I'm* Jace. Jace of Spades, if you care to sometime look into my face. I'm only Mr Al's chauffeur-cum-photographer-cum-butler. You owe me, dude, one mighty expensive new camera. *How*-ever, since *wifey* was so accommodating, and we don't care to see *your* white ass around here no more, you got yourself clean peenicker pawnee.'

Holy Mary, he'd sock him one hard, but he didn't want to be in trouble with the police, or DaWinter. He'd kill Fran for this. 'Come on, let's get out of here.' Keir bundled Francesca up the stairs to sidewalk level.

Out in the street, Francesca jerked her coat around her and refused to walk back with him. It was all he could do to keep up with her. 'Where's your wedding-ring?' he demanded furiously.

'In the doo-doo can, shmuck!'

And he used to think Winnie needed a Dettol mouthwash!

Once inside the apartment, she turned on him, fists pounding his shoulders, 'You dumb mutt! You *humiliated* me in front of those black jacks!'

'You didn't seem to mind taking off your clothes for them. Is money so important to you, you act like a hooker?'

'Watchit, buster. I take my clothes off for recognition from the *real* moviemakers, no other reason.'

'By being a cheap stripper?'

'I dunno what's with you, knuckle head! Some movie director might see my picture and offer me a contract to act. You gotta act wise in this showbusiness biz. Mr Al has contacts everywhere, including the White House. Why! President Coolidge himself might see my picture on his office calendar. And fancy thinking that rat-fink stooge, Jace, was Mr Al!' She flung her hands up temperamentally. 'How dumb can you get!'

'Grow up, Francesca.'

'No, *you* grow up, you great galoot! I can't get a proper job on Broadway because of the hours you keep.'

'What have my hours got to do with it?'

'*Jodi!*' She yelled at him. 'I gotta make arrangements every time for him. And no one likes staying awake till three and four in the morning! You're his father! You might at least do your fair share of baby-minding.'

'And you're his *mother!* You surely can't mean you resent your own child for keeping you out of the limelight? Can't you even wait a few more years until Jodi grows up and is out of your way at school before you start taking your clothes off for the general public?'

For an answer she let fly with her fist and caught him smartly in the eye. 'That's for ruining my career and my life. A few years puts lines on a woman's face, while her tits need surgery. No thanks! You go to your dumb Christmas party with your hospital bedlugs. Me, I'm still in show biz, buster, and that's where I'm staying. With or without my clothes!'

At that moment the door bell buzzed. Keir, his hand over his bruised eye confronted Mrs Guggenheim and her ubiquitous cigarette. Looking a little nervous, she held Jodi's hand tightly. 'I'm sorry to intrude at a bad moment, Keir, but Jodi was sick, and wanted to come home. Momma Bolli left him with me as she had to get back to Mr Cini's delicatessen. Jodi said he'd like to get to bed.'

Keir picked Jodi up. 'Okay, Mrs Gee, thanks for minding Jodi. You let Francesca know how much she owes you for babysitting this week as I'm in a hurry right now.'

'Thanks, Keir. But I could do with the money as soon as possible as Tiptop's been poorly and vets don't come cheap. What've you done to your eye?'

Francesca yelled from the kitchen, 'Tell that old bag of soup bones she ain't getting a cent from me! And she needn't mind Jodi any more, I'll make other arrangements for him. All she needs to mind from now on, is her own dumb business and her goddam noisy flea-bitten skunk!'

Keir shrugged apologetically, thrust a dollar out of his own pocket into Mrs Guggenheim's hand, and hastily shut the door.

He made sure Jodi was all right before returning to the hospital. A steelworker on a skyscraper building had fallen thirty feet from scaffolding onto broken sheets of glass and was presently in Emergency. As soon as his condition was stabilized, he would be coming along to Surgery. The man was in a bad way, multiple fractures, femoral artery severed, possibly requiring above-knee amputation. Dr Devlin was required in the operating theatre, *stat*!

The only time he ever heard Theatre Sister Thoresen make a personal remark was during that operation. 'Dr Sanders who has been covering for you, Dr Devlin, wondered where you had got to. Now we know. Try beefsteak on your war-wound. I believe it works wonders.'

'Can't afford it. Pass the amputation saw — if you please, Sister.'

He wondered if a pair of Macy's dark glasses might not be too obvious at Bentine DaWinter's Christmas party.

Winter, and now again spring, he hardly noticed the changing seasons, the passage of time, himself getting older, let alone his son. The daffodils and crocuses were thrusting their way up in Central Park. Limes and lindens and shagbark hickory burgeoned gracefully while the flock of southdown sheep in Sheep Meadow already had their lambs skipping beside them, and, with the rest of the world, shared the city's grassy space. Spring fever was in the air: he had forgotten what it smelled like.

He and Francesca had settled back into an uneasy domestic routine since he had made it very plain to her he did not want her taking off her clothes for Mr Black Jace, Mr Al, or Mr White House President himself.

Francesca, after the black eye episode, turned over a new leaf. She cleaned and smartened up the apartment, bought new curtains and covers, spent a field day in Gimbels buying clothes and toys for Jodi, whom she had enrolled at a Catholic kindergarten, and was generally behaving as,

Keir felt, a wife and mother should.

And then that niggling doubt assailed him – here he was patronizing her again instead of adding something constructive towards domestic harmony. Was he truly being fair to Francesca despite his own promises to take more responsibility as far as Jodi was concerned? Jodi was his child too. Francesca was doing her best around her own career, so why should she be the one to give up her role each time and not he? Keir was in a dilemma, matrimonial problems never envisaged when marrying a career woman, presenting unpleasant friction now.

He had taken for granted that upon marriage a woman's place was in the home. What he hadn't bargained for was the maternal hand rocking the matrimonial boat instead of the cradle.

But, had he, in his own mind, defined Francesca's role to suit himself and now resented it because she didn't conform to his masculine ideas of where a woman's place should be? Was he confusing his own mother and Francesca with the Virgin Mary? Had he unconsciously placed in a niche the two most important women in his life, reconciling to them that Madonna role he himself had bestowed upon them? Michelle had been pressed into earning a living for her family in the absence of a supportive husband. Francesca, too, required to be independent. Was he, the threatened male, suddenly resentful because of this reversal of roles? Was the son in the first instance, the husband and father in the second, relegating to mother and wife that smiling, simple, loving, caring, unworried, vacant Virgin Mary? And was the cherubic infant – who never needed a father in any capacity other than to be the male in the background, the stalwart dependable breadwinner who, while never expressing his love voluably or tangibly, did it none the less – confused with images of his boyhood without a dependable father?

Perhaps: and perhaps he was still smarting from a lot of things, the fact that independent women made him feel insecure and inadequate, his masculine ego threatened; the fact that maybe there was still a resentful little boy lurking somewhere in his manly soul and body, for had

Joss only once, just once, taken him to the park to fly the superb kite Jacob Schiff had given him for his fourteenth birthday, all would have been forgiven. Joss, however, had been too busy drinking himself to death at that time to spare a thought for the youngster eager to fly his kite, with his father bestowing paternal praise and encouragement beside him.

So, from those memories of a marred boyhood he did not want Jodi to experience, was he, ultimately, demanding too much of himself and too much of Francesca? Possessiveness could be destructive, so he had better watch out; he mustn't be so critical of Francesca, wanting her to be that perfect wife and mother at every turn. And he was probably being overly old-fashioned in his viewpoint, too, concerning career women. Jenny herself, another of this new generation of feisty postwar independent women, would be the first to tell him not to be so boorish.

And, if he saw himself as 'careful' in the exercise of thrift, which Francesca was apt to describe as mean and stingy, it was with a certain amount of caution, born from the fear of debt and poverty casting a shadow over him still. He asked her dubiously, 'Can we afford this new lifestyle? I mean, Fran, Jodi in kindergarten, all this flashy new furniture. I still only earn a doctor's pittance, y'know!'

'Aw shucks, don't rub it in honey! You know I didn't mean what I said. Sure, things cost money, but don't worry about it. I got me a nice little part-time job Mondays to Fridays while Jodi's away in kinders school. It pays well, I'm able to juggle the housekeeping a lot better.'

He didn't like to appear too suspicious. 'Doing what?'

'I was waiting for you to ask me that, Doc, and sure as hell, you never let down wifey. You gotta suspicious nature, you know? I got me a cashier's job in the local grocery store, seven-thirty till two-forty-five, while Jodi stays snug as a bug in a rug under the caring Catholic eye of Miss Deakin. No more worries. You in the mood, Doc?'

'Sure, why not?'

Perhaps Francesca was settling down at last: or was it just spring fever? Keir hoped fervently to be able to count on domestic bliss from now on. An additional bonus would be to know that he had got the job as Orthopaedic Registrar and then, perhaps, Francesca might consider a decent apartment in a decent part of town.

Keir was only grateful that the Chief did not personally operate on Mondays or Fridays, but left it all to his noble little team, because, one Friday afternoon in April, right in the middle of DaWinter's orthopaedic list, he received an urgent summons to the telephone. As he was unable to take the call, he asked Nurse O'Neill, runner that day, to take a message. After the operation, she handed him a piece of paper with Mrs Guggenheim's telephone number. Still in his soiled surgical gown, Keir dialled the operator and was put through to her straightaway.

'Keir? I'm sorry to have called you at the hospital, but I've only just got in from taking Tiptop to the vet. I can't reach Fran, but you'll remember I was given your hospital number to ring in case of an emergency? That's why I'm calling now. I've never wanted to abuse your hospital obligations, but now I feel I've every right to put you in the picture and ...'

'Right, Mrs Gee, what's the emergency?' Keir, impatient to get back to scrub up for the next operation, hadn't got his watch on, and grabbed Nurse O'Neill's arm as she flitted down the corridor. 'Time?' he mouthed, tapping his left wrist.

'Half-six, Doc.'

'Thanks, er ...' Keir frowned at the phone. Mrs Guggenheim could be a real pain in the neck sometimes. But as she possessed the only telephone in the Sloane Court apartment house, he had to be nice to her in case he had to use it in a hurry. Neither did she mind traipsing backwards and forwards between apartments with messages for him, or for Francesca when he required to contact her. Mrs Guggenheim's voice was tremulous and tearful, and Keir was forced to ask, 'Are you okay, Mrs Gee? You're not sick or – what about Tiptop?' He knew how she worshipped her little dog. 'You haven't had to have him put down, I hope?'

'I'm fine, Keir. Tiptop had a back tooth removed, but he's not too bad after the chloroform, a little sick, that's all.

The vet says he'll be able to eat some mashed food tomorrow. Why I'm calling, Keir, is because Yasmin asked me. It's Jodi – I'm not sure how to say this, but he's kindda acting peculiar …'

'What do you mean peculiar?' His voice was suddenly unrecognizable even to himself.

'I don't really know how to explain. He's kindda lying there in Yasmin's place downstairs, rolling his eyes and making funny noises in his throat and …'

'Where's Francesca?'

'She's not here – she's probably working late like she often does …'

'Right, I'll be around as soon as I can.'

He didn't wait to hear any more, Mrs Gee's vague wafflings instilling in him the worst kind of feelings imaginable.

Sister Thoresen managed to find an off-duty team-surgeon who did not mind undertaking the last scheduled operation on the orthopaedic list for that day, despite it being Dr Sanders's only afternoon and evening off in a fortnight. Keir had the feeling that Thoresen knew all about his domestic problems and had taken pity on him – not to mention Sanders himself. Condescension and sympathy from Surgery's ice pick didn't make him feel any better.

He took the subway to West 4th Street station. Sam's General Grocery Store where Francesca worked as cashier, was on the corner of West 3rd Street and Bleecker Street. Keir stopped by and asked for Francesca. She wasn't there.

'Then where the hell is she?' he asked Sam, the proprietor.

Sam shrugged. 'Search me, Doc.'

'Come off it, Sam! You must know if Fran's working overtime or not!' Keir knew full well how money-mad Francesca could sometimes be. He didn't doubt for one minute Mrs Guggenheim's story about Francesca working late. Francesca would most certainly be prepared to moonlight for the extra money – and the new clothes she could buy with every last cent, for Francesca never saved any money.

'I dunno what you're talking about, Doc, sure as hell I

don't. Fran never works here afternoons, or evenings. She goes home a quarter to three, pronto, to collect Jodi from school. Fran left here today, as usual, ain't that right, Meg?' Sam yelled down the length of the store to his wife now doing Francesca's job of taking the money from the customers.

'Sure. She went home like always, never a minute late to put on her coat and get outta here,' said Meg, weighing out some sweet potatoes. 'She's probably lying up at home with a belly ache of her own, Doc. Fran's always in a rotten bad mood when it's her time of the month.'

He felt he was going mad. He wondered what Francesca was playing at now.

He banged on the door at Yasmin's ground floor apartment. Yasmin's Greek husband, Theo Sofádhes, owned a small restaurant on Bleecker Street, and Yasmin herself had two small children who went to Miss Deakin's kindergarten along with Jodi.

Without a word, Yasmin took him to where Jodi was lying on the couch, her children anxiously crowding him out as they sat beside him and kissed and caressed Jodi unceasingly. Jodi himself remained unmoving, his eyes not rolling at all as Mrs Guggenheim had described, but closed. Jodi's breathing was sterterous and uneven.

'Jodi fell all the way down the stairs, from the top to the bottom,' supplied little Greta, trying to do a somersault over the back of the couch. Yasmin caught hold of her daughter to stop her antics in the moment Keir turned a grey, gaunt face to her. In his examination of Jodi, especially in the pinpointed pupils, his worst fears were confirmed.

'Tell me how, Yasmin, why and when.' Keir said in a dull, flat voice devoid of feeling or comprehension in that instant.

She conveyed the full facts. Francesca had collected Jodi, Greta and Petra from school at quarter to three, it being Francesca's turn to do the afternoon school collection. And then Yasmin had to dash off to her husband's restaurant to lend a hand for a few hours. She'd taken her children with her. When she had got back home, just after six o'clock, she found a note from Francesca pinned on the door — Francesca wanted her to mind Jodi until she got back. She didn't know what time Francesca had left the note, it could have been any time between three o'clock and six. Fran's scribbled note, which Yasmin showed Keir, stated that a major part had come up in a Broadway musical which she didn't want to miss auditioning for. She was off to the Playhouse just around the corner. Yasmin had then gone straightaway to look in on Jodi (Mrs Guggenheim had been out visiting the vet with Tiptop at the time), when she had found Jodi lying at the bottom of the second-to-third-floor staircase. Jodi had obviously woken up, clambered over his cot-side after Francesca had left for the Playhouse, and come downstairs by himself, probably in search of Greta and Petra to play with.

Jodi could have been lying at the foot of that draughty and dangerous wrought-iron staircase for anything up to three hours with a fractured skull. Keir was at a loss to understand Francesca. More concerned with herself than making sure Jodi was being cared for, her deliberate neglect of a small boy just so that she could race off to audition for a Broadway musical, was incomprehensible to him.

From Mrs Guggenheim's apartment Keir rang the Paediatric Registrar. 'Dr Keir Devlin from Orthopaedics here, sir. My son Jodi's had an accident. I want to bring him in at once — he's three years, four months — symptoms presented are, continuing comotose, contracted pupils at this stage, bleeding, and the escape of cerebrospinal fluid from the external auditory meatus — what do I suspect? Jesus! That's a painful thing for me, his father, to have to say — yes sure, I'll bring him over right away, thanks.'

Keir wrapped Jodi in a blanket, while Yasmin called a cab. At the last minute, little Greta Sofádhes thrust Jodi's favourite toy under the blanket. It was the colourful Jack-in-the-box with the yellow-spotted bow tie from Macy's Store.

At City Hospital Jodi was admitted at once into a small private ward in the isolation wing, not the children's main ward.

Dr Hart-Rice said in the same language Keir himself was

often apt to repeat to 'the victims', those unconnected patients and families, those ordinary lay-folk out there without the knowledge of hospital jargon, without the knowledge of what constituted life and what death, 'You're quite right ...' as though he, Keir should not be quite right for some reason in his diagnosis. 'Jodi has sustained not only a middle fossa fracture of the skull, but also posterior fossa fractures.'

Numb from grief and shock, Keir nodded blankly.

'We can relieve a certain amount of intercranial pressure through trephination, but, if he recovers, Devlin, I'm sure you'll fully appreciate that your son will be paralysed and mentally handicapped for the rest of his life.'

How do you reconcile textbook prognosis to human hopes? Keir asked himself in that terrible moment. How do you pray for your child to die in the moment you yearn with all your heart that he should live?

'Terribly sorry, but you know we'll do our best for Jodi, although I hold out no great hopes for his recovery.'

Jodi was prepared at once for surgery, and, ironically, it turned out that Zimmerman would be leading the neurosurgical team.

While Jodi was in surgery, Keir telephoned Uncle Brook and little Mo, and they came at once, their grand new Dupont getting them anywhere faster than public transport. His sister Jenny was out on a house call. But as soon as she came back into the agency, the Lilly Wald secretary promised to pass on the message. Momma and Poppa Bolli, Sylvie, Stella, and three of Francesca's brothers arrived at the hospital. One of Francesca's brothers, Angelo, went out again to fetch his sister from the Playhouse after Keir informed the Bolli family of Francesca's whereabouts. Angelo returned without Francesca. Auditions had finished at six o'clock, over three hours ago; neither had Francesca shown up at the apartment in the interim, according to Yasmin.

Uncle Brook had an idea where Francesca might be. But to spare the Bolli family any embarrassment, he despatched an errand boy, not one of her brothers, to go and find her and bring her to the hospital.

When she eventually put in an appearance, Francesca

170

was in tears and gave a very good performance of theatrical histrionics. The iron entered into his soul and Keir wrenched Francesca's arms from him when she flung them round his neck with her motherly renderings. 'Where is he! Where is my baby? What's happened to my Jodi? Why didn't someone let me know what was going on? I made arrangements with Yasmin downstairs to keep an eye on him while I went for an audition. I reminded her about it in the morning when I first got that call through Mrs Guggenheim. Yasmin didn't mention anything about going to the restaurant in the afternoon, she just said okay, she'd mind Jodi. When she didn't answer the door, I left the note, thinking she'd only popped out for a minute or two to Sam's store. Gee! She forgot her promise, didn't she! I *told* her I'd probably be gone a few hours – you know how long auditions take.'

Keir looked at Francesca in distaste. 'Quit lying to me, Francesca. You went off to Lexington after the audition, instead of going home to make sure Jodi was being taken care of properly. I don't believe you even asked Yasmin to look after Jodi. I believe you dashed off to the Playhouse regardless, hoping Jodi would stay asleep or would play quietly in his cot till you decided to return home.'

'Yasmin promised! Gee, you've a nasty suspicious mind sometimes, you know Keir? How was I to know Yasmin was washing up dishes for Theo and forgot all about Jodi! What are they doing to my little boy? Who is this Hart-Rice guy, is he any good?'

Without answering her, Keir stepped away from her to go and stare blankly out of the window. Reciprocal blank stares from the other hospital windows on three sides of him were all there was to look at.

How could he accuse her of neglect let alone downright murder? He was as guilty as much as she. With nobody in the apartment to watch his capricious three-year-old movements, Jodi had obviously done just as Yasmin had said, clambered over his cot-side to go and look for his little playmates. And there had been no one to stop him – or his descent headlong down all those wrought-iron, fancy stairs. No mother, no father, nobody to care for him – why had he put off being that father he had promised himself he would be? The husband Francesca never really had? Was it because he had never truly loved her, but just – just fancied her? Was it because he, to the detriment of all else, including family, loved his career and his own advancement more? Was he now finding excuses concerning his marriage to Francesca simply because he had become disenchanted with it, and with her? He did not know. He was too confused by what had happened to think straight right now.

Someone up there had made a monumental cockup, thought Keir in that desolate moment, and he wished he had been a praying man. And then the paradox presented itself, so that he was left even more bereft when recognizing the fact that Man made his own errors, *not* God upon whom all human errors were cast. Jodi's life! Forfeited by two people who *pretended* to be his loving caring parents. *Mea culpa, mea culpa, mea culpa*, he found himself repeating in the same vein as his Latin memorizations of prescriptions, t.d.s., *ter die sumendum*, three times a day, o.m. *omni mane*, every morning – oh, dear God!

The Bolli family, every one of them, wept and wailed and were destructive rather than constructive as far as his own tattered emotions were concerned. Keir hoped Jenny would come soon: he wished his mother was here – oh how desperately he wished it.

'Francesca, all evening the boys look out for you. Where you been, you naughty girl? Momma and Poppa, they are very angry with you.' Momma Bolli, consumed with grief, mopped her eyes. She shook her head and her finger at Francesca. 'Where you go to after your audition? Why you not go home afterwards, but to some other place without making sure Yasmin is home to take care of Jodi? Why you not tell Mrs Gee, or someone else what you are doing?

'Momma, you don't *understand*!'

'Oh, sure Francesca, Momma understand fine. Myself, I *notta* understand how you an leave your own bambino all the time for some crazy movie-star dream,' Poppa Bolli told Francesca sadly and angrily.

Keir didn't want to be there while they had a full-scale family row. He wasn't even interested in where Francesca had been, in her lies, in her neglect of Jodi, in anything at all about Francesca Bolli.

He went and sat down alone in the little room prepared for Jodi, and waited for his son to come back from the operating theatre.

After he had been returned to the ward, the special nurse attending Jodi said, 'Dr Devlin, I'll let the head nurse know you're sitting with Jodi. Would you like a cup of coffee?'

'No thanks. If my wife wants to come in here don't tell her how critical Jodi's condition is, will you?'

'No sir, of course not. That's Dr Hart-Rice's place. He'll be coming along shortly with Mr Zimmerman to let you know the results of the operation. I've been checking Jodi's vital signs …' She showed him the chart. 'I'm afraid there is now dilation of the pupils.'

'Yes, I know.'

'I'm real sorry about Jodi. He looks such a sweet little boy.'

'Thank you.'

Francesca came in a little while later, green eyes wide and afraid when she saw Jodi in an oxygen tent, his head thickly bandaged, and looking so vulnerable with a respiratory tube in his mouth. 'Gee, I never thought I'd ever have to act the grieving mother off Broadway. Only this time it's really happening, huh, Doc?'

'*Yes!*'

She drew back, startled. Francesca asked nervously, 'Jodi's not going to die, is he?'

'Shut up, Francesca! Either sit down and be quiet, or get out of here.'

Without another word, she sat down on Jodi's bed, and regardless of hospital nursing rules, slipped her arms under the flap of the oxygen tent so that she could hold both Jodi's hands in hers.

Jodi died of irreversible brain-damage the following day.

In the long spring evening Keir walked in Central Park. He looked at things he'd never noticed before.

He tried to come to terms with himself and the way his life was going, something he'd never tried before.

What did he want from life? What did he *truly* want?

Over and over again he was being taught a lesson he didn't care to learn about: life was nothing without people, the core of the universe, those two-pinned human objects wandering alone out there, equally lost and disorientated, programmed for God knew what, acting out shabby lives in an otherwise perfect world, and managing always to foul up another life and the perfect world itself, but blaming it all on God or the Devil: what was it all for anyway? What was this Divine Purpose? Or was he just being ultra-cynical in his outlook? Shouldn't he just accept without question the *problem* of human existence, belief and unbelief centered around a verbal surrogate God, and not try and seek a logical explanation for Jodi's death? Logic and the spirit could never be reconciled no matter which way one tried, so what the hell!

He didn't know any more; he didn't *care* any more.

Delicate white candles on the chestnut trees reminded him of Christmas Eve. Cherry trees were covered in fragile pink blossoms like the sugar flowers on Jodi's birthday cake made by Momma Bolli. He noticed the tulips, crocuses and hyacinths, and the tiny-leaved Chinese elm said to be one of the oldest trees in the park. He noticed how the pink granite was flaking off Cleopatra's Needle, and he noticed the swans and swanboats on De Voor's Pond. He had never walked in the park with Jodi. Never shown him the swans, or the newborn lambs. Never taught him how to skate on the pond, nor shown him the wild birds of the park. He and Jodi had never made a wish under the Chinese pagoda tree, nor listened to the sound of cascading water through the shady shrubbery of the Ramble. He had never walked across Bow Bridge with Jodi, never played ball, never helped fly a kite with Jodi, as other fathers played with, and took a pride in their sons: and now, with all the time in the world, he never would.

And in that moment of heightened awareness, he realized other things too. All that unfinished business when one lived life too fast; the perpetual desire to do more, gain more, earn more, accomplish more, hoard more, until, in the end, you burned yourself out on the whirligig of human desires: and regrets, always regrets, as his father's death had taught him. Joss served only to pinpoint how very late and how futile his own life was apt to be. He had loved Jodi very much, more than Francesca now that he had a chance to analyze his true feelings hewn from deep personal shock, which had brought him face to face with himself. Francesca didn't matter any more, but Jodi did. Jodi had been a part of himself, his firstborn, his own little bit of immortality. To know that Jodi was the victim of his mistake was the death of part of himself; and that was *very* hard to take.

Keir sat down on a park bench and watched them together, fathers and sons, and he nursed Jodi's Jack-in-the-box on his lap: funny how he'd never noticed New York before.

Francesca found him alone on the park bench, and sat down next to him. She put out her hand to take his, but he brushed her off and stood up. '*Don't* touch me, Francesca!'

'You still mad at me? He was my son too, you know.'

He looked at her pityingly. Without another word he walked off across the grass.

Leaving a three-year-old child alone and unattended in a top floor apartment, with a dangerous well of iron staircase outside the open door, to keep some sleazy rendezvous after her audition at the Playhouse, without explanation, and without a thought in her empty head for Jodi, that was what he was unable to forgive. While he himself might not be blameless, might be no less responsible for Jodi's neglect than Francesca, he at least had been trying to earn an honest living for his wife and child. To know that his wife had been spending her evenings in another kind of occupation, one quite unconnected with bona fide Broadway musicals, but rather those sordid and corrupt liaisons for the *love* of money, turned his stomach.

'Honey – come back! Where're you going?' Her voice reached him over a gulf he knew could never be breached again.

And out of his own pain and failure came the accusing voice, 'Out of your life, Francesca, for good.' He stopped, turned and faced her across the open space. 'We have nothing more to say to each other. It's finished. I never want to see you again.'

'Keir! Don't leave me to bury Jodi alone – Keir don't!'
She ran after him, and took his arm, and something inside
him snapped because she touched him in the same breath
that she mentioned Jodi's name.

'You bitch, Francesca! You whore! Perhaps it's just as
well that Jodi will never know what kind of mother he
had.'

'What're you talking about?'

'You know *damn* well what I'm talking about! Uncle
Brook told me what kind of company you've been keeping
lately in a smart apartment house on Lexington. Mr Al's
nothing but a kinky white pervert employing anything
available to make him the rich porno-king he is. Black,
white, and yellow, any sex, and any age! I know all about it
from Brook, including the *pimpmobile*!'

Keir tried to contain his rage.

Brook had somehow discovered that the blue Rolls
Royce that had run down Joss on Fifth Avenue belonged
to this Mr Al whom Francesca had been associating with.
Brook hadn't wanted to tell Keir about it, but Keir had
forced it out of his uncle. After Joss had been accidentally
knocked down on Fifth Avenue, the quick and dirty
getaway was because the occupants of the Rolls had not
wished Sergeant O'Reilly to come poking his nose in. To
know that Francesca had been mixed up with this Mr Al
and the car that had killed Joss, the blue 'pimpmobile' as
Brook had called it, had removed the ground from under
Keir's feet on the night his son had been dying.

But nothing was ever going to bring back Jodi or Joss,
and he had to face facts. Keir got a grip on himself. 'Look
Francesca, I know I'm mostly to blame for what's
happened to our marriage. But honestly, if I didn't work
all the hours God and Chief DaWinter put my way, there
would have been no hope for further advancement with
more pay – not for a long while. I've *had* to do the
dogsbody hours in order to get to the top quicker than
men like Zimmerman, who climb the ladder because of
who they are and who they know. But that's as may be.
What I can't face out of this mess of our marriage and both
our lives is your going off to film cheap movies while I've
been working my guts out to give us a better standard of

living. I understand that you couldn't cope with being the wife of a poor doctor. I understand that you're eager to get on with your own life without being held back by someone trying to make Consultant Surgeon one day. But I'm not the Chief, as yet, earning big money, and neither am I a mogul of Hollywood. So let's both face it, I'm not the one to give you your big break into show business, and we're both very bad for each other. I also know that you were at this – this *Al's* place after your audition at the Playhouse. The facts remain, any which way you care to look at them. You left Jodi dying on a stone-cold iron staircase – yes *you*! Why the hell didn't you use Mrs Guggenheim's telephone to let me know you needed to go out and that Jodi was alone? I was off duty as soon as the list was finished. The latest would have been nine-thirty as I wasn't on call, and then I'd have come round and been with Jodi while you did what *you* wanted.'

'You say that now. *After* it's all happened. And nine-thirty would have been too late. Auditions were over by then. But you never thought to say any of this before, did you? Only now, to make me look more guilty in your eyes. *You* don't need a woman or a wife, Keir. You want a paragon of bloody virtue because of your own screwed up emotions over your father and what he did to you and your mother! You can't accept that people are people and each one has to live life according to himself and not government dictatorship! You're a goddamn puritan – must be your Pennsylvanian streak,' Francesca accused in equal bitterness and anger.

'Francesca, I didn't *know*! I didn't know *what* you were doing or where you were while Jodi was – was dying ...' His voice broke. 'God, I can't believe this is happening – I can't believe ...'

Stuck for suitable words, he also knew nothing more could be said to alleviate the situation. Accusation was all that was left, and the guilt. 'All I know is that while Jodi was either in Miss Deakin's kindergarten, or being taken care of by a succession of surrogate parents, Mrs Guggenheim, Yasmin, your mother and sisters, and a dozen other people besides, you spent afternoons and evenings with Mr Al and his cameras, doing things only a cheap hooker would do. For money or thrills, Francesca, that's what I want to know? Did Harry Vincenti knife your face because he knew something about you I'm only just learning?'

'You bastard!'

'Yeah, maybe, for neglecting Jodi *and* you. I can't blame you entirely for going off to find your thrills outside the marriage bed, but I do blame you for not being honest with me. I also wonder what Momma and Poppa would say if they knew what kind of *movie making* their lovely Francesca has got herself into, uh?'

'Honey, I'll give it up, I swear – but don't leave me now Jodi's gone. We'll get a nice place somewhere, away from Broadway if that's what you want. Even medical quarters. More kids, if that's what you want. I only did it to buy the extras, to give Jodi the nice things we never seemed able to afford on your doctor's salary. It was only until I made enough to put some by, to save to use for a rainy day. That's all, I swear it. I was going to tell Al I was quitting next week.'

Keir took a deep breath, every word she uttered making the raw edges of his life bleed anew. 'You're a liar and you always have been. A liar, a whore and – and the murderess of *my* son!' And even while he hated himself for saying it, he could not help it.

Keir turned on his heel, ready to walk away from her as he had once walked away from Joss. He did not have the stomach to fight Francesca any more. He wanted no more bitterness to be dredged up out of the cesspit of his marriage to her.

She followed him. 'You don't know what it's like to be poor and insecure. Wanting so bad to make it you'd do anything just to get one bite of the apple. You had someone else's money too. *And* contacts to get you through medical school. So don't be so high and mighty in your principles. I've only got my face and my body, not brains like you, Keir. I have to use what I've got to get me on. I've got as much talent as Garbo. And, Al says, I'm better looking than her. Please, Keir, try and understand, only don't walk away from me now when I need you so badly.'

Keir despised her more than ever. Standing stock still on

the grass to confront her one last time, it was like the scales falling from his eyes, the shackles falling from his limbs. For once in his life he had no regrets. Were he right or wrong, for the rest of his life he would have to live with this decision tonight – to cut and run, just like that time with Joss. All he knew, right now, was that he couldn't live with lies, deceit, and with a woman who would sell her very soul, as well as the life of a child, to the Devil in order to further her own ambitions.

'Oh, I know exactly what it's like to be poor and want a bite of the apple, Francesca. But that didn't make me want to stick my butt in the air for pimps and niggers and filthy old men who can't get it up unless the cameras roll. I'd have forgiven you anything, except doing just that while our son needed you. So you'd better get back to Mr Al, since that's where your *talent* lies.'

Quickly he walked away from her, not knowing where his feet were taking him, knowing only that he wanted to get away from her as fast as possible.

He came to the lake. In his hand he still clutched the battered little Jack-in-the-box Jodi had loved so much. He looked at it like a man in a trance, and then willed himself to let go.

It dropped into the water where it floated a while, a grinning face above a cheeky yellow-and-white-spotted bow tie, two arms in the air sticking up from the sides of the rainbow-tinted box, hands together, imploringly. Please save me from drowning, it seemed to be saying: then slowly Jodi's toy sank.

Keir looked up at the darkening skyline of Manhattan and knew he had to get away from New York.

179

PART TWO
Creation Ex Nihilo

'Women have served all these centuries as looking-glasses possessing the magic and delicious power of reflecting the figure of man at twice its natural size.'
Virginia Woolf

CHAPTER FIVE

Vinarosa: August 1929

The weather was so hot it hurt to be alive. Like some vendetta of the sun god riding his chariot across the cloudless sky of Catalonia, day after day the harsh white glare beat upon the thirsty land. Raven felt like a candle in an oven. She cowered for protection under sun hat and behind dark glasses. Prickly pore-jumping heat decimated her senses, ate through the fibres of her being, bathed her flesh in sweat, pure sweat, and left her soul paralysed by inertia; tempers were short, grudges long.

As the endless summer oozed from her sebaceous glands, the only place Raven found to be bearable was the sea. To lie in the warm rockpools, or to float on her back, lulled by the gentle waves of an unruffled tide, she gave herself up as the sacrifical virgin on the alter of Sol: until José put an end to her solitude.

'So here you are! Taking your siesta on the beach instead of in a shady nook,' he accused, one afternoon when he just *happened* to saunter, hands in his pockets, down the cliff path to the sandy beach below Cabo Alondra. From that moment on, the moment when she had peered over her dark glasses at him with her lovely smoky-grey eyes, her neat bottom enticingly tucked beneath the sun umbrella, José forgot about Toril's attractions, and concentrated instead on Raven Quennell whom he had scarcely noticed until now.

José, twenty-one, handsome, tanned, and as brazen as Ramiro, had been spending his afternoons in a bar in Toril with his friends, playing cards and catching up with the local gossip. He was studying Oenology and

Viticulture at the University of Dijon, France, and was in his last year of studies. He had spent the summer vacation at Vinarosa, but would be starting his new semester at the end of the month.

Unfortunately, Roxana discovered that José was suddenly spending a lot of time with Raven, and brought Ramiro along as well. Raven's drowsy afternoon peace rudely shattered, four separate entities had suddenly become two couples and she didn't know how: who had instigated the subtle pairing off, José, Ramiro, or Roxana? At least José was nice to her, but Ramiro's supercilious company Raven could have done without.

One afternoon Roxana and Ramiro decided to take a walk into Toril: and where they found the strength and energy to go walking in such heat, Raven did not know. Above her, high on the cliff top, was the white dolphin shape of Cabo Alondra. She had hoped Roxana would stay there and keep Sonny company until evening. Roxana and Sonny had taken to watercolour painting, and Peedee, no mean artist himself, tutored and encouraged them wholeheartedly, especially Roxana, who was kept out of mischief behind canvas and easel during those hours of supervised creativity. Raven was wondering whether to sneak back to Cabo Alondra while José was swimming, when José decided to get out of the sea.

Smoothing back his sleek black hair, his dark eyes armour-slits against the driving sun, José trod warily on the sides of his feet like a bow-legged mariner crossing a burning deck. In his navy-blue swimsuit he was tanned, skin glistening with droplets of water. He pulled painful little faces and uttered heartfelt little oohhs and aahhs until he reached the shadow of the huge colourful umbrella Peedee had thoughtfully provided for the benefit of his grandchildren, who used the beach most.

José flung himself down beside her. Raven was annoyed, she resented sharing her shady space with anyone, especially José. This was *her* patch, and besides, the way José sometimes looked at her when she was wearing her bathing costume made her feel funny: not exactly annoyed, but uncomfortable.

Raven had discovered over the years that long summer

holidays at Vinarosa could be tedious. She could not wait to get back to the studious serenity of her Swiss school. She loved beautiful Switzerland with its gentler climate and civilized culture. Spain was harsh and vibrant, and at times too cruel for her, a country where, to her dismay, she had seen peasant women, bowed and bent and prematurely aged, dragging wooden ploughs behind them as they endlessly furrowed Don Ruiz's fields.

Raven sighed like an old lady, and tried to concentrate on the book she was reading. She found it difficult, what with José's masculine presence beside her, his attention blatantly upon the back of her neck, her calves, and possibly her bottom too. She sensed what mood José was in; it was all to do with this hot Mediterranean siesta hour.

'What are you reading?' While she was still reading, he rudely lifted up the book to look at the spine. Raven lost her place as well as her temper.

'Nothing to do with you,' she said shortly, slamming her bookmark back into place.

'Is that the title of the book? A woman's romantic novel, no doubt,' he said dismissively. Settling on his back with his hands behind his head, he closed his eyes.

Presently she tossed the book aside. It was impossible to concentrate while José's body sent heated signals in her direction, making her hotter even than had she been lying stark naked under the direct glare of el Sol. José lying on his back like that, all muscle and brawn and masculinity, made her conscious of him as a man she did not know, instead of the teenage boy she had grown up with as closely as a sister during these past five years. Raven reached for her towel.

Without opening his eyes, his hand came down on hers, holding her captive. 'Don't go. I want to know if you will come with us to the cinema in Vilafranca this evening.'

'Who is us?'

'Ram and Roxa.'

'No, thank you.' She pulled her hand away. 'I thought Ramiro had to get back to the factory by five o'clock.'

'Not today. He has taken the evening off to go to the cinema with us.' José opened his eyes wide and came closer. Propping himself on his elbow, he noticed the sultry colour of Raven's attractive eyes, the same colour as his brother Ram's, but not as cold or blank. Raven had grown into one of the most beautiful girls he knew. Tall and slender and graceful, she had even captivated his friend the Civil Guardsman, Marcos Rodriguez.

Marcos sometimes patrolled the headland, and often joined José and the others in an off-duty game of cards in Toril. He had let drop in conversation that he had seen a very pretty girl sunning herself each afternoon on the beach below Cabo Alondra. Marcos had added that he was trying to pluck up courage to say *hola* to her. José had guessed it might be Raven. He had also sensed that Marcos, being a typically Spanish male without the benefit of Señor Peedee's broad education, wasn't used to young women baring all on the beach. José, however, was not going to be outdone by Marcos in overlooking an opportunity like this to get Raven all to himself, and what better place than the beach. He was only annoyed when Roxana and Ramiro had appeared on the scene each afternoon. Fortunately, Ramiro usually buzzed back to Barcelona by five o'clock when the siesta break was over, though not today.

'If you don't come with us, then none of us will be able to go to the cinema.' His tone was bantering, as well as a little accusing. 'You will spoil everyone's fun.'

Raven regarded him with narrowed eyes. 'Meaning?'

José smiled lazily, his mouth a full pink bow of sensuality, reminding her of Ramiro. 'Meaning, my sweet little blackbird, that your grandfather will not allow Roxa to go to the cinema without you.'

Raven bit her lip.

'Come on.' He ran his hand up her warm, sandy arm. Raven had gradually been thawing towards him these past three weeks, and he did not want to force the issue, not just for the moment, anyway: 'Don't be a spoilsport, blackbird. We'll go in Papa's new Boulogne.'

As if that ought to tempt her! 'Don't call me blackbird,' Raven said, and rushed off to the sea, her towel trailing in the sand.

She was unprepared for him. On swift and silent feet José raced up behind her, his impatience suddenly getting the better of him. He wanted an answer from her right now. José brought her down with a thump at the very edge of the water. On the soft sand, the playful waves washed gently over their feet. Half in, half out of the sea, José pinioned Raven's arms and grinned down into her face. 'It's *The Jazz Singer*.'

'Roxa and I have seen it twice already.'

'Then see it a third time, with Ramiro and me.'

José smoothed her bare shoulders, his attention upon the curve of her neck and upper body. Then he kissed her, very carefully.

Raven was so surprised, she could do nothing except stare back with wide-open, astonished eyes at José's half-closed eyelids, while he was in possession of her mouth. She had never been kissed before, not by a boy, and certainly not by a man. Then, because kissing felt so nice, she closed her eyes, put her arms around his neck, and gave herself up to him.

She knew it was her fault; she should not have encouraged him, for suddenly the gentle exploratory kisses while they tested and tasted one another, turned into a prolonged suffocating sensation aroused by José's darting, licking, searching tongue. It was as though the sea had come roaring through her ears and a strange kind of melting desire filled her body to leave her weak and unprotesting. José slipped down the shoulder straps of her bathing costume. Through his knee-length swimsuit his body had an iron strength that was altogether frightening as he pressed himself against her.

The drowsy heat of the afternoon acted like a heady drug on her heightened emotions, while the whirlind of feelings José aroused in her by kissing and handling her with such passion, were confusing, tormenting, and wonderful. Raven felt out of herself, as pliable as Plasticine, softened, melted and manipulated finally to accommodate the shape, the weight and the force of José de Luchar's body.

The plunder of waves on the rocks by her feet suddenly served to remind her that she was treading dangerous water. For a long, drawn-out, ecstatic moment, she had wanted to continue to embrace him, cling to him, and to return his kisses. But now she wasn't so sure. Struggling to be free of him, Raven breathlessly twisted away, at the same time pulling up the straps of her costume. 'José, Grandfather might be at the window with his telescope. He might see us.'

'I am doing nothing. Look, no hands!' José flapped his hands in the air and made her smile. Then he smoothed back her dark hair from her forehead, and gently kissed the ugly scar visible at her hairline. 'How terrible of the Irish to have done this to you,' he said, changing the subject and the mood of the moment.

Grimacing in embarrassment, she turned her face away. 'The Irish didn't do it, only madmen. But please don't remind me of Ireland, José.'

'*Querida*, I wish I hadn't said anything. I didn't know it would upset you like this. It's only because I wish to know all about you. You are the most beautiful girl in the world to me. No scars could possibly detract from your beauty. I think you know I have always loved you; ever since you were a little girl, eh blackbird?' He chucked her under the chin and made her turn back to look at him. 'Don't be afraid of me. I'd never do anything to hurt you. I respect you too much. If you are concerned about your scar, then you should wear your hair in a more mature style that frames your face instead of wearing it scraped back into two braids like a schoolgirl. You're a woman now, and should look and behave like a woman. But I suppose, with only a grandfather to bring you up, you don't know about the things a woman should know.' One hand had slipped back to her breast, pressing and exploring it, sending ripples of pleasure through her. He kissed her salty shoulder. 'You should talk to my mother and see what she says about a proper coiffure. I'm sure she'll be delighted to give you all the advice you need.'

Raven felt better. She desperately wanted to be that woman who could take control of her own life, not the juvenile schoolgirl tagging behind her wayward twin sister the whole time. This afternoon, José had made her feel very much a woman: until he began tickling her.

Laughing together, they rolled across the sands like puppies in play.

José let her go, eyes gleaming, strong white teeth displayed in a wolfish grin while he tried to control his ragged breathing. Conscious of that fragile moment between them, and because she was still only a young girl finding love and sex by degrees, he wanted to stay around a bit longer. 'Have you ever bathed in the sea with nothing on?'

'No, José, I have not!'

'It feels good, almost like sex. Especially if the waves are a little playful.'

'I dare say.' She pretended a cool detachment she was far from feeling.

'Why don't you take off your costume and we'll swim to the other side of the bay? It'll cool us both off.'

'Because I don't want to!' They had rolled back to where she had left her towel on the sand, and retrieving it now, she dropped it over his hot head and shoulders bronzed to the colour of mahogany, before running into the water. She would have to wade a long way out before it was deep enough to swim properly.

José sat on the sands like an Arab, and yelled at her neat girlish bottom. 'I think you would love to swim in your bare skin, blackbird, but you are afraid to let yourself go. You should not fight yourself so hard, Raven, it will only make you … *sentirse frustrado*!'

'Go to Hades, José de Luchar!' She yelled back.

He grinned. 'I will tell Carina and Isaba that the four of us will not want supper tonight.' He got up and left her in peace.

When she arrived back at 'Cape Skylark' in the early evening, Peedee was in his deck-chair among the dried grasses he called his garden. A walnut tree growing in the only civilized piece of 'garden' at the front of the villa, shaded his deck-chair, the rest of the grassy headland stretching away to the cliff edges. Only a line of white stones marked the boundary between terra firma and space. The two cats, Morgan and Le Fay, snoozed contentedly at Peedee's feet. Peedee looked up from his newspaper, took off his reading glasses and picked up his glass of red wine from the small garden-table beside him. Over the rim of the wine-glass he smiled broadly. 'Much

189

more sun and water, dear girl, and I shan't be able to tell you apart from Minnie Mouse.'

'Go and eat coke, Grandpapa!'

'Oh now!' He gave her an old-fashioned look while he sipped his drink. 'Is that what they teach you at l'École Internationale? I would have thought it of Roxa, never of you. I think I shall have to have a word with Eugénie the next time I visit Geneva, and tell her she is corrupting my girls.'

Raven grinned, flung down her wet towel, her novel, and her sun-specs at Peedee's feet. She unfastened the two heavy dark braids that sometimes pulled her head backwards as though she were tethered to a hitching-post. She had wound the braids around her head, Gretel-fashion, while she had been swimming, but now she swung out her schoolgirl pigtails like two damp thick ropes, and sprinkled Peedee with droplets of sea-water.

Her teeth perfectly white against her smooth, tanned complexion, her smile was wide. She was growing into a very attractive woman. Peedee could see that Raven had matured this summer. A good five feet, eight inches, already an inch taller than he, she made him feel very inadequate. The only trouble was that she was still as thin as a caber even though she ate like a piranha. Peedee noticed all these things about her, and commented, 'When are you going to stop growing like a beanpole, dear girl?'

'Oh Peedee! Must you talk about it?'

Raven hated her height to be mentioned, her *bête noire*, just like the scars on her forehead and scalp that she imagined to be more disfiguring than they actually were. Peedee chided himself for teasing her about her height. Raven was becoming increasingly sensitive to critcism only because she was approaching that awkward age between girlhood and womanhood, when all females wanted to see themselves as perfect: so he must watch his tongue more carefully!

Raven flung herself from his presence, and left Peedee grinning insensitively to himself. She knew that he was only teasing, but it had touched a nerve that was still very bruised and battered. Roxana, however, was the worst one for making her feel inferior, despite the fact that she was also able to top Roxa by a couple of inches! But whenever Roxana wanted to get even, she would pass an unkind remark about wrinkled foreheads and scalped maidens, a tactic guaranteed to depress and torment Raven every time.

Raven, looking at herself in her bedroom mirror, tried to smooth out the uneven skin on the right side of her forehead, just above her temple. Other people never seemed to notice her disfigurement, but she was always so conscious of it. The surgeon who had sewn up her head hadn't had much of a delicate touch, she couldn't help reflecting miserably.

Out of a face puckered in woe, two grey eyes stared back at her in commiseration. Then she touched her bosom. Against her tan, she saw two pale bumps that were hard and firm, not soft and tempting, or very large at all: you are *ugly*! the face mouthed back. What can José possibly see in you and your ugly scar-face and goosepimple chest? Even your hair is a mess! José's right. You ought to see a coiffeuse. Perhaps a cosmetic surgeon, too! Wailing and agonizing over her appearance, she wanted, more than anything, to appear attractive in José's eyes: why José? she suddenly asked herself.

The more she stared at her reflection, the more dismayed she became, until, in the end, she reached for the scissors. In two smart snips, the plaits had gone: she was left with the stump ends of her hair. Oh God! Now see what you've done to yourself, Raven Quennell! Cut off your nose to spite your face!

In further anguish, Raven desperately searched around her sparsely-furnished and tidy bedroom, seeking a fashion magazine or some such item to restore her self-confidence. There was nothing to console her, no template for her other image. The only fashionable face in the room was the silver framed photograph of her mother smiling at her from the dressing-table. Raven picked up the photograph and stared at it thoughtfully. Her mother was wearing fancy-dress costume, Robin Hood with neat little cap and quiver of arrows protruding above her left shoulder. The resemblance between herself and her mother in that picture was quite startling, especially in black and white, so that the difference in their colouring was not apparent. Under the Robin Hood cap set at a jaunty angle, what interested Raven most was the hairstyle. Shoulder-length, sleek and straight, it was obviously a wig because her mother's hair had been naturally wavy, and a delicious red-gold colour, not black. But she wore a fringe! Now why hadn't she thought about a fringe before, Raven asked herself, instead of wearing her hair like an old peasant woman? Raven thought that the pageboy style might just suit her.

Once committed, there was no turning back.

Raven undid the amputated stumps of her braids, loosened and brushed her hair fiercely over her face, then tossed the thick swatch of hair back over her head: just as well José couldn't see her now, a wild Macbeth witch, she thought, as she picked up the scissors again. Poised like a nervous barber in front of the mirror, she closed her eyes, took a deep breath before taking the first snip. A horse's tail of blue-black hair came away in her hand. She opened her eyes, and then, having pledged pique to vanity, endeavoured to copy the look her mother carried off with such aplomb.

Half an hour later, Raven stared into another face.

She breathed a hearty sigh of relief; at least she didn't look like a Haitian voodoo doctor any more! Her scarred forehead was now discreetly hidden under a smooth dark fringe. Straight-cut hair was shoulder-level in an easy-to-care-for style. Gone was the heavy waist-length curtain of hair that had to be divided and plaited every morning, a time-consuming, dreary task. Besides, the new hairstyle gave her a touch of glamour, something she had thought she'd never possess. She looked quite grown up, even liberated, a woman now, and not an inky-fingered schoolgirl who wore braids and black stockings!

Satisfied that she had done the right thing, Raven cleared up the mass of hair around her feet, shoving it all into the wastepaper basket. Thrilled with her new image, she started to search through her wardrobe for something appropriate to wear to enhance it. She found a dress handed down to her from Doña Jacqueline; she held it up against her, scrutinizing herself critically in the long, bevelled cheval mirror. The dress was perfect! It disguised her straight shape completely, simply because it had been designed to the dictates of fashion, not figure. Raven thought to herself that she might just go to the cinema in Vilafranca, after all.

But first she would have a bath, wash the salt-water off, shampoo her new hairstyle, and ask Roxana for some of her scent. Roxa, she knew, went around pilfering Doña Jacqueline's expensive perfumes, as she had once done in the old days from their mother.

Raven was unaware of the door opening until Roxana became reflected in the mirror. Looking flushed and rather guilty as she tried to get her breath, Raven couldn't help noticing how brightly blue and sparkling were her sister's eyes. Roxana's unruly curls all over the place, appearing to have lost her hair-ribbon which kept them tidy, Raven said, 'Oh, there you are! Where have you been all afternoon?' Raven began to wonder what Roxa and Ram had been up to all this time alone; she did not trust Ramiro de Luchar an inch.

Roxana stared in amazement. Then she found her tongue. 'Good Lord! What have you done to yourself? You look utterly transformed.'

'Cut my hair.'

'I can see that. Peedee will be livid.'

'Why should he be?'

Roxa shrugged. 'Oh you know him, horribly old-fashioned and all that. He has an aversion to women with short hair, short skirts and frilly knickers.'

Then she thought better of upsetting Raven; she wanted a great favour from her. Upsetting her twin was definitely not the way to go about it. 'It suits you,' she admitted, however grudgingly. Then she picked up the silver-backed monogrammed hairbrush that had once belonged to their mother and drew it through her tangled curls. 'Raven, how would you like to go to the cinema this evening? We can go in the new Hispano. Don Ruiz ...'

'I know all about it. Of course I want to see Al Jolson: "Mammy, how I luv ya, how I luv ya!".' Raven, laughing delightedly, twirled round the room, then dropped backwards onto the bed and kicked a leg in the air.

Roxana, nonplussed, had never seen her sister in such an abandoned mood. 'Golly, thanks, Rave. Peedee said I could go only if you were to accompany me. For some reason he doesn't trust me without you. I didn't think you'd want to see *The Jazz Singer* again, because I know you don't much care for jazz. José said we can all have supper afterwards at a smart little seafood taverna he knows of, further along the coast. It will be a nice evening out for all of us before José has to go back to Dijon and we to the nunnery.'

Roxana always referred to Madame Roget's International School as the nunnery, the cloisters, or Angels' Hell.

'Roxa, have you – have you ever done anything with – with Ramiro?'

Roxana looked surprised. Big sister was asking *her* such things! But she was delighted to show off her superior knowledge and experience in such wordly matters. 'Do you mean sex?'

'Yes.'

'What do you want to know?'

'Whether Ramiro has ever kissed you – with his tongue.'

'Goodness, Raven! All experienced men kiss with the tongue. That's if they like you and you haven't got bad breath. It's to show they want to do other things. It's called French kissing.'

Raven knew, in a kind of vague and disjointed way, what Roxana meant by 'other things'. But she didn't like to show her complete and utter naivety by asking how much further one went before saying *stop, no contacto*! Or if Ramiro had been as demanding as José. 'Have *you* done other things?'

'Going all the way, you mean? Of course! A man – and Ramiro and José are men now, you know – don't want scarebabies. They like *real* women! And Ramiro as well as José can have any number of women they want, so I'm not going to be a silly little fool and say no to Ram who is *terribly* sexy!' She smiled and tossed her head in front of the mirror. 'It *feels* nice!'

'What does?'

'Making love. It makes your stomach feel all funny, like going over a hump-back bridge fast in the Hispano Suiza. Naughty but nice.'

Roxana exaggerated a lot, so Raven did not believe Roxana had done anything other than kiss Ramiro while allowing him perhaps a little more liberty, like José wanting to touch her breasts this afternoon. All this lovey-dovey business was known as 'special relations', because she had overheard Isaba talking to Carina once on the taboo subject of sex. But Raven very much doutbed if Ramiro and Roxana had had any 'special relations' other than Peedee, who would be simply livid if he ever found out that Ramiro de Luchar had done anything to Roxa in the place the Virgin Mary had kept immaculate. He would most likely report Ram to his father, and Ram would not risk that kind of humiliation or embarrassment. Roxa was a mere girl of sixteen, whereas Ramiro was a grown man. Peedee and Don Ruiz between them would take him apart.

Lying on her back on the bed, Raven, in a more sober frame of mind, said, 'Roxa, I think José is nice. A real *caballero*. Perhaps that has been Peedee's influence, don't you think?'

Roxana put down the hairbursh, opened the door to go back to her own bedroom, and from the threshold said, 'If you want my opinion, José is nothing but a Fascist slob, just like Amery Noughton Peel.' She banged the door.

Raven selected her wardrobe carefully, while thinking about Roxana's strange remark concerning José. Roxana had been influenced by Ramiro of course, the two brothers had always been rivals. If Ramiro accused José of being a Fascist, then that was only because Ramiro was a Communist! She had often heard Don Ruiz arguing with Ramiro for taking the side of the socialist trades unionists at the Fabrica de Luchar, instead of being 'management supportive' and backing uncle Salas Rivales rather than opposing him.

Raven chose a frock by Patou in a soft pale blue satin. It was sleeveless, had a straight sheath bodice that plunged daringly to a low V at the back to show off her smoothly-tanned skin, while the skirt began at the hipline and only just covered her knees. It had an undulating hemline of flared godets that fluttered and swayed as she moved. Doña Jacqueline had explained with a good-natured little laugh when parting with her cast-off clothes, that Don Ruiz had thought she looked like a hen dressed as a spring-chicken in that particular dress! Doña Jacqueline, who had no wish to be seen as any such thing, had generously thrust the lovely frock at Raven, and because she was always fair in her dealings, Roxana had been placated with a lime-green and white sheath dress to complement her outstanding colouring, again, another one with an *haute couture* label. Corsets, of course, were terribly old-fashioned, and it was far too hot for stockings. Her satin evening-shoes, with low louis heels, matched the colour of her frock, and her only jewellery consisted of tiny gold-and-pearl-studded earrings from Aspreys, and a neat jewelled wristwatch that had belonged to her mother.

Peedee, predictably, did not approve of the way either of his granddaughters were dressed that evening. Gone were the schoolgirls he had come to recognize and be comfortable with, to be replaced by two young vamps!

Roxana, who had modelled herself on the cinema actress, Theda Bara, wore the lime-green and white sheath dress that revealed too much of her figure, a skirt also with short, uneven godet panels as though (in Peedee's candid opinion) the seamstress had been too tipsy to cut straight, while bare arms and legs and shoulders offended his Victorian sense of values concerning a woman's exposed areas. Roxana sported a green and white silk scarf tied around her head, pirate fashion, which she told him flatly was a bandeau, not a bandage!

'Good lord, you both look – extraordinary!' Peedee remarked wryly. 'And what have you done to your hair, dear girl?' he asked Raven.

'I've cut it, Peedee.'

'What on earth possessed you to do such a rash thing?'

'To cover up my forehead.'

'What was wrong with your forehead, pray?'

'Oh, Peedee, really! Are you so blind?'

'I'm very blind, tonight!' He put on his glasses, rustled his newspaper, and clearing his throat looked at neither of them when he said, 'Mind you're both home by eleven sharp! Otherwise I shall come to Vilafranca after you.'

They did not doubt it for one moment: Peedee was able to travel far and fast on his old boneshaker.

*

José had given a low whistle of approval when he had seen her with her new hairstyle and adult frock, and she had seen the look, too, in Ramiro's eye. 'Santa Maria, you both look stunning!' Then José had murmured in a gallant aside, 'Especially you, with your new hairstyle, Señorita Raven Quennell.'

'Thank you, Señor de Luchar!'

José had held her hand during the film, and sent funny little love-signals through the palm of her hand to make her tingle all over, so that she knew he was thinking more about her than Al Jolson. Then they had all driven to the coast.

The night was as hot as the day. Sitting out under the stars in the glare of the white, hard-faced moon illuminating the sand and the sea, it was easy to forget everything, for desire was with the moment, the laughter, the jokes, the subtle little love-signals and loving touches of people who were rich enough to afford most things and wise enough to want to enjoy them. Raven recalled some words from her precocious past, *Les Nourritures Terrestres*: Father and William Butler Yeats had been discussing it in Waldre's library while she had listened at the keyhole without understanding. Now she knew what was meant by 'the poetry of beautiful experience'.

'What's the matter, Raven?' Jaime touched her arm to bring her back from her reverie.

Raven smiled. 'Nothing Jaime. Just thinking.'

Raven was glad in the end that Jaime and Marta had been included in the party. It made her feel a little more secure. Two Romeos like José and Ramiro de Luchar together would have been hard to handle. Fortunately, Jaime and Marta had wanted to see the fantastic first ever sound musical of Al Jolson in *The Jazz Singer*, all over again. It was a movie whose appeal was guaranteed, no matter how many times one saw it. Raven was only dismayed that Sonny, at the last moment, had refused to accompany them. Raven suspected that, because it was a musical film, Sonny felt disinclined to see it in case it upset him. She half understood his reasons, for Sonny, if a piece of music touched him deeply and personally enough, ended up depressed, so depressed in fact, it was like a black shadow over him for days.

'Rave isn't used to wine, especially *sangria*' said Roxana, holding her crockery beaker out to Ramiro, vigorously stirring the contents of the large and heavy earthenware jug on the table with a wooden spoon. He poured her more *sangria*. José had brought them all to this coastal taverna some miles from Vilafranca, because he knew the owner. Señor Rojo and his wife had hovered attentively all evening, and had given them only the best of the taverna's seafood platter and *sangria*.

'Here's to bull's blood and brandy, oranges, lemons and – and everything else bunged into the jug, and another ghastly term at Angels' Hell,' Roxana said, the potent *sangria* giving her a fit of the giggles.

'Don't you like your Swiss school, Roxa?' Ramiro asked.

'I *hate* it!' Roxana replied with venom.

Raven froze: under cover of the table and its concealing white cloth, Ram was sneakily sliding his hand up her thigh while pretending to be listening to Roxa and her silly giggle-gurgles like a faulty bathtap.

His silvery eyes never wavering from Roxana's face as he pretended to be giving her his undivided attention, Ramiro wondered to himself if Raven would encourage him further, as José had told him she might when he had tried to seduce Raven in the sea and almost succeeded this afternoon, or put an end to his ardour. English girls had reputations for being 'fast' and Roxa was proof of it. At least it was worth a try. He had always fancied Raven and did not see why José should have her. Ramiro wanted to crack Raven Quennell's ice-maiden image, and thus score a personal victory against his brother.

Raven dug her nails deeply into the back of Ramiro's hand.

Swiftly he stopped what he had been doing. He turned to look at her, glowering in silent anger and injury. Roxana had swivelled her attention upon 'darling' José, and asked in real Theda Bara style with a fey look from under her fluttering eyelashes, 'Are you not looking forward then, José darling, to returning to your *viticulture* place in France?'

He was non-committal, and grunted something Raven could not quite catch, as Jaime and Marta joined in the conversation between Roxana and José.

Raven took advantage of their preoccupation to hiss at Ram, 'You do that again and I'll tell your father.'

His grin wickedly calculating, he sucked his knuckles, eyeing her above them. 'Whatever turns you on, Raven.'

Raven brought her attention back to what the others were talking about. She had put Ram in his place, and she could tell that he hadn't liked it. Good! Let him know that she wasn't as fast as he thought perhaps she might be.

Raven gathered that José did not much care for the land or viticulture, but, because his father had insisted that he should gain experience in such matters, as one day he would inherit the vineyards, he had to grin and bear it until he knew as much about the business as the best experts employed by Don Ruiz.

'Your grandfather's fault,' he told the girls. 'He was the one who put the idea in my father's head in the first place.'

Raven remembered the evening well. It had been over five years ago. Now Jaime had also left the schoolroom, and the only two left to Peedee to teach were Carlos and Sonny. Carlos, always mad about aeroplanes, was going to join the Air Force as soon as possible. Jaime worked the land along with Juan, the overseer, while Ramiro was learning all about industry and commerce at the Fabrica de Luchar in Barcelona, although Raven knew that Ramiro spent more time fighting with his uncle, his father, and anyone else who opposed him.

'Raven, what are you smiling about, all to yourself?'

'The moon, Jaime.' He would never understand about the 'poetry of beautiful experience', or know about William Butler Yeats, even had she been able to explain. For her last birthday Peedee had given her a bound volume of WBY's poems which she treasured far more than the old print of a bullfight, his first gift to her when she had been a small, war-torn girl in the Dublin Rotunda hospital.

'Then I will join you!' Jaime raised his glass to the moon. '*La luna!*'

'*La luna!*' They clinked glasses. Raven felt as light as foam, she wanted to dance on the sea.

'I *hate* the moon!' Roxana said fiercely. 'The moon

always gives me the creeps, as though God has a glass eye which he pops in every night so that he can spy on us. Then he'll write it all down in his people-spotting book, you for heaven, you for hell!'

José found Roxana's analogy highly amusing. 'You are no moonflower then, Roxa, if you don't like the moon looking at you.'

'Perhaps she's a mooncalf instead,' Ramiro added rather rudely.

Jaime turned to Raven. 'You look especially nice tonight, Raven. I think it must be the new grown-up hairstyle.'

'Thank you, Jaime.'

'I like your dress.'

Raven liked it too: she also liked Jaime with whom she felt comfortable. She devoted her attention to him in view of the fact he was less shy tonight and had opened up to her so warmly and naturally. Jaime was genuine, she felt she could trust him, unlike his brothers. 'It's one of your mother's frocks from Paris.' She had to be honest about it, Jaime was so earnest.

'The short skirt is nice, it suits you. You have nice legs,' Jaime added.

Jaime was becoming maudlin on too much *sangria*, and Raven flashed him a quick, self-conscious grin as she tucked her long, brown legs out of sight under the table, while preparing to unsheath her claws a second time around should Ramiro not have taken the hint about not touching.

José, noticing that she and Jaime were becoming too friendly said, 'Raven, let's walk along the seashore. I have something I want to say to you.'

Realizing that José was jealous, because Raven was paying him more attention than anyone else around the table, Jaime, who had no wish to upset José whom he idolized, flushed and drew away from Raven. He stared at the dark, open expanse of the sea. The warm breezes from Africa rustling through the palm-thatch roof of this open-air taverna made a swishing noise like the grass skirts of a native dancer. Jaime looked suddenly forlorn, very much the younger brother put in his place by the elder.

Raven resented José's proprietary claim upon him. She had been enjoying her little conversation with Jaime. She was thankful when Marta intervened, her sour-grape face, for once, getting the timing right.

'José, it's time to go home. I don't think Papa will approve of your ordering *sangria* for everybody. The English girls are not used to it. And you should not have dismissed Pedro who should have waited for us while we were in the cinema. He gets paid to drive us, even if he has to walk back to Vilafranca afterwards. You know how Papa hates you boys to drive his motor car.'

José put his sister in her place. 'Marta, you're not a married woman yet. When you're someone's wife, you may become the matron. For now, drink up your wine and then close your mouth.'

Marta picked out another king prawn soaked in garlic from the huge iron dish of seafood cooked over charcoal, *calamares, gambas, langostinos, sepia,* and with her blunt fingers tore the shellfish apart in her fury.

When Raven, swift on Marta's criticism of him, pointed out the time to José, and said that Peedee would not be pleased if they did not arrive home at the appointed hour, José reluctantly forgot about walking her along the seashore. Raven respected her grandfather's wishes enough to want to obey them to the letter.

Jaime drove the huge new Hispano Suiza, which was Don Ruiz's pride and joy. He had acquired the Boulogne 8-litre H6C Sport Model only a few days ago, and Raven hoped Jaime would take care of it as he drove home. She had no need to fear, Jaime was a good, steady driver, and did not race the car along the narrow, winding coast road, nor take the risks that José and Ramiro had taken earlier.

Marta sat in the front beside Jaime. Raven found herself squashed in the back with José, Roxa and Ramiro. José would not hear of her sitting in the front with Jaime and Marta and had almost kidnapped her into the back of the car. Raven was very conscious of Ram's hand caressing Roxana's bare knee, and Roxana's capricious little giggles while she and Ramiro, their heads touching, whispered endearments to one another. Raven was afraid that José would try and become as familiar with her as Ram was behaving with her sister, but she need not have worried. José behaved like a perfect gentleman and did nothing more than lightly hold her hand in rather a sweet and proprietary way.

Jaime stopped the car on the rough unmade road outside Cabo Alondra. Peedee's study-light was still on. It was three minutes to eleven, and Raven breathed a sigh of relief; at least they were not late.

José stepped out of the car with her. 'Raven, I could not talk to you properly this evening, as I had intended. I have something important I want to say to you before I leave for Dijon next Saturday. Please will you meet me tomorrow afternoon outside the Caverna Rosa – three o'clock?'

Peedee stood at the door. He beamed at them in the light of the porch-lamp. Purple and red bracts of bougainvillaea growing around the doorway surrounded him in royal plumage, while insects of the night droned around his head. He flapped at the nightlife ineffectually. 'Oh good, you're home at last. Now I can go to bed. Did you enjoy yourselves, dear girls?'

'Yes, thank you Peedee,' they dutifully chorused.

Over her shoulder Raven whispered to José standing in the shadows, 'I'll think about it.' She fled into the sanctuary of Cabo Alondra.

The following morning, Raven was aware of the solitary figure in uniform watching her from the cliff-top. It was the man who had been prowling around the headland the entire summer. The sinister presence of the soldier annoyed her. She did not know anyone who wore uniform apart from the local policeman; but it was definitely not the portly, moustached, and exuberant little Policeman Albarda from Toril. Albarda never wore a hat like that, nor did he carry a rifle over his shoulder. Besides, Policeman Albarda would have given her a friendly wave had he seen her sunbathing. Raven did not care to be spied upon from the cliff-top, it made her feel as though she was doing something wrong.

Five minutes later, the man disappeared from view, and

Raven dismissed him from her mind. She spent the rest of the morning until lunchtime alone on the seashore. In the afternoon, she decided that she would, after all, keep her rendezvous with José.

In the old days, de Luchar wine production had been confined to one area, the main bodegas situated within the Parque Vinarosa itself. As the de Luchar wine business had developed in volume and size, and the export of wines had increased to the Spanish colonies, Don Ruiz had decided to centralize everything in a more convenient location. Larger, more modern bodegas with hydraulic presses, and a new vinification plant, had been built in the town of Vilafranca, on Commerce Street, adjacent to the railway line, thus facilitating the easier and more efficient transportation of the wine casks to Barcelona and the docks. Some wine production, however, was still undertaken at Vinarosa, though in the slower, old-fashioned way, and mainly wines for the home market.

The Caverna Rosa, where she was supposed to meet José, was situated at the far end of the estate. Here, Don Ruiz's best distilled wines were left to age in huge oaken Limoges casks. Raven had borrowed Peedee's bicycle for the afternoon. Peedee was teaching Sonny extra Latin at Cabo Alondra, as he was very bad at Latin according to Peedee. Raven wore her cycling shorts, a thin white cotton blouse, canvas tennis shoes, and her wide-brimmed straw hat upon which the hot afternoon sun beat down mercilessly. A mile and a half to Vinarosa, she cycled energetically, but was still ten minutes late.

Hot, breathless, and very red in the face by the time she arrived, there was no sign of José. She propped the bicycle against the darkened walls of the Caverna Rosa, and sat down on the grassy verge of the path, hoping he hadn't arrived early, got tired of waiting, and left: she would give him twenty minutes, by which time she would have regained her breath, then she'd go.

Hardly anyone came here any more, except on wine-tasting or feast days, or when a few bottles of something very special were required for Don Ruiz's own table. Raven glanced around nervously. On one side of her was a thick forest of Spanish spruce darkening the skyline, the boundary of the estate. Even in the heat, this edge of the estate always felt damp, gloomy, and mysterious, shrouded as it was in deep shadows cast by the forest. On the other side, where the sunlight reached and the slopes drained well, endless rows of vines, the local white Parellada that grew to high quality in this Upper Penedès area, would soon be ready for harvesting.

Just when she had made up her mind to return to Cabo Alondra because she had missed José, she heard a motorcycle engine, and breathed a sigh of relief when she saw José driving along the rutted and dusty boundary-road between the vineyard and the forest.

José wore dark blue dungarees, a blue checked cotton shirt, and *alpargatas*, rope sandals, on his bare feet. He looked so casually handsome, mature and self-assured, Raven felt dizzy with love just looking at beautiful José de Luchar, while wondering what he saw in her, nothing but a plain, unsophisticated teenage schoolgirl. José turned off the motorcycle engine, and grinned at her without apologizing for being almost half an hour late. 'Do you like my new toy?'

'I don't know much about motorcycles,' she said, dubiously eyeing the cumbersome machine.

'Nor do I, but I'll learn. Although I prefer the comfort of a motor car, I think a motorcycle is much more practical where speed is concerned, especially on our roads. I persuaded Doña Maria to buy me this machine as a Christmas present.'

Raven had to laugh. 'José, you've *cheated* your grandmother! Christmas is another four months away.'

'She doesn't know that. Neither does she know what to do with all her money. Ram has also tumbled to her senility, so I have to beat him at the game of fleecing her.'

'You two are shameless.'

José gave her a hug, before taking a bunch of keys out of his dungaree pocket to open the heavily-padlocked door. 'Come into my parlour, said the spider to the fly,' making her laugh as he extended his hand to help her down the broken, moss-covered stone steps to the caverna. 'Papa wants half a dozen bottles of his finest Imperial brandy, which Cipi is supposed to have left for me to pick up.

Don't tell anyone, but Papa has an important guest coming for dinner.'

'How can I tell anyone when I don't even know the name of this important guest?'

José smiled at her over his shoulder. 'Then I'll tell you, because I know I can trust you not to spill the beans to the anti-monarchist brigade. He is Don Jaime de Bourbon.'

'Who on earth is Don Jaime de Bourbon?'

'A very special man, blackbird. He is a distant cousin of the King, and the pretender to the Spanish throne.'

'Why am I supposed to cheer?'

'Don Jaime is unmarried. He has no children ...'

'I should hope not!'

'The political climate is unsettled at the moment. King Alfonso is not in a safe position. Should anything happen to the King, Don Jaime is his likely successor. That's if his eighty-year-old uncle, who lives in Paris, does not outlive him. It seems unlikely. Now do you understand the situation?'

'No.'

José guided Raven into the unfamiliar darkness. The wonderful chill and scent of the caverna after the glaring heat outside took her breath away. Just inside the door was a table and from it José took up a box of matches and lit a candle. No electric lighting had been installed, for the heat generated even by ordinary lamp-bulbs would upset the delicate temperature balance down here, where the very best distilled wines matured to perfection. José quickly shut and relocked the cellar door to prevent the heat from outside penetrating the cellar. Then he scribbled in a thick ledger like a family Bible, placed beside the matches, candles and the half-dozen bottles of 'El Grandee Imperial Licor de Luchar' Cipi had left out for collection. 'We have to account for each bottle or cask that leaves this place, you see,' José explained with a smile, 'for this is my father's liquid gold-mine.'

'Why should Don Jaime being a bachelor have a special significance?' Apart from the heady brandy scent in the caverna, Raven was beginning to sniff out secrets ripe for her people-spotting book, which she still kept going despite all Roxana's snide remarks.

'If Don Jaime does not marry and produce a child soon, then his eighty-year-old uncle, Alfonso Carlos, will be his successor. Alfonso himself, although married, has no children. What seems far more likely is that both will die before long, leaving our puppet King, another Alfonso, the sole figurehead between democracy and anarchy. Papa is a traditional monarchist, but all the Alfonsists and Carlists preach is *Dios, Patria y Rey*, God, Country and King!'

Raven did not know why, but she got the impression that José was enamoured of such patriotism even though he pretended not to be.

Although she had welcomed the chill of the caverna, Raven suddenly felt colder still for another reason – uncertainty. She began to realize that what was happening in Spain today, had happened in Ireland yesterday, and in all preceding Irish yesterdays that would go on and on into all Ireland's tomorrows: and she did not want that to happen to her adopted country of Spain: she did not want Peedee, Sonny, Roxana, and herself embroiled in someone else's conflict.

José, observing her discomfort, drew her close. His arms tight around her, he whispered, 'Are you cold? Stay here with me, let me warm you up a little, blackbird.'

She clung to him because he was warm and human, because he was flesh and blood, because he was an attractive young man offering her comfort and love, and because he thought of her as a beautiful woman and not a silly schoolgirl. Dispossessed at once of her confidence, self-reliance, and any kind of bravado she might have been feeling, Raven wanted to feel José's arms around her, keeping her close, just like yesterday. 'Oh José, sometimes I think I love you more than anyone else in the world, apart from Peedee and Sonny.'

There! She had said it, the words tumbling spontaneously from her lips like pollen from a flower, and Raven was horrified with herself and her forwardness. José would think her fast, for, after all, it was but a mere twenty-four hours ago that she had been made aware, for the first time, of José's feelings as far as she was concerned: and girls – nice girls – didn't reveal their real feelings concerning a young man. 'Oh José – oh, dear! I'm really sorry. I didn't mean it – I didn't mean to – to tell you just yet. I didn't mean to be so – silly!' Raven felt she could die for shame: José would think her *cheap!*

He was not taken aback by such a revelation, and smiled into her red face. Then he brushed her lips gently with his. 'What is so silly? You must know the way I feel about you. I want to marry you one day. As soon as you are seventeen, I will ask your grandpapa for his permission, and then we can get engaged.'

He suddenly threw her feelings for him into even greater confusion. While she had adored him from afar, and since yesterday afternoon, at great proximity, she had not thought about *marriage* to José. Not just yet. To commit herself to becoming a Spanish grandee's Doña was out of the question at the moment. In theory, she was still only a schoolgirl, and Peedee would jump on that fact at once. She herself had only ever thought about matriculation, never marriage. 'It wouldn't be possible, José, not yet,' she told him candidly. 'Peedee might make us wait. At least until I'm twenty-one. Don't ask him anything just yet, not until I'm eighteen. Peedee might be a little more ready to listen to us then about getting engaged.'

'I understand. Perhaps I ought to get my diploma first from that damnable Viticulture and Oenology College in Dijon before we plan our future together. But, from now on, I want you to know only this one thing, that I love you and that I intend to marry you as soon as it's possible.'

She relaxed. She was only thankful that he had treated her with respect, and had not embarrassed her in any way through her awkward, fumbling schoolgirl admissions of love. Romance was what she had been looking forward to, marriage to José de Luchar was only for a very much later date.

He held her close. 'Do you truly love me, Raven?'

'Yes, José.'

'I love you too, little blackbird, very much indeed. Come, let's sit together for a moment and talk.' He led her away from the shadow-filled glow of the candle, and pulled her down with him in a dark corner on some sacking. His lips against her neck, he murmured, 'Do you see the black marks all over the walls and ceiling of this place?'

'Yes.'

'Do you know what discolours it so?'

'No.'

'Oxidization. We *vinicultors*,' he gave a humourous little grunt, his warm breath ticklish against her neck as he nestled against her, 'call it the angel's share. Brandy you know, has a soul. The soul is the aromatic and volatile part, its true essence. The purer and more noble part is called the heart. You remind me of – you remind me of the angel's share, the spirit of the brandy, for no one knows to where it goes; possibly it returns to heaven.'

Slowly but deliberately, José began to unfasten the buttons of her blouse. When she stopped his hands with the merest hesitancy, he looked at her so accusingly and so hurtfully, she felt she had done him some personal injury. 'Blackbird – oh, I'm sorry, I know how you hate to be called by that name, I'll call you Raven. Please trust me, Raven. I'd never do anything to hurt you, you know that.'

She wanted desperately to believe him.

'Papa, you know, has copied the methods of Jerez. The vinicultors of Jerez themselves learned the technique of brandy distillation from the Arabs. Jaime thinks Papa should try the Cognac method of France. I disagree. I think we should 'individualize' – improve upon our own unique Catalonian methods with our natural Penedès stock. Your grandfather is right. My father should not diversify so much, but rather concentrate, specialize, advertize, but only in selected markets ...'

She hardly heard what he was saying. By now he had opened her blouse fully, and was caressing and looking at her breasts in a way that she would never have believed could be so utterly wonderful. Her tiny twin mounds had always been a sensitive band of flesh, ever since she had discovered them surreptitiously emerging from the flat plains of her barren, fourteen-year-old chest, alarmingly, yet sensitively pushing their way towards the sunlight. But, she was still unprepared for exposure on this scale, and, even if, umm, heaven! to be caressed and loved like this by José, was – was tetra! – she knew she must stop him at once:

'José, I think we ought not …'

He did not pay her any attention, but went on kissing her in a way that deprived her of all power of resistance. The drumming in her ears and her heart, experienced for the first time yesterday and quite unconnected with bombs and stitches in one's head, might have nothing to do with love and everything to do with temptation, yet, thrilled and enveloped in a sweet, ecstatic cloak of the purest emotion, she thought, I love him, he loves me, this *can't* be wrong! The adoration in José's dark eyes, that same look he had bestowed upon the Madonna one Christmas Eve when Doña Jacqueline had taken them all to Midnight Mass at the Cathedral in Barcelona, he was now displaying for her benefit. These feelings flooding her whole body were so wonderful, they must be right. Loving someone seemed so beautiful, it *must* be right! She felt warm, secure, and wanted in his embrace, so why did she feel so guilty?

Raven refused to think about it. The gospel according to St Cassy was again interfering with her enjoyment of life.

She closed her eyes and gave herself up to feeling rather than thinking, remembering only the warmth of the sea and the sand against her skin, and José's hard young body loving her.

Then he began in that smooth, sure way of his to unfasten the side-buttons of her shorts, and had begun to ease them over her hips. 'You have such a slim, sexy body,' he said, adoringly. 'I want to show you what love is all about, Raven. I want to be the one to teach you. You are mine, so it will be all right – I will be very careful with you so that you don't have to worry about anything except relaxing and enjoying yourself.'

'No, José, please don't – I think I must go home now …'

He couldn't have understood her. He went on trying to undress her completely, and touch her in a very personal place, the place Cassy at bathtime had always called the place of the Immaculate Conception …

'You remind me of the essence that escapes from an oaken cask and no one knows to where it goes – the spirit that seeks the air in that mysterious distillation of the heart and the soul and – the body …'

She wasn't listening to him any more. Raven pushed him

away forcefully, her nails digging into his shoulders as they had done into Ramiro's hand last evening. José recoiled from her, the look on his face one of betrayal on her part: after all, she had been waiting for *him*, was the look on his face in that awful moment.

'I shall never meet you alone again, José de Luchar!' she almost sobbed as she got to her feet. 'What do you take me for?' Her chic grown up hairstyle tousled, her whole being dishevelled, she trembled with agitation as she fastened her clothing, not having expected this at all from him, yet knowing she was partly to blame for what had happened.

'I thought you wanted me to,' he said in some confusion. 'I didn't know you were so inexperienced, or such a – a *schoolgirl* still! I thought you knew everything, and enjoyed it, just like your sister.'

'What do you mean?'

'Sexual experience – Roxa's always hot for it according to Ram ...'

She slapped José's face so hard, the palm of her hand stung.

Without a word José unlocked the cellar door and opened it wide. Raven rushed up the steps. Gulping down the sunlight, she grabbed Peedee's bicycle, and did not stop her frantic pedalling until she reached Cabo Alondra.

Mercifully, Peedee and Sonny were having their siesta, and Roxana was nowhere to be seen. Raven went straight to the bathroom, turned the cold water tap on fully, and filled the bath. She set her teeth and sat in the cold water until her insides were numb.

When she came out thirty minutes later, she was as pallid as putty and her legs felt so wobbly, they hardly supported her. She locked her bedroom-door, and, dripping puddles on the colourful Spanish tiles, only then removed her sodden clothes, which she tossed into the back of her wardrobe.

Feeling as though José had stabbed her with an icicle, Raven put on her dressing-gown, lay down on the bed and stared at the ceiling. Mentally tormented rather than physically abused she breathed in short, sharp gulps of pain and nothinginess; she wanted to die.

She began to wonder what physical damage José had

done to her: would she have a baby now? She covered her face with her hands, suffused with guilt and shame. Oh, God, what had she done! How could she tell Peedee she was about to become a mother. Oh God! She thought she would drown herself in the sea if that happened. She had no idea of how far one had to go to conceive a baby, or how many times; she knew nothing! Her instincts told her that José hadn't acutally *done* anything, except *try* very hard to seduce her. He hadn't used any part of himself expect his mouth and tongue when kissing her and his hands that had roved all over her body until the moment when he had wanted to explore her insides! But she was still so unsure of her facts, she still didn't *know*! She dare not ask Roxana how one became fully pregnant, Roxana would only become 'superior' again, or laugh, which would be even worse.

Raven wondered if she ought not to start praying to God about it; he had answered her prayers before, why not again? Please God, she began, not moving from her mummified position on the bed while she prayed to the ceiling, I'm guilty of a bad sin with José de Luchar in the Caverna Rosa this afternoon. We are not married, so I think it's called adultery when a man takes liberties with a woman he's not married to. José has promised to marry me though. You must have been there, watching over us, so you'll know it wasn't altogether my fault, as I didn't understand what José was trying to do. Please forgive me, and not let me have conceived like the Virgin Mary, because I honestly didn't intend to be so wicked. Amen.

Raven turned over on her side. Her face in her pillow, she gave vent to her overwrought emotions.

When Roxana banged on her bedroom-door to say that Carina was tired of holding supper back for her, and even Peedee was getting cross, Raven, in muffled misery, answered, 'Tell Peedee I'm sorry, and to please start supper without me.'

'What's wrong with you?' Roxana demanded rattling the door-handle. 'And why have you locked your door?'

'I have one of my migraines. I don't wish to be disturbed.'

'Then you're starting the curse – you always get a

migraine at those times. I came on this morning, and you know we always get it together. All right, I'll tell Peedee you have the monthly miseries and want to be left alone.'

Raven could hear Roxana clattering back down the polished cedarwood staircase to the dining-room. Then she got off her bed, knelt down, put her hands together, and said simply, 'Thank you God for always answering my prayers so promptly. I know I can't have both at the same time, curse *and* baby, so I promise to behave myself in future. Amen.'

A few days later, Peedee asked to speak to Raven alone in his study. Raven had been busy packing, as the following morning she and Roxana were leaving for Switzerland. Peedee had never acted the inquisitor or the heavy-handed grandfather before, and Raven was terribly perturbed. Could he have found out about her and José?

'I want to talk to you about José,' Peedee said, frowning at her above his spectacles. He took them off, laid his newspaper aside, and then, observing how pale and trembly she had become, said, 'Do sit down, dear girl. There's no need to stand there on the carpet as though I'm going to whack you. Neither am I about to read you the riot act, so don't look so guilty.'

Raven quickly sat down.

'Now then, I know you and José have spent much time together this summer, and I want to ask you one or two questions.'

Raven had difficulty in swallowing the lump that came into her throat. Her extreme pallor turned to rose-red, but if Peedee noticed, he turned a blind eye.

'He, dear girl, was supposed to have shown up at his Agricultural College in Dijon last Saturday, but he never arrived. He has been missing now for five days. The last person to have seen José was Pedro, who drove José to the railway station in Vilafranca. Doña Jacqueline and Don Ruiz are beside themselves. They think that José has been kidnapped by Anarchists wanting money for some useless cause or other. The longer I teach history to Sonny and Carlos, the more I realize what a foolish breed is Man.

212

However, that's irrelevant. Somehow the newspapers got to hear that the pretender to the Spanish throne, Don Jaime, dined at the Mas Luchar while on his way to Paris to see his uncle. Don Alfonso is the other claimant to the Spanish throne. I'm not confusing you, am I?'

'No, Peedee. I know about the Alfonsists and Carlists.'

'Good. Well then, Don Ruiz thinks that might be the reason why José was kidnapped – oh, not indeed, by the Alfonsists, but those opposed to traditional monarchy, the Anarchists, and Revolutionary Communists and suchlike. However, I do not think that our José has been kidnapped at all, because by now we would have received a ransom note. Kidnappers do not sit on their prisoners for longer than twenty-four hours without making their demands perfectly clear to those involved. So, as no ransom demand has thus far materialized, I think José's disappearance is of his own doing. Now, dear girl, while I have not the slightest reason to suspect you of kidnapping José de Luchar, waving a magic wand over him to make him disappear before he pops up again in a top hat, or of any other vanishing trick upon him, have you any idea at all where he might be? Has he ever said anything to you that might give us a clue as to his whereabouts?'

'Nothing. I'd've told you had José mentioned to me about not returning to Dijon. He seemed very happy to be retur … oh, wait a minute, there is something.'

'Yes?'

'The other morning when I was on the beach, a man on the cliff-top was watching me. Well, I thought so at the time. I rather think now, he may have been looking out for José.'

'What did this man look like?'

'A soldier in a green militia uniform and funny hat. He carried a gun.'

'Then he was one of the Guardia Civil relying on his Mauser to keep the peace. The funny hat as you describe was no doubt his black leather *tricornio*. Thank goodness he was wearing a *tricornio* and not a beret – *checas* in the control patrols wear berets and breeches. They are secret policeman who have also decided to keep an eye on this stretch of the coastline. For what reason, I cannot begin to imagine. On the other hand, the Civil Guard might have been posted here for security reasons. All to do with this Don Jaime business.'

'Peedee, why would anyone want to take José prisoner?'

'I've no idea, dear girl, other than for mercenary gain, which seems very likely.' He pondered for a moment, and then said distantly. 'An old Spanish proverb springs to mind: "if you want to let the whole world know your business, invite a saint to supper." Well now, in view of the fact you know nothing about our José's mysterious whereabouts, we had better just be on the safe side and invite *two* saints to supper. Senor Albarda and his dear little wife should arrive here at about ten o'clock. However, you know the Spanish and their timekeeping. It could be eleven or even midnight before they appear. You and Roxana may or may not be present at the table, I leave it entirely up to you girls, as you have an early start in the morning. Don Ruiz has kindly offered the Hispano and Pedro's services to get you to Barcelona, and I think you ought to accept in view of all the luggage I see cluttering up the hall. Now run along, dear girl, I have some thinking to do.'

As she opened the door Peedee cleared his throat. 'By the way, Raven, when did you last see José?'

'Umm – a few afternoons before he was due to return to Dijon. Let me see – when did we all go to the cinema? Was it last Tuesday or Wednesday? Tuesday, I think. So, I saw José the following afternoon, Wednesday. Don Jaime de Boubon came to dinner that evening – yesterday week. Peedee.'

'You met José at the Caverna Rosa?'

'Yes – how did you know?'

'I see. Oh well, just a thought, dear girl. You may buzz off now and leave me in peace,' he chivvied without actually answering her question.

Raven realized she would probably not swim again for another six or seven months, and that the next Easter holidays would be the earliest likely time for her to indulge in her favourite sport, even though the sea was usually freezing in the early spring. She put on her costume and beach-robe, took a towel, and went one last time to take her watery leave of the Mediterranean Sea, stealing across the wonderfully warm, gold-tinged sands of Cabo Alondra.

Now that she thought about it, she would miss the company of all of them at Vinarosa: she would probably even miss Juan the 'woof-woof' vineyard overseer, as well as Policeman Albarda. She always felt the same every year when she and Roxana made their rounds of Vinarosa with their heartfelt farewells amid Spanish tears. At the beginning of the summer holidays in June, time stretched endlessly before one so that old insults, grudges, and sore points could be brought out once again into the open, to be exploited, embellished and relished. But once the last week of August arrived, with a new academic year looming ahead, Raven always felt sad to be leaving. At the end of the holidays, old grievances were forgotten, handkerchiefs were brought out, and it was time to start another new phase of one's life. Her year was monitored by that end-and-beginning month of August.

This year she felt particularly upset about leaving Vinarosa and Cabo Alondra because of what had happened between José and herself. Was she the cause of his sudden disappearance from Vinarosa? Did he blame her for rejecting his love? And now that she had had time to think things over, she felt that she *had* rather over-reacted to that grand seduction scene in the Caverna Rosa: after all, José was a young, red-blooded Spaniard, and even though Peedee might have given the de Luchar boys an English gentleman's education, in the end, she supposed, blood would out. José and Ramiro both had passionate Latin temperaments. They only thought of women as bodies, never as persons with minds or individual rights. She had seen it in the way they treated their sisters and the servant girls around the estate. José had honestly thought she had gone to the Caverna Rosa to have 'sex' with him, and while she burned in embarrassment when she thought about it, and while the two things had curiously separated in her mind, sex and love, she fervently hoped that he hadn't thrown himself in the sea and drowned on account of her violent rejection of him. Raven half hoped that some fanatical political group *had* kidnapped him for a ransom, as everyone seemed to think, for then she would be spared the agony of his suicide on her conscience.

On the other hand, was hē being bullied and tortured at this very moment while she was enjoying herself in the warm, blue sea? That too, would be hard to reconcile. Had he gone off to Paris with Don Jaime? Oh dear, where was he, for goodness sake?

Raven spent half an hour swimming, her thoughts always returning to José. When she came out of the sea, a soldier with a very Spanish moustache was standing on the beach, his elongated shadow thrown over the evening sands. This was probably the same man who had been patrolling the cliff-top the entire summer. His uniform was of a greeny-grey colour, his rifle was slung across his back, and he wore a shiny black three-cornered militia hat, which must be the *tricornio* Peedee had mentioned, as worn by the Guardia Civil. Raven wondered if he had come to arrest her for showing too much leg, thigh, and bosom on the beach. She knew how funny the Spanish were about nudity, and while she wasn't guilty of anything as excessive as that, she rather imagined she *had* exposed rather a lot of bare flesh in public.

His boots planted firmly beside her towel, she immediately took exception. Neither did she like the way he was staring at her. While she was half-afraid of the Civil Guardsman's uniform and Mauser, she was not afraid of the person who wore it, a young man about the same age as José. She spoke to him in Spanish, 'Señor, this is a private beach, please go away.'

He retrieved her towel off the sand, and handed it to her. 'Señorita, you should be careful.'

She held the towel in front of her while she wiped her face. 'What do you mean be careful? Let me tell you, this beach is owned by Don Ruiz de Luchar, and you have no right to be spying on me.'

'I'm not spying on you, señorita. And, I think, the sea belongs to God, as do all the grains of sand we're standing on. No mortal man can own what belongs to God.

However, I'm not here to engage in a philosophical argument.'

'Then why *are* you here?'

'I have a message for you.'

'For me?'

He fumbled in his tunic breast pocket and fished out an envelope.

Raven's heart lurched; so, the ransom note had come at last. Poor José. She was suddenly prepared to forgive him everything.

'It's actually addressed to your grandfather, Señor Peedee.'

'Then why didn't you give it to him? He only lives up there, at that villa you've been hovering around the whole summer.'

'Because I'm afraid of him.'

'Because you ...' she almost burst out laughing. She stared at the Spaniard, her fingers pressed against her lips. And then, against her will, she did burst out laughing because he presented such a comical and harmless picture, 'You're afraid of my *grandfather*?'

'Yes, señorita.' In his discomposure the young man shoved the envelope he was supposed to pass on to Señor Peedee Purnell, back into his breast pocket. From another pocket he extracted a small battered tin and took from it a homemade cigarette. Then he put the tin back in his pocket, lit the pathetically bedraggled cigarette, and inhaled deeply in order to restore his manly image before the young woman he had come to adore from a distance. He did not mind how much she insulted him, it was wonderful just to be standing so close to her, and to hear her voice. He was also a little afraid of her simply because she was so beautiful, so accomplished, and so un-Spanish.

'I'm sorry if you think I've been spying on you, señorita,' Marcos Rodriguez said tersely, his nervousness making him abrupt, 'but I've wanted to tell you for several days now, you must be careful of exposing yourself on the beach as you have been doing. There are many weird characters going around these days, hiding in woods and farmyards, terrorizing innocent people. You have heard of the Death and Freedom Brigade from Toril?'

'Yes, I've read about them in the local papers. Are you saying that they are responsible for what has happened to José de Luchar?'

'I'm saying, señorita, that such hooligans and gangsters are not to be trusted. They would as soon rape, as burn and loot and desecrate holy property, and so you must cover yourself whenever you are on the beach. I am here to protect you, not to spy on you. That is all I wish to say.'

'Don't worry, señor, *no problema*! I'm returning to Switzerland tomorrow.'

For a moment Raven thought the Civil Guardsman had looked almost crestfallen by her announcement. She took matters into her own hands since he seemed to be devoid of words and direction. 'Señor, we're standing here wasting time talking when José de Luchar's life might be in grave danger. Just give me the note for my grandfather, and then get off this beach.'

He fumbled in his breast pocket, produced the white envelope and held it out to her. She snatched it from him, and ran up the steep cliff path that would take her back to Cabo Alondra.

CHAPTER SIX

Geneva, Switzerland:
May and June 1931

The matriculation class of Mademoiselle l'Impératrice alighted from one of the *mouettes genèvoises* that had ferried them to and from Cologny. The eight girls had been to the Byron Fields on the other side of Lac Léman, for the school syllabus included a study of the lives of Lord George Gordon Byron and Percy Bysshe Shelley. Mademoiselle l'Impératrice was upper school's Form Mistress. She also taught French, history and botany.

'What was the name of Byron's last resting place, Roxanna Quennell?'

'Missolonghi, miss – I mean mam'zelle.'

'So you did take in something. I apologize for having thought you'd spent the entire day giggling with Vida.' l'Impératrice, speaking French to her class, stepped up the pace. 'Come along, girls, don't dilly-dally. There are other people waiting for the boat. Vida, if you and Roxana don't stop chattering and watch where you're putting your feet, you'll both end up in the lake.'

'If she doesn't stop squawking so much,' Vida de Martello hissed in Roxana's ear, 'she'll lay an egg in the lake.'

Two or three of the other girls smothered their giggles. l'Impératrice used her index finger to push up her owlish spectacles onto the flat bridge of her snub nose, and smiled apologetically at the other passengers for any inconvenience her girls may have caused. Clapping her hands together sharply, she urged, 'Form a crocodile, please girls – come along, snap-snap! Now then, Head Girl, are we all present and correct?'

Raven, doing a hat check, said, 'Yes, everyone's here, Mademoiselle l'Impératrice.'

'Yes ma'am, no ma'am, three bags full ma'am!' said Vida under her breath to Roxana, and sarcastically wiggled her bottom behind Raven. '*Mon Dieu*, your sister's a beastly little creeper, Roxy. I think we shall tar and feather her soon for being such a goody-goody.' Vida shot her hand in the air, 'What has Mussolini to do with Cologny? That's in Italy, isn't it, mam'zelle?'

'Dear child, Missolonghi, not Mussolini. Lord Byron lived at Cologny, but died in Greece.'

'And in hock,' Vida muttered, and set them all off giggling again.

'Best foot forward, my dears, and march our little brigade smartly back to school,' l'Impératrice urged Raven and Janice Fairchild, the assistant head girl. At the head of the crocodile, they led the upper sixth form matriculation class from the jetty and took the wide path separating La Perle du Lac on their right from the Parc Mon Repos on the left. This would bring them out to the Rue de Lausanne.

Vida and Roxana continued to snigger and whisper together, making l'Impératrice wonder what fresh mayhem they were plotting. She couldn't wait to deposit this unruly mob back to school, and sighed helplessly: the only two worth their salt were Janice Fairchild and Ravenna Quennell, and how the Quennell twins could, in every way, be so disparate, l'Impératrice was at a loss to understand. 'Vida, your hat is not to be worn so jauntily on the back of your head, and your tie is crooked. Please adjust your dress correctly, and pull down your gymslip, which is not supposed to be tucked up under its sash in that untidy fashion. Your knees are showing.'

'Oh, my God!'

'What was that Vida?'

'Oh, my word, mam'zelle, please watch where you're treading. I do believe a nasty little dog has done his business in your path.'

'Dear me – thank you, Vida.' l'Impératrice, flustered lest the soles of her shoes might have become soiled and smelly, spent time wiping them on the grass. She made the girls walk on ahead. She couldn't see anything on her shoes, but then, she was badly short-sighted.

Vida and Roxana almost suffocated with childish mirth at l'Impératrice's expense, and Raven promised herself to deal severely with her sister later! Since the beginning of the last autumn term, Roxana and Vida de Martello had become bosom pals, much to the chagrin of many of Vida's old cronies – the queen of the senior dormitory had found a new favourite. Roxana had even spent the Easter holidays in Paris with Le Comte de Martello and La Contesse III. Vida's father and his third wife had been tremendously taken with Roxana (according to Roxana who had never in her life suffered from an inferiority complex) and liked her better than all Vida's other friends. So they had invited her back to spend the long summer vacation between their château at Fontainebleau and coastal villa at Antibes. Peedee had given his permission, but Raven was not happy at the liberty her well-meaning but naïve grandfather allowed her less than responsible sister: Vida was definitely not a good influence upon Roxana.

Mademoiselle l'Impératrice caught up with her class.

'Oh look, Roxy!' Vida squealed in delight behind Raven and Janice. 'There he is again! Isn't he wild, isn't he sexy!' Vida stopped dead on the path and the four girls and l'Impératrice following, all trod on each other's heels.

'Vida, what *is* the matter now?'

'I have a stone in my shoe, mam'zelle.'

'Then stop and get it out. Wait girls, please – better still, let us make use of every minute that the good Lord puts at our disposal to improve our earthly minds.' (l'Impératrice was a good solid Genevese Calvinist like Eugénie Roget). 'You four come with me – Raven and Janice, you two stay with Vida and Roxana. So tiresome!' she muttered, as she divided the company in half, before adding the simple explanation, 'There is a rare tree over there, that I want you girls to try and identify in order to prove to me that you have managed to assimilate a little knowledge from botany classes. We shall be back in five minutes, Raven, and I hope by then Vida has found the cause of her discomfort. Come along girls – this way, back towards La Perle du Lac.'

'Just because she saw him a few days ago talking to Madame Eugénie in her office, she's made an excuse to stop every time we walk through these parks, and it isn't funny any more,' said Janice to Raven, referring to the irritating Vida who had thrown down her satchel on the grass.

Without the subject of her desire being aware of what she was doing, Vida aimed her Kodak at the man seated some distance away on a park bench. She had been taking pictures all day long, and she gurgled, 'Last photo of the day coming up, girls, and now I can get them developed. I'll let you have a copy of HIM, Roxy, darling.'

'He's hardly Douglas Fairbanks!' Janice scoffed in an aside to Raven. 'But then, we all know how much of a man-eater is *our* Vida!'

Raven agreed wholeheartedly, everyone aware for the fifth time this week of the man who had become Vida's fatal attraction. It had become embarrassing to say the least, and she only hoped the 'man on the bench' wasn't aware of the adulation he was receiving from a crocodile of schoolgirls. Raven could see that he was simply not interested in the gymslip and ankle socks brigade, despite Vida's efforts to attract his attention.

Deeply engrossed in his newspaper, he sat in the same place each afternoon, on a park bench in front of the Villa Moynier with its lovely views of the lake. Painted in Trianon grey, the long windows of the four-storeyed wedding-cake-shaped villa behind him, were open wide on warm afternoons, shutters thrown back. A wrought-iron balustrade flanked steps leading up from either side of a pretty garden full of red flowers in the shape of a cross against a background of white flowers, for the Villa Moynier was the headquarters of the International Committee of the Red Cross.

'I think he works there,' said Vida. 'Must be his tea break. I wonder if he's a doctor, and if he's married.'

'Doctors wear neat suits, ties, and hats, Vida, not red

socks. I expect he's the gardener, and he's bound to be married at his age,' Jan said, giving Raven a resigned look.

Broad-shouldered, athletic, he was hatless, not like the good, solid men of Geneva who wore hats even whilst taking the air in the park. With strong, rugged features, he was more 'interesting' than sleekly handsome – the sort that Vida de Martello usually became crushed on. The breeze off Lac Léman ruffled his wavy hair, dark except for the silvery streaks at sideburns and temples, which were not unattractive, so that he presented the rather distinguished, donnish air of a composer-conductor or absent-minded scientist. He was in need of a haircut too, visible by the way the hair on the back of his neck curled crisply over his jacket collar while his attention was focused on his newspaper. He wore a red tartan shirt, no tie, and his shirt-collar was open at the neck, coyly revealing the manly dark hair on his upper chest. His brown corduroy jacket had leather patches on the elbows, and his fawn trousers had lost their creases. Hand-knitted red socks (they could only *be* hand-knitted in that outrageous shade) and heavy brown brogues completed the picture.

'Not your usual suave, sophisticated, unpatched, glossy, patent leather Valentino type, is he Vida?' Jan smiled.

'I've gone off brilliantine types after seeing *Blood and Sand*. I don't like smarmy or domineering men any more. I'm into my sugar daddy period.'

'He doesn't look much like a sugar daddy to me, only a poor, studious daddy or a Canadian lumberjack with that ghastly shirt,' Jan commented wryly.

'I think he's a struggling maths professor, Vida, not your type at all,' Raven said, knowing that anyone remotely intellectual was enough to put Vida off. 'Have you gone off Monseigneur Paulus too?'

'Yes. So you can have him all to yourself, Raven.'

Adoration of Monseigneur Paulus, the golden priest, was universal at Maison Roget. He who had blushed more times than any other cleric on the Rue de Lausanne, on account of some precocious RC adolescents like Vida de Martello from l'École Internationale divulging untrue and un-innocent things in his ear during the Sacrament of Penance, was aristocratic, refined, genteel, and painfully handsome. Raven considered Monseigneur Paulus to be far more of a heart-throb than the stranger in the park.

Meeting Monseigneur Paulus in the first place had only come about because one Friday morning, when they had all been in the third form, a group of Roman Catholic girls had been unable to make up their numbers to attend confession at l'Église St Raphael, the Roman Catholic Church in the Rue de Lausanne. Many of the girls had been down with influenza at the time, and Raven had made up the numbers in Vida's group, even though she was not a Catholic. Number one school rule was that all students went around in groups of four, and junior and middle-school students had to be accompanied by a prefect. Raven, on that first occasion, had sat at the back of the church, and from then on had been smitten by the golden priest just like all the other girls who attended his church. Monseigneur Paulus had inspired her in a way she was unable to explain.

Then, some months later, Peedee and Sonny had been returning from Belfast where Sonny had had new artificial limbs fitted. They had stopped in Geneva on their customary visit before returning to Spain. While Peedee had been taking tea with Eugénie Roget, and discussing their school reports, Sonny and she had taken a walk along the Rue de Lausanne, Roxana and Janice accompanying them. They had passed St Raphael's open doors, and had heard the choir at practice. Sonny had stopped to listen.

Raven remembered how pleased she had been because Sonny had shown an interest in music again: and because she sensed he wanted to go inside the church, she had offered to accompany him, mentioning the fact that she had often attended services there as an observer though not a participator.

'Why not?' Sonny had replied.

While she and Sonny had been listening to the choir, Roxana and Janice Fairchild (who was staunch Church of England and, therefore, refused to set foot inside a Roman Catholic church) had decided to wait for them in the park. On that occasion, Monseigneur Paulus had actually spent time talking at length to her and Sonny. He had invited them to attend his church whenever they so wished. Sonny had explained that he lived in Spain, but

Raven, since then, had often sat at the back of l'Église St Raphael, not only in her recent capacity of Head Girl and chaperone to the junior RC girls, but for her own soul's satisfaction. Eugénie Roget had ended up as confused as Raven herself as to which denomination she truly belonged.

'He's hardly in the first flush of youth any more, Vida,' Jan Fairchild continued to tease Vida about the man on the park bench.

Vida was undeterred. 'I like older, wilder men with oodles of experience, and he looks *very* experienced to us, doesn't he, Roxy?' Vida, her camera discarded upon the grass next to her satchel, stood on one foot and removed her shoe, while hanging onto Roxana's shoulder to steady herself. 'His face has a kind of "lived-in" look, don't you think, darlings?'

Roxana giggled, 'Lived-in where, Vida?'

'Debauched, darling, debauched.' Vida gave Raven a sly sidelong glance, her lambent dark eyes flashing wickedly. Then Vida fumbled under her school gymslip and took from the pocket of her navy-blue gym-knickers a tiny, flat box of rouge. Her mouth puckered into a tight rosebud, she reddened her lips, dabbed a little on each cheekbone, before passing the rouge box to Roxana. Vida loved to give Head Girl heart failure, for Raven Quennell was easily shocked. 'Sexually depraved, darlings, just like Le Vicomte Arnaud de Pinchat with his sexy smiles and bulging wallet. He took us to the Casino in San Sebastian, you know, Raven. He's at least forty, the sort of *roué* who knows what it's all about and isn't afraid to prove it to the younger generation. You know what I mean, darlings!'

Janice, over her shoulder commented dryly, 'Your heart-throbs are *always* lived-in, Vida. Especially their jackets. Honestly, soon you'll be falling in love with the rag-and-bone man.'

'Perhaps heart-throb's the new odd-job bod at school, Jan, since he was seen being interviewed by Madame Eugénie in her office,' said Raven, tired of hanging around waiting for Vida to stop behaving like an alley cat. 'By the way, Vida, your lips are crooked.'

Vida turned to Roxana, who carefully wiped the

smudgy edges of Vida's lips with her handkerchief. 'That's better – even if he's not quite top-drawer, Raven, he definitely has *something* about him,' Roxana gushed, always siding with her friend who helped her now to paint her lips with illegal rouge.

Whispering and giggling like a couple of children from kindergarten while Vida hopped around on one foot, she and Roxana only drew attention to themselves from other passers-by, while the man on the bench did not look up once. Vida took her time extracting the make-believe stone from her sock, her silly behaviour only encouraged by Roxana. 'Don't you think, Roxy darling, he has a kind of dormant animal ferocity simmering behind that newspaper?'

'Which belies his poor, tramp-like presence in the park, Vida.'

'Oh definitely! Probably hoping to himself that one day we'll come along without several million head girls following us. The newspaper is only a prop, of course. One can almost *feel* his eyes boring through it, burning two little holes in the page to look at us without appearing to be doing anything other than innocently reading the "lonely hearts" column.' Vida clasped her hands and looked skywards: 'Sir, please forget that newspaper and concentrate upon seducing us. We wish to be set alight by your sexual prowess and masculine regard upon our feminine bosoms throbbing away madly behind our *haute couture* liberty bodices.'

Roxana took up the stage. 'Vida – Roxa – you both tempt me beyond endurance! I would lay down my life for you both: never mind the bally "lonely hearts" column. Let we three depart Mon Repos this very minute. Let us go back and bask in the pastoral sunshine of the Byron Fields, where I will tell you the truth of my life. Nay, I am not a humble tramp, odd-job bod, or horse-thief. I am the Grand Duke of the Scrumpitanian Republic!'

'He *can't* be a grand duke of a *republic*, Roxy! Where were you brought up?'

'Ireland.'

'Then that accounts for it, the Irish are as confused as the French.'

'But you're French.'

'I'm not! I'm Parisian.' Vida, on one knee, wrung her hands, 'Come away to my castle on the hill, where I can ravish you to distraction without l'Impératrice's beady eyes upon us, for I do so Miss-a-long'y.'

'Individually or together?' Roxana asked with a giggle.

'Your choice, darling. I'm not a prude about three in a bed – or were you referring to l'Impératrice's eyes?'

'Forgive her, *mes amies*, but she's reading far too much Colette these days.' Roxana gave Raven a quick apologetic smirk. 'Oh Raven, don't look so head girlish!'

'She can't help it. It's the uniform. Raven wears steel breastplates and her knicker-legs are so tightly elasticated it wouldn't matter if she wet herself.' Consumed by her own wit, Vida, hysterical with laughter, collapsed backwards on the trim grass verge bordering the path.

'Vida de Martello, what on earth is the matter with you now? Get up off that damp grass at once!'

'I have a stitch, Mam'zelle l'Impératrice. It hurts.' Vida sat up and clutched her side, her expression rapidly changing to one of agony as Form Mistress stepped smartly across the grass, followed by the four girls who had correctly identified the rare tree as a common horse chestnut.

The others, sighing in disgust, waited for Vida to pull herself together.

'She really has got a stitch, Mam'zelle l'Impératrice. The school doctor thinks it might be a grumbling appendix.'

'Thank you, Roxana, I will be the judge of that. Now then, move aside.' Mademoiselle l'Impératrice knelt down, shook out Vida's shoe and sock, and began very firmly to help Vida on with her sock. 'How old are you?'

'Nearly eighteen, Mam'zelle l'Impératrice.'

'You behave more like a child of five, Vida.'

'Yes, I know. My third mother took me to see a very expensive psychoanalyst not long ago, Professor Carl Jung, do you know him? Well, he and that other man, Mr Sigmund Freud, know all about dreams and things. Professor Jung told stepmother the third that my *irregular* behaviour is all to do with being institutionalized from a very young age, and not knowing who my real parents are, which in turn has suppressed my natural *libido*. That was the actual word he used, *libido*, and also because we have to wear socks and gymslips. Did you know libido is a psychic drive of sexual instinct and energy, Mam'zelle l'Impératrice?'

'Is that so, Vida, how interesting!'

'Were you breast-fed, mam'zelle? Professor Jung is so astute! He said that those people in adult life who like to wear uniforms were usually not breast-fed. It's all to do with this emotional security business. Why are prefects allowed to wear decent skirts and blouses while we have to suffer these beastly, baggy, pleated gymslips? It's not fair. After all, we're nearly all the same age in Mat Group.'

'Because Vida, senior prefects have earned that privilege. You might have qualified for a navy-blue skirt and grey blouse too, had you behaved more responsibly and with more maturity. Privileges have to be earned, my dear, and have nothing to do with breast-feeding. Now, are you ready?'

'Oh, Mam'zelle l'Impératrice, do look at that poor tramp – haven't you noticed him sitting on that park bench every afternoon this week?'

'I cannot say that I have, Vida, simply because I'm not rude enough to want to stare at the poor man.'

'He's always there on that bench, waiting for us to walk past him. But, most of all, mam'zelle, he watches Raven Quennell. Look, there he is now, staring at her again – oh, you missed the sexy look he gave her. He's gone back to reading his paper so you can't see his face. I think he realizes you've noticed what he's up to. But honestly, mam'zelle, he can't seem to take his eyes off Raven. Do you think he's some sort of pervert who only desires to ravish girls in school uniform because he wasn't breast-fed by his mother?'

Vida, nostrils dilating, quickly brought out from the storage place of her school knickers, her handkerchief. She stuffed it against her face, trying to stifle her fit of the giggles. L'Impératrice glanced over her shoulder at the harmless gentleman enjoying the warmth and sunshine of this late spring afternoon, and, because she was so dreadfully short-sighted, did not recognize him as Madame Roget's nephew.

'I swear I'll kill her,' said Raven under her breath to Janice.

'I'll help you. Leave her to us, Mademoiselle l'Impératrice.'

Both of them bent over Vida, one on either side, hands under her elbows, 'One, two, three, *up!*' said Raven as she and Janice hauled Vida de Martello to her feet. Roxana retrieved Vida's satchel and Kodak. Raven hissed in Vida's ear, 'Don't show us all up by your silly childish behaviour.'

'Let's give her five hundred lines of *Julius Caesar* by this evening, Raven. I'll tell Madame Roget to expect them.'

'Typical Britishers, so superior!' the French girl snorted. 'Janice Fairchild, you will be one person in the world I shall *not* invite to my coming-of-age party aboard Papa's yacht!'

'I shall be far too old for it, anyway, Vida.'

Raven admired Jan Fairchild's sang-froid. Jan could always be relied on to back her up to the hilt.

After supper Madame Eugénie Roget gave out the final notices of the day. Her dignified, calm, and unflurried manner was always reassuring to parents, staff, and pupils alike. Tonight, the girls noticed Madame Roget had a slight flush on her cheeks, her eyes were bright, and she seemed as chirpy as a robin finding it hard to keep a juicy worm to itself.

As the head of a very well-respected establishment, Eugénie was proud of her own achievement and desired only to maintain her good reputation. For most of her young life, Eugénie had cared for her ageing Deauvier grandparents. After they died, she married Othmar Roget, a staunch Calvinist himself. He had died of tuberculosis at the young age of thirty-four, leaving Eugénie with a crippled daughter, Lamone. Eugénie soon realized she would have to start thinking about earning her own living, for what little money her husband had been able to leave her, would not last for ever. Othmar had been in a perpetual state of ill health during their short married life, and most of the money had been spent on medical care and nursing fees. She had, however, managed to give individual lessons in her own home, teaching music, drawing, and languages to a few private pupils. After Othmar's death, Eugénie had decided to set up her own girls' school.

Maison Roget had been in her husband's family for many generations, a vast, rambling mansion on five floors. Down the years it had been allowed to fall into a very dilapidated state, Eugénie, Othmar, and Lamone having occupied but a few rooms during this period. Eugénie undertook to renovate and refurbish the house herself, a room at a time, so that she could start a small but very select school for the daughters of respected and financially-sound families. As Eugénie's school became more solvent, so Maison Roget received a new roof, new windows, and an outside coat of paint in Trianon grey, the house colour beloved of the good, solid Genevese-French living in the Rue de Lausanne. As far as the capacity for hard work went, and making money work for her, Eugénie had inherited that same Swiss-Pennsylvanian trait of character evident in her sister Michelle.

Lamone helped out in the school sewing-room, in the kitchens, or wherever she was required. While Lamone could only manage to hobble around awkwardly and painfully on her twisted hips and stunted legs from inherited tuberculosis of the bone, she was able to sit for endless hours mending, ironing, rolling pastry, or peeling huge mounds of vegetables. Any task, no matter how boring, menial, or tedious, Lamone undertook. She never complained about her deformities, she was always happy, always sharing a joke, always laughing. Roget pupils from the youngest to the oldest, whilst adoring unpretentious little Lamone, also shamelessly manipulated her, for she would do anything for anyone, including mounting guard at the downstairs bathroom window to let senior girls in via the back of the building when late Saturday passes ran out: Vida de Martello, and Roxana Quennell being the two worst culprits. Madame Eugénie Roget was well aware of all the little tricks the girls got up to, her own daughter included. But girls will be girls, and so she turned a blind eye (but only on Saturdays) and accepted the fact that Lamone would always be with her, an unmarried, helpless, graceless woman.

But there were compensations: twenty-two years later she was able to look around the dining-hall, and see how fruitful she was in other respects, how her little establishment had multiplied and grown, and how infinitely successful was l'École Internationale that turned out some of the loveliest, wealthiest, and above all, accomplished young women, who could hold their own anywhere in the world.

Madame Roget, standing on the dais at the far end of the dining-hall, waited for absolute silence as she fingered the last gift her husband had given her before his death, a single strand of pearls. Senior girls were at the back of the hall, middle school came next, and juniors sat in the front where Lamone also sat, while Roget's teaching staff were partaking of their own evening meal in the staff common-room.

'Girls, I have a very special announcement to make this evening,' Eugénie Roget began, and thus ensured a modicum of hush in the dining-hall. 'Some of you seniors will remember Madame Michelle Devlin, my sister, who was School Secretary here for a few months when Mademoiselle Opi, the then School Secretary, decided to move on elsewhere. My poor sister was commandeered by me to help us out before she had time to set foot properly in Geneva. When I eventually found my present right-hand person, indispensable and very dear Madame Legant, Michelle left to pursue her own specialized career as a medical secretary-stenographer. The International Committee of the Red Cross snapped her up. She could have stayed here with us, but my sister believed that two women, especially sisters, in the same kitchen, was not a wise decision. I am inclined to agree. We are neighbours without wishing to live in each other's pocket. We have also remained the closest of sisters and the best of friends since her return from America, six years ago. Michelle, I am delighted to announce, is getting married again. Isn't that wonderful news, girls?'

'Oh yes, Madame Roget!' Enthusiastic handclaps resounded from the front to the back of the dining-hall.

'Lucky for some, and there's hope for all of us, even

those with grey hair and wrinkles!' Vida hissed across the senior table. 'What a pity Monseigneur Paulus is not the marrying kind. I'd have bought him off as well as run off with him by now.'

'We thought your *objet d'art* was the man in the park?' a senior girl whispered.

'Shhh!' Raven frowned at them.

'The marriage ceremony will take place at l'Église St Raphael as both the bride and groom are Catholics. The wedding-reception will be held in the dining-hall. You will all be kept very busy with decorating the school and transforming the place as befitting the occasion, a wonderfully exciting way to end this summer term. Michelle will be married on the twenty-third of June, *after* senior students' matriculation!'

A universal groan went up from the senior table.

'Who is Madame Michelle marrying, Madame Roget?' asked someone from middle school.

'A man of course, you silly little zit,' Roxana muttered under her breath. 'Doesn't Klara Blumhardt know the facts of life as yet?'

'She might be marrying a monkey for all we know, Roxy. Retarded Klara's brother, no doubt,' Vida said from behind her hand. Then she and Roxa dived under the table to fidget with their shoe-laces until sober again.

'Roxana Quennell and Vida de Martello will no doubt be confined to sick-bay recovering from asphyxiation unless they both come out from under the tablecloth at once,' Eugénie Roget's unruffled voice continued from the platform. 'Now then, Klara asked me a question. Madame Devlin's fiancé is a Monsieur Albert Contrin, a widower with no children. He is a banker and businessman from Zurich. Michelle's son, Dr Keir Devlin, has come all the way from North America especially to give his mother away …'

'Tramp, tramp,' murmured Vida, muffling her snorts in her table napkin.

'What do you two girls find so funny? Vida de Martello, I am tired of your snorting, sniffling, and coughing when I am trying to make an announcement. Are you suffering from a cold?'

'Yes, Madame Roget. I've had a sore throat for a week now, but Matron refuses to take me into sick-bay.'

'Then I suggest a good dose of castor oil before bed tonight. That should set you right by morning. Head Girl, please let Matron know that Vida requires two tablespoons of it after this assembly. Now, I will continue, if you please Vida, without interruption. My nephew, Dr Keir Devlin, who was here a few afternoons ago to introduce himself to me, will be giving his mother away at her wedding. Michelle has specifically asked for half a dozen girls from the finishing school to be her maids of honour. The names of the girls Michelle has chosen to attend her, will be on the notice board by Saturday.'

Raven remembered Madame Devlin from her early days at the school. She had been the only one patient and long-suffering enough to answer her barrage of infantile questions upon her admission to l'École Internationale; and she had been full of them at the time! Raven, who had liked Madame Devlin very much, still saw her occasionally on her way to or from her place of work at the Villa Moynier. Madame Devlin always stopped for a friendly chat. With a sly smile to herself, Raven thought about the man who had taken tea with Madame Roget a few afternoons ago. So, he was Michelle Devlin's son, well, well! An American doctor, who had been paying his respects to his aunt and crippled little cousin; the man behind his newspaper in the Parc Mon Repos, whose attention Vida had been trying so hard to attract. What would Vida make of him now that his real identity had been revealed? Not a mysterious European prince fallen on hard times, not a Russian grand duke in exile, not a romantic playboy in search of fresh pastures, not a wild gigolo, or sex maniac seeking to ravish school-girls, but a down-to-earth, hard-working doctor, no doubt heading straight back to America as soon as he had given his mother away to her Zurich banker.

In the senior common-room after supper, Raven said to Vida, who had been getting on everyone's nerves when they were all trying so hard to swat up for their final examinations, 'If you're to have castor oil tonight, I'll ask Matron if you can sleep in sick-bay. We don't want to be kept awake all night while you dash to the bathroom every five minutes.'

As Head Girl, she felt quite within her right to lay down the law where Vida and her two tablespoons of castor oil were concerned, and serve her right!

On Saturday morning the list of girls chosen to be Madame Devlin's maids of honour was pinned on the notice board. They were Ravenna Quennell and Janice Fairchild, Arlene Dracourt and Christianne Hohe, Vida de Martello and Anita Marcos. If any of the non-Catholic girls objected to attending a Roman Catholic ceremony, please notify Madame Roget at once, had been the typewritten postcript to the list.

'Very democratic, I must say!' Vida said with a deprecating sniff as she read the names. 'Two Protestants, two Calvinists and two Catholics. It should have been *all* Catholics. I wonder what Monseigneur Paulus will think of the arrangement?'

'Delighted, I should imagine,' replied one of the Calvinists. 'Catholics usually can't wait to claim other religions for the Pope.'

'We know what you *mean*, Prissy-Crissy darling, but you *do* have a funny way of expressing yourself,' Vida sneered.

'Anyway, I really don't know what your Catholic lot are doing here. I thought Catholics all stuck together in their own schools.'

'Vida and her bunch are only lukewarm Catholics, Crissy,' Arlene added.

'Yes, darlings, but even lukewarm Catholics when they're stinking-rich can still inherit the Kingdom of Heaven,' Vida retorted smugly.

Janice refused to have her conscience compromised. She informed Madame Roget that as much as she was flattered to be chosen as one of Madame Devlin's maids of honour, she simply couldn't take part in a Roman Catholic religious ceremony. Eugénie, understanding as always, substituted Roxana, who was delighted to take Jan's place. Roxana told the girls of senior dormitory, 'Makes no difference to me what religion Madame Devlin is. She can be Hindu for all I care, since I don't believe in *any* religion except the Kama Sutra.'

Vida giggled and Roxana went on to add, 'Eugénie has given us permission to discuss the order of the ceremony with Monseigneur Paulus. He'll see us this afternoon, she said.'

'Oh goody,' said Vida. 'I'll wear my new Redfern outfit which is wildly chic and cost a lot of money *oh-oh-oh, mun-ee, mun-nee* ...' She skipped around the room, singing and dancing, teasing the two Calvinists, and generally behaving like an idiot in Janice's opinion: why were the French always so immature, she asked herself in disgust.

Because the girls of the matriculation class were also at the finishing-school level, they were allowed to wear their own clothes at weekends and at private functions. The girls still had to go about town in groups of four or more, unless out with a parent or relative. So, after lunch that day, Madame Devlin's six maids of honour set off together to find out the order of the wedding ceremony from the Roman Catholic priest.

Monseigneur Paulus was forty-six, an Austrian aristocrat whose family had descended from a branch of the Hapsburgs. Any day now he was hoping to be summoned to the Vatican. His term of office in Geneva completed, and with a change of administration at the Vatican, he was looking forward to returning to Rome.

In the sacristy, he outlined the programme of the wedding-service, pointing out to them that Monsieur Contrin and Madame Devlin had both been married before, and even though death had divided them from their previous partners, there were certain alterations in the wording of the service and in the significance of a second marriage ceremony. 'It is a *blessing* of marriage rather than a sacred solemnization for the procreation of children within the marriage,' he explained with a far distant gaze in his lucid blue eyes, to make Raven worship him more than ever from afar: he is so divine, so pure, and so godlike, were her rapturous thoughts as she hung on every word of his.

Vida nudged Roxana in the ribs. 'He means she's not a virgin, so she can't get married in white or have a veil,' she hissed in Roxana's ear, loud enough for Monseigneur Paulus to overhear, and be amused by the remark.

ost of the girls were only half-listening to him, any way, ..d he knew it. Madame Roget's girls had afforded him much entertainment in the confession box, as well as embarrasment, but they were not to know that. 'Any questions?' he finally asked them, hoping there would be none.

There were several questions and he answered them all with that same faraway detachment, that godlike condescension, which set him apart from ordinary mortals. Then, just as they were about to leave the sacristy, he called Raven back, and asked the other girls to wait in the nave. Through the red velvet curtains dividing the sacristy from the main body of the church, Raven could see Vida and Roxana fidgeting and whispering together on the front pew. She wondered what Monseigneur Paulus wanted of her.

'You are not a Catholic, Raven, so why do you come so often to my church? Have you something to confess to me?' His blue eyes twinkled merrily and, beneath his calotte, his fair hair shone like gold and silver threads woven together on an altar cloth.

Monseigneur Paulus, no more cool and detached and godlike, but suddenly displaying a very human side to his nature, Raven was so tongue-tied and shy in the priest's overwhelming presence, she stood like a window-dummy without saying a word.

'My dear child, I'm utterly delighted you do me the honour of coming to St Raphael so often. It means I am not boring you by my lengthy sermons.' The pale pouches of his eyes crinkled good humouredly. 'Neither must you be afraid of me, Raven. I am not a religious zealot out to hound you into the Roman Catholic Church. How is your dear brother Sonny?'

'Extremely well, Father.'

'It's so nice to meet and talk with him, and your grandfather, when they visit the school. Ever since our little chat three years ago, Sonny calls upon me whenever he is in Geneva. A dear, dear boy, a saintly boy. He has the makings of a fine priest, and I'm afraid I told him so.' Monseigneur Paulus smiled like a handsome golden god.

Raven's heart took a flying leap for reasons she was well aware of.

Monseigneur Paulus often had this effect upon her.

Could it be that she had fallen in love with him, and ⬛
respect, she was no different from the other girls in ⬛
Catholic entourage? Raven hoped not; it would be lo⬛
energy wasted, like Vida's libido. Was it love on ⬛
rebound after José's behaviour in the Caverna Rosa tw⬛
summers ago? Was she still suffering from shock, even
after all this time? Was she desiring the purity of love
rather than the profane, hence her desire to fill the space
left by José with this pious priest? Why did Monseigneur
Paulus always make her feel so wretchedly gauche? It *must*
be love, a new kind of love she was just beginning to be
aware of, and one quite different from José's fumbling,
bumbling sexual misleadings that had sent her scuttling
back to a bathtub of cold water.

Miserably, Raven stood in front of Monseigneur Paulus,
trying in vain to hide her discomposure.

'I pray often that your brother Sonny's crude limbs will
afford him less pain and more peace of mind. He told me
how your old nurse Cassy would often take you and him to
your local Catholic church in Dublin when you were both
little children.'

'Yes, that's true, Father.'

'Yet you are a devout Protestant, eh, my child?'
Monseigneur Paulus stooped towards her. But because she
was almost as tall as he, and he found himself peering into
a pair of grey eyes that were so startlingly clear and direct,
he suddenly drew away, disconcerted by the level look she
gave him. She was a pretty girl, a very pretty girl, indeed,
he could not help reflecting in that moment. What a pity
she was not a Catholic girl, a virgin of the Church of
Rome, a handmaiden of Christ called by God himself.

'I am not a devout anything, Father. I have no confessed
religion. Sometimes I don't even believe in God.'

He did not appear to be unduly shocked by such a
confession. 'Then that is sad, my child.'

'Why, Father?'

'Because your religious education has been sorely
neglected. There is no hope for your soul's salvation
unless you are guided by those wiser than you in such
matters.'

'I try to be good. I say my prayers often. My grandfather

oes not have to belong to a specific religion
...ain salvation, for Christ died for everyone,
...nners. God can be found in the temple of our
...ell as in the man-made temples of religion.'
...is true, my child. But we must also subject
...ves to the rules of obedience, submission, and
...pline. Only through membership of God's Holy
...urch are these things possible. For it is written in
Romans, thirteen, that everyone must submit themselves
to a higher power. The authorities that exist have been
established by God himself. Consequently, he, or she, who
rebels against authority, is rebelling against that which
God has established, the Holy Roman Church: "Who-
soever therefore resisteth the power, resisteth the
ordinance of God: and they that resist shall receive to
themselves damnation." You do not wish that upon
yourself, do you, my child?'

'No Father.'

'Then you must not be a slave to yourself and your own
pride, my child, for "rulers are not a terror to good works,
only evil". I perceive that you are a poor, lonely creature
under a great misunderstanding. I want to try and help
you out of your confusion of mind and spirit, for I know,
Raven, that you are searching for a reason and an answer
to that evil bomb which shattered your life, your brother's
life, and the lives of the other members of your family. I
know that your faith in other people, and your ultimate
belief in a caring, humanitarian God has been called into
question on account of what happened in your early life.'

'There is no reason, and certainly no answer, Father, I
have worked that out for myself.'

'But there *is* an answer, my child – forgiveness. As we
ourselves have been forgiven by the highest in authority,
so must we forgive in order to find peace. Peace within
ourselves. Do you not say the Lord's Prayer every day,
"forgive us our trespasses as we forgive those who trespass
against us"?'

'Yes Father. But I say it with a kind of emptiness inside,
not really meaning it, and not really knowing. I say it
because I have been *conditioned* to say it.'

'Everything, Raven, in our universe, is a conditioning

process, which, in turn, forms an orderly pattern. Wit.
an orderly pattern our universe would fall into utter ch?
and confusion and we, ourselves, conditioned in ou.
dependency upon the sun, upon oxygen, water, plant and
animal life to sustain us, would die. The Church of God is
like that, an orderly structure based upon rules for the
perfect pattern to be maintained in order to sustain us and
lead us to everlasting life. You are empty inside for the
simple reason that you belong nowhere.'

'I'm sorry, I can't accept that, Father. God *always*
answers my prayers.'

With a gracious and charming smile, he took both her
hands in his, and turned them palms up. Then he bent his
head over them. Raven, overwhelmed by the intensity of
her feelings for Monseigneur Paùlus, stared down onto
the priest's bowed head. The crown of his embroidered
calotte, patterned with pearl-drops, glistened like real
tears, and the scent of incense around him was like a
heavy, embracing cloak. Reverently, he kissed the palm of
each open hand.

His action was so unexpected, Raven jumped as though
she had received an electric shock. A vibrant current,
exhilarating and strong, surged through her fingertips
and up her arms. It flowed along every fibre, stimulating
her, revitalizing her, touching the core of every nerve-cell
in her body so that another, greater power, a tremendous
lightening and a gladdening of her spirit, awakened a
response in her that was altogether awesome.

Raven felt that that particular kissing of the hands had
been done in the same manner as Jesus washing the feet of
his disciples, to impart to her the significance of those
Pentecostal flames; the flames that touched her now, and,
transmuted, burned her through and through: God's
priest, through his magnetic, hypnotic, powerful touch,
had doused the flame of a pagan love and lit the flame of
holy love by this, his own special benediction! Monseigneur Paulus had not been unaware of her all these years;
she was not the stranger in the church any more, not José's
prisoner any more. She had found something far more
beautiful, far more exciting, far more enduring, than
anything José could have offered her. Yes, she wished to

239

confess everything; she desired only to lay her whole life open like the palms of her hands, to this golden man who had liberated her from all the José de Luchars of the world, and from all the yearnings of the flesh, and from the world itself, and from herself ...

Monseigneur Paulus smiled at her knowingly: '*Creation ex nihilo*, in Latin meaning, something out of nothing. The healing touch brought about by the power of invisible forces, the power of the spirit. I have it, you have it. In this most potent of physical desires given to us by God, the desire of the flesh made holy through the laying on of hands, these God-given tactile impulses of our bodies are telling us to recognize ourselves for what we are. I have already recognized myself as a priest of Rome. You must, through me, Raven, recognize yourself as the handmaiden of those above you, those in authority. Do not waste what is a gift of God, use this, your inner healing-strength to the power of good. You are a wonderful girl, far the nicest in Madame Roget's school. I know, I have seen them come and go from here, but there is always one who will stand out in a crowd. You are that one. You would be a great gift to the Church of Rome. I shall miss you, my child.'

'Why — Father?' Her legs began to give way through an awful, unbearable fear that she would never see him again. In a vague, unrelated way, she had even toyed with the idea of coming back to l'École Internationale as a pupil teacher after matriculation, so that she could see Monseigneur Paulus at least once a week from where she sat at the back of his church.

'Because, my dear child, I shall soon be leaving Geneva to take up an appointment in Rome.' He released her hands and hooked his finger under the gold cross visible in the open V of her blouse-collar. 'If you are not a religious person, why do you wear this symbol of the Christian religion?'

Raven had difficulty speaking; everything that had transpired during these few brief minutes alone with him, had been totally unexpected and somewhat alarming. He had held her in his hands and, in so doing, had illuminated her soul. She wanted simply to stay as an integral part of Monseigneur's life. 'I am — still a Christian. The cross — it used to belong to my old nurse.'

'Cassy?'

'Yes. It was found in the rubble after the bombing. That's how they were able to identify her body. There was not much of her left, you see, Father.'

'Yes, I see, my child. What a terrible tragedy for you to have to live with for the rest of your life. Let us hope that you, too, will receive the Grace of our Lord Jesus Christ, as Cassy did.'

'Grace was Cassy's mother's name, Father.'

'Before I return to Rome, I want to leave you a present, Raven. It is a little book of questions and answers concerning Roman Catholic theology for children to memorize and recite. Of course, you are not a child, but such a catechism might be useful in helping to sort out some of your confusion concerning God and the place he has in our lives.'

'I have no confusion about God, Father, only people.'

Once again he subjected her to his slow, lazy smile, which she found most disconcerting. 'Then what the catechism does not answer, I will endeavour to answer for you.'

'In Rome?'

'I am not going anywhere until after the little wedding I have been asked to preside over. But, when I do go away, I promise to write to you. We will communicate with each other via the courtesy of the postal services, as your brother Sonny and I do. I received a charming letter from him last week giving me all the news from Spain. The situation there is not reassuring since the King's abdication. To be a priest in Spain, at this present time, takes a very special courage. But the fight must go on, good against evil and against those two anti-Christs, Communism and Fascism, which have come to threaten the existence of the Christian world. Now, my dear child, you must leave me, for I think the other girls are getting impatient. But remember, Raven, I am always available if you need me, Geneva or Rome. I promise not to think of you as a Protestant, but as a pure and sweet girl of a Catholic God – Catholic in this instance meaning belonging to the whole body of Christians.' He patted her shoulder comfortingly.

Loathe to leave his shining presence, she smiled tremulously. 'Thank you, Father.' He led her to the others.

Outside the church, Vida hissed angrily, '*Mon Dieu*, it's about time! What were you two doing for so long? We saw you two, holding hands, and Monseigneur Paulus kissing you ...'

'Fair's, fair, Vida, only her hands in a priestly blessing,' Anita Marcos chipped in.

'Perhaps he's trying to entice Raven into becoming a Catholic, just like I said,' Arlene added.

'Just like a couple of conspirators, or lovers!' Vida continued peevishly. 'Wait till I tell l'Impératrice! She'll tell Madame Eugénie, and then you won't be anyone's maid of honour, but a madam of dishonour!'

Raven's exhilaration was unbounded. The fresh air on her burning face, hands, and throat made her aware, more than ever, of Monseigneur Paulus's radiance. Like the Holy Spirit touching her, the power and the purity of his presence enfolded and enriched her; it was as though he still held her in the palms of his hands, captivating and trapping her by his lucid eyes and magnetic gaze into revealing her innermost soul; it was as if he still breathed into her the breath of life, his lips scorching a pathway through her very soul; it was as though his fingers still brushed the flesh of her throat, touching Cassy's cross, and her heart. It was as if a miracle had happened, and she had been healed of all her infirmities.

Raven took a deep breath and said mildly, 'Maybe you should become a Protestant, Vida. Then Monseigneur Paulus will be able to lay his priestly hands around *your* neck.'

Dear Sonny, Raven wrote for the third time. A week had passed since she and Monseigneur Paulus had had that strange talk in the sacristy, with the charade of the laying-on of hands, and she was trying to tell Sonny not to get carried away by the golden priest, who was only seeking to gain more converts for the Roman Catholic religion. She had allowed herself to become momentarily blinded by Monseigneur Paulus's dazzling beauty, not his intent, but once she realized what he had really wanted from her, she had been wary.

Monseigneur Paulus told me that you and he have been writing to each other. Is he trying to entice you into the Roman Catholic Church? He tried it with me last Saturday afternoon ... No that wouldn't do at all, the statement was rather ambiguous. Indoctrinate was the word she had been seeking.

Raven crumpled the letter into a tight ball and tossed her third effort towards the wastepaper basket. Roxana and Vida de Martello were making so much noise in the adjoining bathroom, she wondered if they had been at Vida's secret supply of vodka. Raven got off the bed to investigate.

Roxana, her arms folded along the top of the bath, knelt on the linoleum floor. Head bent, her luxurious red hair tumbled in waves and ringlets into the tub where Vida sat without any water. Fully dressed, but without shoes, Vida pumped together something in her hand that looked like two wet lips: *'Bonjour, mam'zelle*, can I 'elp you?' She worked the rubber lips like a ventriloquist's dummy.

Roxana was having difficulty in not choking to death, while Vida looked up innocently at Raven and added, 'Do you know what this is, Raven?'

'I've no idea, Vida, but can you two kindly tone down the noise. You're making such a hullabaloo, I can't hear myself think.'

Vida squeezed the rubber lips together, let go, and the slippery object sprang open and jumped out of her hand into the washbasin. This set them both off again, howling with laughter, tears streaming down their cheeks.

'Oh Mother!' Roxana collapsed over the side of the bath, 'Oh Jumping Jehoshaphat!'

Janice Fairchild came into the dormitory and joined Raven in the bathroom doorway. 'What on earth is the matter with those two?'

'What is ever the matter with them. They require deeming.'

Vida got her breath back and squealed, 'Oh Jan, darling, retrieve my rubber froggy, will you? He's sitting on a lilypad in the washbasin pond.'

'What is it?' Janice looked without touching.

'I knew they wouldn't know, Roxy! It's a *diaphragm*, Jan darling. Non-clinical name, Dutch Cap, according to the

243

old bat who demonstrated it to me a couple of hours ago. However, you do *not* wear it on your head, but up your vagina, although the old bat put it more delicately and called it your front passage! What a hoot. Sounds like somewhere you keep your Wellies and barometer. Seriously though, this new device is supposed to be the female equivalent of the French letter. In other words, you puritan ignoramuses, a contraceptive thingy for we poor, hard-done-by females. Now we women can be in control of our own baby-free future. Roxy and I are just putting in some practice, sex without stress, although I can't see how. The reason I'm in this inelegant position in the bath, *sans* camiknickers, is because this is the only place my diaphragm won't go shooting off into outer space.'

'It appears that by the time you get *it* up inside, loverboy will be on the *other* side pushing up daisies. Meanwhile, I've come to tell you two that Dormitory Mistress says NO!'

Roxana and Vida stared at Janice in dismay. Vida struggled out of the bath with her lubricated, pink, monogrammed contraceptive device clutched in her hand. 'The old bat! That's three Saturdays in succession she's refused us Saturday passes to go shopping and visit the theatre. Mam'zelle Annette Anis, up your – protractor! Roxy and I hate you!'

Mademoiselle Anis, Maths Mistress as well as Dormitory Mistress, had had enough of Roxana and Vida's surreptitious jaunts through the downstairs bathroom window, disturbing the other girls and constantly outstaying their late passes, and so she had decided to put a stop to them.

'But!' said Janice raising a sage-like finger in the air, 'I persuaded her to think again. Till eleven o'clock!'

'You what?' Roxana said in a manner that would have horrified Peedee when counting the cost of her lady's Swiss education.

'We all know we cannot go into town unless we go as a foursome. Raven and I want to do some shopping this afternoon. We also want to go to the Rachmaninov concert at the Conservatoire this evening, and it doesn't finish until ten-thirty. Nobody else is willing to make up a foursome for the Conservatoire, so we'll go shopping with you, and anywhere else you like, *if* you will come to the concert with us. Late passes until eleven o'clock, *mes amies,*' Janice continued offering the carrot to the two donkeys.

Vida groaned. 'All right. We agree.' She confided to Roxana later, 'Don't worry. After Bon Marché and *les plus grands menus gastronomiques*, we'll give them the slip. I have no intention of sitting through some fiendishly boring concert at the Conservatoire.'

'Rather!' said Roxa wholeheartedly. 'And with the very best that the menu has to offer, I shall have the very best Perlan.'

'Gamay is better for your gastric juices. I myself will order champagne.'

'Then I'll join you!'

'At last, Roxy darling, you are learning to be a Frenchwoman!'

'How do I look, Jan?' Raven asked, bobbing her head from side to side in the milliner's mirror.

'Wonderful. No truly! That hat really suits you.'

'Roxa?'

'Um – I don't know, darling. You remind me a bit of Mama and her famous cloche hats.'

'You mean old-fashioned?'

'*Oh, mais non!*' the milliner hastened to reassure Raven in a typical throaty Parisian voice redolent of the best in the *haute couture* business. 'Eet is never old-fashioned, mam'zelle! Eet is *très joli.* Zis is not ze cloche 'at, eet is called ze 'ead 'ugger. Ze 'ead 'ugger should always be worn with an 'igh collar, which must come as 'igh as your ears – like zis, mam'zelle.' She wrenched down the head hugger over Raven's ears, and pushed up her hair so that none was visible, for the head hugger had been designed to show off a woman's face and nothing more: and the smaller the ears, the better!

Then the milliner tut-tutted in dismay over the flat, uninteresting neckline of Raven's white silk blouse, and the plain gold chain dangling a religious cross. 'You 'ave such a nice chin, mam'zelle and a 'igh white neck which is so smooth and fashionable! You should use your neck for your advantage! A real pearl necklace, no less, and ze monkey fur collar would make for ze much more fashionable look, mam'zelle. I 'ave 'ere, just ze most sup-*erb* monkey fur collar!' With a conjurer's flourish, the milliner produced the monkey fur collar off a hat-stand.

'Oh no! I don't think so,' said Raven quickly. 'I'm allergic to monkey fur.'

'Will it be cash or will I charge eet to your account, mam'zelle?'

'I think I ought to pay cash. Then I don't have to worry about settling accounts at the end of term.'

The milliner's face dropped a mile. 'Very well,' she sniffed. 'As you wish.'

'Oh, just a minute!' Raven searched in her purse and discovered she hadn't enough Swiss francs, only Spanish pesetas, to pay for the outrageously expensive spring-green head hugger she had so admired in the shop window. 'Perhaps you'd better charge it to my account, after all. The name is, Ravenna Quennell, care of l'École Internationale, Rue de ...'

'Do not worry, mam'zelle,' the milliner beamed in delight. 'I know eet very well. Some of my best customers and their mothers come from Madame Eugénie's leetle international school at Maison Roget. I 'ave, through 'er, many famous peoples from all over ze world. Madame Eugénie, she recommends my 'umble 'at shop to everyone. Zeese famous peoples, zey are good for ze 'at business and for ze skiing business, which comes so much into vogue, just like ze 'ead 'ugger.' The milliner fussed around Raven and her new hat. 'Ze 'ead 'ugger, eet looks very well on you, mam'zelle Quennell. *Très charmant!*'

'Thank you.'

'Will you be wearing my leetle 'at, or will you be wanting eet in an 'at box, mam'zelle?'

'I think I'd like to wear it.'

'*Enchantée, mam'zelle.* You are a good advertisement for me. You 'ave such an – 'ow you say, express-eeve face and good neck: *le cou*, as we say in French. Madame Eugénie's sister, she was 'ere only last week with 'er 'andsome son 'oo is a doctor from America. Madame Deauvier-Devlin, 'oo is soon to become Madame Contrin, she buys one of my

246

leetle 'ats for her marriage, and anozzer one for 'er 'oneymoon. And now, 'ere is my leetle card. I 'ope you and your friends will come again – ooops! We 'ave 'ere one already!'

Vida de Martello came bursting into the shop and set the hat-stands wobbling. 'Hurry, darlings, I have a taxi waiting. I've just bought *the* most ravishing beach costume by Schiaparelli. Just you wait and see my skimpy beach suit, Roxy. I'll be the envy of Antibes this summer, *oh-la-la*!'

'I thought you and Roxana were going to Fontaine-bleau,' Raven said, climbing into the taxi with her new spring-green head hugger. A mizzly drizzle had set in, and she was afraid of getting her new hat wet.

'Fontainebleau, Antibes, San Sebastian, it's all the same to my father. One day here, two days there, three days elsewhere, it's no problem. He has many houses all over the world, and his yacht will take us to all of them. Raven, I don't like your hat. If you don't mind my saying so, darling, it looks like a green pea stuck on a fork.'

'Thank you very much, Vida!'

'Oh, take no notice of her Raven,' Janice said, wiping the steamy taxi window with her glove. 'Vida just wishes she had the face to carry it off.'

'I certainly do, darling!'

They all had to laugh at that. Then Vida shrieked at the taxi-driver and gave him the fright of his life, 'Monsieur, *arrêtez*! Stop, stop at once!'

'I thought you wanted to go to the Hotel Carlton, mademoiselle' he grumbled as he slammed on his brakes, and skidded to a sudden stop.

'We've changed our minds, we want to get out here.'

'Why Vida?' Raven asked in bewilderment. 'We've reserved a table for four at the Carlton.'

'I've just seen *him*!' Vida breathlessly thrust some money into the taxi-driver's outstretched hand. 'Monsieur, please take all these parcels to Maison Roget, Rue de Lausanne. Leave them at the school, please.'

'Very well, mademoiselle, but you 'ave not given me enough money to cover the extra fare.'

'Oh, come on, monsieur! It's no distance, *and* it's far

247

quicker to walk than ride in this old rust-bucket. But, if you will be awkward, then put the extra fare on my account at the school, Mademoiselle Vida de Martello ...'

'*Merci beaucoup, Madameoiselle* de Martello, but I prefer cash in advance.'

In the end Janice paid the extra fare. The taxi driver touched his cap, and muttering under his breath drove off with their purchases.

Vida turned round and grabbed Roxana's arm. 'He's wearing a mackintosh – I saw him go into the patisserie.'

'Vida, we're all starving and want a proper meal, not cakes!'

'All right, Jan! You can have your proper meal afterwards. But stop moaning! You sound so beastly middle-class English.'

'Not another word from any of us. Lead the way Vida.' Janice stepped aside for Vida to enter the patisserie. 'I'm just keen to see how you handle the situation once inside this crowded place without a spare table in sight.'

The typical Geneva drizzle had given everyone the same idea, to get indoors quickly. The girls chose and paid for what they wanted from the delicious selection of cakes and pastries, collected their tickets from the counter, ordered coffee, and then looked around for 'Vida's man'.

After a desperate survey of the crowded room, they found him seated at a corner table. The huge plate-glass window on one side of him, his back was to the wall displaying a sunny mural of the city in summer.

Keir wiped the steamy glass with the sleeve of his 'lived-in' tweed jacket, and peered across the Jardin Anglais towards the misty lake and the mountains, barely visible, on the opposite shore. His raincoat was over the back of his chair, a cup of coffee and a journal were by his elbow. He was alone at the table, three empty chairs surrounded him.

'Bad luck, Vida, the three of us bag first places. Now what are you going to do?' Raven said, poised for immediate flight should Vida embarrass them further in such a public place. She only hoped that none of them would be recognized as the Roget schoolgirls in the Parc Mon Repos during several preceding afternoons. Today, however, they wore their own fashionable clothes instead of school uniform, and presented a more sophisticated and, Raven hoped, a more sober aspect. Her new hat, too, helped to bolster her self-confidence. Vida led the way through the deafening hum of sociable afternoon conversation and the mass of hot steamy bodies hugging the crowded tables. Raven, hoping desperately to remain inconspicuous despite Vida's penchant for the limelight, trailed in the rear.

Keir stirred his coffee, his attention returning to the British medical journal, *The Lancet*, whereas a short while ago he had been gazing absently out of the window.

Vida stopped beside him, and with a dazzling smile when he looked up at her enquiringly, indicated the three empty places. 'Excuse me, monsieur, but is it possible we might share your table as the others are all so full?'

'By all means. I'm just leaving anyway.'

Her face dropped, 'But monsieur, you have only just arrived! You must finish your coffee first, so please don't leave on account of us.'

'I'm not leaving on account of anyone, mademoiselle.' He gulped down the rest of his coffee, grabbed up his medical journal, and was about to push back his chair and stand up when Vida sat down beside him, trapping him against the mural and the damp plate-glass. She gasped breathlessly in a throaty and seductive French accent not normally 'pidgin' when speaking English, 'You are Madame Roget's nephew, *n'est-ces pas?* I recognize your face, monsieur le docteur. Please to forgive me for being so bold!'

He looked at her without really seeing her, 'I'm sorry …?'

'An *American* doctor?' Vida's tone was one of hushed reverence.

'Right again,' he flashed her a quick interrogative smile, then recognition dawned. 'Oh sure – now I know who you girls are – you all look so different without your uniforms. Uhmm …' He seemed to have difficulty with what he wanted to say. 'The young ladies from the Parc Mon Repos – I mean, my Aunt Eugénie's school?'

Vida relaxed. So he had noticed them after all! And he

was not half bad when he smiled, and his eyes were the most marvellous blue! She tossed her Eton crop coquettishly, and flashed her dark eyes as only a Parisienne knew how: Janice sighed in anguish while Vida continued to gush, 'We are the matriculation class from l'École Internationale, Dr Devlin.' Vida wanted him to be fully aware that they were also young ladies eager and adult enough to matriculate in other subjects outside the classroom. 'We are soon to be your mother's maids of honour at her wedding.'

He seemed embarrassed, and shifted in his seat, anxious to be off. He looked beyond Janice and Roxana to Raven standing awkwardly behind her sister, and his face changed to the fixed rigidity of a mask. He stared at Raven as though she were a ghost.

Then, gathering himself together, he scraped back his chair, stood up and mumbled, 'Excuse me ladies, I've just remembered an important call I have to make – sorry.' He grabbed up his medical journal, raincoat, and departed.

'Oh my God, Raven, it was the hat!' Vida collapsed into the chair Dr Keir Devlin had just vacated as the others took their seats around the table. 'It must have given him a bilious attack.'

Raven sank down, her elbows on the table, her face in her hands.

Vida said accusingly, 'So, I didn't imagine it! He *did* stare at you in the park when we walked past him. He looked at you then as he did just now, as though you were some sort of zombie from his past catching up with him.'

'Vida, why don't you shut up!' Jan said. 'Can't you see how upset Raven is. You not only embarrassed us, you embarrassed *him*!'

Raven, her hands covering her scarlet face said, 'I could kill you, Vida!'

'Why, what have I done? I didn't know you knew him.'

'I don't!'

'Well the way you two looked at each other just now I thought you'd had a mad, passionate love-affair at some time in your murky pasts and now felt guilty about it.'

'What *rubbish* you do talk, Vida!'

Vida shrugged indifferently. The waitress brought

them their coffee and cakes. Raven pushed her plate away and Vida grabbed the *marrons glacés* Raven had ordered but now rejected.

Roxana said thoughtfully, 'I don't think Vida *is* talking rubbish, Raven. I think Dr Devlin probably *did* think he'd seen you before. I told you in the milliners you looked just like Mama, especially in that hat which covers your hair. You look so much like her. Especially without the hair showing.'

Raven said fiercely, 'You're the one most like her! You and she have the same colouring.'

Vida, wagging her cake fork in the air said, 'Let's not argue about it darlings. The fact remains, Raven was the reason he ran away so fast.'

Roxana agreed, 'I think Vida's right. I think Dr Devlin has mistaken you for someone else – possibly Mama. Maybe he had a love-affair with her in America. You know how often Mama used to skip abroad. America to her was just another love-affair.'

'America, Roxana, is a big country!' Raven said desperately. 'Besides, mother died eight years ago!'

'Well, he's no youngster. He could have been in his twenties when Mama went to New York on that fund-raising lark and met the President of the United States. She could have met Dr Keir Devlin then. You know how Lyra always fancied men a lot younger than herself.'

'Mother was not another Lyra! She loved Father, and I'm sure she was faithful to him even though she might have flirted with men like Amery and William and all the others. But it was just good fun, nothing more.'

'Well, I'm only trying to solve the mystery. Lamone told me he was a bit Irish, too. Perhaps they bumped into one another at an Irish White Cross bazaar in New York.'

'Lamone told you?' Vida stared at Roxana. 'How come?'

'I asked her. I wanted to know all about him. I did it for you, Vida, because I know you have a crush on him. Raven isn't the only one good at people-spotting, you know.'

'Oh Roxy, I do love you sometimes! You're so *sweet*!' Vida grabbed hold of Roxana's head, ignoring the fact that Roxana was still eating as she planted a resounding Gallic kiss on the top of her head. 'Shall we go and see his mama who lives in the Avenue de la Paix? We can always make the excuse we've come to be measured for our maid-of-honour dresses, eh, Roxy?'

'Roxana will do nothing of the sort,' Raven said, as she set down her coffee cup to glare at Vida. 'If you two involve Jan or me in any more of your childish games, or embarrass Dr Devlin again, I'll report you to Madame Roget.'

'Oh, come off it, Raven Quennell! Stop pulling rank. It was your face that gave him the belly ache, not ours. Come on everyone,' Vida thumped her fists on the table angrily, 'it was all just harmless fun. I don't know why you're getting yourselves so worked up over nothing. Anyway, I've gone right off him.'

'Thank goodness,' Janice breathed a hearty sigh of relief. 'Now perhaps we'll all be able to settle down and get some swatting done in peace.'

'You two swat! Roxy and I are off to do some dancing.'

'Aren't you coming with us to the Conservatoire?'

'No, darling Jan,' Vida said sweetly, 'but we'll meet you afterwards at the Place Neuve tramstop, so that we can all go home together like good little crocodiles. By the way Roxy, did you bribe Lamone to keep the ground floor bathroom window open in case we're late?'

'Of course.'

'I knew I could rely on you. I do hope the taxi-driver didn't fancy my Schiaparelli bathing suit and take it home with him.'

They left the patisserie arm in arm. Raven said to Janice, 'Let's hope they get kidnapped and are sold off into the white slave trade.'

'Here, here!' Jan replied heartily.

By the time Raven and Janice began to queue for tickets outside the Conservatory of Music in the Rue Général-Dufour, the niggling drizzle of the afternoon had given way to a steady, light rain.

'I must remember in future that Geneva is very much like England and bring an umbrella with me every time I set off somewhere, even though the sun might be shining at the time,' Janice said, turning her nose up at the weather. She shrank into the broad revers of her maroon and beige Lanvin jacket that matched her flared skirt. She did not wear a hat, and her fair hair, tied back at the neck with a broad black hair ribbon, glistened with a misty film of raindrops.

'Oh, my lovely new hat!' Raven moaned. 'It will start shrinking to my head and then I'll get the mother and father of a migraine!'

She peeled off her head hugger and shook the rain from it, before shaking out her hair. 'Gosh, that feel's better already.' She combed her fingers through her fringe, flattened under her hat. 'I never realized until now how my mother's head must have suffered beneath her fashionable hats. Jan, just look at this queue! Do you think we'll ever get tickets?'

'Well, if we don't, we can always go back and do some revising.'

'Excuse me, ladies – can you use an umbrella?'

They both turned, and Janice said in surprise, 'Dr Devlin! What are you doing here?'

'I fancy the same as you, lining up to hear a Russian native of both Switzerland and America play his piece: Sergey Vasilyevich Rachmaninov is why I'm here, ladies.' He looked over his shoulder and turning back to them, said, 'May I join you? It appears we're at the end of the queue.' He held the umbrella over them. 'Where are the other two?'

'What other two?' Jan asked pretentiously.

'The redhead and the brunette.'

'They don't like highbrow concerts, only jazz.' Janice said.

'I hope I didn't offend …? Oh, darn! I didn't even ask her name.'

'Vida?'

'If it's Vida: I hope I didn't offend her by dashing off so rudely from the patisserie, but I remembered in that instant I had an important call to make on my mother's behalf. I clean forgot about it until I saw your hat …' Apologetically he looked at Raven, and his face fell. 'You're not wearing it! I hope you didn't think I was – oh look, I'm sorry, I don't even know *your* name.'

'Raven Quennell.'

'Raven — that's a bird, isn't it? Have I seen you somewhere before?'

'In the Parc Mon Repos? she said stiffly.

'No — somewhere else besides the park. I'm sure of it. Only I can't think where. Tricks of the memory, a symptom of — well, never mind. I guess I ought to apologize to you too, Raven, for my rude behaviour this afternoon. You see, it was all to do with this cloche hat business. Let me explain. My mother happened to buy one the other day, otherwise I wouldn't have had a clue what a cloche was or anything else. *Cloche* in French meaning a bell, so she tells me, seeing your cloche hat reminded me of a bell, the bells, and telephone bell! Then suddenly I remembered I had an important call to make. An association of ideas, you see, ladies, which made me rush off the way I did.'

Raven, with a little smile, said, 'Dr Devlin, cloche in French also happens to mean dish-cover and blister. I hope I don't remind you of those!' She held up her bedraggled head hugger, and pulled a sorry face, 'My cloche is now the verb, *clocher*, meaning limp!'

He smiled very winsomely, 'You remind me of — did you say your name was Quennell?'

'Yes.'

'I knew I'd seen — no — tell a lie!' He put a hand to his brow and shook his head while he gazed dazedly at her. 'I've seen you before, and I know that name, I'm certain of it. But I'm darned if I can think how or where. It's very annoying.'

'America?'

He quizzed her, 'Have you been to America?'

'No.'

'Try again.'

'Spain?'

'I've never been to Spain.'

'Then, Dr Devlin, I'm afraid I can't help you.'

'Not to worry. I'm sure I'll remember before too long.'

'Probably in the dead of night,' said Janice, and held out her hand to him, 'I'm Janice Fairchild, Dr Devlin, and I'm from London.'

'London, England?'

254

'Where else?'

He shook her hand heartily and raindrops from the huge black umbrella he held over them spattered their shoulders. 'I've never been to England Miss Fairchild ...'

'Janice.'

'Janice, that's a nice name. But I hope to very soon – go to England, I mean.'

'Then you must telephone and let us know when you're coming. We'd be delighted to show you around London.'

'Us? We?'

'Ma, Pa and Charlie, my brother. He races.'

'Horses?'

'Motor cars'

'That's great! A champion?'

'Yes. British Champion three times. Brooklands, Le Mans and Indianapolis.'

'Not the Indy?'

'Yes, last year.'

'Wow! And you, Raven. What about your family?'

'You met my twin sister this afternoon, Dr Devlin. The redhead without a cloche; and no, we're nothing alike. In fact, we don't even resemble sisters, so you needn't feel duty-bound to comment upon the fact. It gets boring after a while. There is also a brother.'

'What does he do?'

'Study. I'm really happy to be your mother's chief maid of honour. I expect she's thrilled to bits you've come all the way from America to see her get married again.'

'I never saw her get married the first time,' his blue eyes twinkled under the sheltering dome of the black umbrella.

Raven, too, smiled. 'No, I don't suppose you did. Was it a long journey from New York?'

'I didn't come from New York, I came from Toronto.'

'I'm sorry. I thought someone said you were a doctor in New York.'

'I was. But then I moved on. I went to Canada. I've been there ever since – ever since!' He sucked in his lower lip, stumbling over the actual time spent in Canada. 'Can't remember how many months,' he concluded awkwardly.

'And will you be going back to Canada when you – when your mother is married?' Janice asked.

'Nope. Coming to Europe for my mother's marriage is a very good excuse for me to stay away from America for a while. The Wall Street Crash which resulted in the recession America's now seeing, is biting hard everywhere. I just wanted to get away from North America. I've got something in the pipeline, and I'm keeping my fingers crossed it comes off.'

Raven said vaguely, 'The rain's easing, and I do believe the queue is shortening.'

'Do you two ladies like music – no, that's a dumb question! Of course you must like music if you queue in the rain for tickets to a Rachmaninov concert. Do either of you play anything, any instrument?'

'Raven plays the piano and violin, oh, and the mandolin and guitar.'

'And you?'

'The church organ on Sundays, Dr Devlin. At home.'

'In London, England?'

'In London, England. Twickenham, actually. And you?'

'Me? I can't sing a note. As tone deaf as a beefsteak.'

Raven and Janice laughed. Raven said, 'An Irishman, tone deaf?'

'Fourth generation, Irish-American, so I suppose the shamrock and the Irish jig don't mean as much to me as they do to you.'

'I've never danced the jig, Dr Devlin,' Raven said. 'And Ireland means nothing more to me.'

'Why do you say that?'

'I live in Spain with my grandfather. Geneva is just my place of education – oh look, we're next for tickets.'

'I'll buy the tickets, so put away your money – no, I insist!'

'But you can't! It isn't right. We hardly know you!' they protested.

'But you do now. I've never known a popular concert line to be so short. That was all the talking we were doing – three tickets, best seats,' he said to the girl behind the glass window of the box-office. Keir smiled reassuringly at Raven and Janice. 'You're doing *me* a favour. I couldn't have wished for better company tonight.'

Halfway through the concert Raven wondered why he

had associated her with Ireland. It couldn't have been her accent, surely? She thought she had lost that, years ago.

The concert ended at ten-thirty. Afterwards he accompanied them to the Place Neuve, only a short walk around the corner, where they were to meet Roxana and Vida. It had stopped raining and the umbrella wasn't required.

'Well, goodnight, ladies.' He shook hands with them. 'Thanks for your company. The pleasure was all mine.' They watched him stride off in the direction of the Rue Treille and Veille-Ville.

'I wonder where he's off to now? The Avenue de la Paix is not that way.'

'Don't be so inquisitive, Jan!' Raven said with a little laugh. 'I expect ten forty-five is a little early for him to go home to mother and so he's off to enjoy the nightlife of the Old City. I wish he wouldn't keep calling us ladies the whole time.'

'What did you expect him to call us, gentlemen?'

'What's wrong with Jan and Raven? Ladies sounds like a public convenience.'

'Americans have their own particular parlance. And he's shy.'

'He's also very vague and absent-minded. Pretending to know the name Quennell, really! He could have played to the gallery a little more plausibly.'

'You mustn't be annoyed with him, he was quite genuine. You made a great impression on him.'

'Me?' Raven looked at Jan in astonishment.

'Yes *you*! He had eyes only for you. All that cloche hat business! Dearest Raven, don't be so naïve! Can't you read a man and his motives, as yet?'

'No, Jan, I can't! Neither have I any desire to. Especially where Dr Devlin's concerned. He's not my type at all.'

By ten-fifty both Raven and Janice realized that Roxana and Vida had had no intention of meeting them in the Place Neuve, and they were, themselves, horribly late in returning to Maison Roget.

In the end they hailed a taxi.

Then they discovered that the ground-floor bathroom window had been locked. 'That's that beastly Vida!' Janice hissed angrily, in the darkness snagging her silk stockings. 'Those two must have got back early, and decided to lock us out in order to get us into Aniseed's bad books. Wait till I get hold of them!'

Old Johann, the school janitor, had retired to bed at eleven o'clock, the time everyone was supposed to be behind lock and key. They had no choice but to ring the front doorbell. Annette Anis, woken from her sleep, appeared with dishevelled hair, bags under her eyes, furiously tying the cord of her dressing-gown. 'You two! The most senior girls in the school, and you are late! You knew you're supposed to keep together, yet Vida and Roxana were back hours ago, saying that you two had gone off on your own. It's *too* bad! What are we to expect from the younger girls when the older ones are not to be trusted? Five hundred lines, each, of *Julius Caesar* by tomorrow evening and two late passes stopped. I thought the concert finished at ten-thirty. Where have you been since?'

'Nowhere. We missed the earlier tram. Ask Dr Devlin.'

'Who?'

'Madame Roget's nephew.'

She sniffed disbelievingly. 'Very well. I can always check up on that tomorrow. You may go to bed now. And quietly please, so that the younger girls do not know of the bad example you are setting.'

Raven and Janice got ready for bed and then Vida sat up, followed by Roxana. 'Five hundred lines of *Julius Caesar* from each of you by teatime tomorrow,' Janice said to them, hoping Aniseed would not check the handwriting too closely, otherwise she and Raven would be in line for losing all their late passes until the end of term. But even that would not be as bad as their reputations being mud with Vida and her unruly crowd.

'Rachmaninov was that awful, huh?' Vida said, smiling like a Cheshire cat.

'For conspiring to make us late. The concert was wonderful.'

'So, tell us, what did you two do with yourselves all evening?' Raven asked them.

'What we didn't do was go to the boring old Exposition

again,' Roxana replied. 'We went to see Dr Devlin in the Avenue de la Paix.'

'Oh really! What did he say?'

'He didn't say anything.'

'*Quelle domage!*' Raven murmured.

'Because he was at the *Conservatoire!*' Roxana, in a red temper, threw her pillow at her sister.

'Go on!' said Raven, catching the pillow, and grinning as broadly as Jan.

'We *hate tisane!* We hate tea, English, Chinese or American! Vida and I spent one and a half hours in his mother's boring company, drinking tea and making small talk, while *he* was somewhere else listening to some beastly, boring man playing the piano!' Roxana threw a tantrum and woke the other four in Mat Group.

'We're trying to get some sleep, you selfish beasts!'

'Oh go to sleep then!' Vida snapped. She turned back to Raven and Janice. 'You might have told us he was going to the concert with you, you sneaky bitches!'

'I thought you said you'd gone off him, Vida,' Raven reminded her.

'That was six hours ago.'

'Of course it was! Anyway, we didn't know he was going to the concert until we ourselves began queueing for tickets.'

'What did he say? Did he ask where we were?' Roxana asked eagerly.

Jan answered, 'He said, I bet Vida de Martello and Roxana Quennell are taking tisane with my mama right now, and eating their hearts out because they're not here with the Grand Duke of Scrumpitania at the Rachmaninov concert.'

'Don't be so childish, Janice Fairchild!' Roxana snapped.

'Oh, Roxy, I'm sorry. Did mama's tisane upset your tummy-wummy, then?'

Vida took Roxana's side. 'I think you're a sneaky bitch, Janice Fairchild. You fancy him too, don't you? Yet try to make out you don't, you goody-goody!'

'I'm *wild* about him after tonight, Vida.'

Vida, sitting up in bed with her arms folded, put on her satisfied smirk. 'I bet he didn't tell you two puritan ignoramuses he's married. Mama told us a lot about her darling boy.'

'Is that so?' Janice said lightly.

'He's also a Roman Catholic.'

'So?'

'Roman Catholics can't get divorced.'

'What's that got to do with me? I'm Church of England,' Jan said airily.

'Just putting you in the picture, perfect perfect, in case you get any ideas about him.' Vida slid down the bed and pulled the covers over her head. 'I'm going to sleep – who wants a culture vulture like him, anyway! Besides, there are plenty more better looking fish in the sea, uh Roxy?'

Keir Devlin almost forgot that he was supposed to give his mother away. He stood staring at the stained-glass window of St Raphael, who just so happened to be the patron saint of physicians, when Keir felt a sharp nudge in his left side. He looked down to encounter the exquisite profile of the girl who was his mother's chief maid of honour. But she stared straight ahead, presumably reflecting upon St Raphael too, and for a moment Keir wondered if he really *had* felt Raven Quennell's elbow in his side.

'Who giveth this woman to this man?' Monseigneur Paulus repeated more loudly.

Raven blinked rapidly and nudged him a second time.

'Oh – I guess I do ...' Keir responded rather too hastily as he stepped forward, grabbed his mother's hand and thrust it into that of Monsieur Contrin. Vida giggled into her bouquet of flowers.

Afterwards, at the reception held in the school hall, noticing that the chief maid of honour's glass was empty, Keir armed himself with a full bottle of champagne to give him courage. Then he approached Raven, fussing around the wedding-cake made by the school chef. She was waiting for the bride and groom to cut the cake, when Keir tapped her on the shoulder. 'Hi.'

'Hello.'

'Can you use any more of this?'

She held her champagne glass out to him, and after

refilling both their glasses, he set the bottle down beside the cake. 'Thanks for bringing me in on cue.'

Raven smiled above the rim of the glass, the bubbles teasing her nose. 'Your mother nearly didn't get married at all! What were you dreaming of?'

'Oh, a very pretty maid of honour in a pink dress, I guess.' His gaze was directed straight at her so that she would be under no misconception as to which maid of honour he was referring to.

'Peach, actually.' To hide her confusion Raven turned aside to fiddle again with the ribbons and silver horseshoes on the cake.

Keir had not intended to embarrass or offend Raven Quennell, and because it had been the champagne talking, he covered his mistake by saying, 'Weddings are pretty things if you yourself are not involved.'

She turned back to look at him then, not quite sure of what he had meant. 'Are *you* married?'

'Yes. I'm still married – after a fashion. I'm still waiting for my *Decree Absolute*. I'm not a practising Catholic, you see, nor was my wife.'

Raven sensed he had no wish to talk about that side of his life, and searched her mind desperately for something else to say. 'Janice tells me you're shortly to visit England.'

'Yup.'

'I hope you enjoy your visit to Twickenham. Her people are awfully nice – oh, goodness, just listen to the orchestra warming up!'

He suddenly smiled, and his whole aspect changed wonderfully. He agreed with her about the sounds emanating from the school's musicians, who were to provide the entertainment for the evening. 'Not quite Rachmaninov,' Keir said, 'but commendable enough. If you're the talented musician Jan tells me you are, then why aren't you in the school orchestra?'

'I am, normally: but I can't be in two places at once,' she teased him.

'No, I guess not.'

'And I'm not really talented. Sonny, my brother, is the one with the real musical talent. I just *like* music, that's all. Except jazz, though. Jazz always sounds to me like José's motor bike on a rough road.' Raven could feel the champagne getting up into her head, she was becoming garrulous.

After a rendering of 'Parma Violets' and 'Oh, For the Wings of a Dove', Maison Roget interpretation with Annette Anis conducting, it was time to cut the cake. While everyone was delving into wedding-cake Keir turned to Raven and took her off guard, 'Tell me about José.'

'José?'

'Your young man. He has a motor bike, I believe.'

Her face cleared and she gave a little laugh. 'Oh, no, no, no! You've got it all wrong, Dr Devlin. José isn't my *young man* in that sense! He's the young man I was brought up with – like a brother, in fact. Oh look, let me explain. Roxa, Sonny, and I live in Spain with my grandfather. José de Luchar's father, Don Ruiz, owns the estate, Vinarosa, where we grew up. My grandfather rents a *casa* on Don Ruiz's land, and is Tutor to Don Ruiz's sons: although José has long since left the schoolroom.'

'So now he's got himself a motor bike. I see. What does he do with it, race it like Jan's brother races motor cars?'

'Oh no. José's a soldier. A legionnaire with the Army of Africa. He ran away on his motor bike – scooted off, to be more precise – to Toledo, where he joined up as a legionnaire, leaving his family wondering where he'd got to. At the time of José's sudden disappearance, nearly two years ago now, everyone thought Spanish Anarchists or Communists had kidnapped him, as he's the heir to Vinarosa, for ransom money to further one of their anti-government causes. In the end it turned out that José had vamoosed of his own accord, because he didn't want to study Oenology any more.'

'What's Oenology, for heaven's sake?'

'The study of wine.'

'So José skedaddled off to become a soldier rather than a potential alcoholic.' Dr Devlin's expression, Raven couldn't help noticing in that moment, was rueful as he stared into his glass of champagne. 'Can't say I blame him,' he added, glancing up at her with a strange, faraway expression in his deep blue eyes. 'Can't say I know much about Spain, either.'

The orchestra suddenly launched into a boisterous rendering of 'The Blue Danube' and again Raven and Keir exchanged mutually resigned glances as well as laughs.

'Oh, *Mon Dieu*, eet is terreeble, *mais non?*' Vida clutching her head, exaggerated the orchestra's awfulness by staggering towards Keir and Raven, still engaged in a desultory conversation beside the wedding-cake, neither of them able to get to the core of the other. Roxana, as usual, was Vida's lady in waiting, trailing in the rear, somewhat glassy-eyed with too much champagne behind Form Mistress's back.

'Dr Keir, if you can recognize the music, will you please dance this waltz with me?' Vida hiccoughed.

'A waltz is about all I can manage,' he confessed, 'but I've already promised this one to Chief Bridesmaid.' Keir took Raven's glass out of her hand, put it down on a table, and twirled her onto the dining-room floor, far away from Vida de Martello.

'Goodness,' said Raven, still catching her breath. 'This *is* sudden! Don't you like Vida, Dr Devlin?'

'Ladies like Miss Martello scare the daylights out of me – sorry, I'm not a very good dancer.'

'You seem all right to me.'

He looked down into her upturned face searchingly. Raven thought he was about to say something else, but he appeared to change his mind and remained silent. They finished the dance. She was sorry it was over. She had enjoyed dancing with Dr Devlin, even though he appeared to be in some other hemisphere. 'Thank you,' she said when he led her off the floor. 'And now here comes Vida, again. This time you really cannot refuse her if you're a gentleman!'

After Albert and Michelle Contrin had set off upon their honeymoon in Lugano (Keir had whispered the secret location in her ear whilst they stood beside the cake), Raven pleaded a headache and retired to the senior dormitory.

None of the others had come up to bed as yet she was glad to see. She wanted to be alone with her thoughts, just this once.

Raven lay on her back in the darkness, staring up at the high ceiling, hands tightly clasping to her breast the little book of rules Monseigneur Paulus had given her. A great sigh of contentment escaped her lips: she was so in love with him, she wanted to go to sleep straightaway so that she could dream and dream about her handsome golden priest, who had signaled her out to be his special handmaiden.

Instead, she dreamt about a tall, dark, mature man in need of a haircut, with a winsome smile, cornflower-blue eyes like his mother's, red socks, and brown brogues, treading on her toes.

CHAPTER SEVEN

Catalonia:
December 1932 – October 1933

It had been an altogether harrowing day! Early that morning Don Ruiz de Luchar had found himself in heated discussion with the Republican Minister of Agriculture about the new Agrarian Reform Law and the expropriation of some of his land at Vinarosa: 'But I play fair with those who rent my land,' Don Ruiz had insisted. 'Even my hired hands are treated well. Through my agent they are paid three-seventy pesetas a day, and at harvest, four-fifty! More than anyone else around here!'

Nevertheless, his 'grandee ownership' was far above the new limits set for the fair distribution of land, that of two hundred and fifty acres.

Don Ruiz tried to win himself more time: certainly until the municipal elections in the New Year. In the free elections of last summer, Catalonia had declared for Home Rule, and an overwhelming plebiscite had resulted in an autonomous government for Catalonia, the Generalidad. The Catalan language would be revived and would be taught in all schools along with Spanish; the culture of the region would be restored after years of suppression; the Catalan people would regain their identity in a Utopia that had been promised by the new Government. So far it had not materialized, for laws and governments were apt to be toppled overnight, as Traditionalists, Radicals, Socialists and Anarchists all set out to prove that might was right: Catalonia had become another Ulster.

Then, at his textile factory on the outskirts of the city at Llobregat, Don Ruiz had had another bitter row with Ramiro over factory management and the unpractical trade union demand for sickness benefit. Ramiro had argued, that in view of no government unemployment benefit, de Luchar textile workers deserved some sort of security when long illness or injury prevented them from working. Don Ruiz had tried to impress upon his son (who seemed to have taken upon himself the role of saviour of abused factory employees) that the production of cloth was not a heavy industry and, therefore, textile workers did not merit the same considerations as those employed in the iron and steel industries.

Thereafter, to calm his agitated spirits, Don Ruiz had returned to the Castillo de Luchar at Montjuic, for he preferred to lunch at home quietly with his beautiful and understanding wife, rather than with anyone else: And after his lunch he usually had a quiet siesta to refresh himself for the second half of his busy day, only today it had not been so. Halfway through his lunch, he had received an urgent summons to the telephone. He had taken the call in his study, just two words from an unknown person: *Remember Sanjurjo?* Don Ruiz stared at the receiver before the click at the other end brought him to his senses.

'*Qué pasa?*' Doña Jacqueline had asked anxiously when he returned to the dining-room.

Pale and shaken, Don Ruiz had pushed away his plate of half-eaten monkfish with almonds. 'Nothing is the matter,' Don Ruiz had reassured her, gathering himself together and giving Doña Jacqueline a weak smile. 'I'm just a little tired, *querida*, that's all.'

Doña Jacqueline poured her husband a tot of brandy to calm his agitation, and while he drank it, she tenderly smoothed his dark curly hair and troubled forehead.

Don Ruiz mentally revived the conversation he had had last summer with an old friend and *caballero* like himself, a turbid conversation that had put him right on the spot. 'I have taken an oath to serve the new régime – yes, I know it is in the interests of the Monarchists. But an uprising will not succeed. You have too many enemies who will bring you down. Yes! I will let you have my answer by this evening ...'

It had been a foregone conclusion in that General Sanjurjo's plot to overthrow the Government would not succeed. As it turned out, Sanjurjo was betrayed by a common Madrid prostitute. Urged by his friends to flee to Portugal, Sanjurjo had been caught and brought to trial; his lands had been confiscated, and those grandees and rebel officers, in what came to be known as the 'Sanjurjo Affair', also had their land and property expropriated: it had been the prelude to pushing through a new Land Reform Act by the Republican Government, which otherwise might never have had a second glance. The power of the grandees had to be broken if the proletariat were to survive in the class struggle, and Sanjurjo had proved the point.

Unable to settle down for a decent siesta, Don Ruiz attended a meeting at his Public Relations Office in the city centre on the Placa del Palau. From here, all the advertising and publicity for the promotion of his wines and his textile business was conducted. He had had another argument, this time with his advertising manager concerning the bad handling of an important and lucrative wine order from Argentina.

At six o'clock, Don Ruiz, as an elected delegate in the Generalidad, went to the Placa de Sant Jaume for a brief private meeting with Gil Robles, the leader of the Catholic Party, CEDA. Gil Robles had offered to support Garcia Lerroux and his radicals in the Cortes, should there be a general election after the municipal elections in the new year.

'I distrust that degenerate son of an army vet,' Don Ruiz's disgust was deep-rooted, 'for he has *never* outgrown his wharf-rat days at La Barceloneta!'

'Don't let your prejudices get the better of you, Ruiz,' Gil Robles cautioned, feeling about the matter as heated and as frustrated as Don Ruiz. 'It is unwise when everything in Spain these days hinges on personalities and the power they wield.'

Don Ruiz relaxed, intemperance achieving nothing except high blood-pressure. He and Robles had the measure of one another, for he was another one who ran with the hare but hunted with the hounds. It was dangerous to openly declare oneself for the monarchy these days, when Monarchists were being blamed for all sorts of things, especially the burning of churches, the suppression of Jesuit schools, and inciting the masses to riot.

Gil Robles said to Don Ruiz in a more rational tone, 'Lerroux is a powerful man in the Government, we *need* his support. He will become the next Prime Minister, I am sure of it. He is also a changed man, Ruiz, for he has disassociated himself from his past and the seamier side of his life.'

'Hmph!' Don Ruiz accepted the bribe in the shape of a Havana from Gil Robles. His smile was cynical as he sucked on the fat aromatic cigar, 'Wasn't it Azana who said that Lerroux without his gun was like a priest without his rosary? I agree, for a leopard cannot change his spots, my friend.'

The compromise had been reached with an underlying rancour, though no more was said openly on the subject of the man pushing himself forward to be the new Prime Minister of the Republic. Don Ruiz had left Gil Robles' presence in that same disillusioned and unsettled frame of mind that had dogged him all day.

But despite all that, he was still right on time to meet Raven's train from Geneva when it arrived in Barcelona at seven-thirty that evening.

Raven was amazed to see the Lord of the Manor, his brand new Hispano Suiza, and Pedro the chauffeur, waiting to drive her home in style. She was accustomed to summoning a taxicab from the railway station to the Castillo de Luchar, so Raven wanted to know how Don Ruiz had known the precise time of her arrival.

'Señor Peedee has dropped so many hints these past few days, I couldn't help but pick up one of them: Miss Raven Quennell arrives on the train from Geneva at the Estacio Franca at seven-thirty p.m. *prontamente!*' he said, 'spangalising' the language to make her laugh as he embraced her with affection. Pedro, meanwhile, considering himself above the menial task of portering, lugubriously eyed all her luggage.

'Peedee is very good at blackmail,' Raven said. 'He's been

practising on Roxa for years. I hope you weren't inconvenienced by being blackmailed to meet me like this. I know what a busy man you are.'

Large, warm-hearted, and constant, he was like the rock of Montjuic. Don Ruiz, his Jaeger camel-wool coat open in the wintry breeze to reveal his smart Savile Row suit, held the door open for her and left Pedro and a porter to sort out Raven's suitcases and boxes.

'Why didn't Roxana come with you?' Don Ruiz settled himself beside her in the back of the car.

'She and her friend are going to Paris to buy their Christmas presents. Roxana is not going to break with tradition, so don't worry. She'll spend Christmas at the castillo as usual.'

He shook his head in trepidation. 'Doña Jacqueline has always maintained that Señor Peedee is marvellous with the boys, but where his young and beautiful grand-daughters are concerned, he is blind. Too much liberty for Roxa without a chaperon is not good. She'll fall into the wrong company, and then there will be *much* trouble.'

Raven only wished Roxa were here to take note. Yet, she was loyal enough to her sister to want to set the record straight. 'Roxana has a chaperon in La Comtesse de Martello the Third, otherwise Peedee wouldn't have allowed her to go to Paris on her own.'

Pedro battled with the city traffic. From the Placa del Palau where Don Ruiz had visited his main offices earlier in the day, past the Columbus Monument, Pedro then took the Paral-lel to Montjuic.

Don Ruiz, still in a very gloomy frame of mind said, 'Montjuic will never be the same again. The International Exposition has turned the Placa d'Espanya into one big funfair. But, I suppose, there is something to be thankful for. I still have the sea in front of me even if the tourists are able to peer into my back garden from the top of the Palacio Nacional.'

Raven smiled, 'Oh come now, Don Ruiz, don't be selfish! You've become part of the attraction: *El Grandee*, living his right royal lifestyle within high castellated walls, while the rest of the world lies at his feet, what more could you want?'

'Do I detect a note of criticism there, Señorita Raven? You are not becoming a Communist like Ramiro, are you?' he asked as he patted her hand.

'No indeed!'

'No indeed! Huh! If I wished to live with the world at my feet, then I would shift my castle to the other mountain which Jesus Christ himself was tempted to buy from the Devil.'

'Then why don't you?' she teased.

'Because, my dear Raven, it doesn't matter where one lives in Spain nowadays, someone is always looking for a reason to remove the ground from under one's feet. If Montjuic has become a tourist attraction, then, next time round, the entrepreneurs and city fathers will fix their green eyes upon the magnificent Tibidabo and the rest of the Sierra de Collserola. Soon the whole Mediterranean coast of Spain from San Roque to Port Bou will resemble one great big fairground *full* of tourists baring all to *el sol*!'

'You think so?'

'I *know* so.'

'How?'

'Oh, it will come, it's bound to. Landowners, *latifundistas* like myself have been too long entrenched in our feudal way of life. The land must be given back to the people. I, from my elevated position can see what is happening better than those who live at ground level.'

He sounded weary. As though he had had a very hard day at the Fabrica de Luchar.

'Has there been more trouble at your factory?' She almost hesitated to ask.

Don Ruiz glanced out of the darkened window. 'There is always trouble, Raven. I seem to spend my whole life, these days, arguing and fighting with other people, my own sons especially. The factory is now divided into two warring factions, the Socialist trades unions and the Anarcho-Syndicalists, and neither side will agree on anything. Salas Rivales is in a difficult position. Raw cotton from the West Indies is rotting at the dockside while we waste more time in stoppages and arguments about sickness benefits, holidays with pay, eight-hour days, and minimum wages, than we do in manufacturing the cloth that will pay for all that the workers are demanding. Sometimes I think I will do what your grandfather once suggested.'

'What's that?'

'Specialize instead of diversifying. I should concentrate on one thing or the other, wine or cloth, not both. The only reason I am loath to part with the textile factory is because it came with my wife as part of her dowry. Before our marriage it was supervised by her brother. In those days it was called the Fabrica de la Rance. After Robert de la Rance's death in the Great War of 1914, Salas took over. At one time it was possible to have a finger in many pies. Nowadays it is *all* trouble since major industries are being collectivized by the Government.'

It was all too complicated. Raven had no idea of the machinery of commerce so that she could sympathize, criticize, or even ask the appropriate questions. The nearest she had ever got to monetary headache was when Peedee himself became nervous about the amount of death duties owed after their parents' deaths.

'And you, Raven, I detect that you do not like very much being a pupil schoolteacher at l'École Internationale and I would like to know why.'

'One should never return to a place of good memories.'

'Why not?'

'Memories tend to tarnish if revisted twice over.' She thought about her golden priest and the ghost of Dr Keir Devlin sitting in the Parc Mon Repos, and because all her contemporaries had left Maison Roget, Geneva was not quite the same city as it had been when she was younger. 'Sometimes I wonder if I was as silly, gigglish, and empty-headed when I was twelve.'

'To wonder about it at all must surely be a sign of growing older and wiser. What are you teaching these silly gigglish twelve-year-olds?'

'English and Spanish.'

'Then they should do very well.'

The long black Hispano Suiza drew up gracefully in the courtyard of the Castillo de Luchar. The castle and its environs always appeared so pretty at night. Lights of the sprawling city flickered and twinkled all around and below them, for Barcelona, seduced by the embrace of high mountains, rainbowed the sea while the eyes of the mountains themselves winked back like abundant fireflies. Somehow, this time, Raven felt it was good to be back in Spain.

Sonny and Peedee rushed out to greet her after her absence of three months.

'Dear girl,' said Peedee, enthusiastically grabbing up her hockey stick from the luggage Pedro was pulling out of the boot of the car, 'there is a bullfight on Sunday. I have three *huge* placards in readiness. You, Sonny and I will take a picnic to the Place de Toros to do our duty where the bulls of Spain are concerned.'

Tradition to the de Luchar family was as sacred as the Catholic Mass. The Feast of the Nativity was as much a part of Castillo de Luchar as it was of Bethlehem. Even Roxana thought twice about breaking with that tradition. She arrived in Barcelona a week before Christmas, and telephoned from the railway station to ask Doña Jacqueline whether or not she could bring a friend, and could Pedro and the Hispano Suiza be sent to meet them.

Raven felt that it was a bit much of Roxana to take such liberties, especially when the friend in question was already in tow.

Doña Jacqueline was not at all put out, apparently delighted to have another house guest for the Christmas period. '*Si, Si*, Roxa – but of course – *si querida*! I will despatch Pedro to the station at once, for we will have need of the Hispano in about ...' she glanced at her tiny jewelled Cartier wristwatch, 'in one hour, so don't delay your arrival.'

'I wonder if you will say the same thing if the friend turns out to be one of Roxana's raffish boyfriends,' Raven said when Doña Jacqueline replaced the receiver with a bemused expression.

'A raffish *rich* boyfriend,' Doña Jacqueline replied with an indulgent smile.

'He's bound to be rich,' Raven replied wryly. 'Roxana has to maintain her style.'

'Then so much the better.' Ever practical, Doña Jacqueline's thoughts turned to the more mundane. 'Now, where is Conchita? I must ask her to prepare another guest bedroom before I have to leave for the grand reception.'

Don Ruiz and Doña Jacqueline were off to the Palace of the Generalidad in the Placa de Sant Jaume, where a year ago Francesc Macia had proclaimed the Catalan Republic after King Alfonso XIII went into exile. Doña Jacqueline, looking wonderful in a peach and cream satin Vionnet evening gown, her heavy salt-and-pepper chignon caught into a sequined net snood on the nape of her neck, paused for a moment on the threshold of the oak-panelled grand salon to regard Raven perched on the windowseat, her faraway gaze intent upon the turbulent sea.

'You look sad. What's the matter, my dear?' asked Doña Jacqueline.

Raven looked up then and gave Doña Jacqueline a bright, reassuring smile. 'Oh goodness, nothing! I was just thinking, that's all.' How could she tell Doña Jacqueline that Christmas and New Year always made her feel sad and lost because for her it was a time of painful memories rather than joyful celebrations; a time to die by Irish bombs and partisan hatred. A time to reassess one's own life; a time to ask why.

When Doña Jacqueline had gone in search of the housemaid, Raven took from her pocket the letter she had received at the Maison Roget, and re-read it. A hastily-scrawled and almost illegible message on the back of a thin Christmas card read, *Thanks for the memories, and the pleasure of your company during my brief stay in Geneva last June. Thanks also, for being such a great maid of honour at my mother's wedding. I now have Rachmaninov beside me, courtesy of a second-hand HMV portable jungle phonograph which is also a darned temperamental one! However, it only cost me five dollars, cheap at the price, so I can't complain. One can buy anything in Guatemala City. But the maestro will never be quite the same here, as at the Conservatoire. Best wishes for Christmas, 1931, Keiren Hunter Devlin.*

In the school library Raven had taken a geography book and looked up Guatemala City, Central America. It had

273

been completely destroyed by an earthquake in 1917. The capital was slowly being rebuilt. The region was volcanic. Main exports were fruit and coffee. There were traces of an ancient Mayan civilization in the area. Raven wondered what he was doing in such a remote and primitive place. Keir Devlin had kept his private life very much to himself when in Geneva.

Raven had also been left wondering about the date of the postmark on Keir's belated Christmas card: December 1931 – a year ago! Who had been to blame for a Christmas card arriving a year late, Americans or Spanish? And what had he meant about Rachmaninov not being quite the same as at the Conservatoire? In what way was it not the same? Was it to do with his second-hand jungle phonograph, or was it something to do with his Geneva interlude: was he thinking about Jan, or her?

She would write at once to Jan Fairchild in London and ask if she, too, had received a belated Christmas card thanking her for services rendered in the summer of 'thirty-one!

To Raven's dismay, Roxana's friend turned out to be none other than the obnoxious Vida de Martello, who had been the bane of her life at l'École Internationale. Vida's schooldays over, she had failed all her matriculation subjects, which hadn't worried her a bit as her father's wealth compensated for her lack of brains. Vida and handsome Ramiro, however, appeared to have made a very good start as far as the spirit of Christmas was concerned. Two days after the girls' arrival at the castillo Ramiro invited Vida to go with him to a Barcelona nightclub, the invitation not extended to Roxana.

'It's because she's filthy-rich and that creepy-crawly Communist knows it!' Roxana fretted and fumed as she chewed her red-varnished fingernails. 'He hasn't wasted much time, has he? But I know what he's hoping to achieve. He's hoping to sweep Vida off her feet before she has time to realize what his little game *really* is!'

Raven waited for flashpoint. It came soon enough, but from a totally unexpected direction.

Christmas Eve was the holy day. It was a day spent mostly in church. Meals were frugal and presents were opened quietly and without fuss around a beautiful Christmas tree cut from the spruce forest bordering the Parque Vinarosa. Decorated with red ribbons and white incense candles, it reached to the ceiling of the grand salon.

Vida said to Roxa, 'Doesn't the Christmas tree smell divine! All that pine and incense reminds me of the scent the Virgin Mary must have used. Ramiro gave me some for a Christmas present — no doubt a last minute Bon Marché bargain.' Vida gave a little gurgle of fun while unwrapping one of her presents. 'Oh look, another Cartier diamond bracelet from Papa, how nice. He's still trying to buy my affection, you see. Probably hoping I'll stick around to nurse him in his old age when he's past giving his wives and mistresses what they want. Would you like to have it, Roxy?'

'Why?'

Vida shrugged, indifferent to diamonds and people alike. 'I have enough diamond bracelets.'

'Well, if you don't want it, I'll certainly have it.'

'I hope you'll take out an adequate insurance policy, your own, to cover its value,' Peedee remarked, having overheard their conversation while he unwrapped yet another dotted bow tie. 'Why do people imagine I even *like* yellow polka-dot ties!' He grumbled. 'Maroon, purple, blue, yes, but never *yellow* which is such an *insipid* colour!'

That night the entire family was to attend Mass at the cathedral in the Placa de la Seu as in previous years. When Raven asked Peedee if he intended going to the cathedral with them, he looked at her over his new, very bold, horn-rimmed spectacles and said, 'Since when have I been a Roman Catholic?'

'Well, I only asked. Vida, Roxana, and Sonny are coming.'

'Then that is up to you, my children.' He smiled at her worried expression. 'Dear girl, that was not meant as a criticism. You must all please yourselves where you wish to celebrate the birth of Christ. I myself am off to La Barceloneta, where I will partake of red wine and mass

275

with a lot of Catalan troubadors. I'll see you tomorrow afternoon no doubt, at the grand de Luchar banquet. Say a decade of prayer for me, dear girl.'

So Raven, too, went to the Catholic Mass, while Peedee set off on his bicycle for the waterfront to keep his rendezvous with his friends, the poets and fishermen.

On Christmas Day, family and guests congregated by tradition in the vast dining-room with its panelled walls, stained-glass windows, and heavy baroque furniture. The Christmas feast was a gargantuan affair that lasted from four o'clock in the afternoon until, as in previous years, sometimes eight or nine at night. José's absence was conspicuous. Jaime, Carlos, Marta, Nina, and Sonny kept their usual places, and Ramiro contrived to be seated next to Vida.

Doña Maria and Tía Leah, the Rivales family – Uncle Salas and his wife, Tía Isabella, their son and daughter, Tomas and Amparo – were also present as on other family feast days. Ramiro openly flirted with Vida, but every now and then glanced Raven's way, his eyes containing a brooding, unfathomable darkness. Raven could never be certain of Ramiro. He always left her with a strangely negative and empty feeling, yet, at the same time, with the feeling that he cared about what she thought and felt and that somehow, whatever her feelings, they mattered to him. Meanwhile, she could also see how furious Roxana was becoming because Ramiro had ignored her since Vida's arrival at the castillo. Then, the next hint of trouble came with the first course of *pescado relleno*, when an argument arose between Ramiro and his father.

'Uncle Salas tells me that you are encouraging the Confederacion Nacional de Trabajo to gain a foothold in our factory. When you return to work tomorrow, Ramiro, I do not want to know that you have appointed another Communist shop-steward to cause unrest and discontent among the workers. We are slowly seeing an upward trend and a far greater output from the factory than we have done for the past few years, and I want that trend to continue.'

'How can you say the CNT are causing unrest and discontent when you've admitted to a substantial rise in our output, and an increased order book?'

'That is nothing to do with the workers or trade unions and you know it!'

'No I don't! Surely it's only through the workers' efforts that the cloth is produced? When the workers are happy and contented, they work better. Can't you see that? The unions, no one else, least of all Central Government, have brought about better conditions for the labourers. Trade unions are a good thing, not a bad one, Father.'

'Communists are bad. State control, as in Russia, is bad. And why there is now a boom in the Spanish textile industry is nothing to do with trade unions or workers producing more, it is just that we have a better purchasing power all round, thanks to our own efforts.'

'More likely, thanks to a bumper harvest, which has helped to sustain us through a bad period. But, overall, we still have to consider the losses made by the olive-oil producers and orange-growers: and what about the slump in the iron and steel industries? And what about half a million men unemployed without government benefits? Who supports *their* hungry families? So where is this upward trend we're supposed to be experiencing?'

'That is all to do with the American recession, a depression that is hitting England, France, and Germany, as well as many other European countries. Spain has not as yet fully experienced such a recession, simply because we produce most of our goods for our own consumption and do not rely on foreign markets to the extent that America and Britain do.'

'Half the time you argue against yourself, Father! You are like the politicians who twist the point to suit themselves. It is *you* who do not fully understand the situation. The reason why we are doing well at the Fabrica de Luchar, is because I, myself, as recruitment and staff-management supervisor, keep the peace between the Socialists and Confederacion Nacional de Trabajo!'

Uncle Salas thoughtfully prodded his hake fish with prawn and olive stuffing. His drole voice, habitual long face, and downward-drooping moutache, presented *his* viewpoint, 'Labour legislation has also managed to stabilize wages after the last few years' unrest. But as soon as we move towards an upward trend, we seem to go down again. And that, Ramiro, is because the Communist workers' parties demand that all profits should go to the workers instead of realizing that profit must be ploughed back into the industry in order to make it even *more* efficient and profitable. We are desperately in need of new and modern looms before sickness benefits can be considered. Without looms there will be no employment for anyone, sick or well.'

'That is my point exactly!' grunted Don Ruiz, glowering at Ramiro.

The next course was brought to the table, and the rest of the family kept remarkably quiet.

'The Communists alone are responsible for undermining everything, so I don't want any more of them to be brought into the Fabrica de Luchar. Do you understand, Ramiro?'

'Oh, I understand, Father. You would rather give jobs to outsiders – immigrants from Asturias and Andalusia who come to Barcelona looking for work. You are ignoring the terms of *Terminos Municipales*.'

'How so?'

'You are not offering jobs to the residents of your own town first before taking on migrant workers.'

'Because migrant workers are the only ones willing to do the job, Ramiro!'

'For the pittance that is offered, yes! Anything is better than nothing when one is starving. While I sympathize with the Asturians and their plight, I still think the Catalans should come first.'

'Don't I know that!' Don Ruiz growled.

'I don't think you do, Father,' Ramiro emphasized quietly. 'What about *Labrero forzoso*? You deliberately brought in new methods of farming the vineyards on Jaime's recommendations,' Ramiro turned an accusing look upon his younger brother, who had taken over the administration of the land in José's place, 'in order to confuse and thwart people like Juan and your other labourers who have been loyal to you for a quarter of a century. But no, in typical grandee fashion, you hold down their wages by fair means or foul in order to keep them subservient to you. And when they rebel, you give their jobs to others.'

'You *dare* to question my methods? You, who are a

grandee yourself, and, let me emphasize, not a grandee through his own efforts, but through the efforts of others! You, Ramiro, are only able to sit there in a position of wealth, education, and inherited privilege to give *me*, your father, the benefit of your advice, because you are *my* son. Pah! I spit on you and your senseless talk. Better it came from someone born without your privileges. Through me and my forefathers, who pumped their sweat into the ground that nurtured such an ungrateful whelp, you are able to advise me! Do you, everyone, just listen to the gall of this son of mine!' Don Ruiz thumped the table with his fists to set everything rattling.

Doña Jacqueline whispered to Ramiro, 'Please, for my sake, Ramiro darling, don't antagonize your father any more.'

Peedee concentrated on the mushroom flan that came next and began a desultory conversation with Tía Leah seated next to him.

Roxana added *her* glowering glances upon Ramiro, not because of what Don Ruiz was saying about him, but because of what she felt about him. Ramiro sat on the right of Doña Jacqueline, at the opposite end of the table from his father; fortunate, thought Raven, for otherwise Don Ruiz might have struck his son. Vida, on the other hand, her red lips open wide, but only spasmodically remembering to shove a little food between them, the whole time had her hot little smiles upon Ramiro. Raven and Roxana could see that she was full of admiration and adoration as she hung onto every word uttered by him.

His face very pale, Ramiro took a deep breath, jousting for the last word with his father. 'Father, you are a traitor to your own Catalan people.'

There was a terrible silence at the table.

Then Don Ruiz flung down his napkin and stood up. His finger shook as he pointed to the door. '*Leave my table*! You dare to call me a traitor in my own house, at my own table at which you partake of *my* food and *my* wine!'

'Oh no, please, Ruiz! Leave him alone. Please don't send him away.' Doña Jacqueline, in tears, laid a restraining hand on her son's sleeve. 'This is a family meal, Ruiz. Can't we stop talking politics and Communists, and eat our food

279

in peace and harmony on this Christmas Day?'

His face still purple with rage, Don Ruiz sat down and picked up his napkin. 'Jacqueline, *tell* him what I am!'

'Oh Ramiro, you should not have called your father a traitor to the Catalan people. He has done more to support the Generalidad than anyone after King Alfonso abdicated.'

'*After* supporting General Sanjurjo's Carlist attempts first, Mama, to buy arms from Germany in order to overthrow the Republic. By upholding the extreme right-wing Catholic Party, who are nothing but Fascist sympathizers, he has endorsed just that! I should like to know which side he's *really* on!'

'Please Ramiro!' Doña Jacqueline rarely raised her voice.

'No, Mama! I will say what I have to for the benefit of Uncle Salas and Father, and then I will leave. Father might profess love and loyalty to Catalonia, and he might want to see independence for the Catalan people, but he would do better not to woo Prince François-Xavier de Bourbon-Parme ...'

'Oh, I know him!' Vida piped up, a bright smile on her face. 'He has stayed many times at my father's château at Fontainebleau.'

Ramiro barely glanced at her, his grey stare blank, and then he resumed what he had been saying to his father. 'As he used to woo Don Jaime! All these Bourbon Royals are good at is saving their own skins at the expense of the Spanish people. Anti-republican plots are not the way to win the hearts of the people of Catalonia ...'

'I have *never* supported an anti-republican plot, Ramiro!' Don Ruiz shouted, while his food lay on his plate, forgotten.

'Oh no! then what about the Sanjurjo affair last August?'

'I had nothing to do with that, and well you know it! Had I been involved in such a military and political takeover to undermine the Republic, my lands would by now have been confiscated by the Socialist Trade Unionists, or the Anarcho-Syndicalists, or some other *radical* party inundated with Communists whose hands are always itching to confiscate the so-called wealth of the grandees and use it for themselves!'

'You are *obsessed*, Father, by this British and American fear of Red Communism. What is this paranoia with you and Uncle Salas?'

'Because Communists are dangerous. Because they commit regicide and patricide, and ult ... ultimately *unicide*!' roared Don Ruiz finding his own word. 'As they trample over the established order of things, they even murder God!'

'Calm down, Papa. You are becoming carried away by this mass hysteria disease suffered by the Nazis.'

'They burrow blindly, Ramiro. They infiltrate, just like little moles. They spread their invidious propaganda to make the unthinking, uneducated, illiterate masses yearn to live in a world where everyone shares and shares alike, and where everyone *doesn't* have to pull his own weight because the State will prop him up – as long as he's obedient to Party rules, eh, Ramiro? Only the poor peasant doesn't know that. He is too foolish to realize that all he'll ever get in return for his Communist vote is a dictator, the force of arms, and a six-foot-by-two plot of ground in a grey and shabby world. His epitaph will never be at the *top* of the mountain, but in the gutter and in blood, for that is what Communism is all about! You are a *nothing* party, my son.'

'And you, Father, are a right-wing capitalist flourishing to this day on inherited wealth, who can afford to talk like a Fascist.'

'Communism doesn't work, Ramiro, proven by Russia and its Stalinist régime ...'

'You cannot say that, Father! Stalin has turned Russia into a leading industrial nation.'

'With graveyards from Ekaterinburg to Erimbet!'

'Propaganda.'

'From the Dead People's Republic, no doubt. It still takes private wealth by private enterprise to create jobs, to give to the poor, to put food in their mouths, to generate the energy to plough the land and weave the cloth to make more wealth for greater output – you follow my reasoning, eh, Ramiro? Life, by the simple method of earning it, it's as logical as that.'

'Do I hear my *father* talking? He who has never laboured

with his hands, but only with his tongue and his grandee coat of arms? You betray what you say you stand for, Father, by bringing in outside workers to till your fields and by conspiring to bring the Republic to an end through your association with that traitor Sanjurjo.'

'I am still in possession of Vinarosa, so I think that exonerates me from the Sanjurjo affair and vindicates my position as a loyal member of the Republic. You and your young hotheads from the Communist Youth Movement are no more than a bunch of undisciplined loud-mouths who are the ones undermining the credibility of the Republic. You would all be better off living in Stalingrad with the Anarchist Youth Vanguard! And now you may leave my table.'

Ramiro tossed aside his table-napkin and made for the door.

'Anarchists, Communists and Stalinists! I know your activities with The Catalan Socialist Party, Ramiro, and Partido Socialista Unificado de Cataluña is only another name for Communists! A house divided against itself will *fall*! I want my house to be a unified house!' cried Don Ruiz in a broken voice.

'Tell that to José and his Fascist Hitler Army!' said Ramiro, his steely eyes burning with resentment as he turned on the threshold to confront his father one last time.

Raven could see that Ramiro was blaming his father for splitting the loyalties of the family. Doña Jacqueline scraped back her chair. Her heels tapping noisily on the tiled floor, she hurried out after her son.

Don Ruiz shouted wrathfully, '*Don't* bring him back! I never want to see him again. Not unless he can apologize to his father for calling him a traitor to the Republic and to the people of Catalonia whom he serves. Does Ramiro not realize that I am the one who feeds him plus several hundred other mouths? What is to happen to the workers should I decide to close my factory and uproot my vineyards because I am unable to meet their outrageous demands? Who will feed Republican wives and children then?'

The Christmas spirit was not the same after that

harrowing scene, and lunch finished soon afterwards in a muted and unhappy atmosphere: first José, and now Ramiro. Then Roxana and Vida de Martello.

Because Ramiro had been ordered out of his home by his father, Vida decided to curtail her visit when she had intended to stay until the New Year. She wanted, instead, on a typical Vida whim, to go skiing in the Catalan Pyrenees where her father was holidaying, not with La Comtesse III, Vida said, but with his new eighteen-year-old mistress. Roxana, at the last minute, decided to accompany Vida to Andorra, and Peedee was powerless to stop her.

The final blow came when Sonny announced his intention to leave Spain at the end of January to enter a Benedictine monastery in Ireland.

'Oh no, Sonny! Not Ireland. Stay in Spain. What about the Benedictine monastery at Montserrat? It's only thirty miles away. You'll be close to us.'

Sonny shook his head, 'No Raven. I want to go back to Ireland. I feel I *must* go back. I've already written to the abbot of the monastery to inform him of my arrival at Rosscarbery. I've been accepted into the order on the recommendations of Monseigneur Paulus who is now at the Vatican.'

'But we weren't brought up to be Catholics, Sonny!'

'Yes we were, Raven. Think about it carefully. What Mother and Father, and later on Peedee *didn't* teach us in our Protestant chrysalis, Ireland did. I am Irish, and so, I think, forgive me if I'm wrong, are you.'

Raven almost wept: so Sonny, too, was now running away.

Peedee kept his face turned to the window with its panoramic vista of the stormy sea whipped by the frenzied winter winds gusting along the coast.

'Is it a closed order?' Raven asked, a dull headache starting through tension.

'In so far as I know. But I dare say there are modifications to the rule, depending upon the circumstance.'

'I just wish you weren't going so far away, that's all.'

'Darling Raven, I'll always be near you. We won't ever be

separated, not by land, sea, or air, you know that.' Sonny, at seventeen, stood only as high as her shoulder. Peedee had often joked in the past about Sonny's stationary stature, remarking that he was growing downwards like a cow's tail. Sonny put his arms around her, his coppery mop of curls pressed to her cheek. 'Without you and Peedee I don't know where I'd've been all these years. I don't know what I'd've done with my useless crippled life. You and Peedee have made everything bearable.'

'You could always make music again, Sonny.'

'I could, but I don't want to. Music only makes me feel sad — sad and lonely and very depressed. I leave that now to you, Raven, you and the guitar, and the mandolin you pinched from me — the one with the ghastly transfers of Spanish dancers and fandangos all over it. No offence, Peedee.' He looked across at his grandfather standing solemnly in the bay-window.

'None taken, dear boy,' said Peedee distantly, who then murmured, 'What a lot of complications all you young people make of your lives.'

The feeling of gloom and anti-climax that had prevailed after the disastrous family get-together the afternoon before dogged Raven for the rest of the Christmas holidays. After Ramiro had stormed out of the castillo, the Rivales family decided to go back to the Carrer Sarrià, and Pedro was ordered to drive them home. Doña Jacqueline had wept all evening in her bedroom, while Conchita, the maid, danced attendance on her. Then Roxana and Vida demanded household attention before being whisked off to the railway station in the Hispano Suiza, again driven by poor, long-suffering Pedro. Raven couldn't help reflecting that none of the de Luchars, except Ramiro, seemed to appreciate that Pedro and the other servants had families who needed them on festive occasions and holy days. For the first time ever, Raven empathized with Ramiro and what he had been trying to put across to his father.

Peedee's voice cut across her thoughts. 'Every year this Christmas tradition of spending the so-called 'festive season' here at the castillo with all the family fills me with horror.' He glanced over his shoulder at Sonny and Raven standing forlornly behind him. 'Oh, I'm not talking about my own family – you two and Roxa, I'm referring to the de Luchars and the Rivaleses. Don Ruiz, I know, would be greatly offended were I not to continue with a tradition going back long before you children arrived – my being here on Christmas Day. However, I am too old now for family feuds, so I think I shall go home to Cabo Alondra this afternoon.'

Everything was again quaking under Raven's feet, revealing, once more, dark chasms of uncertainty. She wanted the stability of Peedee's flamboyant yet stalwart presence. The touchstone of their lives for the past ten years, he constituted the security, the comfort, the permanence of life amid the changing patterns of their world. But, for the first time ever, Peedee was unable to offer her the reassurances she required, all taken for granted from the day he had walked into the Rotunda Hospital to pick up the fragile pieces of three little Quennells after a bomb had blown their lives asunder.

'All at once I feel very old and very sad,' Peedee went on to add with a weary complaint to his voice Raven had never heard before. 'My grandchildren have at last found their wings and are flying the nest I once so begrudgingly feathered. I feel redundant as never before: rather like a tea-clipper at a naval review. So, dear people, I must get back to Cabo Alondra before this feeling precipitates me any further towards the breaker's yard.'

'I'll come back with you and spend the rest of my holiday at Cabo Alondra, Peedee,' Raven said firmly. 'I prefer it there, anyway, even if the gales are vicious at this time of year.'

Sonny remained silent, and they did not press him to fall in with their plans.

In the following months at l'École Internationale, Raven came to terms with herself, she positively *hated* teaching! After weeks of agonized indecision, she admitted to herself that she was simply not cut out to be a schoolmarm!

As a Roget pupil from the ages of twelve to eighteen she had loved every moment of her schooldays. Returning in the capacity of a pupil teacher was a vastly different experience altogether. All her friends had left, married by now or engaged like Jan Fairchild, or they were off around the world enjoying themselves like Roxana. Monseigneur Paulus was not at St Raphael's any more, and the priest who had taken his place was not as interested in her spiritual welfare as her golden priest had been. Besides, every time she walked into the dining-hall she saw it festooned with colourful ribbons, balloons, bunting and orange blossom for the wedding of Michelle Devlin and Albert Contrin. She remembered Keir Devlin's arms around her as they had danced to what was supposed to be 'The Blue Danube' and his voice saying over the champagne, 'Weddings are pretty things if you yourself are not involved.'

She had begun to think a lot more about him lately. She did not know why.

Raven battled with herself.

At the end of the summer term, 1933, Madame Roget understood the reason for her resignation. 'I know: I understand completely. Teachers, like musicians, artists, and writers, are born. They cannot be bludgeoned into performing their art. In whatever you next choose to do with your life, Raven, be happy.'

The next few weeks Raven spent in idling her time.

She visited Sonny in Ireland, as well as the people of her childhood, Cathal Swilly and Eileen Hyde, Lockwood, her old governess, and Lyra and Amery Noughton Peel, both of them now gin-swigging, fat, flacid fifty-year-olds. She even popped into the local library, where Clare Fenchurch (still a spinster) had become Chief Librarian. Clare had been really delighted to see her, and afterwards they had had toasted muffins at the teashop around the corner.

After Dublin she had visited Jan. She had been introduced to Jan's fiancé, Archie Cunningham, who spent his time between bowling on Westerham's cricket green (Archie's habitat when not at the Foreign Office) and asking her an inordinate number of impertinent questions about herself, her grandfather, her life in Spain, and why Sonny wanted to be a Benedictine monk. Archie was *really* eccentric, Raven couldn't help thinking, not Jan's type at all. He had even asked her how many languages she spoke fluently and whether or not she would like to join the Civil Service since she had the qualifications and was unemployed and unmarried. 'I'll put in a good word for you with the Chief,' he had said, but she had turned down Archie's offer. The Civil Service was the last thing she had in mind, even if she were 'unemployed and unmarried'.

On her return to Spain, she continued with the idle life, swimming, sunbathing, strumming on a guitar or on Sonny's discarded mandolin, drinking wine, and memorizing lengthy stanzas of poetry with Peedee in the wild *jardin de Cabo Alondra*, while they both picked over the *langostinos*, the *gambas* and the troubador poets, English and Spanish. She was happy as never before.

'The fact remains, Raven, you are a Bohemian like myself,' Peedee put her in the picture one starry night.

'It's a lovely feeling, Grandpapa.'

'I agree. And *don't* call me Grandpapa! Even if I am in semi-retirement as Doña Jacqueline's part-time secretary, I'm not yet ready to depart this life.'

'Glad to hear it,' she retorted.

'Despite all I said when Sonny went off to Rosscarbery, I have discovered, after all, that there *is* life after death. He tells me in his letters, the abbot has put him in charge of the Benedictine silkworm population, so now he's engaged on a never-ending rota of planting mulberry trees to feed the greedy beasts. They eat all day long – the silkworms, not the monks.'

Raven grinned and sniffed her hands. 'Pooh! All this garlic the Spanish put in the food is insufferable. It's a good job I haven't a lover either.'

'And what is that 'either' supposed to mean?'

'Well, you're loverless like myself, aren't you?'

'Carina is sufficient unto my needs, dear girl. She keeps me fed and watered like a good English lawn.' He got up to feed Morgan and Le Fay the titbits of their fish supper.

The soft September night air, de Luchar red wine, the soothing sound of the sea, the intelligent company of a kindred soul, never mind that he was her grandfather and half a century older than she, Raven breathed the rich fragrance of Cabo Alondra, the magic of Cabo Alondra; and it all seemed too beautiful to last.

'Peedee, will there be a war in Spain as everyone seems to think?' Raven reminded herself of the old days, Cassy question-time, the hot-water cylinder in the bathroom Sonny had insisted was a salvaged German torpedo, Roxana pinching scent and sex from everywhere, and she herself, always wanting to poke into tomorrow's unmade bed.

'Yes, dear girl. If you don't get your feet off my chair, there will be a mighty big war.'

'Sorry.'

She shifted her long legs and he sat down. 'What you want me to do is reassure you. I cannot. I can only tell you what I myself think and feel. Yes, it looks like war. No, it will not be so catastrophic we cannot pick ourselves up afterwards and start again. That is what we human beings always manage to do. In the same way that the male and female sex-drive is the regenerative power of our species, so are wars the regenerative power of our fragile world. The greater the war, the greater the urge to take survival measures afterwards. Rather like gamekeeping: a big shoot, a big cull and a big preservation order for next year. Do you want some more wine?'

'No, thank you. I'll get a headache.'

'A hangover, dear girl, is therapeutic. It gives one the excuse to throw up and start again.'

'I said headache, not hangover.'

'One should always live for the moment. That's how I've arrived at this ripe old age of sixty-six, having enjoyed every mile of the journey. Tomorrow your hangover and headache will bring you to your senses, and life will resume its normal pattern of disasters outside our control, which, when you have lived as long as I, you will learn to take in your stride.'

Looking back on those few short weeks at Cabo Alondra in Peedee's company, with not a cloud on her horizon, Raven knew that they were the best in her life.

Shopping in Vilafranca one morning, Raven felt she was being followed. The driver of the black Citroën kept the car creeping close to the pavement. He was annoying her and she was about to tell him to stop pestering her otherwise she would call a policeman, when the car drew to a halt a little ahead of her. Poking his head out of the nearside window, Raven could see now who it was. 'Ramiro! What are you doing in Vilafranca?' Raven paused beside his car.

Ramiro turned off the engine. His light eyes dancing, the habitual cynical smile on his sensuous lips, he moved into the passenger seat to talk to her. 'Señorita Raven! You're a sight for any man's eyes as well as my sore heart. Tell Mama I'm homesick. Would you like a lift to wherever you're going?'

'Pedro is picking me up from the San Pedro Hotel to take me back to Cabo Alondra. Your father has gone to a meeting at his bodega this morning, so Pedro will take me home again as soon as he is free.'

'I'll save him the trouble.'

'Thank you Ramiro, but I'm sure you have other things to do with your time and don't want to chauffeur me around town.'

'If I didn't want to, I wouldn't be asking.' He hesitated. 'I know you don't care for jazz and prefer the blues or classical music, so I thought you might like to go to the Wagner festival drama. *Parsifal* is being performed at the Palau de la Musica in Barcelona this evening. I could meet you at Cabo Alondra and take you home again afterwards – and no hanky-panky! I promise.' His invitation and his smile were disarming to say the least.

She tempered her refusal with a gracious, yet regretful smile of her own. 'Thank you, but no thank you, Ramiro.'

'You are still afraid of me?'

'No, Ramiro. I'm busy this evening.'

'You are afraid of my politics, then?'

'No.'

'You are braver than my father.'

'Am I?'

He raised his arm in a carelessly dismissive and impatient little gesture from where it rested on the window frame of the Citroën. 'Oh, I just wondered if all that talk of Papa's last Christmas about Communists had got to you, too. You may have heard, I've been elected as a deputy for the United Catalan Socialist Party.'

'Congratulations, Ramiro.'

His eyes narrowed and dulled as he surveyed her critically. Hurt and a little angry that she had chosen once again to snub him when he had set out to be nice to her, Ramiro tried to justify himself in her eyes. 'We are *also* anti-Stalinists.'

'I'm sorry, but I have no interest in Spanish politics, Ramiro.'

'Then you should have, Raven, because Spanish politics is what it's all going to be about, pretty soon! Shame about *Parsifal*. Never mind, I'll resist your kiss and cast my lance about elsewhere. Is Roxana home?'

'No.'

'Then I shall have to find the secret of the Holy Grail by myself.' He moved back into the driver's seat and started the engine. 'Are you sure you won't change your mind?'

'Positive.'

'*Adios*, Raven.'

'Goodbye, Ramiro.' She watched him drive off. Now she knew what Ramiro was doing in Vilafranca. No longer his father's deputy at the Fabrica de Luchar, Ramiro was busy drumming up support for the local Communist Party.

Raven assisted with the grape harvest. Not since that first autumn at Vinarosa when she was eleven and a half years old had she helped in the vineyards, for normally she would have been in Geneva during the months of September and October. So, while she was coming to terms with herself and what she was going to do with the rest of her life, Jaime put her to good use.

During those harvest months Raven spent a lot of time with Jaime in and around Vinarosa, Toril and Vilafranca. They wined, dined, danced, and went to the cinema to see films starring Fatty Arbuckle, Harry Reed, Carol Lombard, Greta Garbo and Douglas Fairbanks – who was quite a swashbuckling hero in *The Thief of Bagdad*! Sound movies had made the world of difference, although Jaime sometimes had difficulty with the fast-talking English spoken by American movie stars and got her to translate, while everyone behind them in the cinema shushed and hissed. Raven enjoyed Jaime's company tremendously. She felt unthreatened by him: and this time there was no José, Ramiro, or Roxana to disrupt the happy and contented atmosphere that prevailed.

At the de Luchar bodegas in Vilafranca, Jaime took her on a tour around his father's winery, because she had never been to the actual vinification plant before. She was curious about many things. 'Why can't it all be done at Vinarosa, this pressing and fermenting business, as in the old days?'

'Wine production has increased since the turn of the century. But, having said that, these last two years have seen a drastic fall in our foreign market sales compared to three years ago. Papa blames it, as he blames everything, on the world recession.'

Raven didn't put it into so many words, but thought to herself, and you, Jaime? Who and what do you blame? She thought of José and Ramiro and how they had turned their back on their father and his dominance of their lives. Would Jaime one day turn around and do the same?

'Nowadays competition from other markets, especially France, is fierce, so one must always be one step ahead. In 1918 these more modern bodegas were built by my father. It's more convenient to have the main bodegas here in town where we have the railway line direct to Barcelona going practically past our winery doors. With most of the vine growers centralized in this one commercial area, the whole process of wine production from beginning to end is made more efficient – from the moment the grapes are picked, crushed, pumped, pressed, skinned, pipped, and poured into casks. That's rather over-simplifying the whole process, Raven, but I don't want to bore you. To me, Vinarosa and everything associated with the land is my whole life,' Jaime said unpretentiously.

'José told me fertilizer comes from grapes.'

'Yes. Nothing is allowed to go to waste. The skins and pips of the red grapes go to give red wine or rosé its colour. Red grapes can also make white wine. The *must*, which is grapejuice before fermentation takes place, is another by-product of wine-making.'

'If it's more convenient here, why is there a bodega still in operation at Vinarosa?'

Jaime smiled. 'Sometimes the *rabassaires* are reluctant to switch to new techniques. The little bit of vinification we still do at the Parque Vinarosa is mainly concerned with young red wines for local consumption, done by an intercellular method as in the old days. The harvest is put intact into underground tanks so that a gentle and subtle fermentation takes place within the grape berries themselves. Then, after a few days, the *oenologist*, myself ... his smile broadened at his grand name, 'decides when to proceed with the normal pressing of the grapes.'

Raven flung up her hands in mock exasperation. 'Juan always grumbled when I put stalks and junk-bits in my basket, and now you tell me *everything* goes into the Vinarosa fermentation tank!'

'Well, only in the case of young reds, as I said – and really, it's not quite as simple as that. Stalks do make the wine taste harsh and abrasive if there are too many. But I don't suppose Juan meant you to take his criticism personally.'

'Neither can I understand why, if the Spanish wine-trade has a great future ahead of it, men like Juan are always fighting with men like your father and causing disruption in the vineyards so that everything comes to a standstill.'

'Oh, it's all very complicated, and one can't actually blame the vine-cultivators. Under the Unio de Rabassaires, who are backed by the left-wing CNT, we have to pay attention to the statutes and laws laid down by the cooperatives for the benefit of their members. Then there is this new law, the *Ley de Cultivos*, which enables tenant farmers with vines, the *rabassaires,* who have cultivated their land for more than fifteen years, to gain the freehold. On the other hand, landowners like my father are reluctant to give up *their* rights to the land which has belonged to them for generations.'

'Yes, I suppose there's a lot that goes on behind the scenes that is hard to understand.' They had walked out into the sunlight, and under a gigantic pergola of vineleaves and other trailing plants to create a cool and shady place adjoining the bodega, scores of greyish-green bottles squatted on the earth like tiny plump men. 'What are these funny shaped bottles doing in the ground?' Raven asked.

'They are called *bombonas*. Wine in them matures by the *solera* method in order to produce brandy, the sunbasking method. Look Raven, let's change the subject from wine-making to wine-drinking. At the party tonight, will you be my partner for the *Sardana*?' The *Sardana* was the national dance of Catalonia.

Raven laughed. 'You'll have to teach me how to dance the *Sardana* first, Jaime.'

Underneath the stars, Jaime asked her to marry him.

'Goodness, Jaime! This is totally unexpected! You'll have to give me time to think about it.' Raven, out of breath after all their energetic dancing, flopped down on the grass so that her red skirt fanned around her in a circle. She looked up at him, her expression changing from one of laughing, happy exhaustion to one of gravity when she met his eyes. They were so serious, and yet so sincere. The circle of dancers behind them continued to whirl and twirl, clap and sing, so that the whole world seemed to revolve upon the axis of Vinarosa, its music, and its sons.

In her black silk blouse and red skirt Raven reminded Jaime of a solitary red poppy alone in a vast field of thistles. He wanted to pluck her up and keep her for himself before the thistles claimed her.

He dropped to his haunches in front of her, his expression intense and tragic, while never daring to hope she felt anything at all for him. 'Raven, since you came back from Geneva, my world has changed. I can't remember a time in my life when I've been so happy. I think – no, I *know* I'm in love with you. I will work all my life to make you happy and give you the things I want to give you if you would consider marrying me.'

Raven wanted to put her arms around him and hug him tight. Not as a lover might, but as a mother might. She looked past him to the dancers, her palms flat on the grass, her arms supporting her weight as she leaned away from him. 'Jaime, you've made me very happy, too – but you'll have to let me think about it.' She couldn't look at him.

He touched her cheek and made her meet his eyes. 'Is there someone else? Someone in Switzerland, perhaps?'

'No one.' Half-laughing, half-tearful, she answered only half-truthfully, for way back in her mind someone had indeed replaced José; someone whom she must never think about seriously. 'After all, Jaime, we haven't even kissed …'

He leaned towards her and took her in his arms. He kissed her for so long, she lost track of time and place until an amused voice above them said with sarcasm, 'I can see that the wine you are now producing for Papa is potent stuff, eh Jaime? It gives you extra courage. And Raven, you don't lose much time yourself, do you?'

Raven looked up to see José standing watching them with a sardonic little smile. In that moment José presented a terrifyingly handsome figure in his equestrian-style khaki uniform of a Spanish legionnaire.

Jaime scrambled to his feet, smoothing down his hair before embracing his brother. Overawed by José's uniform, Jaime couldn't refrain from admiring his brother's appearance. 'You look wonderful, José! A real soldier …'

'An officer, not soldier, Jaime. *Regulaires* are soldiers, I am a *capitán* of the Army of Africa!'

'Of course – a captain too! Raven and I were just – were just talking, a little.'

Raven, knowing it was a foolish thing to say, murmured, 'What a surprise, José! Why are you here and not in Tetuan?'

'Vinarosa is still my home, Raven.' José stooped, and putting out his hands, pulled her up off the grass. In that one split second he caught her unawares and, drawing her close, embraced her. 'Raven, you are more beautiful than ever. I've *really* missed you.'

'Don't lie, José de Luchar! If you'd missed me that much, why didn't you ever write to me?'

'I *did* write, but you never replied – or perhaps our letters got lost. Camel-post is not that reliable.'

'Excuses, José!'

'You look truly stunning tonight, Raven. So much more mature and interesting than last I remember. I can hardly bear to think of what I've missed these last four years – lucky Jaime!' Without releasing her, he turned and punched Jaime playfully in the chest. 'What have you been doing with yourselves while I've been learning to be a legionnaire?' He came between them and, draping his arms over their shoulders, drew them towards the house and the soft-coloured lights of the lantern-lit garden.

'Does Father know you're back?' Jaime asked, trying hard to be brotherly in spite of his huge, yearning disappointment: José was home again, handsome and smart and cocksure in his grand military uniform. As always, José's dynamic presence made him feel inferior and terribly insecure. Just when he had Raven all to himself, he felt he was about to lose her.

'Of course! My sins are forgiven. I've been welcomed back into the fold. Papa already has the champagne on ice. Tonight is to be a double celebration, the return of the Prodigal Son to drink the last of the summer wine!'

'Why did you come back, José?' Jaime asked, his manner and tone, unlike him at all, were suddenly belligerent.

José had never heard gentle Jaime so harsh and calculating: poor old Jaime must be falling in love with little blackbird, and that wouldn't do, were José's thoughts. He had come back to Vinarosa for Raven, and for no other reason. A fellow might spend his days bedding the more willing señoritas, but when it came to choosing a wife, he always wanted something extra-special. José tightened his arm around Jaime's shoulders. 'I heard about poor old Ram and how he was chucked out of the castillo by Father last Christmas for being a Communist. I would have come before, but I didn't have long enough leave. I heard that Raven had returned to Cabo Alondra, and, as I wanted to put things straight between us, I decided that the *Fiesta Vendimia* was as good a time as any to spend a little holiday with my family.'

'How did you know I was home?' Raven asked.

'Oh, another little bird told me.' He turned back to his brother. 'I'm not staying long, Jaime, so don't look so miserable.' Then, his gipsy smile designed to seduce sooner rather than later, he caught hold of Raven's arm. 'Raven, I saw you dancing with Jaime, now it's my turn –

oh, don't pull away from me, Jaime won't mind.' Over his shoulder, while he led her firmly away to the dancers, José said, 'I'm only borrowing her for a little while, brother. She was my girl first, you know!'

Raven saw Jaime disappearing in the direction of Juan, the overseer, and his family, and she was angry with José for ruining such a pleasant evening. 'How dare you assume that I was ever *your* girl!'

'Weren't you?'

'No, never.'

'Then what were you doing alone with me in the Caverna Rosa all those summers ago?'

'I was doing nothing with you. You enticed me there. I knew nothing about sex or what a man can do to a woman and her feelings. But I do now! So let go my arm, if you please, so that I can go back to Jaime.'

'Why?'

'That's none of your business. You're assuming too much after four years, José.'

'It *is* my business. Has he asked you to marry him? I think he has a soft spot for you by the look on his face just now.'

'It's nothing to do with you.'

'What a fortunate girl you are, my little Raven – my tall and beautiful Raven.' He stood back, and Raven hated the way in which he admired her, as though she were some kind of brood stock! 'I always remember your legs – fantastic legs! And those wonderful little shorts you wore when cycling around the estate, they were designed for the temptation of Christ himself. Two proposals in one evening: I was about to ask you the same thing as Jaime, please will you marry me? I came home specifically to ask you a second time to be my wife and to apologize for – for what happened between us in the Caverna Rosa. I didn't mean to frighten you as I seemed to have done. I honestly didn't know you had had no previous experience with men. I thought you knew the facts of life like Roxa. I also assumed you liked me more than just a little. In fact, I know you *loved* me! You said so, quite sweetly if I remember rightly.' He touched her hair, his hand smoothing the straight blue-black satin. 'Just like a raven's wing,' he murmured poetically. Then, tightening his hold around her waist, his expression evinced tenderness and consideration. 'Raven, dearest Raven, I still love you very much. I thought I could get you out of my system once I took up soldiering. You were the reason why I went to Toledo to become a legionnaire. You drove me to it by your cold rejection of me. But I want you still. More than any other girl in the world. Please will you marry me and come back with me to Tetuan?'

She had to stop herself from applauding. 'No, José.'

'Why not?'

'Because you have the most monumental cheek, and because I don't want to be your wife.'

'If you marry Jaime, I will kill you both.'

She gave a short laugh, '*Olé!*'

'Yes really! Nobody steals you from me. Least of all my younger brother.'

'Then you shouldn't have run away from me.'

'I didn't run away. *You* ran away! But let's not argue about it. Now that we've both had time to think about ourselves, I know that I want you to be my wife and the future chatelaine of Vinarosa.'

Raven just wished that Jaime hadn't been so ineffectual in front of José and had put up more of a fight on her behalf. But it was not in Jaime's nature to fight anyone, least of all José whom he had always idolized. Jaime would rather lose her, despite what he had said about being in love with her and wanting to marry her, than go against his elder brother and what *he* wanted. José's nature being notoriously fickle, Ramiro's sadistic, and Jaime's weak, she took the de Luchar males in her stride; she had learned her lesson.

'I'm not going to marry Jaime, either.'

José grinned, then suddenly bent his head and kissed her fiercely on the mouth without caring who was watching.

She was so taken aback by his unexpected action, rather like that time Monseigneur Paulus had kissed her hands, she didn't even struggle. They danced out of step and rhythm to the fast music while the people of Vinarosa and Toril swirled happily around them, laughing, smiling, clapping, and waving scarves and handkerchiefs, and clicking castanets like over-exuberant cicadas, until Raven, held far too tightly in José's embrace, thought she would faint from the heady atmosphere.

In the shadows Raven knew that Jaime had been watching them, and had seen José kissing her. She felt sorry for Jaime, because he cared for her, and because he also cared for his brother. And, Spanish loyalties being what they were, she had hoped not to compromise him.

However, Jaime would have to sort out where his priorities lay, woman or brother. José, of course, had no such handicap. He took what he wanted. And, in that respect she grudgingly put him a notch above his brother: yes, she had to be perfectly honest with herself, she was still attracted to José de Luchar, the first man who had ever kissed her and taught her that love had many different facets, even if most of them were blurred and badly cut: even after he had killed off her finer feelings towards him, she was still stirred by his physical presence and hated herself for being so carnal: even after all this time, even after his betrayal, his conceit, and his audacity, seeing him again and being near him again, she was still drawn to him, this worthless inconsistent charming philanderer who thought the world was his special playground!

José made her stand still with him in the circle of dancers. He took something from his pocket and held it up to the stars. 'An engagement ring of diamonds and sapphires, as I think there is still a chance for me now that you've forgiven me for leaving you without explaining why. But love between two people doesn't have to be explained in so many words, eh, blackbird?'

'Not a chance.'

'I don't believe you. Why are you dancing like this with me?'

'Because I'm trapped by you, and don't want to make a scene.'

'Because you *want* to be trapped by me?'

'What makes you think that?'

'I know you, Raven. If you wished to go to Jaime, I would not have been able to stop you. In the same way that you keep Ramiro at a distance, you would be doing the same with me. But you are not. And so I think you still care for me in your secret heart. I also think that these past four years have done us both good. It's given us a chance to grow up and examine our feelings for each other. I am certain about you Raven, and I think, I'm sure your feelings for me have remained unchanged despite the fright I gave you in the Caverna Rosa.' José, having established to himself that brother Jaime was no threat, added, 'I really did come back to marry you, you know, Raven, and here's the ring to prove it.' He took hold of her hand firmly and slipped the engagement ring on her wedding finger. 'See how well it fits? Do you like it, blackbird?'

She held up her hand to watch the flashes of fire from it. Diamonds and sapphires by starlight, not something that happened to a girl every day of her life; Raven knew in her heart she could never accept José's tempting offer. Sexual attraction alone was no foundation for marriage, and neither were she and José temperamentally suited to each other. She would forever be wondering what other pretty woman José was courting behind her back. Beside, she wasn't even perfectly certain she didn't hate him!

Raven, therefore, firmly resisted the charismatic pull of José de Luchar: 'Yes – it's very pretty, José, but you shouldn't have gone to so much expense, or such extremes …' She began to ease the ring off, but before she was fully aware of what José was doing, he had stepped with her onto the floodlit patio, where his family were congregated on garden chairs.

His arm tightly and possessively around her waist, José said, 'Papa, Mama, Doña Maria, and Tía Leah – oh, and Jaime, Raven and I are going to be married before I have to return to Morocco.'

'Oh bravo, José!' Don Ruiz was ecstatic. He embraced them both and pounded José on the back. 'Fetch more champagne, Cici,' he shouted to his cellar master, 'José's getting married to our own *querida*, one who is already like a daughter to us. Señorita Raven Quennell has consented to join her own ancient and noble family name with the de Luchar family name: I have no words to describe my happiness and joy for this marriage. This is the happiest day of my life!'

Raven could tell that Don Ruiz, like his sons, was also under the potent and euphoric spell woven by the last of the summer wine.

Doña Jacqueline, tears in her eyes, kissed Raven. '*Chérie* — as a Frenchwoman who has lived her whole life in Spain, I have not used such an endearment for a long time. Now I use it for you. I am so happy that my eldest son has chosen you to be his wife. I could not wish for anyone better for my José. One day, Vinarosa will belong to both of you and so I shall die happy knowing that my grandchildren's future is secured. Come, here is Doña Maria and Tía Leah to kiss you also. Afterwards we four will go away together and have a little talk by ourselves and make our wedding plans.'

Then Peedee, wheeling his bicycle, his straw hat still on his head even though the sun had long since set, pushed his way through the crowd of well-wishers. Peedee came right up to her, and drawing her to one side, whispered fiercely, 'Are you, drunk?'

'No, Grandpapa.'

'Did you let his pretty looks in that dreadful military uniform go to your head so that your decision was purely an emotional one?'

'No, Grandpapa.'

'Were you fully aware of what he was asking you when you said yes to his proposal of marriage?'

'No, Grandpapa.'

'And I suppose you were moonstruck when you gazed into his eyes and said yes?'

'No, Grandpapa.'

'Do you know what you are doing?'

'I'm not sure.'

'You are throwing your life away on a man not worth your little finger! You deserve a husband far more worthy of you than José de Luchar. Do you know where Tetuan is?'

'Yes, Grandpapa.'

'It's in the desert! In God's name, Raven, why have you consented to marry José of all people?'

'I don't know that I did.'

'Are you going to break down and weep? Because you'd

better do that at Cabo Alondra, not here amongst all these foreigners. What made you consent to marry him, Raven?'

'I didn't – at least, I don't think I did. Jaime also asked me to marry him tonight. I got confused.'

Peedee took a deep breath. 'You'd better sleep it off at Cabo Alondra, Raven. And tomorrow morning I suppose I'll have to explain to everyone that my granddaughter was rendered temporarily insane after receiving two proposals of marriage all in the space of one evening. I do so *hate* the *Fiesta Vendimia*. It makes everyone so *utterly* irresponsible!' Peedee turned around and said in a loud voice for the benefit of everyone, though he addressed himself to José in particular, 'Young man, you might have forgotten who I am while you've been away, but now I'm reminding you. You require *my* permission to marry *my* granddaughter since she is not of age until next January. You have not asked for it, and so I am not obliged to give it!' He got on his bicycle and pedalled off to Cabo Alondra.

During the next two days Raven pleaded an incapacitating migraine. She let everyone know that she had red spots jumping in front of her eyes, which made her feel weak, nauseous, and very ill. All she wanted was to be left alone to die in peace. Outside her bedroom door a *Do Not Disturb* notice was pinned. The shutters of her bedroom windows were kept closed and she sweated miserably in the darkness, wondering what she had let herself in for. She would just *have* to tell José she couldn't marry him because she was not a Roman Catholic but an under-age Protestant. She sent a message to the Mas Luchar via Carina.

No problema! José wrote back, *I'll get in touch with my friend and confessor, Father Gabriel, the priest at the Basilica in Toril who'll come and make you a Catholic in time for the wedding – although, these days in Spain, it isn't necessary for a couple to be religious. I hope your headache soon gets better*, querida. *I didn't think you'd drunk quite so much at the* Fiesta Vendimia. Amor siempre. *José*.

Then on the second afternoon of her self-induced indisposition, Roxana, to add to Raven's confusion and misery, arrived at Cabo Alondra.

Roxana rattled the door handle. 'Let me in, Raven! Why do you always lock your wretched door?'

'Goodness gracious, what are you doing here?' Raven opened her bedroom door and let Roxana in.

'I saw Peedee painting the pine trees at the top of the drive and he told me you were ill in bed.'

'Painting the pine trees?' Raven looked blankly at Roxana who herself appeared very distraught.

'Watercolour.'

'Oh – oh, I see.'

'Where is he?'

'Who?'

'You might well ask, *José*!'

'He's certainly not here. Why?'

'Where is he?'

'Don't shout at me Roxana, I already have a headache.'

'I *will* shout at you – how *dare* you try and *sneak* off with José behind my back! Let me see the grand engagement ring he gave you.' She grabbed Raven's hand.

'I'm not wearing it. It's in the drawer.'

'I bet it's a diamond and sapphire one! The same one he gave me a year ago, Oh, my God, I'll kill him, the *swine*!' she finished through gritted teeth.

'Roxana, will you kindly explain what is going on? *What* are you doing here and *why* are you shouting at me about diamond and sapphire rings?'

'*One* sapphire and diamond ring – *the* one! An *engagement* ring! Carina told me over the telephone yesterday that you and José had got engaged the night of the *Fiesta Vendimia*. I rang up to speak to Peedee because I needed some money to be transferred into my Spanish bank account. If I hadn't, I'd never have known about you and José, and you'd have gone off quite merrily with him to North Africa ...'

'I would not. I have no intention of going with José to North Africa. It has all been a frightful mix-up.'

'Leaving me in pod.'

'I beg your pardon?'

'Preggers, darling, preggers!' Roxana sat down heavily on the end of Raven's untidy bed, pulled off her hat, tossed it away, took off her shoes, and said, 'God! What a hell of a soup I've landed myself in, and it's all José's fault! The bumpy old taxi here was no help either, practically giving me a miscarriage on the way – but that would be too much to hope for.'

Raven sat on the edge of her bed in her nightdress and, white-faced, tried to elicit some sense from Roxana. 'You are going to have José's child?'

'Yes, yes, yes! I'm almost *three months*!'

'You're sure?'

'Positive.'

'Does José know?

'No, of course not! Otherwise he wouldn't have become engaged to you. I didn't know myself until I went to see a gynaecologist in Paris. He told me in no uncertain terms, that I was ten weeks gone. So I took the overnight train from Paris with every intention of going straight to Toledo where I knew José would be on leave – he used to have a girlfriend in Toledo. Anarchists demanding their rights, however, stopped the train at Gerona by attempting to derail it. We were stuck at the station for hours while the doddering old stationmaster was left to sort out the points and the bombs further down the line at Llagosterra. That was when I telephoned here to speak to Peedee about more funds, and Carina told me about you and José. The last place on earth I expected to find him was at Vinarosa. I'm only glad I ran out of money and those Gerona Anarchists decided to get bolshy before you ran off with José, otherwise I don't know what I'd have done.'

'I think, Roxana, you'd better start at the beginning and tell me all about you and José, and why he thought he could come back to Vinarosa to make me look a complete fool in front of everyone.'

'He's made us both look fools. But he's not getting away with it. I'll *make* him marry me and assume responsibility for his child. Otherwise I go to Don Ruiz to let him know what a bastard his son is and what a bastard his grandson will be. That ought to do the trick. And I thought Ramiro took the prize for being a bastard!'

'When have you been seeing José?' Raven, suddenly suspicious about the truth of Roxana's story, found that nothing made sense – least of all Roxana's liaison with José of all people, who was supposed to have been chasing Rifs in the desert for the last four years. 'José's been in North Africa.'

'So have I. We've been seeing one another more or less regularly ever since I left l'École Internationale.'

'But where?'

Roxana shrugged indifferently, 'Tetuan, Toledo, Cueta – not to mention San Roque and Marbella.'

'How come? I thought you were in love with Ramiro?'

'Ramiro doesn't love anyone except himself. He only wants sex without committment on the back seat of motor cars – preferably Hispanos.'

'And what did José want?'

'That, too. But at least José offered me an engagement ring once we started getting serious. He paid for an apartment in Tetuan so that we could see each other more often. We were going to get married as soon as he got his promotion and new orders. Then things started to go wrong about two months ago, and it was all the fault of that lesbian!'

'What lesbian?'

'Vida de Martello, who else?'

'Go on.'

'I don't want to talk about her.'

'You're *going* to talk about her, Roxana, in view of the fact that you've so thoughtlessly managed to mess up *my* life as well as your own.'

'Oh dear, you're angry. I can tell by that big-sister voice, and when you start pacing the room like a black cat. Carina told me you had one of your bad migraines.'

'Shut up, Roxana!'

'I thought you wanted to hear my story?'

'Then get on with it.'

'Vida and I, and a lot of other people you don't know, spent May and June in Antibes. Then Vida and I and a few of her French friends went off to spend some time on her father's yacht. We had a fabulous time. José got eight days' leave and joined us in cruising the Mediterranean coast. We circled the ports from Marbella to Melilla. We even went down as far as Casablanca! The old Comte is a fabulous host, so obliging. He would do anything for me.'

'How nice for you.'

'Yes, it was. It was such a heady cruise, José and I made love all the time during his leave. Then Vida started getting nasty. She tried to get her claws into José, just as she had tried with Ramiro last Christmas before Don Ruiz bundled him out of the castillo. On that skiing holiday in Andorra, Vida was in a funny mood and I thought it was on account of Ramiro. Anyway, she soon got over it when she sprained her ankle and was laid up in bed for a fortnight. I, like a fool, gave up my skiing time to sit with her and keep her happy, and because there were no boyfriends around – men, I've discovered, fight shy of a female sick-bed – Vida was her old self again. She was as nice to me as in our last term at Angels' Hell when we had such fun trying to flirt with Monseigneur Paulus and Dr Keir Devlin.' Roxana lay back across the foot of Raven's bed. Hands behind her head she stared up at the ceiling. 'And talking about him, did you know he sent me a Christmas card from Guatemala?'

'No.' Raven said short-temperedly.

'Oh well, it was ages ago. I haven't heard from him recently, even though he promised to keep in touch when we were in Paris together. It must be lonely all by yourself in the jungle without a woman to take your mind off the mosquitoes.'

'What are you babbling about now?'

'Keir.'

Raven stopped pacing and biting her nails. She turned to Roxana. 'Keir – and you? You never told me all this before.'

'I didn't think you were interested.'

'I'm not ...' she resumed her pacing, her arms crossed over her chest, hugging herself. 'How ...' she seemed to have a frog in her throat and cleared it. 'How was that?'

'How was what?' Roxana, her wavy red hair spread out on the counterpane, wagged her right foot in the air. She next regarded her slim ankles and new suede shoes critically.

'How did you two become so pally? You said Paris. I thought you only knew him in Geneva.'

'Oh, that! It all began when I went to his mother's apartment ...'

'Why?'

'I can't remember the exact reason. Maybe about a

dress-fitting.'

'We were fitted for our maid-of-honour dresses in the school sewing-room.'

'I don't know the real reason. Why was I not supposed to go out with him in Paris if he asked me? Does it matter all that much to you?'

'No, of course not. It's your life.'

'Exactly. Anyway, the first time I went to Madame Devlin's apartment in the Avenue de la Paix, I went with Vida and we took tea with her – but you already know all that, because Vida and I told you when you came back late after the Rachmaninov concert. What I never told you was that Keir and I met the following day. We looked around Expo '31 together; it was a Sunday afternoon I remember. I know we were supposed to be a foursome, Roget girls I'm talking about, but Vida and the other two, Anita Marcos and I forget who else, disappeared to meet their boyfriends after I happened to bump into Keir by the fountains. He was trailing around all by himself, and it went from there. He asked me out to dinner. Then, on the night of his mother's wedding when she and her new husband had left for their honeymoon in Lugano, you had gone up to bed, so Keir asked me back to the Avenue de la Paix. He had had a lot of champagne to drink and was feeling a little lonely after his mother's departure. I was also sozzled, and so were Aniseed and l'Impératrice, who never knew what time I hopped over the windowsill of the downstairs bathroom: Lamone left the window open for me. Keir and I made love and ...'

'I really don't want to know any more!' Raven said sharply, not knowing why she felt so let down and so demoralized by what Roxana had just told her. It was nothing to do with Roxana's behaviour, only Keir Devlin's behaviour with her *sister*, of all people! She had imagined him to be a man of principle. 'No wonder you're in trouble, Roxana. You simply can't behave yourself, or stick to one man, can you?'

'That's not altogether my fault: men are fickle and can't be trusted. Besides, every man that I took a fancy to, Vida also wanted. Looking back, it was all subterfuge on Vida's part. Anyway, getting back to the subject of José, Vida became wildly jealous because José and I spent so much time together on that cruise. Then, when we stopped at Martil to drop José off because he had to get back to Tetuan, Vida, very squiffy on champagne, I might add, wanted to have sex with me. The others had gone to the casbah and only Vida and I were left on the yacht.'

'You *and* Vida disgust me Roxana – anyway, how could she? I mean, she hasn't got the parts for it.'

'Precisely.'

'Then how could she want – you know, from you?'

Roxana flung up her hands. 'Oh, most of it can be the same. Touching and kissing and fingers, the sort of thing which can make you feel good without going the whole way. She has this *thingy*.'

'Not another rubber frog! Spare me your childish sense of humour, Roxana!'

'Not a contraceptive thingy, silly, a dildo!'

'What on earth's a dildo?'

'An artificial device to give a woman sexual pleasure without a man being involved.'

'Like her diaphragm you mean?'

'No, not like her diaphragm at all, Raven! That's flat and uninteresting – God, where have you been for the last twenty years? Like a man's you know what.'

'No, I don't know *what*! But I am beginning to understand. You're nothing but a cheap – cheap tart! But your morals are nothing to do with me, I only want to get to the bottom of this José business. What did you do next?'

'I told her I preferred the real thing, and ran a mile – several in fact, back to Tetuan in José's wake. I should have known it years ago.'

'I could have told you that.'

'You could?'

'Yes.'

'And I always thought you were as dim as Purity Virgin. How did you know Vida was a lesbian?'

'I didn't. I never knew about lesbians until Jan told me – her brother Charlie had told her, you see, to look out for 'odd bods' in boarding school.'

'Oh well, that's what I'm trying to tell you – about Vida and her dildo. I never knew about Vida either, until one day she crept into my bed in dormitory two at l'École Internationale and said, "Shall we have a do?" Well, at twelve years or thereabouts, I didn't know what a "do" was until she came on top of me and started messing about. She told me she knew all about sex, because she'd seen her father and his various amours together. Only during these past few weeks have I had the sense to realize that what she was at twelve, she is at twenty.'

'How ghastly. What did you do – when we were twelve, I mean?'

'I pushed her off and told her she was suffocating me. She never liked me for terms and terms after, until – well, until our last year at l'École Internationale, as you well know. And I thought her fatal attractions were Monseigneur Paulus followed by Dr Devlin. How stupid can one be!'

'What happened between you and José when you got back to Tetuan?'

'That was all my fault, and I admit it. When José returned to garrison duty, I went out for a couple of evenings to a nightclub with another officer whom I happened to meet through José himself. Captain Vittorio Broué's half-French, half-Spanish and very nice looking. In fact, he's super. Terribly generous and great fun to be with. But there was nothing serious in our relationship, because he had a wife trailing him around everywhere. She'd even put on purdah just to catch him out in the old casbah with someone else.'

'I don't blame her, with you around.' Raven was angry, annoyed and disgusted with Roxana.

'So I behaved myself and only ever mildly flirted with him, because I didn't want to get myself into trouble with a married man. Keir was different, he was separated from his wife. Anyway, José found out and became very angry, jealous and abusive, because he thought I was sleeping with Vittorio. I lost my temper, flung Jose's ring back at him, told him I never wanted to see him again, and our engagement and marriage were off. And I really meant it. I didn't want to be saddled with a jealous pig-headed husband with no sense of humour: it might not have been so bad had his accusations been true. So I left Tetuan, took a ferryboat to Gibraltar, hitched a lorry-ride over the border into Spain, and caught the train to Paris. That was at the end of July. I had no idea I was starting to pod then, otherwise I'd have kept my mouth shut and stayed put in Tetuan.'

'Is that where you've been these past three months, in Paris?'

'Paris, Rome, Monte Carlo, anywhere with friends – but not if Vida was there. I was thinking of buzzing off for a while to London and then Ireland. I thought of looking Sonny up at Rosscarbery.'

'I don't think the Benedictine monks would have you.'

'True. But I'm still baby-bound and husbandless, and the awful facts won't go away. I'm sorry, too, Raven, about you and José.'

'Don't be. To tell the truth, I was looking for an excuse to get out of the arrangement. Now I've got several. I'll tell Doña Jacqueline, Doña Maria, and Tingalinga that José has very bad eyesight and couldn't tell us apart in the dark, and that's how he managed to get himself engaged to the wrong twin.'

'Why did you agree to marry him, Raven, if you don't love him?'

'I can't remember agreeing to anything. José came home unexpectedly, and I was rather amazed to see him – stumped for words, actually. He at once assumed I was still in love with him and would swoon at his feet the moment he offered me his legionnaire's body backed up by diamonds and sapphires. I was admiring the ring at the time, holding it up to the starlight and not listening to José's moonshine, and I believe the word yes cropped up in connection with my agreeing that yes, I did like the ring when he asked me. That's all. José never listened to what else I had to say and immediately jumped to the wrong conclusion. Some men are so conceited, it's quite incredible. He obviously thought you would never go back to him, so decided to reclaim old second-best, Raven Quennell!'

'I don't think you were ever second-best with José. You were always first, Raven. I'm the one who is second-best.' She gave a rueful little smile. 'But I'm not worried as long as he makes an honest woman of me.' Then she added the finishing Roxana touch, 'That's if you don't want him yourself.'

'Good God, Roxana, what do you take me for?'

'I know that you and José always had a special thing going between you, and that you always thought more of him than any other man who came into your life.'

'Whatever gave you that idea?'

'Then I'm not doing you out of your man?'

'All I want to do to José de Luchar is pull his hair, slap his face, kick him where it hurts most, and tell him what a dirty double-crossing swine he is. But I'll leave that to you now that you have priority claim upon his person. Here's your ring ...' She went and took it out of the dressing-table drawer and handed it to Roxana. 'I hope you'll be very happy with a military man rather than a filmstar, or a playboy Casanova, a prince without a princedom, or even the Grand Duke of Scrumpitania. I hope that you'll enjoy living in a tent in the desert, and now get out of here and leave me in peace. I feel my migraine coming back.'

'Gosh, you're a brick, Raven.' Roxana came to her and, for the first time in her life, put her arms around her in genuine sisterly affection. 'Thanks, Raven, you're a real true warm-hearted Irish Colleen.'

'I'm a real brickhead, Roxa. Now please stop behaving like Vida de Martello and release me.'

As soon as Roxana went out of the room and closed the door behind her, Raven opened the shutters, flung her arms to the waning sun on the sea and smiled at heaven. 'Thank you, God, for saving me from the clutches of that double-crossing, two-faced Nazi called José de Luchar!' Feeling so much better, her migraine miraculously gone, she decided to have a bath.

A few days later, having borrowed Peedee's bicycle, she met José in Toril's main street. He looked very sheepish, pretending he hadn't seen her until she almost ran him down as he crossed the road.

'*Hola*, José!' she said brightly. 'Roxana's back, you know.'

He ignored her facetiousness, for everyone had been aware of the scene between Roxana Quennell and José de Luchar, related via Isaba and Carina on the kitchen grapevine so that the strange case of the double engagement of the Quennell girls to the heir of Vinarosa assumed episodic proportions in and around the estate.

'*Hola*, Raven! What are you doing here?'

'I imagine the same as you, José. Looking for a priest to listen to my confession about leading someone up the garden path. Or were you requiring your friend, Father Gabriel, to turn Roxana into an overnight Catholic before your marriage? And congratulations, too, about your approaching fatherhood. I hope it will be a bonny, bouncing boy who will one day punch you on your double-dealing nose. What did you take me for, José de Luchar?'

'You must let me explain ...'

'Don't bother, Roxana's explained everything. Were you hoping I might never find out whose ring you put on my finger, or were you as blind drunk and short-sighted as I was on the night of your Prodigal Son return? I should have got Jaime to punch you on the nose. Better still, I should have done it myself. When is the wedding?'

'Mother is trying to get it all arranged before the end of my leave in ten days' time.'

'Be good to Roxana, José, or Peedee and I will knock your front teeth out.' She got on the bicycle and started cycling off. José yelled after her:

'Raven, I honestly didn't know about Roxa having my child when I asked you to marry me.'

'That's very obvious,' she shouted over her shoulder. 'But I'm the lucky one.' She rang Peedee's bicycle-bell loudly. 'I was saved by the bell, just in time!' She went whizzing down the hill.

He was not to know that she was referring to the convent bell of the Camillus Order of the Dames of the Blessed Charity, to whom she had just paid a very special visit.

A month later Raven said to Peedee, 'Can I talk to you?'

'In just one moment, dear girl.' He twiddled the knobs of his wireless set. 'The news is on – I just want to listen to the general election results'

Raven fell silent.

'Do you hear that, dear girl? CEDA seem to be gaining

the most seats: Lerroux looks likely to be voted in as Premier in order to keep Gil Robles out. Oh now! Did you hear that? What nonsense!'

Yes, Raven heard it all right: the Left were accusing the Right of rigging votes by counting the dead in the cemetery!

'It looks as though the Left have lost: a blow for Largo Caballero and the Republic. The Catholic Party have gained the most seats, though not an overall majority in the Cortes. The President of the Republic, Alcala Zamora, secretly does not like Gil Robles or his pro-monarchist Falange Party, and so he has asked Lerroux, leader of the Radicals, who are the second largest party, to become Prime Minister. This really is going to put the cat among the pigeons. Don Ruiz, who is more of an orthodox Monarchist than a Carlist *Requeté*, you know, dear girl, is going to have to ask himself that burning question of whether or not he is anti-Republican as well as anti-Fascist.'

Raven was exasperated. Peedee kept pace with Radio Valencia.

'That articulate young barrister and Andalusian playboy, José Antonio Primo de Rivera – have you noticed how all men called José are handsome playboys, Raven? Anyway, this particular José has been at the Nuremberg Rally recently, and has come back full of Hitler propaganda. José de Rivera has won more votes than ever for his new Fascist Party Falange Española. However, we must await the final outcome – Oh, listen, here is Robles himself on behalf of the Right:'

We must conquer Spain – we must give Spain a true unity, a new spirit, a totalitarian policy. It is necessary to defeat Socialism inexorably. We must found a new state, purge the Fatherland of Judaizing Freemasons …

'Oh dear,' said Peedee in response to Gil Robles' voice over the air waves, 'I do believe Don Ruiz is a Freemason: I might be wrong, but he always shakes my hand in a certain way – by the way, something of interest to you, Raven, women of Spain have been given the vote.'

'I'm Irish.'

'So you are. I think, dear girl, the electorate are sick and tired of violence, anarchy, free love, permissiveness, and Godlessness embodied in the burning of crucifixes, and want to return to a more moderate and responsible way of life. I read in the newspaper the other day about an Andalusian priest being fined by the Socialist mayor of the town for having said Mass in public, thus breaking the law. The priest had actually said Mass within his church walls, but because the roof had been burned off by Anarchists the day before, he was accused of conducting his services in the open air. I ask you! Spain has had a military junta since 1923 when General Primo de Rivero, our barrister play-boys's father, instigated his dictatorship with the conni-vance of King Alfonso, it cannot …'

'I'm leaving Cabo Alondra, Peedee.'

He took off his horn-rimmed reading-glasses, laid them on the newspaper in his lap, and looked at her curiously. 'Leaving? Must you?'

'I think so, Peedee.'

'You must do what you feel is right for you, dear girl, but would it be too much to ask where you're going?'

'Not far.'

'Well, that's a blessing. How far?'

'Toril.'

'Toril? The one just down the hill?'

'Yes.'

'But why can't you still live at Cabo Alondra if you wish to teach in Toril? I'm not that much of a nuisance around the house, am I? I do admit to gargling rather loudly first thing in the morning, but I'll tone it down a bit if that is what is upsetting you.'

Raven took a deep breath. The last thing on earth she wished to do was upset him, and she knew that what she was about to say was going to wound Peedee as much as Sonny's departure had done. 'I'm going to live in the Mother House of the Camillus Order of the Dames of the Blessed Charity.'

Peedee's newspaper rustled as he switched off the radio. He sat up straight and stared at her. 'A nun?' he croaked.

'Yes, Peedee.'

'Good God!'

'I'm sorry.' She wasn't sorry at all, but could think of nothing else.

'For how long?'

'All my life. But first Reverend Dame Olivera told me I must spend a year as a postulant while I get used to everything. Then I enter the Novitiate. Some years after that, when the Church thinks I'm ready, I take my final vows.'

'This is disastrous!'

'No, it's not. I want to dedicate the rest of my life to God, Peedee.'

'Dearest girl, can you not reconsider? I do think this is rather a sudden decision which you cannot have thought about at all properly. This business with José and Roxana has obviously upset you more than we all realized. You feel rejected, it is understandable. But please don't become a nun just because Sonny became a monk and Roxana ran off with handsome José de Luchar. One day you'll find someone else, and you'll be glad you never married a Fascist soldier or gave up a decent English husband and a family of your own for the sake of an ebony crucifix or a misshapen ideology. Raven, listen to me, you can't do this! It's – it's running away from life.'

'I've thought a great deal about it, Peedee. It's what I want to do.'

He sank back into his chair, and shook his head. 'No, Raven, not in Spain. Look what happened to the whole clerical order only two short years ago. The burning, looting, and desecration of churches and monasteries, the murder of priests, assaulting of nuns. It is insanity to join the Roman Catholic Church of Spain at this time. It's all happening again at the hands of Anarchists and disbelievers. I will not see your life destroyed in such a fashion without making my views on the subject perfectly clear. I honestly don't think you know what you're doing.'

She had never seen Peedee so worked up, or quite so adamant about preventing her from doing this one thing she most wanted. He had not protested so vociferously when Sonny decided to go to Ireland to join the order of Benedictine monks.

'Please, don't make it harder for me. I'm not destroying my life, I'm preserving it.'

'Poppycock, if you'll forgive my saying so. Raven, for

God's sake, if you're intending to be a nun, then I beg of you, go to Ireland and be near your brother. Don't become a nun in Spain. What you will suffer here will not be martyrdom for your beliefs, but sheer suicide!'

What had Monseigneur Paulus said a few years ago – it took a special kind of courage to be a priest in Spain these days? Well, the same applied to nuns. She would find that special courage despite all Peedee's fears.

However, she did think he was over-reacting to the whole business. 'Peedee, this is not a decision I've made on the spur of the moment, nor one I've taken lightly. I've given it a lot of thought: years, in fact. As far back as my childhood in Dublin, long before Sonny wanted to enter the priesthood, I wanted to be a nun. The day Father Donahoe put into my hand Cassy's gold cross picked out of the ruins of Quennell House, I felt I was being given a special sign by God. It's just that it has taken me this long to find the courage of my convictions, because I didn't want to leave you. Now I must.'

'Sentiment, nothing more, just pure sentiment.' He leaned back in his chair and closed his eyes. 'All my life I've tried to steer clear of two things, religion and politics. Religion and politics destroyed Ireland, and they are going to destroy Spain. Now, once again, I find my past catching up with me. I'm getting too old for shocks like this. I must sleep on it, Raven. I will let you know how I feel about it in the morning.'

She kissed him gently on his freckled forehead. 'Goodnight, Peedee.'

'Goodnight, dear girl.'

PART THREE

In Limbo

'...so he shall never know how I love him, and that not
because he's handsome, Nelly, but because he's more
myself than I am.'

Emily Brontë
Wuthering Heights

CHAPTER EIGHT

Catalonia: October 1934 – April 1935

Raven could make no impression on the hard earth.

Her thoughts were upon her future and not upon what she was supposed to be doing. She felt as though she were back in the glass-bubble existence of Quennell House, disorientated, limbless, and without identity: in limbo.

Drenched in perspiration despite the cold weather, her knee-length postulant's workrobe of heavy black serge chafed horribly as it clung damply to her skin. The tail end of the Levanter whipped dust and sand into her eyes, got under her clothes in gritty particles, and aggravated her sore body. Raven wiped her eyes on her kitchen apron, rested on her hoe, and thought again about Sunday: This Sunday I shall become a bride of Christ and will have renounced the world for ever. I will lose my name and my identity: Miss Ravenna Mealdow Quennell will cease to exist: *Veni Sponsa Cristi.*

Sister Jeanne, arthritic and bent, battled with a stubborn root. She squatted on the ground, her gnarled and crippled hands tugging and pulling with all her might. Her damp habit, chilled by the sharp wind off the sea, caused her old bones to ache miserably. She was a liaison nun, an extern. The vows she had taken were only simple ones, so she provided the contact between the outside world and those nuns who had taken solemn vows. Sister Jeanne lived within the convent walls, and cared for the community of Camillus nuns by undertaking all the odd jobs, opening and answering doors, paying the tradesmen, shopping, and running errands. Raven, for the last four months of her postulancy, had, in turn, been Sister Jeanne's extern.

'In Barcelona,' Sister Jeanne said, 'they're putting everyone in prison after the recent street battles between young Socialists and the Falangist assassination squads.'

Today I must not answer her, even if she tries me to the limit. Yesterday I succumbed to the noonday devil. Tonight I don't want to have to ask myself those questions at the *examen*. Did I keep custody of the eyes today? Have I told any lies today?

'Did you know, my child, the day before yesterday *policia* Albarda discovered his poor nephew with his throat cut?'

Silver-fish, like the origins of man, crawl out of dark damp places: we don't know why or how, only that it *is*: some things are inexplicable, Sister Jeanne. Raven made the sign of the cross over her body.

'Why are you doing that? Are you praying for the soul of Marcos Rodriguez while weeding? *Jesus, Mary, Joseph*, here we have a saint truly called by God! I know about your presecution at the hands of Dame Rosemarie, dear child, but please don't let her trouble you. She's God's cat to everyone. And I won't tell a soul you opened your mouth while gardening, not even Father Gabriel in the confessional. Lord God,' Sister Jeanne muttered resolutely, 'give me strength for this menial, mortal task, for someone will have to do the same for me when my grave is dug in stony ground.'

Here let me do that for you – *I pray, dear Lord, for strength to remove this non-nourishing root from the earth in order that we may plant more onions*; you see, I never even spoke aloud then, and God straightaway answered my prayer, for here is the stubborn root in my hand, Sister Jeanne.

'Thank you, my child, God will bless you. It must have been a truly horrible discovery. The assassins had propped up young Marcos's body against the stone wall of the bullring for everyone to see and take heed. They had gouged out his eyes, slit his throat, and cut out his tongue.'

Please, Sister Jeanne, I'm dying to talk to you, but I have this daily penance to do for one hour every day this week. Only that today I must be silent for *two* hours as yesterday I twice fell from grace and must make up for my double sin of tongue-wagging and disobedience: all on account of Dame Rosemarie who reported me to Postulant Mother for singing and playing the guitar – the communal one from the music-room which is only allowed to be played as a special indulgence on feast days. But this was not a feast day and it was after compline. Please God, forgive me for thinking badly of another nun, and give me, I pray, the gifts of the Holy Spirit such as grace, patience, kindness, and understanding: sorely lacking in so many of us.

'We are cursed with mad, bad men everywhere. I cannot believe that man created in the image of God is so evil he would kill a fellow human being for doing his vigilante duty.'

Not you as well, Sister Jeanne! I have it – used to have it – from Peedee and the whole de Luchar caboodle. I'm simply not interested in what is happening between Republicans and Nationalists, Communists and Fascists, Catholics and Anarchists, the Asturian miners and Catalonian fishmongers.

'I pray every day for the redemption of those green-shirted rich young *escamots* given the power to terrorize innocent people on the streets of Barcelona, Toril, and Vilafranca. It's *unforgiveable* that President Companys should have made that ex-convict and assassin, Badia, who tried to kill King Alfonso, Chief of Police. So now the *escamots* are able to perpetrate their horrible crimes with Badia's blessing. We live in a terrible age, my child. Corruption is rife.'

Yes, Sister Jeanne, that is why I came here. I am beginning to feel, however, that I'm not as safe as I should be.

'Those devils who call themselves the Death and Freedom Brigade gave me the fright of my life the other day. I was buying tomatoes in the market for Dame Rosemarie, who had run out in the middle of making chutney. They roared past me in their big, rusty motor car with no roof, poked fun at my twisted shape and almost snatched off my head-dress. And the racket they made! Hooting, blowing, whistling, jeering, screaming obscenities, and throwing fire-bombs into the crowd gathered in the plaza. It was disgusting!'

Oh, that must have been simply awful, Sister Jeanne! I, too, must have all my hair cut off when I profess my vows, so I would hate anyone to snatch off my veil after next Sunday.

'His mother is a widow you know – Señora Albarda's sister, Pilar Rodriguez. She lives in Vilafranca. Marcos was her only child. He was only twenty-two years old. He used to be in my class, years ago, when I was at the Convent of the Sacred Heart in Vilafranca.'

I wonder what it would be like to have a deep and meaningful sexual relationship with a man. Now I suppose I shall never know as José has married Roxana and I am the spinster sister left on the shelf. Get thee behind me Satan ... I must not think about men any more. But why do I keep thinking about *him* quite often recently, Dr Keir? Especially after what Roxana told me about having been to bed with him. That should have put me right off him, not made me think about him all the more. Perhaps I am too ugly and tame for him. Perhaps he prefers redheads. Perhaps I'm not in my right mind.

'Dear child, you are not listening to me. What are you thinking, with that deep, faraway look in your eyes?'

I don't *blame* him for making love to Roxana, Sister Jeanne. I'm only jealous. I wonder why I should be jealous, Sister Jeanne? After all, this is a new feeling that has crept up on me since he left for Gautemala. Am I going mad, do you think? The madness that sometimes comes upon a lonely woman left on the shelf so that she begins to fantasize about *any* man?

'You have a *very* mysterious look about you sometimes, my child. The look an old man might have when he broods over past wars in which he was a hero. A cool detachment from life that sets you apart from the world so that no one knows what is going on behind those smoky grey eyes of yours. You will make a good Mother Superior one day, I am sure of it.'

When he sat next to me at the Rachmaninov concert and the music was flowing all around us, somehow I couldn't breathe, because all my thoughts were pinpointed on him and upon his hands holding the programme for me to see, so that I couldn't see a thing apart from dizzy spots in front of my eyes. I wonder why? It wasn't anything to do with starting a migraine. You see, I was madly in love with a golden priest at that time, so why should I have felt this way about another man? Am I as fickle as Roxana? I don't think so. I really can't explain it, Sister Jeanne, but it was as though there were an unspoken chord between Keir and me that had nothing and everything to do with Opus 30.

'Spain is dead!'

No Sister Jeanne, I don't believe it is. I believe it's only just awakening. Raven screwed up her eyes tightly, her lips firmly pressed together. Then she opened her eyes and fiercely reattacked the stony ground with the hoe. Why are we doing this I wonder? No vegetables will grow in this impoverished soil that has been overtilled for donkey's years. It's about time the Church of Rome sent we poor Camillus nuns of Lellis some fertilizer. I wonder if I should write to Monseigneur Paulus about it? But then, Reverend Dame Olivera might not like my going over her head. Next time I see Jaime while I'm out shopping in Toril for Dame Rosemarie, I'll ask him for some squeezed pips and stalks from the leftovers of the grape harvest that make fertilizer. Poor Marcos Rodriguez. Why did those young thugs take out their revenge on him? He couldn't help what he was, he was only doing his duty. He looked so harmless – although gormless would be a better description. I rather think he had his eyes on me and not on his duty that day on the beach during that long, hot summer when José ran off to become a legionnaire. No matter. Marcos was a decent enough chap with his sad brown eyes. Besides, I would rather *he* looked at me any day, instead of Dame Annunciata in the Infirmary. No one is safe these days, not even in a convent.

'Why aren't you talking to me, Raven? You're only a postulant you know. You don't *have* to be quite so hard on yourself. You won't burn in hell forever for disobeying the rules. Not until after you take your vows on Sunday. Have I done something to offend you?'

No, not you, Sister Jeanne, never you. Yesterday I broke my initial penance of silence, because Dame Rosemarie came out into the kitchen garden to ask for spring onions and I told her there were none as yet, this being October. I wonder why Dame Rosemarie dislikes me so much and is always trying to trap me into breaking my vows? It's like a game with her. I know the penalities will be far greater after Sunday when I disobey the rules. But Dame Rosemarie should *not* have asked me anything when she knew very well I was supposed to keep my mouth shut – I mean keep silent, between twelve and one o'clock – two o'clock today.

'You will love little Madre Estelle Calmar when you go to live with her in the Novice Cloister. She is gentle as a kitten, a truly saintly woman. The novices all adore her.'

Yes, Madre Estelle is more of a pet than either Dame Rosemarie, or Dame Annunciata, who is more like a lynx than a kitten and likes rubbing one's back with methylated spirit and talcum powder. She was the other one who got me into trouble with Postulant Mother at the beginning of this week, hence all this extra silence imposed upon me. Dame Annunciata asked me to sing, and play the guitar to cheer up Dame Barnabas dying of an unknown disease in the Infirmary. I had to obey the rules, Sister Jeanne, for Dame Annunciata is Infirmary Mother, and she wanted me to take poor Dame Barnabas's mind off her pain and miseries. But the request was made during profound silence and so I didn't know what to do: I was in a great spiritual dilemma. Music seems to revive Dame Barnabas no end, so that she forgets about her terrible pain. She loves to hear an old Spanish melody from her youth, 'Juanita', and will even hum while I strum. It was after that, Dame Rosemarie reported me: not just once either, but twice, for breaking the rule of silence. I seem to be getting into awful trouble these days on account of some of the older nuns who are testing my strength and faith beyond endurance – including yourself, Sister Jeanne.

'Did you listen to the radio last night?'

No, I did not, Sister Jeanne! I went to bed after compline because my back was breaking after working hard in the garden all week. Dame Annunciata again wanted to rub me up the wrong way with methylated spirit but this time I firmly refused. I also felt a migraine coming on. I had no wish to let her know that, not after the first time I was laid up in the Infirmary soon after I came here. Dame Annunciata, you see, likes touching. She won't keep her hands off her patients. Neither do I find it easy to wake up at two o'clock in the morning to have my breakfast: but I love reciting the vigils once I'm awake.

'We were in Reverend Dame Olivera's house last evening, listening to the broadcast from Philip the Second's Monastery at El Escoril, where the Catholic Action Youth Movement held their rally. It was sleeting in Escoril – we'll get it soon. Everyone was chanting, *Jefé! Jefé! Jefé!* just like the Italians with, *Duce! Duce! Duce!* Then their leader, Gil Robles, got up and said that he had an army of citizens willing to give up their lives for Spain, and that power would soon be theirs. Reverend Dame Olivera didn't switch him off as some of the republican Sisters wanted her to. She said the right-wing parties and the pro-Monarchists, the *latifundistas* like our own Don Ruiz de Luchar, are the only ones who will save Spain from irreligion and revolution.'

I not only love the vigils, I love *Veni Creator Spiritus* which makes my toes curl with the majesty of the music. I'm sure that's why Sonny became a priest, for the holy music. And Sonny has a wonderful voice. I'm glad he has become a chorister. I thought nuns weren't supposed to take sides, Sister Jeanne? I know they do, but they shouldn't!

'Don Ruiz de Luchar and the Church between them own all this land around here. His mother, Doña Maria, and I went to school together, right here in the convent school. We sat next to each other in class, but she was always so much better off and better connected than I. Her father was Mayor of Toril. When she married Don Ruiz's father, the old grandee, everyone thought she had done very well for herself – which of course she had. She still remembers me, though, and often sends word from the Mas Luchar asking me to come and chat to her about the old days. But I simply don't have the time, what with Dame Rosemarie and her everlasting chutneys. I told her she ought to market some on behalf of we poor nuns and then perhaps we could afford some new tea-towels.' Sister Jeanne crossed herself. 'I hear Ramiro has become a Communist. Thank goodness he's not an Anarchist or a Falangist. They are truly the violent ones, always blowing up people and trains.'

Sister Jeanne, you are not supposed to think about the world. Why must you dwell on the macabre the whole time? At your age you should be growing old gracefully by leading a quiet, cloistered life of beatitudes, doxology, and infallibility, not bombs, cut-throats, and politics. I came here to get away from such things. I want to live in peace and quiet, prayer and meditation, do you understand that, Sister Jeanne?

'I don't know where we poor nuns would be if we didn't have the Catholic Monarchist parties to stand between ourselves and total anarchy. Why, only three or four years ago, a wave of such hatred against the Church of Rome swept this country. It was an Armageddon just like Tragic Week thirty years ago. It's happening all over again. I don't know why the workers and peasants hate us so much. I remember Tragic Week very clearly – that was way back before you were born. They disinterred the corpses of nuns from convent cemeteries and paraded them through the streets of Barcelona. I myself was forced to witness a dear old saintly sister who was with me in the Convent of the Sacred Heart, dug up before my very eyes by the leftist-workers and given to the local schoolchildren to play with. She was mocked by the mob and none of us could do anything about it. Poor dead soul in her rotting habit and shroud, bones and teeth all to show that she was ever human.'

Why are you telling me all this, Sister Jeanne? Are you trying to make me see the error of my ways before Sunday?

'The radio broadcasts are so interesting these days. Much better than reading the newspapers. I'm almost blind, you see, dear child, but I'm not deaf as yet. In the old days we were kept very much an ignorance without the modern conveniences you young people enjoy today. No motor cars, no telephones, no gramaphones, no aeroplanes.'

No CEDA, no POUM, no JONS.

'That old reprobate himself, Lerroux, cannot govern the Republic any more, because everyone's in prison.'

Ramiro too, Sister Jeanne. Carlos has taken his place at the Fabrica de Luchar, disgusted because he can't fly his little aeroplanes any more. I can see him threatening a walk-out, too, very soon. Don Ruiz has this habit of upsetting his sons without meaning to. I am sure Carlos will be much more of a loving son winging his way over the Pratt aerodrome, than tied to a loom all day. It's just like ten little nigger boys disappearing one after another.

'Neither is Luis Companys President of the Generalidad any more. He's in prison along with everyone else. Serves him right for putting a villain like Badia in charge of the police force. Now the General Union of Workers have called a mass strike. It's all *very* unsettling to one of my age, who has seen it all before and knows what's coming.'

Please do shut up, Sister Jeanne – ye gods! Oh dear, *mea culpa, mea culpa, mea culpa*! Postulant Mother told me I must learn to control my thoughtless tongue: although, in this instance, I suppose it's my tongueless thoughts getting the better of me.

'All this Catalonian left-of-centre, and Castillan right-of-centre politics is highly confusing to one of my age. It shouldn't be. I used to teach social history and religion to my students in Vilafranca when I was a young lady before I became a nun. But even Reverend Dame Olivera, who is clever enough to have a degree in everything, says she does not understand Spanish politics any more.'

Who does, Sister Jeanne? And how can someone have a degree in everything? Reverend Dame Olivera is Portuguese with a degree in theology and the Pastoral Epistles of Paul, Timothy, and Titus, so she wouldn't know much about CEDA or POUM or CNT, would she? I am frightened, and there is no one to hear me, least of all you, Sister Jeanne, who just love to put the wind up me with all your horrible tales from the past. I came here to be safe, but there is no safe place left in the world: Barcelona and Madrid, just like Dublin and Belfast all over again.

'They say the tortures one party inflicts upon another are truly barbaric. Men go mad in prison just listening to their neighbour being mutilated in the next cell.'

I know the feeling, Sister Jeanne. Especially when Postulant Mother, in the cell next to mine, chastizes herself daily with a leather strap for being too harsh on me. If she feels so bad about it, then she shouldn't give me profound silence every five minutes. I *hate* profound silence more than any other penance. I don't even mind cleaning the toilets as much as having to hold my tongue. When I'm not allowed to speak, I start thinking. And sometimes my thoughts deserve an even greater penance than speaking at the wrong time. But I know I must learn tolerance as well as grace: I'm trying my best. At seventy-eight, I will probably be just like you or even worse. I know you're only trying to be kind by keeping me from breaking my vow of silence by chattering nineteen to the dozen, so that I can't get a word in edgeways, but I wonder if your lack of tact was the reason why the Church kept you as an external nun all your life?

'Nuns and priests were tortured all through Tragic Week. They would push rosary beads into one's ears until the eardrums burst. Or they would pour holy wine down one's nose into one's lungs until one choked to death or drowned – it never happened to me, otherwise I wouldn't be here now telling you about it. But many of our poor nuns were martyred by the Republic for the Republic. It was a terrible time for us. Some nuns went quite mad.'

Marcos, Marcos – et tu, Ramiro! I never thought I'd ever feel sorry for a murderer of fieldmice. I hope they don't pin him to a cactus plant in order to make him change his mind about Stalinist, Marxist, or Trotskyist politics. He'll probably go to Russia if he ever gets out of prison. But I mustn't think about what Ramiro might be suffering – if what you say, Sister Jeanne, is true. Somehow I think you imagine a great deal because you are old and forgetful, and sometimes downright annoying. I have my own tortures to think about. Postulant Mother reproached me severely yesterday and we went through the whole rule-book all over again: blind obedience, self-denial, discipline, custody of the senses, and perfect self-control. I ask myself during *examen*, am I here because I've been called by God? Am I here for Christ's sake or Mary's or my own? I am still waiting for divine inspiration, Sister Jeanne.

'It's all so different from the old days. If Queen Isabella had behaved herself in the first place, and hadn't decided to confess her sins whilst in bed with her confessor, they wouldn't have got rid of her to put Bourbon puppets on the throne of Spain. Why do you want to be a nun, Raven? You're such a clever, pretty girl, you ought to get married to a good, wholesome Catholic man, not the Church of Rome. You can still be a good Catholic as a wife and mother who will bring up her children to be good Catholics in their turn. There is still time, you know, to change your mind. I was talking to your grandfather outside the bullring the other morning where he does his *ban bullfighting* campaigning. He's heartbroken because of your sudden decision to become a nun.'

It wasn't sudden. I have been chosen by God, Sister Jeanne. Someone chosen by God cannot change their mind. Three years ago a handsome, saintly man kissed me in the sacristy and forever nailed me to the cross of holy frisson. FL – Forbidden Love, Sister Jeanne, as taboo as PF – Personal Friendships – and now I shall have to reveal my sins at the next Chapter of Faults, for, while standing here silently hoeing this piece of holy ground, I have already broken all the rules in the book while committing many more sins, adultery in the mind being as bad as adultery in the bed. I have lacked understanding; I have been guilty of impure and unkindly thoughts; I have lacked perfect self-control, and my senses have not been under strict custody. I am also weak and cowardly, for if Postulant Mother imposes upon me another profound silence today, I think I'll go mad listening to her mortifying her flesh for being harsh with me; if I'm not already mad.

'After your Reception, my child, you'll find it harder than ever to come to terms with yourself. The temptation to cling to a particular person, a sister, or a father-confessor, who are there only to influence one's religious formation without providing the comfort that all human beings, including nuns, sometimes crave, can be lonely and unsettling.'

You are speaking from experience, I take it, Sister Jeanne? How many years ago did you have a particular friendship? And was it with a priest or a nun? But don't worry, I'm a heterosexual woman. I first fell in love at the age of six with Cathal Swilly, Butler, who used to let me slide down the staircase at Quennell House on his large silver butler's tray. He also gave me all the newspapers to read when they were inexorably destined for the shoe-cupboard. Then I fell in love with Mr William Butler Yeats, who was a poet and a member of the White Magic Circle. But I was too young for him. Then came Monseigneur Paulus in my adolescent years, and José about the time a female is supposed to blossom. They say a girl never forgets her first kiss or her first love. I will never forget José, for it was rather a shock to my sixteen-year-old system to have my underwear and anatomy suddenly under scrutiny on the dank floor of the Caverna Rosa. Then, of course, there was dear Jaime, very briefly, last year. I don't suppose I can really count Dr Keir Devlin, because he never stayed in one place long enough to become trapped by another woman. He's a separated married man, you see, Sister Jeanne, guilty of a matrimonial offence in the eyes of God and the Church for being a runaway Catholic.

'What you must guard against, my child, is the rule governing particular friendships. It is so easy to succumb to temptation and desire.'

Yes, I know. I keep thinking about him more and more often when I shouldn't. So you see, Sister Jeanne, how I keep on getting myself into the wrong kind of situation where men are concerned? I'm a born loser of lovers, whereas my twin sister, Roxana, hasn't a conscience-stricken cell in her whole body and always gets the man she wants.

'One must not get close to anyone except God, lest we lose custody of our senses.'

I adore God, truly Sister Jeanne; He's the only one who ever listens to me. Sometimes He even answers my prayers – though more often than not He also gives me what I don't ask for. And the only time I can truthfully admit to having lost custody of the senses, apart from this week, was at l'École Internationale. I drank champagne with Dr Devlin and he held me tight while we danced 'The Blue Danube', and I felt so secure and contented in his arms I wanted to stay there for ever and think about nothing except Monseigneur Paulus ... Keir was such a *nice* man, I used to think, until he seduced my sister. There I was in my peachy, flowered, chiffon, figure-hugging dress with drooping sleeves, so that I knew I looked nice under my summery picture-hat, because he said so, and I lost. I came in second – or third or fourth or fifth: I don't even remember because I was intoxicated by Monseigneur Paulus and his catechism at the time, and so I went off up to bed and left Keir to dance with the rest of Mat Group, including Roxa. It was then that I lost him to my sister.

'Before you came into the convent, Raven, did you ever have a particular relationship with anyone?'

It was of no particular benefit to anyone, because it was all over before it had properly started, that was *my* particular friendship, Sister Jeanne. Standing beside a wedding-cake – Keir's mother's, not mine – out of which a big chunk had just been sliced, crumbs of fruit cake and marzipan between us, he said that weddings were pretty things if you yourself weren't involved. I wonder what he meant by that? And I wonder what he's doing now? I don't suppose I shall ever know. I don't suppose I'll ever see him again.

'A deep, meaningful adult relationship, dear child, is like dying inside a honeycomb.'

Gooey and painful you mean? When you look up at me like that from the ground, your eyes round and childlike behind those ridiculously old-fashioned pebble-lenses of yours, are you asking me that question out of simplicity or sensuality? Supposing I said yes, Sister Jeanne? Would you ask me to describe what went on in the Caverna Rosa one summer when José put his hand inside my cycling-shorts before trying to insert himself into places even I cannot reach? I can't really tell you much more than the kissing of the aureola bud bit, because I ran away. If you are left wondering about sex and seduction, Sister Jeanne, so am I, and I am a quarter of your age – a mere child in this game of holy love, sexual love, and profane love. But I am still a virgin, if that's what you want to know. If ever I fall in love, *real* love, not the petty fumbling-and-fiddling sex that boys indulge in, and José was an *immature youth* when I come to think of it, I'll let you know how it feels. However, I don't suppose there's much time left between now and Sunday.

'Dear child, I used to dream a lot when I was younger. Sometimes they were naughty dreams that would make me feel very peculiar the moment I woke up, *dripping* with anxiety. I was wracked with guilt, and wondered if, through talking and thrashing in my sleep, the other nuns would find out what was going on in my tortured mind and would report me to Reverend Mother. I would lie flat on my face in self-mortification all through the night, stretched out on the cold stone floor in front of the chapel altar, just to avoid going to bed and dreaming.'

You're lucky, Sister Jeanne, to be able to wake up again at your age after such bad dreams. But I know what you mean. Sometimes I dream of a man in a tartan shirt, red socks, and brown brogues taking his shirt, socks and shoes off. I dream of his strong athletic body wrapped around mine and I dream of him loving me in a way to make my heart stop, because it cannot cope with all the feelings and emotions God has put into one complicated lump of muscle and blood – and I'm talking about my heart now. But there is no substance, Sister Jeanne, no reality, no climax to our love-making, for when he kisses me we are both lifeless creatures captured for ever inside a glass bubble of a fantasy world, where, out of a clear blue sky, a snowstorm rages across a garden full of summer flowers. Am I making sense to you, Sister Jeanne?

'Once, long ago, when I was straight and firm and untwisted by arthritis and rheumatism, my Novice Mistress undressed me, undressed herself, and then touched me in a very personal place. Then she made me take a cold bath with her. The cold baths continued, but she never again touched me in that certain place. It was her way of exorcizing her innermost devils. She would look at my undressed figure longingly, but never again succumbed to the sin of touching. But she aroused in me my own devils by those looks and that first touch of hers: and, from those days of cold baths and self-denial from all physical contact, I sleep with both wrists tied to the crucifix above my bed.'

Oh my God – *poor, poor you, Sister Jeanne*! What torture! Suddenly, we are not talking about love and human relationships any more, but the absurdity of life! What am

I doing here? Is this what goes on in every Mother House throughout the land? How does Sonny cope with frustrated Benedictine monks? Is he one himself? Dear God, what would Peedee think I've got myself into? Is this a temptation of the Devil who is trying to sidetrack me from taking my vows on Sunday? I have come here to dedicate my life to God, and yet I have thought more about men and sexual involvement than at any other time in my life. Am I like Roxana, after all? Is there a latent lust in me that requires exorcizing by cold baths? I thought I'd said goodbye to the Vidas of this world when I left l'École Internationale: it appears not, for where one or two are gathered together, there shall one find another de Martello, sometimes several together.

'Dear child, are you ill? You've gone quite pale. What is the matter, you look as if you've seen a ghost?'

I wish we could have made real love just once so that I knew what it felt like before dying without knowing what life was all about. I said LIFE, the bit between living and dying. What life, with whom? HIM! The casually-dressed, mature, masculine man in the tartan shirt, red socks and brown brogues sitting on a park bench reading a newspaper while the breeze off Lac Léman ruffled his hair. He looked so – so attractive, so – detached, and interesting, lonely, too – so kind, so lost, and so haunted! I don't mean to romanticize or fantasize about him, Sister Jeanne, that would be an insult to his and my intelligence: besides, I don't really know him. It's just that I wonder sometimes why God puts temptation in our way and then says, *thou shalt not*! That's rather cruel, isn't it? I mean, look at you with your hands tied to your crucifix while you sleep. It isn't really fair, is it, Sister Jeanne, to create us with emotions and sexuality only to deny us experimenting with them? It wouldn't matter about cold baths if only – if only – Oh dear God! Does everyone get into a panic about their wedding-day? I don't think I want to be a spouse of Christ. I think I'd prefer to marry Dr Keir Devlin, who is much more human – and I think I'm going to faint any minute now …

'Dear child, you're muttering to yourself. Speak up, dear.'

Raven sank down on her heels, and doubled over with the agonizing pain that shot through her, from the tips of her breasts, right down her legs, gripping her in the place of the immaculate conception, which Sister Jeanne had unwittingly invoked by all her talk concerning particular friendships. She squatted for a moment with her face between her knees until the iron fist of unrequited love was removed from her gut. Convent bells were chiming Nones, summoning them to afternoon prayer – or was she hearing God calling her again? Joan of Arc hearing voices and bells, God in mortal shirt and shoes, the breeze ruffling his hair, trying to make himself heard through the drumming in her erotic ears: was she just another oversexed Joan of Arc seeking to belong to an over zealous holy army because she was miffed with the world and out to prove she didn't care? Was she another Roxana, hatched from the same egg? She shook her head to clear her senses and spoke. 'Sometimes – I think I'm going crazy – what was I talking about, Sister Jeanne?'

'Something about feeling faint and needing a cold bath. Have you one of your bad headaches, dear?'

'Yes, Sister Jeanne.'

'Poor child. Anyway, you managed to get through two hours of total silence, and made up for yesterday's fall from grace, so now you may talk freely until we get to the chapel.'

But Raven did not feel like talking to anyone any more, least of all herself. She felt drained; drained of energy, and drained of life. Raven closed her eyes: was profound silence always to be like solitary confinement? Were self-discipline and total custody of the senses always to be a prison-sentence to drive her insane? Don't think about the years ahead, just think about Sunday, she told herself. She wanted to get quickly inside the cool, dark chapel, where the smell of incense and the peace and serenity of the Marian devotions and the Gregorian chants exorcized her inner devils. She wanted to prostrate herself full-length on the floor, her face on the cold, ancient flagstones before the altar, just like Sister Jeanne all those long, lonely years ago: *mea culpa, mea culpa, mea culpa*! I am guilty for thinking about a man I should not be thinking about, and not only thinking, but wishing to seduce him when I should be concentrating on becoming a bride of Christ: *Veni Sponsa Cristi*.

Raven was relieved to know that the angelic voices issuing over the garden wall for the past two hours were definitely earthly voices. The choir was practising in preparation for her Reception Day. She lived for the music, she would die for the psalms, they restored her faith in herself and in those around her. She rehearsed the whole scene over and over again in her mind: she would be dressed in Doña Jacqueline's wedding-dress, borrowed for the occasion of her Reception into the Roman Catholic Church. The Bishop of Vilafranca and Toril would stand before the monstrance with Father Gabriel beside him. The Bishop would intone *Veni Creator Spiritus*. Then he would bless her habit, and those of the two Spanish novices who were to share her Reception Day as brides of Christ. Then Father Gabriel would give the sermon and itemize the vows she had to take: vows of poverty, obedience, and chastity. She would repeat them: detachment from things, detachment from self, detachment from persons. Then the Bishop would ask her what she wanted and she would reply that she wanted to take the habit above all else.

After she had renounced the vanities of the world and had promised to live by the rules of the Community of the Dames of the Blessed Charity, she would receive her novice's habit, which was already laid out in Madre Estelle's linen-room: a robe of white linen, white guimpe, the starched cloth covering neck and shoulders; the cincture, a cord belt to gather the habit around her waist, scapular, a short grey cloak worn over her habit, covering the shoulders at the back and at the front; novice's white veil and strange winged head-dress of the Camillus Order of Lellis. Black shoes and stockings, and of course, plain white unfashionable underclothes. Her crucifix and rosary of the decades of Paternosters, Aves, and Glorias, would complete her wardrobe.

After her shoulder-length hair had been cut to the scalp by Madre Estelle, revealing the ugly scars on her head and forehead, she would don her habit and return to the chapel to receive her new name; she wondered what it would be. Suspice would follow, the most solemn prayer of all in the Mass, symbolizing 'Receive'. Bread and wine would be changed into the body and blood of Christ. Then, and only then, would she be able to meet and talk with the friends and relations who had promised to attend her Reception Day: Peedee, Doña Jacqueline, Doña Maria, Tía Leah, and Nina. Don Ruiz had said he would if he could. Jan Fairchild, now Mrs Archibald Cunningham, had also promised to come, provided she and her husband were not hosting some social function at the British Embassy in Paris.

But the person Raven most longed to see was Sonny, now Brother Bernard. He and his confessor, Father MacCree, were in Spain, not solely for her Reception Day, for she doubted Sonny would have been granted permission to come all the way from Ireland just for that. According to Peedee, on the last visiting Sunday she had spoken to him, Sonny and Father MacCree were on a special ecclesiastical mission arranged by the Church of Rome. When Peedee had told her all this, Raven suspected Monseigneur Paulus's invisible hand somewhere in this arrangement, though she did not know the details of the mission. Sonny and Father MacCree would reside at the Benedictine monastery at Montserrat, thirty miles way.

To know that Sonny was already at Montserrat was a deeply comforting thought, and Raven could not wait to see him in three days' time. Roxana, of course, would not be coming. Her baby daughter, christened Pauline Inés, diminutive Pippa, was only six months old, and it would be far too much of an upheaval for mother and child to travel all the way from Tetuan, just to attend her Reception into the Catholic Church. *Besides*, Roxana had written, *I don't approve of your becoming a Roman Catholic nun. It's a stupid thing to do and you'll regret it one day.*

After Sunday Raven knew her life would be inexorably changed. She would live in the Novice House in another part of the convent with Madre Estelle and the other novices. Her jaunts into Toril on behalf of the Camillus nuns would come to an end. She would only be able to see Peedee for two hours a month on visiting Sunday, for she would be forbidden all contact with the outside world, unless Reverend Dame Olivera decided to send her into the community as a teacher, nurse, or welfare worker. That did not seem very likely for several years yet: at least not until she had learned self-discipline and total custody of the senses.

Sister Jeanne laid aside her trowel. 'Come child, let's go and refresh ourselves with some lemonade. I'm parched after all this hard labour in such a biting wind.' Sister Jeanne struggled to get up off the ground.

Raven did not extend a helping hand to assist Sister Jeanne. Personal contact between nuns, unless forced by circumstance, was forbidden. She, instead, collected up the gardening tools and put them away in the shed, while Sister Jeanne struggled with her infirmities.

Raven followed Sister Jeanne's bowed figure along the thyme path back to the kitchen adjoining the Infirmary. 'Carob-beans, carob-beans, carob-beans,' sang Sister Jeanne in her thin, wavery voice. 'Carob bee ...' her voice faded away into silence when she saw Dame Rosemarie rushing towards them.

Dame Rosemarie, who supervised all the housekeeping in the convent, was not actually running, for that was strictly forbidden within the cloister, but she was certainly moving fast. Her long grey habit worn by fully-professed nuns was tugged at by the strong winds from the sea, and the gull-wings of her white head-dress flapped and lifted in the air so that she resembled nothing so much as a ruffled grey bat: 'There you both are – why aren't you two already at prayers? Reverend Dame Olivera wants us all in the chapel immediately.'

'Why?' asked Sister Jeanne who never let anything or any one ruffle her, least of all Dame Rosemarie who was half her age. She took off her steamy glasses and wiped them on her scapular before replacing them. She peered short-sightedly at Dame Rosemarie. 'Reverend Dame Olivera, who is habitually unpunctual herself, is not usually so fussy about time.'

'She wishes to organize relief operations. Once again we are asked by God to play our role as the Dames of the Blessed Charity. I am to be part of the team that is to go to Asturias, praise be to God.' Dame Rosemarie, crossed herself. 'Reverend Dame Olivera is sending a body of nuns to help the wounded and the refugees during the emergency ...'

'What emergency?'

'No, I don't suppose you've heard the news as you've been in the garden all morning. It was on the wireless just now: the President put one of his insignificant little generals in charge of this striking Austrian miners business. In order to stop the revolution from the north spreading across Spain, this Fascist general – I believe his name is Franco – yesterday ordered in Moroccan troops as well as the Spanish legionnaires of the Army of Africa. They sent tanks and aeroplanes from Tetuan. Oviedo has been bombed. Oh, those poor working-class miners and their families! As though starving the labourers and peasants to death hasn't been enough, they are now bombing people out of their homes. Come sisters, let us go and pray for the souls of the living and the dead, and that all this insanity might soon end.'

I must not pay attention to the world and its problems. I must forget about Dublin and Belfast, about Barcelona and Madrid, about Oviedo. I must not think about the Lithuanian refugees and the Jewish pogroms of Russia, Poland and Germany. I must think only about this Sunday when I shall renounce the world for ever to become a bride of Christ. I must not think about Keiren Hunter Devlin. I must think only about myself – and about God of course. I will lose my name and my identity: Miss Ravenna Mealdow Quennell will cease to exist; she will become as obsolete as any refugee dependent upon God's will: '*Veni Sponsa Christ*: Come Spouse of Christ.'

She looked at him in utter amazement. 'You can't really be serious, Archie Cunningham!'

'Life and death serious, I'm afraid.'

'Whose life and death?'

'Yours and mine – and a whole continent of people.'

'What people?'

'European people.'

'Oh! I'm not really hearing this! Did Jan put you up to this?'

'Good Lord, no!'

'Does she know anything about it?'

'No. And don't ever tell her. This is strictly between ourselves.'

'I thought so. Who is behind all this, Archie?'

'I can't say.'

'But you would risk *my* life. Why?'

'Because you are *perfect*, my dear. You speak Spanish like a native, you know the country well, and nobody would suspect a thing.'

'So, you've already checked up on me: I don't like that, Archie. It makes me feel *very* nervous and angry.' And in that moment, too, she even forgot about custody of the senses.

'There is no risk involved, I assure you. Holy cloth is easy to buy – especially when it's Spanish.'

'Utterly ludicrous, Archie! I've dedicated my life to God! *Inside* convent walls.'

'Walls have ears, *especially* convent walls.' He jingled some coins in the pockets of his dark, striped, ill-fitting suit, and grinned like an outsize schoolboy. Archie's pale, rather heavy face and vague washed-out blue eyes did not fool her for an instant. 'I know I can depend on you to er – gather ye posies along the way as I – er, believe you are an expert people-spotter?'

From under her novice's white head-dress, Raven eyed Jan's very British husband in alarm. 'What has my grandfather been saying to you?'

'Nothing. Fascinating telescope he has at Cabo Alondra. Jan just loves the house; fascinating place.'

'Archie Cunningham, don't you *dare* get my grandfather involved in any of your British tactics, either!'

'Never entered my head.'

'The answer is no, Archie. I have just become a nun and a nun I intend to remain. I wouldn't be able to live with myself if I did as you ask.'

'Well, you know where to find me if you ever want two strings to your bow, my dear Raven – I beg your pardon, Sister Justina.'

*

Six months later, Reverend Dame Olivera sent for Sister Justina.

Wondering what she had done wrong now, Sister Justina knelt before Reverend Dame Olivera's office desk, head bowed, eyes upon the cool tiles.

With a calm dignified grace, Reverend Dame Olivera rose from the beautifully carved Castillan chair that complimented her heavy, dark oak desk, and went and stood before the young woman who used to be called Raven, and who, to all intents and purposes, would still be called Raven by the people who had known her all her previous life.

With a wise and discreet smile, Reverend Dame Olivera placed her two hands on the novice's white veil. A gold wedding-band on her left hand glinted in the sunlight shafting through the high arched window in front of her. 'Bless you my child. Don't look so afraid. You may get up off your knees and sit in that chair over there so that I can see your face while we talk. I would like to know how you are coping with your formation.'

Reverend Dame Olivera (also called Reverend Mother by her nuns) resumed her place behind her desk.

Raven, on the low, straight-backed, plain wooden chair, felt uncomfortable. For a novice to be asked to sit in front of Reverend Dame Olivera was an indulgence one received rarely. Either that, or she was politely being discharged from the convent, Madre Estelle Calmar no doubt having told Reverend Mother that Sister Justina was not a suitable candidate for the Church, and would never make it to her final vows as she was a real Doubting Thomas. 'I am – finding it hard, Reverend Mother.' She bit her lip, her eyes downcast upon her hands, which she tried to hold still in her lap without fidgeting, as Madre Estelle had instructed her; it was called custody of the senses.

'That is a good sign, my child. The harder a task, the more one must devote oneself to master that task before it masters us. There is no gain without pain. There is no joy or appreciation in anything unless it is striven for. As Christ struggled with His conscience in the Garden of Gethsemane, so must we, and, in taking up the burden of the cross, bought salvation, so must we. Now then, I asked you to come here to see me, for a twofold reason. I have a special little task for you and Dame Concepción which necessitates your going outside these four walls for a few days at a time.'

Raven's heart lurched with excitement, then she took custody of her senses. To get away from convent walls for a little while should not be generating in her such a sense of relief, as though she were being let out on parole. She had become a nun voluntarily, no one had pressed her to become one. She had wanted to shut herself off from the world and its bombs, so why was she so pleased to hear these words from Reverend Dame Olivera, who was about to throw her back into the real world? Was this God's will, His mysterious way of working through her? Or the Devil's way through Archie Cunningham?

'I think that you and Dame Concepción are the two nuns in this convent most suited for the task I have in mind, as a complete grasp of several languages, especially English, is absolutely vital. The Bishop has approved my choice. We are not the only convent who have been approached by those in higher authority to do this thing. Many other religious houses throughout the Republic have been asked to cooperate in the survival of the Roman Catholic Church in Spain. Therefore, you and Dame Concepción have been chosen to become smugglers for the Church of Rome.'

'*Smugglers*, Reverend Mother? Did you say *smugglers*?'

Reverend Dame Olivera smiled at Sister Justina's expression. 'Well, perhaps that over-dramatizes the role a little. What we have been asked to do is to collect and distribute Bibles in the Spanish language to those churches, monasteries, universities, nunneries and other religious institutions that are suffering persecution at the hands of disbelievers. So much has been destroyed, burnt, and confiscated; Bibles, prayerbooks, religious works of art, holy translations, let alone the solid-material looting of precious religious artifacts. There is now a great dearth of God's Holy Word in Spain. The little task assigned to our convent by the Bishop, via the Vatican, is to fetch from the main religious centre of Spain, Bibles for redistribution throughout this part of Catalonia.'

Doubt and fear assailed Raven as never before. She swallowed the lump in her throat. 'Montserrat, Reverend Mother?'

'That is correct, my child.'

'Forgive me, Reverend Mother, I know I oughtn't to question one in higher authority, but from where are the Benedictine monks at Montserrat getting their Bibles? If every one of them worked for twenty-four hours a day translating the Scriptures, they'd never have enough to go around in such a wide-scale programme of distribution, especially as most of the Church's printing presses have also been silenced.'

'I'm glad that you have had the good sense to realize that, Sister Justina. Intelligence as well as common-sense will hold you in good stead in what you are about to do for us; and that's why I feel I've chosen well, even while realizing that you are the youngest and most inexperienced of our order. The Bibles, already translated into Spanish, will be arriving from Ireland.'

'I thought so! This is something to do with my brother Sonny — I mean Brother Bernard, isn't it, Reverend Mother?'

'Yes. I am unable to deny it. He and Father MacCree came here for an express purpose. They were requested by the Vatican to make contact in Spain for the distribution of God's Holy Word. Your brother, having lived in this area like you since childhood, understands the language and mentality of the Catalonian people. The monks of Ireland have become the life-line of Spain's religious freedom. We are asked to assist them in their literary crusade.'

'Monseigneur Paulus! I knew it!' Raven murmured.

'*Lo siento*, I am sorry?'

'Reverend Mother, if Dame Concepción and I are caught with the Bibles, will we be imprisoned?'

'Yes, my child, if you are caught by those who oppose the Church and its teachings. The Nationalists are more favourably disposed towards us.'

'But we are in the Republican part of Spain, Reverend Mother, who look *dis*favourably upon us.'

'In that respect, therefore, your task will be more

difficult and far more dangerous. The rewards, however, will be far *greater*. For every Bible you and Dame Concepción are able to bring out of Montserrat, you will be saving one soul for God's Holy Church.'

Reverend Dame Olivera stood up again, and went to kneel in front of the huge wooden crucifix on the bare white wall behind her desk. Her back to Raven, her rosary in her hands, she stared at the crucifix for fully three minutes. Raven had no means of knowing for what she was praying as she passed her rosary beads through her hands, she could only guess. Reverend Dame Olivera made the sign of the cross on her body, touching her fingers to forehead, chest, and shoulders. Then, getting back on her feet, her smile radiant, she looked as though she had just received divine inspiration. 'In order to eliminate the danger to yourselves, you and Dame Concepción, for this special purpose, will become English tourists.'

'I beg your pardon Reverend Mother?'

'English tourists, my child! That is why it is necessary for you both to have a good grasp of the English language. It was Dame Concepción's idea, and a grand one it is! She knows all about this assignment and has agreed to cooperate to her last ounce of breath. You are the only Irish nun in this convent, and one whose grasp and knowledge of the Spanish language is second nature. You have all the qualifications to make you the obvious choice in this matter – indeed, even the Spanish Nuncio, through the Vatican itself, highly recommended you to become Rome's young handmaiden despite your being only a newly received novice. That is why you have been chosen.'

'Chosen?'

'God has chosen you for this purpose, this *holy* purpose, Sister Justina. Dame Concepción is another one who comes highly recommended. She will be your chaperon and guide throughout all this. You will be mother and daughter and ...'

'Forgive me again, Reverend Mother, but two tourists, even if they are mother and daughter, cannot smuggle many Bibles out of Montserrat in a suitcase or rucksack without being crippled by the sheer weight of them.'

'My child, you question and question! You really *must* learn blind obedience. Have you no faith in your elders? The Bishop of Vilafranca and Toril, Father Gabriel and I, together with Madre Estelle, have worked out all the details of this holy venture in order to ensure the maximum safety of our order and the precious lives entrusted to us. Dame Concepción has accepted the task in the same way that Christ accepted His cross. You will become British tourists. You will make your pilgrimage to Montserrat in the Bishop's car, his little Citroën, which he has very kindly placed at our disposal. From the monastery you will collect your assignment of Bibles, hide them in the boot of the car and in every other hiding-place available: the Citroën will be adapted accordingly. Then you will drive direct to Barcelona. At the Jesu María Convent of the Dames of the Blessed Charity, who are part of our Camillus Order, you will leave the Bibles. There is a Franciscan monastery practically next-door to the convent in the Puerto del Angel. The Franciscan friars will redistribute the Bibles after our little part of the assignment has been completed. It's as simple as that.'

'Reverend Mother, why can't the Franciscan friars themselves take the Bishop's Citroën to Montserrat to collect the Bibles?'

'Because their task, once they receive the Bibles, is far more dangerous. They will be required to redistribute God's Holy Word in and around the city itself. Too much activity outside their monastery walls, especially as far as Montserrat, will only arouse the suspicion of those anti-clerical agents operating within the city, atheists, Anarchists and all other Godless groups. The priests are needed in a far more strategic capacity, while we nuns are asked to fetch and carry in our lowlier office.'

'How often are we to do this trip?'

'As often as the boat from the West Coast of Ireland is able to cross the seas with its blessed consignment of God's Holy Word.'

'I see. And has Brother Bernard a greater part in all this, that I know nothing about?'

'My child, I cannot answer you. We must not question, we must obey – blind obedience, which you have not as yet learnt as part of your religious formation. Tomorrow morning, first thing, you and Dame Concepitón are to go to the sewing-room, where you will have English clothes made for you so that you can pass off as genuine tourists. Father Gabriel knows someone who will obtain the appropriate identity documents. This evening, you and Dame Concepitón must attend a special service in the chapel, which the Bishop himself will conduct. You will be granted *exclaustration*, permission while you are still under vows to live and work outside the community in a manner approved of by the Church, for the benefit of the Church. That is very important, for you must have God's blessing on what you are about to do outside these convent walls. The first consignment of Bibles will arrive in San Sebastian from Ireland in two or three weeks' time. They will then be brought to Montserrat, where your task will begin. It is a holy crusade, assigned to us by God during these irreligious times. You will be blessed, so have no fear that what you are doing for the Church of Rome, you are doing for your suffering country.'

'I'm Irish, Reverend Mother.'

'Then do it for Ireland, part of the light of the Roman Catholic world. That's why you have been chosen by God, Sister Justina!'

God, Monseigneur Paulus, or Archie Cunningham? Ravena asked herself.

'Reverend Mother never even asked me if I could drive,' said Raven.

Three weeks had passed since her astounding interview with Reverend Dame Olivera, and now, here she was, playing holy charades for the Church of Rome!

'But she knew I could!' Dame Concepitón kept her eyes on the road, the noonday light of the bright spring sun through the windscreen, catching the gold-rimmed frames of her spectacles, which she wore not as a disguise, but because she actually did have bad eyesight. She concentrated hard on the steep serpentine road descending from the strange mountain of Montserrat to the valley.

Raven gave Dame Concepción a sly sidelong glance: she looked so strange and so awful in her English hat with a feather stuck in it, and her Liberty cotton print dress and open white sandals. Only her white lace gloves seemed in any way normal as she clutched the steering-wheel of the Bishop's Citroën. Raven supposed she didn't look much better, either, in 'homemade' English clothes that were functional rather than fashionable! Thank God, too, that manly hairstyles were in vogue, while shaven heads were only for Buddhist nuns, thought Raven as she settled her little skull-cap more firmly over her short, ragged-urchin crop, thanks to Madre Estelle Calmar, and what price vanity!

Having collected several boxes of Bibles from the dour-faced monks, who had helped load the Bishop's car with the illegal literature, the Bibles were now in the boot, covered over with fruit and vegetables destined for the Camillus Covent of Jesu María in Barcelona. Other, less bulky Church literature, had been concealed under the seats and behind the fabric-lined doors. The monks of Montserrat had been very busy adapting the Bishop's car to their own design.

'I wonder why those poker-faced Benedictine monks refused us permission to worship at the shrine of the Black Madonna?' Dame Concepción said. 'It's something I've always wanted to do, but never had the opportunity, until today. Now, when I had the chance, they said no! After all, *real* tourists are allowed to see the Black Virgin and kiss her robes.'

'Maybe they didn't like our disguise. I mean, they know we're really Franciscan nuns, and so perhaps they thought it would be sacrilegious.'

'I mustn't grumble. I'd rather be doing this than participating in what happened in Asturias a few months ago: but thank God it's all over.' Dame Concepción made the sign of the cross over her bosom while her left hand remained in command of the steering-wheel.

'Is the fighting in Asturias really over?' Somehow, Raven was not so sure; she had lived in Ireland for the first decade of her life, all through the crucial years of a Republic and a new country in the making, so she was well aware that

346

violence bred only more violence.

'Yes, I think so. I think that the brute force used to put down the uprising shocked everyone, even the Government, who has since taken a more lenient view and has started to release political prisoners. Perhaps Asturias was a good thing in a way, in that everyone will now be less eager for a full-scale civil war after what happened to the Basque towns of Oviedo and Gijon.'

'Were the legionnaires really responsible for the violence that was reported?' Raven was thinking of José, hoping *he* had not been sent to Asturais.

'Legionnaries, *regulaires*, some of them were beasts! Especially those sent to relieve the garrisons of Oviedo and Gijon. For fifteen days they just brutalized the population. I never believed it could happen. They forced the men who had taken part in the insurrection to give themselves up by holding to ransom their families, even babies and young children, at the end of a bayonet. I had to rescue a nine-day infant from a Moor who was about to dash its head on cobblestones. They set fire to peoples' homes, they killed farm animals, domestic animals, pets, and even destroyed childrens' toys in their fanatical 'purge' of the country. That Fascist soldier, Colonel Yagüe, has a lot to answer for.'

José was with Colonel Pedro Yagüe's Army of Africa. Raven kept her fears to herself. Perhaps José had remained behind in Tetuan when all this was going on: she certainly hoped so.

'The Butcher of Asturias, as he's now called,' continued Dame Conceptión. 'He and that other man they've recently appointed to the Ministry of War, what's his name – ah yes, General Franco, were responsible for slaughtering thirty thousand Asturian prisoners. Only the Communists went on fighting, the others soon gave up, and no one could blame them.'

They conversed in English, for Dame Conceptión, by birth, was Scottish. Miss Isabella Tarbat before she became a nun, she had spent the first eighteen years of her life between Aberdeen and Valencia. Her father had been a Scotsman, an entrepreneur who had struck lucky with fish-canning factories in both Aberdeen and Valencia, the hometown of Isabella Tarbat's mother. She took a language degree at Edinburgh University and after her father's death, returned, with her widowed mother, to Valencia, where she completed her studies at the University of Valencia. After her mother's death she had decided to enter a religious order, and had chosen the Camillus Dames of Lellis. Dame Conceptión had been a nun for thirty-five years.

'Now then, turn that map the right way up, daughter, and tell me where we're supposed to go. I've never driven a car through Barcelona before.'

'I've never navigated before – oh, do watch out dam – mother!' Raven hadn't meant it to sound like a blasphemy, drawing in her breath sharply and with some confusion as they narrowly escaped collison with a donkey-cart on a level-crossing. Mercifully no train was in sight.

They delivered their consignment of Bibles safely to the Convent of Jesu María in the narrow street of Puerta del Angel and, with a great weight lifted off their minds as well as the car chassis, Raven and Dame Conceptión left Barcelona's old Gothic Quarter, and headed back for Toril.

That first Bible-smuggling trip was an adventure and great fun in Raven's opinion, and she looked forward to the next one.

After many more such crusades, having become professional tourists in every way, even down to the Pond's cold-cream, they began to get a little blasé about the whole thing. On one occasion Dame Conceptión even went so far as to ask the Barcelona civil guard directions to Gaudi's unfinished cathedral, the awe-inspiring Sagrada Familia. 'One has to keep up appearances, my dear,' she joked as she drove away from Angel's Gate and the Plaza de Cataluña towards the Rambla, this time wearing huge jaunty-framed glasses in the latest vogue, the more sober gold-framed spectacles kept for her nunly countenance.

'You're flirting with death,' Raven said, laughing now, after having gone through several swings of mood, the loss of courage, hysterical nervousness, exhilaration, icy determination, and resolution, to this present abandoned mood of light-hearted carelessness induced by outwitting the law. 'And that is what Lyra used to do!'

'And who is Lyra, pray?'

'Oh, she was just one of my mother's numerous friends. But Lyra never prayed, only partied. Now she's permanently pickled, poor Lyra – oh, watch out, wretched control patrols ahead – stop, *STOP*!' Dame Concepción had not seen the barrier.

'Not the first time, don't panic.' Dame Concepción said slamming on the brakes. She fumbled in her handbag, looking for the *rouge à lèvre*. She began making up her face in the driving-mirror. 'Exclaustration has taken on a whole new meaning, and the Bishop would have a fit if he could see me now!'

An unshaven carabineer mounting guard at the barrier flung his cigarette-butt down in front of the car before walking round to the driver's window. Dame Concepción remained calm. 'Praise be to God we've surrendered our Bibles,' she muttered fervently in the absence of her rosary beads.

The carabineer tapped on the window, and she was forced to wind it down. He poked his head through, and Dame Concepción, in jerking her head back, dislodged her fancy glasses and her feathered hat, revealing her extremely close-cropped grey hair. Shorter even than the fashionable Eton crop, she looked like a man with make-up. Raven closed her eyes and sent up a silent prayer to heaven that the carabineer would not pry deeper into their business.

'Officer, you made me jump! There is no need to get quite so close …' She flapped her hand in front of her face. 'Garlic offends my senses. Why have you stopped us?' Hastily Dame Concepción readjusted her hat and glasses.

'*Lo siento*. Please speak Spanish.'

She sighed in exasperation, and said in broken Spanish, '*Soy inglesa* – I am an Englishwoman! If you must interrogate me, then do it in English.'

'What is your business?' he asked in Spanish.

'*No comprendo*, my good man. And neither does my daughter.'

'*Qué?*'

Dame Concepción pointed to Raven, stuck out her tongue, her finger on it as she shook her head in the

349

simplest of sign language. With a sigh of disgust the carabineer turned away, and said in Spanish to the man with him, 'She does not speak Spanish, nor does the daughter. It's hopeless asking them anything. But they can't go until they have been cleared. Where's Goded? He speaks English.'

'Listen comrade, let the *ingles* go. Look at the Englishwoman's pasty face and that hat! They're foreign tourists, that's all. Ugly ones, too.'

'They might be spies. Look, I'll fetch Goded. Otherwise I might find myself in prison for not obeying orders.'

Meanwhile another black Citroën had drawn up behind them, the driver impatiently hooting at the delay. The guards took no notice, so the disgruntled driver got out of his car and started to argue with the carabineer, insisting that the barrier be lifted as he was in a hurry. Then, before Dame Conceptión was aware of what she was doing, Raven, in one of the swiftest and most graceful somersaults Dame Conceptión had ever seen, tumbled over the front seat into the back, and covered herself with the travel-rug up to her nose.

'Goodness! What's happened?'

'Don't say a word, Mother, but I'm feeling extremely ill all of a sudden.'

Before Raven could explain further, the driver of the other Citroën came round to Dame Conceptión's window: 'I speak English, I will translate for the carabineer. Who are you and what is your business in Barcelona?'

'My daughter and I are on holiday. We are touring Catalonia. Why have they stopped us, señor?'

'The militia are looking for informers and spies.'

'Do we look like informers or spies?'

'What nationality are you?'

'British. What sort of spies are you looking for?'

'Fascists, Nationalist sympathizers – passports please and your *salvos conductos*.'

Dame Conceptión handed over two impressive blue and gold passports and safe-conduct passes, one issued in the name of Mrs Maud Smith and the other, Miss Molly Smith. Without a glance at them, the Spanish driver passed the passports and other papers directly to the carabineer.

'Where are you from?'

'I've just told you, señor. England.'

'I know that. Where in England?'

'London.'

'Where in London?'

'Mayfair.'

'Whose car are you driving?'

'We have hired it for a few days so that we can do a lot of sightseeing.'

'Where did you hire it?'

'Vilafranca – as you can, I'm sure, tell by the registration plate, señor.'

'Which garage?'

'The main one – on the Tarragona road.'

'I see. What is wrong with your daughter?'

'She has a stomach upset on account of the water in which your hotel vegetables are badly washed: if they are ever washed in Spain. And all that garlic in the food hasn't helped. Sēnor, is it always so hot in Barcelona in April?' Dame Conceptión fanned herself with a glove. 'I'll be glad to get back to England, what with militia men and Spanish tummy-bug all over the place.'

Passports and *salvos conductos* were handed back. 'Very well, you may continue with your holiday. *Buenas tardes*, señora, happy holiday. I hope your daughter will soon be better.'

'Thank you, señor, most kind of you.'

When the patrol and the officious Spaniard were out of sight and they were on their way back to Toril, Raven emerged from under the travel-rug, 'He knows! He *must* know … Oh, mother, oh – what does it matter when we're soon to be imprisoned! The driver behind us was Ramiro de Luchar! He asked all those questions to trap us. He knows full well this is the Bishop's car – the Bishop used to drive it over to the castillo or the Mas Luchar when he dined with Dona Ruiz and Doña Jacqueline. I wonder why he didn't tell the carabineer we were imposters? Perhaps the secret police will be waiting for us at the convent in Toril. They'll lock us up now, I'm convinced of it!'

'Calm down, my child. We are merely borrowing the Bishop's car to do our convent shopping in Barcelona –

where we can get better value and selection than either Toril or Vilafranca.'

'In disguise, after telling lies? You told Ramiro we hired this car from a *garage*!'

'The Bishop's car *was* undergoing repairs at the garage. We picked it up from there. The disguise was used as a protection, a safeguard against brutes from the Death and Freedom Brigade who make life purgatory for we poor nuns. I, perhaps, did not make myself quite clear. And that will be my defence. *No problema*.'

'Try telling that to the Communists, Dame Concepción! Ramiro is not that gullible.'

'What will be, will be, my child. If it's God's will we are to suffer punishment now, then we must accept that burden. All saints must suffer first before they attain heaven. I myself will have to resort to mortifying the flesh again for having told those lies. But I knew I should have to suffer many penances when I consented to do this thing. I can blame no one accept myself.'

'Oh, this is all so silly! It has got out of hand. We can't go on with this ridiculous charade. Now that Ramoir knows something fishy is going on, next time we'll be arrested as soon as we stop outside the Convent of Jesu María – with the Bibles still on us!'

'You are clearly overwrought by the whole incident. I'll let Reverend Dame Olivera know that we are er, "uncovered". Will that satisfy you?'

'No. You don't *know* what Ramiro is capable of! He's a murderer of baby fieldmice among other things.'

'Then we must pray for the redemption of his soul.'

'It will take more than prayer – oh dear, I don't mean to be blasphemous, Dame Concepción, but I know Ramiro of old, and he can be devious!'

'Don't worry, my child, God will find a way out of all this for those who are his faithful servants.'

When Dame Concepción laid their case before Reverend Dame Olivera, impressing upon her that the Bishop's car had most certainly been recognized on the streets of Barcelona by a Communist deputy, and, what's more, a member of PSUC, who were so anti-religion, Reverend Dame Olivera said, 'Then it will have to be a donkey-cart.

Our holy work cannot be halted for the sake of Communists who recognize Sister Justina or the Bishop's car. That is the danger of entering a convent close to home, one can always be recognized by someone at the wrong time, something I, the Bishop, and Madre Estelle Calmar, had not taken into consideration when selecting Sister Justina for a divine office of this sort. However, there is always the devil's alternative. You will just have to change your disguise. Let us see – ah, yes, I know! Two peasant women selling fruit and vegetables grown by the monks of Montserrat for the benefit of the poor villagers of the Llobregat valley. What better!'

'Only to receive illegal Bibles and a prison-sentence in return,' Dame Conceptión muttered fiercely on the way out of Reverend Dame Olivera's office. Remembering that she was back within convent walls, she tucked her hands into her wide grey sleeves, her eyes behind her gold-framed spectacles not sparkling with a sense of adventure any more, but keeping lowly custody upon the cloister stones. 'I'm sorry, Sister Justina. I did try my best to get Reverend Mother to relieve us of this dangerous assignment.'

Raven sensed that Dame Conceptión was rather glad Reverend Dame Olivera hadn't done any such thing; and so was she. Excursions into the unknown gave an invigorating dimension to her pristine life amongst certain older nuns, who were either going through virginal menopausal breakdowns like Dames Rosemarie and Annunciata, or their protracted death-throes like Dame Barnabas.

'It's not your fault, Dame Conceptión. Blame it upon the times in which we live. No doubt the Bishop will be very glad to get his car back before it's confiscated by the Communists.'

CHAPTER NINE

Guatemala: August 1935

Father Silvestre's greatly abused open-backed Fageol truck splashed through the puddles and drew up with a scrunch of gears in a side street off the Avenida 6, Zona 10.

He pumped the klaxon religiously for fully half a minute to let everyone know he had done his shopping and had arrived to pick up *El Americano*. The middle of the rainy season, everything steamed under the bonnet of his overheated truck. But the heavy shower of an hour ago had temporarily ceased and bright sunlight glinted off the long, low, recently whitewashed buildings of the Clinica Unida Comercial.

In the parking area, there was one bay left out of the three reserved for two ambulances, and the grace and favour car of *El Medico General*. Father Silvestre tried to squeeze his wide truck between company Buick and company ambulance, the spare bay shaded by a leafy banana tree growing over the hospital wall. He managed to scrape both vehicles at the same time, but conscience did not intervene, for Father Silvestre was a law unto himself.

He shifted his weight equably on the torn leather seat, happy to be of service to United Commercial Fruiterers of Guatemala. From under his wide-brimmed black priest's hat on the passenger seat beside him, he retrieved a finely chased silver flask. *El Americano* was never ready on time, and always managed a last-minute hiccough to delay them, so Father Silvestre consoled himself by whiling away the time with his flask of tequila and intermittent klaxon blowing.

Keir heard the truck horn blasting away.

Anxious to tone down the noise of the Roman Catholic priest's exuberant arrival for the sake of his patients, Keir stuck his head under the green jalousies at his office window, yelling, 'Cut that out, Father, I'm coming!' Keir gave some last-minute instructions to Dr Philippe Delvalo, the locum who took over during his time off. 'Right, I'm off. Sure you can manage?'

'Listen Doc, no one's indispensable. Wasn't I running this outfit single-handed before you arrived?'

'That's true. Well, you know where to find me if you need me, Santi …'

'Yeah-yeah, we know.' Philippe Delvalo, sitting on a corner of Keir's desk, took a toothpick from the jar on the desk. 'No sweat. If they die, they die.'

'Thanks a million! I haven't sweated my guts out for four years to get this place up to scratch, only to hear such words of discomfort from you.'

Philippe Delvalo grinned. 'Look Doc, most of the *mestizo* in here now, are the same ones who were here four years ago. They come, they go, they come, they go. Now you get your tail out of here, otherwise I quit and go back to my private clinic where I make more *quetzales* in one day than you do in a month. You'll be the one to lose out, not me: and I know how you look forward to your fishing trips with that old reprobate who calls himself a priest!'

'Make sure Papa Taca gets his tobacco. Without tobacco he won't take his treatment. Don't forget to get the nurses to change Lilly's dressing every day, and don't cover up Pico's ulcers with thick bandages. Light dressings are enough. Oh, and Mamma Galindo is due her tenth, any hour now. The contractions are fairly evenly spaced, but the midwife knows and …'

'Sure, sure! Go, will you!' Dr Delvalo put out his hand, palm up.

'Buick keys, hospital keys, drug-cupboard keys, safe keys,' Keir dropped them all into Philippe Delvalo's plump pink palm. 'Anything else? Nope, well, that's it then. *Adios amigo* … oh, and don't forget to telephone Central Medical Supplies. We're very low on glucose and dressings. 'Bye.' He picked up his rucksack beside the desk. Out on the verandah, the hospital sweeper trailed his bamboo broom

355

between the beds. 'Don't kick up too much dust, Peppy.'

In ragged singlet and shorts, long, lanky shanks and feet dusky-brown and bare, Peppy grinned widely. The smile was contagious despite a mouthful of broken black teeth. A bedraggled cigarette drooped forlornly from Peppy's bottom lip. 'I do as you say, Doc. I damp down everything so dust does not rise in air like volcano ash to make blue devils in hospital ward.'

'Good man.'

'Make happy holidays, Doc.'

'Thanks, Peppy. I'll be home in four days' time.'

'Sure thing, Doc.' Pepito rested his broom against the wall and carefully took hold of Keir's fishing-tackle in a corner of the verandah. The fishing-rod had come to symbolize the final moment of Doc's departure into the *Cordillera* with Father Silvestre. 'Everyone need vacation sometime. All work and no play only for donkeys and sweepers.'

'Sure, Peppy.' Keir smiled to himself, the warm-hearted, unsophisticated yet fiercely proud Mesoamerican Indians he had come to know during the past four years had broadened his horizon considerably, even if he did have to keep on reminding them to *do* things! While he knew he often sounded like Moses, Keir also knew nothing would get done unless he constantly drew his staff's attention to the Ten Commandments.

'Make happy holiday, Doc, we'll miss you!' a dozen voices sang from hospital beds pushed out onto the verandah early that morning. Pepito walked solemnly behind Keir, carrying Doc's fishing-tackle as though he conveyed the Ark of the Tabernacle. Pepito handed the tackle over.

Keir slung his rucksack and fishing gear on top of the steaming tarpaulin covering drums of cooking oil, gasoline and water, sacks of flour, sugar, coffee, and chick peas. Father Silvestre shopped once in every four months for the entire village of Santiago Atitlán, coinciding his shopping expedition with Keir's four days off so that they could drive back together.

Pepito, tears in his eyes, held out his hand. The ritual was always the same. '*Adios*, Peppy. Make sure they run things properly while I'm gone.' Keir shook Peppy's hand.

356

'Sure thing, Doc. You bring me back more tobacco and rum.'

'Bad for you, Peppy, especially with your chest.'

'My parents plant me in wrong season, Doc, that is why my chest sound like cracked corn. But you bring me more rum and tobacco, okay?'

'Okay, Peppy,' Keir smiled. Everything bad, according to the *mestizo*, originated from planting in the wrong season. Keir climbed in beside Father Silvestre who started the engine. 'You're parking illegally, *mío amigo*.'

'Who says so?' Like an elephant in a suburban garden, Father Silvestre reversed the truck out of its confined parking-space.

'I say so – and mind my car!'

'I wouldn't need to park at all if you didn't require half the morning to say your *adios amigos*.' Father Silvestre turned the wheel energetically as he tried to get his huge truck to face in the direction of Avenida 6. 'Thought you were never coming. I've a busy schedule. Now you've delayed me.'

'The never-ending story, I take it?' Keir relaxed in the passenger seat. Hands behind his head, he took a deep breath to unfasten his knotted muscles. After four months of hard and unremitting labour, on call day and night, he felt in need of the breaks Father Silvestre offered, and was ever grateful.

'My *history* of Mesoamerica, Americano, not story! And it's slower by twelve days a year lost through ferrying you around instead of getting on with my important writing.'

'You'll eat your words and enjoy them when I catch a giant Atitlán bass you happened to miss. How are the piles, Father, the scurvy, thrombosis, heart-failure, ulcers, and you name it, you've got it?'

'Bad as ever.'

'Uh-huh. Laid off the tequila yet?'

'Not for the Virgin Mary, and certainly not for you.'

'Life is life, eh, Father? What busy schedule?'

'I have an important game of *vingt-et-un* with my clients, and have to be back in Santiago by six o'clock. Besides, there are cracks in the ground again and you know what happened last time we got a wheel stuck in a rut.'

357

'Last time, the tyres melted on the road before they located the ruts. We were travelling on bare rims for hours, if you care to remember!'

'God's fault.'

'You might say that. It was one God-Almighty fault opening up on the Santiago road up the mountain.'

Father Silvestre grinned: 'Guatemala never stops fizzing, you ought to know that by now.'

'Oh, I know it, I just can't get used to it. Or the smell of bad eggs that hits one as soon as we leave the city. Volcanoes have put me off eggs for life. Please stop at the Correos in case some of my mail has got diverted to strange places: as usual,' he added slyly.

'I already did that on the way. I left home especially early just to accommodate your lordship – and I thought getting up in the middle of the night was something I left behind me when I dispensed with the Church's services. But I suppose I wouldn't do it if I didn't like you just a li'le, eh, Americano?'

'Thanks.'

'Just move aside that holy hat of mine you're squashing, and you'll find your letters underneath.'

Keir took them from under Father Silvestre's hat. 'I hope none fell by the wayside this time.'

'Still blaming me for those letters I forgot to post, uh?' Father Silvestre shot Keir a sideways glance. 'In future do your own dirty work. I'll have nothing more to do with your correspondence or your love-life. You're becoming an imposition, and I did away with those a long time ago.'

'Then why do you still wear the cloth?'

'Because I'm human underneath and I don't like anyone finding out.' Father Silvestre, with a broad and engaging smile, pushed his silver flask towards Keir. 'Want a snifter?'

'No thanks, I'm navigating.'

'You ought to have been a priest, my son, since all you do is work your guts out for the *mestizo* population. Just like me.'

'I *am* a priest!'

'Don't I know that. No drinking, no smoking, no swearing, no womanizing, no fornication, so tell me, what *is* your vice, Doc?'

'When I want to confess, I'll find another priest, right?

Meanwhile, I don't need you, rocked, defrocked, or downright crocked to pry into my private life.'

'Point taken, I never bear a grudge. Whose the special letter from? The girlfriend in Spain?'

'I haven't a girlfriend in Spain.'

'London?'

'Nor London.'

'Geneva, Paris, Monte Carlo?'

'Ditto.'

'New York?'

'My sister Jenny. She likes to mother me by spending her nights knitting socks. Any day now I should be receiving another dozen pairs, so .... *Whoa-whee*!'

'*Mestizo* fool – get out of my way with your fowl pest!' Father Silvestre swerved round a truck conveying large circular baskets of chickens to market, and narrowly escaped hitting the local bus. He slammed his heavy foot on the brake and Keir shot forward, almost hitting his head on the windscreen.

'Hell! You almost ran into the back of the bus, Father! Slow down!'

'Didn't touch him – tell me about this Spanish señorita of yours.'

'I haven't *got* a Spanish señorita, how many more times!'

'That didn't prevent you from getting holy mad with me when I forgot to post your Christmas card the year you first got here. So I don't believe you. But I did post it in the end, eh, *mío amigo*, so you can't say I haven't got your welfare at heart?'

'A year too late, Father.'

'I have a bad memory. I mention the subject, only because I – er, hmmm!' he cleared his throat, 'only because I have some more for you. Not my fault, you know. Solola found them on my desk two days ago when she was dusting.' He fumbled in a deep pocket of his soutane and withdrew three belated letters.

Keir snatched them from Father Silvestre. One letter from Barcelona was postmarked January 1933! The other two letters, one from Geneva and the other from New York, were more recent, only three months late. 'Bloody hell, Father!'

359

'Don't swear, my son: It's a sin – ten paternosters. When an envelope is addressed simply to Dr Keir Hunter Devlin, Guatemala City, Central America, one can't expect the *mestizo* postman to be a mind reader, and nor am I. There they were lingering in the Oficina de Correos, until I happened to go in for my post some – er, little time ago, you know what a busy man I am. I must have picked them up with my own letters, dumped them all on my desk, and promptly forgot about them, because I make it a rule never to answer anything official. Neither can I be expected to remember the affairs of someone I see only twelve days a year. Don't you ever put your correct address, especially zone number, on any of your correspondence?'

'Nope. Like you, I don't want my past catching up with me.'

'So, I *was* right!' Father Silvestre held up a finger in glee. 'I perceive little chinks of vice in that impeccable armour of yours. You *have* got a little Spanish señorita your wife knows nothing about.'

'I haven't got a wife.'

'God says you have.'

'Stick God.'

'Blasphemy. Fifteen Ave Marias.'

'And stick your Ave Marias.'

'You're living dangerously.'

'And so are you.'

'You're angry with me?'

'Right.'

'*Very* angry?'

'*Damn* right!'

Father Silvestre grinned. 'That's all right then. Anger is a clean plaster for a festering wound. You'll get over Francesca in time. Meanwhile you're slowly learning to be human again. Who is she?'

Keir gave a little whoop of joy and waved one of the letters under Father Silvestre's nose, 'Now I'll get over her a lot better – guess what this is?'

'Your *Decree Absolute*.'

'Yup! Eight years, and now at last it's for real! I'm a free man again ...'

'Not in the eyes of God or the Church. Once married, always married.'

'I'm not a practising Catholic, nor was Francesca.'

'As you still have a living spouse, if you consort – or even cavort, come to think of it, with another woman, your children will be bastards in the eyes of God and the Church.'

'Then they shouldn't feel left out since most of the world is made up of bastards.'

'You are a cynic, my son, who will one day strangle himself with his own halo. Who is that other letter from?'

'Mind your own business.'

'Aha – another woman, and so soon! Spanish?'

'Irish.'

'Where from in Ireland?'

'Hollyberry House, County Kil ... bloody hell!' Keir smacked his hand to his head.

Father Silvestre shot Keir another oblique glance. 'Twenty Hail Marys. What's up? Bigamy caught up with you at last?'

'That's her, that's the daughter!'

'Whose daughter?'

'Daphne's, – Lady Quennell's! The one featured in *Bona Dia*. The fund-raising Anglo-Irish lady who did charitable things in America on behalf of Ireland. She was married to a Judge of the High Court of Ireland, a baronet or something – Sir Francis. Yep, Sir Francis.'

'Drake?' Father Silvestre quipped.

Keir took no notice. 'They all got blown up by an IRA bomb one New Year's Eve; at least, that was what the magazine article said.'

'You're making no sense to me, Americano.'

'All these years, lurking in my deep subconscious, was *that* face. I *knew* I'd seen her before – only it was the mother's face, not Raven's! Raven Quennell under the green cloche hat, just like the mother before her. The photograph of the children, the little girl sitting on her pony in front of that great Irish mansion called Hollyberry House was none other than Miss Ravenna Quennell, who sat next to me at the Rachmaninov concert at the Conservatoire in Geneva!'

'Are you feeling all right, my son?'

'Yes, perfectly, why? In Geneva faint stirrings of my brain

cells told me that I'd seen Raven before, that she was someone from my past. Yet how could she be? I myself being a generation older than she. I never wanted to pry into her background as it was none of my business, and the two girls told me nothing about themselves apart from having a grandfather and a brother living in Spain; she has a sister, you see.'

'Another of your fancy ladies?'

'No. I prefer – never mind. I only knew them as a couple of rich and privileged young ladies at my aunt's girls' school. It's all suddenly come back to me, though: while Jodi was sitting on his tin pot in the Sloane Court apartment, I remembered thinking that the beautiful face of the woman staring up at me from the magazine on the coffee-table was blasé and incomplete. Yet, somehow, the *essence* of that face had been captured by the photographer. Even though I was not aware of it then, not until this moment, I was really seeing someone else, the face behind the face, so to speak – if you follow my drift. Behind the mother's impeccable glazed image for some glossy story on how the rich are different, the cameraman had also managed to capture and embody the future adult daughter, still only a young, immature girl sitting on her pony outside the family country mansion in Ireland.'

'Go back to sleep, Americano. I prefer you when you're sober.'

'It's the girl, Raven! The one who has been lying dormant in my subconscience, the angel waiting to be resurrected by my tardy brain all these years. *She* is the woman, the *new* woman, the essence, the substance, the *real* person, not Lady Quennell – the Honourable Daphne, or whatever. Just Raven Quennell, the lovely, unpretentious, self-contained young lady who happens to be the daughter of a baronet.' He slapped his forehead again. 'Fool! Why didn't you know who she *really* was in Geneva!'

Father Silvestre sniffed deprecatingly. 'But still only a woman.'

'One who has haunted me for a very long time.'

'I'm utterly intrigued. Tell me more, Doc.'

'Don't be facetious. A pure and incorruptible Irish Colleen, that ...'

'All purity is corruptible. God made women corrupt.'

'That's true. It would still be interesting to find out how pure or how corruptible.'

'After all this time, what made you connect the two – this mother and daughter?'

'I don't know. I don't often look through women's fashion magazines, and so nothing in particular registered except a woman's face – not even the name Quennell. The row with Francesca afterwards overshadowed everything in my mind, because she had left Jodi alone in the apartment. Maybe I've been suffering from amnesia since Jodi's death.'

'That's very obvious.'

'Maybe I've gotten careless in my relationships with the human race because I don't want to become involved with anyone again.'

'That's *most* obvious! So what are you doing in Fruit Bat country?'

'Maybe it has taken me all this time to face up to facts and now that I'm facing up to them, the truth hurts less even while memory still agonizes.'

'That's too deep and philosophical for me. I know only the simple facts: women are trouble, God is trouble, religion is trouble, drink is trouble, smokes are trouble, friends are trouble, buggery is trouble, gambling is trouble, food is trouble – especially to one big ulcer like me. So, what is there left in life, Americano, *but* temptation?'

'Would it be a crime, Father, for an incorruptible man to woo a corruptible lady for the sake of her wealth, beauty, and purity?'

'Depends which order you do it in, my son.'

'Lead us not into temptation.' Keir settled back and closed his eyes. 'Now I'm going to sleep.'

'Your comic and highly entertaining company, Doc, is what keeps me going twelve days out of three hundred and sixty-five.'

'Take me to paradise, Father.'

'Hmmm!' Father Silvestre, who always drove like a maniac, changed gear with a great deal of clutch-scraping, and took the high road out of town. 'Let's hope it'll be before six o'clock. I have a lot staked in this game.'

'Just as long as you can get up at dawn tomorrow to go

fishing at Santa Ana. Otherwise I go alone. Paradise, here I come.'

Four hours later Keir was rudely awakened by an almighty thumping, juddering, and hissing. The truck was at a standstill. Steam enveloped him, and darkness was lit only by the two headlights of the truck. Father Silvestre was not in the driving seat, so Keir stuck his head out of the window and knew by the smell of bad eggs permeating the air, that they were in the shadow of the eleven and a half thousand foot Atitlán volcano. 'What's going on?'

Father Silvestre, standing in the beam of full headlights, kicked the radiator grille of the Fageol. 'This unreliable metal monster will be the death of me! Americano rubbish!'

'I hope you're referring to the truck and not me.' Keir switched off main beam before the battery went flat.

'Put those lights *on*!' Father Silvestre bellowed.

Keir ignored the priest's bellicose tantrums and jumped out onto the rocky, lava-strewn and utterly barren road. It might be hours before anyone came along to tow them into the Indian village of Santiago Atitlán. Immense boulders were strewn along the margins of the road, and an occasional little tail of steam could sometimes be seen, pushing up through the hot ground beneath their feet. 'Why don't you try feeding it with gasoline from time to time, Father? Or at least remember to carry some spare parts like a can of fuel and a spare tyre.' Keir took his powerful torch from his haversack and illuminated the site of inspection under the truck bonnet.

'It's not gasoline, oil, or water this Californian trashcan needs. Got a silk stocking on you?'

'Yeah, I wear them all the time. How about a pair of elastic braces?'

'*Está mucho mejor!*'

Two and a half hours later the truck, with its makeshift fanbelt, jounced into the village of Santiago Atitlán. Under normal circumstances the journey from Guatemala City to Atitlán ought to have taken no more than four and a half to five hours. But in Father Silvestre's company, nothing proceeded normally, and two and a half hours later than presurmised was unremarkable.

Keir was only thankful that they had arrived at all. Often in the past the Fageol had let them down in the most awkward of spots, in the most barren of landscapes, and they had had to walk miles for help: Father Silvestre's fault, he treated the Fageol as he treated himself, with utter recklessness!

Solola, an olive-complexioned, attractive, slant-eyed Tzutuhiles Indian girl who kept house for Father Silvestre, showed Keir into the guest-room he usually occupied when he came to stay at the Santiago Mission Inn.

'How are you, Solola?' Keir asked while she poured water from a jug into the cracked china basin on the washstand.

'*Muy bien*, Doc.'

'No more earthquakes?'

'Two little ones, nothing bad.' She handed him a clean face-towel and smiling shyly, backed out of the door that hung askew on its hinges. It was a job to keep the door closed, as it had a tendency to swing open silently and eerily when least expected. But Keir had mastered the art of keeping it secured by sticking chewing-gum between the jamb and the edge of the door.

Repeated earthquake damage had rendered the rock and bamboo edifice decidedly unsafe. Nobody cared, least of all the proprietor who had bought the deconsecrated land and premises off the Roman Catholic Church. Father Silvestre had immediately set about turning the former mission house into a rowdy, bawdy, card-playing, hard-drinking hostelry, where cock-fights and dog-fights provided day and night entertainment. Tzutuhiles Indians in their purple-and-white-striped *pantalones*, bright sashes, embroided and woven shirts, and incongruous cowboy hats, rubbed shoulders and often fought with the itinerant poncho-draped Mexicans stealing across the border. But, at the end of the day, Father Silvestre still clung like a drowning man to the old order of things, and would have been greatly affronted had someone *not* prefixed his name with Father, or forgot to call his hostelry the *Mission* Inn.

Keir's room, identical to all the others in the Mission

Inn, was a small, dark cell, walls badly cracked, stained, and in urgent need of a fresh coat of whitewash. A bare, dim light-bulb dangled from the cracked ceiling, herbage sprouted throught the cracks in the once brilliant blue and gold patterned ceramic floor, while lizards scuttled everywhere in neighbourly proximity and fell with regular plops from the ceiling onto the bed. A prison window with an elaborate wrought-iron grille looked onto a higgledy-piggledy yard, where cacti grew like trees.

Every time Keir came 'up country' to stay in fascinating Santiago Atitlán amidst mountains and water, with its winding, cobbled streets, its bamboo and stone huts, its lava boulders, and cactus gardens behind rundown bamboo fences, he marvelled that the Indian village, clinging to the dark volcanic slopes like a prickly green burr, had managed to stay where it was without slipping into the wide, deep lake from which it drew its name and trade.

In the bowl of water Solola had provided, Keir soused his head to rid himself of volcanic dust, refreshing himself after the long and tiring journey. By the chuckles, the clinking of bottles, and the strong smell of tobacco wafting through the open window Keir guessed that Father Silvestre was already at his nocturnal amusement. Towelling his head dry, he went to the open window and said through the grille, 'What a pity you weren't around four hundred years ago, Father. Had Cortés made you his military leader instead of blood-thirsty Pedro de Alvarado, the Church of Rome might have canonized, not excommunicated, you.'

'They'd have *cannon-ized* me all right, Doc. On the end of Montezuma's blunderbuss.' Father Silvestre, with a brightly woven shawl around his immense shoulders as the night air was chill, sat on an up-ended orangebox around a plankboard table in company with five Tzutuhiles Indians. His mangy crossbred dog, Jaguar, lay lovingly on his dusty sandalled feet. Father Silvestre always made a candle and starlit night of it with his parishioners, to whom he had introduced the evils of strong drink and gambling, while also managing to convert them to Christianity of a kind.

'That's. true. Inquisitorial thumbscrews apart, we all

know the Indians only had to be introduced to the Knave of Hearts to convert them to anything. But oughtn't you to be writing instead of gambling if you're aiming to go down in literary history?'

'Later. The words only start flowing at two in the morning. I have to get loosened up first to become inspired.'

'Don't get too loose, Father. We've an early start and I've a lot of bass to catch.'

'Go trepan an ape, Doc, I'm busy.'

Keir felt better already. At long last he was away from the pulsating city and his never-ending, mundane, and non-challenging duties at the Clinica Unida Comercial. Nothing was capable of destroying dedication faster than no expense account: not that he wasn't dedicated to being that doctor he had come out here to be. But somehow the enchantment had gone. The routine was always the same, hardly taxing his skills or his mind at all. He had committed himself body, soul, and spirit to his *mestizo* patients and staff, and felt reluctant now to return and rejoin the rat race of North America.

He stretched out on the shaky bed with its bright woven bedspread, and picked up his letters. He had post office-box numbers in Guatemala City, Antigua, and Santiago Atitlán, simply because he didn't want his post or his past catching up with him. If nobody knew where he was, Francesca wouldn't be able to hound him, had been his reasoning when first taking up residence in Guatemala City. Now it didn't matter any more, Francesca and he were no more man and wife, no more one flesh, despite all Father Silvestre's gloomy religious moralizings on the subject. A new start to his life, that's what today was! He might even celebrate with a bottle of beer later on.

Keir began sifting through his correspondence, looking at the envelopes and stamps first, while thinking about the letter Raven had written him two and a half years ago, the one Solola had discovered underneath all the accumlated rubbish on Father Silvestre's desk. It had been brief, telling him only that she was working as a pupil teacher at his aunt's school, teaching English and Spanish to twelve-year-olds. She thanked him for his Christmas card, received a year later than she thought he had intended it to reach her: 'And thanks again, Father!' Keir muttered to himself. 'For being so downright irresponsible! No wonder you came to a bad ending in your parochial life!' Keir was only sad to think that Raven had bothered to reply to him at all, yet had never received an acknowledgement from him. A promising relationship had fizzled out for lack of proper communication. In future, Keir promised himself, he would collect, as well as post, his own letters at the Correos.

Perhaps it was just as well though, he then mused, for he would have hated to have let her down. Destiny had its own reasons and fate was something one couldn't argue against. Someone as lovely, as accomplished, and as charming as Miss Ravenna Quennell was bound to be snapped up by now by a discerning young man: she was no doubt married to some chinless wonder doing his bit for the British Empire, just like Janice Fairchild's husband. Forget the lady!, Keir told himself, she's of another generation as well as from another planet!

He *must* put her out of his head once and for all.

Keir looked at the letter in his hand, postmarked in Geneva, not Zurich where his mother was now living since her marriage. He wondered if this was another letter from Raven, though it was typewritten, not handwritten. He opened it eagerly and was vaguely disappointed when it turned out to be not from Raven, but from Max Huber, the President of the International Red Cross:

Dear Keir, I wonder if you remember our meeting in the summer of 1931? The occasion was your mother's wedding to Monsieur Albert Contrin. You and I spoke briefly about the work of the International Red Cross, and I remember at the time that you told me you were searching for a new challenge in your career. Before I had a chance to recontact you, your mother informed me of your appointment as General Medical Officer to one of the large fruit operatives of Central America. At the time I remembered thinking what a wonderful asset you would have been to our little team of Red Cross representatives who go all over the world in the capacity of 'the third combatant'. To quote a very good friend of mine, Marcel Junod, himself a Red Cross delegate, we are the 'warriors without weapons', the liaison officers in two theatres of war. Right now, war has broken out between Italy and Abyssinia, and our Red Cross delegates are once more stretched to capacity around the globe. Should you ever feel jaded with your medical role in the field of industry, and want to participate as a 'third combatant' on another kind of battlefield, I would be glad to consider you with your experience, qualifications, and, according to Michelle, your conscientiousness, as well as itchy feet, for a place on our team of International Red Cross delegates. Addis Abbaba needs you as soon as possible. Yours sincerely, Max.

'Jesus! Why did this letter have to arrive now?' Keir asked himself.

Anchorless after Jodi's death, his personal life and emotions in tatters, his future bleak indeed, he had yearned to move on, a step always beyond himself, something he couldn't explain even to himself. After New York he had gone to Toronto where his Canadian registrarship had been rewarding, both from a job satisfaction point of view, as well as salary. But that had not been enough. His mother's marriage plans to a Zurich banker had come as a pointer to his future, and so he had accepted the invitation to go to Europe for the wedding, with something akin to relief in his heart.

One day, in the Parc Mon Repos, Geneva, whilst reading an English newspaper, the *Daily Herald*, he had come across an advertisement asking for English-speaking doctors to practise in Central America. Only a box number was supplied and he had written off that same evening with his curriculum vitae, requesting a job description. A week later he received a reply from London. United Commercial Fruiterers, Guatemala, wanted a fully-qualified doctor to supervise their sixty-bed clinic in Guatemala City, run for the benefit of their employees, who were mainly *mestizo*. Salary would be commensurate with age, qualifications, and experience. Together with a staff of thirty nurses, two recently qualified doctors and five *mestizo* student doctors working in a fully-equipped modern building in the heart of Guatemala City, he, as *Medico General*, would be responsible for the care and welfare of the Fruit Company's employees. *Mestizo*, Keir had duly discovered, was a term used to describe the descendants of Central American Indians and Spanish colonials.

Having seen his mother safely married to her plump and portly Swiss banker, reassured in his heart that she had steered herself into calmer waters, he had entrained for a week in Paris, followed by a visit to London.

His view of the Thames shrouded by river mist, and the grimy office windows of United Commercial Fruiterers, Guatemala, the excitable and friendly Spaniard in the interviewing chair opened up a whole new world far removed from the murky vistas of his life so far. Señor Barras went over the top in declaring how impressed he was with his qualifications, his credentials, and experience. 'But most of all,' said Señor Barras, enthusiastically kissing his fingers, 'is the weather of the country they call the Land of Eternal Spring, *molto benévolo*!' He made a deprecating gesture at the fog outside his windows. 'This is English summer, pah! In Guatemala it is Spanish springtime all the year. You will be very happy there, I am sure, Dr Devlin.' He stood up and held out his hand. 'You are very welcome to be in our company, and the job of *Medico General* is yours if you wish to take it. All travelling expenses will of course, be paid by the company, plus one month's salary in advance. Oh, I was forgetting!' Señor Barrass, behind a fat cigar, beamed at Keir. 'There is a big handsome company car that goes with the job, a Buick.'

Guatemala suddenly seemed like the Promised Land.

It took him just three days to make up his mind to accept the job. He sent a cablegram to his chief at the Toronto Hospital, resigning his post and giving a month's notice. He had four weeks left of his vacation before he would have had to return to Canada to resume his duties as Orthopaedic Registrar, so Keir felt everything had slotted into place very nicely. Afterwards, he telephoned Jan Fairchild, and accepted her family's invitation to spend a long weekend with them. Keir enjoyed that weekend enormously, and was grateful to the Fairchilds for their warmth, hospitality, and real 'British spirit'. He was introduced to an English breakfast, ploughman's lunch, and English tea, and, at the end of the day, real English beer in a real English pub. Janice's brother, Charles, was racing on the Sunday. Keir went to Brooklands. He also met Archie Cunningham, Jan's fiancé.

From London to Southampton next, and the transatlantic crossing to New York to see his sister Jenny. He filled her eager ears with details of their mother's wedding and let her keep the photographs. Painful memories of Jodi and Francesca returned with a vengeance, so that he couldn't wait to get away again. From New York, the banana boat, *Cuchumatanes*, belonging to United Commercial Fruiterers, Guatemala, transported him via the Caribbean to Puerto Barrios.

At the smelly fish-and-fruit-laden Atlantic port a battered Fageol truck waited on the tarmac to take him the one hundred and sixty miles overland to Guatemala City. Keir vividly recalled that first meeting of his with Father Silvestre, even the musty, bookish smell of Father Silvestre's soutane that had seen better days.

His round, black wide-brimmed priest's hat pushed to the back of his grizzled head, Father Silvestre had put away his silver pocket-flask, and through the open truck window had shaken Keir's hand heartily. 'I'm Father Silvestre, your chauffeur, Doc.'

'Pleased to meet you, Father, but how did you know who I was?'

'I can smell a doctor a mile off! *El Medico Americano*, you wear your tie like a stethescope instead of a lasso like the other Yankees getting off here, and you'd be wearing a bowler if you were a plummy Britisher – the only kind of Britishers we get around here. Hop aboard, Doc.'

Keir smiled appreciatively. 'They never told me a priest would be doing the honours.'

'Fruit Bats never tell anyone anything except lies. Sorry about not being able to give you a hand with your gear, but I have a little problem that keeps me in my seat.'

'Something wrong with your legs?'

'No, Doc, I have these wretched piles, you see. They give my bum a rough time, especially with all that papaya Philippe Delvalo keeps shoving into me as a cure for bum-ache. That's why I'm in the Fruit Bat hospital.'

'You mean, you're a patient?'

'You might say that.' Father Silvestre took out some leaf-tobacco and rolled himself a crude-looking cigarette. 'Do you fancy Latin?'

'Latin?'

'Food, my son. Or you might prefer Chinese, eh?' Father Silvestre had looked under his bushy white brows at Keir. 'There's a whole recipe book to be found on this waterfront, and whatever your stomach fancies is yours for the asking. The only trouble is, I'm er ...' he rubbed his fingers and thumb together, 'a bit short of the ready, having left my billfold in Santiago.'

Having given it swift thought, Keir discovered he was rather hungry after all, and that he wouldn't mind getting to know a lot more about Father Silvestre before setting off on the long journey to Guatemala City. Besides, it would soon be nightfall. Overnight travel in a bruised and unreliable-looking truck held together with bits of string, wire, and sticking tape, with a priest who secretly tippled while he steered, seemed a decidedly risky proposition.

'I guess I might as well get used to Latin. Don't worry, Father, I think I've got enough *quetzels* on me to pay for our supper.'

'Bravo, Doc! Chitre has the best *enchiladas* and *tortillas* on the whole of this Atlantic coast, so follow me.' Father Silvestre stepped down with agility from the truck, the discomfort of his haemorrhoids having disappeared with amazing rapidity at the mention of food. He assisted the Negro porter, who had jumped on Keir as soon as he had stepped off the *Cuchumatanes*, to toss the doctor's luggage into the back of the Fageol.

Keir tipped the Negro and followed the giant figure of the priest to one of the Latin-American restaurants on the waterfront. Keir mused upon the fact that he had thought he was big at six-three, yet Father Silvestre topped him by another three inches!

A neon sign in English, flashing spasmodically in the early evening sunshine, *Chitre's Café. Enchiladas and Tacos like Momma Make!*, seduced Father Silvestre to take up Chitre's offer. 'Drink?' Father Silvestre asked when they were seated on a long, low bench at a long, low table under the palmy roof of Chitre's open-air restaurant.

'Beer.'

Two bottles of beer were set before them. Not quite what Keir was used to, or had expected, the first gulp robbed him of the power of speech and the next and following deprived him of the lining of his throat.

'*Pulque*,' said Father Silvestre.

'Sorry?' Keir had difficulty controlling his choking fit.

'From the maguey plant which you Americans call aloe. Comes from Haiti.'

Keir wiped the back of his hand across his mouth. 'Strong stuff.'

'You might say that. You speak any Spanish?'

'One word, *mestizo*.'

Father Silvestre grinned. 'I'm a writer of *mestizo* history.'

'That's great. I don't think I've ever met a writer before.'

'An historian, actually. The book is entitled *A Diversified History of Mesoamerica*.' Father Silvestre lunged for the dish of *enchiladas* filled with highly spiced meat, chilli beans, and chicken which Chitre, in his grubby chef's apron, set down in front of them. 'I'm on page two thousand and ninety-six.'

'Oh boy!' Keir, his eyes watering, wished he hadn't been so hasty in choosing to go Latin so soon, for by now, not only his tongue and throat were on fire, but also his eyes and stomach.

'Before anyone else tells you, I'm not really a priest any more. They excommunicated me for writing a book called *Fornication Within The Vatican*.'

'That was very brave of you er – um ...'

'Father Silvestre, if you please, Doc. The Church might have seen fit to abandon me for telling the truth, but I have not seen fit to abandon the Church of Rome – not yet. You'll pick up Spanish soon enough, though it isn't vital. Many Indians speak good English. I'm Creole, that's an upper-class *mestizo*. My father was Spanish, my mother a classic highland Maya Indian. The Mayas don't usually inter-marry, but I think my mother was already having me when her father tièd mine up to a sacred Maya tree with a gun to his head. That's why I was born up in Maya country in the month of Gettysburg, in the year the French invaded Mexico and made Maximillian of Austria Emperor.'

'Is that right!'

'What makes you want to be a banana doctor?'

'I was intending to do more than operate on only bananas, Father.'

'Forget it. None of your predecessors stayed more than six months. Holy awful job. VD's the worst part of it.'

'You mean the *mestizo* have a lot of venereal disease?'

'Voltage disturbances. Electricity's always failing when you least expect it. Get a lot of earthquakes, you know. Last one in 1917 completely levelled Guatemala City. I was a parochial priest in those days, and spent two weeks digging my parishioners out of the rubble so that they could be given a decent Christian burial.'

Keir became more out of his depth than ever. He had never seen anyone eat or drink like Father Silvestre, let alone talk! But unlike Joss, Father Silvestre could hold his *pulque* and appeared none the worse for it. The meal lasted nearly three hours and afterwards Father Silvestre took out a pack of cards, pushed aside the dirty dishes still on the table, and began laying out the cards, face down on the smeary, chilli-stained oilcloth. He was soon joined by interested individuals of diverse nationalities haunting the waterfront, and patience turned into an all-night session of pontoon. Keir dozed off at the table, his head on his folded arms, while the boisterous Indians and Mexicans gambled the night away with the priest. At length Father Silvestre had shaken Keir's elbow. 'Want some more *aguardiente* to revive you, Doc?'

'No thanks, I've had enough.' Keir turned his glass upside down on the table. *Aquardiente*, he had discovered, was a fiery and caustic sugar-spirit liquor Father Silvestre drank to wash down the *pulque* beer. As for himself, he could no longer stand straight, or even sit straight. Paralytic from exhaustion and feeling decidedly ill after what he had eaten and drunk, Keir murmured something about finding a hotel for the night.

Without waiting to finish the game, Father Silvestre gathered up the cards amidst a roar of protest, thrust them back into the pocket of his soutane, rammed his hat on his head, and said, 'Let's go, Doc. We might make it in time for breakfast.'

'What?'

'Banana city where the Fruit Bats operate. Remember,

374

my son, everything in Guatemala, including volcanoes, is owned by the giant fruit companies. Isn't that what you came here to do, *Americano*, play at doctors and hospitals on behalf of the UCF? Or are you another one of those danged American Intelligence agents they send out here from time to time to spy out Communist-backed drug cartels?'

'I'm just an ordinary guy doing an ordinary job, Father.'

'Right. Let's go find the ordinary hospital, then.'

He had remembered nothing more until the Fageol's radiator dried up and two tyres, shredded to pieces on the rough lava-strewn road, had to be changed. Mercifully Father Silvestre knew of a garage a few hundred yards ahead, to which they pushed the Fageol. Father Silvestre collapsed on the tailboard of his truck and Keir had to revive him with the silver flask which Father Silvestre had filled with tequila before he had left Chitre's chilli restaurant. Sunrise was touching the cactus plants, and the black volcano looming on the horizon looked distinctly menacing as red-gold reflections from the rising sun haloed the crater-rim.

'Holy Mary, the Fageol will be the death of me,' Father Silvestre re-entered life along with the dawn.

'It won't be the only thing, Father. Strong liquor doesn't help.'

'Yes, it does,' Father Silvestre growled above the flask of tequila.

Keir put away the stethoscope he had managed to find among his luggage. 'You've got a heart-murmur, and it's a wonder to me you're not dead from pushing that truck up this steep road. Bed-rest as soon as we get to the hospital. I want to do some check-ups on you, and maybe get an X-ray of your irreplaceable parts.'

Father Silvestre was highly amused. 'X-ray you say?'

'What's so funny?'

'Wait and see, my son.'

Keir didn't like the sound of that at all as he helped Father Silvestre back into his truck, by now fully operative again after the loving ministrations of the garage owner, Kanek. 'Try filling radiator with water sometime, Father. Truck don't go without gasoline or tyres.'

'Don't be cheeky, Kanek,' Father Silvestre fanned himself with his priest's hat.

'He do this every time he go to Puerto Barrios to pick up officials of Fruit Company, Doc. He only do this pick-up run because they let him stay for nothing in Fruit Bat hospital. Otherwise he have to pay insurance money like everyone else, and he never has no money. He and his truck both in state of collapse because he look after neither. Last time he not pay me, Doc, for repairs to truck.' Kanek put out an oily hand. Beneath his thick, straight black thatch of hair, Kanek's black eyes were soulful, his expression mirroring the poverty line.

As with the Mexican restaurateur, Chitre, Keir had no option but to pay Father Silvestre's outstanding bills. He climbed into the driver's seat and prayed for no further mishaps before they reached Guatemala City.

'Stick to the Ruta al Atlantico, and you won't go wrong.' Father Silvestre's large head with its cap of tight iron-grey curls, sank down on his chest and he snored all the way into the city suburbs. Keir had to shake him awake for directions to the clinic. 'Avenida 6, Zona 10,' mumbled Father Silvestre, rubbing his bristly chin.

'Thanks for nothing. Which zone are we in now?' said Keir, who also felt in dire need of a shave, shower, and at least six hours' good, solid sleep.

Father Silvestre opened one eye and glanced out of the nearside window. 'Zona 4 … we've passed it. Keep going in a circle, Doc. When you get to Zona 1, you're in the heart of the city. Zona 10 is on the outskirts. My ulcer hurts bad, Doc.'

Keir, by a miracle, found Zona 10, Avenida 6.

The sixty-bedded clinic with thirty nurses, two qualified doctors, and five student doctors turned out to be a figment of Señor Barras's London imagination. Keir could only assume that the man had never set foot in Guatemala, or else company bosses were suffering from illusions of grandeur. So desperate to find a qualified doctor, who also happened to be a masochist with only half a brain, Señor Barras had gilded the lily, and how!

Señor Barras, however, had not lied when he had said the building accommodated sixty patients, for all sixty were squashed into one ward. Medical and surgical cases jumbled together, male, female, adults, and children integrated. Ages were mixed, and not everyone had a bed to sleep on. Mattresses end-to-end on every available inch of floor-space, Keir had to pick his way carefully through bodies to reach the administrative office.

There he had met Dr Philippe Delvalo having a nervous breakdown. 'Santa Maria Madre, *gracias*!' He had clasped his hands together and Keir thought Delvalo was about to kiss him for sheer joy. 'I began to think you were not coming and had changed your mind like they all do. But I was expecting you yesterday, Doc, so what happened?'

'Transport problems, sorry.' Keir looked around him helplessly.

'Now that you are here at last, Americano, I quit. Goodbye. I am supposed to have been gone two months ago. Father Silvestre will show you the ropes.'

'I thought Father Silvestre was a patient?'

'He is. Anything you need, you'll have to get yourself. Anything you want to know, you'll have to find out for yourself. I quit, and good riddance to this den of infection. From now on, I treat only patients able to pay good money, not company peanuts!'

Delvalo had picked up his medical bag and walked out of the shabby office where everything was filed either in cardboard shoeboxes or not filed at all. The mass of messy paper work did nothing to reassure Keir.

He made a dash after Delvalo, 'Hey-hey! Don't walk out just like that! I haven't slept all night. I need to settle in here first. I need to know a lot of things. I need to familiarize myself with the layout of the place.'

'Won't be difficult, it's what you've already seen.'

'One mixed ward?'

'Unless you want to use the earthquake-damaged storehouse at the back.'

'No operating theatre?'

'Surgical cases are transferred to Guatemala City General Hospital.'

'No X-Ray unit?'

'Guatemala General.'

'Supplies?'

'Central Hospital Supplies, Zona 2.'

'What is this place?'

'Death row, Doc.'

'How many nurses?'

'Five, including night shift.'

'How many doctors?'

'One. Yourself.'

'Orderlies?'

'Two, and Peppy.'

'Who is Peppy?'

'Sweeper and Lavatory Cleaner.'

'Oh, that's a relief, they actually have lavatories here! What about kitchens?' Keir, in a definite panic by now, had followed Delvalo into the pit-holed yard that also served as hospital car park for the company Buick and one extremely ancient, battered and rusty Standard 6 Dodge converted for hospital use. Without its roof and stripped of its passenger seats, this lumbering contraption was no doubt the one and only ambulance, since it sported a roughly-painted red cross on the hood.

'Cookhouse in the yard, if the cook hasn't quit again. That's a regular occurrence. If that happens, the walking wounded cook the grub, or else the relatives bring in the tacos.' Philippe Delvalo turned round and flung Keir several bunches of keys, one after the other. 'The Buick's all yours, Doc. They can't get me to stay another minute, not even for that perk! *Adios amigo.*'

'What happens if I decide not to take the job?'

'Then that's a *mestizo* problem.'

'What happens if I need a day off?'

Philippe Delvalo smiled cunningly. 'Then I'm available, for a fee. Fruit Bats are very generous. You're allowed twelve days a year with pay, taken in any order you want. Altogether, far apart, or one day a month. When I stand in for you, the difference in my private capacity to your company capacity is subtracted from your monthly salary. In other words, whichever way you look at it, Doc, you come off worse. Welcome to Fruit Bat country.'

'Thanks a lot!'

In disgust Keir had walked back into Clinica Unida Comercial, wondering how he was going to cope with such a shambles.

Father Silvestre, meanwhile, had turfed out an intruder who had crept into his bed during his chauffeuring activities to Puerto Barrios, and was sitting up, still wearing his soutane and hat, and grinning like a huge black killer whale. 'Don't drink the water, Doc. We ran out of purification tablets a fortnight ago. Oh, and I should check the emergency electricity generator just in case of an earthquake. X-Ray!'

'Get lost, Father!'

Surprisingly, he had coped, the challenge, if anything, spurring him on. He had sorted the place out into five smaller wards, male and female surgical, male and female medical, and one childrens' ward. The infection rate dropped to one per cent when it had been forty-five per cent blue pus under Delvalo's administration. He had found reliable new staff to assist him, and, more importantly, loyal enough to go through thick and thin with him in order to set the place to rights. Peppy, of course, had stayed. He had even managed to get a portable X-Ray machine installed at the company's reluctant expense, as well as two decent and reliable ambulances. He had threatened to do a Delvalo on them, and the X-ray machine turned up within a month, both ambulances within a year. The Fruit Bats could not afford to lose Dr Keir Hunter Devlin now, for he was getting his patients back to work fitter and faster than any other *Medico General* United Commercial Fruiterers had previously employed! Keir was justifiably proud of his unique achievement.

Father Silvestre he had been unable to cure. Keir showed him X-rays of his internal workings. 'You're a walking medical disaster, Father.'

'I've known it for years, Doc. Will I have time to finish my book?'

'Not if you don't give up *tequila, pulque* and *aguardiente*.'

'Then you'll have to finish it for me.'

'I'm flattered, but my vice is medicine, not writing.'

'I'm leaving tomorrow, Doc, so you can have my bed.'

'I haven't discharged you yet. You have a sub-diaphramatic lesion.'

'What in Holy Mary's name is that?'

379

'An ulcer that needs time, rest, and diet in order to heal properly. You also have gall bladder problems. It ought to be whipped out.'

'I'm homesick, Doc. Listen, tell you what. I'll go back to Santiago, and you come and join me when you get your four days off. We'll go fishing and shooting together in the Sierra Madre. That'll do my ulcers, piles, bowels, and bladder more good than papaya or scalpel.'

'Only if you promise to take better care of your health.'

'I promise. Hail Mary, Mother of God, I promise. Now can I go home?'

'Fill that truck of yours with gasoline, oil, and water, so that you don't have to push it home.' Keir had said in despair, knowing that Father Silvestre would otherwise walk out in the middle of the night.

The pattern thus established, Keir spent twelve days a year with Father Silvestre and the Tzutuhiles of Santiago Atitlán, and Father Silvestre spent an inordinate number of days as a reluctant inmate of Clinica Unida Comercial, bemoaning the effects of papaya upon his gut. The History of the Central American Indians progressed by five pages, and Keir became a good shot, as well as an excellent fisherman who had learned to speak Spanish like a native.

The only time Father Silvestre changed out of his soutane into an ordinary man's clothes was to go fishing or hunting in the mountains. Keir came to learn, among the other odd quirks in Father Silvestre's character, that the great man without his priest's robes was uncomfortably naked. Father Silvestre displayed, therefore, a demure shyness not usually apparent, and kept his priest's hat by his elbow on the breakfast-table to compensate for the gaudy Indian *pantalones* and rawhide cowboy shirt he sported.

Desayuno, breakfast of golden maize and cheese potato-balls called *buñuelos*, strong coffee, and fruit served by Solola at five o'clock in the morning, fortified a wide-awake Father Silvestre before setting off.

He was the most amazing man Keir had ever known. 'How much sleep have you had after your night of drinking and gambling?'

'Two hours. What's it to you, *mío amigo*?

'Just checking up on *your* health and the truck's. While you've been munching your way to a brand new ulcer, I've been giving Fageol his breakfast gasoline. The tank was empty, Father, so I could only assume you were setting off the day after tomorrow for the bus station at Panajachel on the breath of an angel's promise. However, the tank is now full, engine checked, tyres inflated, radiator attended to, fanbelt reinstated, and so now I need fear nothing when it's time for me to depart.'

'Hmm!' Father Silvestre piled more *buñuelos* onto his plate. 'You were never a priest.' He spoke with his mouth full. 'Had you been, you would eat at any hour, anywhere, anyhow. Hunger is an enemy more powerful than bullets, Doc, and matins was invented by an insomniac Italian.'

Keir finished his cup of black coffee, all that he was able to face at that time of the morning. 'I hope you realise it will be almost six o'clock by the time we walk around to my favourite fishing spot?'

'I'm coming, Americano.' Father Silvestre wiped his mouth and left the table. 'Solola ...' he bellowed into the back regions of the inn, '*dondé esta la mochila ...? Gracias,*' he said coyly when Keir handed him the rucksack that had been beside his chair all along. 'It's just that I have my one and only soutane in it and so I wouldn't like to lose it, especially when Solola has washed and ironed it for me – wait a minute.'

'Now what?'

'We'll take the dog with us.'

'Why?'

'He's missed me. He's fretful and crochety. He's a man's dog, and lately I've left him too much with women. I don't want a pansy dog.'

'You'll be back tomorrow night.'

'Maybe. Nothing is certain in this life, Americano. I might fall into the lake and drown.'

'As long as you don't poison the fishes. Must he come?' Keir looked dubiously at mangy Jaguar. Evil-smelling, fleabitten and scratching himself to death, Jaguar would be more of a nuisance than he was worth.

They followed a thickly wooded hill-trail to Keir's

favourite fishing spot on the lake. Fishing-rod and rucksack over his shoulder, he whistled a happy tune. The morning was wonderfully fresh and clear and in the distance the impressive peaks of two giant volcanoes, San Pedro and Tolimán, loomed menacingly. Keir did not care for volcanoes, they always made him feel uneasy. At the little Indian village of Santa Ana, unpretentious and remote in its amphitheatre of rock and water, mountains surrounding them, volcanoes on the horizon, they went firstly, according to custom, into the local hostelry run by a Mexican couple, Deena and Rancho. Father Silvestre ordered his usual pre-fishing *soupçon*, called *atole*, which Keir considered to be a truly diabolic drink and one he had never touched after the first time. It was made from maize, fruit, sugar, and instead of the usual chocolate, Father Silvestre took it with a dash of chilli. He maintained it set him up for the day. They hired two *cayuco*, dugout canoes, from Rancho, as one small canoe would not have been able to accommodate both of them adequately.

In the clear sunlight the fishing was good. While the Indians spear-fished, and even Father Silvestre was no mean expert in the art, Keir preferred the conventional *Americano* way with hook, line and sinker, and ignored Father Silvestre's ascerbic comments drifting across the water.

'What measly bluegills you're catching, Americano! Throw them back – ah-ha! Now look here at the size of this smallmouth black bass.' Proudly he held it up on the end of his bamboo spear for Keir to examine. 'This is what you call a *real* fish and a proper-sized meal for a real man's supper.'

'Don't talk so much or so loudly, Father. You'll frighten off every other bass in the place.' Keir lolled back in his boat and relaxed, only disturbing himself to reel in a carp, perch, or bluegill, leaving the bigger game-fish rippling the waters of this enormous and very deep lake to Father Silvestre and his spear. 'This is the life, eh, Father?'

'One can still find weeds in paradise, my son.'

'Yeah, and angels are ordinary folk in heaven. I've heard it all before.'

'Life is life, my son. So tell me, why are you thinking of

quitting paradise? Have they recalled you to the Pentagon?'

Astonished by such a calculating remark from Father Silvestre when he had never intimated a single thing about leaving Guatemala, Keir said gruffly, 'Bloody hell, you're like a bloodhound always looking for ulterior motives when there aren't any!'

'Aren't you getting restless? I know you by now Doc, and you're trying to let me down gently. Where are you off to next?'

'I'm not off to anywhere! I'm committed to work in Guatemala for five years. I signed a contract.'

'Means nothing. Oh well, maybe my intuition was wrong this time, and American Intelligence didn't send you to spy on me.' Father Silvestre yawned loudly, sound carrying clearly over the clear blue water. 'I'm off to get some shut-eye among the reeds. See you anon, Doc.' He put away his spear, made himself comfortable in the bottom of his canoe, paddled into a natural mooring-bay of high, stiff reeds, and was lost to view.

As the morning progressed Indian women and their young children came down to the edge of the lake to wash the family laundry. With their bright red head-dresses, elaborately woven skirts and *huiples*, long, beautifully embroidered overblouses, and woven shawls, they were like a flock of eye-catching rainforest birds. Chattering, laughing, and bashing out the linen on the huge boulders at the water's edge while the children splashed happily at play, they shattered the peace of the lake and fishing was over for a little while at least.

Keir followed Father Silvestre's earlier example and paddled his canoe into the reeds. He slept soundly for a couple of hours and only awoke when the first large drops of rain began to splatter on his face. He sat up and stretched, aware that the low rainclouds shrouding the tops of the volcanoes were there to stay for the next few hours. Keir resumed his fishing. The best time to catch the big ones, he had discovered, was when it positively bucketed.

Father Silvestre presently emerged from the reeds, and along with all the Indian fishermen gliding silently across the vast pock-marked surface of Lake Atitlán, they spent a glorious afternoon catching fish in the rain.

By the late afternoon, rainclouds disappeared and the sun came bursting through. Keir and Father Silvestre went back to Deena and Rancho's hostel to change out of their wet garments, dry clothing in their rucksacks. The white shell-strewn, sandy shore was the hostel's front garden, a banana grove its back garden, restaurant and amusing liquor-bar somewhere in the middle; this was what Father Silvestre had meant when he had talked about paradise.

After a couple of drinks and lively conversation at the bar, Father Silvestre, back in his soutane, took out his pack of cards and started a poker game with some Mexicans. Then, underneath the stars, with the lulling motion and soft sounds of lapping water on the sand, they lit a campfire on the beach and cooked a feast of fish. Afterwards, replete, Father Silvestre hauled out from his rucksack his gigantic manuscript to continue his history of Mesoamerica by firelight. Keir fed the campfire with driftwood and found himself once more thinking of Raven Quennell: it was a bad sign, and he knew it. Perhaps he ought to consider Abyssinia after all.

'Know anything about Beatriz de la Cueva?' Father Silvestre asked out of the blue.

'No, should I?'

'Pedro de Alvarado's widow.'

'The faceless Big Boss of the worthy Company of Fruit Bats?'

Father Silvestre knew very well that *El Americano* was 'sending him up' and ignored the facetiousness in his tone; the Doc knew exactly what he was talking about. 'Spanish lieutenant in the wars against Montezuma. Cortés put him in charge of the army and told him to subdue this land, so Alvarado immediately obeyed orders and slew Tecún Umán, the great Maya-Quiche warlord – an ancestor of mine.'

'Interesting.'

'Beautiful Beatriz was only twenty-two, the first woman to rule Guatemala. Shortest ruler in Mesoamerican history.'

'She was a dwarf?'

'Her reign lasted approximately thirty-six hours, ten minutes.'

'That *was* short.'

'She declared herself Governor and Supreme Ruler of Guatemala, Alvarado, meanwhile, having been crushed under his secretary's horse while pursuing Montezuma up a Mexican volcano. He was very philosophical about it as he lay dying, blaming himself for having taken a fool like his secretary with him to Mexico. Unfortunately – fortunately for the Mayas who didn't like her – Beatriz soon joined her husband on the other side. She was swallowed up in a great earthquake, followed by a flood, while she knelt praying for his soul in her private chapel. Volcan Agua erupted and that was the end of her. Part of Maya prophecy. For superstitious reasons, the capital was moved into the Panchoy Valley and in the next two hundred years grew to become the most magnificent city in Mesoamerica. Not much left of it now, I'm afraid.'

'How so?'

'Earthquake levelled it to the ground in 1917.'

'Oh yes, now I remember you have mentioned it before – quite often.'

'I guess the next big one will be about the year – um, let me see, in the year 1976.'

'How can you be so sure?'

'Maya prophecy, my son. They calculated with zero one thousand years before we even knew how to use zero. There is a mysterious power that moves us poor human ulcers upon this earth in the same way as a seismic fault moves *under* the earth. Nobody knows how or why such an advanced and powerful civilization as the Maya-Quiche suddenly disappeared off the face of the globe during the ninth century. It wasn't a Beatriz earthquake, flood, or volcanic eruption. No one knows. Only the ruins of their colossal cities are testament to their existence at all. I am still working on it.'

'What have you found?'

'Not a lot. But I believe that creation and disintegration are part of a powerful motivating force within ourselves, and are nothing to do with God and the Devil, who are no more sinister than the creative good and the destructive

385

bad at work within man himself. Self-sufficiency on earth, and total harmony with ourselves as well as our environment, Doc, so forget about heavenly harps or hellfire and brimstone.'

'A strange anti-establishment philosophy for a priest, surely?'

'Ex-priest; *dismembered* in more ways than one on an act of heresy and treason against the Church of Rome.'

'That figures.'

'I believe the Chinese, not the Church, have got it almost right: Yin and Yang.'

'Yin and Yang?'

'Similar to ancient Mayan philosophy: creation through power and energy, the worship of the elements, fire, sun, earth, water, air. Yin is growth above the ground, Yang is growth below the ground. Yang is *power* and *energy*, the motivating force in the process of creation. Yin is passive harmony with one's environment, the female side of it all.'

'You've lost me, Father.'

'Let me put it this way: a big earthquake is Yang, power and energy; the Yin bit is the bright new jewel of a tropical island pushed up from the ocean bed by the forces of Yang, the birth process. I joined the FBI after the Church threw me out,' continued Father Silvestre, going off at a tangent.

'Oh yeah!' Keir was used to the priest's flights of fancy, and took them in his stride.

'They wanted to smash a big drug cartel operating from Antigua – Mexicans, bringing in the stuff over the border. Banana boats were then taking raw heroin into the United States. I helped put away Pedro Domingo – you may have heard of him, a big Fruit Bat boss and gang leader. He was caught and sentenced to twenty years, but only served seven before they let him go. He's up to his old tricks again, pushing drugs, violence, and vice on the streets of San Francisco, New York, Antigua, and Guatemala City.'

'So you've reoffered your services to the FBI?'

'Yep. Pedro Domingo and I are old friends turned enemies. We grew up in the same village, so I know all his devious little ways, as well as his hideouts. Poisoning the simple *mestizo* with drugs, just so that he can get fat and rich and live in style in Acapulco and New York, makes me angry in a way that even the Church of Rome never made me angry. Besides, life gets a bit monotonous wearing a soutane all the time. It's the ideal disguise though. Confession boxes are better than thumbscrews, especially in Catholic countries.'

'Just to change the subject, Father,' Keir jogged the old priest back to reality, Father Silvestre sometimes getting carried away on his own heavenly cloud. 'What happened to my gramophone and records that I lent you?'

Father Silvestre frowned in abstraction. 'Holy Mary, how should I know?'

'You didn't forget, and leave it all behind on your last sortie into the jungle by yourself, eh, Father? Rhapsody on a theme of Paganini by Rachmaninov was a favourite of mine. A darned expensive one too, since it was the maestro's most recent composition recorded on HMV.'

'You have a technically suspicious mind, Americano. But now you mention it, it must be around somewhere, along with all your other Master's Voice rubbish. I'll get Solola to look for it tomorrow.'

'Tomorrow we fish again.'

'Then the day after. You're nit-picking tonight, Americano!'

'Sorry. I'm a bit tired. I think I'll turn in if you don't mind.'

'Why should I mind? I'll be able to get on with my writing. I hate long faces around me, and yours is long tonight, Doc.' Father Silvestre took out his flask. '*Buenas noches, mío amigo.*' Father Silvestre smiled to himself. He watched Keir amble off up the beach back to Deena and Rancho's hostel, where they would be staying the night, and shook his head in bemusement while thinking to himself that *El Americano* badly needed a woman or a war to take his mind off himself.

The following day the programme was repeated. But the evening proved to be far more lively than the one before. Local fishermen gathered around the campfire and started grilling the catch of the day. Someone fetched a crate of *pulque* from the hostel and presently everyone was making a night of it, singing, laughing, swapping far-fetched yarns and shaggy-dog stories, while Jaguar and another dog had a fight on the beach.

The fishermen took bets while the dogs snapped, snarled, and sprang at each other. Half Jaguar's ear hung off. Then Jaguar went for the other dog's throat. It fled, tail between its legs, followed by Father Silvestre's fishing spear. He had won his bet and Jaguar was rewarded with the remnants of everyone's fish supper, while Keir came to terms with the fact that he would never get used to how animals were treated in this country.

In the early hours, beneath an umbrella of bright, cold stars, they took the long trail back to the Mission Inn at Santiago Atitlán, where Keir dropped wearily into bed, and even Father Silvestre went quietly to his room.

The following day, Keir's last free day for four months, he and Father Silvestre spent the morning fishing in home waters, Solola cooked a special 'going-away' lunch for him of *tamales*, pancakes with fillings and sauces only she knew how to make. Then he and Father Silvestre set off to the main lake resort of Panajachel, where Keir bought Peppy his special tobacco and rum. From here Keir would take the bus back to Guatemala City, ninety-six miles away, and Father Silvestre would return to Santiago Atitlán in his truck.

'*Adiós amigo*,' said Father Silvestre, waving his hat out of the window. '*Muchas gracias* for the pleasure of your company, and when I see you next time at Christmas, we go big-game hunting in the Sierra Madre, eh, Americano?'

'You bet, Father!'

Six weeks later, Keir was in his surgery performing a minor operation for the removal of nasal polyps, thinking to himself he would be better off giving his job to a first-aider while he himself went back to what he was trained to do, when Peppy burst unceremoniously into the surgery.

'Get out of here, Peppy!' Keir shouted behind his mask. 'You know you can't come in here while I'm operating ... Nurse, hand me those septum forceps, next size ... You still here, Peppy? I thought I told you to buzz off.'

Peppy's inverted rib-cage heaved with effort and fright as he wheezed gustily, 'Come quick, Doc, much trouble with priest.'

'What priest?'

'Father Silvestre.'

'He's not back again, already? Okay Nurse – that's it I think. Don't remove the pressure pads till I tell you … What's wrong with Father Silvestre?' Keir straightened his aching spine to look at Peppy.

'He dead drunk, Doc. He park truck through wall of hospital yard. Everyone think earthquake come when bricks crash everywhere. Then Father Silvestre, he fall out of truck into middle of car park.'

'Right, I'm coming.' Keir stripped off his gloves and mask, and still in his white surgical gown followed Peppy into the back yard where everyone was gathered around the prone figure of Father Silvestre. Keir was perturbed to see Solola, who never left her village, kneeling beside Guay, another familiar figure from Santiago Atitlán, for Guay was the local garage owner who had serviced Father Silvestre's truck on Keir's last visit to the village.

Solola, cut and bleeding from the impact with a solid brick wall, was mercifully not more seriously injured. She wept and wailed, and, in general, was making so much fuss over Father Silvestre, who lay flat on his face and out for the count in the yard, Keir, at first, thought he was dead.

"All right everyone, back to work, clear a space. What's he been up to now, Solola? I thought I told you to lay off the tequila, Father,' Keir said angrily as he turned the priest's large head to one side so that he wouldn't smother or choke himself to death.

Solola agitated Keir's sleeve, and shook her head. 'He sick bad, not drunk Doc. That is why I come this time with him to hospital. Guay, he drive truck from Santiago without knowing the way, and only in city, Father Silvestre drive when Guay get lost. Father Silvestre, he fight and sing and say he can drive truck, but all the time he like crazy man. Then, when he get here, he finished, and truck smash into hospital wall.'

Keir tried turning the hefty priest onto his back so that he could examine him properly, but Father Silvestre remained as rigid as a board. Face-down in the dusty yard, he mumbled insanely while refusing to cooperate.

'Bloody hell, Father! You've probably gone and given yourself a perforated ul ...' Solola again shook her head emphatically, and tugged his sleeve, trying to make herself understood.

'Not tequila this time, it *Jaguar!*'

'Jaguar? His dog?'

Solola nodded. 'He shoot Jaguar which make him unhappy.'

'Why did he do that?'

'Dog, he go very funny — he bite Father, he bite me. Jaguar like mad dog, so Father must shoot him.'

'When?'

'Maybe two week ago.'

'Miguel, Jimmy ...' he called the two sturdy orderlies. 'Get a stretcher and get him inside quickly.'

Father Silvestre, upon movement, began thrashing about with such violence, in the end it took three orderlies and Keir to get him into bed in a small isolation cubicle. Keir examined Father Silvestre carefully, and was perturbed by his condition. He found partially healed wounds and scar-tissue on the back of Father Silvestre's hands, ankles, and calves.

Keir asked the nurse to fetch Father Silvestre a drink of water, and as soon as the priest saw the water, his mental confusion increased, he had difficulty in swallowing, and began foaming at the mouth. His worst fears confirmed, Keir was devastated; all that could be done now for Father Silvestre was to keep him isolated, tranquilized, and comfortable.

Solola had been bitten on the heel by Jaguar, a deep puncture-wound, which Keir had to treat by soap and water surgical debridement, and afterwards, a strong solution of nitric acid. Guay claimed he had not been bitten by Jaguar, the dog had only licked his head, but to be on the safe side, Keir sent off blood and saliva samples to the pathological laboratory at Guatemala City Hospital from both Solola and Guay.

Rabies had a lengthy incubation period. Immediately Keir undertook Pasteur treatment on Solola and Guay.

Serological tests taking too long – at least a week to give a positive diagnosis – they both might be dead in that time, so it was a difficult decision for Keir to have to make regarding whether or not to give rabies vaccine to his patients without a positive serological result. To give rabies vaccine to Solola, especially, without being perfectly certain that she *had* actually contracted the disease – and she had a four to one chance of *not* – was a risky business. Should it transpire that she was incubating the disease, then she would invariably end up the same way as Father Silvestre. Without having seen the severity of Jaguar's symptoms, Keir was not to know the extent of the risk involved; he could only go by Father Silvestre's condition. Therefore, prevention rather than cure, he reassured himself, was the treatment to undertake in this instance.

Keir telephoned Guatemala City Hospital, asking for more anti-rabies Pasteur serum to be sent over at once, as he hadn't sufficient in stock to treat two people.

'Neither have we enough, Dr Devlin, not all that you require …'

'That's great – then just find me *enough* prophylactic serum from *somewhere*, in order to save *someone*'s life!'

Keir was convinced now, that the vicious stray dog chased off the beach that night at Santa Ana six weeks ago, had been the rabid dog that had bitten Jaguar, who, subsequently infected with rabies, had passed it on when he had bitten his master.

Already desperately ill when he had been brought to the clinic, Father Silvestre was not as lucky as Solola and Guay, who were prevented from contracting the disease because of early systemic treatment and immunization by the Pasteur method.

One night Peppy crept into the priest's room, dried tears in salty runnels on his leathery brown cheeks. 'Wan' a cigarette, Doc?' He offered Keir a brand new packet of cigarettes that Keir knew Peppy had gone out especially to buy for him.

Terribly touched by the old man's regard, and the fact that Peppy had spent his hard-earned money on him in this fashion, and memories of his night vigil by Jodi's bedside eating him away, Keir said to Peppy, 'Thanks Peppy, I don't mind if I do.'

Father Silvestre died at four o'clock that morning, seven days after he had been admitted to the clinic. Keir, who had sat beside him all night, staring out of the darkened window to the starry sky above Guatemala City, realised how close and dear a friend Father Silvestre had become.

And even though there had been no one in the end to give him extreme unction, Keir hoped that a final salvation would not be denied the old, rugged priest, glutton for life and self-confessed reprobate of the Roman Catholic Church, by a power beyond any man's vain and punitive hypothesis.

He also knew that the time had come for him to move on.

PART FOUR

The Third Combatant

'Who is the Happy Warrior? Who is he, that every man in
arms should wish to be?'

W. Wordsworth
'The Happy Warrior'

CHAPTER TEN

London, England: July 1936

Mrs Archibald Cunningham ducked her head from the eagle eye of the waiter hovering nearby with the menu in his hand. Jan thought fiercely to herself, I shall give Archie hell for being so late!

Archie had promised to meet her at one o'clock in the restaurant of Simpson of Piccadilly. It was now a quarter past two, and she was starving. She promised herself she would wait only fifteen more minutes, then leave. In the meantime, she turned back to the parochial gossip in the *Westerham Parish Magazine*, but with one ear tuned to the conversation at the next table. Sipping the last of her Simpson's pre-lunch fruit cocktail, Jan shamelessly listened to the name-dropping taking place. She would not normally have taken any notice of the foreign-looking men in deep discussion, and, at times apt to be a little hot-tempered and loud-voiced, had she not recognized the attractive red-headed Englishman in their midst. Captain Cecil Bebb, an RAF pilot, had been at the same prep school as Archie and her brother Charles. Cecil and she had also met up at a couple of parties since.

'Will he do it?' was the question put to Cecil.

'How can I say?

'This is an undertaking upon which the whole future of Europe depends: indeed, upon which the whole civilized world depends. We deserve some sort of cooperation.'

'Then why don't you ring Hugh Pollard yourself and ask for *his* cooperation?'

'He has a blonde daughter, hasn't he?'

'Yes, Diana. What's that got to do with it?'

'We need three platinum blondes.'

'Why?'

'To make this whole thing look – like a holiday jaunt.'

'But *three* platinum blondes! They don't grow on trees, y'know.'

'We *need* three.'

'All right! Hugh has one, his own daughter. And there's her friend, Dorothy Watson, who is a blonde. She might even be persuaded to come along. However, I can't vouch for a third.' At that moment Cecil Bebb's roving eye caught Jan's at the next table. 'Wait just a minute – maybe I'm being a trifle hasty.'

He came across to her, his face creased in a deep smile of belated recognition. Taking up the hand Jan had extended in greeting, instead of shaking it, Cecil raised it to his lips with calculated charm. 'Jan Fairchild! Well I never, what a small world! How's old Charlie?'

She didn't trust this sauve young RAF pilot an inch. Twenty-six years old, the same age as Charlie, Cecil Bebb seemed very sure of himself. 'He's very well, Cecil. Charlie has won most major racing events this year and is all set for the British title. And I'm now Mrs Archibald Cunningham.'

'Well I never, lucky old Archie!'

'How's the cricket going these days?'

Cecil Bebb's eyes lingered upon Jan's delicate fair features beneath the fashionable white hat with upturned front brim: bobbed hair sleek and golden, curling under, she wore a suit of Prince of Wales checks with padded shoulders and pencil-slim skirt: just the sort of classy young blonde he was looking for. 'Not much time for cricket, I'm afraid – listen Jan, you wouldn't want to do me a favour would you?'

'What favour Cecil?'

'A little holiday – with your husband's approval, of course,' he added hastily.

'Where to?'

'Africa.'

'Why?'

'For the pleasure of your company. Hugh Pollard might be bringing along his daughter. You and Diana know each other, I believe.'

'How clever of you to remember, Cecil: and I'm very flattered you would wish for my company. Africa is a big country. Whereabouts in Africa?'

'Morocco.'

'Morocco? That's Spanish, isn't it?'

'Bits of it.'

'Then why Morocco? I mean, Morocco is hardly fashionable – unless, of course, one is talking about Casablanca.'

'Casablanca, my dear Jan, is *the* place this summer, haven't you heard!'

'No. Archie and I usually spend two weeks in Penzance.'

'Are you still living in London?'

'Off and on. We've recently managed to acquire a dear little cottage in the country, at Westerham. I'm only sorry we spend so little time there. But I must admit, London is awfully dull in July.'

'Oh, awfully dull, Jan. You'll like Casablanca much better. We'll also be stopping off at Biarritz.'

'As tempting as it sounds, Cecil, and as much as I'd have loved to go flying off to Casablanca with you, I have to accompany my husband back to Paris tonight.'

'What sort of work does Archie do?'

'He's in the Diplomatic Corps.'

'Really! I had no idea Archie was … yes, well. I always knew he'd go in for something Empire-building like the FO. Starchy Archie we used to call him at school.'

'Yes, I remember.'

'Has he anything to do with issuing passports and visas and things?'

'Why?'

'Just a thought. It's sometimes nice to have friends in high places.' He smiled tightly. 'Well, anyway, it was worth a try, and I'm sorry you won't be joining us. Be seeing you Jan.'

'Good luck with your platinum blondes, Cecil.'

'Thanks, Jan.'

Cecil Bebb returned to his table and Janice heard him saying something about business to attend to. Shortly afterwards he left the restaurant and the three men at the table ordered more coffee and Cognac.

Ten minutes later Jan looked up as her husband threw a shadow over the *Westerham Parish Magazine*. 'Darling, I'm sorry I'm so late!' Archie leaned over, and placed a husbandly kiss on her cheek. 'Couldn't get away. Everyone's buzzing over what to do about this Edward and Mrs Simpson affair. The PM is desperate for a solution. He even went so far as to approach our Paris office for advice in case the King decides to abdicate and buzz off to France to live his life of exile.'

'Oh no, Archie! They don't honestly think King Edward will abdicate just for Mrs Simpson, do they?'

'Just for Mrs Simpson? Jan, old girl, he's head over heels in love with the American woman, and everyone fears she might even be the next Queen of England. Unless Baldwin digs in his heels and says an emphatic, N.O., England is in for a rough ride monarchy-wise.'

'The sanity of the British public will prevail in the end.'

'That's what Baldwin is banking on. An American queen would be rather too much to swallow. Have you ordered?'

'I didn't know whether to order lunch or tea, this being the in-between hour, as you will see by your watch.'

'Hint, hint. So let's do both. Let's order a three-course lunch, followed immediately by a three-course tea?'

'Why not? That's why I think I married you, Archie.'

'Explain yourself, dear woman?'

'For your down-to-earth practicality.'

'Only because I fear we shan't have anything to eat once we're airborne.'

'Airborne?'

'We're flying back to Paris instead of taking the Golden Arrow: Ambassador's orders. A plane will be waiting for us at six-thirty at Croydon airport to fly us straight to Orly. Sir wants me to be there at the crack of dawn so that I can organize the press, as well as a suitable residence in the Bois de Boulogne for the King and Mrs S., if and when they should decide to marry.'

'Then you think they really will get married after all?'

'Not I alone, but everyone.'

'I do wish you would qualify who this everyone is, Archie!'

'The Government and Buck House, who else?'

'Blow the Government! Governments have been proven wrong in the past. Queen Mary will never allow her son to let England down so badly.'

'Dear girl, love is love, and King Edward won't be the first man to give up a kingdom for it. Now, getting off the sentimental side of things, do you prefer roast beef and Yorkshire pudding, or *boeuf à la mode*?'

'Anything. Whatever you fancy. Archie, Cecil Bebb was just talking to me.'

'The RAF chap? Not terribly *au fait* with him, even though we went to the same chapel stairs on occasions.'

'Chapel stairs?'

'Naked-bum thrashings in public – for major preppy misdemeanors.'

'How primitive. He and those three over there are plotting something, I know it.'

'Calm down, old girl, and stop jumping to conclusions.'

'Don't patronize me, Archie! I know those three are up to something.'

He glanced over his shoulder. 'Cecil isn't with them.'

'He left shortly before you arrived. I'm surprised you didn't bump into him.'

'He was with Jerrold and his cronies?'

'You know them?'

'I know *of* them.'

'Oh honestly, Archie, you're exasperating. Who are they?'

'The one in the middle is Douglas Jerrold, an English right-wing Catholic. The one looking like wet tripe is the unlikeable Luis Bolín, London correspondent of the Spanish pro-monarchist daily newspaper, *ABC*, which is run by the Marqués de Luca de Tena. And the wrinkly third is a Spanish grandee, Juan de la Cierva y Peñafiel, Minister of the Interior during Spain's Tragic Week way back in 1909.'

'Archie, you know things you're not telling me about.'

'Have you heard from Raven lately?' With deep concentration, Archie sawed a piece of meat. 'Darling, I wonder if the chef knows this is really roast beast and not roast beef.'

'You're changing the subject deliberately.'

'Well, have you?'

'Only through her grandfather.'

'Remarkable fellow. Great Englishman. Wasn't looking forward one bit to her initiation ceremony or whatever the Catholic Church call it, until I sat next to Raven's grandfather in that morbid convent place in Toril and he told me all about his campaign to ban bullfighting in Spain. He showed me his remarkable telescope that could not only search out the stars, but also every ship that passed up and down the coastline. A real crusader, the old boy.'

'You never told me all this before, Archie.'

'It's taken me twenty-one months to pluck up courage. What did he tell you?'

'Raven is training to be a nursing sister.'

'I thought she wanted to be a nun.'

'She is still a nun. But apparently Camillus nuns have to pursue useful occupations like teaching, nursing, or housekeeping. She didn't want to teach: she was doing that at l'École Internationale, when she gave up as a pupil teacher because it didn't suit her. Peedee wrote that she had turned down Reverend Mother's offer of housekeeping duties: a certain Dame Rosemarie used to make poor old Raven clean the convent toilets when she was a postulant, and so she chose nursing as the lesser of the three evils, although I can see no difference between cleaning convent toilets and convent bedpans. A women's hospice is affiliated to the convent, I believe.'

'And I thought nuns lived idle, genteel lives praying around their rosary beads all day. Convent life sounds just like the Foreign Office.'

'Full of nuns you mean?'

'Hmm-hmm.' Archie wagged his head, chewed, swallowed, and sipped some water. 'Mind you, I don't hold with her becoming a nun. Dashed bad waste of an intelligent woman.'

'It's her life.'

'There you are then. What did Cecil Bebb ask you?'

'He wanted me to accompany him to Casablanca.'

'Why?'

'He didn't explain, only that three platinum blondes were required to make up the party.'

'What party?'

'He didn't explain that, either. He merely mentioned Diana Pollard and her friend Dorothy Watson. He was hoping to rope Dorothy in as well on the Casablanca run, with myself as the third blonde in the party.'

'Diana Pollard – Major Hugh Pollard's daughter?'

'I presume so. She's blonde, though I don't know if she's a platinum blonde. I wonder what this obsession is with platinum blondes?'

'Kinky, I must say. What else did you overhear?'

'Something about an aeroplane being chartered from Croydon airport, a Dragon Rapide, I think, in the name of Luis Bolín. They were going to telephone Hugh Pollard for his cooperation in the matter.'

'They? Who are they, be more specific, darling.'

'It's that important?'

'It might be.'

'Well then, Luis Bolín did most of the talking. He seemed to be the organizer, while getting Cecil to do the dirty work. He asked for Cecil's cooperation to fly the plane to Casablanca. Jerrold said he would telephone Hugh Pollard and ask him to bring along Diana and Dorothy and one other blonde to add the necessary authentic touch to their holiday jaunt.'

'Bolín, Bebb, Jerrold, and three blondes: all sounds very fishy to me.'

'That's your suspicious mind working overtime. I received another nice letter this morning apart from the one Raven's grandfather sent me.'

'Who?'

'Another extremely nice man. Guess?'

'Couldn't possibly. You have so many beaux, darling, I sometimes wonder what you saw in me.'

'Idiot! Dr Keiren Hunter Devlin, Archie darling.'

'Who is he?'

'You know very well, so don't pretend otherwise.'

'Oh, your American chappie. What did he have to say?'

'I'm not telling.'

'I'll divorce you.'

She dug the toe of her shoe into his shin.

'Ouch, that hurt!' Archie said, leaning down to rub his leg. He picked up his knife and fork again. 'Go on, old girl, spill the beans.'

'Well, then, you know he left Guatemala and went off to Abyssinia with a Red Cross ambulance corp?'

'Did I? I feel you must have told me, but I've forgotten. But doesn't the silly fool know the war's over? Addis Ababa was occupied in May by Italian troops.'

'He's staying on a bit, to help clear up the mess left by mustard-gas burns on the Emperor's barefooted warriors.'

'That's brave of him. The Italians aren't interested in *any* Articles laid down by the Geneva Convention.'

'I know. He mentioned the bombing of Dessie and the Red Cross ambulance convoys, as well as their hospitals. He wanted news of Raven – don't look now, Archie, but our friends the Spaniards are leaving. We'll probably bump into them on the runway this evening if they're flying off from the same aerodrome as we.'

'I hope not … Is he interested in her?'

'Keir and Raven? Oh, I think he's always been interested in her – ever since Opus 30 – never mind, Archie, it's not that important. But although he had separated from his wife, he was still technically married to her when he met Raven in Geneva. He couldn't pursue the relationship for Raven's sake. At least, that's what he told me when he visited London that time. Besides, he always felt that Raven would think him far too old for her. But he's got his *Decree Absolute* now – not being a practising Catholic and all that.'

'That's why I'm good sensible Church of England – although poor old Eddy Eighth is having his own problems with Mrs S and *her* divorce.' Archie chuckled roguishly and rubbed his hands together. 'However, peasant that I am, I can always divorce you when I'm tired of you.'

She jabbed him sharply a second time under the table. 'Too late, Archie. We're going to have a baby.'

He blinked a couple of times and then a slow grin spread across his bland and heavy-jowled face. 'Good Lord. Well done, old girl! Oh gosh, do you think you're fit to fly? I mean, in your condition, will it be safe?'

'Don't fuss, Archie, it's only the size of a pea at the moment according to my gynaecologist.'

'Well, you and he know best, old girl.'

'Archie, should I tell him about Raven?'

'Your gynaecologist?'

'Keir. Should I tell him about Raven?'

'What about her?'

'Oh, Archie, you can be so obtuse sometimes! Should I tell him Raven has become a nun so that he knows it's no good contemplating a Wallace and Edward act as far as Raven is concerned?'

'Bit of a blow to his hopes, poor chap: especially with all that mustard gas around him. One never knows what might happen. I should let him cling to at least the thought of love for the time being. Anyway, Raven could – possibly change her mind about being a nun in a year or two. Besides, it's really not your business, is it? She has a sister to do the informing.'

'That's true. Roxana is bound to dash Keir's hopes if she feels threatened by Raven in any way. But he was wondering why she hadn't replied to a couple of letters he'd sent her, and so I felt I should let him know that she is not allowed to have worldly contact … Goodness! Just look and see who the cat has just brought in – oh Archie! For heaven's sake, I didn't mean you to turn around and stare quite so blatantly! I wonder what she's doing here? And who on earth is that handsome creature with her?'

Archie had swivelled right around in his chair to stare at the couple being shown to a table in a discreet corner of the restaurant. 'Who is she?'

'Vida de Martello, Archie.'

'Not the millionaire Comte de Martello's daughter? Even I've heard of the famous gun-running Count.'

'Does he really do that? No wonder he's so rich. Vida was at school with Raven, Roxana, and myself. She's always in Antibes at this time of the year, so I wonder what brings her to London – excuse me, Archie, I really *must* go and find out her business. I shan't be long.'

'Jan, you are shameless!'

'Yes, I know, but I'd like to discover who her Rudolf Valentino is.'

'Listen, old girl, while you gossip with your old school chum, I'm popping along to do a little chin-wagging of my own in a private telephone booth. I've just remembered something I ought to have told the boffins before I dashed off to meet you. Shan't be long. Maybe they'll bring us tea: order it would you, darling.'

In exasperation Janice watched Archie in his dark pin-striped suit, jacket flying open in his perpetually harassed and absent-minded manner, weave his way in and out of the crowded tables, before presenting herself at Vida's table.

'Janice Fairchild!' Vida, as temperamentally French and efferverscent as ever, flung down the menu she was studying and stood up. She wrapped her arms around Jan and enthusiastically kissed her on both cheeks, and the mink coat around her shoulders slipped to the floor.

The waiter picked it up, 'Shall I take it to the cloakroom, madam?'

'No, we'll keep it here,' the bored-looking Valentino, who had risen to his feet, put out his hand for it. The waiter handed it over. 'Thank you. July in England,' said the foreigner to the waiter as he took the exquisitely soft and wildly-expensive mink coat and draped it over the back of Vida's chair, 'is just like December in Andorra.'

'Indeed, sir. I can't say I've ever been there.' The waiter bowed and then scurried away to serve another table with the look on his face implying that this was England and why didn't foreigners realize afternoon tea was served at three o'clock, *not* lunch!

Jan noticed that Vida de Martello's adolescent puppy fat had given way to a heavier, bustier kind of weight: a contented weight, Jan couldn't help thinking, which somehow did not look ill-at-ease on affluent Vida. 'How nice to see you again, Vida.' She glanced meaningfully at Vida's latest acquisition.

'Oh, please meet my husband,' Vida thrust out her hand. 'Look Jan, a wedding-ring. We got married this morning at Chelsea Registry Office.'

'Congratulations – er …'

Vida's husband shook Jan's hand, his cold light eyes and supercilious smile making allowances for his wife's exuberance. 'Forgive her, please. She's a little over-excited after all the champagne at the Registry Office, and so she has forgotten to make the proper introductions. I'm Ramiro de Luchar.'

'How nice to meet you, Mr – er, Señor de Luchar. And congratulations to you both. I'm also married, Vida. I'm now Mrs Archibald Cunningham.'

'Oh-la-la! You are married, too! I didn't know it, Jan.' Vida squealed in delight and said in short staccato bursts of nervous energy, '*Ram chéri*, Janice was Raven's best friend at school. Jan was Deputy Head Girl. Oh, do you remember what fun we had, Jan! Do you remember the Parc Mon Repos? Do you remember how terribly in love I was with Dr Keir Devlin? Mademoiselle l'Impératrice and everyone else used to be so disapproving of everything I did! In my opinion, Raven only became a nun on account of her crush on Monseigneur Paulus. Do you remember him, the gold-plated god? But I suppose he never meant as much to you as he did to us because you're C of E. I wonder if Keir really did go to Guatemala after his mother's wedding?'

'Yes, he did. But he's now in Abyssinia: well, he was a month ago.'

'Really! What's he doing there?'

'Working for the Red Cross.'

'I wonder if he's still married? Wasn't there something about him being separated from his wife? He was hoping to get a divorce, wasn't he?'

'Yes. He's divorced now. He happened to mention it in his letter.'

Ramiro de Luchar tried to get a word in for himself, all this banal schoolgirl talk making him impatient. 'Mrs Cunningham, what a small world, so you are a friend of Raven Quennell?'

'Yes, I am.'

'Is it not a tragedy that your friend has become a nun? – Oh please sit down with us – how ill-mannered of us to keep you standing.'

'Only for a moment, Señor. My husband has just popped out for a moment to telephone his office, so I can't be too long.'

'Your husband is here with you?'

'Yes, Señor de Luchar. I don't like eating alone if I can help it.'

'Then why do we not all get together later? We could

meet at the Ritz Hotel where Vida and I are staying, and have drinks before dining.'

'Thank you, but Archie and I are flying back to Paris this evening.'

'Jan darling,' Vida gushed, 'do you have Roxana's address?'

'All I know about her is through snippets of news her grandfather lets slip from time to time in his letters. But I believe Roxana and her daughter are in Santa Cruz de Tenerife since her husband has been made a temporary staff officer to the Military Governor.'

'That is very interesting, to know about my brother's military activities through an unrelated third party – no offence Mrs Cunningham.'

'Do you not have any contact at all with your brother, Señor de Luchar?'

'No, Mrs Cunningham.'

'José is the enemy, like Roxana,' Vida said hastily. 'That is why we are in London, to organize a proper army against the Fascists. We have been to lots of communist rallys in and around London, to gain support for the ...'

'Mrs Cunningham,' Ramiro impatiently interrupted his talkative wife, 'do you hear anything of Raven these days?'

'Not a great deal, Señor de Luchar. I only know what her grandfather cares to tell me. Raven is a nursing sister at her convent. I would have thought, however,' said Jan with a crafty little smile, 'that you would know more about Raven than I, as the Camillus Convent at Toril is right on your doorstep.'

'The sad thing about Spain these days, Mrs Cunningham, is that brother and sister all too often have become the enemy of brother and sister – and I have always looked upon Raven as a sister. Nuns and Communists have very little in common, I'm afraid.'

'Yes, I suppose so.'

'You say you and your husband are off to Paris this evening?'

'Yes, he has to get back to the Embassy.'

'*Oh-la-la!*' Vida squealed again. 'Jan, if your husband is attached to the British Embassy in Paris, I have a Jewish friend who desperately needs an exit visa to get her out of

Nazi Germany and into Fra ...'

'Please, Vida,' said Ramiro stiffly, 'do not embarrass Mrs Cunningham, or her husband.'

'*Pardon*! Never mind then, Jan. Perhaps when my husband goes back to Barcelona, Roxy will join Papa and I on the yacht. That is why, Jan dear, I want to get in touch with her again. Roxy is such fun. We quarrelled, you know, last time we were on the yacht together. But now I have forgiven her, and so I think she will forgive me when she knows we are now related.'

'Ah, here comes my husband,' said Janice with a sigh of relief. 'We have to get back to Westerham to pick up our suitcases before dashing headlong to Croydon to catch our plane – Archie, this is Señor and Señora de Luchar. Vida, I mentioned to you, was at school with me, while Señor de Luchar practically grew up with Raven and Roxana. Or should it be the other way around?' Jan smiled at Ramiro, who got to his feet and shook hands with Archie.

Jan added in a rush, 'They got married just this morning, Archie!'

'Is that so?' Archie said. 'Well I never. Congratulations! So pleased to meet you. Grew up with Raven, eh? What do you think about her becoming a nun?'

'She is a crazy girl, Mr Cunningham.'

'Absolutely! Darling – I hate to rush you but ...'

'Yes, I know, Archie. We have a plane to catch. Do excuse us please. Vida, I'm sure you'll be able to get in touch with Roxana again if you approach the military garrison at Santa Cruz de Tenerife.'

She said goodbye to them, and in the back of the official car taking her and Archie back to Westerham, Jan said, 'Goodness me, now I know what Raven meant when she once mentioned something about living life "face to the sun". I should think she was in danger of becoming barbecued, especially in the presence of someone as prickly as Ramiro de Luchar! He, of course, only married Vida for her money.'

'And she, of course, hasn't a brain between her diamond lobes. Could tell that right off. Why would a Communist marry a millionaire's daughter unless he's a Spanish Communist and she's a ...'

407

'Millionaire lesbian Parisienne who has today signed over all her father's gun-running money to the Communist cause?'

'Has she?' Archie looked startled, then they both burst out laughing.

'Archie, darling, if I told you half of what went on at l'École Internationale, between so-called "nice" girls, you wouldn't believe me, so you just tell me who you telephoned at the Foreign Office, and why.'

'That would be giving away State secrets.'

'I'll divorce you.'

'In that case, I told the Chief about your eavesdropping on Luis Bolín and his cronies. The old overhead wires, at this very moment, are doing overtime between here and Barcelona, not to mention Gran Canaria. It's widely believed in our green acres of diplomacy, confirmed by the Spanish attaché in Paris, that civil war is about to break out in Spain.'

'Tell me something new, Archie. There's been talk of civil war in Spain for the past five years.'

'True. But it's pretty well confirmed this time. There have been so many murders of prominent politicians lately, one side against the other, the situation has gone out of control.'

'Why do you suppose Luis Bolín, a Spaniard, is getting an Englishman like Cecil Bebb into mischief, as you so obviously think?'

'The purpose of this innocent holiday trip to Casablanca organized by Luis Bolín, might not be as innocent as it appears. I only wish you had complied with Bebb and taken him up on his offer about flying to Casablanca with Diana Pollard and Dorothy Watson.'

'Oh, for goodness sake, Archie. Why?'

'It might have revealed the real truth behind Bebb's journey to Casablanca.'

'What truth?'

'MI6 believe it to be an attempt to get General Franco out of Tenerife and back to the mainland in order to instigate a military coup to overthrow the Republican Government of Spain.'

'Heavens! First we have pro-Russia Reds like Ramiro de

Luchar under our English beds, and now we have MI6! Come on Archie, live in the real world, will you.'

'Darling, there is only one real world, the survival of the fittest. If I told you that right now, in Paris and Barcelona and Madrid, people are queueing for false passports, or that Jews are being interrogated for selling arms, expensive, *dud* arms, to help the Communists gain a foothold in Republican Spain, or that Mussolini's Blackshirts are organizing themselves to help the Spanish Fascists, or that in Vienna, Monarchists are going on bended knee to get Alfonso Carlos back to Spain, or that Prince Xavier de Bourbon-Parme is being asked for his support in a Nationalist military uprising in Spain, would you ask me again if I'm living in the real world?'

'Dearest Archie, I can only wonder at what goes on in every telephone booth between Piccadilly and Portugal. I thought you were a conventional little British attaché liaising between Whitehall and Paris, not someone engaged in espionage activities! MI6, really!'

He grinned. 'Listen, old girl, even though every diplomatic department is a watertight compartment, and nothing dovetails, there are moments in one's career when everything lands on one's plate together. Today has been one of those days. And I *am* rather sick of issuing passports and visas all day long.'

'It seems like it. So what has happened today, Archie, to make you like a cat on hot bricks?'

'Only a quick briefing by those in the know. Our Government wants to pursue a policy of non-intervention should civil war break out in Spain. Hitler and Mussolini support Spain's Nationalist cause, while France is in a stew because she doesn't want a third Fascist state on her borders. However, while Britain is opposed to Fascism overrunning Spain, and perhaps the rest of Europe, we're not going to intervene. Eden wants Mussolini's army stretched to its limits between Addis Ababa and Madrid. So, while Russia sends Republican Spain her men, Moscas, and Katiuska bombers, and Hitler and Mussolini pour in their Panzers, Heinkels, and Junkers to help the Nationalists, Britain stays out of it, and prays for a stalemate. It's called the waiting game.'

'But that can be dangerous, can't it, Archie?'

'Very dangerous. From the sidelines, we are apt to get hit in the face by ricocheting bullets from all sides.'

'Darling, isn't it going to be awfully dull looking for a suitable house in the Bois de Boulogne for King Edward and Mrs Simpson if they think of marrying, when you've a real war brewing only eight hundred miles from your doorstep?'

'Oh, awfully dull. But I'll manage somehow. I rather fear, however, that from where I stand in all this, if there is civil war in Spain, France will close her borders, and my job at the British Ambassador's right hand in Paris is going to get awfully hectic with all sorts of people trying to get in or out of Spain via Paris. Meanwhile, what are we going to call our son?'

'Diplomacy?'

'Oh look, Jan, I'm sorry to be such a bore, but honestly, I do think this Spanish thing is frightfully important.'

'Do you, Archie, why?'

'For our own survival, old girl.'

'In what way?'

'Fascism versus Communism.'

'And which side are you on?'

'Good Lord, Jan, I'm on no one's side. Both the ultra right and ultra left are not our kind of politics. Britain, thank God, is neutrally level-headed in all this. However, that Ramiro de Luchar fellow is a real hard-nosed Communist, don't you think? I wonder what such a Red is doing in London at the very moment he should be in Spain?'

'Drumming up support for the Spanish Communist Party. Vida hinted something about the Republicans being very short of arms, with no organized army to speak of. That's why the honeymoon was combined with her husband's political activities. He's recruiting British Communists to fight for Spain.'

'Is that so, by jove! What *would* I do without you, old girl, and your international Swiss education.' Archie squeezed her hand tightly.

In the honeymoon suite at the Ritz Hotel, London, Vida de

Luchar tossed her new pair of Italian high-heeled shoes into a far corner, followed by her Fifth Avenue mink coat. She bounced down on the springy bed that was so large one could have a dinner-party on it. She picked up the receiver of the ormolu telephone set placed on the bedside-table, and began dialling the outside number of the International Exchange operator. 'Ram, darling, please grab the internal phone in the other bedroom and get room-service to bring us some more champagne.'

'I have already done that. Can't we get rid of some of these flowers?' He flung out his arm in an expansive gesture of disgust, and added, 'It's like a graveyard in here, and flowers always make me sneeze.'

'You really are a sourpuss sometimes, *chéri*. But very well, I'll telephone the concierge to come and remove them before I speak to Roxy.'

'*Roxana?*'

'Yes. Have you some objection?'

'You heard that Cunningham woman. Roxana is in the Canary Islands.'

'So what?'

'Do you know how far the Canary Islands are from London?'

'What does it matter? You are not paying the telephone charges, but Papa – hello, hello? Is there anyone there? Yes, I am waiting to be connected to the International Exchange!' She sighed in exasperation, 'Why does it always take so *long*!' Vida examined her scarlet fingernails while she waited to be connected.

Ramiro bit his lip. 'I'm going out if you insist on insulting me.'

'We have only just come in, *chéri*.'

'And now I am going out again.'

'Before we've made love? This *is* our honeymoon. Papa will be upset if he knows you've upset me. I'll do *anything* you want of me ...' Languidly, Vida dropped the telephone receiver back on its cradle and slid down the bed. Her eyelids heavy, she held up her arms to him, and gave a wicked little smirk. Her nose crinkling in lambish play, she stuck out the pink tip of her tongue. 'And you can have *all* the money in the world you want, *chéri* as I am now a millionairess in my own right on the marriage settlement Papa gave me.'

Against his handsome, tanned features, Ramiro's smile was broad and white and infinitely sensuous. Vida was reassured. She had bought him for a price, and as long as her fortune lasted, so would her husband. She wriggled out of her dove-grey Dior silk dress in which she had been married, and waited for him to do the rest.

An hour later Ramiro left the Ritz.

Vida again asked the International Exchange operator to put her through to the military garrison of Santa Cruz de Tenerife, but was told that might not be possible as lines and main telephone exchanges on the Spanish mainland, through which connections had to be made, were in disarray.

'Then go through Gibraltar, that's British, isn't it?' Vida snapped.

'I will do my best, madam, but it will be a very long time before you can be connected, if at all. Why don't you send a cablegram? It will be cheaper and easier.'

'Because I want to speak personally to Señora Roxana de Luchar, you fool! I don't care how long it takes, or how it's done, just do it!'

'Very well, madam,' replied the cool, detached voice of the international operator, 'I will keep on trying for you.'

At one o'clock in the morning, Vida, naked and asleep on her stomach in the wide bed, was startled into consciousness by the telephone ringing shrilly beside her pillow. She put out a sleepy arm, and felt around the bed. Ramiro was not there. Disgruntled, Vida sat up, pushed back her wayward and springy brown hair from her eyes and picked up the telephone receiver, '*Oui?*'

'Your telephone call to Santa Cruz de Tenerife, Señora de Luchar.'

'I'll take it now.'

A great deal of clicking on the line followed. Then a man's voice in Spanish said, 'Who is it you are wishing to speak to, señora?'

'Señora Roxana de Luchar – and be quick about it.'

'Personal messages are not being received unless they are of a vital nature.'

412

'This is very vital, Señor Who-Ever-You-Are.'

'Are you a relative? Has there been a death in the family?'

'Yes and yes. This is her sister-in-law. I have news from her husband's brother about what the Communists are doing in Barcelona and who has been put to death ...' And just be thankful you aren't nearer to the mainland yourself, Señor Army-Riff-Raff, Vida muttered to herself as she reached for her cigarettes.

'Then, if you will wait, señora, I will try and locate Señora de Luchar. She will be in married quarters, and midnight is not a good time to find anybody on the island.'

'Neither is one o'clock in the morning in London, señor, so please just hurry yourself.'

Vida lit her cigarette and inhaled deeply. Smoking a 'Kensitas' instead of eating between meals was supposed to make one lose weight according to the advertisement – well she was trying! The minutes ticked by and then the faint but distinctly husky voice of Roxana answered, 'Si? Who is calling, please?'

'It's Vida, Roxy!'

'Vida de Martello?'

'Who else, you silly chump!'

A short silence followed.

Vida said breathlessly, 'Roxy, don't hang up! Please don't be angry with me for contacting you. I just want to say how sorry I am for our quarrel three years ago. Let's be friends again.'

'You're lucky to find me here, Vida. We were at a party, but José was called away to attend to some personal business on behalf of General Franco, and so we left early. I'd only just stepped into the apartment when I heard the telephone ringing furiously. You woke Pippa and her nanny. Where are you?'

'The Ritz Hotel, London.'

'Lucky you. Tenerife is purgatory. It does nothing but rain in the north and broil in the south, and all the time it's just boring-boring! I'm sick of looking at banana plantations and playing tennis with dull foreigners and ugly military wives. Vida, why are you in London? I thought you'd be in Antibes at this time of year.'

'I'm going to San Sebastian as soon as Ramiro goes back to Barcelona, so …'

'Ramiro – Ramiro de Luchar?'

'*Oui, chérie, Ramiro de Luchar!*'

'What's he doing in London? He's supposed to be in prison.'

'Not any more. I have – er, secured his release. He was freed a month ago. So Ramiro and I are now on our honeymoon.'

Another weighty pause followed, and Vida knew Roxana was chewing over all this fresh and stunning news. Vida stubbed out her half-smoked cigarette in the ashtray, and immediately lit another which she inserted into her fashionable cigarette-holder. She inhaled with deep satisfaction, and smiled serenely.

'You and Ramiro are *married*?' Roxana asked disbelievingly.

'*Oui, chérie*, this morning, at Chelsea Registry Office.'

'Does his father know?'

'No one knows, only you, darling, oh, and Jan Fairchild who is now Mrs Archibald Cunningham. I ran into her this afternoon in the restaurant of Simpson of Piccadilly.' Vida, spying a bottle of champagne in the ice-bucket on the floor beside the bed, leaned over and picked it up. She squinted at it in the light of the bedside lamp. At least half a bottle of flat champagne left, she poured some into the empty glass on the bedside-table and wondered whether to drink it or use it as a mouthwash; she also wondered where Ramiro had got to. The ashtray overflowed, she and Ramiro both using it to capacity earlier. But with the unsubtle 'Do not Disturb' notice on the door, no chambermaid with dustpan and brush had dared risk entry into the honeymoon suite. Vida smiled to herself yet again. 'Are you still there, Roxy?'

'Yes, I'm here.'

'What are you thinking?'

'That I'd like to strangle you, Vida de Martello!'

Vida laughed in delight. 'Oh, Roxy, come to London.'

'I think I just might! I want to know what's going on between you and Ramiro.'

'You are still attracted to him?'

'Yes always – he has *much* more gumption than José! You're a bitch, Vida. You only married him to get even with me.'

'Why would I do that?'

'You know damn well.'

Vida gave a little chuckle. 'Darling, you don't only want one man, you want them *all*! I wonder why? Are you, by any chance, darling, still searching for the *right* man?'

'Go to hell, Vida.'

'What about a woman, if your *husband* doesn't come up to your expectations?'

'You haven't changed a bit, have you Vida?'

'Nor have you, Roxy.'

'How do you know?'

'I *know*! If you *really* had wanted nothing to do with me, you would have put down the telephone by now. But, darling, if you want some excitement in your dull life, leave your husband on his banana island, come to London, and I'll tell you all about it. I'll wait here until you arrive.'

Vida replaced the receiver with a definite click and a smug look of satisfaction.

When Ramiro returned, he found his wife sitting up in bed smoking a cigarette, while flicking through the fashion pages of Riviera designs in *Harper's Bazaar*. *The Tatler* also lay beside her, plus a magnum of Roëderer Cristal Brut in an ice-bucket on the bed. Vida had taken a bath, made up her face, put on a fresh silk nightdress, and it appeared room-service, at two-thirty in the morning, had also been busy. The ashtrays had been emptied, bridal bouquets removed, the room tidied, and two supper trolleys crammed with silver entrée dishes stood beside the bed. 'Hello, *chéri*, was she good? Which position did she most favour, fore, aft, or all sails unfurled?'

He didn't deign to reply.

'Where have you been – or need I ask?'

'Stepney.'

'Where is that?'

'In the East End of London.'

'I see. You have been meeting with more English Communists, I take it?'

'*Sì!*'

415

'To raise yet more money and men to turn Spain into another Russia?'

'*Si, si querida!*'

'Ramiro, I'm not going back to Spain with you, because I wish to spend a little more time in London.'

'As you wish.'

Vida stretched arms to the ceiling like a sensually satisfied cat basking in the sun. 'I have made provision for you to be able to draw upon my account at the Bank of Vizcaya whenever you wish, *chéri*. I still wish to be a free woman in spite of the wedding-ring.'

'Thank you. That is most generous of you.' Ramiro took off his tie and shoes. 'Would you mind if I slept on the couch? I'm tired, and I don't fancy lying on chicken bones all night.'

'That's nice of you, *chéri*. I thought I'd been putting on a little weight recently, not taking it off.'

Despite his tiredness, he grinned. 'Sometimes, French lady, I'm glad I married you rather than anyone else.'

'Because no one else you know is as rich as I, uh, Romeo of mine?'

'Very true. But also because you desire me as an appendage, not a person. It's an arrangement that works well from my point of view also. Possessiveness and jealousy, I could not live with. That is why I never asked Raven or Roxana to marry me.'

'You're conceited, Ramiro.'

He came beside her, sat down on the bed, drew down the bedclothes, and drew up her nightclothes. With some amusement he leaned over her and watched her expression glaze over a few moments later. On her gasp of delight, he stopped titillating her, his wry comment, 'I've never known anyone get such maximum pleasure out of such minimum performance.'

'We all have to lower our standards sometimes, *chéri*.'

He didn't know how to take that remark. In the morning, he promised himself, it would be his turn to enjoy his rich and greedy wife, but not now. He'd had enough of women for one night, shrill-voiced, anti-Communist hecklers making him squirm with desire to slap coarse, working-class faces and silence their glottal stops from airing any more of their ignorant opinions on behalf of their witless, out-of-work husbands. However, the blonde East End barmaid afterwards had compensated for the rigours of holding a political rally in a place he would normally have avoided like the plague. He just hoped she hadn't anything that could be passed on besides information.

'What's the matter, Ramiro?' Vida asked sulkily as he walked off, leaving her alone in the big bed. 'Can't you rise to the occasion?' she added with a viperish smile.

'I couldn't screw a barrel of treacle tonight, *chérie*.' He smiled sleekly through the gap in the communicating doors between bedroom and sitting-room, before closing them in her face.

The cheap perfume lingering in the air and on his clothes reminded her of funeral lilies stuck in a tankard of sick. Vida thumped her pillow savagely, and muttered to herself, 'You couldn't even screw a lid off a jam jar, you two-faced Commie bastard!'

Five days later, Roxana arrived at the Ritz Hotel, London, just as Vida had anticipated. With Roxana was Pippa and the Spanish nanny, Annuala. 'Where's Ramiro?' was the first thing Roxana asked.

'He has returned to Barcelona, darling, because two Republican officers have been murdered in the last week by the men who support all you snobbish Nationalists. In reprisal, Ram's lot murdered the revered rightest leader, Calvo Sotelo. But then, I suppose you know all that.'

'I'm really not interested in all that political stuff, Vida.'

'All right then. Ramiro, with the light of battle in his eyes, went hot-footing it back to Barcelona after getting what he wanted in London – English Reds to fight for Spanish Reds. Now tell me how you got here when Spain is seething with so much trouble.'

'Oh God, you might well ask! What a palaver!' Roxana sighed, and threw herself on Vida's double bed, while Pippa and the nanny slept off the effects of the past few days' constant travelling in a suite of rooms on another floor. Roxana helped herself to one of Vida's cigarettes.

She took her time to fit it into an ebony and silver holder that had once belonged to her mother. 'Any champagne around here to quench my thirst, Vida?'

'Of course, darling.' Vida poured some out for Roxana who lay back, relaxed, and said: 'The night that you telephoned me, Vida, everything was at sixes and sevens on the islands. Early that morning Amado Balmes, a friend of José and mine, shot himself in the stomach. He was Military Governor of the Islands, so you can imagine what a scandal *that* kind of accidental suicide caused. José, not I, was invited to his funeral by General Franco – an upstart! I was livid! Anyway, to cut a long story short, I kicked up rather a fuss, I must admit, by refusing to be left on Tenerife without my husband. So I asked my nice and charming friend, General Franco y Bahamonde, if I could attend Balmes's funeral along with my husband. He refused again. So I hopped aboard a pleasure-boat hired by some holidaymakers sightseeing around the island. Do you remember Diana Pollard?'

'The dotty one?'

'That was her friend, Dorothy. Anyway, Diana's father – an ex-major in the British army, Diana herself, and friend Dorothy, were skulking around the black beaches of Tenerife in their boat, eventually to sail back to Las Palmas. I decided to join in the fun. While the tug-boat conveying General Franco and the rest of his important staff officers, including José, plied between Santa Cruz and Las Palmas, I trailed in their wake with the Pollards and Dorothy. Well, once on Gran Canaria, the plot thickened – oh, please excuse me, I've just remembered, I'm dying to go to you-know-where. I haven't had time to get my bearings until now.'

Roxana dashed into the bathroom. Vida, reclining on a chaise longue at the foot of the bed, her rose and black lace negligée trailing on the luxurious *vieille rose* carpet, lit herself a cigarette and gave a self-satisfied smirk.

Roxana said in despair when she re-entered the bedroom, 'Tomorrow I really must get a facial and a manicure at Harrods. Seawater is a killer. Where was I?'

'Telling me about your part in General Franco's coup.'

'Oh yes. Seems funny to me poor old Balmes, who was

an excellent shot, often inviting José and me to go squab-shooting with him on the islands, managed to shoot himself in the broad expanse of his stomach with a pistol he was testing. I can't imagine how a man as good as he with a gun can misfire to such a degree.'

'A political murder like Calvo Sotelo's?'

'Who knows? But it happened at a very convenient moment – for General Franco, that is. However, Franco arrived at Las Palmas for the funeral, while I, still keeping company with the Pollards, met that delicious red-headed man, Cecil Bebb, with his Dragon Rapide. Diana, naturally, got the best of Cecil, while José was furious with me for following him to Las Palmas where I was not wanted. But what seemed funny to me, General Franco asked José to swap passports with him.'

'Did he? Has José come to resemble Franco then?'

'Of course not – are you being facetious, Vida?'

'Of course not, darling. I just wondered, that's all.'

'He had no choice but to obey his commanding officer. General Franco had succeeded in General Balmes's place, as Governor of the Islands, and now he just wanted to skedaddle on *anyone*'s passport, even a camel's if it could get him to the mainland. He was in exile, remember.'

'Intrigue, intrigue!' Vida clapped her hands in delight. 'What happened next?'

'After Balmes's funeral, General Franco, by bribery and corruption, or prearranged intelligence, I don't know what, because I didn't see José again to ask him, suddenly hopped aboard Cecil Bebb's Dragon Rapide and they both flew off to Tetuan before you could say *Arriba Español*!'

'They never did!'

'As sure as I am here now, Vida, the crafty General and the English pilot debunked from Gran Canaria for the garrison at Tetuan. And that, I learned from Diana Pollard herself!'

'Why Tetuan?'

'I only knew the full facts when the plane was airborne, as did everyone else, for suddenly the Moroccan garrisons mutinied. It turned out that Franco was returning to the mainland via Agadir, Casablanca, and Tetuan. A few hours later a military coup at the garrison of Melilla heralded the uprising on the mainland. José had orders to join his command immediately in Tetuan from where troop-ships were leaving for Spain. I took the ferryboat from Las Palmas back to Tenerife. Then I managed to get Nanny and Pippa and myself into Gibraltar on a charter boat. From Gibraltar we went via train to Portugal. I couldn't travel through Republican Spain despite my British passport, because of being married to a Nationalist soldier. Then, from Lisbon to Porto, back into Nationalist Spain where, in Corunna, we were lucky enough to get passage on a British Naval vessel straight to Portsmouth. So here I am at last.'

'Good for you, but what a roundabout journey, poor darling! I tried to get in touch with my father at San Sebastian to go and pick you up in Tenerife, but he was a bit tied up at the time and for once couldn't oblige us.'

'That's all right. I didn't mind the journey apart from Pippa and Annuala being seasick all the way from Corunna. But I simply could *not* stay in the Canary Islands another day, while the world was passing me by. So here I am, in dear old London at last. Your telephone call, Vida dear, was my salvation.'

'I'm so glad I was of some use after all, darling. And now you're here, what shall we do and where shall we go to do it?'

'Vida, why did you marry Ramiro?'

'Why did you marry José?'

'Because I was expecting his child.'

'Well, I'm not expecting Ramiro's child, that's for sure. I married him because he asked me, Roxy.'

'He's a very good lover, was that your reason? To satisfy your sexual fantasies, or simply to get even with me – or both?' Roxana lit up another one of Vida's 'Kensitas' and gave her an amused glance above the gold and onyx lighter.

'All those reasons, Roxy. And José?'

'Fantastic – when he has time.' She pulled a face. 'No, that's a lie, really. I think the *Tercio* is more important to him than anything else in his life – including Pippa.' Roxana put down the lighter and rested her head back on the pillow with a sigh. 'Life is immensely dull all of a sudden.'

'Same with me, now that the wedding is over. Roxy darling, Ramiro came after me in Andorra each winter, not so much to enjoy himself skiing with me, but for what he could get out of me. I've always known that. And I also know he is more in love with La Pasionaria than with me.'

'La Pasionaria?'

'That's what the Spanish call her. Her real name is Dolores Ibarruri. She's supposed to have sold sardines in the Basque village where she was born. Her enemies say she once murdered a right-wing priest by sinking her teeth into his neck and severing his jugular vein – mind you, I've felt like that about Ramiro this past week. However, she *is* like a female Hitler when you hear her public addresses and see the way she can incite the masses to a frenzy of patriotism – the anti-Fascist kind, though. Anyway, Ramiro thinks she's the Virgin Mary all over again, and only talks about *The Passion Flower*, Communism's saving grace! Roxy, let's go sailing on Papa's yacht and forget our husbands for a little while.'

'You've only been married to Ramiro for a week, Vida. Don't say you're tired of him already?'

'I'm not tired of him, I don't get enough of him. The honeymoon was an utter disaster, and for that I blame the Spanish Civil War, which decided to break out the very week I managed, at last, to drag Ramiro to the altar – even if it was only a registry office altar. Now he's gone rushin … oh!' Vida giggled, too much champagne bad for her. 'Get it, darling? Russian? Never mind, Roxy!' She reached for the Röederer Cristal Brut, her favourite champagne, which made the world look pink instead of black. 'Ramiro's gone back to Spain as if I don't exist. He and his little *Passion Flower*, at this very moment, are no doubt making impassioned speeches all over Republican Spain to raise even more money for guns and soldiers to fight their Communist cause – egged on by Stalin, of course. Come on Roxy, be a sport like the old days and say yes.'

'Yes to what, Vida?'

'New boyfriends on Papa's yacht? We'll invite some nice, sexy Frenchmen aboard, instead of these war-mongering Spaniards we've somehow got ourselves involved with.'

'It sounds very tempting. But I now have a daughter to think of.'

'Bring Pippa and her nanny with you. Annuala is

attractive enough since she's under fifty and endowed with good mammary glands, so there's no fear Papa won't welcome her aboard. As for Pippa, he'll simply adore her. He'll pretend it's me, all over again. He has this thing about children – oh, but nicely! Papa adores children and always wished he had more than just me: he always wanted a son to inherit his title and fortune. Instead, he got me. But Papa's just like Santa Claus where children are concerned.' Vida drifted off into a private reverie.

'I'll have to think about it, Vida.'

'What a pity we can't get that sexy man aboard Papa's yacht as well, now that he's free and uninhibited by a wife. But he's also at war, I believe.'

'What sexy man?'

'Dr Keiren Hunter Devlin.'

'Oh, him! I'd forgotten about him. I don't even know where he is. The last time I heard anything about him, he was supposed to be in Guatemala.'

'He's in Abyssinia now.'

'How do you know?'

'Jan Fairchild told me.'

'Jan Fairchild?'

'Well, she's become Mrs Archibald Cunningham – didn't Raven ever tell you her best friend is married? I met Jan the other afternoon. I told you over the telephone, but I think you were probably too squiffy to understand. Keir apparently keeps in touch with her.'

'What's he doing in Abyssinia?'

'Red Cross work.'

'Sounds riveting.'

'Shall I telephone him in Addis Ababa and ask him to join us?'

'He'll only say, "Sorry no thanks, duty calls" or some such chilling stuff to put a woman off. Men like him are such dreadful bores for allowing their moral consciences to rule them. My father was like that, so frightfully austere with his war medals and holier-than-thou approach to life. Raven's a bit like him. Even the servants trembled at his approach, let alone terrorists. I was so afraid of my father I'd run a mile in Mama's high heels when I saw him step through the front door. But Mother was a sweetie. She never boasted about her good works on behalf of the Irish White Cross. She was able to enjoy herself thoroughly, while spreading her light-and-love policy all around her … Vida, we've run out of champagne.'

'Plenty more from where that came, darling, we've only got to shout down to night-service. Come on, Roxy, don't be so frightfully boring yourself. Say yes, and let me cable Papa now to tell him we're joining him and his new mistress gambling their nights away between San Sebastian and Biarritz. He just loves it when someone younger than his current mistress pops up on the scene; and you know how he adores you.'

'Oh, very well then. Spain at the moment sounds simply awful. José is welcome to it.'

'Darling, you're a real friend. I shan't forget this in a hurry. I'll make it worth your while, I promise.'

'As long as you don't come near me again with your artificial devices.'

'*Chérie*, I'm a reformed married woman! Now that I realize what a *man* can do for a woman, I prefer the real thing.'

'Let's hope you don't change your mind.'

423

CHAPTER ELEVEN

Andalucia and Extremadura:
August – October 1936

Captain José de Luchar was tired of hanging around Tetuan docks. Time had gone by and all they had been subjected to was General Franco's interminable soul-stirring broadcasts to the Spanish people, ending as always with, *Arriba Español!*

José paused by a couple of *regulaires* seated on orangeboxes. Intent upon a game of checkers, the squared board and checkermen set out on another orangebox used as a table between them, the *regulaires* looked up at José, who, hands clasped behind his back, absent-mindedly watched them.

'What's the delay, *Capitán*?' one of the *regulaires* asked. 'We thought the General was dying to get us to do the same for our Fatherland?'

José prodded a checkerman into king row, and the soldier to whom it belonged, promptly crowned it with a crow of delight while the other one moaned, 'Hey, *Capitán*, that's not fair! He never was any good at this, and I've got a bet on with the blokes that *I* win this game.'

'Franco's waiting for the *Lepanto* to leave Gibraltar before we cross the Straits,' José informed his soldiers.

'The *Lepanto* can't do us any damage, *Capitán*. She's badly holed and laid up in Gib, thanks to the Ities who dive-bombed her decks a few days ago.'

'Well, General Franco isn't too happy about her being in Gibraltar. He doesn't trust the British.'

'I thought we were fighting Reds, not British.' The soldier José had aided by crowning his man added, 'The

424

Lepanto's Republican, isn't she, *Capitán*?

'That's right.'

'So what's it to do with the British?'

'The *Lepanto* is undergoing repairs in Gibraltar and the General is worried, that the moment we begin crossing the Straits, she'll come out of her bolthole and start blowing our troop-ships apart.'

'So what's the old man going to do about it?'

'He's going to send a message today to the British Governor in Gibraltar to tell him that the *Lepanto* is a pirate ship, her officers having been slaughtered by her Red crew.'

The *regulaires* grinned. Then the soldier who was not very clever at checkers, with a deep frown, asked, 'What happens if the British bloke doesn't take any notice of our jumped-up little General?'

'Then we'll be stuck here another week. By which time you should have learned how to play checkers, eh Costa? Take my advice, just move on the black squares and jump Centelles whenever possible.'

'A bit like the way we treat the Moors, eh, *Capitán*?'

'*Exactly* how we treat the Moors.' José moved off along the quayside to see what the rest of the troops under General Yagüe's command were doing with their bored selves.

The following day they heard that the Governor of Gibraltar had issued orders for the expulsion of the *Lepanto* from British waters. Soon after, the news was that the damaged Republican destroyer had been forced to sail to Málaga. The Straits at last clear for the Army of Africa, a rousing cheer went up from the troops bivouacking on the beach and dockside, and immediate embarkation began from Cueta and Tetuan for the mainland.

Weeks of intense negotiations between Berlin, Rome, and Santa Cruz de Tenerife had produced results at last: transport planes from Germany and Italy arrived almost immediately. German JU 52 maximum capacity transports, Heinkel 51 fighters, Lufthansa Junkers, and the Italian Savoia-Marchettis provided the air-transport necessary to move an army. Adolf Hitler had made the deprecatory comment to his friend, Benito Mussolini, upon receiving General Franco's request for aid, 'It is *I* who first suggested to this Spanish Señor he needed *transport* for his army *before* guns! He was only concerned with weaponry without realizing that a war is won in the first place by swift and correct disposition of one's troops. However, we will wait and see what happens now in Spain, thanks to our *German* armaments factories!'

Herr Hitler had taken a further step towards implementing his thousand years of the Third Reich.

Within weeks, fifteen thousand soldiers of the *Tercio*, the Spanish Foreign Legion, and tons of weaponry and supplies were air-lifted from north Africa onto the mainland of Spain. More came across the Straits of Gibraltar aboard troop-carriers.

General Franco flew to Seville. To greet his triumphal entry, the city was awash with colourful red and gold Nationalist flags replacing the red, yellow, and purple of the Republic. General Franco met the suave and genteel Sevillian *caballero*, General Quiepo de Llano, who had declared over Seville's captured radio station, 'The rabble who resisted will be shot like dogs!' Shortly afterwards, José, with the rest of Colonel Yagüe's Army of Africa, heard that the Divisional Headquarters of the Burgos Junta had declared General Francisco Franco y Bahamonde, Chief of Staff.

'Our paunchy little bourgeois has come a long way fast from nowhere!' said Colonel Yagüe to his staff officers in an after-dinner exchange of confidences induced by a little too much excellent French brandy.

José took a cigar from the box of Havanas being passed around the mess-table. 'Yes, sir, just like us. But now, sir, the Moors are complaining that they are thin on boot-leather, and some are even walking on the soles of their bare feet.'

Colonel Yagüe, known as the Butcher of Asturias, polished his spectacles, his smile very much like General Quiepo de Llano's had been when Seville had finally fallen into his hands and he was able to shoot 'Red Dogs'. 'Then, *Capitán* de Luchar, as they are not used to marching along hard roads but soft sand, our savages will have to take Madrid barefooted.'

Further orders came from General Franco at his newly established headquarters in Salamanca. Colonel Yagüe's army was by now encamped to the north of Seville. José could see each one of them arriving in Madrid without boot-leather on account of the speed with which Franco and Yagüe were pushing them. Colonel Yagüe informed his officers at a briefing, 'We are to meet up with General Mola's Army from Corunna, as well as the Nationalist Army of the Centre. Colonel Monasterio, who commands the Army of the Centre, will cover our left flank. German and Italian fighters will provide air-cover against any Republican attacks while we are to make a concerted assault upon the capital. As soon as Madrid falls, Barcelona will also be ours.'

He hopes, thought José, who, a Catalan himself, knew that Barcelona would not be taken without a very tough fight indeed. The Catalonian Separatists would not give up easily, and nor would the Communists, not by a long stretch of Yagüe's or Franco's imagination.

Colonel Yagüe studied the map of Spain laid out on his camp table. 'We are to meet Mola and Monasterio here …' He pointed to the Province of Extremadura. 'The two halves of the Nationalist army are to join up at this old Roman town, Mérida, which is right here.' The Colonel jabbed his finger on the ordnance map. 'Then, from the Tagus valley we take southern Castille, follow it up with a pincer-movement upon Navalmoral, merge again, then on with our final push towards Madrid. Meanwhile, Varela, in the south, will be subduing Granada. Any questions? No? Then you had all better be aware of what you are doing, otherwise there will be tail-feathers flying everywhere.'

Before those orders could be acted upon fully, poised as the Nationalists were on the brink of capturing Mérida, a second set of instructions from Salamanca negated the first. Colonel Yagüe was to turn around again and march south to capture the capital of Extremadura, Badajoz.

Close to the Portugese border, Badajoz was a hotbed of Republican sympathies. This action, General Franco explained to a confused Colonel Yagüe over the telephone, would clear up the last pocket of left-wing resistance west of Madrid and give the Nationalists control of a broad triangle of the country, from Cadiz in the south-west, to Corunna in the north-west, and Navarre in the north-east.

'The trouble with *Our General*, gentlemen, is that he thinks just like a woman,' said Colonel Yagüe in disgust, when again briefing his officers regarding the General's change of plans. He breathed on his glasses, his heavy, pasty face decidedly put out as he wiped the lenses vigorously. 'He never knows whether to enjoy a rape or try and put it off. We have been diverted to Badajoz, so make the most of it when you get there, because it will be a long time now before you enjoy the rape of Madrid.'

José de Luchar, Captain Legionnaire, trained under a hard and ruthless *Africanista* soldier such as Colonel Yagüe, was used to the atrocities committed by the Rif tribesmen of North Africa on any captured legionnaire, and, in turn, reciprocal acts of violence by the Moors upon the enemy. Having taken part himself in the Asturian campaign two years ago, when the Army of Africa had been sent in to relieve the garrisons of Oviedo and Gijon, José knew what to expect. But, for the first time in his military career, he was sickened by what happened at Badajoz.

After several hours of savage fighting, the city walls were breached and the Nationalist Army entered the capital. Resistance continued until Colonel Yagüe ordered all captured militiamen to be taken into the bullring and shot.

Then the Falangists, the Spanish Fascist Party whose doctrine, in José de Luchar's mind, seemed as confused as the Civil War itself, hovering between Monarchism and Fascism, right-wing Nationalist ideology and totalitarian concepts, and were to José, were like maggots in cheese, crawled out in their patrol cars. They started rounding up the last remnants of the Red Army of Extremadura. Falangist confusion finding its very expression in the label of their leader, *El senorito!*, José Antonio Primo de Rivera, had been taken hostage by the Republican Government and imprisoned in Alicante gaol. While the Falangist leader was occupied with reading Kipling's *If* and issuing orders to his Party from prison, the Party itself was out for revenge. Falangists everywhere engaged upon a terror campaign.

The dead buried, the wounded attended to at the casualty clearing station or the field hospital, José and the men under his command were taking their ease in the shade of the ilex trees. As a superbly trained fighting force the legionnaires realized what was expected of them, and, as tired as they were after very heavy fighting all the way north from Seville, knew there would be no respite until Madrid was in Nationalist hands. They made the most of the short lull in the fighting, smoking, chatting, playing cards, or quietly snoozing with their backs to the hubs of their truck-wheels. Extremadura was under Nationalist control, just as the Generals had ordered.

Peasants were returning from the outlying fields. Groups of *braceros*, labourers and field-hands stood on the street corners eyeing the Nationalist soldiers warily, for word had preceded the Army of Africa regarding the black Moors who ate babies and committed unspeakable atrocities upon women.

Not everyone in Badajoz was afraid, especially the children. Courageous enough to risk being eaten, they crossed the road to ask for sweets and chocolate or even a piggyback ride on a soldier's shoulders, as some children were getting.

Watching the children being spoiled with luxuries they were starved of, less timid adults started wandering up to the convoy. They offered tomatoes, oranges, a melon, or peach in exchange for a cigarette or two, and information concerning in whose favour the war was going. José, standing in the roadway beside the communications vehicle, waiting for Colonel Yagüe's orders on whether to move out, turn around, head further north, head for Madrid, or stay where they were, was approached by a *bracero* with a handful of walnuts. '*Capitán*, go away, for the sake of God and for the sake of Spain!'

José shook his head, only half-aware of the stupid *bracero* as he turned his back on the man to concentrate on the babbled sounds in his earphones.

A Falangist patrol car came speeding down the main street, so close to the convoy, José, like everyone else, had to jump out of the way. Anxious parents grabbed up their children who began screaming for the sweets dropped in the gutter.

The Falangist squad car stopped further up the street.

'Stupid bastards!' José spat and went after the driver.

Half a dozen Falangists in their distinctive blue shirts had already jumped out of the car. With sub-machine-guns they herded together people lingering on the street.

José had witnessed this ritual many times before, a favourite sport of the JONs, or Blueshirts. Any discolouration on the shoulder of a man or woman and the suspect was as good as dead.

A group of men and women, their arms and faces streaked with mud and perspiration, clothes darkened by sweat, had just come from the hot, dry summer fields around Badajoz. Made to stand in line with their hands above their heads, shirts and overall-straps, blouses or frocks were ripped aside revealing the nervous pulsation of a fear never encountered before. José couldn't help but be affected, couldn't help but feel an empathy with these poor peasants who were supposedly the enemy; these people who were not Rifs, but his own Spanish people protecting their town.

Three old women and two *braceros* were released. No shoulder bruises had left the tell-tale evidence of a recoiling rifle. The redeemed stood meekly aside, while eight of their comrades, six men and two young women were marched off to the bullring.

'Hey!' said José to the Falangist leader. 'Stop!'

The Blueshirt turned around and gave the open hand Fascist salute.

José returned the salute.

'What do you want, soldier?'

'Captain to you, *cojon*! Who was the driver of your car?'

'That one over there.' The Blueshirt pointed to the man leading the column of labourers off to the bullring, 'Maurice – the *Capitán* of legionnaires wants a word with you.'

The other Blueshirts paused long enough in their shepherding activities to turn around and grin at José. '*Arriba Español, eh, Capitán?*'

José walked up to the man called Maurice and punched him straight in the mouth so that he staggered back, ending up in the dusty road. 'That's for not looking where you were going.'

The men and women standing in line for the bullring shuffled their feet uncomfortably, unsure of how to react. The Blueshirt sitting in the dust fingered his cut lip. He regarded José in amazement, never having expected such treatment from someone on the same side.

In the next instant the rat-a-tat-tat of sub-machine-gun-fire was devastating as the rest of the Blueshirts opened fire on the *braceros*.

José turned pale.

While he could believe it, he was still unable to accept the bloodiness of this war.

Eight bodies lay in the roadway, one of the men twitching horribly until the driver, Maurice, put a final bullet through the *bracero*'s head.

People who had been watching the drama from shop doorways and kerbsides fled in silence, dragging screaming children with them. Blood from the bodies streamed across road and pavement as the flies began to settle.

José, jaw and shoulders set, but his stomach heaving like a butter churn, walked back to the convoy under the ilex trees without betraying what he felt about such a swift and mindless act of reprisal by the Falangist JONS.

The radio operator, noticing José's pale, grim face, said consolingly, 'Never mind, *Capitán*, it wasn't your fault. They were going to be shot anyway.'

'*Basta*, enough! Have you heard anything yet?'

'Nothing, *Capitán*. Yagüe's probably sleeping it off on his mistress.'

'Shut your stupid mouth, Corporal. Just get on with your job.'

'Yes sir.'

José walked off to the head of the convoy. Getting into the staff car, he instructed his driver, 'Get out of here. Anywhere! Drive as far away from this town as you can. I want a beer that doesn't taste of blood.'

All through the night the machine-guns in the bullring kept up their incessant noisy revenge upon the people of Badajoz.

At two in the morning José returned to the town. He felt compelled to go to the bullring to see for himself what was happening; perhaps to discredit what his ears and his brain were telling him. When he saw the carnage under the spotlights he had the grand idea of countermanding Yagüe's orders. But there was a major, a lieutenant-colonel, and a colonel in superior command and he, as a mere captain-legionnaire, could do nothing! Rank always took precedence over humanitarian principles – machine-gunners in the centre, people to be shot gathered in a circle around their executioners, the scenes were always hellish. The condemned with their pale, round faces, luminescent in the artificial light under a black night sky, about to die like their comrades in whose blood they stood, without trial, and without protest, it was – it was apocalyptic!

But what appalled José de Luchar most of all was the passive acceptance of death on the faces of these simple people.

Affected by the chilling dignity displayed by those facing the spotlight and the machine-guns, he asked himself, Who did they think they were dying for, God, Spain, King, Community, or Communism?

The victory of Badajoz seemed inglorious, almost shameful, after that.

When orders came at last to move out, the sun was high and strong in a cloudless blue sky, marred only by huge black clouds of droning flies. The city was strangely silent after the incessant chattering of machine-guns over the past few days and nights while the battle for Badajoz was at its height. The stench of the city wafted high on the hot still air and reminded José of the abbatoir close by Toril's own bullring, only that the meat slaughtered there had not been human.

The convoy of army trucks had to pass along the lane

running beside the bullring. It was as though it had been raining all night. The lane was churned into a sticky river of mud, and lorries skidded, flinging up clumps of red dirt onto the bonnets and windscreens of the vehicles following.

'Jesu Maria! said the driver of the staff car. 'What *did* they do last night?'

They had come to a standstill behind the lorry in front, its wheels spinning. Gullies of blood from the bullring mingled with army petrol to catch the bright morning sunlight. Deep irridescent red pools formed under the stationary wheels of the convoy.

'Captain!' Someone banged on José's side of the car, his face thrust against the closed window. José wound down the window.

Only then did the man produce his press card, which he brandished in front of José's nose. José quickly tried to wind up the window again, but the man had thrust his elbow in the gap: 'I'm from the *Chicago Tribune*. There are other reporters here from the Portuguese newspapers. What have you to say about last night's massacre by your Nationalist soldiers, Captain?'

'*Lo siento. No hablo inglés,*' José lied.

'Then I will speak Spanish,' said the persistent newspaperman. 'Do you know that in all, one thousand, eight hundred men and women, citizens of Badajoz, were machine-gunned here during the past few nights?'

'I think you're mistaken, señor,' Jose replied, keeping his eyes straight ahead and concentrating on the blood-spotted windscreen.

'Is it true that the Army of Africa takes no prisoners?'

'No, it's not true.'

'Have you not noticed the bodies left on the streets in the wake of your advancing army, Captain?'

'Yes, I have noticed. They are the victims of Republican atrocities. I am a soldier following the orders of my commanding officer, señor, I am not an undertaker investigating death statistics. I dare say the same thing is happening to Nationalist soldiers caught behind Republican lines. If you want to know anything else, speak to Colonel Yagüe.'

'But those were innocent men and women in that bullring, Captain, non-combatants!'

'No comment, señor. Now, if you will move aside, please, so that we can pass.' The lorry in front began to move off and José wound up the window. 'Drive on, Corporal, and next time, don't stop for *anyone*!'

Back at General Yagüe's headquarters at Talavera de la Reina in the Tagus valley, the volleys of gunfire went on and on, and there was no respite in the mass executions of the townsfolk, just as in Badajoz: and in countless other towns and *pueblos* throughout Spain, Nationalist and Republican. José, angry and disheartened, never having dreamt that this war, this *small* war of partisan loyalties as everyone had believed in the beginning, would hack Spain into so many terrible, bloody pieces, found Colonel Yagüe in a foul temper when he went to him with his report of the success of the Badajoz campaign. 'It was appalling, sir, and can have done our cause no good whatsoever. The internatioinal press have got hold of the story and will no doubt embellish the whole thing to ten times its enormity.'

'What does everyone expect me to do? Am I expected to turn the enemy loose again so that they can creep up behind us and recolour the map of Spain bright red to suit the Russian High Command?'

Colonel Yagüe began pacing the floor of the bullet-scarred farmhouse that had become his headquarters. He would let no one get a word in edgeways as he began to rant and rave against General Franco, who had decided to postpone the assault on Madrid.

José suspected Yagüe to be on the verge of a breakdown. He encountered the looks of the other staff officers who had been summoned to make their individual reports, most of whom held similar views, that Yagüe was out of control of the situation as well as himself.

'He is mad! Air Force Commander, General Kindelán, has told him he is mad and so have I. It is *mad mad mad*! Utterly ludicrous when we have come so far, to divert us off course like this. General Franco will lose the war on account of it. He changes his mind time after time, so that it has become a feminine joke. I am to divert my troops to Toledo of all places! I am to send in as many *banderas* of legionnaires and *tabors* of Moors as it will take to relieve the Alcazar. Pah! Am I now Moscardo's nursemaid?'

Colonel José Moscardo was the Nationalist Military Governor of Toledo. The Alcazar was an impregnable fortress-palace perched on a crag of solid rock high above the River Tagus. Colonel Moscardo had barricaded himself inside the fortress with thirteen hundred people, most of whom were citizens of Toledo, civil guardsmen, officers, cadets, right-wing militants, five hundred and fifty women and children of the city plus another one hundred Republican hostages. The Republican army was assaulting the Alcazar, day after day, night after night. Colonel Moscardo had telephoned General Franco to inform him that they had more than enough weapons to withstand the Republican onslaught, but not enough food. One hundred and seventy-seven horses had already been slaughtered, only one remained, a thoroughbred racehorse that not a single Nationalist soul could bring himself to kill and eat as the horse had become somewhat of a mascot: as long as the racehorse lasted, so would the Alcazar. *Viva Español*!

Colonel Yagüe rounded on José who had insisted on interrupting him by asking the question, 'Excuse me, sir, could you clarify the position we're supposed to take?'

'Indeed! Since you're familiar with the Alcazar, *Capitán* de Luchar, having done your early training inside the Gymnasium and along the whore-streets of the city like all good legionnaires, now is the time to prove yourself. I give you full permission from General Franco to go in and get Moscardo out!'

'Single-handed?' José asked a little uncertainly.

'You can have a *tabor de los Moros y regulaires*. Major Dorada can take the north and you, de Luchar, the south face of the Alcazar. All battle stations will report to Lieutenant-Colonel Bogatell, who will kick the Reds out of the *Ayuntamiento* and hoist the Nationalist flag in place of that devilish Anarchist rubbish fluttering from the balcony.'

'Thank you, Colonel!' José saluted and went to find his battalion of two hundred and twenty-five Moors and Moroccan regular soldiers. And good luck to Bogatell! he muttered to himself. Let's hope he manages to capture the Town Hall without having a nervous breakdown like Yagüe.

Colonel Yagüe's staff officers, having feared the worst concerning their commanding officer, who had been pushing himself and everyone else to the brink of disaster, were not let down by him. That very day, Colonel Yagüe collapsed from nervous exhaustion and his command was given to General Varela of Seville.

Asturian miners were sent in by the Republican Government to blow up the Alcazar with Colonel Moscardo still inside. With fire-hoses, they sprayed petrol on the walls of the fortress and then set it alight. But very little damage was done, the walls of the Alcazar were over ten feet thick so that nothing, not even fire, could penetrate.

Nationalist airmen dropped food supplies into the Alcazar and then, finding themselves short of bombs until the next armaments supply arrived from Italy or Germany, dropped huge melons on the Republican soldiers marching along the Toledo road.

The Republican Air Force retaliated by dropping leaflets on the loyal people of Castillan and Extremadura, declaring General Franco's intention to see the nation's capital, like their very own city of Toledo, razed to the ground rather than occupied by Marxists: every loyal Republican must fight for Madrid, to the last man, woman, and child. *Viva España!*

Militiamen from Asturias this time tried underground dynamiting of the Alcazar, crawling along sewers to lay their explosives. The Republicans partially succeeded in their intention to reduce the Alcazar to rubble, and one tower was destroyed, the one José's Moors had been instructed to breach.

Colonel Moscardo still refused to surrender to Republican 'Bolsheviks'.

Bombardment of the Alcazar by Republicans was stepped up. Street fighting between the two sides was fierce and brutal and to José, who had lost account of time, seemed to last for ever.

Still the bespectacled little Colonel refused to surrender

to the Reds, while Nationalist soldiers could make no serious indentation on the determined militiamen holding Toledo. Then, Colonel Moscardo's twenty-four-year-old son was captured by the Republicans and taken hostage, his life forfeit unless the Military Governor surrendered the Alcazar within ten minutes of Luis Moscardo being brought to the telephone to speak to his father.

Colonel Moscardo told his son to commend his soul to God for the sake of Spain.

Luis Moscardo was executed in front of the Tránsito Synagogue a month later, not on account of the seige of the Alcazar, but in reprisal for a devastating air-raid by the Nationalists.

The day after the air-raid, which had reduced whole streets to rubble, José and a handful of Moors wearing their colourful uniform of tasselled fez, baggy pantaloons and tunics, were in hot pursuit of some Reds in possession of a vital radio transmitter.

'Rif-eaters – get those bastards! Don't let them get away otherwise they'll try and make contact with their Red comrades who enjoy raping nuns and executing children. *Arriba Español!*' José, light-headed from lack of food and sleep, and euphoric with the excitement of hand-to-hand battle in endless skirmishes with militiamen while his Moors cut the throats of Republican soldiers on the steeply winding and narrow cobbled streets of Toledo, felt in his pocket for a grenade. He discovered he had used all the good German ones.

Left as he was with two unreliable hand-bombs picked up from a dead Anarchist, José cursed his luck. Homemade bombs called FAIs, which in his own mind José referred to as FAItal-futiles, as they either went off in your hand, or didn't go off at all, were as good as useless. The lever, instead of being held in place by a pin, was secured by a piece of tape. José peeled off the tape and quickly lobbed the bomb away.

Predictably, the FAI hand-bomb fizzled out. It rattled back down the steep street, bouncing from boulder to boulder until it came to rest against a wooden street-barrier: oh well, José thought to himself, it was just as well, since it had been intended for him anyway. '*Olé!*'

José gave chase up the winding, rubble-strewn street, the second homemade Anarchist bomb in his hand, his Moors close behind the militiamen with their radio transmitter. 'Don't let them get away! *Arriba!*'

The last thing they needed now was for the Reds to get through to their air-base. The Nationalist camp and Yagüe's headquarters had had a thorough blasting early that morning in retaliation for yesterday's air-raid on the town. José's orders were to put the militiamen's radio out of action before they could send any more information on the deployment of Nationalist soldiers in and around Toledo.

A young militiaman, no more than seventeen, carried the radio equipment in his backpack. In a last defiant gesture he turned at the top of the demolished street. Bringing his rifle waist high, he opened fire on José, who didn't even bother to get out of the way. José had discovered that it took something in the region of a thousand bullets from one militiaman's rifle to hit its target, so bad were the Russian weapons the militia had been supplied with by their Red friends in Moscow. With the end of the FAI tape in his mouth, he jerked his head, peeled away the tape, and released the lever of the bomb. José flung it at the Reds and prayed this one would go off, though he held no high hopes.

Reds had formed a firing-squad at the top of the street. The small explosion from the FAI hand-bomb found a target, an empty wine barrel which sent only splinters into the air. Scree, disturbed by the ineffectual blast, rattled loosely down the street and a little dust was all there was to show for Anarchist efforts to compete with the Germans in ballistics.

The young militiaman stood up. Silhouetted against the skyline he waved his rifle above his head and jeered, 'Now whose weapons don't work, rebel!'

José took careful aim and got the young soldier in the foot. Not a serious injury in itself, because the soldier wore heavy-duty army boots, and the bullet lost penetration. But the militiaman lost his balance on the crest of the rubble strewn slope and pitched forward from the weight of the pack on his back. José went for the backpack containing the wireless equipment, the militiaman presenting an easy target as he scrabbled for purchase on the slippery slope. Several well-aimed shots found their mark and the soldier's body jerked grotesquely until José stopped firing, revolver empty. The Red was dead and so was his field radio.

Bullets still whined around his head, snipers firing from ruined buildings. José flung himself sideways into the doorway of what had been a butcher's shop. A militiaman's bullet glanced off the broken iron shutter in front of the partly demolished shop doorway. The bullet creased the back of José's left hand. José continued laughing at the enemy's efforts, in themselves so ineffectual as to be a constant source of amusement. 'Bad shots!' He yelled as he dodged from building to building. 'Couldn't hit sitting ducks if you tried! Who manufactured your guns, your Russian grandmothers?' He ducked low and waited for the right moment. Then, flinging himself across the cratered street, snaked across on his belly. A few feet, and then another few feet forward, using the wooden street-barrier as a shield, while the militiamen continued sniping from the top of the incline.

A hard, ovoid lump of metal was in his side, and too late José realized he had rolled onto the FAI bomb that had not exploded when thrown at the Reds.

Through his legionnaire's khaki Zouave tunic José felt a nip on his left side, no worse than an amorous mistress's seductive love-bite. But when he sat up, his hand going to his side as though he had a bad stitch, his palm came away sticky with blood, and a smoky black tear in his tunic showed him that the Anarchist firecracker had indeed belched a little. But his wound couldn't be anything to worry about, José reassured himself, otherwise he'd be feeling a lot worse. Nothing felt broken, anyway. Relieved to know how useless were the enemy's weapons, he managed to get to his knees, and crawled into another shop doorway. 'We'll get you yet, Red scum!'

'*Maricons*! Nancy-boys! Fascist salami, arse-lickers!' came back reciprocal taunts from the militiamen.

'After the bastards, Rifs!' José urged on his men. 'We'll slit their gizzards, and stuff their Red throats with their own

Communist sausagemeat!'

Several hours later, grinning, black-faced Moors finally caught up with the remnant of the Red army holding out in a cellar. Their remaining few German hand-grenades, taken from their pouches, were tossed in through an outside hatchway. Inside the confined space the grenades went off with a resounding explosion. Flames guttered through the ruined building. Blinded, wounded, cursing militiamen tumbled out into the street like a colony of ants. José's Moors put the Reds out of their misery.

Not far from where the Reds lay with their throats cut, José himself finally collapsed, unconscious from loss of blood. The ineffectual bomb he had rolled on had managed to perforate his spleen.

On that same day General Varela from Seville began a fresh onslaught with Nationalist reinforcements. Republican resistance had at last been wiped out after heavy fighting, the exhausted remnants of the Red army fleeing Toledo to leave behind them a valuable powder factory. Colonel Moscardo, still grieving over his son's death at the hands of the Reds, stepped into the bright afternoon sunshine of Toledo and said solemnly, 'Nothing is new in the Alcazar.' He had been under seige for sixty-eight days. Eighty-four defenders of the citadel had died, and typhoid had broken out among the survivors.

José was not at the final relief of the Alcazar, but undergoing emergency surgery at the San Juan Military Hospital, which had been badly shelled and damaged during the worst of the fighting.

José survived the operation for removal of his spleen. Then, forty-eight hours after his operation, he sustained a massive internal haemorrhage. A blood-transfusion was at once commenced, and tubes were inserted all over his body. He was given oxygen, and the Roman Catholic padre was summoned to give José de Luchar the last rites. A telegram was despatched at once to Señora de Luchar from the San Juan Military Hospital, Toledo, via the War Office, Salamanca, informing her of her husband's critical condition.

But José de Luchar was made of sterner stuff – he was not going to die!

He rallied, slowly but surely.

One day, opening his eyes blearily with the feeling that he had indeed returned from the dead, José saw two beaming Generals standing beside his bed.

Moscardo, who had recovered after his long ordeal within the Alcazar and, for his courage, had been promoted to the rank of General, together with General Varela, his new Commanding Officer in place of Yagüe, reminded José of Peter and Paul in the mural of the Last Supper in the dining-room at the Mas Luchar. José felt unable to smile back, though he did his level best.

'We have come to bestow upon you the Laureate Cross of San Fernando by order of General Franco,' said General Moscardo, draping the cross on its length of ribbon over the metal transfusion-stand and bottle of blood beside José's bed, the nursing sister having warned the generals about disturbing the patient too soon.

José noticed that Moscardo's own Laureate Cross for the defence of the Alcazar was proudly displayed on his tunic. But General Moscardo's medal, José learned later, had been pinned on him by the hands of General Franco himself when he had visited Toledo soon after the town had surrendered.

'*Capitán* de Luchar,' said General Varela, 'General Franco wishes you to join his staff at Salamanca Headquarters as an ADC. You will be unable to fight for a little while on account of your gallant battle-scars, and so he wishes to make good use of your talents in another direction.'

'Thank you, sir.'

'It is a high honour for you, *Capitán* de Luchar,' said General Moscardo.

José, unable to bear being embraced by the two victorious Generals, lifted his right hand that felt like a jellyfish and feebly shook hands with them.

A few days later, his strength returning by degrees, thanks to several pints of Red Cross donation blood, José opened his Red Cross parcel and read his letters. There was one from Biarritz, the neat italic script on the envelope unmistakeably Roxana's.

José read about his brother Ramiro's marriage to Vida de Martello, a French socialite and heiress to her father's fabulous fortune. Roxana was having 'a teeny holiday' aboard the Comte de Martello's luxury yacht cruising the Cantabrian coast. She had run out of money and wondered if he, José, could possibly transfer some 'housekeeping' into her depleted bank account. *Pippa costs a fortune to keep. Little girls need all sorts of things, especially pretty clothes and shoes, hair-ribbons and dolls. However, Pippa and the nanny are with me on the cruise, and the Comte is spoiling Pippa to an unhealthy degree. I am fortunate to have such understanding and loving friends. But I cannot depend on their generosity for ever. You must take your fair share of Pippa's unkeep, José. I shall await your remuneration forthwith. I do hope you are fully recovered after your little ordeal fighting the enemy. The War Office notified me of your temporary setback. But as I was not at Vinarosa, Peedee cabled Le Comte de Martello, who then contacted me on the yacht radio. Your loving wife, Roxana.*

José's thoughts were that if nothing was new in the Alcazar (a catch-phrase on everyone's lips since Moscardo had made it one), then certainly nothing was new in the Quennell camp either! Apart from that begging letter, Roxana's news was scant.

Even to his own daughter, Pippa, he felt himself a stranger.

José looked up from his correspondence and his introspection when Captain Vittorio Broué, who had briefly come between him and Roxana in Tetuan, pulled up a chair beside his bed and said cheerfully, '*Salud*, José!'

'*Salud* yourself, Broué.'

'I didn't bring you flowers, but my congratulations instead.' Vittorio crossed his legs in his impeccable legionnaire's khaki cavalry twills, a cigarette between his fingers. He noticed José's longing look, 'I would offer you one, but the nursing sister says it's forbidden after the fright you gave everyone. They all thought you were about to become cemetery meat.'

What José said in response to that remark was uncommented upon by Vittorio who, with a grin, brought out a packet of Gauloise. He lit José's cigarette with an indolent flick of his lighter. 'So! You are joining the High

Command while I am to take my Moors to the University of Madrid where the Reds are holding out despite all odds.'

'I'd rather fight than write,' said José morosely as he inhaled. Immediately he felt nauseated and dizzy by that first deep glorious inhalation of tobacco after long abstinence, and reluctantly had to extinguish the cigarette in the urine bottle beside his bed. 'I'd have been promoted to Major had I been able to command a *bandero* of men. Instead, I am still only a staff *capitán* despite the medal.'

'But now you'll be able to command a *bandero* of secretarial mules, so I shouldn't despair. Men and mules are much the same I've discovered. In your present mood, however, I think I'll commiserate with you rather than tender my congratulations. Why are you so down in the mouth after you've been awarded such glorification as the Laureate Cross? As a wounded *Africanista* who has saved Toledo from the infidel Reds, you should be proud of yourself, not suicidal.'

'Franco has probably only just tumbled to the fact that my father is a grandee from an ancient and noble house, and so he had better start wooing the de Luchars for their moral support in Catalonia. And, for another reason, because my father did not support Sanjurjo in that affair four years ago to oust Azaña from the Government to make Sanjurjo Commander-in-Chief. I also know that there's no love lost between the President of the Republic and General Franco, because Azaña dislikes Church *and* Army! But that doesn't make me feel any better. I'm still being overlooked for *real* promotion.'

'Terribly tragic about Sanjurjo though, don't you think?' Vittorio blew a smoke ring in the air.

'What about him?'

'Oh my God José, where have you been for four weeks?'

'Fighting for Spain you bastard, not fucking! I know you've only just got here from the last Las Palmas party. While I've been marching on my belly and getting shot in the gut for Miss Canary Islands, never ask me where I've been! What has happened to Sanjurjo?'

'Plane crash in Portugal. At a very convenient moment for Miss Canary Islands,' replied Vittorio using the name the legionnaires had given General Franco. 'Four weeks ago the Puss Moth ordered by General Mola to bring Sanjurjo back from Marinha to Burgos as Head of the new Spanish State, crashed into some pine trees on take off. Ansaldo was the pilot. That young Carlist, and extremely inexperienced pilot to whom Mola gave the assignment, escaped with bad injuries. The old man of Spain died in the flames. They found his diary though, extracts of which have since been printed in some scurrilous Red newspapers.'

'What are you talking about, Broúe?' José sighed.

With a mischievous grin Vittorio brought out a scrap of paper from his pocket. 'I cut out the obituary diary for you. It makes amusing reading concerning the northern front. I thought I might cheer you up a little since everyone else found it so funny, especially the Reds who, as legend would have it, are starving to death in Barcelona.'

'Go on then, read it if it's so amusing. But I doubt I can raise a smile or anything else, even for you, Broué.'

'Well then, just pretend I am he, the great man who ended his days in a pine tree at a very crucial moment in this peculiar way. I am having breakfast at eight-thirty, according to the diary. Then, at nine-thirty, I depart for the front – God knows where the front *is*! A little bombardment of enemy batteries follows, then machine-gunning of trenches and convoys. At eleven I partake of a little golf at Lasarte, and afterwards I *sunbathe* on Ondarreta beach. I indulge in a little swimming, beer-swigging, and shrimp-picking, before setting off home for lunch. At three p.m. I have a short siesta followed by my second war-mission similar to that of the morning. At six-thirty I go to the cinema to see Katharine Hepburn, followed by an apéritif and a real Scotch. Dinner at Nicolasa's, some war songs, and good company followed by bed at ten-thirty. I am fighting the *war*, my friend!' Vittorio tore the Republican newspaper cutting into shreds and tossed them into the air. They fluttered down onto José's white hospital counterpane like grubby snowflakes. 'Do you think we'll win this war, José, when one considers what arseholes are in command?'

A kind of tragic irony to his humour when he realized how long and how hard he had fought without even Kathleen Hepburn to help him, José, his hand pressing his left side, said, 'You've made it all up you stupid *Africanista*!'

'I swear I have not! You ask anyone. It's a standing joke in the *Tercio*. God! What those Red bastards must think of our Nationalist army! Right pansys!' Vittorio lit another Gauloise. Leaning towards José's bed, he whispered conspiratorially, 'What isn't a joke though, is that Sanjurjo's death coincides with the *exact* moment when Miss Canary Islands has been proclaimed by the Burgos Military Junta of *los amigos*, Kindelán, Mola, and Orgaz, *Generalissimo* and Head of State in Sanjurjo's place!'

'Really?' José fingered his Laureate Cross, 'You mean to say our funny little Humpty-Dumpty General is now *Head of State*?'

'Supreme Commander, no less. Come back Alfonso, all is forgiven! Make-believe, second-rate 'royals' are not quite the same as the real thing, no matter how much of a pain in the neck those royals might have been, eh, José? You who are of the ruling class yourself. Convenient time for Sanjurjo to hit the pine trees, though, don't you think? While the poor dazed pilot doesn't know what hit him.'

'*C'est la vie*, as the French say. And, talking of the French, my brother has just married a *very* rich French woman whose father owns an armaments factory just outside Paris, and possibly several more elsewhere. Not only that, but my wife is aboard my new sister-in-law's father's yacht: the Comte's gun-running yacht, which, at this very moment I dare say, is basking in sunshine off the coast of Biarritz, San Sebastian, or maybe even Santander.'

'Then, when you get to Salamanca, you should whisper all your family secrets in the ear of our dumpy little *Generalissimo*, and he will no doubt give you another medal. Meanwhile, I'm glad to be back in Toledo. When you're fit again, we'll do the town as we used to when we were raw volunteers, with no idea at all of what the Foreign Legion really meant, eh, my friend?'

'If you say so, Vittorio.'

'You don't sound too enthusiastic, José. It's understandable. I forgive you in view of your morbid condition induced by your emergency spleenectomy. I, too, have to be careful. My wife happens to live in Toledo you'll remember. And now that I've saved the town for her, she's so grateful, she won't let me out of her sight for one moment. Right now she's downstairs in the main hall awaiting my departure from your bedside in case I slope off quietly to some den of iniquity. So come on, José, hurry up and get out of that bed and rescue me from my wife. Think of all the liberated girls out there.'

'It'll be a long time yet, Vittorio, before I feel like performing any acrobatics for anyone, no matter how pretty the belly-button.'

'You're growing old, José.'

'And you're all balls Vittorio, you fornicating, hen-pecked *Africanista*!'

CHAPTER TWELVE

Barcelona: November 1936 – January 1937

Three months later, and five hundred miles from José de Luchar in Salamanca, Raven was keeping watch over women patients in the infirmary at Toril's Camillus Convent of the Dames of the Blessed Charity.

Almost asleep, she dug her nails into the palms of her hands to keep herself from dropping off. Then she got up and walked around the ward.

She knew she ought not to take notice of what was going on outside convent walls, but she couldn't help it; after all, she had a great deal of practice in minding other people's business, even though she had long since relinquished her people-spotting book. These days, it was too risky to commit anything to paper, unless it was a ward report for Infirmary Mother.

Raven picked up a Republican newspaper lying at the foot of Señora de Xeno y Maragall's bed. The wife of a lawyer and local Government Minister, Señora de Xeno y Maragall was one of that rare breed of Spanish women who could actually read. In the next bed, Señora Zamora was snoring loudly. Raven gave Señora Zamora a guilty glance before picking up the newspaper belonging to her neighbour. The Civil War was now into its fifth month, and the fighting was becoming increasingly bloody on both sides. Moors and legionnaires were indiscriminately murdering peasants from small villages. Prisoners were forced to dig their own graves before being shot. An account of the brutality of Franco's 'Army of Repression' detailed the sordid death of Garcia Lorca, the revered

Spanish poet, playright, and actor.

Raven knew very well that Peedee had deeply mourned his friend's cruel and shameful death in Granada. Big, burly, handsome, and charming Garcia Lorca, who had his own travelling theatre company, had been accused of homosexual practices and of being a 'leftist intellectual pervert' by his Falangist executioners. On that same day, his brother-in-law, the Socialist Mayor of Granada, had also been executed. Together with nearly six hundred Reds, the poet had been forced to dig his own grave before being shot in an olive grove, the bullets aimed into his buttocks.

'We live in the blinkered age of *Era Azul*,' had been Peedee's sad comment on one short visiting afternoon when she had only been able to sympathize through the convent grille, without understanding.

She put aside the newspaper, and went back to her lonely night vigil. The long, narrow ward had twelve beds on either side, with a carved crucifix on the whitewashed wall above each bed. Illuminating her immediate field of vision, the desk-lamp cast a feeble glow across the duty-book in which she scribbled down the treatment each patient had received during her hours of vigil in much the same way that she had recorded her juvenile observations in her people-spotting book. Ireland seemed so far away now, distanced from her present existence through time and the pace of living, the greedy eating up of her life while men waged war and women gave birth.

Most of the women slept peaceably, but there would always be one person during the long night who would remain uncooperative. Señora Zamora had woken up again. She tossed and turned, shouted, and wept as her pains returned. Raven was afraid Señora Zamora would wake the other patients. She put down her pen and went to Señora Zamora's side for the umpteenth time in two hours. 'Please try and relax, Señora Zamora.' Raven whispered frantically. 'It will help to ease the pain.' She held a brown paper bag over Señora Zamora's nose and mouth. 'Breathe deeply into this bag. It does help, I promise!'

'You're trying to suffocate me, Sister Justina!'

'I'm trying to help you.'

Disturbed by the noise Señora Zamora was making,

Señora Xeno y Maragall turned onto her back. In the lay-infirmary because she suffered from severe diabetes, Señora Xeno y Maragall had been in a deep coma on admission, but her condition had now been stabilized by Dame Annunciata's qualified ministrations. She whispered, 'Sister Justina, Señora Zamora does not understand what the paper bag does.'

'It does nothing except reassure Infirmary Mother,' Raven whispered across the dividing space between the two beds.

Señora Xeno y Maragall smiled sleepily. 'Most things are in the mind, Sister Justina, but try telling that to Señora Zamora.' She turned over and went to sleep again.

'What does the bag do?' asked Señora Zamora fretfully.

It was no good explaining to the simple peasant woman about carbon dioxide and air, so Raven said, 'Just think of it like your husband's loving arms around you. It will help to focus your mind on what is happening to your body to make your premature labour easier to bear.'

'Sister Justina, you're quite right. This brown paper bag *does* remind me of my husband – not only his arms but his whole body, which is brown and baggy and full of air. I am only like this because of *him*!' Señora Zamora sent up another painful howl.

Above the woman's anguished cries, Raven stiffened and paid closer attention, her head on one side: was that the Angelus bell? But it was far too early for matins. She ignored it. Having heard it all too often, it had become a token sound, a summoning to prayer, meditation, or time-check, as consistent, as reliable, and as uninteresting as her own heartbeat, nothing more.

But it did not stop, it went on clamouring out its urgent message into the night.

A few minutes later, Dame Annunciata and two extern nuns walked into the ward. 'Be calm, Sister Justina. The convent kitchen is on fire and it will spread to the infirmary in no time.' Dame Annunciata switched on all the electric lights, hooked open the double swing-doors leading to the main corridor, and started issuing instructions to each patient in turn as she hastened down the length of the ward. 'You can walk Señorita Pestana, so can you Señora Xeno y Maragall. Please take the other ambulant patients with you. Go and wait in the main cloister where Reverend Mother will tell you what to do. Sister Justina, this woman needs a helping hand, and this one is a wheelchair case. Help the externs please to evacuate the patients. Come along, Señora Esposa – here are your crutches. Hurry please, dear ... No, you haven't got time to look for your knitting, the convent is on fire.'

Dame Annunciata chivvied the ambulant patients out of the ward, and then helped Raven to remove the bed-ridden cases, dragging the women out through the double doors on their own mattresses if necessary. Other nuns came to their assistance until the smoke began to choke everyone half to death as it spread before the flames, and Dame Annunciata insisted they stay away for their own safety. There was only one patient left in the ward now, and she and Sister Justina were quite capable of dealing with her, she told her helpers.

In the thickly congesting atmosphere Raven asked, 'How did it happen, Dame Annunciata?'

'I've no idea ... Señora, what is the matter with you, *why* can't you move?'

Señora Zamora tried to keep her face averted but Infirmary Mother peered closer still. 'Sister Justina, what is Señora Zamora doing here?'

'She's miscarrying, Dame Annunciata. The bleeding and pain are severe.'

'Does the doctor know?'

'Yes. I called him out from his bed two hours ago when she was first admitted. That was at nine o'clock – you were at Devotions.'

'What was his prescription?'

'He told her that if she lost the baby, it was God's will, and if she kept it, that was also God's will.'

'What have you done to help her?'

'I've given her one of your treatments – her own respiratory carbon dioxide to slow down the contractions while she breathes into a brown paper bag.' And why it had to be brown, Raven never really knew.

'How many weeks is she?'

'Umm – twenty-six according to her calculations.'

'No wonder she's in so much pain, poor woman! The child must be almost viable. Have you packed her?'

'Packed her?'

'Cotton-wool plugs, Sister Justina! Dear-dear-dear! If you are going to be a nurse, you ought to start learning the fundamentals of first-aid. She can't be allowed to lose the baby after carrying it for so many weeks. Go and fetch a dressing-pack. We'll attend to her before we move her.'

'But …'

'Don't argue with me, Sister Justina! If you and I are to die in the performance of our duty, then that, too, will be God's will.'

With no choice but to resort to blind obedience, Raven, her hand over her nose and mouth, ran into the treatment-room to fetch a pack of cotton-wool and dressings.

Storage, sterilizing, treatment- and sluice-rooms led off from that one long corridor with its coffered ceiling. Already the smoke was suffocating as it crept under the double rubber swing-doors leading to the main kitchens at the far end of the corridor. There were no exit doors except onto the corridor and only one external door halfway down the corridor that led to the kitchen gardens, through which the infirmary patients had been evacuated. She prayed that fire wouldn't cut her and Dame Annunciata off from the corridor exit before they'd attended to the patient. Raven rushed back to the ward with the dressing-pack.

Dame Annunciata, wide sleeves rolled up above her elbows, took her time in plugging the mouth of Señora Zamora's womb, while the Spanish woman screeched in more terror of the fire than the thought of losing her ninth child.

'Please, Dame Annunciata,' Raven implored, 'we must hurry if we are to get out of here alive.'

'Sister Justina, we have a duty towards this woman's unborn baby. It is not time for it to arrive in the world as yet, so we must do our best to prevent its premature birth. I think, at twenty-six weeks, the foetus will have every chance of survival if we plug the cervix and stop any further placental bleeding. Hand me that dressing-pad.'

A few moments later a tremendous explosion ripped plaster off the corridor walls and sparks showered down outside the entrance to the ward like the Aurora Borealis.

'Jesu Mary Joseph!' said Dame Annunciata turning pale and crossing herself with the pair of forceps in her hand. 'That was the oxygen cylinder in the treatment-room – praise be to God you weren't still in there looking for the dressings, Sister Just ...' A ball of flame and thick black smoke suddenly leapt through the open infirmary doors, for neither Dame Annunciata nor Raven had thought to close them.

Hypnotized by the greedy orange and red tongues of fire licking around the wooden framework of the ward doors, terrified yet fascinated by the compelling beauty of fire, Raven was rooted to the spot. She was reminded of standing too close to a huge garden bonfire at Hollyberry House, the gardeners raking together the dead branches of trees and mounds of bright, damp leaves, tossing the débris of autumn onto the flames, while admonishing her to stand further away from the blaze: she was reminded of Samson and Delilah, of Soloman and Sheba, part of her past, the bombs and the flames of Ireland and the scars left by an Anglo-Irish war ...

Only Señora Zamora's screams brought Raven back to reality. The Spanish woman tossed everything aside, sent the dressing-trolley flying, and, putting her legs together despite Dame Annunciata's determined administrations with forceps and cotton-wool, struggled out of bed. She tried to stand, but collapsed when another gripping contraction drove her to her knees. Gasping, she clutched her pelvis with one hand, the other tugging Dame Annunciata's long white apron covering her grey habit, almost wrenching it off. 'I'm going to die – where is my husband?'

Flames took hold of the avenue of beds and the feather mattresses began to burn. Electric light-bulbs popped one by one in the heat building up in the room, leaving them on the edge of a darkness lit only by fire getting ever closer. The Spanish woman fainted. Dame Annunciata crossed herself again. She and Raven, both almost overcome by the suffocating smoke, supported Señora

Zamora's dead weight between them. The heat from the flames drove them back against the far wall, and they were unable to reach the exit.

Only an arched stained-glass window relieved the blank nothingness to which their backs were pressed, the wide stone window-ledge far too high for them to reach even had they stood on chairs.

Raven, in that moment, recalled a certain history lesson, and Mademoiselle l'Impératice's vivid description of Joan of Arc burning at the stake. Raven prayed she would not feel the flames licking her feet before she became unconscious, nor that the blood would boil in her veins, her eyeballs bursting, before she suffocated to death. She had a dread of fire stemming from a childhood spent in Dublin.

Fighting for every breath, feeling that a hot, heavy pillow had been thrust over her face, Raven faced the flames snaking along the avenue of white beds, licking and tasting and finally devouring the bed-linen like greedy red reptiles. Wooden ceiling-beams began to smoulder and then flare, showering sparks everywhere. For a wild second Raven wondered if they could not rush the wall of fire and gain the burnt-out entrance before being consumed by fire on the spot where they stood.

Dimly conscious of the sound of breaking glass somewhere above their heads, she turned and looked up. Dame Annunciata also turned her back upon the flames, and a spark caught her flowing veil. Raven did not have time to help Dame Annunciata whose head-dress and habit swiftly caught fire. Raven tried to lift the unconscious weight of Señora Zamora towards the man whose top half had appeared through the smashed window, reaching his arms down to them. The effort was enormous. Her throat and lungs seared by the suffocating smoke, tears blinding her, Raven, too, lost her grip on reality.

Raven opened her smarting eyes, and for a long time couldn't see anything at all. She panicked and flung out her hand. Someone held it tightly and she sank back again in relief when she heard Peedee's reassuring voice, 'Dear girl, rest quietly. You're going to be all right.'

Her blurred vision gradually cleared. Raven registered the fact that she was lying on the ground in one of Toril's side streets with a blanket over her. Not only Peedee was peering anxiously at her, but a whole host of friendly Spanish faces. She wanted to ask, 'What happened?', but she couldn't speak. She coughed so much, she felt sick. Someone gave her some water to drink.

'Good gracious, dear girl, the fire brigade rescued you just in the nick of time! Only your veil and the hem of your habit were in any way singed. And, as you have no hair to speak of, that too, is still intact. The harassed Spanish doctor doing his emergency rounds of all you poor burnt-out nuns, looked at your hands and feet just now and pronounced them to be still useable. Can you feel yourself burning in any other place he did not examine?'

Raven managed to shake her head.

'The firemen had to fight their way through a narrow stained-glass window with their ropes, ladders, and stretchers to get you three out of the infirmary inferno,' Peedee went on to explain, 'otherwise I might have been minus one granddaughter.' Peedee, who was seldom sentimental, squeezed her sore hands lovingly.

In the cool, refreshing night air, the clamour of the fire engines, clanking buckets, and gushing hoses, with the jangling of ambulance bells, and a multitude of babbling voices sounding curiously detached from her immediate existence, Raven breathed deeply and was glad to be alive.

After a little while she was able to croak, 'Dame Annunciata – Señora Zamora, are they all right?'

'Señora Zamora was hauled to safety first. Her hefty husband was lowered down a rope-ladder. He managed to get up it again with his unconscious wife slung over his shoulder. Infirmary Mother, poor soul, was last in line to be rescued and came off the worst. She and Señora Zamora have been rushed off to Barcelona in an ambulance.'

'I must go to them ...'

'Do lie still, dear girl, and stop being heroic. There's nothing you can do. They are already on their way to the main hospital.'

'Does anyone know how the fire started, Peedee?'

'Sad as it is to even contemplate such a thing, I should think the same way as all such convent and monastery fires start these days.'

'Deliberate arson?'

'Chief Fireman, Señor Tajo, and Policeman Albarda seem to think so.'

'Poor Policeman Albarda. Especially after what happened to his nephew two years ago – his sleepy little bull-fighting town seems to have turned into a hotbed of hatred. Is the convent badly damaged, Peedee?'

'All but destroyed, dear girl. The only thing left standing, as far as I can see, is the chimney of the laundry.'

'Poor Reverend Dame Olivera. I wonder what will happen to us now?'

'No idea. I myself only knew what was happening in Toril when I looked through my telescope for the constellation of the Great Bear, and found the whole sky lit up like a heavenly fairground. I was about to telephone the Royal Observatory, when, to my horror, I saw that the convent was ablaze. So I hopped on my bicycle, just in time to lend a helping hand with a water-bucket. Otherwise I fear, dear girl, you might have ended up as a burnt offering.'

'Oh, Grandpapa! I love you and your wonderful down-to-earth approach to life. I love you because you are the most human human being in all the world!'

'Obviously you are overwrought and your nerves are in a state of abradement. You need to get away from the cloister for a little while. Shall I ask Reverend Mother if you can come back to Cabo Alondra for a respite from your nun's duties?'

'Peedee,' said Raven, who tried, cautiously, to sit up, 'I somehow feel, that a great many nuns will be sharing Cabo Alondra with you tonight.'

'God forbid! What have I, a mere bachelor, done to deserve all this? Listen, dear girl, if you're sure you're feeling all right, I'll just get back to my fire-fighting duties. I don't want the blaze spreading to Cabo Alondra. Now, promise me you won't get up off that stretcher until I come back for you with Juan's truck?'

'I promise nothing.'

Cabo Alondra as well as the Mas Luchar were turned into hasty overnight refuge centres for homeless nuns suffering from shock. Madre Estelle Calmar, the two Spanish nuns who had shared Raven's Reception Day, Sister Jeanne, and one or two other veteran externs spent the rest of the night under the sheltering roof of Peedee's Spanish villa, while he himself fire-fought the night away.

Raven firmly refused to get into Juan's truck with the rest of the Dames of Charity. She insisted quite emphatically that there was nothing wrong with her and so she would stay in Toril to help Reverend Dame Olivera and Dame Rosemarie rehouse everyone. Madre Estelle Calmar had, in the end, capitulated in the face of Sister Justina's persuasive argument, she herself had enough problems to attend to in resettling the novices and externs.

The following day, when the convent was just a quietly smouldering mass of blackened beams and sad rubble, the nuns returned to examine the débris of their home.

Peedee, wearing a navy fisherman's jersey and gumboots, a spotted navy and white scarf around his neck and his beloved straw hat on his head despite it being mid-December with a cold wind blowing off the sea, cycled energetically along the avenue of Monterey pines. He met Raven halfway down the avenue. She had come from the direction of Cabo Alondra.

Peedee braked sharply and got off his bicycle to walk beside Raven, who had hoped to meet him, if only briefly, to say hello and reassure herself that he was all right before she returned to Toril.

'Did you manage to get an hour or two's rest at Juan's house, Peedee?'

'I've spent an appalling night, dear girl. At four-thirty this morning, the hour at which Juan and I returned to his cottage after our fire-fighting activities, Cipi was waiting for us with more bad news: Don Ruiz was arrested while everyone was away fighting the convent fire.'

'Arrested?' Raven stared at him blankly. 'Why?'

'Who knows?' Peedee shrugged despondently. 'These days there does not have to be a reason for the most outrageous things to happen.'

'Has someone betrayed him?'

'Dear girl, the dreadfulness of this war is that friends betray friends. Brother will kill brother, while fathers suffer for the sins of their sons and vice versa.'

'Do you think Don Ruiz might have been arrested because of José being a Nationalist soldier on General Franco's particular staff?'

'Who knows?'

'But Don Ruiz cannot be held responsible for his son's politics. José is a grown man with his own mind.'

'This is *civil* war, Raven.'

'But isn't there anyone who can help him? I mean, he must have friends in high places. What about members of the Generalidad? The President himself?'

'President Companys, who spends half his life in prison, is in an awkward position, dear girl. Socialists and Communists together are at least trying to restore law and order to stop the spate of murders going on around here. The Communists, Anarchists and the President himself, have formed a Central Committee, although the Communists are in overall control. President Companys has become merely a figurehead dictated to by people like Ramiro, who has, by the way, cleverly had himself elected to the Generalidad as a delegate for PSUC. The United Catalan Socialist Party are really Communists under a sweeter-smelling name. Our handsome and ambitious Ramiro has been very clever. That spell of his in prison has served only to sharpen his wits more than ever. He has succeeded to a position of power towards which he has always yearned, even as far back as the schoolroom.'

'Then surely, he'll be able to secure his father's release from prison?'

'I would like to think so,' said Peedee. 'However, I hardly think Ramiro is about to lay his head on the chopping-block even for his own father. He and Don Ruiz have always been at loggerheads, and there is no love lost between them. Ramiro isn't going to throw away a golden opportunity to paint Catalonia red by saving Vinarosa for the sake of family loyalty or the Monarchists.'

'What about Jaime?'

457

'From this month, big estates like Vinarosa are to be handed over to workers' cooperatives, who are dividing up the land into small-holdings. Jaime was going to stay on here and run the vineyards while trying to keep the peace between the family and the *rabassaires*. Everything, however, has changed because of this latest suspension in the law concerning land and land-values, the *Ley de Cultivos*, which has given rise to a new spate of aggression. I feel the utmost sorrow on Jaime's behalf. He, out of all of them, is the most level-headed, but is now torn between loyalty to the Republic and loyalty to Vinarosa. The two cannot be resolved. They are, on account of this evil war, on opposite ends of the pole. Poor pacifist Jaime!' Peedee shook his head sadly. 'The de Luchar family has fallen between two stools. Don Ruiz was right, this really has become a house divided.'

'Poor Doña Jacqueline! Where is she now?'

'Well, dear girl. It has all become terribly complicated and I wasn't going to say anything to you in case you, as a nun, were held by the wrong sort of people and forced to tell the truth.'

'What are you talking about, Peedee?'

'Yes, I am waffling on a bit, am I not. But I'm rather tired as I haven't been to bed all night.' He took out his spotted handkerchief and wiped his perspiring, smoke-begrimed face despite the coolness of the weather. 'Doña Jacqueline, Nina, Doña Maria, Aunt Leah, and Jaime, are in hiding.'

'In hiding?' Raven echoed. 'Where?'

'In the Caverna Rosa.'

'In the Cav …'

'Please, dear girl, desist from repeating everything I say: it's most irritating.'

'I'm sorry. I've had a strenuous night, too.'

He patted her shoulder reassuringly. 'We are both suffering from strain and lack of sleep, so let's both try and be less touchy. You and I are going to need each other more than ever in the coming months, dear girl. The family are hiding in the brandy cave because they are afraid of what might happen to them at the hands of angry labourers demanding the land that their families have

458

tilled for generations on behalf of the *latifundistas* like Don Ruiz.'

'This new commune and community rule thing, you mean?'

'Exactly. Leaderless mobs, especially since the Army of Africa have captured all the small *pueblos* around Madrid, and displaced men are wandering indiscriminately throughout the countryside, another menace to our erstwhile peaceful existence. Everyone, it appears, is merging on Barcelona.'

'Peedee, surely all those with a real or imagined grudge against the de Luchar family will know where they're hiding. They'll guess about the Caverna Rosa in no time.'

'They might guess about the Caverna Rosa but finding the family is another matter. Have you ever explored those underground tunnels? Yes, I believe you have. Dare I say it, one summer with José de Luchar?'

She did not blush gracefully as he thought she might. 'I never discovered any *tunnels* under the spruce forest, only the one, the Caverna Rosa.'

'That's what you think, dear girl. Don Ruiz's father, the old grandee, had many more tunnels built long ago when he feared a French invasion during the Franco-Prussian war. He was a little senile at the time and feared that the French, or Bismarck, might run off with his distilled wines. He built himself a catacomb of secret tunnels radiating off the main cellar, in which vintage de Luchar spirits are still being stored, as you well know.'

'Peedee, I don't know! José never gave away *any* family secrets.'

'Well then, he probably didn't know himself – just testing your intelligence, dear girl, forgive me. However, it's so complicated, a map was made of the underground network which covers, I believe, miles. It has been in Doña Maria's possession since the death of the old grandee himself. She is the one who told me in the first place about a secret network in existence below ground. Three of the tunnels actually come out on the beach just below Cabo Alondra. In fact, from my overgrown kitchen garden there is an airshaft that leads directly down into one of the sea-tunnels. One can live happily underground and undiscovered for years as long as one has food.'

'Good gracious, you kept that all to yourself, didn't you, Grandpapa!'

'Sonny knows about it. In fact, Sonny and I spent a busy time exploring them before he decided to go off to Ireland. However, I'm digressing. What I really want to say is, that before the cooperative takes over, Cici and his cellarmen are going to try and shift as many barrels from the Caverna Rosa, into the secret tunnels until after the war. What that will do to the 'ageing' process of the wines I dread to think, but only in that way itinerant Nationalists, vandals like the Death and Freedom Brigade, and militant *rabassaires* won't get hold of the best stuff. That would only be an awful waste of such an antique liquid fortune. Cipi will then fill the Caverna Rosa with less valuable wines. Jaime is hoping to go along with the vintage stuff.'

'Jaime? What on earth are you talking about, Peedee?'

'Jaime is hoping to reach Cadiz by sea. He hopes to join up with the *Requetés* – those dashing red beret Carlists who have finally fired my pacifist boy's imagination.' Peedee gave a heavy sigh of regret. 'Oh dear, how all our young men do glorify war and yearn towards acts of heroism. The trouble is, most of them are not there in the end to count the headstones or the final cost of war. Carlos has already left the nest. You remember how he loved to indulge his little hobby of gliding airplanes around the Pratt airfield in Barcelona? Well now, I hear he has got himself his fighter pilot's wings and has said goodbye to the Fabrica de Luchar, where he absolutely hated working after Ramiro's banishment. Carlos, I suppose, is now off to drop bombs on brother José and his Laureate Cross, possibly upon Jaime too.'

Peedee shook his head sadly. Raven remained silent.

'I never thought,' said Peedee, 'that when I instructed those four good-looking de Luchar brothers in the horrors of the Great European War, they'd end up killing each other before the first lesson was barely ended.'

'How long is Doña Jacqueline intending to stay in hiding, Peedee? She surely can't spend the rest of the war underground?'

'I don't know, dear girl. As long as it's necessary I

suppose.'

'Franco seems to be gaining the upper hand,' Raven murmured.

'Raven, you mustn't breathe a word to anyone, because one never knows who might denounce one these days. But I do know that a big offensive is shortly to take place. The rebel armies of the Nationalists are seeking to cut off the Madrid-Corunna road and trap the Republican army in the Guadalajara mountains, where the rebels hope the Reds will freeze to death. But now that the International Brigades have joined the Republican forces, things might go the other way. I'm not in favour of any extremist party, Fascism, or Communism, gaining the upper hand, that's too dangerous. The International Brigades just might restore the balance of power a little. One must always maintain a balanced view of things, I feel, and that's why I'm glad to know the lads from other lands are here at last. I'm not being white-livered about all this, but really, this is one war where there will be no glorious victorious side.'

'Peedee, look after Jaime, don't let anything happen to him.'

'Jaime, I hope, will get away safely tonight, so don't worry. I'll do my best to give him and his chums a good send-off. The German battleship, *Graf Spee*, is lying off this coast – yes, I know, you want to know what *I* know about the *Graf Spee*! Admiral Karls and the commander of the German torpedo boat, *Ildis*, have been standing by to take the Falangist leader, José Antonio, to Germany. Unfortunately, José Antonio was shot in Alicante prison two weeks ago and now ... oh! just wait, don't go yet ...' He drew her back into the shadow of the thick stone wall of the bullring where they had stood together so many times in the past protesting the cruelty of bullfighting. But since it appeared that most bullfighters were Nationalist, and had left the town, Peedee was out of a job.

'What's the matter?' Raven whispered anxiously, wanting to know more on the interesting subject of the *Graf Spee* and José Antonio Primo de Rivera.

'Stay out of sight, don't move.' Peedee stood in front of her, shielding her between the wall of the bullring and his bicycle.

Half a dozen men were being marched down the main street, hands on their heads while they were prodded along at gun-point by labourers wearing dark overalls, their flat caps jauntily set on the side of the head.

'*Checas*,' Peedee whispered back.

Checas were a newly formed pseudo-secret police unit set up to fight left-wing groups, and were greatly to be feared. They went around in plain clothes, disguised as humble *braceros* or bourgeois butchers, bakers, or furniture-makers. Raven, although she knew she ought not to hate anyone, hated and feared the *checas* like nobody else, for they were the unseen ones who made people disappear overnight, never to be heard of again. The *checas* had probably been responsible for Don Ruiz's sudden disappearance, and would no doubt put the rest of the family away, too, if they discovered them hiding in the Caverna Rosa.

'How do you know, Peedee, who they are – oh, look! There's Father Gabriel – he doesn't belong to any political group …!' Peedee silenced her at once, his hand over her mouth.

One of the men standing beside Father Gabriel raised his right hand with a clenched fist salute and was immediately knocked to the ground by the stock of the *checa's* rifle. Raven's tiny cry was muffled by Peedee's hand and his fierce whisper in her ear, '*Shut up!*'

The prisoners were taken into the bullring. Ten minutes later the frightening staccato bursts of rapid gunfire made Raven put her hands over her ears. 'Oh no!' She crossed herself, '*Hail Mary, full of grace, the Lord is with thee* – oh, please don't let anything have happened to Father Gabriel – let him be there in the capacity of confessor for the redemption of the souls of those other men – let him – let him be alive …'

She said her prayers even while in her heart she knew that Father Gabriel had been shot by the secret police.

Raven pushed aside Peedee's bicycle.

He grabbed hold of her cincture to stop her headlong flight towards the closed gates of the bullring.

'Where are you going?' Peedee cried.

'To help Father Gabriel …'

'You can't help him now, Raven!'

'I can pray for his soul.'

'God in heaven, dear girl!' Peedee let fall his bicycle and ran after her. 'They'll *shoot* you if you interfere! Please, Raven, go back to the convent and find out from your reverend mother what is to become of all of you. I will see to Father Gabriel and those other men. I'll try and find out why they were shot and let you know so that you can tell your bishop. Inform Reverend Dame Olivera what has happened, but please don't go anywhere near those men in their present vile mood.'

Helplessly Raven turned to him. 'This is unbelievable. It can't be happening in Toril. It's like a nightmare that haunted my early years in Dublin – a repeating nightmare that just goes on and on in cycles of brutality and killing in whatever country I live. When will it stop?'

'I know, I know, dearest girl!' He took hold of her hands to calm her frenzy. 'Please go back and find the other nuns. It isn't safe for you to be alone on the streets. Just get back behind your convent walls, I beg you.'

'What convent, Peedee? There's nothing left.'

'The boundary walls are still there, Raven. Get back onto your own consecrated ground before anything else happens to give me more grey hairs.'

'Promise me you will take care of Father Gabriel's body and not let them abuse him?'

'I promise. Now go and say your prayers – I'll see you across the road, I don't want anything else to happen to you. The sooner you are away from here the better. Why don't you consider going back to Ireland?'

'No, Peedee.'

'Very well then, I won't play the heavy-handed grandfather as yet, but please watch your step, dear girl.'

'You mustn't call me Raven or dear girl, but Sister Justina. I've renounced the world, remember?'

'I know, I know. But I was your grandfather long before you were a nun, and disrespect does not enter into it, only the humble love of an ageing relative.'

She smiled wanly, and because she wanted to clasp his hand and feel the reassurances of that love, put temptation aside by tucking her hands firmly into her wide

463

sleeves. Raven was thankful when Sister Jeanne arrived to unlock the gates.

She said goodbye to Peedee and watched him cross the wet and blackened road still displaying signs of the Fire Brigade's activities in and around the convent until the early hours of that morning.

Raven dreaded facing Reverend Dame Olivera with the news of Father Gabriel's assassination so swift upon the tragedy of having her convent burnt to the ground, while Dame Annunciata lay in agony in a hospital in Barcelona.

'Thank goodness it's you, Sister Justina!' Sister Jeanne said breathlessly as she struggled with the heavy padlock and chain. She swung open one half of the gate and admitted Raven, before hastily relocking it. 'You are the last one to arrive back and Reverend Dame Olivera was getting anxious. She was going to send out a search party, but guessed you might still be with your grandfather. You must never stay out alone like that again, Sister Justina.'

'I'm sorry, Sister Jeanne. I had to find my grandfather as I was worried about him. They have arrested Don Ruiz.' She refrained from mentioning what had happened to Father Gabriel, for Reverend Dame Olivera was the first person who should know about such a dreadful thing. Such an act of barbarism by Spaniards against Spaniards Raven was unable to fully comprehend: until she remembered Ireland.

'I'm sorry to hear that. We will include Don Ruiz in our prayers. Now hurry along, dear child, we have plenty to do. We have to salvage as much as we can from the mess. Reverend Dame Olivera is trying to get us rehoused in other Franciscan convents. I'm to accompany her to the Convent of the Sacred Heart in Vilafranca until everything is under control again – and to think I shall probably end my days where they first began, fills me with a great inner peace and solace I have not had for years, for I believe that God *does* move in mysterious ways.'

'I'm sure He does, Sister Jeanne,' Raven murmured, only half listening.

'I think you and Madre Estelle Calmar and a few others are going to the Convent of Jesu María in Barcelona. As soon as I ring the Angelus bell we're to meet in the cloister

464

walk so that Reverend Dame Olivera can tell us what is to become of us all. The chapel is completely gutted and looks frightful. Everywhere beams are still smouldering and fizzing, so we can't go inside any part of the building as it's too dangerous.' Dame Jeanne did not let up in her chattering all the way to the cloister walk.

On the hard, bleached flagstones scrubbed clean again by Dame Rosemarie and her helpers, trampled grass and kitchen gardens black and wet and ruined all around them, Camillus nuns knelt in prayer for two hours. The humbling of themselves, and their prayers, were for the soul of Father Gabriel, followed by the simple recitation of the beatitudes and the Latin texts of the Gregorian chant. Even without an organ, the refrains were filled with the solemn melody of the nuns' voices soaring high above gutted convent walls.

Keir hoped to renew his acquaintance with Dr Marcel Junod, who had been in Spain since the outbreak of hostilities the previous July.

Keir and Dr Junod had met for the first time in Abyssinia when they were both engaged in assuaging the horrors of modern warfare wrought by the Italian soldiers and airmen on Haile Selasse's primitive warriors. But now the President of the International Red Cross Committee in Geneva, Max Huber, had asked Keir to assist Dr Junod in this new theatre of war, where Communists and Fascists had divided the map of Spain so that thousands of refugees were pouring into France. In his neutral capacity with the International Red Cross team, Marcel Junod and others like him had already brought great relief and hope to prisoners, soldiers, and refugees on either side of the fighting lines.

Keir found his journey prolonged by a visit to the Spanish Embassy in Paris to gain the necessary documents to enter Spain. Whilst in Paris, Keir made brief contact again with Archie Cunningham in the Consular Section of the British Embassy, but Archie was so busy, he could only spare Keir a few moments of his time. Keir had been hoping to meet Jan, and to prize from her any informaion about Raven, but Archie told him that Jan was spending the last three months of her pregnancy in England busily furnishing the nursery at their home in Westerham. Any news of Raven would have to wait a little longer, Keir reassured himself, for he had no wish to ask Archie about her: besides, Keir thought happily, he would, in any case, soon be seeing Raven for himself.

From the Gare d'Austerlitz Keir had taken the train to the Spanish border. He had been warned by Archie that delays were considerable and confusion supreme at all the border towns, and he might have to find an alternative way to enter the country. Keir had decided to risk it. As soon as he arrived at the Spanish border town of La Jonquera, Keir realized how right Archie Cunningham had been.

La Jonquera bristled with an odd assortment of Red officials and anti-Fascist militiamen. Subjected to an interminable delay while Republican border guards argued his status, Keir could see himself being imprisoned as a spy in the indomitable fortress on the spruce-covered crest of the pass between France and Spain. High above the gorge, the fortress was frighteningly visible from the barred window of the border guards' office. Should it transpire within the next few minutes, God forbid, that the Nationalist Air Force were to blow it up, Keir felt sure that he and his interrogators would go the same way as the ugly, orange-roofed town, crushed to powder beneath the red rubble of the fortress of La Jonquera tumbling down the hillside on top of them.

His American passport, Red Cross identity papers issued in Geneva, as well as the *salvo conducto*, safe conduct pass, stamped by the Spanish Embassy in Paris, were totally disregarded by the officials, many of whom sported the black and red neckerchief of the Anarchist militias. Most of the men could not read. After much futile argument, Keir finally lost his temper with the Spaniards.

'*Dr Marcel Junod, Calle Lauria, novento-y-cinco!*' he shouted in exasperation. 'Telephone him for Chrissakes! He'll tell you I'm not a Fascist spy or any other kind of goddamn spy!'

At that show of temper from *el Americano*, the pompous little *carabinero* behind his rifle and desk beamed like a spotlight, stood up and shook hands vigorously after having hindered Keir for so long.

'You are a friend of Dr Marcel Junod? Why did you not say so in the first place, comrade! It is a pleasure to meet any friend of *El Medico Junod* whose name is in all the papers, for he has done much good work in July to release our women and children from the clutches of the Fascist pigs! You are here to fight for us with *los Americanos* from the Abraham Lincoln Battalion, eh comrade?' he asked, slapping Keir jovially on the back.

Keir thought it best to nod.

The *carabinero's* grin broadened and he shouted, 'Hey, André, find some reliable transport for *el Americano*. He is from the Abraham Lincoln Battalion and has joined up to help us fight the Fascist pigs. *Viva España!*' Then he asked with less bolshy overtones, 'You have some "Lucky Strikes", Americano?'

Keir dropped four packets on the desk. The *carabinero* grinned broadly, swooped them up and put them into his own pocket before anyone else grabbed them. He proceeded to stamp Keir's papers with gusto, issued him a new *salvo conducto* to Barcelona, and ushered him out into the wintry sunshine with the added adjunctive, 'Book in at the Lenin Barracks when you get there, comrade, they serve the best food.' He disappeared back to his desk and Keir could hear the Spaniard through his teeth whistling the catchy tune of the 'Red River Valley' song, the marching song of the Lincoln Brigade.

The absence of protocol and discipline, as well as the odd assortment of mud-brown garments purporting to be a uniform, knitted caps and berets and neckerchiefs denoting the various trade unions forming the militias, amused Keir considerably. He couldn't help thinking what an undisciplined and inefficient mob these *carabineros* were, allowing for their final good humour when they had satisfied themselves he was not one of Franco's spies. But he couldn't imagine them winning any war, not unless someone, before long, seriously took them in hand.

'You know Mickey Mouse?' asked the young militiaman,

André, who was to be the driver of the requisitioned and all but clapped-out Fiat. Keir thought the lad could not have been more than fifteen and Barcelona, nearly two hundred kilometres away, was surely going to be a further voyage of discovery.

'Yeah, I know Mickey Mouse,' Keir replied laconically.

'You have some chewing gum like all Americanos?'

Keir took out a packet from his pocket and handed it to André who grinned happily, then, as further indemnity, Keir slapped a bar of chocolate in the lad's hand. By the look on André's face, Keir realized he had just passed muster as the genuine article, a real Mickey Mouse Americano.

Keir had been hoping to close his eyes for at least a couple of hours like the two elderly passengers travelling to Barcelona with him, now snoring loudly in the back seat of the Fiat. Instead, he was engaged by André in a lively conversation about American cinema and Al Capone. Keir also made the startling discovery that the two citizens in the back were André's parents who lived in La Jonquera. André went on to confess that he was taking them on a 'little outing' to Barcelona because they had never been to a big city before. His parents were hoping to see caged monkeys in the Rambla as they had never seen monkeys before. This was André's first important military assignment on behalf of the Republic. He had only driven a motorcycle before, never a car. 'But the steering is all the same, and to know when to stop, eh comrade?' André had flashed Keir a charming grin. André himself had been ordered to bring back some rifles from the Lenin Barracks because there were only sixteen rifles at La Jonquera, which everyone had to share in relay on sentry duty. André was hoping to go to the Aragon front shortly with the men of the POUM militia. 'POUM-POUM!' The young man simulated gunfire. 'We will soon make short work of the Fascist pigs, comrade! They will be sorry they ever started this war on we working men.'

Keir told himself he must remember in future three names to get him safe conduct passes through Republican Spain, Dr Marcel Junod, Abraham Lincoln and Mickey Mouse.

After a harrowing journey at André's inexperienced hands wrapped sweatingly around the steering-wheel, they arrived in the middle of the night at Calle Lauria 95, a typical shuttered building of wrought-iron, burglar-proof windows against a flat, square grey façade fronting the main street. The noisy Fiat leaked oil and reeked of petrol, and seemed hardly capable of making it back to La Jonquera with rifles for the border patrol. The last time Keir remembered a similar journey, was going up a volcano in Guatemala with Father Silvestre.

Thankfully Keir said goodbye to André and his parents, and hoped they would enjoy the caged monkeys in the Rambla – whether to see or to eat, remaining a matter of reckoning.

Keir discovered that it was just as well the Anarchist officials and *carabineros* at the border had not tried telephoning Dr Junod to establish his Red Cross identity, for Dr Junod would not have been found. The Spanish Red Cross representative informed him that Marcel Junod could be anywhere between Valencia and Salamanca. Valencia had become the Republican seat of government in the face of the advancing Nationalists, and Marcel Junod, in his capacity as arbiter between Franco's Spain and President Azaña's Spain, spent his time negotiating between the two capitals.

And next Sunday, Keir promised himself as he at last flung himself down to sleep in the cramped and makeshift accommodation found for him at Red Cross Headquarters, he would take a little excursion out into the country. He was looking forward to renewing his acquaintance with Raven Quennell, surprising her (nicely, he hoped) at her home in Cabo Alondra. He might even invite her to the cinema – though not to see Mickey Mouse, but something a little more subtle and suited to his mood.

When Keir, on the following Sunday, took a bumpy bus ride from Barcelona to Vilafranca, and thence to Cabo Alondra, he was disappointed. Apart from a few peasants tilling barren fields ready for the spring planting by a most antiquated method, to his American eyes, of donkey and wooden plough, he met no one who was in the least helpful. Certainly neither Raven nor her grandfather were anywhere in the vicinity.

The villa was closed and shuttered for the winter. But a sullen-looking fisherman, his nets spread out on the sands below Cabo Alondra, tersely muttered, 'I don't know when Señor Peedee will be back. Ask at the Mas Luchar.'

There was nothing as dreary and as depressing as a stormy sea and brow-beaten coastline in mid-winter, so Keir put the fisherman's unfriendly mood down to the weather, for it was far too rough to take a small boat out today, let alone try to catch fish for a living. '*Muchas gracias, señor.*'

Keir, his hair teased by the fierce wind, took the cliff path back to the peculiar-shaped house on the headland, Cabo Alondra, where he had hoped to have been invited in for a cup of coffee and a friendly chat with the girl whose raven-dark hair, soft grey eyes, and sweet smiling face had so beguiled him in Switzerland. But it was not to be.

He found the Mas Luchar set in the middle of fields where small, skeleton vines looked strangely forlorn. A few weatherbeaten *rabassaires* were half-heartedly prunning brittle stems into shape. The farmhouse had the closed and shuttered look of Cabo Alondra. The de Luchar family, according to the elderly cook, who was as forthcoming as the fisherman on the beach, were living in Barcelona.

'But what about Señor Purnell and his granddaughter?' Keir asked, his eyes watering as the woman peeled strong Spanish onions at the kitchen table.

She shrugged, non-committal. 'Try Barcelona.'

'Thanks, señora!' he said, and walked away from the sombre, sprawling farmhouse.

From one of the small windows two women watched his departure.

Doña Maria hissed, 'He looks a nice man. Isaba says he is American and works for the Red Cross in Barcelona. He might be able to help us. Go fetch him back, Nina.'

'No Grandmother! It might be a trap. Isaba said he was also enquiring after Señor Peedee and Sister Justina. You know how Señor Peedee helped Jaime and his friends get away on a German battleship, so the secret police might be

470

after him for that reason. Also because Sister Justina is a nun. One never knows who to trust these days. He might have been sent here by the *checas*.'

'I don't think so, silly girl! *Checas* don't wear shirts and ties like that man, they dress like pigs!' Doña Maria snorted contentiously. 'Only foreigners wear ties these days. Go fetch him. I think he may be able to help us, or at least bring us news of the others, especially if he is with the Spanish Red Cross who are able to get information about anyone.'

'I won't risk it, Grandmother.'

'Santa Maria, you disobedient girl, then I will!' Determinedly Doña Maria began rapping on the windowpane with her walking-stick, but Keir was too far away from the farmhouse to hear.

Making his way back to the main road along the avenue of Monterey pines whipped to a frenzy by the strong, cold wind, Keir was downcast. His carefully laid plans to meet Raven on her own home ground had misfired badly, and he could not help reflecting, somewhat philosophically, whether or not it was an unkind fate keeping them apart deliberately, since it would be foolish to start anything romantic, especially in war-torn Spain.

He turned at the sound of softly running footsteps behind him. A breathless voice said, 'Señor, please stop.'

The young Spanish woman, pale and agitated, a headscarf tied around her head, a shabby blue woollen cardigan wrapped hastily around her thin shoulders, confronted him. 'Are you really who you say you are?'

He smiled at her obvious distrust. 'I'm Keir Devlin, an American doctor who is not fighting on any side, señorita, so don't worry.'

'Isaba told us you were an American doctor working with the Spanish Red Cross, but I didn't know whether to believe her.'

'Isaba?'

'Our cook and housekeeper. I am Nina de Luchar. My grandmother, Doña Maria, and I are the last ones left. But we are under house arrest and cannot leave Vinarosa.'

'I was given to understand that none of the family were at home, Señorita de Luchar.'

'Isaba was afraid, as we all are. That's why she lied. She, too, must be careful in case she is seen to be more on our side than on the side of the workers. She's in the middle, and it's often difficult for her. My grandmother made me come after you because she thought you might be able to help us.'

'Who is keeping you prisoner in your own home, señorita?'

'Junto de Pueblo, señor, the War and Defence Committee of Toril, who, in turn, receive orders from the Committee of Workers now running things around here. Under new laws Vinarosa is run by a Rabassaires Cooperative, the land divided into small-holdings. The army enjoys our wines now, no one else.'

'What has happened to the rest of your family?'

'Two of my brothers are fighting for the Nationalists. The other two are on the side of the Republic: Carlos is in the Republican Air Force, and Ramio is a Communist delegate in the Generalidad in Barcelona. My eldest sister, Marta, has become a militiawoman and has gone to the Aragon front. My father, Don Ruiz, disappeared one night shortly before Christmas – no one knows what has become of him. My mother, grandmother, aunt, and myself hid in one of the wine cellars until my brother Jaime got away to the Nationalist side. When we thought it safe, we came out of hiding. Then, two weeks ago, my mother and Aunt Leah were arrested when they were returning from a secret Mass being held in Vilafranca. The saying of Mass and public worship you see, Señor Doctor, are banned. I do not know where they are being held.'

Keir took a deep breath. 'And what has become of Señor Purnell and Miss Quennell?'

'No harm has come to them because they are Britishers. Señor Peedee went to Barcelona to try and find out what has become of my father, and why my mother and aunt are being detained by the Communist authorities.'

'And Miss Quennell?'

'If you are talking about Roxana, she married my eldest brother and is ...'

'I'm talking about Raven.'

Nina gave Keir a guarded look, 'I'm sorry, señor, don't you know about her?'

'What about her?' he asked somewhat impatiently.

'The Camillus nuns were burned out of their convent in Toril a few weeks ago and Sister Justina was rehoused with a sister order, the Dames of Charity of the Jesu María Convent in Barcelona. You will find her there.'

'Sister Justina?' His voice discordant even in his own ears, Keir was perturbed by what this Spanish woman was trying to tell him. An ominous foreboding creeping over him like an unwelcome rash, he stared at Nina disbelievingly, 'You mean Raven has become a nun?'

'Yes, Señor Doctor, did you not know?'

It took him a long time to answer. When he did, he turned a haggard face to Nina. 'No I did not, señorita. No one ever told me.'

'*Lo siento*, I am sorry.'

'So am I – *Muchas gracias*, Señorita de Luchar.' Keir began to walk off down the avenue of pines.

Raven Quennell had come to represent a shining star on the horizon of his loneliness. During his long years of devoted medical work in Guatemala and Abyssinia he had thought about her often. Now, more recently, he had even dreamt about her, begun to envisage a whole new world opening up for him, a world of promise borne on a sweet smile given long ago in Geneva – weddings are pretty things if you yourself are not involved, he had remembered saying at the time, and now regretted. Insidiously, despite his resolution never to get involved with any woman again, Raven Quennell had managed to edge her way into his mind and more lately his heart; he was unable to edge her out. He had been prepared to accept her marriage to someone else, had faced up to that possibility, but having caught up with her at last, only to be told that she had become a *nun* was absolutely devastating. All hope of any long-term commitment between them had been cruelly dashed – he couldn't have her: Mother Church had won again!

Father Silvestre had been right; the promising smiles of pretty women meant trouble, as troublesome as the cold grey ashes Francesca had left for him to clear out of the

473

empty grate of their marriage once the fires of passion had died the death of deaths.

'Señor Doctor, please,' Nina's anxious voice called to him, 'won't you come back to the Mas and refresh yourself? My grandmother wishes to talk to you.'

'Some other time. Thanks all the same, Señorita de Luchar. I've got to get the last bus back to Barcelona.'

CHAPTER THIRTEEN

Euskadi and Catalonia:
January – April 1937

Roxana was once again spending the winter season in the tiny picturesque principality of Andorra in the Pyrenees mountains. She had become expert at the fashionable and exclusive sport of alpine skiing. Pippa was now nearly three years old. The Comte de Martello, a devil at all times, had dragged young Pippa and her nanny onto the training slopes, and despite Annuala's protestations that Pippa was far too young to ski had said, 'Nonsense, girl! Three years of age is the best time for a child to learn to ski. By the time Pippa is her mother's age, she'll be an Olympic champion.'

'Or a cripple: and she is not three until April, Monsieur le Comte!' Annuala had hotly declared, flatly refusing to be coerced by the Comte de Martello to don a pair of skis like her protégée.

At the end of the skiing season Roxana encountered a difficulty that had never presented itself before in all the years she had been to Andorra with Vida and her father. She didn't know how to get home – home this time being Salamanca. Roxana, a little bored with Vida and too much of the good life, which had become a trifle stale to her jaded palate, felt it was high time she joined her husband again: and no doubt the delicious, witty, handsome Vittorio Broué would also be in Salamanca as a change to the scenery.

'*No problema*, Roxy darling,' said Vida who let nothing

daunt her capacity for enjoyment. After all, money could buy *anything*: jewels, houses, yachts, fine clothes, and champagne; it could buy politicians, friends, and traitors; guns and wars and freedom; and it could buy lovers and husbands. The whole world was her lotus-land. 'We will go back to St Jean de Luz and sail to Corunna, where you will be with your own side again. So don't worry that the Reds will have your beautiful body for themselves!'

The Comte himself and his mistress were not joining them on the cruise to Corunna. He told Vida he had urgent business in Paris. From the small airport at Seu d'Urgell he and his younger-than-young Romanian mistress left Andorra in his private Puss Moth for Paris.

Vida, in the absence of paternal restraint, ordered the crew of the *Al-gandura* (the Comte's winter residence in Andorra, also called *Al-gandura*, an Arabic word meaning Wanton Woman) to sail from St Jean de Luz to Biarritz, not Corunna.

'We simply *must* have a little spring holiday in the casino before you insist on getting back to city life and your stuffy husband: and why you must, I *don't* understand, Roxy darling.'

'I've run out of cash, Vida. I can't afford the casino, not unless my husband remits me some money or Peedee parts with what my parents left me. The trust was handed over when Raven and I were both twenty-one, but even so, Peedee, who sees to our financial affairs, can be a real mealy-miser! He's always telling me that to make inroads into one's capital is a foolish thing to do. My money is supposed to last me until my decrepitude, you see.'

'Oh, how stuffy of him! Who needs money when they're old! Darling, my inheritance will *never* run out, so you can always help me spend it long after we are both decrepitudes haunting the casinos of Monte Carlo, San Sebastian, and Biarritz. I'll lend you the money and, because I know how proudly British-minded you are, you can repay me, if you want, when you've won it all back.'

Roxana fell in at once with Vida's suggestion. Six of Vida's friends joined the yacht party at St Jean de Luz. From there, they sailed along the French coast to Biarritz where Roxana tried to recoup her losses.

In the middle of April they left Biarritz and sailed back along the Cantabrian coast, this time intent upon taking a very out-of-pocket Roxana home to beg her husband for more 'pennies from heaven'.

'Which is all it will be knowing him,' Roxana disgruntled, divulged to Vida. She had lost an awful lot in the casino, the chips being definitely down in her case. She owed Vida a fortune (not by Vida's standards of course, only Peedee's), although Vida had said to forget it. Roxana dared not telephone Peedee for more funds to be transferred into her bank account because he had done so when she was in Andorra. He had told her then over the telephone to make it last at least six months. She found it impossible to live decently on such a penny-pinching basis.

'Come on, Roxy darling,' Vida said, 'cheer up. Look, it's market day in Guernica, let's get Gérard to stop at Bermeo. We can spend the morning buying some of that lovely crochet work in the market, have a seafood lunch in Bermeo, and then explore the caves of Santimamine.'

'You'll have to buy the lace, Vida, I'm flat broke.'

'I've never seen you so down, Roxy. What else is wrong besides being flat broke? You've never let money bother you before.'

Roxana burst out sulkily, 'Damn Sonny for inheriting it all! He promptly disposed of everything to the monks! Hollyberry House has become a Catholic hospice for ageing Benedictines, and Quennell House a printing works for Bibles, yuk!'

'Oh, my poor Roxy, you really *are* down!'

'And I *hate* being dependent upon José. If it weren't for my own private funds, he'd keep me like all Spanish wives, a prisoner to his masculine ego.'

'Ramiro, too. Spaniards are *such* chauvanist pigs.' Vida sighed regretfully. 'Ramiro ignores me, but doesn't want me to ignore him.'

'Then won't he be wondering where you've got to if you don't return to Barcelona?'

'Oh, I'm tired of him. We only ever screw once in a blue moon since he's more intent on screwing everyone else on behalf of the Communist Party. I think I might even divorce him if he insists on playing Bolshevik games at my expense.'

477

'What do you mean?'

'The Republican side is very short of weapons – strictly between ourselves, darling, because Ramiro made me promise not to tell because it's bad for morale – Communist morale!' She gave a little gurgle of fun. 'So, Papa is going to supply the Communist militias with badly needed weapons. My father might be a millionaire but he's still *very* French and socialist in his attitudes.'

'Then why does he keep his title?' Roxana enquired.

'Double standards, Roxy darling, which is why the rich are different. Papa has no desire to see a Fascist regime sitting on his doorstep and backs Spain's Republican cause to the hilt. If it means supplying the Communists, or the Socialists with guns to keep the Republic going, he'll do it, because neither has Papa got a very high moral conscience. It also means more money in his pocket. As it's Communist money in this instance, he's quite happy keeping Ramiro happy to keep me happy. Papa is only receiving back from the Communists what my Red husband takes off me, clever, huh?'

'Very clever.' Roxana murmured, not caring one way or another *how* Ramiro got his guns.

'A huge supply of armaments will arrive in Andorra in a week's time,' Vida continued, hoping to take Roxana's mind off her financial worries, for she hated miserable people around her. 'From Andorra they'll be taken by the Communists to dish around among their PSUC comrades in Barcelona. I really don't know who is fighting who in this war, only that Ramiro appears to be fighting not only Franco, but everyone else, including me.'

'After all this is over I think I *will* divorce José. The only trouble is I haven't found another lover to take me on. Franco's war has truly gone and messed up everything. Every man I know is now more concerned with fighting either Facism or Communism instead of making love. The man I could have worked on since he's utterly adorable, is completely dominated by his ugly little Spanish wife.'

'Who?'

'Captain Vittorio Broué. You don't know him. I met him in Tetuan. Vittorio's a legionnaire and José's best friend. The only trouble is, his wife follows him everywhere.'

'Never mind, darling,' Vida said placatingly. 'I'm sure you'll meet your heart's desire one of these days. Someone who is madly handsome, a fabulous lover, stinking-rich, fancy free and faithful – to you. Meanwhile, the world is our oyster, so stop thinking about gloomy things and enjoy Papa's generosity.'

'A man as wonderful as that, Vida, simply doesn't exist.'

'Then no one else can have him either, Roxy darling!'

Roxana smiled, somewhat mollified by Vida's practical advice. She helped herself to more breakfast champagne and then got herself ready to comply with Vida's wishes and her programme for the day.

Annuala and Pippa were to stay aboard the yacht with Captain Gérard and the crew, as Roxana feared Pippa would get tired of walking any great distance. In the lee of the pine-slopes of the Mundaca valley rising above wonderfully secluded, sandy coves, they could swim and sunbathe. Roxana would have wished to swim and laze around on the sands like some of the others in the party, but Vida appeared to be in an energetic mood and demanded her company on the shopping spree. Roxana felt indebted to Vida over the casino affair, so she reluctantly accompanied Vida and three other friends to the sleepy market town of Guernica lying at the head of the estuary. They spent a busy morning shopping for souvenirs and lace and the kind of knick-knacks Vida so loved. Afterwards they lunched at Bermeo, its seafood restaurants among the best along that stretch of the Cantabrian coast. The caves of Santimamine, where they headed next, were five kilometres east of Guernica.

It was late afternoon by the time the whole party returned to the *Al-gandura*, thoroughly exhausted and flushed with success because no one had apprehended them. Captain Gérard asked Vida, 'Everyone doing the same as they've always done in the Basque country, fishing, weaving, and milking cows?'

'Of course. I told you they would be. It's not like a real war. It's only a peasants' war and nothing to get worked up about, so relax, Gerry darling!'

'As long as they can see our Tricolour, Vida *chérie*, and *don't* start firing on us, and as long as we *don't* run into any mines.' Relieved that everyone was back safely, Captain Gérard ordered the engines to be started.

'*Mon Dieu*, Vida!' Louis-Jou, a fashion photographer beloved of Vida, who had accompanied them to Guernica and the Santimamine Caves, groaned as he flung himself into a deck-chair and closed his eyes. 'I thought this was supposed to have been a nice leisurely cruise until we dumped Roxy off with her husband. Instead, I find myself on army fatigues!'

'The precise reason why I didn't go with you,' yawned Axël de la Motte from a hammock. Axël had been sunbathing and taking it easy all day.

'You ought, Axël darling! It would have been good cross-country training for when you have to run away from the Basques.' Vida, who had changed into a Schiaparelli bathing-costume, smiled and unpeeled a banana with her red talons. She bit into it seductively. 'But don't worry, boys, Gérard is an excellent skipper.'

'He has to be to take some of the orders you give him. No offence, darling. But I don't blame him for feeling a little uneasy.'

'Rough water under the bows, David darling.'

'Well, it's a wonder to me we haven't been fired on by the Basque Navy for getting in their way,' Louis-Jou said, agreeing whole-heartedly with David.

'I think it's terribly exciting dodging the mines and warships.'

'Yes, isn't it, Sylvie darling.'

'I'm serious, Axël! David bought a Spanish newspaper in Guernica this morning. There was supposed to be a fight three days ago between a Nationalist warship and three Basque fishing trawlers. They were blown sky-high out of the water.'

'Who?'

'The Basques, of course.'

'Franco must have got a lot of fish to eat in Salamanca that day.'

Vida tossed banana peel into the sea. She picked up her champagne cocktail, sipped it, put it down again, and then moved her fleshy legs off the unoccupied deck-chair in front of her to turn over the record that was making a scratching sound on the turntable. The strains of 'My Funny Valentine' echoed across the sea.

Vida's phonograph was still churning out Vida's favourites, the holiday party lounging about the decks and drinking numerous champagne cocktails, when a low droning from the south caused Captain Gérard to alter course and head out towards the open sea. He had been keeping the Cantabrian coastline in sight, and was hoping to reach Santander by nightfall.

'Why have you altered course?' Vida stormed angrily into the wheelhouse. 'I thought we were heading for Santander.'

'It's a bombing raid, Vida.'

'On us?'

'I hope not. *Mon Dieu*, what a good job you weren't still buying your lace in the market place, *chérie*. Your father would have given me as bait to the fishes had I taken home your ashes covered with a crocheted tablecloth.'

'Guernica? Don't be ridiculous! There's nothing there except an old oak tree and some market stalls – here, give me those binoculars.' Vida snatched them from slim, trim Gérard in his sailor ducks.

Through the glass he had been scouring the coastline without approaching too near for fear of running into trouble. 'You're looking in the wrong place. About five kilometres east – all that smoke in the air,' he told Vida. 'Now we'll just have to ride the waves a little, I'm afraid.'

'Oh this ridiculous war! It's getting on my nerves. Well, don't go too far out into the bay. I don't want to be seasick. Why on earth should anyone want to bomb Guernica?'

'For their handmade lace, perhaps?' Gérard said.

Vida's party crowded the rails, sharing the crew's binoculars. Captain Gérard had shut down the engines, and the yacht gently rocked on the swell of the waves, while everyone aboard observed the air-bombardment taking place on the coast.

'I expect they're trying to bomb the Renteria bridge over the Rio Oca. It's probably of strategic value to Franco.'

'Why, David?'

'So that he can keep the Basques cut off from the rest of the Republican side, Vida darling.'

'The trouble is,' added Louis-Jou, 'the Spaniards aren't very good at aerial bombardment and keep making drastic cock-ups. Shame about Guernica, though. *Someone* seems to be terribly off target if they want to hit the bridge.'

'Louis, go fetch your camera.'

'Why on earth should I want to become a war photographer, Vida *chérie*?'

'Might make your reputation one day in the absence of other talents, not to mention fortune, my sweet.'

'What? Selling pictures of Spanish fighter-planes rather than skimpy bathing-costumes or delectable nudes?'

'Mother of God!' said Gérard a little while later as the whole coastline between San Sebastian and Cape Machicaco gradually blackened as though that part of the world had its own eclipse. The sight of all those bombers and fighter-planes made Captain Gérard want to take the *Al-gandura* even further out into the *Mar Cantábrico*. 'I think the only bargains anyone is going to be able to pick up in the market square tomorrow will be some matchsticks – that and a lot of dead bodies.' He shook his head regretfully.

'Those aren't rubbishy Spanish planes, they're German! Here Gérard – you look,' David handed back the binoculars.

'Heinkels – and Junkers,' murmured Captain Gérard. 'Hardly precision bombers when the Germans have got Stukas.'

Louis did run to fetch his camera then: 'Isn't it exciting, darlings!'

'What's happening?' Roxana came indolently to the stern rail, a glass of champagne in her hand. 'Why is everyone gazing so intently at all that smoke?'

'Roxana *chérie*,' big blond Axël breathed in her ear, 'they are dropping bombs on Guernica.'

'Go on! Is that what they are? I thought they were having a grand firework display for Easter!' Then she asked seriously, 'Why Guernica?'

'Precisely, Roxy.' Axël patted her bottom. 'Unless, of course, Hitler has become tired of waiting for his coal-mines and has decided to bomb the Basque countries as an act of reprisal.'

'What are you talking about, Axël?'

'Hitler's *Unternehmen Feuerzauber* – Operation Magic Fire. Franco, it appears, has promised Herr Hitler Asturian coal-mines in return for military aid. All those Heinkel One-Elevens you see up there are German aid in exchange for Spanish coal-mines. The Fascists want the Basque Separatists and Reds out of it, you see.'

'How do you know all this?'

'My father is attached to the French Embassy in Berlin and has many contacts in the Nazi Ausland-Organization – Germany's Foreign Affairs Department.'

'What a bore! I hate politics like I hate men with consciences.'

'I am half-German myself. I went to school in Berlin. My mother is a German baroness …'

'*Aix*-cel darling,' Roxana said flippantly, 'I'm really not interested in your pedigree.'

'Then what other part of me are you interested in, Roxana, my sweet?' he asked with a sleek smile as he fingered her cleavage revealed by her skimpy bathing-costume.

She coiled a long, bare leg around his warm, thick thigh and draped her arms around his neck. 'You made me promises last night you couldn't keep, *Aix*-cel, you naughty boy.' She put a finger on his lips.

'You were squiffy, darling, and couldn't tell a totem pole from a damp squib …' He nipped her finger with strong teeth. 'Still can't by the look of you,' he added, while his hand surreptitiously pumped her hot little bosom.

'I'm never squiffy, *Aix*-cel! Only choosy,' said Roxana uncoiling herself from him. She did not care for his Superman braggings that were only hot air, nor his politics. 'Seems like I made a bad mistake last night – damp squibs being the operative word. Darling boy, you have *such* a lot of growing up to do!' She brushed the soft golden down of his cheek with a languid hand. 'You really ought to get back to Herr Hitler's Nasty Youth Movement. I believe they just *love* golden boys like you. Vida has a theory about you, especially your fella-felon-fellatio conjugations. She said that you were probably not breast-fed by your German mother.'

'Bitch!' he murmured, still smiling.

'Was she, darling? I would never have guessed.' Roxana smoothed his golden shoulder. 'I just love *real* red corpuscle men with muscle!' She sighed as she ran her hand up and down his arm. 'What a pity you're still only a boy.'

'I forgive you, Roxy darling, since you're such a wonderfully amusing hogbitch yourself. And I know you don't mean it. Are you going to give us another naked little performance of the dance of the seven sins like last night? Highly original, I must say. Old Gérard nearly popped his cork – didn't you Gerry!' He slapped Captain Gérard on the back. Intent upon the bombing-raid over the Mundaca valley, Gérard almost lost his binoculars in the water.

Roxana turned away, 'Go play tiddlywinks with Lucy and Clarissa, Aix-cell-ent, my darling. You'll be safe with them as they're your age – mentally. Vida, can't you get the music and the party going again?'

'Darling Roxy, of course! How about a little Cole Porter?'

'Bliss! Better than listening to a Geman air-raid, or Axël de la Mooch!'

Vida put on, *'I've Got You Under My Skin'*.

Roxana grabbed Pippa out of the deck-chair where she was sipping lemonade. She began twirling Pippa round the deck so hard and so fast, Pippa got hiccoughs. Vida joined in the fun.

Annuala frowned disapprovingly. Vida pulled her out of the deck-chair. 'I order you to dance with me, Señorita Stuffy Nanny!' she laughed crazily, and twirled the embarrassed Andalusian girl around remorselessly. 'Come on, we've got something to celebrate! Had I not chosen this morning but this afternoon to buy my lace, we might all now be *dead* under an oak tree. Huh, Roxy?'

The next moment a salvo of shots across the bows of the *Al-gandura* put an end to the party atmosphere.

'*Merde*!' Captain Gérard scrabbled for his revolver while a naval gunboat bore relentlessly down on them. 'Shit!' he swore again. 'It's flying the Basque flag. It might not have been so bad had we met the Republicans.'

'Better still had they been Nationalists, eh, Gérard? And what good is a revolver, *chéri*, when they have machine-guns?'

'I knew we should have headed straight for Corunna

without messing about in Biarritz, and sightseeing along the way. Your father is just going to *love* his precious yacht being shot up in the crossfire between Reds, Whites, and Basques.'

'Calm down, Gérard,' Vida said coolly. 'Keep out of their way, that's all.'

'I am trying my best, Vida, but we're in Spanish territorial waters, and not in the non-intervention patrol area.'

'Why aren't we?

'For a whole host of good reasons why we oughtn't to be here at all! I'm trying to avoid naval warships, mines, Reds and Basques, all at the same time. *Merde*!'

'Don't say it too often, Gérard, it might bring you good luck!'

'*You* wanted to go sightseeing this morning with a war on, remember? We ought to have gone straight to Corunna. Not mess around in ports where there's a war going on. So that's why *chérie*!' he said in heated exasperation. 'I was stupid to listen to you, my lovely.'

'You *are* temperamental, Gérard!'

The young radio officer, Gaston, interrupted, 'They want us to go to Bilbao, sir.'

'Why?' Vida snapped.

'For questioning, Vida.'

'Tell them we're neutral French. Can't they see our flag? They can't detain us. *I'll* tell them so, if you don't.'

'According to the Basques we're in their war zone. They want to know our business.' Alain, using sense, cautioned her, 'Unless we do as they say, they'll blow us out of the water.' Alain was First Officer, and Captain Gérard's deputy.

'And I think they mean it, Vida, *chérie*.' Captain Gérard breathed down the barrel of his revolver. Methodically he placed bullets, one by determined one, into the multi-chambered cylinder of the gun he had not used since the Anglo-American reprobation with French participation way back in 1919.

Vida became edgy. 'Gérard, tell them we're not going to Bilbao. You're forgetting Roxana and Pippa.'

Captain Gérard said through his teeth, 'I'm trying to

preserve your father's several-million-franc yacht and a dozen French lives.'

A Basque coastguard vessel drew up alongside, and the Basque gunboat proceeded on its way towards Guernica, anti-aircraft guns finding the range of the German bombers overhead. The Germans had been concentrating on Guernica, otherwise Captain Gérard feared that the *Al-gandura* might have been bombed out of the water from both sides. As it was, they were still in the danger zone, and he made haste to get out of the way by obeying coastguard orders to sail down the Nervion River to Bilbao.

Vida said to him, 'Can't we pretend we're heading for Bilbao, Gérard, then give the coastguard the slip? We can get out of their six mile zone or whatever, and into international waters where they can't touch us.'

'It's too risky, Vida. The coastguard boat is bristling with guns and I dare say there are shore batteries trained on us as well.'

'But we can soon outstrip them, you know how fast the yacht is.'

'I don't know,' he said dubiously, while stroking his chin. 'They can still inflict an awful lot of damage on us. The yacht might be fast, but she's also flimsy. A few bursts from the coastguard's guns and we'll keel over or blow up. And don't forget the mines we might run into. We'd be better off putting ourselves in their hands.'

'You're a damn coward, Gérard! Roxy's life's in danger!'

'I thought you told me she was Irish, with a British passport.'

'Do you honestly think the Basques will give a damn when they find out she's married to an enemy soldier? Just *look* up there, Gérard!' Vida flung out an arm towards their view of the coastline. 'See what the Nationalists are doing to Guernica with their bombs and fighter-planes and then tell me Roxy isn't in danger of being imprisoned as a Nationalist *wife*! José is on Franco's staff, and you can bet your sweet life that the Basques will hang on to Roxy as a hostage after what is happening here today.'

Captain Gérard had to see the wisdom of Vida's argument. 'All right,' he muttered ungraciously, his expression clearly implying that he had enough to worry about without having to think about Roxana de Luchar and her politics. 'Just get her out of sight – and the other Fascist woman too, the nanny.'

'Supposing they want to search the yacht, *mon Capitain*?'

'Then we will entertain the Basques right royally, Vida!' he snapped irritably, feeling that his ulcer was about to flare up again. 'We'll give them as much champagne as they can drink and you can bare all for them, just like last night when you and Roxy entertained everyone so wonderfully well! They'll be so happy, they'll forget about searching anything except you.'

'I hope you're right, Gérard! Because I'll have your balls if Papa doesn't, for getting us into this mess in the first place. You should have taken us straight to Corunna as I ordered, and kept well away from the Basque coast.'

Captain Gérard knew better than to argue the point with her. He only hoped the Basque authorities in Bilbao wouldn't give him as much trouble as had the boss's daughter.

Sister Justina and Sister Barbara kept close to the walls of buildings. They had just finished their tour of nursing duty at the Roman Catholic Hospital of San Berenguer, and were returning to the Camillus Convent of Jesu María in the Puerta del Angel. It was seven-thirty in the morning.

Sister Barbara, a Spanish nun who had shared Raven's Reception Day, and had entered the novitiate at the same time as she, said in a whisper. 'Even though the streets of Barcelona are pitch-black when we leave for duty, I still prefer walking out at night rather than in the day.'

'I agree. At least we don't have the loudspeakers blaring away at night. Nor are we able to see all these red and black flags and the awful posters.'

Posters were stuck everywhere – *Industry for Peace: No industry for War!* The colourful picture depicted an orange cannon in front of grey industrial chimneys blasting smoke into the atmosphere; *What have you done for Victory – Y tu?* bombarded them in the face. Yet another Socialist trade union poster showed a priest with a Nazi swastika on a ribbon around his neck sowing a field with wooden crosses, the slogan, *How the Church has sown its religion in Spain*. The snake of Fascism was being chopped to pieces by loyal Anarchists next to the poster of the priest sowing death. Someone in return, had scrawled in red capitals underneath that particular poster, *Reds Crucify Nuns*.

Sister Barbara crossed herself whenever they drew abreast of the unknown person's chalky scrawl over the bullet-scars in the wall, a reminder of the fierce fighting on the streets of Barcelona last July when the dead lay in droves throughout the city. Raven hated passing that particular piece of wall, and averted her eyes, keeping them upon the ground with good custody of the senses. She had come to refer to this part of their walk through the city as the 'Screech of Propaganda'.

Relying on the red crosses on their armbands and aprons to speak up for them, Raven felt that they were less likely to be apprehended, engaged as they were in hospital and welfare work around the city, than nuns without that sort of immunity hiding behind their solid convent walls, for even an Anarchist might one day require a nurse to save his life.

'They say that thirty-seven churches have already been destroyed in Barcelona.'

'Is that so, Sister Barbara?'

'I hope that tonight won't be as dreadful as the one we've just spent.' Sister Barbara was always a little nervous and talkative when walking back to the convent in broad daylight.

Raven agreed. Last night had indeed been awful. They had been working at the San Berenguer Hospital since December, shortly after the convent at Toril had been burned to the ground. Each case that came into the San Berenguer these days had its own horror story to tell. A priest had been admitted to the men's ward. The regular lay-nurses of the hospital were assigned to male wards, while she and Sister Barbara nursed the women and children. But last night, Matron Gonzales had sent for both of them to try to pacify the becrazed priest. They had been unable to get near him or to reason with him and had spent half the night dodging tins of talcum powder, spirit, jugs of cold water, and anything else he could find to throw at them, the sight of two nuns seeming to drive him into a worse frenzy.

The priest's case history was tragic. He had been tortured by some extremists and was found half-dead in the road suffering from severe shock. He had been brought to the hospital and soon after his admission, had gone into renal failure, which had exacerbated his mental condition. He had almost wrecked the male ward. In the end he had taken out a pistol he had managed to get hold of somehow, hidden away under his soutane, and had started firing at random. Two orderlies and the ward sister had been severely wounded, and then the priest had shot himself in the stomach. He had died slowly and painfully of his injuries four hours later.

Now, after such a terrible night, all Raven wanted to do was to get prayers over and done with so that she could snatch a few hours sleep before further convent devotions and duties claimed her weary body.

But as soon as she entered the convent, Reverend Dame Infanta, the Reverend Mother of the Jesu María, sent for her. Raven was always perturbed when having to face Reverend Dame Infanta, who was forever scolding her for one thing or another. The last time it had been over a rose! She had picked a perfect pink, sweet-scented rose from the garden to give to Dame Annunciata whose face and body had been so badly scarred by the Toril fire, that the shock and the pain of it all had made her lose her eyesight. Raven had taken Dame Annunciata's blindness as a blessing in the same way as Cassy's death had been a blessing, for now Dame Annunciata would be unable to see the extent of her gross disfigurement even while she fingered her scars and rambled in her mind. But when Reverend Dame Infanta had found out, she had taken the rose away from Dame Annunciata's bedside-table, where it had been perfuming the air of the nuns' convalescent bay. She had then imposed a severe penance upon Raven for having indulged her senses as well as blind Dame Annunciata's.

Raven was still not quite able to grasp the reasoning behind such thought – how the beauty of creation perfected in a flower had to be ignored as though it didn't exist, and in the deprivation of the senses, one took a step nearer to God: it didn't make sense to her.

Raven was astonished to see Dame Concepción in Reverend Dame Infanta's office. She hadn't seen Dame Concepción for several weeks as she had been rehoused in another part of the city. Dame Concepción had been working with Red Cross and Quaker organizations for the relief of orphan children and refugees from Málaga, which had finally fallen to the Nationalists two months ago.

Reverend Dame Infanta came straight to the point. 'Tonight, Sister Justina, you will not be reporting for duty at the San Berenguer Hospital. I will send another nursing nun in your place. I have already telephoned Matron Gonzales to inform her that you will be unavailable for the next few nights. Rather than give anyone new and inexperienced the assignment, since you are both so well acquainted with the routine, the Bishop has asked that you and Dame Concepción should collect more Bibles from Montserrat.'

Raven took a deep breath. 'I thought Bible-smuggling had been halted, Reverend Mother, in view of the fact that there are hardly any churches and convents left in Barcelona and the surrounding towns.'

'You have a habit, Sister Justina, of always questioning those in authority. I have received instructions from Dame Superior Olivera, who has, by the way, been promoted. She is no more just the Reverend Mother of a specific convent, but is now *Dame Superior* under the auspices of the Bishop of Vilafranca and Toril. From now on, Dame Superior Olivera will be responsible for the whole administration of the Franciscian Camillus nuns in this area. She has asked me to convey this order, which comes from the Bishop, who himself receives his orders from the Vatican. We have been told that it is more than ever vital that God's Holy Word reaches the people, for there is soon to be a religious revival throughout Spain.'

'How …' Raven swallowed, but pushed on with her next question despite the rule of obedience, 'how are we to set about it, this time?'

'Explain to Sister Justina, the plan, Dame Conceptión,' Reverend Dame Infanta intoned frostily.

Dame Conceptión beamed, took off her gold-framed spectacles and polished them vigorously before replacing them. 'We will be joining a Red Cross convoy leaving Barcelona docks this evening, Sister Justina. The plan is in readiness, it just needs us to put it into operation.'

The April evening was warm and smooth, like brushed velvet, the sort of long spring evening that in peacetime would have drawn out the noisy, gaudy crowds onto the streets: the sort of evening, too, Raven nostalgically reflected, she had loved to sit outside Cabo Alondra and watch the moon light a silver candle to the sea, while Peedee recited gems of Spanish verse, given added zest by a bottle of *vino tinto*. But that, she reminded herself sternly, was in another time, another life. She must forget the past in the same way that Dame Annunciata was not to be reminded of the sweet scent of God's roses.

'What did Reverend Dame Infanta mean by an upsurge of religious zeal throughout Spain?' Raven asked Dame Conceptión. 'Persecution of nuns and priests is as bad as ever.'

'If the Nationalists win, then of course there will be an upsurge of religious zeal once again throughout this Catholic land. It cheers my heart to hear that Nationalist soldiers, before a battle, have to attend Mass by orders of General Franco.'

'Propaganda, Dame Conceptión.'

'The Roman Catholic Church of Spain will never die! The Nationalists *must* win, since Franco is on our side.'

'You have forgiven him then for what he did to the Asturian miners?'

'Yes, I *must* forgive him – and so must the Basque people. Forgiveness is what salvation is all about if religious tolerance is to become the new order of things. The Anarchists and Communists have decided that it is no good burning us out of house and home and suppressing the Church, because that sort of thing doesn't reflect them in a very good light with the rest of the world. Especially now that the Internatioinal Brigades have come to help them whip the Fascists. I agree with Reverend Mother, we *are* about to witness a new era where a nun or priest can walk safely down the street without fear, whether it be a Fascist or a Communist street.'

They had arrived at the docks and Raven saw the long convoy of grey-green trucks, each with the symbol of the Red Cross painted boldly on sides and roof. The trucks were being loaded with Geneva-organized parcels and medical supplies that had just arrived by ship from Marseilles. Dame Concepción brought the Bishop's Citroën, flying a *Cruz Roja* pennant, to a halt a little distance from the convoy. In the shadow of the Moorish arches fronting the quayside they waited for the right moment to tag themselves to the tail of the last truck.

Raven was intrigued. 'How did you manage to get hold of all those Red Cross parcels in the back if they are only just being unloaded?'

'Monks and nuns have been busy all week in Vilafranca, according to Dame Superior Olivera. They have been copying the parcels identically.'

'So the Red Cross know nothing about our part in all this?'

'Good heavens, no! If the eye doesn't see, the heart will not grieve.'

'Aren't we endangering the lives of Red Cross personnel should we be caught smuggling Bibles instead of genuine food parcels and bandages?'

'The parcels are all genuine, spiritual food as important as physical nourishment, and don't worry about not wearing Red Cross uniform, either. There are so many nuns and priests helping. The Spanish Red Cross in Barcelona, they are an accepted part of the team. Only the other day I and three other nuns were asked by one of the Red Cross officers in the Calle Lauria, to take Red Cross parcels to Las Cortes Women's Prison.'

'But if the wrong people find out what we're doing, they're going to close down the Red Cross in Barcelona, and that would be an awful shame, don't you think?'

'Blind obedience, Sister Justina.'

'Even when it puts innocent and valuable lives in danger?'

'If you would rather be relieved of this mission because you are afraid of the consequences, then I will relieve you of it now. You may return to your duties at the San Berenguer. I will explain to Dame Superior Olivera the situation.' Dame Concepción pinned her attention outside the windscreen, to the Red Cross convoy waiting to depart.

'I'm not afraid for myself, Dame Concepción, only for the Red Cross nurses and doctors we are using as a shield for our own ends.'

'Sister Justina, listen to me. The Bishop, Dame Superior Olivera and I have given this matter great consideration, and it is a perfectly safe and straightforward procedure. We will follow at the tail-end of the Red Cross trucks to get us out of the city without suspicion, then we will head for Montserrat while the convoy goes off without us to Lérida.'

'Isn't someone going to get suspicious and check our identity – a Red Cross official or patrol control when we return with identical parcels from Montserrat? Because, all I can assume is, that the monks of Montserrat have their own kind of Red Cross parcels which they will substitute for ours – not milk, sardines, and chocolate, Dame Concepción, but *Bibles*!'

'I've been working for the Spanish Red Cross and so I managed to get all the necessary papers we need, including safe conduct passes, so that we could mingle with Red Cross personnel without arousing suspicion. I also know their routine. Every time we return to the city with our Bibles concealed in the Red Cross parcels – below the dried milk, chocolates, and the sardines, or whatever else the parcels are packed with – we will use the same checkpoint. The official will then get used to seeing us working on behalf of the Red Cross and after a while will just wave us through the barriers. Food parcels are arriving all the time in Barcelona to distribute among prisoners and other needy persons. The symbol we are both wearing in our nursing capacity, the *Cruz Roja*, is the safest identity there is at the moment, so there's nothing to fear, I promise you. If we are stopped and questioned, then we will show them our Red Cross badges and tell them we, as nuns, have been recruited to work together with the Spanish Red Cross as many other religious organizations are doing, especially the Quakers. Any more questions, my child?'

'Yes. Why is the convoy travelling overnight? Red crosses aren't going to show up in the dark, are they?'

Dame Concepción sighed gustily. 'Oh dear! I see what Reverend Dame Infanta meant about the questions. Convoys leave in the dark, and they also leave by daylight. It makes no difference, they go when the going is good. In the dark red crosses might not show up and in daylight it seems to make no difference, either. Those above us in the sky still bomb convoys of lorries whether they display the *Cruz Roja* or not. Now *this* particular convoy we are to follow leaves at the same time every Tuesday and Saturday. It arrives in Lérida at nine or ten o'clock at night, and continues to Zaragoza in the morning. We are following *this* convoy because it falls in nicely with our own Bible-smuggling operations. Now are you satisfied, Sister Justina?'

'Satisfied perhaps, but not happy to use the Red Cross as a shield for our own private ends. Blind obedience cannot be right when it endangers the lives of innocent people.'

'If you are unhappy about this you may return to the Jesu María Convent, Sister Justina. I am happy to do this thing alone. I do not want to be the one responsible for compromising your conscience.' Dame Concepción's fingers on the steering-wheel tapped out an impatient little tattoo.

After careful consideration, Raven made up her mind. 'No, I can't leave you alone. This is far too important and dangerous an assignment. I'll just have to relearn the first rule of blind obedience by accepting the orders of my superiors. But I would still have preferred our donkey-cart and peasant women disguise to this kind of deception.'

Dame Concepción smiled happily. She did not really want to undertake this mission by herself or with another nun who had not Sister Justina's Bible-smuggling experience. She had become very fond of Sister Justina, and would have missed her company. 'We must obey our superiors, Sister Justina, as we must spiritually nourish

494

those hungry and thirsty Christians who rely on us to bring them God's Holy Word. And because we serve the Lord, He will not let us down. He will be our shield and our armour in this fight of good against evil.'

'Then let us *charge* into battle, Dame Conceptión! I see the Red Cross are moving off at long last,' Raven concluded on a wry note.

Captain Gérard of the *Al-gandura*, Alain, First Officer, Gaston, Radio Officer, plus Vida and her party of six French holidaymakers were detained for questioning by the Basque authorities at Bilbao.

Submitted to intense interrogation for twenty-four hours, their papers and passports examined and re-examined, what had begun as a carefree holiday jaunt turned out to be anything but. The Basque authorities would not believe they were not spies, especially when it was established that the hostess of the party was married to a prominent Catalonian Communist. Basque Separatists were not fully in sympathy with the Government of Catalonia, nor its Communists who ran things for the good of Communists in *Cataluña* and not the Basque people.

Meanwhile, Roxana, Pippa, and the Andalusian girl, Annuala, were hiding on the *Al-gandura*, undiscovered by the Basque authorities when they had officially stepped aboard the Comte de Martello's luxury ocean yacht.

Then, quite unexpectedly, the Basque officials, having satisfied themselves that Señora de Martello de Luchar's party were who they purported to be, just innocent French people caught up in a war that was not theirs, released them.

'Señora, you and your party are free to go. Return at once to St Jean de Luz and stay in French waters if you do not want to get into trouble again.'

Vida, who always had difficulty understanding the Basque dialect, even though she spoke fluent Spanish, understood the word 'freedom'. '*Muchas gracias, señor.*'

Apart from the smartly dressed trio of the crew in their white sailor ducks and gold-braiding, the young people were all wearing an odd assortment of clothes – but expensive clothes, for one could tell quality! The Basque official who had returned their passports watched the French holidaymaking socialites with a curious detachment while thinking to himself that it would be nice to be *so* rich nothing mattered in the world, not even a war: holiday shorts, bathing-costumes, safari shirts, one young woman wearing a scanty nightdress, another in an equally revealing evening dress, and a couple of men in fancy dress, it appeared anything was fashionable as long as it was worn by the right people.

Personal documents returned to them, ten people rushed for the door at once. After having been detained in the hot and smelly domains of the port authorities for a night and a day, Vida and her friends wanted only to taste the sweet, fresh air again. But they had not gone ten yards in jubilant procession when they saw Roxana, Pippa, and Annuala being dragged along the quay from the direction of the *Al-gandura*'s moorings.

'*Oh, merde!*' Captain Gérard said in horror. The very fact that Roxana, her daughter, and the nanny were discovered hiding aboard the *Al-gandura*, would *look* guilty! were his anguished thoughts in that moment. None of which was going to do any of them any good now. 'I told you, Vida! We should have braved it out. They couldn't have touched us, or Roxy, who would have had the British authorities on her side. Now we're all undone. The Basques will never believe another word of ours.'

'Why don't you *shut up*, Gerry!'

The four Basque Port Control officers who had, for the second time, searched the yacht so thoroughly, were armed.

Once more Vida and the others found themselves surrounded by hostile Basque officials in no mood this time for French lies and interference after what the Germans and Franco's Nationalists had done to the little Basque town of Guernica twenty-four hours ago. Instead of being detained in the port buildings overlooking the murky polluted water of the Nervion, they were all, including little Pippa, bundled into police vans which took them straight to Bilbao gaol.

In the van Pippa buried her face against Annuala's

breast and cried noisily, her tattered doll in one hand, the other arm clinging around her nanny's neck. Vida noticed Roxana's sundress was torn. She had hastily donned it over her bathing-costume when they had been arrested by the coastguard. Roxana's face was bruised and streaked with dirt. 'What happened, Roxy? How did they discover you?'

'Simple really.' Roxana's tone was resigned. 'They found a book of love poems under my pillow in our cabin. I'd forgotten all about it. Vittorio Broué – the man I told you about – had written a little dedication to me in the flyleaf, *To Roxa, much love and thanks for the good times, Vittorio, Tetuan 1934*. So they assumed this gift must be from a legionnaire – and you know what kind of reputation the legionnaires have around here after Oviedo and Gijon. The Basques then went into a frenzy looking for this mysterious Fascist "Roxa" from Tetuan not in the French party being questioned. Annuala and I could hear them all the time on the other side of the panelling while they tore the whole boat apart. Once the galley had been smashed to smithereens, they found us in the false hold behind the salon your father had made for his smuggled goods. It was not a nice experience to suddenly find oneself face to face with a lot of evil-smelling Basques wielding axes.'

Vida, ever the cheerful opitimist said, 'All is not yet lost, darling. We must get a message to my father and your grandfather. My father will be able to work for our release by making the Basques an offer they can't refuse. Your grandfather can get the British to intercede. After all, even if you are married to a Spanish Fascist, you still have a British passport.'

'For what it's worth,' Roxana replied with gloomy foreboding.

'Cheer up, darling! The Nationalists will soon take Vizcaya. Just think, San Sebastian surrendered to Franco's side without any trouble, afraid he'd otherwise blow her lovely casino apart. Papa was terrified lest his beautiful summer villa at Mont Urgull would also go sky high along with the casino. But all is well. After what we saw happening to Guernica, the Basque Government will surrender to Franco, and then you'll be saved. *No problema*.'

'And where will that leave you, Vida? You're on the

497

opposite side to me, remember?'

'We'll never be on opposite sides, darling. We're the love and light brigade, so how can we possibly be on opposite sides? You needn't worry about me. I can take care of myself. Papa's name and money see to that. I've never had so much fun in all my life.'

In prison, Vida, Roxana, Annuala, and Pippa were kept isolated from the other women. Periods of intense questioning were interspersed with days of intense starvation. Pippa started to vomit whenever any food did come their way. Then, ten days later, Vida was told she was being released.

Through the Spanish Red Cross in Bilbao, a message had found its way via Captain Gérard to the Comte de Martello in Paris. Gérard had notified the Comte about the detention of the *Al-gandura* and her party, including Vida herself. Through further negotiations, the Basque Government were offered five million French francs for the release of the Comte's daughter and the French people aboard his yacht.

Vida, when eventually told about the transaction, told the Basques where they could put her father's money.

'Very well, señora, in that case stay in prison with your Fascist friends. The French people in your party are free to go.'

Prison meant a variety of places, at one point a filthy hold on one of the prison-ships in the harbour, occupied by forty other people. Then, Roxana, Vida, Annuala, and Pippa were removed to another prison-ship, the *Menor*, moored at the mouth of the estuary. Shoved into a tiny hold no larger than a kitchen pantry, the prison-ship was in danger of being blown out of the water by Nationalist warships now blockading Bilbao harbour.

'Don't worry, darling,' Roxana said, smoothing Pippa's tangled hair, 'we'll be out of here soon. They're only trying to scare us and break our spirit.'

'When will Papa and General Franco come?'

'Soon, Pippa.' She didn't tell Pippa that it was Daddy's side bombarding them at this very moment.

Pippa sucked and blew down the cigarette holder her mother had given her to play with. An ear-splitting whistle from it made Annuala clamp her hands over her ears. Pippa giggled and did it again. 'Why won't they put a light on? I don't like the dark.'

'It's better than having one of those horrid bright lights shining in our eyes all night, darling.'

'Rats like the dark. I felt one sniffing my hair last night. It was nice and friendly. Like a big pussycat. I was going to stroke it but it bit my finger and ran away.'

Annuala burst into tears.

'Vida,' Roxana asked in a small voice, 'why did you choose to stay with us when the Basques were willing to release you?'

'All my life, Roxy, Papa has bought me for money.'

'Is that so very wrong if he loves you?'

'He only loves the power his immense wealth brings him. I'm the appendage to his otherwise carefree existence, the reminder that life sometimes has its obligations. He feels he owes me something for having sired me in the first place. Now that I have become a nuisance to his less salubrious activities, he thinks he'll buy me, and everyone else off. Like he always does.'

'But he loves you, Vida. He loves you very much. Can't you accept that?'

'Not as much as I love you and Pippa. You are the sister, the mother, the friend and the family I've never really had. So I would rather be here with you than in St Jean de Luz, Paris, Antibes, or Barcelona without you.'

Three days later they were taken off the prison-ship *Menor*, which miraculously had survived the bombardment of Bilbao harbour. For the next month they were held in Bilbao prison. But at least the four of them were still together, and her child hadn't been taken from her. For that concession, Roxana was thankful. As long as Pippa was with them, she knew the Basques would not do anything really outrageous. They were just trying to break her spirit, that's all.

Then, one night, they were again moved to another place.

'Where are they taking us now?' Annuala whispered, hardly recognizable as the smart young nanny Roxana had engaged to look after Pippa. None of them was

499

recognizable any more, or indeed even human. Every day had become just one more day to chalk up on a prison wall, one more day to tell yourself that this was an impossible nightmare and you would wake up soon; one more day to tell yourself that tomorrow the Nationalists would arrive and you would be free; one more day to tell yourself it wasn't really the Basques who were to blame for all this, that it was all a big mistake; one more day to tell yourself that your name and number wouldn't be called out at six o'clock tomorrow morning, and soon after to hear those shots in the prison yard, and know there were bodies lying out there, dead, and tomorrow it could be you. One more day to tell yourself that tomorrow you'd be able to wash your hair and get rid of the lice – tomorrow!

'Does it really matter, Annuala?' Roxana said listlessly.

Pippa had fallen asleep in Vida's arms. Driven in a police van to the Church of St Zavier, Roxana, Vida, Annuala, and Pippa were shepherded together along with other Nationalist prisoners, all women with their children, down into the vast tomb-like crypt of the church.

Then Pippa was taken away from Roxana.

'Bring her back!' Roxana shrieked, tearing at the man who had picked Pippa up. Basque men with rifles stood behind him, their guns poised menacingly.

'Don't do anything foolish, Roxy, they'll shoot you!' Vida said, grabbing hold of the hem of Roxana's tattered sundress. 'They won't hurt Pippa, they daren't! The Spanish love children.'

'Basques aren't Spanish!' Roxana said savagely. Her split and dirty fingernails found their mark, gouging the face of the man abducting Pippa, drawing blood. 'Let her go, or you will be *shot* when General Franco gets here!'

The man dodged head and shoulders from side to side in an attempt to avoid Roxana's heated slaps and painful scratches. 'Basques don't hurt children as Fascists do, señora, by dropping bombs on them. The child will be better off where she's going.'

The awful truth began to dawn on Roxana. 'Oh God, Vida, they're going to shoot us for what happened at Guernica ...'

'Don't be silly!' Then Vida herself began to understand.

'Let her go, Roxy. *Let her go with him!*' She dragged Roxana away from Pippa.

Roxana, afraid, terribly afraid, and too drained to protest any longer, fell back beside Annuala and Vida. Other children of suspected Fascists and Franco insurgents were also being taken out of the crypt. For almost an hour the scenes were chilling as distraught mothers clung to their children.

When the last child had been forcibly removed from its mother's arms, a group of militiawomen with sub-machine-guns entered the crypt.

A man's voice full of sombre undertones echoed through the pillared cavern of the great church like the voice of God, 'Women of Euskadi, remember Asturias, remember Guernica. Do what you will to the women of those who have deprived you of *your* loved ones.'

'Oh my God ...!' Roxana took hold of Vida's hand. Annuala, on her knees, thrust her face against Roxana's stomach, wrapping her arms around her waist. Roxana held Annuala's head against her with one hand, the other clinging to Vida. She closed her eyes.

One by one the women around them began to fall on their knees. Weeping, crossing themselves, or simply silent, they offered up their prayers to a partisan God Roxana was unable to approach, '*Hail Mary, full of grace, the Lord is with thee, Blessed art thou amongst women ...*'

Then the Church of St Zavier echoed to the confused screams and clatter of sub-machine-guns like a score of pneumatic road-drills boring through the ancient stones of Bilbao.

The silence settled at last, punctuated here and there by a soft sob, until, eventually, even the sobs were extinguished and only the silence, vast and absolute, remained.

CHAPTER FOURTEEN

Barcelona: May 1937

From all over the world Red Cross ambulances, tents, medical supplies, and food, continued to arrive in Barcelona, the relief operation co-ordinated from Geneva. Regular Red Cross convoys left Barcelona docks for the various battle-areas throughout Spain – Guadalajara, the Basque countries, Aragon, and Madrid, the capital still holding out desperately against Nationalist rebel forces.

San Sebastian and Irún had surrendered to the Nationalists at the outbreak of the war. Now that the rest of the Basque countries were capitulating to Franco's side, it was far easier than at any other time for Bibles to be brought from the north coast to the administrative centre of Montserrat for redistribution throughout Catalonia.

The symbol of the Red Cross held in esteem by all parties on both sides of the fighting lines, the Bishops's Citroën flying the *Cruz Roja* pennant on its bonnet was always waved through the same checkpoint in and out of the city. No one asked any questions and no one, after the first couple of sorties distributing Red Cross parcels in the area, bothered to examine the parcels filling the back of a car flying the official Red Cross symbol. If the two nuns in their strange winged head-dresses were engaged in open acts of humanitarian kindness throughout the city, rather than in secretive ones behind their convent walls, the Communists, Anarchists and Trade Unionists were quite happy to see the nuns come and go freely in the line of duty.

Fifty kilometres from Barcelona, the Citroën left the Red Cross convoy making its way to Lérida where it would halt overnight before resuming the next stage of the journey to Zaragoza. Raven, who had become a commendable driver under Dame Conceptión's tuition, turned sharply off the main Barcelona-Lérida road, leaving behind the official convoy, to take the tortuous mountain road to Montserrat. 'We're being followed,' Raven, said, glancing into the driving-mirror.

'Nonsense!' said Dame Concepción, turning in the passenger seat to look out. 'There's nothing behind us, only long evening shadows. Tricks of the imagination, Sister Justina, that's all.'

Raven said no more, but concentrated on driving to the summit of the strangely pinnacled mountain.

At the monastery, one set of Red Cross parcels was exchanged for another, the switch taking place smoothly and efficiently by the monks helping to load the Citroën with the most economical use of space.

The pure, clear voices of choristers from the Escolania, one of the ancient music schools of Europe, sang the '*Virolai*', the 'Hymn of Montserrat', the mountain that the Catalonians believed had been riven into pieces at the time of the crucifixion. Echoes of those lovely voices rang across the deep valley on this Saturday evening.

The Abbot of Montserrat, personally supervising the 'Bible' operation, came forward when the two nuns were leaving. They were not of his Benedictine order, but they were still his Franciscan sisters helping to distribute God's Holy Word throughout Catalonia like so many Benedictines, Cistercians, Franciscans, Augustinians, Carmelites, and Dominicans: but one of these nuns, he remembered suddenly, had a brother who was a Benedictine monk in Ireland. And so the Abbot bestowed his blessing and his personal benediction upon them. 'Thank you Sisters. Another thousand souls have been saved today through your wonderful efforts.' He made the sign of the cross over them, before returning to his private apartments with his little band of personal helpers.

'Five thousand souls, Sister Justina!' said Dame Concepción happily, 'not bad for five nights' work. My turn to drive, I think.' Dame Concepción climbed into the driver's seat.

It had grown dark by now, the long May twilight displaced by a starry night as Dame Concepción pulled out of the courtyard fronting the Abbot's apartments. The two Benedictine monks in their black robes holding the impressive wrought-iron gates open, immediately clanged them shut again, padlocking them as soon as the Citroën had disappeared from view.

One and a half kilometers to the bottom of the mountain as they descended into the Llobregat valley, at the junction, a Renault was drawn up across the road.

A man smoking a cigarette leaned against the radiator grille of the car.

'I told you someone was following us!' Raven whispered anxiously.

'Don't worry, he seems to be alone. One man can't do us much harm.'

'I wouldn't be too sure. The car is probably full of secret police keeping their heads low.'

As they drew nearer, Raven thought there was something remarkably familiar about the tall, broad figure standing in front of his car in such an unconcerned attitude while he smoked a cigarette. She immediately dismissed her fantasies as just another trick of the imagination.

The man moved his position. Raven saw the white pennant with a red cross on the bonnet of his car. Undoubtedly an official Red Cross car: far more official than the Bishop's Citroën. Her worst fears were confirmed, 'I knew we'd gone too far this time! Someone was bound to catch up with us sooner or later.'

Dame Concepción remained unruffled. 'Don't panic, Sister Justina.'

Raven ducked low, her hands in her lap, while relying on Dame Concepción in her supreme equanimity, to get them out of *this* fix.

Dame Concepción braked, turned off the engine, and got out of the Citroën, slamming the driver's door so that Dr Junod's delegate wouldn't pry too closely into the car. 'Dr Devlin! What a surprise,' she said in English. She had encountered Dr Devlin on several occasions during Red Cross work with refugee children and prisoners, he being the man who had asked her to help out by taking Red Cross parcels to Las Cortes Women's Prison.

'Likewise, Dame Concepción,' he said levelly.

'Have you broken down, Doctor?'

'No, Dame Concepción. I was waiting for you.'

'Me?'

'I wanted to put you on the right road. The convoy went *that-a-way*!' he indicated the direction. 'To Huesca and Zaragoza, via *Lérida*, Dame Concepción, *not* Montserrat.'

Raven wished she knew what Dame Concepción was saying to the Red Cross official, especially when he pointed with his cigarette in the direction the convoy had taken two hours ago. Standing as he was in shadow some distance from the Bishop's car, she was unable to see his face, only the red glow of his cigarette.

Keir continued tantalizing Dame Concepción. 'I'm going to Lérida myself. How about following me so as not to get yourself lost again, uh, Dame Concepción?'

'Er – thank you, Dr Devlin. But doing such a foolish thing like losing oneself up a mountain road in the dark has rather eaten up the petrol ration I fear. The Citroën only has enough to get us back to Barcelona.'

'Then let me relieve you of all those parcels on your back seat. I've room enough in the Renault. We don't want some poor soldier at the front to be deprived of his knitted socks and chocolate, do we Dame Concepción?'

'Indeed not, Doctor.' Dame Concepción felt well and truly trapped. She searched her mind desperately for a plausible excuse to get her and Sister Justina out of such an awkward situation.

'Is something the matter, Dame Concepción?'

'Um, yes …' She put a hand to her forehead where the tight band of her winged head-dress cut her thoughts in two. Why had she to meet *him*, of all people, on this lonely moutain road? she asked herself. 'I feel a little faint – I must sit down, Doctor.'

'Oh, forgive me! Is there anything I can do?' He took a step towards her but she waved him away.

'Oh, no, no no! I shall be perfectly all right if I sit down.'

'How thoughtless of me to keep you lingering by the roadside when you're feeling so unwell. Go and sit in your car. The nun with you, I'm sure, will help me transfer the parcels into my car. You just take it easy, Dame Conceptión.'

'Thank you, Dr Devlin. I'll tell Sister Justina to lend you a hand.'

His head jerked up and he gave her a strange look. 'Sister Justina? Did you say *Sister Justina?*'

'Yes, Doctor. She's my co-driver. Let me call her ...'

'No, it's all right.'

Dame Conceptión thought that Dr Devlin's voice had lost its familiar, bantering tone of a moment ago and had become nervous and jerky. She wondered at his sudden change.

'On second thoughts, Dame Conceptión, if you're not feeling well, you'd best get back to your nunnery as soon as possible. Goodnight.'

'But the Bi ... the Red Cross parcels, Dr Devlin?' She was gambling with the Devil and knew it. For a moment, riveted as she was to that mountain road, Dame Conceptión waited for God's answer to her prayers.

'Take them to the Calle Lauria, Dame Conceptión. They can be distributed some other time.' Keir flung his cigarette into the roadway.

Raven, from the front seat of the Citroën, saw the faint shower of sparks like bright pink stars when the Red Cross officer's cigarette hit the ground. She saw him stamp on the cigarette-butt before getting into his car and quickly driving off along the Lérida road. With an enormous sigh of relief she asked Dame Conceptión, 'What was all that about?'

'God working on our behalf, Sister Justina!' Dame Conceptión replied triumphantly. 'Dr Devlin changed his mind about taking our Red Cross parcels to Lérida with him. I've no idea what made him change tack so abruptly. It's as though I said something to upset him.' She suddenly became aware of the look on Sister Justina's face, as though she, too, had just bitten into heartbreak pie. 'What's the matter, dear child? You look as though you've seen a ghost.'

Raven said, 'Dr Devlin? *Keiren Hunter* Devlin?'

'Well, his intials on his Red Cross *mochila*, are K.H.D., so

506

I assume it must be Keiren Hunter, if you say so. I only know him as Dr Devlin. We've bumped into each other on one or two occasions during the course of my work with prisoners and refugee children. Do you know him?'

'Yes,' said Raven in a small voice.

'Then why didn't you say so? I'm not Reverend Dame Infanta about to upbraid you for past personal friendships ...'

'I didn't know who he was – just now – it was too dark to see properly. Besides, I didn't know he was in Barcelona – or that he smoked. He never did in Geneva. I'm not doing this again, Dame Concepción.'

'Then that is between you and our Council of Superiors. It is up to them, Sister Justina, whether or not to relieve you of this holy mission, and whether or not you are to suffer the consequences of disobedience to an order that comes directly from Rome. But whatever happens, at least we have managed to deliver five thousand more Bibles to the lost souls of Barcelona.'

Raven said nothing. Her thoughts concerned Monseigneur Paulus at the Vatican, a staunch supporter of powerful Cardinal Pacelli, Secretary to Pope Pius XI. Raven hoped she would be forgiven her uncharitable thoughts concerning Monseigneur Paulus. He, no doubt, was earning blessings and heavenly promotion from God and the Pope's Secretary for having organized this Christian mission in the first place, while *she* risked imprisonment at the hands of Communists and other anti-religious organizations; while Sonny and other monks risked death should their boat ever sink in heavy seas when bringing those Bibles printed in Ireland to San Sebastian, or alternatively, imprisonment were he to be caught by those not favourable towards the Roman Catholic Church; while Dame Concepción, too, ran the risks that came to all small people caught in the net of those more grand and more powerful.

Raven struggled with herself and her self-imposed penances. She went about her nursing duties protected by that special immunity furnished by the universal symbol of humanity, the Red Cross. Because it was not the Red Cross of Geneva, but of the San Berenguer Hospital, her heart stayed riddled with the bullet-holes of bad conscience.

*

One morning, Raven and Sister Barbara were hurrying back to the Jesu María Convent after night duty at the San Berenguer Hospital. It was still early, seven o'clock, and bright spring sunshine warmed the uneven paving stones of the city streets. Fingers of sunlight crept into doorways and touched the peeling paintwork of window-shutters. A bent and bow-legged woman dressed in black dusted a doormat on the front wall of her house. A cat, tail poker-straight in the air and disdainful of humanity, minced across the plaza in pursuit of its own business.

A grand funeral procession had set off from one of the buildings. The mourners, trailing silently in the wake of the handsome ebony and brass coffin borne on the shoulders of six sturdy Spaniards, solemnly crossed the square. The person who had died was obviously well-to-do and important, for in most instances, city funerals these days were hurried, shabby affairs over pine coffins.

Then, all at once, shots rang out from the roof of one of the buildings close by. An answering salvo spluttered from the windows of another building. Flashes of rifle-fire like dashes of sunlight burst from all around. A number of flower-pots hanging from iron balconies went crashing to the pavement below as bullets smashed into them. Bright trailing geraniums like wounded lizards lay bleeding on the streets. Coffin-bearers dumped their burden in the middle of the vast plaza and, with the rest of the mourners, scrambled for cover. The cat fled, and the old woman grabbed up her doormat and disappeared behind her solid front-door.

'They have started again!' Sister Barbara sighed in rueful acceptance of the situation as they scurried into a shop doorway where they were soon joined by other people getting out of the line of fire. Exasperated, but resigned to the delay, they saw that the coffin had become isolated in the middle of the square. Bullets struck the brass fittings, whining and 'zipping' as they ricocheted. Slivers of black wood jumped into the air like astonished stick-insects. Expensive flower wreaths lay abandoned and bedraggled, torn to shreds in the crossfire.

'What's going on? Has Franco's rebel army got here already?' a housewife wanted to know. She had been determined to be at the head of the bread queue this morning, and had taken her stance outside the baker's shop before anyone else. Now she had lost her place. The baker, having only just raised his shop-front, had slammed his steel shutters down again the moment he heard the gunfire. The housewife doubted the bakery would open again that day, and she had no rations left to feed five hungry children.

'Since yesterday afternoon Anarchists and Trotskyists are fighting the Guardia Civil for the Telephone Exchange, and now the fighting is spreading all over the city between the various trade unions,' a man explained for the benefit of the little crowd gathered in the baker's doorway.

'Fighting the Guardia Civil?'

'I heard it on Radio Valencia last night. The Guardia Civil have been sent in by the Government to get the Anarchist unions out of the Telephone Exchange.'

'Why?'

The man shrugged. 'Trade unionists have been accused by the Government of not doing their job properly. The Anarchists are only putting through and receiving telephone calls which suit them. Such tactics are causing widespread disruption in the communication system. Now the Communists are trying to get the Anarchists out of all the key positions in the city.'

He said no more. One had to watch one's tongue carefully these days, for there were informers and Fifth Columnists everywhere. He himself could see that this was just what the Government of Valencia wanted, to take complete possession of Barcelona and thus bring the self-governing region of Catalonia once more under the firm thumb of Central Government.

Sister Barbara nudged Raven. 'Shall we risk it? The shooting seems to have stopped for the moment.'

Raven, dropping on her feet, was anxious to get back to the convent. She still had two hours of devotions to do before she could possibly take to her bed. Her hopes of getting three or four hours' sleep before the rest of her convent duties was a fast-diminishing dream should the shooting continue.

'We'll have to stay close to the buildings and not venture across any open spaces, Sister Barbara.'

As soon as they emerged from the shop doorway, a sporadic burst of gunfire greeted them, and though the shots went wide, they hastily dodged back into the safety of the doorway.

Two hours elapsed before they could venture out into the street again. Raven spent those two hours with her eyes closed, asleep where she stood with her back pressed up against a drainpipe. A weary nun, she discovered, will even sleep standing up.

Working-class men were laying seige to the various buildings around the square, while others had started building barricades at the street corners. Ordinary citizens began helping with the barricades, hastily digging up the paving-stones and transporting them in prams and wheelbarrows to the workers.

In the Plaza de Cataluña the Revolutionary Communists had their Party Headquarters, and from the surrounding buildings, fighting was fierce.

At nine o'clock that night, Raven set off from the Jesu María Convent with Sister Barbara for their routine night duty commencing at ten, at the San Berenguer Hospital. They avoided the Plaza de Cataluña altogether and took an alternative route from the Jesu María Convent in the Puerta del Angel, along the Ronda Universidad. This would bring them into the Via Layetana, and to the San Berenguer Hospital. The barricades had been completed, and were now head-high. Reinforced with sandbags, mattresses, tables, and anything else solid, men were still taking pot-shots at one another from behind their defences.

Barcelona had always seemed far-removed from the actual war taking place in and around an area referred to as 'the front line'. Bedraggled columns of militia returning from the front to spend their leave in Barcelona, talked about trenches or mountain dugouts, about the intense cold, the mud, the rats, the lack of everything – weapons, food, blankets, boots, clothing, cigarettes. Now, without warning, it appeared that the front line had shifted to Barcelona itself. To Raven nothing seemed to make sense any more. A huge battle was still going on for Madrid, for the Basque lands, for Catalonia itself, and here were militiamen fighting among themselves in Barcelona, centre-point of Republican loyalties.

In the ensuing days the fighting intensified and frightened pedestrians kept off the streets, while working-class men of the same inclination sniped at each other from the roofs of buildings, from doorways, from alleyways, and from behind their barricades. Hand-bombs were rolled down the Rambla as though the Civil Guard and anti-Stalinist Communists were engaged in a game of French boules, while the food shortage increased dramatically because all the shops stayed shut. Radio Valencia blasting over the loudspeakers in the Rambila stated that the Communists running the Government had decided to put an end to Anarchist control in strategic public services in the city and that was why squads of Civil Guardsmen had been ordered to take the Barcelona Telephone Exchange out of the controlling hands of the Confederacion Nacional de Trabajo.

After three days the fighting abruptly stopped. Shopkeepers pushed up their steel shutters and normal trade was resumed. As soon as the militants had replenished their bread and wine stocks, and with their pangs of hunger temporarily assuaged, down came the shop shutters again and everyone went back to fighting each other.

On the fifth evening of this fierce conflict, Raven and Sister Barbara were following their diverted route to the hospital when the electric tram was brought to an abrupt stop in the Via Leyetana by a bunch of youths firing indiscriminately from an office building. People fled screaming from the tram, while several passengers and the tram-driver were left injured inside.

'We must go and help,' said Raven, hurrying across the road to where a crowd had gathered around the stationary tram-car. The firing appeared to have ended as suddenly as it had started. Raven could see two bodies lying slumped against the shattered windows. Blood-spattered shards of glass glittered in the road.

'Out of the way, I'm a doctor.' Keir had been on his way back to the Calle Lauria. He never travelled these days without his doctor's bag, and retrieved it now from the Renault flying the Red Cross pennant. He pushed his way through the knot of shocked and hysterical passengers, while the tram-driver remained slumped in his seat. The dazed conductor sat on the platform of the tram, muttering. 'I was only doing my duty, I was only doing my duty, I was only …'

It was by now dark in the Via Layetana, street lighting dim in case of air-raids, and the tram-lights were also out. In the beam of a torch someone held for him, Keir examined the injured passengers, but knew immediately two of them were dead. One was a fragile, white-haired old woman. Her meagre bread ration had been trampled bloodily into the centre aisle during the mad stampede by the rest of the passengers to get out of the tram-car before it was over-turned. The other was a handsome dark-haired little boy, no more than five, whose mother screamed dementedly while she held her dead child close to her. The tram-driver had been hit in the arm and shoulder, but would live.

Keir put a tourniquet on the driver, who was bleeding heavily, then placed the old lady full-length down on the seat and covered her face with his handkerchief. He left the Spanish woman alone for the time being, and let her nurse her son: *Jodi, Jodi, Jodi*, always there was Jodi in the back of his mind.

He turned around when two nuns boarded the tram car.

By torchlight Keir looked into the face he had searched for so often in the Barcelona crowds, yet had dreaded finding. It was a face he found even more beautiful, mysterious, and moving as he gazed at that cameo of Raven Quennell held in the framework of her nun's white head-dress.

He looked away again, haunted and taunted by her and what she had done with her life. A hollow emptiness was all he could feel in that moment of seeing her again. He released the rubber tourniquet on the tram-driver's arm.

Raven told herself to keep calm, that this was what was meant by custody of the senses. 'Is there anything we can do, Dr Devlin?'

'Yes, Sister Justina. Try explaining to that Spanish mother her boy is dead. Then if you wouldn't mind accompanying her to the hospital, I'd be grateful. She'll have to be treated for shock.'

'We're on our way to the San Berenguer.'

'Then you've got yourselves a free ride in an ambulance,' he said in a flat, detached tone.

A few days later the Republican Government of Valencia despatched the élitest unit of the Assault Guards to put an end to the fighting between the warring factions of the trade unions. The city resumed some semblance of normality, the Assault Guards doing their job well in keeping the peace, and control of the capital.

Raven saw Peedee, still in possession of his bicycle, standing in one of the long bread queues. While oranges were in abundance, bread was as precious as gold. 'Dear girl! I was hoping you'd pass this way today – come on, follow me. I've got something to tell you.'

'But won't you lose your place in the queue, Peedee?'

'I'll have to make do with goat's cheese without bread – I was only standing there in the hope of seeing you. I've got some miserable news …'

'Sonny? Something's happened …'

'Sonny is fine,' Peedee quickly reassured her. 'Keep walking … Good morning Sister Barbara. I trust you're keeping well?' He peered round Raven to the nun on the other side of her.

She nodded cheerfully. They walked together down the broad palm-lined avenue of the Rambla, Peedee, looking just like an habitué of La Barceloneta in his fisherman's jersey and gumboots, pushed his bicycle through the crowds out in their numbers (even at this early hour) after the recent street battles. Raven thought she saw Salas Rivales's pretty daughter, Amparo, on the arm of a good-looking, off-duty Assault Guard as they both went into a café for breakfast. Only the dug-up cobblestones and the pock-marked tree-trunks bore evidence of the recent street fighting, while the loudspeakers were fully operational and blared martial music across the bay.

If it was not Sonny then it must be Uncles Salas or one other of the Rivales family with whom Peedee was lodging. Uncle Salas Rivales still ran the textile factory, now making utilitarian army uniforms on behalf of the Republic. He was also responsible for the wineries in Vilafranca and Vinarosa during Don Ruiz's absence and, to this end, he had Ramiro's full backing. Salas's son, Tomas, had joined the newly formed Popular Front Army while Amparo's flirtation with the Valencian soldier, apparent just now, seemed a little disconcerting. 'Has Salas Rivales been arrested?'

'The Rivales family are doing quite well for themselves out of this war, dear girl. Didn't you notice that wanton hussy, Amparo? Salas has promised to back Ramiro up to the last inch of cloth and cask of wine. You know that Ramiro has ascended even further up the scale of the Communist hierarchy, and has turned the Castillo de Luchar into a kind of hammer and sickle club?'

'What do you mean?'

'Dear girl, it isn't important. What *is* important is that Roxana is a prisoner of the Basques.'

Raven tucked her hands into her wide sleeves so that Peedee wouldn't notice her sudden agitation. 'How do you know all this?'

'In the same way that I know that four hundred Chato fighters, three hundred Moscas and one hundred Katiuska bombers, not to mention a few more Rasantes and Natashas came off the deck of a Russian battle-cruiser in Barcelona Harbour a few days ago. I keep my ears and peepers skinned. I talk to people, especially Russian generals, as well as Communist delegates and Red Cross personnel, and anybody else able to furnish me with *answers!*'

Raven had, for a long time, suspected Peedee of being a Fifth Columnist working behind the lines, and now she was certain. 'Is this how you know about Roxana? Through the Red Cross?' Raven put into effect her own strategy.

'Not in this instance. Apparently, Roxana and some young friends of hers did a very foolish thing. They strayed, or rather, the pleasure-boat they were aboard strayed into Spanish waters, well within the limit of the Basque war zone. Everyone is disputing Spain's claim to neutral waters, including Great Britain. The Spanish Government has claimed for itself, instead of the customary three, six miles of marine territory. Vida and her friends impinged Spanish restrictions and suffered the results. They were arrested and imprisoned in Bilbao.'

'Was Pippa with her?'

'Pippa and the nanny.'

'Now tell me how you know all this.'

'Through a *very* reliable source, I assure you – Ramiro.'

'Ramiro?'

'Ramiro's wife was with Roxana when they were all captured by the Basques.'

'Vida de Martello?'

'Vida de Luchar.'

'Very well, Peedee, but why should Ramiro put himself out for us?'

'He wants his wife back. She's rich, while her father supplies him with weapons via Andorra – the tax exile's haven where the Comte de Martello happens to have a convenient mountain retreat – and *don't* ask me how I know all this, please, because I do not wish you to know. Ramiro certainly did not mention his private and secret armaments deal with his father-in-law. However, getting back to the crux of the matter, Ramiro *did* inform me that the Count has put up five million French francs to secure Vida's release. But the silly woman turned her nose up at being ransomed, and chose to remain in prison with Roxana.'

'Why would Vida want to risk her life for Roxana?'

Peedee shrugged. 'From what I'd gathered by your schoolgirl letters to me over the years, Vida always was a strange young woman with the oddest sense of values. But I must say, I admire her pluck and loyalty where Roxana is concerned. However, the Comte de Martello then increased his offer to ten million, which now includes Roxana, Pippa and the nanny. But the Basques aren't playing anyone's game except their own. As far as they're concerned, Roxana is married to a Nationalist soldier and so she stays in their hands as a political prisoner and hostage. I'm afraid that the deliberate air-bombardment by the Germans upon the small undefended Basque town of Guernica, which the papers have reported in all its horror, has not helped Roxana's case one bit.'

'What can we do, Peedee?'

'Nothing much for the moment, dear girl. I have registered her case with the Red Cross. I hope that Dr Junod, or one of his delegates, can at least get Pippa and the nanny released. If I hear anything more, I'll let you know at once. I'll be in Señor Fabian's bread queue between six and seven o'clock every morning, so that when you come off duty we'll be able to meet for a few minutes to sort out our family problems.'

'Peedee, did Ramiro mention anything about – about Roxana's treatment? I mean, the Basques wouldn't ill-treat Roxa, or Pippa, just because of José's involvement in the Asturian campaign, would they?'

'That, I cannot answer. This war has brought out the oddest quirks in human character, and so we must just hope for the sake of Roxana and her child that the Basques will treat them well.'

Raven, under the trees, watched Peedee wheel his bicycle down towards the harbour. After what Yagüe's Army of Africa did to the populace of Asturias when they took Gijon and Oviedo, and after hearing about Guernica, she did not think her sister was in a very good bargaining position at all.

Sister Barbara, who had tried to shut her mind and her ears from the conversation between Sister Justina and her grandfather by walking a little apart from them, had still been aware of the substance of their low-voiced conversation. And she sympathized greatly in the family's hour of need. 'This is truly a tragic war.' Sister Barbara crossed herself. 'I'll forfeit my sleep today, to pray to the Virgin and her child for the safety of your sister and *her* child, Sister Justina.'

'Thank you, Sister Barbara. I'll spend the hours of vigil with you.'

Raven faced the people who controlled her life. They were gathered in the tiny office of Reverend Dame Infanta of the Jesu María Convent. The extraordinary Council had been

516

convened because Raven had asked for holy guidance in the matter of Bible-smuggling.

The Bishop of Vilafranca and Toril was an elderly and kindly man who turned a blind eye when it came to the rough treatment of his official car by the nuns in his diocese. Half-asleep in the padded chair kept only for his use, his heavy-lidded eyes focused blearily and somewhat ruminatively on the young novice who stood in compliant attitude before Reverend Mother's desk. In her white habit and veil, her well-shaped feet and legs confined in black shoes and stockings, Sister Justina reminded him of a slender lily arrayed more wonderfully than Solomon in all his glory; she reminded him that the virginity of a bride of Christ was the loveliest flower of all in Rome's varied bouquet. He sighed in contentment: an asset to God and the Church. Indeed, they had chosen her well – if only she would speak up a little. The Bishop placed his hand behind his ear. 'My child, speak louder, I cannot hear you!'

'Your Reverence. I'm unable to continue deceiving the Red Cross Organization.'

'Deceiving, deceiving? What is the child talking about, does anyone know?'

Dame Superior Olivera, who had accompanied him from his residence in Vilafranca, said gently. 'Your Reverence, Sister Justina feels we are using the Red Cross to our own ends.'

'Well, we are, aren't we?'

'Indeed, Your Reverence, but what Sister Justina is trying to say is that she no longer wishes to continue using the Red Cross as a shield to our Bible-smuggling activities.'

'But Rome has ordered it.'

'Yes, I know they have ordered us to get the Bibles to the people, Your Reverence, but no mention was made of the Red Cross – that is what is at issue here. I myself feel, as Sister Justina does, that it is not fair on the Red Cross doctors and nurses, who have served us very well on five occasions now, to use them any longer.'

'Very well then, let Dame Concepción and Sister Justina go back to their donkey-trap and fruit and vegetables.'

Raven heaved a sigh of relief.

Reverend Dame Infanta of the Jesu María frowned.

'Not nearly as many Bibles can be brought from Montserrat in a donkey-cart as in the Citroën, Your Reverence.'

Plump little Novice Mother, her soft melodious voice like a bubbling brook, said breathlessly, 'But they can do the journeys more often. They won't have to rely each time on a Red Cross convoy leaving the docks in Barcelona. Instead of, perhaps, two journeys every week, they can carry vegetables and fruit *every day* of the week!'

God bless Madre Estelle Calmar, were Raven's thoughts, even while Madre Estelle had no conception of how far it was to Montserrat on foot!

'It is settled then,' said the Bishop, anxious to get back to his ecclesiastical residence for lunch. Diocesan affairs, which consumed so much of his time, he found tedious. 'I shall be glad to have my car back, Sister Justina. Public transport is dismally unreliable these days, not to mention downright dangerous.'

'Yes, Your Reverence.' She took a deep breath and plunged straight in with both feet, 'Your Reverence, there is just one other thing I should like to say.'

'You have permission to speak, my child.'

'Every Friday I confess to Father Avda, my confessor since Father Gabriel's death, my transgressions regarding this Red Cross business. In his forgiveness he tells me that I'm keeping Christianity alive in Spain during this dark age of her history. However, I would also like to confess my part in using the Red Cross to provide the cover for our Bible-smuggling activities to the people I've deceived, the Red Cross themselves. Only in that way can I truly be at peace with myself.'

Reverend Dame Infanta of Jesu María looked at her aghast. The Bishop looked as though he had not understood one word, Madre Estelle Calmar seemed astonished, and only Dame Superior Olivera looked in any way sympathetic.

'Sister Justina,' said Reverend Dame Infanta, 'why stir up a hornet's nest when there's no need?'

'It will relieve my conscience, Reverend Mother.'

'So you must unburden your conscience to the detriment of the whole Franciscan Order, of which we, as

518

Camillus Dames of Charity, are only a small and insignificant part?'

'I unburden my conscience each week upon Father Avda, Reverend Mother. The man I can speak to at the Calle Lauria would never denounce us.'

'How do you know he might not?'

'He's an American Catholic doctor I knew in Switzerland before I decided to take Holy Orders. He's also of the highest moral conscience and would keep faith with us.'

'You are certain of this?' asked the Bishop.

'I'm positive, Your Reverence.'

'In that case, my child, far be it from us to poke into the dictates of your private conscience. You have my blessing Sister Justina. Confess your sins and *tell the truth* if it brings you solace. Perhaps it was wrong to use the Red Cross, but the error was not intentional, merely expedient at the time. Now we will seek another route to bring the Bibles to the people. If it transpires we are all to suffer on account of it, then it is God's will. But at least I know your heart is in the right place. Sister Justina, now tell me before I must go rushing back to Vilafranca, when will you be taking your final vows?'

Reverend Dame Infanta interrupted swiftly, 'Your Reverence, I don't think that the time or the climate of things is quite right for Sister Justina to proceed with her final vows. She's not yet ready to become fully professed despite her religious zeal, for she doubts the codes of the Canonical Laws far too much. She hasn't yet learned to accept God's Holy Will without question.'

The Bishop turned to Madre Estelle Calmar for her opinion.

Madre Estelle Calmar, with a sadly apologetic look at Raven said, 'Your Reverence, I'm inclined to agree with Reverend Dame Infanta. Sister Justina is not yet ready to take her final vows. She must be wholly certain that what she is doing is the right thing for her – and sometimes I feel she is not sure herself.'

Only Dame Superior Olivera came to Raven's defence. Her distinctive Portugese accent even when speaking Spanish was more pronounced than ever because she was trying to emphasize an important point. 'I beg to disagree, Your Reverence. Sister Justina questions more than any other novitiate simply because she is interested enough in what she is doing to want to know the answers. Blind obedience is what we are taught, but blind obedience can also mean that we are labouring in the dark. Knowledge is essential, especially to one who must have all the answers at her fingertips if she is ever to become a Dame Superior herself – one who is completely sure of herself when she is called upon in the future to counsel her own nuns.'

The Bishop beamed, and stood up. His stomach was rumbling horribly. 'We will leave Sister Justina's final vows in abeyance for another year.' He blessed them and, fingertips still in the air, scurried towards the outer door.

He and Dame Superior Olivera returned to Vilafranca in the Citroën, Madre Estelle Calmar went back to the Novice House and Reverend Dame Infanta asked Raven to remain behind in her office. 'Sister Justina, if you are to unburden your conscience by confessing your sins to this Catholic American Red Cross doctor, then you must include Dame Conceptión in this confession, which I can only see as a betrayal of all we have been striving to do here. You are putting at risk the lives of a great many nuns should this American Catholic doctor give us away to the Communist authorities.'

'I promise you, Reverend Mother, he would never do that. Neither would I want to go behind Dame Conceptión's back when she, too, is involved in such a moral issue. Ask her yourself. She knows Dr Devlin of the International Red Cross with whom she has worked. She will agree with me. But it will make us both far happier to wipe the slate clean and start again without any guilt. To ask for his forgiveness as a representative of his organization is the least we can do.'

'But if he does not know about it, what does it matter?'

'He knows. I'm sure of it. He stopped us one night on the way from Montserrat, but then let us go free again. I think that was because he really knew what we were doing and was hoping we might own up to it.'

'Hmmm ... very well. I'm not happy about it, but I've been overruled in the matter. I just hope that you are right, Sister Justina. I rather feel, however, that sometimes our Dame Superior, being Portuguese, rushes in where even angels fear to tread.'

Raven knew that there was no love lost between the Spanish Mother and the Portuguese Mother. Reverend Dame Infanta had coveted Dame Superior Olivera's elevated position, and would not forgive her easily for having 'pipped her to the post'!

Calle Lauria 95 was like a madhouse.

The refugee problem was the worst. Málaga had surrendered to the Nationalist insurgents in February, aided by the Italians who, angry at encountering no militiamen to fight because the militia had deserted the town, had used their air force to strafe innocent civilians. Hundreds had died on the road from Málaga, hundreds more were still pouring into Barcelona three months later. The battle of Jarama, swift on the heels of the fall of Málaga, added to the refugee problem.

Against an incessant background noise of clicking typewriters sounding like a forest full of cicadas, the ominous presence of the Civil Guard with bayonets, wandering through the premises to keep the peace between Nationalist wives in search of their husbands, sons, fathers and brothers, and Republican wives in search of their husbands, sons, fathers and brothers, Keir was at his wits' end. He had thought Abyssinia was a chaotic shambles, and now he faced another shambles. He looked back with nostalgia on the peaceful days he and Father Silvestre had spent together fishing on Lake Atitlán, dodging the chickens and goats and donkeys in the abused Fageol truck as they rumbled through Guatemala City, his first taste of Mexican food in Chitre's Restaurant at Puerto Barrios, cock-fighting in the shadow of giant cacti, the scent of *aguardiente* ...

"'If I should die think only this of me,'" he found himself reciting to himself one morning as he recalled a soldier's fevered mutterings at the Aragon Front. An English poet of the Great War would never have gained his attention had it not been for the wounded Englishman

521

in the International Brigade spouting war poetry in a field hospital at Alcubierre: "'That there's some corner of a foreign field that is for ever' ... Guatemala ...'"

'Guatemala, Doctor?'

Keir, unaware that he'd been muttering out loud while rifling through a card index in search of a name, looked up at two nuns wearing the distinctive winged head-dresses of the Camillus Order of the Dames of the Blessed Charity. Both the nuns he recognized with pleasure. Behind them the endless queue of suppliants stretched out into the Calle Lauria itself.

'Rupert Brooke, Sister Justina. Substitute England for Guatemala since I misquoted, and there you have my exact sentiments. And isn't it strange that the only three countries recognizing Franco's State of Chaos happen to be Germany, Italy, and Guatemala? I bet you didn't know that. Now, what can I do for you two reverend ladies other than furnish you with the timetables of Red Cross convoys leaving Barcelona docks?'

'I must talk to you ...' Raven glanced over her shoulder at the pressing queue behind her, '... in private, please, Dr Devlin.'

'Not possible. We are up to our ears in war work. You know the kind of thing, rescuing refugees, prisoners, soldiers – Red Cross parcels.'

'That's what I want to talk to you about. Dame Superior Olivera has given me permission.'

'*Dame* Superior, well I never!'

He rocked back in his office chair, two legs of which were dangerously inclined to slip on the floor lest he watch out, thought Raven. In that very chaotic moment as he regarded her with wry humour she wanted to snap a question. What's so funny, Dr Devlin? 'And the Bishop,' was all she added with abject humility, her eyes downcast upon her shoelaces.

'And the Bishop!' He sucked in his lower lip, and turned his attention to her companion, 'Dame Conceptión, is this to be your confession, too?'

'Good morning, Dr Devlin. Indeed it is. But I'll let Sister Justina do the talking since you know each other from the days of Sister Justina's past life.'

'Very poetically put, Dame Conceptión! So, you're both going to confess to me?' He seemed to be deriving some sort of gross pleasure from all this, as well as great satisfaction.

'Please don't mock us, Doctor, this isn't easy.' Raven tried to attach as much *sang froid* to her remark as she could muster, knowing that everything about this meeting had gone sadly awry.

'It isn't easy for me, either, Sister Justina, believe me. Very well, let's go back there and talk.' He indicated a door behind him. 'It's the kitchen cupboard, but it will have to suffice.' He led the way.

In the cramped kitchen-cum-staff room Keir took up the jug of coffee on the hotplate. An eyebrow quirked in Dame Conceptión's direction, he pointed to the jug held high. 'Coffee? It's only ersatz, but at least it's hot ersatz.'

'No, thank you, Doctor. It's our hour of fasting.'

Raven, too, shook her head.

'Then you won't mind if I do? I'm hooked on caffeine since my intern days – and nights.' He eyed them over the rim of the jug. 'Okay, I'm all ears. Confess away.'

Raven began, 'I don't know how you know I'm Sister Justina, but …'

He interrupted at once. 'I went to Cabo Alondra to look for you. I was going to ask you to accompany me to the cinema, with dinner afterwards. I had hoped, you see, to get to know you better. Nina de Luchar told me you'd become a nun. If she'd told me you'd become a paid assassin, I might have accepted the truth a lot better.'

Dame Conceptión cleared her throat awkwardly and looked away. Not wishing to compromise Dame Conceptión, or herself, Raven said hurriedly, 'Dr Devlin, I came here to tell you that *I'm* Dame Conceptión's accomplice in smuggling Bibles, not Red Cross parcels, between Montserrat and Barcelona.'

'I know.'

'You know? Then why didn't you say something or – or apprehend us that night on the road to Montserrat?'

'I was waiting for you to make the first move.'

'I don't understand.'

'After the second time of being tailed by a gleaming

Citroën, a polished, well-cared for car, a rarity in itself these days, and two nuns who did not appear to be on my list as part of my Red Cross team, I paid closer attention. I know very well what you and Dame Concepción have been up to on behalf of the Roman Catholic Church. I was waiting for you to give yourselves away.'

'You were so certain we'd give ourselves away?'

'Yes.'

'How?'

'Because you are nuns, and presumably honest ones who, while being totally misguided and hopelessly naïve females, are also not without scruples.' He looked sharply at Dame Concepción, but she kept her eyes downcast.

'Now you're deriding us again, Dr Devlin,' Raven said helplessly.

'Damn right I am! Didn't you know what would happen to the Red Cross Society in Barcelona had the Communists or Anarchists found out Bibles were being smuggled under the Red Cross flag instead of food, clothing, and medical supplies?'

'Yes. That's why we're here now, to apologize to you.'

'Apologies not accepted. Why? That's all I want to know.'

'Because we were ordered to by the Church of Rome. Oh, not to use you, of course. The method of collection and distribution of the Bibles was left to we nuns. It was an idea hit upon by our superiors – to – um – to ...'

'Hide behind the *Cruz Roja*?'

'Well no, not exactly – well, yes, I suppose so – something like that. There's a rule we must obey called blind obedience.'

'Why did you become a nun was what I really meant.'

'I've always wanted to be one: since I was very young, very frightened, and totally under my Catholic nurse Cassy's influence in Dublin.'

'Religion, you thought, would buy you immunity from God's further wrath?'

'Something like that.'

In his doctor's white coat, the *Cruz Roja* armband on his sleeve, Keir turned his back on Raven and Dame Concepción and in frustration dashed his coffee-cup into the stone sink. He had been alone with Raven, he could have spoken his mind. Dame Concepción with her full, maiden-aunt aspect behind her golden glasses beaming holy disapproval, hampered his style. Keir took a deep breath, summoning courage to say what had been on his mind for a long time.

He turned back to face her, and to hell with the other nun beside her – and then, suddenly and despairingly, Keir realized he could not say one single word to Raven of what was contained in his heart: how do you take an illusion you've created for yourself and turn it into reality?

What *could* he say to her? What could he possibly say that would change both their lives so irrevocably she would say yes, yes, yes to everything he could ask or could want from her? Sleep with me? Marry me? Let's run away together to Guatemala where we can live in blissful sin for a million years? Let's forget the past and face the future, together? Let's found an empire of our own with kids who don't have to worry about war or vice or disease or death or a million other destructive forces taking possession of their souls; let's forget about holy fanaticism in your life and a million miserable memories in mine? Let's – let's just make a new world for ourselves, let's just do it! What then?

What he desperately wanted to say to her was, I love you, Raven. I want you to know it even while you have chosen to renounce such a thing as wordly love between a man and a woman. I want you to know that there comes a certain point in one's life when a decision has to be made between what is right and what we want – I want you. When I realized who was with Dame Concepción that night on the Montserrat road, I realized that I wanted you more than ever. And what I felt in that moment for you made me afraid to face you, because I was suddenly taken unaware by the strength of my feelings for you.

I think I first fell in love with you during Rachmaninov's concert at the Conservatoire. Love at first sight might be fodder for the romantics and the sceptics, but I know it can happen. With Francesca it was different – it wasn't love at first sight, but lust. I was a fool to think that love grows out of lust. But as we grow older, we live or die by those mistakes of our youth. Francesca was part of my finding myself again after Joss's death.

On my last day in Geneva I couldn't tell you what I felt about you when you and Jan saw me off on the train to Paris, because it wouldn't have been fair to you – my broken marriage, divorce, and all that sort of messy thing being involved. However, I've thought about no one except you since those Geneva days – over six long years. I had hoped, you see, to be able to strike up some kind of relationship through writing to you while I was in Guatemala, but it wasn't to be because someone forgot to post my letters. I suppose, had I really persisted in keeping contact something might have come of it – if only to prevent your becoming a nun. But I've always been very lazy when it came to writing letters. At that time, too, I had no wish to embarrass you, or myself.

When I was asked to come to Spain on behalf of the Red Cross I jumped at it, only because I thought I might meet you again. And I prayed like hell that you wouldn't be married to someone like Jan's Archie. So I went rushing off to Cabo Alondra to look for you and to reassure myself about you. I was devasted to learn that you had become a nun. I just wish that, after all this time, there was a way for us, you and I, my darling. But I know that that is an impossibility because of the way things stand at the moment. So there you have it, my confession to you, for what it's worth …

But he said none of those things; it would have been like turning the thumbscrews on her.

Dame Conceptión, her face grave, *feeling* the chord of unspoken things between these two diverse people, said, 'Dr Devlin, I'm truly sorry for putting you in this awkward position. I apologize. But I always think that everything has a purpose in life. Even the smallest, most insignificant happening is a pointer towards our future life. What will be, will be.'

'Thank you for apologizing, Dame Conceptión – and you, too, Sister Justina. I'm flattered that you should have chosen me, and not Dr Junod or some other person in higher authority, to come to – to, er …' he rubbed the side of his nose, 'to confess your sins. However, let's put it behind us. And don't let it happen again!'

They were being treated like naughty schoolgirls, and

Raven knew it. He must think to himself that she had never outgrown her days in the Parc Mon Repos with Roxana and Vida, and, truly chastized in this unbecoming fashion, she turned to go. 'Everyone will think you are lost, Dr Devlin, so we must let you get back to your duties.'

A frog in his throat, and a smile that hurt, he answered her with equal detachment while fighting to keep his arms from wrapping themselves around her despite the presence of Dame Conceptión and everyone else at Calle Lauria 95. 'I'm just one of a whole nation of displaced persons out there looking for a place to settle, Sister Justina.'

CHAPTER FIFTEEN

Barcelona: June 1937

Against the lesser darkness of the night sky, the mountains resembled black serrated teeth devouring the moon. There had been a thunderstorm earlier, but now the storm had abated, the rain had almost stopped, and only a mizzly vapour cloaked the valley. Scudding clouds looked as though they had finally shredded themselves to pieces on the high pinnacled crags of Montserrat.

Disguised as peasant women in black, with rope sandals on their feet, Raven and Dame Conceptión were soaked to the skin. Struggling with the donkey and its overloaded cart, Raven would dearly have loved to shake off the thick black scarf wrapped around her head and shoulders, letting her short crop blow free in the storm. But she knew that Dame Conceptión would not have approved of her indulging her senses to such a degree: meanwhile saints had to suffer.

Rain-washed earth, pine trees, damp leather and donkey hide reminded her of the smells of Ireland and of Hollyberry House in particular, where the turf of Kildare grew emerald after the rain. Spanish summer rain, though, was not Irish rain, peaty and gentle, without malice and pure enough to sell in tin cans for the tourists. The downpour had been fierce and heavy, causing flooding. It also caused their small leatherbound Bibles to get very wet when they slipped into the deep puddles every time the tail-gate of the cart was jogged open.

The mountain road was pitted and uneven, and loose scree had been washed down by the deluge. Dame Conceptión sighed gustily as she slammed shut the tail-gate for the umpteenth time.

The newly printed Bibles, a dozen in each brown paper parcel over which waterproof sheeting and then straw and manure had been heaped, had been too well-disguised, for now the Benedictine farmyard's liquidized part in all this could be sniffed a mile off. Dame Conceptión wrinkled her nose fastidiously. 'Oh, for the Citroën and the dignified comfort behind the *Cruz Roja* banner, Sister Justina!'

'Suffering is salvation, Dame Conceptión,' Raven reminded her as she walked beside the steadfast little donkey resembling a polished carving with its gleaming wet hide. Raven added to herself for her own salvation, so they keep telling me!

'I don't know which is worse, going uphill with our melons and oranges tumbling out of the cart, or downhill with this smell,' said Dame Conceptión, not grumbling so much as searching for God's hand in all this. 'Dealing in manure for the convent garden is not my idea of fun.'

'One good thing, though, we can rest assured the anti-Bible brigade won't get too close!'

'That's true. Whoever receives these versions of the Latin Vulgate will *definitely* detect a certain odour about them.' Dame Conceptión wiped her wet glasses on her wet skirt. 'Before we do this tedious journey again, Sister Justina,' she put her glasses on, 'I shall ask one of our Franciscan brothers to fix a new tail-gate on this wretched cart.'

'I don't think it needs a complete new tail-gate, merely two new wooden pegs fitted to a couple of longer chains. The pegs are so worn, they don't fit tight any more, so, when they fall out, the tail-board flops open.'

'Not only spiritually blessed, but practical with it!' Dame Conceptión said, marvelling at Sister Justina's many gifts.

Through the Llobreget valley they heard the echo of the monastery bell chiming midnight. This was a pilgrimage that usually took forty-eight hours to complete on foot as the journey, via the mountains, was so steep and hazardous.

At the bottom of the range, Raven said, 'And now that we're on the level again, we'd better walk a little faster if we're to reach Barcelona at all.'

Dame Concepción sighed again. 'Dear little Madre Estelle Calmar who hardly ever steps beyond her four walls, was talking about doing this journey every day of the week!'

'When I apply, very shortly, for another pair of *alpargatos*, perhaps Madre Estelle will realize what kind of pilgrimage we're forced to do,' said Raven as they splashed through the puddles. Her rope sandals had shrunk, and cut painfully into her feet and ankles. As soon as they gained the smooth main road she promised herself she would go barefooted just like the Discalced Franciscan Tertiaries of old, obedient to the rule of bare feet.

They were in the shadow of the strange mountains where even the rising sun could not make its presence felt. Raven and Dame Concepción stopped to rest and refresh themselves at a little roadside shrine.

Hours later they set off once more along the straight road and only stopped for a siesta during the hot afternoon. Under cover of summer darkness they continued on their way. Raven marvelled at Dame Concepción's fortitude when she herself, thirty years younger, was flagging, longing for even a bed of straw upon which to fling her aching body.

The pattern of their journey was repeated the following day. Humble peasant women, with less than fresh market produce stinking in the heat, they prayed at wayside shrines and rested in the olive groves.

Forty-eight hours later, and in the heat of the night, Dame Concepción dragged the stoic little donkey through a side gate in the covent wall, and sighed on a plaintive bleat, 'Oh, for the Citroën!'

Raven was worried. 'Dame Concepción, why is the side gate open?'

'I expect some absent-minded extern forgot to lock it before she went late to prayers.' Dame Concepción, panting from exertion, was only half listening to Raven. The donkey had never played up so stubbornly before with its haunches down. It stuck fast just inside the wrought-iron gate and refused to budge. Normally, it couldn't wait to get to its stable and nosebag. 'What is the matter with the wretched beast?' asked Dame Concepción.

Exhausted, hungry and irritable, she too was dropping on her feet, and had no patience left.

Raven thoughtfully relocked the side gate with the chain and padlock lying on the ground. She helped Dame Concepción get the capricious animal into the stable, Dame Concepción pulling on the leading rein, while she shoved from behind. They unfastened the donkey from the cart and fed him, then swept off the dirty straw in the cart. The covering layer of manure was a hard-baked crust on top of the waterproof sheeting that had been covering the Bibles, for the June sun had been fierce during the day. They stacked the Bibles on the stable floor.

Then, arms full, Raven, her chin pressed on the top package to keep the heavy load steady, followed Dame Concepción across the courtyard to the convent library where they hoped someone would offer to fetch the rest of the consignment left in the donkey stable.

'I don't like this – it's so quiet! Why aren't we hearing *Salve Regina* as we normally do at this hour?' Raven mumbled over the top of her stack of Bibles weighing down her arms.

'Perhaps compline is being held back for us,' said Dame Concepción, and then, with a hoarse cry of fright, dropped her load of Bibles onto the cloister tiles when the shadows moved with frightening intensity.

'Caught red-handed! And the lying bitch in charge of this little lot pretends she doesn't know what we're talking about,' a man's voice cut vengefully through the shadows.

Another made a grab at Raven's black scarf. 'Disguised as peasant women! Come on then, let's see what your head looks like, *nun*!'

Raven tried to keep calm. The third man in the shadows, with the butt of his rifle, knocked the Bibles out of her hand, and she and Dame Concepción were prodded at gunpoint towards the chapel.

Inside, everything had been smashed and overturned and torn to shreds. Vandals were looting the valuable items. Chalices, crucifixes, old and rare statues and paintings, the monstrance of solid gold that received the host on special feast days, handwrought incense burners in filigree silver and gold, gold plate and a host of other precious church artifacts, were being heaped into the centre of the altar cloth embroidered by the hands of devoted nuns a hundred years ago from precious threads of spun silver and gold.

The beautiful carved and painted sandalwood statue of the Virgin Mary and child, normally standing in an alcove in which prayer-candles were lit, had been placed on the bare altar. The Virgin had been beheaded, her head had been put next to her feet. A lighted cigarette protruded from the partly-open smiling mouth of Mary, who had once gazed lovingly upon the infant in her arms. Up against the altar a brutal game was being played.

A group of men and youths armed with guns and knives were taunting the nuns and some Franciscan priests from the monastery next-door. Six priests had been stripped of their grey robes and made to stand against the altar.

Before the naked priests, the nuns were forced to kneel. Deprived of their winged head-dresses, cropped boyish heads revealed, they were being asked to kiss the priests' genitals. If the nun refused, or the priest prevented her, he was mutilated and shot. The rest of the rabble jeering, laughing, and blaspheming, rosaries and crucifixes torn apart and desecrated, a youth urinated on an alabaster statue of Santa Camillus of Lellis, patron saint of nurses, and of the convent.

The low murmur of nuns and priests on their knees, praying despite what was being done to them, filled the chapel in a dreadful dirge.

Dame Concepción fainted. She was left on the ground.

In front of the high altar, Raven saw Reverend Dame Infanta with her face slashed. She was sprawled out on the blue majolica floor, her head-dress and veil ripped off and smeared with blood. A priest, stripped of his robe, sat slumped against the altar, a rope of saliva and blood hanging from his open mouth to his shoulder like a slimy umbilical cord. Knife-marks covered his white body. A black jagged hole through his chest marked the bullet that had killed him.

Sister Jeanne's terrible stories of Tragic Week thirty years before had never prepared her for this. Had he, that poor dead priest, been the first one, the warning of what was to come because Reverend Mother had been unable to do as they had wanted of her? She would kiss him – *she would, she would, she would*! She would kiss them all, only please God don't let anyone else die in this terrible fashion! A man gripped her cropped hair tightly, his lips pulled back over his teeth in an animal snarl as he snapped her head back and forced her to her knees before one of the priests.

Raven closed her eyes, unable to pray, unable to do anything except blindly obey. The scene behind her closed eyes penetrated into her mind, a vision black with blood and hatred.

'You like living off the fat of the land, eh, *nun*?'

Dame Rosemarie, half-conscious, on her knees beside Raven, moaned and shuddered uncontrollably while muttering in a mad voice, 'Hail Mary, Hail Mary, Hail …' Dame Rosemarie shook her head as the man held a knife under her chin. Through ritual rather than an awareness of her actions, she lifted her hands, making the sign of the cross over her body, and her assailant slit the front of her habit.

'God's parasites, eh Vergara? What shall we do with this one?'

'She's not bad looking, and has big tits – we'll keep her for later, after we're done with these traitorous priests.'

A voice in Raven's ear whispered, 'Marry me, nun!'

She shook her head, her lips unable to frame the words.

He snapped her head back a second time so that she thought her spine would crack: 'I can't – I am a bride of Christ – promised to the Church …'

A raucous burst of laughter came from the throats of mocking men. The man breathing heavily in her face traced his tongue around her ear and said thickly, 'But I would *like* to marry you. You are very beautiful – young and luscious – unlike these other fat sows.' He clutched her breasts. 'And you have nice tits, too!' He pushed her head forward against one of the priests. 'Do it then, if you don't want to marry me. Go on, *peasant* girl, show us you really like it despite what your dope of a Pope makes you believe – and this one, and this one – they will all go the same way unless you do as you're told.'

The priest above her raised his hands, blessing her, saying something she couldn't hear as he prayed and forgave. 'Courage, Sister,' he repeated more loudly. Raven began to cry. She knew that the priest was going to die anyway.

'Good! Now this Christ can be shot so that you'll be rid of your holy husband. That makes you nearly free again, doesn't it nun? How many husbands for Christ's sake does one nun have?'

The laughter, the insinuations, the vileness of such men was something alien, loathesome, contemptible to her. Were such men really created in the image of God, as Sister Jeanne had once asked? Raven was at a loss to understand.

'This one is coming out with me. I fancy a virgin tonight. These other baggy cows are all too ugly, fat, and wrinkly.'

'That's good living, comrade! The Church has fed off the backs of suckers since Christ was supposed to have been born.'

Half carried, half dragged out of the chapel by the sturdy Spaniard, Raven heard a shot being fired and knew that the priest who had asked her to keep faith was dead. The Spaniard slammed her up against the inside cloister wall where the shadows were deepest. 'Don't please – don't,' she whispered, too terrified to do anything except beg.

'Shut your mouth, nun! I want to fuck, not talk …'

Dimly she was conscious of more gunshots in the distance, remote from her existence as the man pulled up her skirts, clawed and pushed, panted in her face and kept her pressed hard against the wall. She struggled with him, fighting him every inch of the way. 'Damn you, nun!' He held her face tightly between strong fingers, crushing her jaw and squeezing the air out of her as he forced himself on her.

Then all at once his head jerked back, as though someone held him by the roots of his hair. His grip relaxed and he let her go. In the gloom of the cloister he seemed to stare at her as though suddenly surprised to see her there at all, before slowly sliding down the length of her body with a soft gurgling sound, to lie at her feet.

There was blood on her, and on him. Someone was sobbing, like the low mewing sounds of a tortured kitten, and she knew it must be herself.

The man who had come so stealthily through the cloister faced her. She cowered back, her breath harsh, sobbing, painful to listen to, and accusing, wondering who this new assailant could be. She stared down at her hands, and then up again at him, asking the silent question.

'I would have shot him,' he said, 'but I was afraid the bullet would go through you as well. I'm sorry I had to cut his throat in front of you.'

The voice she recognized. In the silver finger of light suddenly tracing the courtyard as someone held a torch behind him, the man wiped the blade of his knife on the dead man's shirt. With a flash of white teeth as she smiled fiendishly in the darkness, he resheathed the knife.

'*Ramiro?*' Raven whispered.

'*Si*, Raven, it is I.' His eyes were like cats' eyes in the dark, reflecting the light. Her knees giving way, Raven slid down the wall to sit on the cloister tiles next to the dead man. Ramiro crouched down beside her. 'Are you all right?'

She nodded. Numb and weak and still terribly afraid of him, she felt she would never be all right ever again. She could only stare at the person she had hated and feared during their years of growing up together at Vinarosa; and, just as in the past, she wanted Ramiro to go away and leave her alone.

'Some stupid bastard put the lock back on the side gate, and because I had to shoot my way through it, I think they know we're here and will have disappeared like the sewer rats they are. I'm sorry you're involved in all this, Raven.'

'How – how did you know it was me?'

'I didn't. I just saw this POUM bastard doing the obvious and guessed it might be a nun he was trying to rape. Normally, I wouldn't have bothered to stop him, but just lately POUM members have been giving me a headache and so I wanted to get rid of as many as I can. Tonight I have a good excuse. Why are you dressed like that, instead of wearing your habit? Have you wisely decided to renounce the faith?'

Raven was confused, she couldn't think straight. It hurt

to think and breathe. All she wanted to do was remain quietly in the darkness until Jesus Christ himself reassured her that what was happening here tonight was for a specific God-given purpose. Her arms rigid, hands pressed down on the flagstones of the cloister walk, her chin lifted to the dark heavens, she breathed as though they were the last droplets of salvation she would ever inhale. Ramiro gripped her wrists, trying to calm her. 'Conservar la traquilidad, Raven ...'

'Go away – please go away.'

He would not leave her alone. His whispered conversation in the eerie shadows was one of real urgency, and had an unreal quality. At length Raven listened to him, and began to unravel truth from fiction. 'So you and your Communist friends are not the ones responsible for terrorizing us?'

'This time, no. Sorry to disappoint you. We are after these radical revolutionaries who are creating so much havoc everywhere. The POUM Party has recently been outlawed, and is now an illegal organization. Today it has become certain that their leader, Andrés Nin, has been murdered, and so they are taking their vengeance out in the kind of reprisals you see here tonight. But now your ordeal is over. My men, who are hiding everywhere in this garden, since I managed to get the gate open, will end it.'

'But why – why us? Why the Jesu María? Why the Camillus nuns and those poor Franciscan priests?'

'Falangist priests, not Franciscan! You know, Raven, Communists and Anarchists aren't the only ones responsible for killing religion in Spain. Catholics have persecuted non-Catholic communities and deprived the people of a basic education in the schools – deliberate ignorance so that the masses are unable to read for themselves, and have to go to the Catholic priests for enlightenment – their own Roman version! Now they smuggle it to the people. I know you're involved in all this Bible-smuggling business, and, I suspect you are involved in many more underhand activities it would be interesting to find out about, eh, querida?' He forced her head up, the cold light back in his eyes.

'Sister Justina,' she corrected him defiantly.

'No never. I do not believe in that kind of thing. But since you want to know how and why – though I suspect you already know – I will tell you how much *I* know of what nuns and priests get up to behind their cloistered walls. Many of your Fascist priests are Fifth Columnists, secret agents working on behalf of Falange. They have also been trying to undermine my party, PSUC. In a Gerona bookshop we found some of your Catholic Bibles printed in Ireland. Not all the Bibles contained merely the word of God, some also contained the coded word of certain political and military groups, *agents provocateurs* and Fifth Columnists working against us. Your order was going to be closed down because of this – though not in POUM's brutal fashion. You were all going to be disbanded, made illegal like POUM, as soon as we'd established the truth about these Bibles and how they were getting here. Unfortunately, the other party arrived before us because they also felt betrayed by your holy brethren. What was discovered in that Gerona bookshop led to the death of the leader of the POUM party, Andrés Nin. Many more anti-Stalinist communists, Marxists, and Anarchists were tortured and put to death because of this incident. Now do you understand the implications of your Bible-smuggling activities, my innocent little nun?'

'Am I to go to prison like your father and mother and Aunt Leah?'

'My advice, Raven, is to leave Spain and go back to Ireland where you belong. As false as it may sound to you, I retain great affection for you and don't want to see you personally harmed in any way. I would like to have married you instead of Vida, but you and I are worlds apart. I myself would be the first to own that there would have been no happiness in our relationship, because we are two of a kind: strong-minded, self-seeking individuals – oh, don't deny it! You are nothing but an adventuress, *querida*, despite the pious habit. However, I knew you felt more for José than for me, and because he ended up marrying Roxana, you decided to do this crazy thing by giving yourself to a misbegotten Christ instead of a flesh and blood man.'

Ramiro paused, took a deep breath and continued in the face of her accusing and fearful silence. 'I'm not going to mention your name concerning illegal Bible-smuggling, because you will be imprisoned, if not shot if it's proved that Andrés Nin's death, Catholic Bibles, secret messages, and military documents discovered in Gerona are in any way connected. I think the Fransciscan priests guilty of conspiracy have been dealt with tonight by POUM. Now that brings me to your brother Sonny. I know that he and his monks are smuggling Bibles from Ireland via San Sebastian and Irún, which, fortunately for him, are in Nationalist hands. If you don't get him to stop, then I will have your grandfather arrested in his place.'

A spark of life flared from her shattered spirit. Indignation replaced fear. 'Up to now I felt indebted to you for having saved my life. You've just cancelled out that debt. If you ever touch my grandfather I'll personally see to your downfall, Ramiro. I'll go to the British Ambassador. The British aren't sympathetic towards the Communist cause. They'd prefer to see Franco at the head of the Government of Spain rather than Stalin, Dr Negrín, or – or even Ramiro de Luchar!' Raven got to her feet. Horribly dizzy, she clung to the cloister pillar. Ramiro stood up beside her and put out a hand to steady her but she shrugged it off. 'Don't touch me!'

'For someone who is not supposed to take sides, you're getting yourself pretty worked up over all this, eh, Sister Justina?' Then Ramiro added a brittle-edged warning. 'I should keep away from your chapel for the rest of the night. There's bound to be a lot more throat-cutting going on in there.'

Raven, her heart in her mouth, kept to the shadows of the cloister until she reached the infirmary close by the Mother House. She knew that those nuns not at Devotions when the terrorists struck, would be with their sick sisters, praying for the souls of the dead nuns and priests, and for the lives to be spared of those captured.

What she did not know was that Ramiro had followed her at a distance to make quite certain she reached a place of safety around which he afterwards placed his own cordon of security guards.

*

At the Mas Luchar on the Vinarosa estate, Keir faced Doña Maria and Nina de Luchar across the newly scrubbed kitchen table. Isaba stood at the stove, stirring some concoction in a saucepan.

Doña Maria said querulously, 'I hope it isn't beans again, Isaba. Beans give me wind.' She turned to Keir. 'Beans, beans, beans, that's all we ever have to eat these days, and if it isn't beans, it's chick peas. I feel I'm turning into a budgerigar.'

His eyes always watering in the presence of Isaba's cooking, Keir had brought them good news. 'I've found out the prison in which your mother and Aunt Leah are being held, Señorita de Luchar ...'

'Dr Devlin, my name is Nina.' Her eyes lighting up with anticipation, she awaited his news eagerly. After so many months of misery, each day that went by undermining her courage and spirit, despairing of ever seeing her parents and aunt alive again, the Red Cross doctor had awakened fresh hope.

With her walking-stick, Doña Maria tapped imperiously on the heavy wooden table. 'Coffee – proper coffee, for the doctor, Isaba! And don't interrupt him, Nina. Let him get on with what he's come to tell us.'

'Doña Jacqueline and Doña Leah are in Las Cortes Women's Prison.' Keir heard Isaba at the stove suck in her breath and he quickly reassured the women. 'It's all right. I've been to see them, and they are not being ill-treated.'

'You've seen them?' Nina's voice was breathy with excitement. 'When?'

'Yesterday.'

'How are they?'

'Fine.'

'Do you know why they were arrested?'

'They tell me that your mother and aunt have Nationalist sympathies, two of Doña Jacqueline's sons being insurgents. They also broke the law by attending Mass when it's forbidden.'

'So the Communists in the Government won't release them, is that what you've come to tell us Señor Doctor?' demanded Doña Maria who had difficulty with her hearing.

Keir grabbed up the steaming mug of coffee Isaba placed in front of him before Doña Maria could upset it with her stick. It smelled like the real thing, too. 'As a matter of fact, I've been promised their release very shortly ...'

'Oh Señor Doctor!' Nina jumped up and flung her arms around his neck, smothering his face with kisses. 'Señor Doctor, you are wonderful, simply wonderful!'

'Stop that, silly girl, don't embarrass the poor man!' Doña Maria prodded Nina back into place with the brass ferrule of her walking stick. Red-faced by her own exuberance, Nina sat down again shyly, and Keir mopped his tie.

He smiled at Nina. 'Barcelona prisons are overflowing at the moment, and with five thousand enemy mouths to feed the Government are desperate to release or exchange certain categories of prisoners – especially the women. Your mother and Aunt Leah will be free in a few days' time. But they are to remain here under house arrest, their activities to be controlled by the Workers' Committee.'

'The Workers' Committee, pah!' Doña Maria spat contemptuously. 'You know what they wanted me to do the other day, Señor Doctor?'

'No, Doña Maria.'

'They only wanted me to knit socks for the Anarchists! Pouf! I have never knitted in my life and they insult me now, at my age! I told them what they could do with their balls of wool, for I would as soon put a hole in an Anarchist sock with one of their own bombs! They took away my ration cards for a month. It made no difference, I still have sugar and chocolates in a secret cask in the Caverna Rosa.'

Keir was glad to hear it, especially as the delicious coffee he'd just sampled no doubt came from the same stockpile.

'And my father? Have you heard anything about him?' Nina asked.

'Sadly no. I can't get anything on him, yet, but I'm still trying,' Keir reassured her.

'It would kill my mother if my father has been executed without a fair trial.'

Keir stood up, ready to take his leave. He patted Nina's shoulders. 'Your mother is tougher than she looks. As soon as I get a permit for her release from Las Cortes I'll let you know. It shouldn't take more than a few days, so you can start putting the flags out.'

'They only have black ones here,' Doña Maria said with another spitting pah! directed at the floor. 'But then, that is to be expected when there are such black-hearted devils running the country. Ruining it, too. Who would ever have thought friends could become traitors so easily.'

Nina de Luchar saw him to his official car. 'Thank you so much for your help Dr Devlin ...'

'If I'm to call you Nina, then you must call me Keir.'

She smiled and shook his hand. 'I received a letter from Jaime. Señor Peedee brought it to me.'

'Good news, I hope.'

'Yes, he's well. But Jaime doesn't care to go around killing his own Spanish people. He doesn't agree on what politicians say are the *opposite sides* in this war. So he has transferred to the *Requeté* catering corps, where he feeds others and is well fed himself.'

'He'll probably be safer that way. Goodbye Nina. I'll bring your mother and aunt home in a few days, so don't worry.'

'I know you will. *Adios*, Doctor Keir.'

Standing in the avenue of pines, she was sad because he was so nice, and because she had to keep lying to him about certain family matters; but this was a Spanish war in which America had no part. It was a question of the survival of Spanish families – the whole fabric of Spanish life.

Nina waved goodbye to Keir until he turned left for the Barcelona road, and was lost to view.

On his return to the Calle Lauria, Keir found a message from Bilbao on his desk. It was from Dr Marcel Junod. Bilbao had fallen to the Nationalists two days ago. The city was in chaos since Franco's troops had entered, and he couldn't get any sense out of the Basque authorities concerning Nationalist prisoners still in Basque hands.

The last that had been seen or heard of Señora Roxana de Luchar, her child, and the nanny, and Señora Vida de Martello de Luchar was when they had been removed from the prison-ship, *Menor*, moored in the mouth of the Nervion River. They had been taken to another place of internment somewhere in the city, possibly Bilbao prison itself. Thereafter, the two de Luchar women, the child, and the nanny seemed to have disappeared off the records, along with many other political prisoners.

In a way it was good news, even if it wasn't *definite* good news. If the Nationalists had taken the town, then Roxana and her daughter, Keir felt sure, would be released very shortly.

Later that evening he went to the Rivales house in Carrer Sarrià in the exclusive Pedralbes district. He rang the doorbell. While he waited, he took in his surroundings. The impressive front door with its elaborate carved panels and wrought-iron fittings could have withstood a battering-ram. The courtyard of Spanish tiles with a fountain in its centre, was surrounded by carefully tended borders of bougainvillaea and oleander illuminated by subdued and expensive electric lighting concealed in the shrubbery. A barrow of new potted-plants for outdoors as well as indoors had been left in a discreet corner, obviously awaiting the gardener's ministrations in the morning. Even though so many others were not doing so well, Señor Rivales was obviously prospering in this war, Keir could not help reflecting wryly.

The smartly-attired maid who eventually answered the door informed him that Señor Rivales was not at home, neither was Señora Rivales – nor the English lodger, Señor Peedee.

'Do you know where I might find Señor Peedee?'

The maid shrugged. 'No, Señor Doctor, I do not.'

Keir decided to go to the Jesu María Convent, and leave a message for Raven concerning her sister. It was a good excuse, anyway, and, with luck, the Reverend Mother might allow him a few minutes alone with *Sister* Justina! He turned up his nose ruefully at Raven's determination to be that bride of Christ, while refusing to be put off by such a fact; nuns had been known to retract upon their vows.

At the Jesu María Convent in the Puerto del Angel, Keir

received a shock. Communist guards occupied the premises. An ominous notice had been pinned to the main gates of the convent, a warning to other religious orders still within the city: *in terrorem* was the Latin inscription. *This Franciscan order of monks and nuns has been disbanded and exiled from the city.* The scrawled signature at the foot of the notice was illegible.

'On whose authority has this order been disbanded and exiled?' Keir demanded of a portly little Spaniard who appeared to be in authority as he strutted up and down behind the gates, a rifle slung on his back.

The Spaniard shrugged. 'The Government.'

'Where have they been sent?'

The man eyed Keir's Red Cross armband on the left sleeve of his jacket and flung his cigarette butt into the courtyard before spitting on the ground. 'How should I know, comrade? They are dispersed all over the place. If they are wise, they will go to France. However, these creatures of religion are not wise, otherwise they would not have aided and abetted the Fascists. They are traitors to the Republic, comrade, and all traitors must be exterminated.'

Keir's thoughts immediately went to Raven and her Bible-smuggling activities – aided and abetted by Dame Concepción and the rest of the Roman Catholic hierarchy. The cold iron fist of reckoning clutching his heart, he asked, 'Who is the man in charge here?'

'I am, comrade. These religious buildings are now a prison for political adversaries of the Government. I am the new Prison Governor.'

'I want to talk to someone responsible for the closure of this convent. Someone in *real* authority, señor!'

'Then you must speak to Commissar de Luchar.' The Communist picked his teeth with a dirty fingernail. 'He is Deputy Secretary General for Internal Security Affairs, and is the *real* Party Leader.'

De Luchar again! Would he never get away from this family who straddled both sides of the fence? Keir demanded of the guard, 'Where can I find him?'

'Castillo Palomar out at Montjuic – it used to be called the Castillo de Luchar, but that was not a good party name, and so now it is changed to one that suits everybody.'

Huh! was Keir's further comment to himself as he drove off to the Castillo Palomar, wondering to himself what next he would encounter at the Castle Dovecote!

The old de Luchar family residence shared the same coastline as Montjuic fortress which had, like the Jesu María Convent, become a prison for political offenders. Keir knew Montjuic well; on several occasions lately he had visited the prison authorities as well as many of the internees held in Montjuic without trial, and he did not like what he had seen there. Keir doubted he would find any doves in the shape of Communists residing at the newly christened Castillo Palomar, either.

It was eleven o'clock at night. To his great good luck the Deputy Secretary General for Internal Security Affairs was at home.

Ramiro and Keir met in the lovely old dining-hall with its stained-glass windows, where, at the Christmas party in 1931, Vida and Ramiro had first begun their liaison, and Don Ruiz de Luchar had banned Ramiro from his own home on account of his Communist politics. But Keir was not to know about that. He knew only the exigencies of this Civil War and saw the suffering caused by it: sons against fathers, and vice versa, friends against friends, lovers on the opposite sides, and politics that destroyed.

At the same table around which the family had gathered on that ill-fated Christmas Day over six years ago, Ramiro invited Keir to be seated in an antique carved Castillian chair. 'Would you like some brandy, Señor Doctor?' Ramiro smiled smoothly, reminding Keir of a handsome brilliantined tomcat. 'It is one of our very best.' He held the crystal decanter up to the crystal chandeliers so that rainbow diamonds sparkled in the electric light. 'My grandfather named it for my grandmother, so, in English, it is very impressively translated as *The Imperial Milk of Doña Maria*!'

'Then I can't very well say no, Señor de Luchar.' Keir was in need of a fortifier; he was worried about Raven and could only sense bad tidings concerning her.

'You are here because you have news of my wife, Dr Devlin?' Ramiro began.

'In a way – I have heard from Dr Marcel Junod concerning the fall of Vizcaya ...'

544

'Vizcaya is only a temporary setback, Dr Devlin. We will oust the insurgents from Bilbao before too long.'

'That is not my concern, Señor de Luchar. My concern is the Two Conventions, the protection of the wounded and the protection of prisoners of war – under which category innocent women and children come. Such prisoners are from both sides of the fighting lines, Reds and non-Reds.' Keir, casually seated at the table, the patina of which defied modern abuse, and upon whose glassy surface Ramiro had placed the decanter and coasters, nursed his brandy-glass in his hand. 'Dr Junod informs me that your wife and your sister-in-law were last seen and heard of on the prison-ship, *Menor*, moored in the estuary of the Nervion River. When the Nationalists bombarded the city the women and children were taken off the ship for their own safety. However, no one knows what has become of your wife, sister-in-law, niece, and nanny, since then.'

Ramiro contemplated the deep gold of his grandfather's brandy. 'I'm sorry to hear that.' He set down his glass on a silver coaster, stood up and began pacing the length of the dining-room, his hands behind his back. 'A friend of mine, Dolores Ibarruri – perhaps you have heard of her?' He glanced over his shoulder at Keir. 'She is more commonly referred to as "The Passion Flower" because of her impassioned speeches.'

'Yes, I've heard her on the radio.'

'Discount the rumours, Dr Devlin. She is not a bride of the Devil and she did not suck the blood of any priest. She has the cause of the working-class people close to her heart and wants to see justice done for the poor people of Spain. Autonomy for the Basques, as well as a continuing autonomy for the Catalans is essential for the future peace and prosperity of the Spanish mainland. If Franco grabs power over the whole of Spain, then I fear that people like the Catalonians and the Basques will lose their national identity, heritage, and independence, and, contrary to the belief of Franco supporters, he will suppress *all* religion in Spain. We will become a country afraid to look in the mirror for what we will find there. I am not one of those Communists who wants to give Spain to Russia, Dr Devlin. All I want is Fascism to be kept out of Catalonia. I want to

545

see the faces of the Catalonian people bright with hope for the future – which cannot be, under the likes of Franco y Bahamonde, for he is only another Nazi.'

Ramiro paused, sensing Keir's impatience to get on with matters more dear to his heart than the internal politics of a country not his.

'However, I know you haven't come here to listen to me, Dr Devlin, so I will just say this. Because Dolores Ibarruri is a Basque woman, I have asked her to intercede in this matter. She will talk to the Basques of Bilbao who have had a hand in my wife and sister-in-law's detention. Let's hope there will be a happy outcome to an unhappy situation. Vida is now the woman in danger since the insurgents took control of the city.'

'The fortunes of war, Señor de Luchar.'

'Indeed, Dr Devlin, and all too often the price. But I hope Roxana and Vida are both safe. Communists, contrary to popular belief, do have hearts as well as ideological aspirations.'

'What I really came here to ask you, Señor de Luchar, since you are in charge of security matters, and, I believe, the one responsible for disbanding the Camillus nuns at the Jesu María Convent, is where is Raven Quennell?'

'She is at Vilafranca, at a small and insignificant Franciscan convent: The Convent of the Sacred Heart, I believe it's called. You will find it off the Rambla Francesc, hiding away behind its high brick walls next to the more imposing Diocesan residence of the Bishop of Vilafranca and Toril, and the Eglesia de la Trinitat. Raven is quite safe, I assure you.'

Keir remembered certain words of caution from Max Huber in Geneva: never take sides, always remember that you are a non-combatant, a warrior without weapons, an officer of peace, not war.

But Keir would dearly loved to have received reassurances from the likes of Ramiro de Luchar for the protection of people from all walks of life – not the glaring evidence of the firing and terrorizing of religious orders, and other groups the Communists wished to eliminate: how long before you bastards drive the nuns and monks out of Vilafranca, too? was what he really wished to ask.

'I'm glad Sister Justina has found sanctuary,' he found himself saying. 'Perhaps, Señor de Luchar, you also know where her grandfather is?'

Ramiro turned away and studied a portrait of one of his grandee ancestors on the panelled wall of the dining-room. 'I've no idea, Dr Devlin. That old Englishman is a law unto himself.'

Keir stood up. 'Thank you for your cooperation, and your time, Señor de Luchar. Now I must get back to the Calle Lauria.'

Ramiro half turned to look at Keir. Over his shoulder, he said, 'You and your colleagues from around the world are doing good work on Spain's behalf. I should be thanking *you*, Dr Devlin.'

'We do our best.'

Ramiro turned around fully to face Keir. Hands behind his back, Ramiro's eyes were coldly calculating. 'I hear you have managed to secure the promise of a release for my mother and aunt?'

'That's right.'

'When will they be going home?'

'In a few days.'

'Who signed the order?'

'Dr Negrín.'

Ramiro smiled. 'The de Luchar family is indeed fortunate to know so *many* powerful people – royalty, presidents, Prime Minsters and the Red Cross officials themselves, all working on their behalf. You are honoured to have got the ear of Dr Negrín, Señor Doctor. The Prime Minister is such a busy man these days. But my poor father though, we're all so worried about him: I'm still trying to find out what has become of Don Ruiz for my mother's sake.'

'Tell me, Señor de Luchar,' Keir said, taking up a stance on the threshold, 'why did you do nothing to release your mother and aunt from prison when you had it within your power to do so after they were whisked off by the control patrol early one morning, just as they were coming from Mass?'

'I'm not the ultimate authority in these matters, Dr Devlin. My mother and aunt were becoming a danger to themselves on account of their wilful flouting of the law on, not just one occasion, as with this participating in the Catholic Mass, but on many occasions ...'

'Forgive me, Señor de Luchar, I have not come here to argue the ethics of this war but ...'

Ramiro held up his hand and ignored Keir's interruption. 'So, rather than seeing them put away permanently by members of a popular tribunal or *Casa de Pueblo* committee formed by people who hate my family and who are looking for an excuse to remove them for ever from Vinarosa, I prompted their arrest and internment in Las Cortes. My mother may not think so now, but she'll have cause to thank me when this war is over. I would hate to see her suffer at the hands of illegal tribunals controlled by the Anarchists, and so I had her put out of harm's way – right in the belly of the whale, so to speak. Ask her yourself. She and my aunt are very well treated in prison, and even have their own gramophone as well as exceptionally good food. In fact, they can have anything they wish. Our old chef here at the castillo takes fresh food to them every day.'

Keir also knew that Doña Jacqueline gave it all away to other less fortunate prisoners, because she thought Ramiro was the person instrumental in her husband's disappearance, possibly right into the hands of torture-interrogators. She and Leah de Luchar had spilled out their grief to him when he had interviewed them in the grim confines of Las Cortes.

Thoughts of Raven paramount in his mind, and what she, too, might be undergoing at the hands of the Communists and Anarchists, Keir took his leave of Ramiro, who at the door said, 'I know you have acted out of compassion and regard for my family, Dr Devlin, and I thank you for that. But I am perturbed. By releasing my mother and aunt back into the hands of Anarchist *Casa de Pueblo* dogs working against the Government of Catalonia, I hope your humane action won't be regretted by you, or by my family later on in this war.'

Disturbed by such words of counselling, Keir went back to the Calle Lauria, determined to set off at the crack of dawn to find Raven who was supposed to be at Vilafranca.

But it was not to be. A message awaited him when he returned to the Calle Lauria, and an order that could not be easily ignored. A huge offensive had just been launched on the Segovia front, and both armies were massing around Madrid. Urgent medical supplies and blood were required to be sent up at once to the battle-areas. Through the main branch office at Valencia, he was to coordinate this work with Geneva, with a full report on the situation facing the Red Cross.

It was one month before Keir was able to return to Barcelona, while the battles raged around Madrid. The battle of Brunete in which the American battalions, the Washington and Lincoln, had to merge as one battalion because of appalling losses, was fought in July. Both Nationalists and Republicans were now firmly dug into their trenches. Both sides were not giving an inch and both sides were claiming victory over the city. But it was to be many more months, with many more bloody battles taking place, before Madrid finally fell.

Keir, after reporting back to the Calle Lauria, went straightaway to Vilafranca. Dame Superior Olivera greeted him in her spartan office. 'Good morning, Dr Devlin. We have not as yet sung lauds.'

'I'm sorry I'm so early. I wanted to come here a month ago to talk to Sister Justina, but the Segovia front, I'm afraid, drew me away from Barcelona.'

'More Red Cross work, Dr Devlin?'

'First and foremost, Dame Superior Olivera.'

'Thank God there are still right-minded men like you and Dr Junod in this crass world of machine-guns and bombs, Dr Devlin.'

'I think you're giving me more credit than I deserve. Dr Junod does the real work of salvation. Why I'm really here is to talk to Sister Justina concerning her twin sister and young niece.'

'Of course! *No problema.* I will, at least, allow her that humane concession. But first I must tell you, Dr Devlin, that Sister Justina is going through her own dark night of the soul.'

'Pardon me?'

'Personal desolation, Dr Devlin. Since the dreadful night a month ago when the Jesu María Convent in Barcelona was ransacked and desecrated, Sister Justina has been unable to pray, to confess, or to talk about her experience at the hands of – I don't know who! Some said they were POUM Anarchists, others say the Stalinist Communists were to blame, others again claim the Falangists were responsible. All I know is, Sister Justina was so distraught after that incident, she was unable to get out of the clothes of her capture – peasant garments, black and bloodstained, which she clung to for five days and nights as a fashionable woman might cling to a mink stole. I was at a loss. For the first time in my life I was unable to communicate with one of my nuns. I am still at a loss. Even though four weeks have passed, Sister Justina is finding it difficult to settle back into convent life. I can only call it spiritual dispossession, a blackness and a blankness, Dr Devlin, as she hovers on the fringes of her calling. For no more is she that truly dedicated and inspired young woman who first came to me in Toril, determined to give her life and her whole self to God.'

Keir suddenly felt a lightening of his own soul; he couldn't begin to explain how glad he was to hear such words from the Dame Superior of the Camillus nuns: Raven was wavering in her faith, there was hope for him yet.

Dame Superior Olivera turned away from him. She faced the crucifix on the white wall, her hands confined within the embracing sleeves of her grey habit. 'The Papal Nuncio has condemned what took place at the Jesu María in Barcelona, but he is powerless in the light of present political events. The Pope himself has denounced the Republic. Meanwhile, we all have to be sheltered, fed and sustained in faith.' She paused, her back still turned to him, her eyes upon the crucifix on the wall as she told him the appalling truth. 'Seven of my nuns were raped by terrorists and revolutionaries. Five Franciscan priests were murdered in the most horrible way. They were found with parts of their bodies, with rosary beads, with torn pages from the Holy Bible, and with Communion wine thrust down their throats. It is so hard to pray for forgiveness against those who perpetrate such crimes. I want you to report this to Geneva as an atrocity of war so that the world might wake up and take notice of what is happening in Spain today – which could so easily happen to the rest of the world tomorrow.'

'Was Sister Justina raped?'

Dame Superior Olivera turned back to face him. 'No. She was out of it for most of that horrible night as she and Dame Conceptión were on a special mission outside convent walls. They both arrived back at the convent just before some PSUC men came on the scene, bent on arresting the Anarchist POUMs. She tells me that she was saved by prayer and the hand of the Lord interceding on her behalf. Her faith in God is still strong, you see, Dr Devlin, although she needs her faith in herself and in mankind, restored.'

Keir found his earlier hopes concerning Raven eroded by Dame Superior Olivera's words. But he told himself not to despair.

Dame Superior Olivera, impaled on the horns of a dilemma, said, 'All my nuns are in grave danger while they remain here, and neither is the convent big enough to house all of us for any length of time. I'm trying to reallocate them in the safest possible way. It is *not* an easy task. I have so many homeless nuns to deal with, while the Bishop himself is frantic to rehouse his Franciscan friars, who have become displaced persons like ourselves. Many of them are having to go abroad, to France or Italy, which is a tragedy for Spain and her future spiritual welfare. Sister Justina's welfare is also close to my heart. That is what I meant just now about having her faith in herself restored. Her inner strength has diminished. She needs to find herself again. A nun who is only half-certain that there is indeed a God of love at all, is no spiritual asset to any community let alone a religious one; that is what has happened to Sister Justina following the events at the Jesu María, so that now she even questions the existence of God. And where all this brings me, Dr Devlin, is to ask you to take off my hands half a dozen nuns, Sister Justina being one of them, in order to make my task six times easier.'

'I'm sorry – I don't understand.'

551

'No, of course you don't: I'm getting carried away by my own enthusiasm. You require nursing staff, do you not?'

'Yes, always.'

'Then take six of my nuns with you to the front lines.'

'That's too dangerous.'

'Why?'

'Military nursing personnel are trained to accept the horrors of the battlefield, your nuns are not.'

'My nuns have had to accept some very dreadful horrors so far.'

He could not deny that. 'If you are talking about the battle for rehousing refugees, prisoners of war and displaced persons, then yes, I do require volunteers. So what are you suggesting Dame Superior Olivera?'

'I offer you the free nursing services of Sister Justina and five other homeless persons like her. Nuns are people, after all, Dr Devlin, and they require to be housed, fed, and sustained in their faith and in their duty to the rest of mankind as well as to God.'

He hesitated, but only for a fraction of a second. 'How? How am I expected to handle such a tall order?'

'Administering, rehousing, stringing food parcels together, chauffering, nursing – right *on* the battlefield if that is where they are needed. Anything at all, just send them where they are most needed.'

'You want me to dispose of them to the front line?'

'If that is God's will.'

'Both sides of God's will?'

'Now you are questioning my motives.'

'Absolutely.'

'You are an agnostic, Dr Devlin?'

'I'm a realist, Dame Superior Olivera.'

'Then, as a realist, will you not see your way to relieve the situation that faces my Camillus nuns who are as persecuted as any refugee or prisoner of war whom the Red Cross goes out of its way to protect and help?'

'Whose conscience will that relieve, yours or Rome's?'

'Yours, too, Dr Devlin.'

'How do you mean?'

'I mean, Dr Devlin, that Sister Justina might find herself again, given the exigent needs of war. And you, too, might

552

find yourself.'

He looked at her in alarm. Then he said, 'You're an extraordinary lady!'

'Perhaps. But you cannot deny the truth, Dr Devlin!'

'I'm going uphill all the time, Dame Superior Olivera.'

'Take Sister Justina with you.'

'Why?'

'Because I believe you care deeply for her, and that she knows it. Because I think she requires to look again at her life, and because I want her to sort out her innermost thoughts and feelings before becoming a fully-professed nun. It is too serious a step for any woman to take unless she is absolutely convinced in her heart that she is doing the right thing. Novice Mother and the Bishop do not think that Sister Justina is at all ready to take her final vows. The other day I would have thought them wrong. However, after what took place at the Jesu María Convent, I think that Sister Justina needs more time to herself in order to come to terms with herself and her religious undertaking. I pride myself on the fact that every novice I have personally recommended to take her final vows has never let me down. I want Sister Justina's faith in herself and in her calling to be restored. At the moment she is a *dry soul*, lost between two worlds, her faith shaken, her belief in a caring, loving God almost suspended. I want her to go into the world again, and when she is tired of it a second time, then to reaffirm her vows of poverty, chastity, and obedience!'

'You mean she wants a dispensation of her vows?' He could hardly keep the jubilation out of his voice.

'No, Dr Devlin. Sister Justina has not taken any solemn, binding vows as yet. She requires leave of absence, in this instance meaning a period of time away from a religious community for some specific purpose. Sister Justina's specific purpose is to find herself again through the errors of this Spanish war, as well as her own inward war of the mind and soul.'

'But you'll lose out, Dame Superior Olivera.'

'In what way, Dr Devlin?'

'Because, in her heart of hearts, Raven is not cut out to be a nun, a Dame Superior, a Reverend Mother, or – or any other religious zealot as you and she might think.'

'You are so sure, Dr Devlin?'

'I'm sure.'

The handsome Portuguese nun, with a quirk of a black eyebrow into the starched white band of her head-dress, smiled. 'Dr Devlin will you or will you not take six of my nuns off my hands, and perhaps save their lives?'

'I'll take them, but *only* if Sister Justina is included in the deal, and she'll always be Raven to me. Now may I talk to her, please?'

But when Sister Jeanne showed Raven into Dame Superior Olivera's office, it was as impossible to talk to her as on that other occasion in the Calle Lauria with Dame Conception hovering in the background. All these dames were beginning to become a bugbear, an unnecessary anxiety in his life when he had thought he had shrugged off such impositions, especially where the female of the species was concerned. After Sister Jeanne had closed the door Keir found Dame Superior's presence restrictive, and his own manner and speech towards Raven, were therefore, stilted. He could tell her only what he himself knew about the *Menor* episode from Dr Junod's report a month ago. There was no further news concerning Roxana, but the search was still going on through Red Cross channels.

'Thank you, Dr Devlin,' was all she said, her eyes downcast, her hands contained within her wide sleeves. 'I appreciate the fact that you've come in person to tell me this when you must be so hard-pressed for time.'

Dame Superior Olivera said, 'Sister Justina, I have a new assignment for you. As you know, we are all rather crowded together in this small convent that has offered us temporary sanctuary. However, Dr Devlin is going to place six nuns with the Red Cross until the war is over. You are one of those nuns. Dame Conception will go with you as your chaperon and spiritual guardian.'

And then she did look up at him, her eyes, far from containing that blankness and spiritual deprivation Dame Superior Olivera had been talking about, were angry! Keir could read in Raven's accusation, also the humiliation – So! Now you and she have bartered me like a slave to serve your respective interests; well, I'm not ready for my soul to be bartered by you or by Dame Superior Olivera!

And while she stood there like an alabaster image of the Virgin Mary unable to open her mouth in her own defence, all he could do was make his apology in equal silent anguish: *I love you, and I want to help you by taking you away from behind the bars you've erected around yourself. I want to prove to you that the world can be a better place. I learned again through the simple eyes of Peppy, and others like him. I know that you and I together can fight the world. We can vanquish the scars of war and the brutality and what happened to you in Dublin, Toril, and at the Jesu María, by replacing the bad memories with our own good ones so that we don't have to live for ever in the shadow of other people – all those other people who have destroyed us. We can do it through love …*

But even while temptation trembled on the tip of his tongue to speak his mind despite Dame Superior Olivera's overpowering and dominating presence, salvation was not going to come so easily, not now, not now …

Oh God! He stared at the crucifix on the whitewashed wall: how do you tell a nun you're love-crazy for her, body and soul, and that she'd only know the reality of a relationship once she had experienced it, not with Christ her Saviour or with her gaoler Dames, but with him, the man who loved her: and if I tell her I love her and she still denies me for the sake of this holy fanaticism, what do I do then? Bleed to death from her denial as from those wounds inflicted by Joss, Francesca, and Jodi?

'If it's God's will, Dr Devlin,' was her stony reply before he left her presence.

Keir, on his return to the Calle Lauria, was devasted to learn that Doña Jacqueline and Doña Leah were not, after all, to be set free. The order for their release had been countermanded.

The signature on the note lying on his desk was that of the Basque Republican Minister of Justice, Manuel de Irujo y Ollo, who had overriden the Prime Minister's previous pledge regarding the release of the two de Luchar women. It clearly stated, '*Lo siento. Hay que prever todos los resultados* – Sorry, but one has to foresee all possible outcomes – and these two women are dangerous.'

Keir felt he could never face Nina de Luchar, or her indomitable grandmother, with shattering news like this.

CHAPTER SIXTEEN

Aragon and Navarre:
August and September 1937

Keir managed to place two displaced Camillus nuns with a St John's Ambulance blood-transfusion unit, and two more with a Red Cross hospital behind the Republican lines at Alcubierre. Dame Concepción he found amusing and useful. She and Sister Justina, partners in crime, as far as he was concerned they both had a very big personal debt to pay off to the Spanish Red Cross!

After hearing about Raven's 'dark night of the soul' and her request for leave of absence from the convent, Keir had half expected Raven to turn up at the Calle Lauria dressed in ordinary clothes (the lovely fashionable young lady of Geneva days still haunting him). But when he saw her still clinging to her novice's habit and utilitarian black shoes and stockings, his heart sank.

'I thought you were getting out of your order for a little while?' He half accused, even while noticing that her nun's head-dress had been replaced by a hospital head-dress of plain white linen displaying a red cross, without any holy trimmings of angel's wings favoured by the Camillus nuns.

Raven smiled. 'You want me to?'

'Want you to what?'

'Stop being a nun?'

'Right first time.'

'This is the uniform of a Camillus novice engaged in nursing the sick and I'm sticking to it – all except the head-dress and veil which Dame Superior Olivera said I

556

should compromise upon. The head-dress, you see, Dr Devlin, is extremely important. It signifies a nun's commitment to renounce the world, utterly.'

'Have you – utterly?'

'No. Hence the compromise.'

'Why?'

'I'm still searching for the truth.'

'The truth, Raven, is that there is no truth. Truth is a myth, same as the unicorn.'

'I still believe in fairytales, unicorns, and truth.'

'Truth can' always be distorted, as in the case of unicorns.'

'And Camillus nuns. I'm of two minds these days. Rather like a Siamese twin born with two heads and two hearts, but only one inclination.'

'What's that?'

'To survive the point of this exercise.'

He grinned, his heart light because they were both able to speak freely at last. 'I'm not entering into my religious argument with you because you're totally confused – and we'll argue about *that* at some future date when you come to your senses and realize how you're wasting your life. Politics, religion, and women have been the downfall of mankind, and today, as a mere man, I want to live life as it comes. Which means you and I have to name-tab three hundred children to be evacuated to stately homes in Belgium. And then we are going to Bilbao.' He handed across two Red Cross armbands for her and Dame Concepción to wear, as well as two regulation *mochilas*.

Raven draped both military-looking khaki knapsacks with red crosses, over her shoulder. She did not know where Dame Concepción had got to, and then espied her a little distance away engaged in conversation with a group of Spanish women who had come to the Red Cross for assistance. Poor Dame Concepción appeared properly tied up, what with all the weeping, wailing, and wringing of hands going on. Raven turned back to Keir. 'Why Bilbao?'

'To find out what has become of your sister, your niece, and many other political prisoners like Vida de Martello de Luchar. I've also got to make an inspection tour of Red Cross hospitals supported by American donations to see that they're being run efficiently, and the money is going where it should. Bilbao is on the agenda.'

'I thought Dr Junod was taking care of Bilbao and the Basques?'

'Dr Junod has gone to Salamanca to negotiate the freedom of Arthur Koestler.'

'Who is Arthur Koestler?'

'An Anglo-Hungarian journalist important to everyone, Nationalists, Republicans, British, French, Germans, and Russians alike.'

'Why?'

He shrugged. 'How should I know? I'm only an American doctor doing my bit for world peace. The only people who communicate directly with me are the International Red Cross officials. Now are you ready?'

'Ready when you are, Dr Devlin.'

'Can't it be Keir again?'

'A policeman is not allowed to drink on duty.'

'What's that got to do with us?'

'Flippancy aside, Dr Devlin, there are still serious issues to be taken care of which require our full attention. I am on loan to you only as long as this war lasts and nurses are required by the Red Cross. That's all.'

He chewed over that fact as they headed for the yard in which his car was parked.

Dame Concepción, following them, said breathlessly. 'Oh, those poor women with their husbands and sons missing. War is destructive, but civil war is just *self*-destruction. Sheer madness.'

'You're so right, Dame Concepción. Now then,' Keir added with a straight face, 'you drive, since you're so adept at finding your way in the dark.'

'Where to, Dr Devlin?' Dame Concepción climbed into the driver's seat, then wiped her steamy spectacles.

'The School of Our Saviour, in the Pedralbes district. There are three hundred refugee children awaiting evacuation on a Belgian ship sailing from Barcelona this evening. Tomorrow, you and Sister Justina will be required to tail a Red Cross convoy – officially this time – taking medical supplies and blood to hospital units between Lérida and Zaragoza, and then on to Bilbao.'

'Your word is my command, Dr Devlin,' said Dame Conceptión cheerfully as they set off. 'Dame Superior Olivera assigned me to you, and I am obeying my vows of blind obedience.' Over her shoulder she added, 'I suppose the next best thing to a Citroën is a Renault, Sister Justina.'

'And the next best thing to Bible-smuggling must be children-smuggling!' Keir added darkly.

Raven did not answer. She had asked Dame Superior Olivera for leave of absence to sort herself out; but she had not envisaged spending that leave of absence in Keir Devlin's disturbing company.

Late August, when sometimes an early fall came to the Catskill mountains, would have been a sight for sore eyes: Keir could not help reflecting that changing seasons in the mountains of Alcubierre did not resemble the environs of New York State in the least when trees arrayed in their turn-of-the-year colours, bronzes, yellows, browns, and golds, would have clad the mountains skirting the City of New York like banners of American glory. Here, in the Spanish sierras, mountain-slopes were bald, denunded by successive generations of impoverished peasants, by goats and sheep, and more recently by soldiers in search of fuel for their cooking-fires, so that the landscape, irrevocably changed, resembled nothing so much as the sparse surface of the moon. The heat was intense, the landscape by daylight baked to a harsh, glaring, bone-dry whiteness so that one had to reach for the sunglasses before the eyes became fried to the road.

Keir had managed to catch up with the Washington and Abraham Lincoln Battalion at last, the two having merged after the battle of Brunete in July. The Republicans had suffered appalling losses during the offensive on the Madrid front, and the International Brigades had rebelled against their incompetent officers. The British had threatened to clear off to Madrid to sit it out there, if their brutal commanding officer, a Hungarian by the name of Janos Galica (or Gal as he was unpopularly called) wasn't promptly relieved of his command. The Lincolns on the other hand, flung into battle after battle by their over-zealous commanding officer, an Englishman with illusions of grandeur, had lost one hundred and twenty men at Brunete out of a brigade of five hundred. A great many more had been wounded. They mutinied, refusing to go back into line until they elected their own American commander. Peace was restored when Martin Hourihan from Pennsylvania took over from the English 'Hussar', who had narrowly escaped being lynched by the Americans.

'The Red River Valley' ditty did not figure as much as the banging of spoons against empty pannikins or the friendly accents of gum-chewing men from 'back home'. Black, white, and coffee-coloured, they put into perspective the strange vagaries as well as the compelling issues at stake in this Spanish war.

'Hi Doc, you'll never guess! There's a señorita back there who plays the *gi-tar*!' The accent was definitely familiar even if the surroundings weren't.

That the 'gi-tar'-playing señorita was none other than Ravenna Quennell, lately a nun, and, even more lately a disturbing influence to the men at the Aragon front, did not console Keir in the least.

A borrowed guitar, her haunting songs and her smoke-eyed Irish beauty, conveyed the brutality and the futility of war as nothing else could. The soldiers were not starved of the sight of a female. There were many women to be found at the front, militiawomen fighting beside the men, and the wives of Spanish soldiers providing a voluntary catering corps behind the scenes of conflict. Sister Justina's presence only served to boost the morale of the soldiers in quite a different direction: unless he felt this way about her for more personal reasons? You're jealous! Keir told himself.

'Hey, Sister, you know, "On the Banks of the Ohio?" What about "Irish Eyes?" Or this one that goes – "A little pretty nightingale, sings outside my stony gaol: but 'morrow morn she sure will cry, when she knows I'm goin' t' die …".'

No, she didn't know that one, but she had a good ear for music, and could soon pick out a melody.

The entire moutainside was honeycombed with natural

bomb-shelters into which the International Brigade had dug themselves. Sentries were taking up their night positions behind the protecting walls of the terraced olive-groves, lines of ready-made fortifications able to keep an army snug for months. Campfires of the two opposing armies skewered the darkness. The Nationalist camp on the other mountain was only a stone's throw away, across a narrow, dry, but very deep ravine separating the two sides. The voices of the Nationalist soldiers could be clearly heard, amplified by the acoustics of the sierras. The 'scrunch' of Nationalist shells half-heartedly fired on a range that was hopelessly ineffectual, usually landed way off mark, around eleven o'clock, when both sides would 'turn in' and hope to sleep as best they could. But tonight, the Nationalists on the other side of the deep gorge remained quiet – quiet in so far as they stopped hurling missiles and abuse across the valley to join in the singing.

A voice in English echoed across the ravine from the Nationalist camp, 'Hey there, Irish Eyes, you ever thought about joining a *real* army?'

'She's with us, rebel!' one of the Lincolns yelled back. 'Who'er you?'

'O'Duffy's Irishmen.'

'Blueshirt traitors.'

Keir felt a tight restriction in his chest, her repertoire disturbing him: 'You took the east from me: you took the west from me. You took the gentle moon and stole the staring sun. You've tattered the heart that beats in the cage of my breast. and even denied me Christ, the Virgin Mary's Son ...'

And because Raven had innocently invoked such tragic memories in that moment of singing 'Donal Og', an Irish lyric his own father would sing accusingly in his whiskey hour on Jefferson Street, Keir, out of the blue, and out of the pain, was curt with her, 'Why don't you go the whole hog? How about "I know where I'm going, and I know who's going with me?" ', just so that she might take the hint! It was an Irish-English folk song Joss also used to sing – the old man having had a good voice, too, drunk or sober!

The spell of the jolly evening broken, knowing she had

plucked a broken string in Keir Devlin's heart, and was sorry that she had, Raven handed back the guitar to the soldier from whom she had borrowed it, and rejoined Dame Conceptión and the Red Cross nurses who had been listening to her, as well as participating from the entrance of the hospital tent.

Keir sat motionless in the darkness, a terrible sadness and inertia holding him prisoner to regret: what was the sacrifice all for, anyway? He wasn't even doing what he had been trained to do when this war needed so many skilled surgeons like himself ...

'Oliver Law's dead, Doc, killed at Brunete.' The voice cut through Keir's reverie.

'Sorry to know that, soldier,' Keir replied. Oliver Law had been the huge Negro commander of the Lincolns who had taken over from the Pennsylvanian Hourihan.

'Here's to Major Merriman!' someone said, and the Lincolns echoed the reply, 'Here's to Merriman. Long may he live!'

'It was so bloody hot at Brunete you could kebab a Fascist on a bayonet, Doc.'

He knew: he had been there himself. But he didn't tell them.

'You'll never guess what they did to El Campesino's captured men at Brunete, Doc.'

'What, soldier?'

'Cut off three hundred pairs of legs, the Fascist bastards!'

'Yeah, Orville, but then El Campesino shot four hundred captured Moroccans to get his own back, remember?'

'How can I forget. Uncle Sam sending you enough mobile transfusion units and good-looking nurses, Doc?'

'Plenty thanks.'

'That's great organization, Doc. Good to know that if we bleed to death for the Dagos, there's a bottle of democractic Yankee blood waiting to revive us.'

'Why did you volunteer for this war, soldier?'

'So democracy never dies, Doc.'

'That's right, man! The people voted, the people have a right to their choice of government without any danged Fascist *junta* stepping in to take it all away.'

'Believe us Doc, those Fascist swine kill their own side if

they so much as find them with a red pimple on the chin. They even shoot fifteen-year-old kids for desertion when the little beggers are so screwed up about the guts and noise all they want to do is get back home to momma.'

'Who's the classy Red Cross dame who can play the guitar, Doc?'

'The blue-blooded one you mean, Orville?'

'Yeah, she's a lady all right. and real cute, ain't she fellers?'

'Ain't she jest!'

'Sings like my Wisconsin canary in a good mood. She one of ours?'

'She's Irish.'

'Near enough, eh, Doc? You wanna Lucky Strike?'

'Thanks soldier.' Keir lit up, and smiled to himself. He couldn't help reflecting that this Spanish war was a funny business: there was not just one Spain any more, but several, the whole map of the country cut out into little patchwork pieces of red, red and black, red-yellow-purple, red and gold, red-yellow-red, that somehow had to be stuck together again. One laughed and cried for all sides: today issuing blood to the Lincolns, tomorrow saving someone from a firing-squad, the day after getting his eyes scratched out by a distraught housewife because he hadn't got any news about her husband or son on the other side, and the day after that maybe drying the tears of a three-year-old orphan kid on its way to France. Tomorrow they would be crossing over into Nationalist-held territory and heading for Zaragoza, and the process would be repeated under the colours of another partisan flag.

Keir went to his own bunker, the physical aspects of love as acute as hunger pangs, but far more dangerous, were eating him up because he could neither voice his love for Sister Justina, nor even contemplate it.

It was warm, beautiful, a velvet night loaded with sensuality, a night ripe for love. Danger enhanced the moment as desire and lust crept willingly into the rock shelter of his heart.

She was so very beguiling. Her white garments

reminding him pointlessly of the image she had created for herself, maddening him to such a degree, he wanted only to tear the traitorous clothes off her, expose her to the real image of herself – a woman made for love as opposed to the cold vestal virgin sacrificed on the altar of fearful religion. Yet, he also sensed her indecision, her desire to taste the apple just like Eve, and he took advantage of her weak moment: he reached for her, this time with determination. The game she had been playing was as old as time, as old as the Book of Genesis. It was called the temptation of man. She lifted her arms, unpinning her veil first. He could only watch, fascinated by the slender white body as she slowly divested herself of clothes. He wanted her so badly, he would kill for her – bishops and Papal envoys, nuncios, the Pope himself. Having her would be like a heavenly dream, drawn through his hands as smoothly as silk, slipping through them like a cascade of sunlit water slips over the edge of a mountain, soft and cool and fleeting. Kissing her would be like a second awakening, her body eager to be taught the lessons of love, touched, awakened and relished by him, her dark place of virginity still to be aroused by a communion that had nothing to do with Christ. To take her down, wrapping himself around her until the pain of love and the fierceness of desire were assuaged, he wanted it to last and last, to turn and twist and be tormented by the sweetness of this new kind of love-making, a knife turning in the wound of his sordid past, cauterizing his marriage to Francesca. '*Raven!*' he cried out in anguish …

Shielding his eyes from the cold reality of another battling day, torment returned a hundredfold when awakened harshly from such seductive dreams: someone was frantically shaking his shoulder. 'We've got to go, sir!'

'Go where?'

'The convoy's ready to move off to Zaragoza.'

Keir opened his eyes fully, his senses dulled by the dream that came to him so often. 'Zaragoza?' His mouth felt thick, gritty, unable to formulate the word.

'Yes, sir, it's almost daylight. Franco's lot are kicking up an awful shindig this morning, so we'd best get out of here before the mountain falls on our ambulances.'

Slowly Keir orientated himself. A dream, nothing more. Why had he expected more? Life was a series of craters filled with muddy water, so why had he thought for a moment back there that he had found the crystal clear dew of an Irish girl's pure love? Father Silvestre had been so right: there was no such thing as a perfect woman, so don't even bother looking. But he still shuddered at the loss of the night and the woman he had held in his arms. The longing was still with him, even more acute in the half-asleep, half-awake dawning of another battling day. Was the night's passion to be just an empty taste in his mouth, after all?

The Welsh Red Cross driver, Tom Coles, removed himself from the bunker. They were late setting off. He wondered what Dr Devlin had been dreaming about so vividly. He had even shouted the name of a bird out loud!

Keir reached for the packet of cigarettes on the rock shelf behind the camp-bed, and thanked Peppy the Spanish Indian for getting him hooked on tobacco on the night of Father Silvestre's death.

It was so hot in the bunker, he was wet through with perspiration.

So this was what it felt like to be under real Spanish fire! Grimly he fastened his shirt-buttons. Yellow dirt showered on his head, and got in his mouth and eyes. His empty belly hungered after a decent breakfast of hash browns and eggs easy-over, while his heart and loins still hungered after that unreal woman he had spent the night with.

'*Mea culpa*,' he muttered half to himself, his cigarette between his lips while he searched for his boots in the semi-darkness. This filthy little dugout where he had been forced to spend the night was strewn with stale food and tin cans left by previous platoons of soldiers. Trench warfare was always an unhealthy mixture of bad food, excreta, urine, caudite, rats, and the sickly-sweet odour of death. Keir didn't think he'd ever get used to the smell of war, and in that moment wished he was back in the antiseptic confines of Chief DaWinter's sterile operating theatre at New York City Hospital.

Keir stood up and banged his head on a wooden pit-prop shoring up the tunnel and a chunk of roof fell in on him. He'd die like a rat if he didn't get out of here quick, he told himself.

He emerged into the dawn light and a burly Negro soldier held a pannikin out to him.

'There you go, Doc! Get that inside you before you head off to do more good deeds for the day. My patrol is off to cut the piped water supply to Quinto, right under the noses of the Fascists holed up on Pulburrel Hill.'

'Thanks,' said Keir. 'What's this hash, soldier?'

'Chilli beans.'

'Great! I've had chilli beans at a Guatemalan christening, but I've never had chilli beans for breakfast.' He dug in with the soldier's spoon.

'That's what the Irish señorita said. Only it wasn't any christening she was referring to but the fact she ain't never had chilli beans for vigils. She's one heck of a singing lady, Doc. The Lincolns sure hate to see her go.'

'Duty first, soldier, even for nuns.'

'She's a nun?'

'Umm-umm. Sometimes. She's not too sure herself lately.'

'Boy oh boy! What a waste! You can sure knock us down with a feather. We all thought she was an ordinary Catholic nursing sister in that white uniform.'

'She's never ordinary, that Irish señor-ita! Thanks for breakfast, soldier – and good luck.'

'Thanks, Doc.' He took back his pannikin. 'Ring the Liberty Bell for me if you get home before I do.'

'Sure thing, Lincoln!'

The soldier saluted, his grin wide.

The route to Zaragoza cut across high, barren plateaux with only occasional glimpses of the green fertile valley of the Ebro. The white ribbon of road which the Red Cross convoy followed must have shown up from the air like the Great Wall of China. Keir could not help feeling that they were extremely vulnerable to air-attack as he drove the Renault behind the last ambulance. The *Croix Rouge* (as he still mentally referred to the Geneva Red Cross) was emblazoned on the top of each truck and ambulance. Keir recalled the Italian Air Force's devastation of the Swedish Red Cross unit on the road to Dessie, and he wouldn't put it past the Italians from repeating the same action all over again on the road to Zaragoza.

He told himself to stop being paranoid about Italians. Francesca wasn't here today.

Seated next to him in the front, Dame Concepción tried to make sense of a military map. 'One day, when I'm old and grey and incapable of moving down the cloister walk, I shall sit in my cell and draw some decent maps of the unchartered interior of Spain especially for the Red Cross, Dr Devlin.'

'And then I shall put your name forward for the Nobel Prize for Cartography, Dame Concepción. You will have done humanity a great service. I have never yet been able to make sense of a Spanish map.' He glanced over his shoulder. 'Are you asleep in the back there, Sister Justina?'

'Almost, Dr Devlin.'

'A bad night, eh?'

'A very good night. I'm half-asleep reading about the history of Zaragoza. In particular the Virgin who is the patroness of the Guardia Civil, who call her the Captain General of Zaragoza.'

'Why?'

'Because she has withstood repeated Republican air-attacks.'

'Santa Maria!' said Dame Concepción, crossing herself.

Keir glanced at her in amusement and flicked his cigarette-ash out of the open window. 'Don't you approve of Sister Justina doing her homework like a diligent novice?'

'A bee has become lodged under my scapular, Dr Devlin. I call upon a saint to protect me from its sting. Neither have I any wish to squash it flat as it is entitled to its bumbling bee's humble life, as much as I am to mine.'

Keir thought that the old Dame was indeed a game one, and enjoyed her company. 'Which town are we approaching, Dame Concepción?' The convoy was almost at a standstill and Keir wondered why. Crawling along at this speed, they would never reach Zaragoza by nightfall.

The nun turned the map the right way up. 'Osera de

Ebro – a village, not a town, about five kilometres from here.'

Farm-carts, donkeys, and pedestrians blocked Keir's view of the road ahead. 'Things look as though they're getting a little busy to me.'

'There's a strategic bridge at Fuentas del Ebro. Perhaps these people are from the other side of the river.' Dame Conceptión frowned. 'I think we're in trouble, Dr Devlin.'

The convoy had now stopped altogether to avoid running over peasants and their donkeys packing the road. Household items were piled high on carts. Small boys and old women in black carried baskets of scraggy chickens or vegetables. Pigs squealed among the wheels. Goats and domestic pets constituted a motoring hazard along with the children who ran amok in the road. Some very small children were perched high on mountains of straw, old and beloved quilts and rugs, on cupboards, kitchen tables, rocking-chairs. Everyone appeared to be in transit, but in the opposite direction to the Red Cross convoy. Keir was used to the sight of refugees by now, yet they still filled him with alarm. He stuck his head out of the driver's window. 'What's going on?' he yelled down the line.

The driver of the ambulance in front, the Welshman Tom Coles, yelled back, 'They say the Republicans have launched a huge offensive against the Nationalists trying to cross the Ebro. The road ahead is blocked for miles.'

Keir got out. He pushed his way up to the head of the convoy to find out for himself what was happening, but distraught villagers caught between two opposing armies, clamoured for his attention. Old women, housewives with small children, grandfathers, and grandsons, handcarts bumping his shins, imploring arms held out to him, clutching his sleeve, stroking the Red Cross armband, the peasants restrained his movements, bullying him to come to their assistance. 'Señor Doctor, our village has been bombed by the airplanes – my son, my father, my husband, my lover is dead, is missing, is injured, a prisoner – our daughter has been taken away, we don't know what has become of her ...' They fell upon the Red Cross convoy like swarming ants upon honeyed paper, while all

Keir could do was wipe the sweat from his brow: the migration of a nation, and he was supposed to be the signpost to salvation.

Minutes later the sky was filled with German Messerschmitts and Russian Chato fighters converging from the opposite ends of the sky.

Refugees scattered in all directions, scrambling for cover under the Red Cross vehicles, diving into the olive-groves on either side of the ribbon of road stretched tautly straight between the Sierra de Alcubierre and the Los Monegros.

Keir was only glad that the Red Cross of Geneva plastered everywhere, would show up like branding-marks to the fighter-planes overhead. But he still gave instructions for the convoy to pull off the road and get into the protection of the olive-trees. Dessie and the bombing of the Swedish Red Cross unit was still too vivid in his mind to trust implicitly in the humanitarian spirit embodied in the written word of the Geneva Convention; certain pilots could be notoriously short sighted.

He was not wrong. In the wake of the Messerschmitts and Chatos, a cloud of heavy German bombers lumbered across the skies, from the north, heading south-west. Some twenty bombers, and at least the same number again of supply-planes, they were escorted by Fiat fighters and Italian Savoias 79s.

Russian Sun Chatos and Supermoscas came in pursuit of the Messerschmitts and fascist Heinkels. The fighters came low, swooping over the main Zaragoza-Lérida road, curving up again like swallows on the wing.

Then, out of the bright, blinding sun, Italian Savoias and Fiats, commanded by the hero of the skies, the Spanish air ace, Garcia Morato, met the Republican Air Force, who could not even see them as they headed into the sunlight. To the people on the ground, as Russian and German war planes fought in the skies above the Ebro valley, heaven had turned into hell.

In the next instant the unbelievable happened. Whether or not the Heinkels had misjudged their timing, or had deliberately targeted the refugees and Red Cross convoy, bombs started dropping into the olive-groves and onto the road.

Raven had been standing beside the Renault parked at the edge of the olive-grove when the air-attack started, and was caught unawares. She could only stand and stare at the devastation as ambulances were being blown to bits, as people, animals, household furniture, were flung down like scattered confetti all along the Zaragoza road.

Total confusion reigned in the air and on the ground as the bombs fell, while the screaming engines of fighters in the sky were only surpassed by the panic on the ground. One of the ambulance drivers grabbed her, forcing her to get out of sight. 'Get down!'

She found herself lying in the deep inverted-V of a rainwater conduit between road and field after one of the German bombs fell into the olive-grove. Earth and rocks and what she did not know then to be human débris, showered down on the heads of those who were cowering in the ditch.

Dame Conceptión had been shepherding small children to safety, ushering them urgently into the safety of the trees. Raven, realizing what had happened, scrambled out of the conduit, tearing her nails and stockings, cutting her knees and hands in her desperate bid to reach Dame Conceptión and help her with the children. Someone clutched her skirt, holding her back. People were still screaming everywhere in the background of her mind. She ignored the hands trying to keep hold of her, pulled herself free and struggled up the conduit into the olive-grove.

A vast circle of olive trees had gone from the middle of the shady grove. The smoking, blood-spattered ground all around the bomb-crater was covered with blackened branches and the bodies of the dead.

'Oh – no …!' Her cry caught in her throat. She tripped over a tiny torso and went sprawling headlong beside it. It was a little girl, her thin clothes blasted away, the lower half of her missing. An elderly nun lay some distance from one of the children she had been taking to safety, recognizable only by her scorched and bloodstained grey habit and the shattered, twisted frames of her spectacles lying beside her. Raven was unaware she had picked up the mutilated child. She nursed her in her arms, clutching the girl to her breast like a bundle of rags.

That was where Keir found her, rocking back and forth on her knees in the olive-grove, a child's mutilated body in her arms, while pitiable sobs all around the olive-grove filtered through his consciousness like acid, drop by drop, eroding the rest of his numbed senses. He had been shouting her name along the road, like a madman searching the faces of the dead, terrified that she, too, had died like Tom Coles and so many others. 'Raven! Jeeze – thank God ... oh, thank God you're okay.'

She looked up at him, her white habit torn, blood- and dirt-stained as she tried so hard to keep calm while all the time her world was spinning and spinning – just whirling away upon the rims of fear, down into the craters of death ...

Keir looked down at Raven as though he could not quite believe it was she. Then he dropped to his knees beside her. 'Here, let me have the kid.'

'Don't hurt her,' Raven said.

'I won't.' Gently he took the Spanish child away and laid her down beside the nun.

'Dame Conceptión is dead,' Raven said in that same dull, resigned voice he recognized as deep shock.

He had difficulty speaking: hell was only ever for the living, never the dead. And all he wanted to do was hug her close in relief and thankfulness because she was alive and unharmed, and because sometimes he, too, needed the comfort of another human being's arms around him. 'Are you all right Raven? I mean – you're not hit by shrapnel or anything, are you?' He did not know why he had asked such a dumb question when he could see that she wasn't.

'I'm perfectly all right, so don't worry about me. I'm a veteran of bomb-attacks.' She looked down at the Red Cross knapsack still draped around her neck. 'This isn't much use now, is it? I mean, cotton-wool and bandages and iodine aren't going to heal this kind of war-wound, are they, Doctor?'

Across the lush valley of the Rio Ebro the 45th Division of the 5th Army Corps, under the command of General Lister, held fast the north of the river while the 35th, together with the British Battalion, held the south. The Spanish front line extended for 1,000 miles, while twenty-seven divisions of the Army of the Ebro launched the Republican offensive against Franco's Nationalist forces.

The main road to Zaragoza cut across the high, dry plateau of the Ebro, with the *pueblo* of Quinto lying some forty kilometres south of Zaragoza.

The Ebro offensive was to cut Nationalist communications, and rejoin the two halves of Republican Spain. Zaragoza was a Nationalist stronghold, so were Quinto and the hill of Pulburrel lying to the east of Quinto and joined to the plateau by a high neck of barren land. The British Battalion had been ordered to take Pulburrel Hill out of Nationalist hands. The Americans had already cut the vital water supply to Quinto and Pulburrel Hill.

Barbed wire, revolving gun-turrets and concrete emplacements made what was supposed to be a lightly guarded hill a suicide mission. Nationalist soldiers were entrenched on their impregnable hill-fortress and couldn't be shifted by repeated British ground-attacks.

Badly wounded in the stomach as he and his men, in the most appalling heat, tried to assault the Fascist position, Commissar Daly of the British Battalion later died in hospital. The new Commissar realized how deeply the Fascists were dug in and withdrew his men until adequate air-cover could be provided over the open ground surrounding Pulburrel Hill.

Early the following morning, before the sun reached its zenith and scorched the hide off them as on the previous day, the British moved forward again, this time with artillery support and anti-tank guns. The Lincoln Battalion provided covering fire.

Luck and the smiling gods were on the Republican side that day.

The Nationalist Air Force repeated their mistake of the day before and bombed the wrong target, Pulburrel Hill this time. The Fascists on Pulburrel Hill surrendered, blasted out of their stronghold by their own side, and ravaged by thirst on account of their water supply being cut off by the Americans.

The burly Negro soldier from the Lincoln Battalion who

had shared his breakfast with Keir the day before, never made it home: the Liberty Bell tolled for him right there on Pulburrel Hill.

The battle for the tiny villages of Quinto, Pulburrel Hill, and beleaguered Belchite was over. The Nationalist advance had been stopped, the Republicans had gained valuable ground, and the road to Zaragoza was now open for the Popular Front Army to follow up their overwhelming victory.

There was little consolation or respite for Keir in the long hours that followed. Only afterwards did he realize what had happened. The German bombers had dropped their loads five kilometres too far short of the strategic bridge of Fuentas del Ebro to stop the Republican advance towards Zaragoza.

He sent out stretcher-bearers to bring in the wounded. Together with three other Red Cross doctors and a few qualified Red Cross nurses, he operated all through the night by the light of car-batteries in a makeshift hospital hastily set up in the olive-grove. Casualties were enormous. Fortunately, the blood-transfusion unit which had been on its way to Zaragoza when the bombs dropped, went unscathed. He put Raven in charge of finding willing donors, a blood-bank desperately needed in the face of this kind of blind blunder made by the Nationalist and Republican Air Forces alike, the kind of blunder that had been made so often during this war as far as helpless civilians were concerned.

The Republicans, he learnt, had begun attacking on eight points: three offensives had been launched north of Zaragoza, two between Zaragoza and the village of Belchite, and three offensives to the south. Belchite might have been a strategic military target on the map of Spain, because the red beret Carlists were at Codo and other units of the Nationalist Army were pushing forward, but Belchite was twenty-five kilometres from Osera de Ebro, while The Red Cross convoy travelling towards Zaragoza was five kilometres from the Bridge of Fuentas del Ebro. Someone somewhere, Keir couldn't help feeling, had got their sights and their readings all wrong again. He wondered at the price of war while he amputated more limbs and stitched up more heads and bellies in one night than he had ever thought possible.

Only after twenty-four hours of standing beside his operating table, made out of an old farmhouse door laid on top of four wine barrels, did he pause in his labours. Under the olive-trees, standing on the perimeter of the crater that had become Dame Concepción's grave, Keir smoked a cigarette. His hands were shaking just like DaWinter's, his vision was blurred, and he felt more than a little unsteady on his feet. A voice beside him made him jump.

'I've brought you some soup before you collapse from exhaustion,' said Raven, unaware that in another field kitchen twenty-five kilometres away, Jaime de Luchar of the Carlist *Requetés* lay dead amidst his battered pots and pans. Against two thousand Republicans, two hundred Carlists had valiantly held their position at the *pueblo* of Codo, until overwhelmed by the sheer force of Republican numbers.

'Thanks,' Keir said. Taking the bowl from her, he sat down stiffly under an olive-tree, its leaves and fruit blasted away by yesterday's bombs. His aching back against the gnarled grey trunk. Keir pulled a face as he gazed into the contents of the bowl, which reminded him of what had covered his hands and surgeon's gown for the past twenty-four hours. 'Rhesus positive or negative?' he quipped.

Raven, too exhausted and still too shocked to smile back, said, 'It does look a little bit like that, doesn't it? But it's the best our chef could do in the circumstances. He's Polish and called this concoction *borsch*. Beetroot was all he could find around here.'

'Oh well, here goes.' Keir tipped the bowl to his mouth and drank just like a French peasant. Afterwards he shared a bar of chocolate with her, followed by another cigarette.

'I feel I can be of more help to you,' Raven said, adding, 'Bandaging and splinting is something any woman who isn't trained as a nurse can do, and your surgical nurse must need a break. Do you require a relief nurse to help you with your operations, because I'm willing?'

He looked at her steadily, and then said with the utmost integrity, 'What I require right now is relief of the neck muscles. You any good at massage?'

'I don't know, I've never massaged anyone before. But I can try.'

After a little while he grunted in satisfaction, 'I bet there aren't many guys who can say they've been given a massage by a nun.'

'I don't suppose there are many nuns who can say they've lived as dangerously as I.'

'That's true. But just think of all the sin-things you'll have to tell your father confessor.'

She stopped. The rhythmic movements of her hands on his neck and shoulders were beginning to convey other kinds of messages. 'Now you're mocking me – and right beside Dame Conceptión's grave. I don't think that's very nice.'

'Perhaps I am – not a nice person.' He caught hold of her hands and drew her round to face him.

Raven knelt down as he refused to get up, and what he had to say to her was both wonderful, and alarming. 'I *love* you even if that's not a very *nice* thing to say to a nun! I've been meaning to tell you for a long, long time. Yesterday proved to me how close to death we all are: and I'm not prepared to go to my grave without a fight, or revealing my true feelings for you. I love you and I want to live the rest of my life with you. Will you give up the convent and marry me when this war is over?'

She was so dumbfounded, all she could think of in reply was, 'You're already married.'

'I was married – once. Long ago.' He released her hands and looked away to the blackened trees. 'But that's all over and done with now. Francesca is out of my life for ever.'

'Why did you marry her if you hate her so much?' Raven asked, sensing it in his voice and his manner, while feeling closer to him now than she had ever felt before, closer even than at the Conservatoire in Geneva.

'I don't hate her, I despise her for what she did to Jodi and me.'

'Jodi?'

'My son.'

575

'Oh!' After a moment or two she was able to say. 'I'm sorry, but I didn't know you had a son. You've never talked about him before. But that must surely make you and your wife – I still call her your wife because the Roman Catholic Church does not recognize divorce – have some sort of bond. A child can only be a bond uniting the parents, no matter what their differences.'

'Jodi died.'

Again she was at a loss for words.

His son: and all those children who had died here in the olive-grove yesterday … at last she found her voice, 'But you must have loved your wife once, to have asked her to marry you in the first place?'

'She was going to have Jodi. We got married because of Jodi. Lust, Raven, not love.' Then, aware of the pain and the embarrassment he was causing her, Keir squeezed her hand. 'It's all right. You don't have to say anything. There's nothing *to* say. Francesca was all silk to slime. She tainted everything she touched. No sooner had I married her than I realized I had made the most monumental mistake of my life.'

'How – how did Jodi die?'

'Through neglect. Mother's *and* father's! Jodi was farmed out to other people who never cared two hoots about him, only the babysitting money. Francesca and I were always too busy trying to make money to spare our own child a moment of our adult time. And so Jodi became the human sacrifice to other people's errors, *mine* most of all. That's why we must find your young niece, Pippa. Children are so very vulnerable to the mistakes we adults make. They carry those mistakes with them their whole lives through – that's if they ever get to be adults.' Despairingly, he indicated the olive-grove.

'How old was Jodi?'

'Three years, four months.'

Why is life only ever so *sad*, Raven asked herself, as she, too, searched the olive-grove for answers. Raven thought about Dame Concepción, her rosary beads in her dead hands beneath the yellow earth. She thought about a grieving Spanish mother kneeling beside her small son on the perimeter of that crater. Only a small dark spot, like a

576

graze on his temple, showed how the little boy had died.
Keir had said a metal splinter had penetrated deep into
the child's brain. The pretty little boy had lain on his back
beside all the other dead children for burial last evening.
He wore a white shirt and grey shorts, white socks and
shiny black shoes with shiny buckles. His eyes were closed,
his dark thick lashes half-moons on his plump cheeks. He
looked just as though he were too sweetly lazy to get up
and go to school. Had he reminded Keir of Jodi? The little
Spanish boy's mother would not allow her son to be
buried, but kept putting on and taking off his shoes and
socks time and time again, while lovingly coaxing him to
wake up because it was time for *deysayuno* and he would be
late for school.

It was a sight Raven knew she would never forget.

Keir's voice from far away penetrated her thoughts. 'I
asked you a question just now. Will you give up the
convent and marry me?'

'I can't. You should not even ask me such a thing.'

'Why not?'

'I've dedicated my life to God.'

'Then why did you ask your Dame Superior or
whatever, for leave of absence from your convent?'

'She thought I wasn't totally committed to being a nun –
not after – after …'

'The Jesu María?'

She looked down at her hands. 'Yes – and so she gave
me time away from the convent to come to terms with
myself.'

'*She* thought? What about you? What about *your*
thoughts?'

'I think Dame Superior Olivera made a mistake.'

'Why?'

'Had she left me where I was, my thoughts and feelings
about God and the Church might have had a chance to
heal over in time. After what has happened here, I think
it's going to take me a lot longer to come to terms with my
spiritual life.'

'You are calling into question your faith?' Keir
demanded.

Raven gave a forlorn little smile. 'Now you sound just

577

like Monseigneur Paulus! No. Not my faith, *myself*. I know I shouldn't question, I should just accept things with the simplicity of a child – that is what blind obedience means. But I can't. Not any more. I am fighting my conscience and my commitment all the time.'

'Maybe that's because you don't love God as much as you love *life*, the *only* one you'll ever get! Maybe that's why you keep challenging it. Maybe that's why you keep questioning your conscience and your commitment, because you've *become* unhappy for having chosen the wrong thing for you – all this nun business. Maybe you need someone who *really* loves you quite apart from God Almighty. And maybe I'm presuming too much by shooting my mouth off in this fashion when we've work to do. Come on.' He got to his feet and, reaching out to give her a helping hand, hauled her off the stony ground with the added plea. 'I love you, Raven. Think about it.' Then he strode off, back to his makeshift operating theatre.

She helped with the sterilization of surgical instruments by first washing them in a bowl of water, then transferring them into the field sterilizing unit, which looked just like a fish-steamer plugged into an emergency generator. The four doctors operating, included Keir, Red Cross nurses and ambulance-drivers, voluntary anaesthetists and stretcher-bearers under that canvas awning marked with the Geneva cross, where transfusion-bottles were suspended on olive-branches, individual human endeavour was at its height.

In that moment, too, Raven began to see Dr Keir Devlin for his true value: she listened to him patiently instructing and encouraging a stalwart old man, an obliging refugee roped into holding the chloroform sponge over the patient's nose, while Keir himself never paused once with the suturing needle in his hand, and she knew why he was the man he was.

Then, as though her intent gaze upon him had triggered off a morse message, he lifted his head for the surgical nurse to wipe his streaming brow. His eyes met hers, and above the heads of everyone else in that olive-grove hospital, his message was for her alone.

I love you – think about it.

Raven smiled back. She wondered if he had ever heard of tetra perception.

The Republican victory was short lived because it was not followed up.

In the Spanish Parliament, the Cortes, the Socialist Minister of War and Finance, Indalecio Prieto y Tuero, wanted to know how a few insignificant *pueblos* in Aragon warranted such a massive and expensive campaign under Generals Lister, Walter, and El Campesino. It was argued that too many Russian generals were at the front, who treated the soldiers like vassals of Russia or dogs of war, not Spaniards fighting for their country.

The Republicans lost the ground they had gained and Zaragoza remained in Nationalist hands. The Army of Africa crossed the Rio Ebro, leaving behind them a burning testament of victory. The whole of northern Spain now under Nationalist colours, yet pockets of resistance continued.

The remnants of the Red Cross convoy had crawled on towards Zaragoza. Raven was not with Keir but conveying the wounded to hospitals around the city after the bombing-raid over Fuentas del Ebro, when Keir, trying to get some petrol for his battered yet reliable little Renault, stopped at a *pueblo* garage en route. On the other side of the road, in the village square, a large crowd had gathered. 'What's going on?' he asked the garage proprietor.

The Aragonese shrugged indifferently. 'A trial and execution.'

Keir was wary of these *Casa de Pueblo* trials, which usually turned out to be bloodthirsty tribunals hastily convened for the satisfaction of a few individuals in authority with imagined grievances. He crossed the road to investigate for himself.

Half a dozen Nationalist soldiers had been lined up under the trees, their hands tied, eyes blindfolded. A group of militiamen sat at tables in front of a kiosk bar, drinking beer, and smoking, while others with bayonets guarded the prisoners. The lethargic owner of the kiosk, in his vest and dungarees, sweated profusely behind his sticky counter, and from time to time scratched his armpit, while listening to the radio giving news of General Mola's progress through the Basque countries. Some of the soldiers were paying attention to the news, those with the bayonets prodded and goaded the captured Nationalists, while peasants and villagers abused and spat on them, some even kicking and hurling stones or rotten vegetables.

This couldn't be right, thought Keir as he bought himself a bottle of Coca-Cola at the kiosk. He took note of the soldier who seemed to be in charge of this rough *pueblo* group. Designated the rank of Major by the badge on his sleeve, he wore a black neckerchief as part of his uniform, whereas the six Nationalists tied up had these Anarchist scarves around their eyes.

'I'm Dr Devlin, a representative of the International Red Cross. I'd like to know what battalion you serve and what is going on here,' Keir said to the Major.

'Piss off, Señor Doctor!'

'Not until I know what you are going to do with these Nationalist soldiers,' Keir said, calmly swigging back warm Coca-Cola from the bottle.

'Then, if you really want to know, Americano, we are from the Durruti Column and this business is nothing to do with you. This is a Spanish matter.'

Remnants of the tattered Durruti Brigade, for Buenaventura Durruti, the Anarchist leader, had been shot dead in Madrid, Keir was now certain these Anarchist militimen were not acting officially, but taking out private vengeance on prisoners of war. 'If these Nationalist soldiers have committed no other crime other than that they are on the opposite side to you, Major, they are prisoners of war and you have no right to treat them in this fashion. If they have committed some other crime deserving of punishment, then they are entitled to a fair trial.'

'This *is* a fair trial. We're giving them thirty-six pesetas each to desert to our side: more if they had their rifles on them when we captured them to prove they weren't fucking at the time. Franco's *caballeros* will *all* decide to desert, otherwise we'll shoot them in their noble private parts, eh, my friends?' The Major turned to his men for support. They began to laugh, nudging each other and making derogatory comments about Keir's Red Cross armband.

Most of the soldiers were very young and very rough. Keir forgave them their stupidness, they couldn't help that. What he wasn't prepared to put up with was their taking the law into their own hands. 'What you are doing, Major, contravenes the Articles of the Geneva Convention in relation to the treatment of prisoners of war. I will make out a full report of this incident unless you stop this sham trial at once.'

The Major grinned fatuously, and threw away his cigarette. Then standing up, he flung up his arms in a temperamental gesture and almost knocked over his bottle of beer. 'Listen to him, friends! He thinks he is Jesus Christ just because he sports that bandage on his arm. Come with me, Señor Doctor, come!'

Keir followed the Major to some cattle-trucks drawn up on one side of the square. The Major opened the sturdy wooden doors. Half a dozen militiawomen were laid out on the floor of the truck like a row of sardines. All were in various stages of undress, all were dead. Keir could see for himself what had been done to them. The Major strolled to another cattle truck.

Nationalist soldiers, some wounded, all tied up, starved of air, thirsty, hungry, and broiled in the mid-afternoon heat were herded together like animals on the filthy, straw-strewn floor. Convinced that they were all about to be shot in batches of six by the Anarchists when the wagon doors were suddenly opened, they blinked in the bright sunlight, and saw Keir's armband. A little cheer went up. It was cut short by the Anarchist Major.

'Shut up, rapist pigs! Otherwise we shoot first then talk!' He turned to Keir, militiamen gathered behind him. 'Señor Jesus Christ, since you have appeared like a miracle to save the lives of these cowardly pigs who surrendered to us after they'd abused our women, you can have their bacon. Now you owe me one thousand, five hundred and twelve pesetas. We'll forget the interest on the rifles because we're keeping them.'

Keir found himself on the receiving end of Anarchist

guns, and knew they would not hesitate to shoot him as well as the prisoners if he said or did the wrong thing. But he was determined to have the last word. 'How do you know these Nationalist soldiers are responsible for what happened to those women?'

'Because, Señor Jesus Christ, we captured most of them with their bums in the air. Which side of this atrocity will you report to your newspapers, Señor Red Cross Doctor? Murder before or after rape? But it doesn't really matter, does it, as the dead don't talk and Spanish atrocities aren't *really* what's important to you, eh, non-combatant Americano? So cough up, or we open up!'

Thinking to himself what a stroppy little bugger the Major was, Keir handed over thirty good American dollars, his expenses for the time he was committed to stay in Zaragoza.

Durruti's men went off whistling and laughing to their vehicles and he was left to sort out what to do with forty-two captured Nationalist soldiers, some of whom were wounded, in a hostile village with no amenities, plus six dead militiawomen. Keir heard the Major chuckling to himself whilst tucking the money into his breast pocket. 'Jesus Christ was on our side today, my friends. Not a bad profit, heh? Thirty American dollars, which is a better exchange than one thousand, five hundred and twelve falling Republican pesetas. We've also got ourselves a truckful of German weapons, and no Fascist pigs to feed or bury tonight!'

The Red Cross ambulances had been a gift from the Swiss people to the people of Zaragoza. Those that were left and in functioning order after the bombing of the convoy were handed over to the Nationalist mayor of the town in a ceremony outside the *Ayuntamiento*. The ambulances were immediately put into service, while some of the nurses and doctors that had been attached to the convoy on the journey from Barcelona, were assigned to Zaragoza's hospitals or the Red Cross mobile services unit.

Raven was billeted with medical war services personnel in a small hotel close to the Town Hall. Her first wish had been to take a hot bath to cleanse herself of all the blood of the past few days, but the plumbing did not work, and all she was able to get from the bath-taps was a feeble trickle of yellow water. Removing the worst traces of what had happened in the olive-grove, she took from her one small piece of hand-luggage a change of clothing. She put her old soiled habit in the dustbin. In a clean white habit and head-dress, she went purposefully to the cathedral, the Basilica de Nuestra Señora del Pilar, where she spent the whole night in prayer.

Raven did not encounter Keir again on a personal basis for several days. He arrived in Zaragoza forty-eight hours after everyone else who had been with the damaged Red Cross convoy, muttering something about some Nationalist soldiers he had had to transfer to a prisoner-of-war camp. Raven knew how extremely busy he was, and kept out of his way. He had official meetings to attend, reports to make out concerning prisoners, missing persons, displaced persons, refugees and orphans, all such compilation and documentation having to be passed through the appropriate Red Cross channels in order to be acted on. He had to make a general inspection of Red Cross hospital units in the area, note their needs, their complaints, their shortages, as well as replenish stocks of medicines, food, blood, and bandages.

In the meantime she was asked by the local Spanish Red Cross official to help out at a nearby St John of Jerusalem orphanage while she remained in the city, and she turned to the task willingly.

Returning late one evening to the Hotel Don Quixote after a tour of duty at the orphange, she ran up the stairs to her room on the top floor, and bumped into one of the Red Cross nurses coming out of the bathroom.

Nurse Freya, a Norwegian girl, was jubilant. 'It works, it works, Sister Justina! The plumbing has been restored. I have just had the most delicious bath of my life, and if you're quick, you might be able to grab some hot water for yourself before it all disappears.'

Raven smiled in equal delight, and made haste to take her towel and tiny precious piece of soap and grab the bathroom before anyone else came in from duty. Twenty minutes later she unlocked the bathroom door after her glorious bath, peered round the door to make sure the coast was clear, and dashed back across the landing into her room before anyone saw her in her underclothes.

Keir was in her room, peering out into the darkening street below.

Startled to see him there uninvited, she stood by the closed door with damp hair and in her wet petticoat that clung to her like second skin. Feeling horribly self-conscious, she was only thankful that the room was in semi-darkness and he couldn't see her properly with her urchin crop and schoolgirl blushes.

He turned around from the window, equally astonished to see her standing there like something that had been dredged out of the Ebro. 'I'm sorry. I didn't know you were having a bath. I was told you weren't in yet from the orphanage and so I decided to wait up here for you rather than in the lobby, where I only get pestered.'

'What do you want?' She had not meant to sound quite so ungracious or accusing.

He held her in his glance. 'Don't make it sound as though I'm violating a nun's cell.'

'You are.'

'I came to tell you that I've done what I have to do in Zaragoza, and our next port of call will be Logrono, where I'm to exchange one set of important prisoners for another. We set off again tomorrow morning.'

So the surgeon was once again an official delegate of the International Red Cross; what a waste of his skills, she could not help feeling.

He saw the look on her face. 'What's the matter?'

'You were brilliant in the olive-grove. You saved so many lives that might otherwise have been lost. Why did you give up scalpel for Spanish pen and ink?'

'And now I have a question to ask you,' he countered. 'Do you always take a bath in your petticoat?'

'Yes.'

'Convent rule number ninety-nine, I suppose?'

'Yes.'

'I'm going. I promise not to peek at you as I creep past on my way downstairs. Go back to praying for God's guidance,

Raven. And sweet bloody dreams!' He swept past her in a couple of strides, and could be heard clattering down the linoleum-covered stairs.

Raven did not travel with him now that Dame Concepción was no longer around to chaperon them. Instead, she travelled in another car to Logrono with three Red Cross nurses, while Keir went in the official Renault with two other delegates on Red Cross business. The political prisoners for exchange were transported in a police van to the uninspiring town of Logrono, the capital of Là Rioja. There the exchange was to be made in the presence of the Red Cross delegates.

Raven, who had become used to sleeping rough, and had learned not to feel squeamish when eating out of the same pannikin in which she brushed her teeth, was pleasantly surprised when she and the other Red Cross nurses were decently housed by the local authority in a pretty little pilgrims' hostelry on the banks of the river Ebro. Vines covered the pergola over the terraced restaurant, and later that evening Keir and the other two delegates from Zaragoza joined the nurses for dinner. Raven, who was still tied by her vows of chastity, poverty, and obedience, could hear them all out on the terrace below her window, laughing and joking and generally imbibing a great deal of Rioja wine.

Suddenly she felt an outcast, and slightly rebellious.

No sooner had that emotion taken possession of her soul than she got down on her knees and began a decade of prayer. She couldn't find an answer, a solution, and certainly there was little solace in praying to the Virgin Mary when the one person who occupied her mind right now was enjoying himself in a worldly way in other company.

'*Hail Mary, full of grace, the Lord is with thee ...*' she continued to whisper in the darkness. 'Hear my prayer. Suddenly I want the good things of life when before they meant nothing at all to me. Suddenly I feel I'm missing things I am not supposed to miss. Suddenly I feel I don't belong in my novice's robes any more, and can't wait to be rid of them. Is this the way a novice on her way to becoming a fully-professed should feel? I know that a short time ago, while standing beside Dame Conceptión's grave as I said goodbye to her, and thinking about her as another Cassy, the right answer seemed to present itself – to become his wife if and when it becomes possible. Then, when the moment of disbelief and despair following Dame Conceptión's death left me, and I watched him saving lives in that olive-grove, I knew that I had a lot more thinking to do. We both of us have to do the right thing for us so that we won't, decades from now, hate each other for thwarting each other's lives when the passion and the spirit wear out. That's why I want to keep things the way they are now, and the way I am now. But I know that is not possible, for I have to make a final choice. I want him, and I want the peace of God's blessing through His Church, but I know I cannot have both. What am I to do?'

From Logrono they went to Pamplona in Navarre. Life had become a travelling circus, a never-ending voyage into the unknown. The only thing that made it all bearable was the man on the perimeter of her existence. Raven knew she was losing her ground: I love him, I love him not, I love him, I love him not – she plucked the petals of her confusion.

And more horror, so much horror in this war, Raven felt she could not turn around but be faced with the stark, staring eyes of death. And always the atrocities seemed to take place in an olive-grove.

The day was thundery, humid and thoroughly miserable for travelling long distances. Soaked in perspiration, dusty, irritable, tired, travel-sore, Raven was 'finding herself' the hard way. She, Keir, two nurses in the Renault with them, two Red Cross delegates and another nurse from Zaragoza following in the car behind with an official driver had stopped for a breather. Their small party of seven (the Red Cross driver having stayed with the cars) had wandered off the main road, into the shady grove to rest awhile and refresh themselves from the packed-lunch and flasks of cold drinks that had been provided for them, and there were the bodies dangling from the trees.

'Don't look!' Keir had said sharply, as he pulled her round to face him, forcing her head against his chest. Even his comforting hand on the back of her neck was a trespass upon her emotions, for the warning had come too late. Raven, filled with revulsion and disbelief against the close hand of murder and savagery in relation to her own life, was once more faced with the brutal extermination of something inside herself, for here again was a personal reckoning.

Keir had been unaware of the identities of the bodies, but to Raven the shock was all the greater for it was as though God, fate, an unseen hand, the Devil himself, was forcing her to look and look and look again into that mirror of life with all its childhood reflections of death and sinister uncertainties. Marta de Luchar was one of the three militiawomen hanging from an olive-tree.

Raven, choked to death herself in that carefree moment turned to tragedy, knew that she could have gone all over the world, over the rest of Aragon, Navarre, and Catalonia, and she might never have stopped to have a drink and a sandwich in an olive-grove anywhere, so why just outside Pamplona at five-thirty in the afternoon, so why now, why? She had only wanted to sit beside Keir and talk to him about happy things: no more olive-groves, no more, no more – and afterwards she had cried bitterly. 'I wonder what crime she committed other than to be on the wrong side?'

Keir said nothing; there was nothing to be said. He could only share in Raven's dark night of the soul while the bodies of the Spanish women were cut down and laid on the hard, stony ground and he was left to file away yet another official report on atrocities committed by one party upon another. Now where was the oval green-topped table in the Villa Moynier? And the terrible picture of the battle of Solferino to remind the world that war was evil not glorious, or the name of Henry Dunant that had first inspired the principles of humanity and the Red Cross emblem? And where the hell was the text of the Two Conventions all nations of the world had been asked to ratify?

The weather changed. Torrential rain set in, making travelling even more miserable. Soldiers on the move, Nationalist and Republican, all locked into the mountains, struggled on in bedraggled columns, weary and demoralized by a war that dragged on and on, while a second bitingly-cold winter in the sierras was all they had to look forward to. And what was it all for, anyway? Who could care less about Franco, Stalin, Mussolini, or Hitler, was the question bandied around among them.

Since the evening when she had found him in her room at the Hotel Don Quixote in Zaragoza, Raven realized Keir was avoiding any further personal contact with her. She found it practically impossible to talk to him alone without someone demanding his attention, or he himself made some excuse to keep out of her way. She knew his motive, he was giving her time to come to terms with herself, and to give him a firm answer before they reached Bilbao; yes, I will give up the convent; no I won't give up the convent, even for you.

On her last night in Pamplona Raven was in another dilemma.

The death of Dame Concepción on the road to Zaragoza had posed many more problems for her. She had no wish to embarrass Keir or herself, now that the three nurses who had been her constant companions for the past few weeks were leaving to join a refugee centre on the other side of the Navarrese Pyrenees. That would mean having to travel in her novice's robes, in the company of three men – four if one included the driver of the second car – all the way to Bilbao, for the delegates from Zaragoza were also going there. Raven doubted that even broad-minded Dame Superior Olivera would approve of that kind of liberty granted on a leave of absence. So she 'borrowed' a Red Cross uniform from Nurse Freya who was her size, with the excuse that she had lived in her remaining habit far too long and it would never survive the journey to Bilbao.

'You're welcome to it, Sister Justina, I've a spare issue. One thing easy to get hold of in this war is a uniform. That's all they make in Barcelona. Besides, now that you're on your own since Dame Concepción's death, you'll be better protected by a Red Cross outfit while travelling, rather than your nun's robes. I hope you manage to find your twin sister and niece soon.'

'Thank you. I hope you all have a safe journey to Pied de Port.'

In the morning Keir hardly batted an eyelid when he saw her in the navy dress, coat, and hat of an official Red Cross nurse. 'It suits you better,' was his only comment as he ushered her to the Renault.

'Where are Drs Marronettés and Réyes? Aren't they travelling with us?'

'They've gone on ahead with their official driver. I want you alone, all to myself on the last lap of our journey. Do you want to drive, or shall I?'

'I don't mind.'

'Lady! One day you're going to be able to make up your own mind. You drive. I'll sit and scribble notes beside you and take time off to gaze longingly at your knees.'

Her skirt was shorter than she was used to. She took pains to cover her stockinged legs, feeling very exposed as she took the wheel, and set off towards las Vascongadas.

'Don't worry,' said Keir beside her, 'I won't look – not deliberately, even though you've got lovely legs, which I haven't had the opportunity to admire since Geneva. I promised Dame Superior Olivera I'd take care of you until you'd sorted yourself out, and I'm a man of honour – I think. Why are you wearing Nurse Freya's uniform?'

'How did you know it was Nurse Freya's?'

'She told me before she left to expect a different woman today.'

'Gossip-mongers!'

'Have you made up your mind yet?'

'About what?'

He put his hand on the curve of her knee and disturbed her considerably. 'If you want to play it that way, I'm willing.'

'Dr Devlin, just because I'm out of my novice's habit, and there is no Dame Conceptión to act as chaperon, don't treat me as though I were Roxana.'

Startled, his hand came off her knee like a man scalded. 'Stop the car.'

'What?'

589

'Stop the car I said!'

'Why?'

Without warning he turned off the ignition. The Renault coasted to a jerky and grinding halt by the side of the main road. 'Now, what's this about Roxana?'

'Roxana told me that you and she had an affair in Geneva. I'm not prepared to be made a fool of a second time.'

'She told you that? I wonder why?' He seemed half-amused by it. Her militant yet healthy response was something else to make him smile.

Because of his negative reaction, Raven was suddenly not sure of her facts. 'Why – why should she want to make it all up?'

'Ask her. And why should I lie to you when I love you to distraction? Even though you do say and think the utmost garbage, *Sister* Justina!'

'Then – Roxana means nothing to you?'

'I love *you*! Since the very first day I met you in a hot and steamy cakeshop! Roxana and I mean nothing to each other. I have not had an affair with her, I have not been to bed with her, I have not made love to her, I have not seduced her even up a gum-tree, if that's what you're implying.'

'I'm sorry. I have no right to pry into your private life. But Roxana told me that she went to the Avenue de la Paix one evening just before your mother's wedding to try on her maid of honour dress. Your mother was not at home, but you were. She said you invited her in for coffee, and then you asked her to go to bed with you. After your mother had gone away for her honeymoon, at the end of the reception at Maison Roget, you again asked Roxana to keep you company because you were lonely.'

Keir's deep infectious laugh reverberated off the Renault roof. 'Is that what's been bothering you all this time, Raven?'

'Sister Justina.'

'Bullshit – no apology, either. Answer me.'

'I just want to be sure, that's all.'

'And what the hell was all that about "a second time"? Who made you look a fool the first time?'

'It doesn't matter.'

'Yes, it does – Oh, I guess I know. The guy with the motorbike – José, your *youth*-ful lover who tossed you aside. That's why you decided to become a nun, huh?'

Raven was determined to keep control. 'José de Luchar asked me to marry him – he never had any intention of fulfilling his promises, but I never knew that at the time. He and my sister were lovers. They had a child, Pippa. José married Roxana from necessity, not love. If you and Roxana were lovers, I'd like to know about it in view of the fact you say you love me and want to marry me. I think I'm owed that much.'

'With my fine, upstanding mother about to return to her apartment any moment and discover your sister's imaginative maid of honour appearance in my bed, you want to be sure about *me*?'

'Not about you. About Roxana. I know that she tells lies. I just had to be certain that this was just another one of her lies.'

'And now that you know, why is it so important to you if you're still the touch-me-not nun you make out you are under that very warm exterior of yours?'

'Because passions can either overcome us, or we can overcome them.'

Keir took a deep breath, and diverted his gaze to the long, wet, deserted road stretching away into the distance. 'My passions the night Roxana tapped on my mother's apartment door in the Avenue de la Paix went as far as offering her coffee before chucking her out. Not a very gentlemanly thing to have done, I admit, but I was still working Francesca out of my system. Roxana reminded me too much of my ex-wife. Besides, I also had other things on my mind at that time. Now tell me something. What are you aiming for by embracing all this nun and religion stuff?'

'Equanimity and contentment of spirit.'

'What will that achieve other than an unholy inward frustration?'

'At the moment I can't explain anything of myself to you, Kier.'

It was a start in the right direction: she had called him

Keir after a very long time. 'Were you in love with José de Luchar?'

'I *thought* I was when I was sixteen, seventeen and eighteen. But the answer is no.'

'Good. Then, *when* you've decided whether or not you want to be a Dame or a plain Mrs, let me know.'

She had to smile. But she also had to say, 'Right now I'm not ready for compromises, Keir.'

'But you expect me to be?' His voice was more a croak than a question.

She shot him a sidelong glance. 'I expect nothing except honesty from you.'

The woman behind the face that, long ago, had captivated him from a fashion magazine called *Bona Dia*, this was the Devil catching up with him yet again, denying him the angel's share. Raven Quennell had become the substance, the essence, the captivating creature spirited from the ghostly womb of his past; and he refused to relinquish any part of her, past or present, she was his future! But he also had to remind himself of his promise to Dame Superior Olivera, otherwise he might just sweep this mixed-up nun off her feet and straight into his arms. After that, it was anyone's guess what might happen.

He reached up and took off her brimmed hat and tossed it onto the back seat. 'Now I can see your face properly. I am not anyone. I am the man who loves you to distraction and yet you give me nothing in return.'

She didn't answer. She couldn't.

'Drive on,' he said abruptly. He picked up his file of notes lying by his feet under the dashboard. 'Guatemala,' he added presently, 'is paradise. One day, Raven Quennell, I'd like to take you to paradise and wipe out all conscious thought and phony notions from your silly little head.'

CHAPTER SEVENTEEN

Bilbao and Salamanca:
October – December 1937

One hundred and thirty kilometres further on, they reached Bilbao, a grim, grey, sluggish city overlooking the Nervion river. Kier stopped the car along the river embankment, switched off the engine, and said to Raven, 'Looks just like Pittsburg.'

'Cork,' said Raven, remembering some scenes of Ireland in an old picture-book from her childhood.

'I've never been to Ireland.'

'I've never been to America.'

'Tell you what, let's do a deal. You marry me and we'll do both. Now then, shall we eat on the east bank, the west bank, or in my room?'

'I'm surprised you've got any time off. Haven't you been invited to some official reception tonight by the Basque officials waiting to welcome you to their city?'

'Tomorrow night. I've arrived a day early.'

'A hero's welcome again!'

'Not really. Usually Government officials and house-wives only want to tear me limb from limb for not being able to deliver as promised. Most RC delegates, Red Cross in this instance and not Roman Catholic, have this great communication problem.'

Raven, leaning over the passenger seat as they had swapped driving places halfway, took her hat and bag from the back. 'Where am I billeted tonight?'

'Where do you want to be billeted?'

'Since I'm homeless and chaperonless, I think I ought to book in at the nearest Mother House and explain my position to the Mother Superior.'

'No deal, Raven. I'm not putting you back in any cloister now that you're halfway to coming out of it. How about driving out of town again and finding a little Basque farmhouse, where I promise not to seduce you over dinner unless you ask me.'

'What a pity we weren't nearer to San Sebastian!' she sighed.

'Why? Would that make a difference?'

Ignoring his teasing, she explained, 'Le Comte de Martello has a villa there. We would have found immediate accommodation.'

'We can find immediate accommodation right here in Bilbao. The best hotel in town, if that's what you want.'

'No, I don't think so. It wouldn't be right. I ought to try and find a convent to give me sanctuary for the night.'

'What're you afraid of, Raven? Me, sex, God, or the Devil?'

'None of those.'

'Then what?'

'Happiness. It's too fleeting even to be captured. I'm half-afraid to capture it.'

'So you want to spend your whole life being miserable, making me miserable, too?'

'I would like to be able to spend my life with you once I know that is the right thing for both of us. At the moment everything in my life is incomplete. Completeness in our lives is what I want, and, I think, is what you want. Besides, I am still tied by my vows of poverty, chastity, and obedience, and even though I'm alone and without another nun to keep me on the straight and narrow, I must obey the rules. I'm half-afraid to even talk to you.'

'Oh Raven!' He clasped her hand tightly and then let go as though unable to bear the contact. He stared out of the darkened windscreen to the city lights flanking the Nervion River. Raven and God, Francesca and the Devil: there must be a moral there somewhere. He turned on the engine and let in the clutch. 'We'll go straight to Red Cross Head-quarters.'

Keir spent days and days sorting through card indices and files, trying to build up a picture of what had happened to Roxana de Luchar, Pippa, Vida de Martello de Luchar, and so many other women and children on the last few nights of Basque resistance before the Nationalists entered the city.

Always he encountered a blank wall.

The Basque minister informed him that all Nationalist women and children captured between 26 April and 26 July had either been released or taken to a place of safety.

'What safety?' Keir insisted.

'Where orphan children were concerned, Dr Junod arranged for the British ship *Exeter* to evacuate them to France.'

'But I cannot find any names on these lists to correspond with the names of the people I'm looking for!' Keir, in exasperation, knew he was getting nowhere fast. 'Look here, señor. *Someone* must know what happened to a little girl called Pauline de Luchar, diminutive Pippa, aged three when she disappeared off the records in Bilbao along with twenty-five women and their children.'

'Then Señora de Luchar and her daughter, together with her sister-in-law, the Señora de Martello de Luchar, and the child's nanny, must have been sent home,' the Basque minister replied pedantically.

'They are not in Salamanca. I have checked.'

'Then you must ask the governor of the prison-ship, *Menor*. You must understand, Señor Doctor, that Bilbao was in a great state of chaos just before the Army of Africa arrived. It has continued to be in a state of chaos ever since.'

Keir grit his teeth and contained his frustration. Although Bilbao was in Nationalist hands, the Basques still retained a certain amount of autonomy in the handling of their own internal affairs. so it was with great difficulty he was able to extract any information at all from Basque officials, who had become very close-mouthed since the arrival of Franco's forces. But he persevered, painfully. 'The governor of the prison-ship, *Menor*, has since been shot by the Nationalists. And before you ask me to turn my attention to the governor of Bilbao prison, I have already checked the prison records. Nothing of what went on between 26 April and 26 July has been officially recorded, and I can get no sensible explanation from the new prison authorities. Now, I want someone who can furnish me with proper answers, otherwise I file this incident as a Spanish atrocity.'

'Guernica was also a Spanish actrocity, Señor Doctor, despite what General Franco and his high Command and the newspapers have told the whole world. The town was *not* heavily defended, it was not a centre of resistance, they did not shoot down Nationalist planes simply because there *were* no weapons in Guernica. It was an ordinary, everyday market town, its citizens leading quiet, peaceful lives, that is all. Saturation bombing for the first time ever, by German planes on an undefended town, upon innocent people taking their afternoon siesta, can be nothing else but a deliberate act of aggression. Where were our humanitarian rights on that day, Señor Doctor? Where were the articles laid down by the Geneva Convention for the protection of human life on that day, Señor Doctor?'

'That is why I am here, Señor Vincenté. To document such atrocities in order that they may never be repeated.'

'You think that is so?'

'I can only *hope* that it will be so in any future conflict.'

Keir left the *Ayuntamiento* without any satisfaction whatsoever. Nothing, absolutely nothing, had he learned about the *Menor* affair. But he was more than ever determined to find out the real truth behind the mysterious disappearance of women and children from that prison-ship.

And always in the back of his mind there was solitary Raven. Each day that passed, resolution multiplied. He would extract the truth from the Basques as he would undermine Raven's resistance. He would *make* her break with the idea of being a Catholic nun to become a Catholic wife and mother instead. She wanted love, she needed love, He wanted to give it to her – romance, love, passion, sex, marriage, kids, the lot, so what the hell!

*

One night, Keir went to a bar in the Casco Viejo. Bars, he had discovered since his days in the company of a defrocked Jesuit priest by the name of Father Silvestre, were marvellous centres of intelligence.

After his fifth night of hard drinking, he was rewarded. He was in a little dockside taverna swigging down his umpteenth warm Coca-Cola and picking over the *tapas, calamares, anchoas, langostinas* and garlic meatballs, when a horrible little urchin with a gap in his front teeth dragged at his jacket sleeve, '*El Americano*! You look for a woman?'

Keir, from his superior height on the bar-stool, looked down into two golden eyes as beguiling as fudge and said in Spanish, 'Don't tell me. You're a starving-to-death apprentice pimp ... Care for some squid, kid?'

'Señor Doctor, I am serious. You want a woman?'

'What sort of woman?'

'She sees you on your first night in another bar and knows you want something more than just sex.'

'*Is* there anything more than *just* sex? Gee, kid, you're great stuuff, you know that! So tell me, what do I want if it isn't sex?' Keir skewered a garlic meatball with a toothpick.

'Information.'

'Who from?'

'This woman I am talking about.'

'What woman?'

'This woman I am talking about.'

Keir gambled his disadvantage. '*Calamares* or clear off, niño.'

His sleeve was wrenched again. 'Señor Doctor, this militiawoman knows what happened in the church of St Zavior on the night the Nationalist women and their children were taken there. She knows you want information.'

'How much?' Keir concentrated on his *tapas*.

'Two thousand, one hundred-twenty Republican pesetas.'

'Get lost, *niño*!'

'To you rich Americans that is only fifty dollars – give and take a few cents. I am being generous.'

'I said, get lost.'

'What is ten pounds to a rich man?'

'Plenty.'

'Then I cannot help you, Americano. Information has its price.' He struck his right fist into his left elbow and drew his arm up in a gesture that would have made Keir clout him round the ears had the urchin not reached the door.

'Hey, wait a minute!'

The boy accelerated back to Keir's side. 'Okay. A deal?'

'A deal. And a bar of chocolate if you take me straight to her with no messing.'

The militiawoman wanted the money first.

She tucked it away down her bosom. 'I am a hunted woman since the Nationalists occupied Bilbao. This is not my town, and I hate it.' She spat contempt.

'From where do you come, señora?'

'Guernica.'

'She lost everything so has become a collaborator,' the boy interrupted.

'Shut up! I'm telling this story to the American doctor!'

'Who is this boy, your son or grandson?' Keir asked.

'He is an orphan. We have adopted each other. His family were killed at Guernica. My husband and six children were killed at Guernica. What else do you want to know, Señor Doctor?'

'What were you doing in the Church of St Zavior the night the Nationalist women and children were shot?'

'I was defending the liberty of the Basque people. But the Nationalist women were not shot – none of them. Though we all felt like it.'

Keir took a deep breath. At last he was getting somewhere. 'Tell me what really happened, señora.'

'The women and children from the prison-ship, *Menor*, were taken to the main prison in the town. Then, on a certain night, they were transferred to the crypt of the Church of St Zavior.'

'On whose orders?'

'Orders, orders, Señor Doctor!' The Basque woman waved a hand in the air derisively. 'Who obeys orders in this war? Even the People's Army do not have generals but all are equal in rank. Some foolish commissar or other might have given the order, who knows? Anyway, you want to know what happened to these women and children and I am trying to tell you. They were not killed, though many of us from Guernica wished to see them dead. But what does revenge achieve, Señor Doctor? We are simple people. We live by our families, and our livestock, our sheep and goats and pigs and green grass, the fish in the river and the sea. To kill more women and children does not bring back all that, it only serves to make double trouble. We took away their children first, just to let them know what it felt like to be deprived of their loved ones. Then we lined them all up against the wall. They thought they were about to die, and so they fell down on their knees and began to pray to the Virgin Mary.'

She paused and wiped her pale, dewy face with a grubby handkerchief taken from her uniform overalls. Keir didn't dare interrupt for fear of losing her altogether.

'Then we opened fire on them. But we fired above their heads, at the pillars of the crypt, not at the women. We wanted to frighten them, that's all. We wanted to teach them the lesson we had learned at Guernica.'

'What about the blood-stains soaked into the stones of the crypt, and the bullet-scars everywhere? I have seen them, only today.'

'*Semana Trágica* – Tragic Week thirty years ago, Señor Doctor. I was a girl of ten and saw what happened then, and I never thought to see it happen again. There was so much blood that time, those stones will never be clean again. That is why I and others like me could not kill the Nationalist women despite what they had done to us.'

'But those women did nothing to you, señora,' Keir reminded her gently.

'Yes, they are guilty!' she replied fiercely. 'Marriage is a combination of two souls as well as bodies! Two hearts and minds and ambitions, Señor Doctor! Those Nationalist women were as much a part of their legionnaire husbands' atrocities in Asturias as I am part of the death of Guernica.'

Once again he had no answer. His plea was simple. 'I am here on a peace mission, I take no sides. Tell me what happened to those women and children and I'll leave in peace.'

'Then you are an extraordinary man, Señor Doctor. Most men want war. They want to fight each other, to dominate and subjugate and dictate. But now that I know who you are and what you are, let me tell you this. The women in the crypt were allowed to go free. After their little scare at the receiving-end of our sub-machine-guns, they were left alone. What happened to them after that was their own business. The church doors were left open. There were no guards or guns. They were free women.'

'And the children?'

'They went back to their mothers. If they could not find their mothers, then they were shipped to a refugee camp in Mexico.'

'Thank you señora.' At the door he hesitated, then turned back to her. 'Do you know what became of Señora Roxana de Luchar and her young daughter, Pippa?'

The Basque woman shrugged indifferently. 'The names do not ring a bell. If she was in the crypt of St Zavior that night, she was not killed. I tell the truth. Try elsewhere.'

'*Muchas gracias*, señora.'

'*De nada*: it is nothing, Señor Doctor. I still have to live with the ghosts of Guernica.'

The Nervion river was like the boy's eyes, golden-brown, deep and polluted as the life artery of Bilbao. The night air smelt of dead fish.

The boy tugged his sleeve. 'You want to know more?'

'How much more?' asked Keir.

'Only one thousand and sixty pesetas. But this time Nationalist pesetas, you understand.'

'How old are you?'

'*Ocho*.'

Only eight! By the time he was ten he would be a right little swine. But then Keir pulled himself up short. Hell, no! Bastards and saints were not selected at birth, they were given a free choice. Keir said grimly as he hauled the urchin up by his ragged pullover front, 'Listen good, Sonny Jim! If you've got anything more to say to me, I'm not paying. But I'll tell you what, you do me a favour, and I'll do you one. No pesetas, only you and me, *entiendes*?'

The boy with his feet off the ground, grinned his gap-toothed, engaging smile, 'How do I know that, Americano?'

'I'll drop you a postcard from time to time if you leave me your address. Okay, Mickey Mouse?' He set the child back on his feet and held up his palm.

The boy slapped his hand down in the big friendly palm. 'Okay, Americano. You give me chewing-gum and I'll take you to another lady. This one is *really* crazy! She likes many men, but lives only with a Swedish one who is crazier than she. She does her business when he is not at home, you understand. I hope we don't bump into him tonight. He'll *kill* you.'

Eleven-thirty at night, and the nightlife of war-torn Spain was only just beginning. Keir, finding himself ascending the filthy wooden staircase of another shabby riverside apartment house, much like the one he had just left, wondered what else was in store for him this night.

He was totally unprepared for the sight of the woman with nicotine-stained fingers and a grubby dressing-gown who opened the door after his fervent bashings on the wood. '*Roxana!*'

'Keir! Holy Moses – what are you doing here?' She peered over his shoulder and discovered the boy. 'Out! *Viajazo!*'

Keir raised an eyebrow in surprise.

The boy wagged his finger at Roxana. 'Tomorrow morning I will not bring you *churros* and chocolate.'

'*Va, quitamotos!*'

Again Keir looked at a loss, standing there on the landing like a fish out of water, while wondering from where Roxana had picked up her descriptive vocabulary.

'I told you she was crazy,' said the boy, screwing a finger to his head before scampering down the dark stairwell.

'You mustn't stop long, Keir, I'm expecting someone.' Roxana drew him into the room and quickly shut the door. 'Who's with you?'

'No one. I'm by myself.'

'Darling Keir, have you a cigarette?'

He offered his packet of Lucky Strikes and she took one. He lit it for her. The room was awful, smelling of onions and garlic and other unnameable odours. Claustrophobic and gloomy, a small, curtainless window overlooked the river where a hundred such apartments flapped their dingy washing from the windows and balconies, and refuse was flung straight into the Nervion. The remnants of a meal for two, and a half-finished bottle of red wine remained on the table. Saucers, bottle-caps, anything that could be used as an ashtray, were everywhere full. Cobwebs hung in tatters from the ceiling and from a greasy bare light-bulb. A couple of other doors which led off from the living-room Keir assumed were bedroom and kitchen. It reminded him too much of Francesca's higgledy-piggledy apartment in Sloane Court, New York City.

Perched on the arm of a fireside-chair drawn up to the window, Roxana inhaled deeply before turning to him. She regarded him over her shoulder with hostility. Her red hair was touseled, her nail-varnish chipped. She was thin, dishevelled, distraught, and looked twenty years older than when he had last seen her in Paris. She smoked nervously while she monitored the window.

'Roxana,' he began, but she cut him short.

'I know why you've come, Keir. Her father sent you, didn't he?'

'I don't know what you're talking about. No one *sent* me. I came here of my own accord.'

'Why?'

'Because we wanted to find you.'

'We?'

'Your grandfather, Raven ... all of us.'

'You too?'

'Me too.'

'She's dead, if that's what you came here to find out.'

'Pippa?'

'Vida – though Pippa might be too, for all I know.'

'Vida de Martello – de Luchar – how?'

'The Nationalists shot her when they took Bilbao. I don't want to talk about it.' She turned resolutely back to the window and began picking off what little paint was left on the sill.

'Roxana,' he said indulgently, 'I'm here to help you. I

want to know the full story so that I can make out an official report about what really happened.'

'So you're not really here because of me but because of your official report?' She blew smoke at the steamy widowpanes. 'Thanks a lot, Doc!'

'Of course I'm here for you. We all thought you were dead.'

'I *am* dead. I am *dead, dead, dead* in this awful place!' She banged the windowsill with the flat of her hand in angry frustration.

'Then why do you stay?'

'Because there's nowhere else for me to go, and I have no money.'

'There's Salamanca with your husband, and Cabo Alondra with your grandfather.'

'I don't ever want to see José again! Look, Keir,' she turned back to him, 'you really will have to go now.'

'Roxana, where is your daughter?'

'They took her away – the Basques – I can't talk to you tonight.'

'Tomorrow then?' He could see how agitated she was and he didn't want to upset her any further.

Roxana got off the arm of the chair and went to the sideboard where she poured herself a full glass of cheap brandy. 'Do you want some?' she remembered to ask as she turned to him.

'No thanks.' Then he repeated his question. 'Will you promise to talk to me tomorrow, Roxana?'

'Yes,' she said in abstraction. 'Yes, come back tomorrow afternoon.'

He got up from the tattered sofa and Roxana asked, 'Can I cadge another cigarette from you?'

He left the packet with her. He had no doubt in his mind as to how she kept herself, or the brandy on her sideboard.

Raven thought she heard a sound outside her door. She still had the light on. It was almost one-thirty in the morning and the last time she had gone down to the reception desk to check if Dr Devlin was back, the night porter had given her a funny look. The whole building, of what had once been a grand hotel, had been commandeered by the Nationalists for use as offices. The Red Cross had been assigned part of the building. Sleeping accommodation was in the former servant-attics and Keir's room was further along the dark corridor. She hoped nothing had happened to him in his search for Roxana. She knew he was trying to glean information by haunting the less salubrious areas of the city.

Raven opened her door and peeked around it into the lonely corridor, and the shadow outside moved. She jumped back in alarm and Keir said, 'Don't worry, it's only me.'

'Keir! What on earth are you doing skulking in the dark like that?'

'Trying very hard to hold back my desire for you ...' He came inside quickly, closed the door, turned, and before she knew what was happening, had taken her into his arms.

He was only glad he had given neither of them a chance to pause for breath because he would have hated to lose out on the moment.

If just holding her in his arms and kissing her could feel so bloody marvellous, what would the rest feel like? God! he mustn't even think about it.

He released her and flung himself down on the hotel bed and lay there like a dead man, his arm across his eyes. He couldn't touch her or look at her any more and remain in control, not while she wore only her thin nightdress. 'I've found Roxana,' he said just to take his mind off what his body was telling him it wanted from the woman he loved. 'I couldn't sleep – and so I went for a walk. I saw your light was still on when I got back – heard you were asking for me.'

Raven hardly heard him. She was still shaking from head to toe by that brief contact with him, his mouth crushing hers, his arms enfolding her so closely she had felt soldered to his body and his will. She hadn't wanted him to let go of her quite so abruptly. She didn't want to know about her sister or anyone else: she regarded him stretched out on her bed in an attitude of despair and neglect. She wanted to go to him, put her arms around him, and to welcome thereafter whatever might come of the moment, but she reminded herself when she was almost seduced by her own thoughts, you have relinquished the world and all hope of a personal relationship with a man; you have taken holy orders and made holy vows to that end ...

Yes, but vows you've broken a million times over, she again reminded herself. This time you have failed miserably, and behaved abominably in so far as you *are* still under vows, however temporary. *Mea culpa, mea culpa, mea culpa* ... I'm sorry Dame Superior Olivera, and you too, God, for I have succumbed to the temptations of the flesh, and now I will have to tell my confessor of it – but it's just that Keir gives me back my identity so that I'm *only fully alive* when he's around. I know I've relinquished my wordly identity, but sometimes it keeps returning to tempt me: and a flesh and blood man as nice as Keir Devlin is so much easier to love than an intangible spirit floating around in the heaven of my mind.

Raven took a long, deep gulp of air. Never had she felt so happy, so liberated! José hadn't made her feel anything but guilty and inadequate: Monseigneur Paulus had never made her feel anything but pious and virginal. But Keir – Keir made her feel worthwhile and wanted: Keir made her feel that sitting beside him in a rocking-chair after the passion and the spirit wore out wasn't such a bad proposition, after all; that holding hands in the darkness of night amidst one's own inner darkness, and without a word being spoken, but to know that you were loved despite all, would be oh so comforting and worthwhile!

I am so confused: the windmills of my mind keep turning and turning, forcing me first in this direction and then that one, so that I'm not sure where I belong! Blow Dame Superior Olivera for making me lose track of my spiritual aims by involving me in all that Bible-smuggling in the first place!

Where was the Holy Spirit in all that earthly business? she asked herself. And really, flesh and blood was what it was all about, wasn't it? All that 'touching' nonsense forbidden between Rome's chosen people just wasn't natural, not when God had intended it in the first place. It had just been proven to her how very weak and willing was *her* human flesh, because she wanted Keir to kiss her again … 'Roxana?' she asked, her voice sounding funny in her ears. 'How is she?'

'Just the bitch she's always been. Her sister-in-law is dead. Shot by the Nationalist's for being a Communist. And in answer to your next question, no, I have not discovered the definite whereabouts of Pippa de Luchar, but I believe her to be in Mexico, at some refugee centre or other. If so, we'll get her back after the war. Thirdly …' he said as he heaved himself off the bed, 'if I stay here much longer, I shan't be responsible for my actions. I just came to tell you that there's *no problema* as far as your sister is concerned. She didn't say much, but she'll talk to us tomorrow.'

He turned to the door, ready to take his leave. Because she wanted to keep him a little longer to herself, Raven found herself delaying his departure in the turmoil of her emotions. She said simply, 'Thank you, Keir, for what you've done for Peedee and me.'

'*De nada* …' And then, because she looked so sweet and lost in that moment, he was caught up in his own welter of confused emotions, so that he almost threw caution to the four winds. But he also knew that any physical act between them now would mean a lifetime's compromise thereafter, and he didn't want that: he wanted every part of her to cherish fully without restrictions of any sort. 'I love you,' he told her. 'I love you with wet hair or dry, long or short. I love you whether you bathe in your petticoat or not. I love you in your Geneva head hugger, your nun's holy wings, Nurse Freya's uniform, and especially this nightdress.' He touched her forehead tenderly, brushing the lumpy scars of her childhood with a surgeon's fingertips and eye for detail, searching her face and the truth of what he had just heard from her own lips to make him feel all his persistence had been worthwhile: and he loved her imperfections most of all because they were the most human part of her. 'I live in hope,' he said, before making himself scarce.

The following afternoon Keir parked the Renault outside

the dockside flats where Roxana lived. It was a murky grey afternoon with mist settling on both banks of the river. The hills above the city were occluded by industrial pollution from the factories, steel and shipbuilding works, as well as the sooty twilight drizzle. The Nervion River was like a thick swathe of oily milk, jammed with all kinds of craft, mostly naval warships. Above the east bank the strange spire of the Viscayan holy shrine of the Basilica de Begona had a little light burning on the top to warn low-flying aircraft.

Raven pulled a face. 'What a sordid area.'

'I warned you, didn't I?'

'I wonder why she doesn't want to go back to José?'

Keir didn't answer, but opened the car door for her.

They ascended the wooden stairs that hadn't been swept in a decade. Cigarette-butts, hair, dust, and spittle were everywhere. On the top floor Keir knocked on Roxana's door, but there was no reply.

After five minutes a little voice behind them piped up, 'She is not at home.' Two fudge eyes and a cheeky face peered at them through the banisters, the boy's chin on a level with the landing floor.

'Where is she, niño?'

'At the pictures, Americano.'

'Cinema?' Raven looked at Keir enquiringly.

'The Englishwoman always goes to the movies with him in the afternoon,' the boy said.

'Who's him?' Keir asked.

'Her Swedish amorcillo. Best you come back tonight when he is away on his new boat, otherwise he will kill you. He does not like her seeing other men – but sometimes she does, when of course he is not looking.'

'Why don't you go jump in the river, little boy,' Keir said angrily as he followed Raven's hasty descent to the street.

'I am only telling the truth, Americano. Many chulas operate from this building.'

Keir, in passing, took satisfaction in swiping el niño across the ears.

On the quayside Raven took several deep breaths.

'Hell honey – don't get upset, there's a war on.'

'Don't call me honey, ever!' Raven got into the front passenger seat of the Renault and slammed the door.

Keir lit a cigarette before he got in beside her. He was trying hard not to smile. The force of her feelings were extremely human! And *twice* in twenty-four hours, when he remembered her long, slender legs and beautiful body against his and the heady eager kisses she had returned in the early hours of this morning. It all added up to the fact that Sister Justina wasn't quite as frigid as she tried to make out behind her holy habit: he was glad to know.

Raven said, '*You* can go back there alone! From now on I don't really care what happens to her. She doesn't care about anyone except herself. Not her missing daughter, not her husband, not Peedee, or me, no one, so let her get on with her own life *whoring*, if that's what she wants!'

Keir sat on the draughty, dirty stairs smoking a cigarette while waiting for Roxana. When she arrived back it was past midnight, but she was alone. He did not think she would have been without an escort, had not Gappy-Gob with the fudge eyes warned her of his presence outside her apartment door.

'Raven and I came here this afternoon to see you,' he said tautly.

'Lars was home so we went to the movies. He's a sailor and does the night run between the French port of St Jean de Luz to Bilbao or Santander. Foreign boat owners, you know darling, can earn themselves one hundred per cent profit for conveying essential supplies to blockaded Spanish towns. Anyway, we have all night to talk, so don't be angry with me. I just couldn't face Raven, that's all. She's so censorial of everything I do.'

'Christ, Roxana! She has every right to be! She has risked everything to find you and Pippa.' He turned to face her on the dimly-lit landing. 'Why did you not let your family know that you were safe and well? A hell of a lot of people have been worried sick about you.'

'That's nice! But I haven't been safe or well, and that's the truth.' She turned the key in the lock and let them in. 'Let's talk inside. I'm glad you're here to keep me company tonight.'

'Because you've warned off your other customers?'

She went to the sideboard and helped herself to a drink. 'You're *really* pizzicato about sex, aren't you darling? Just like Raven. You two make a good pair.' Standing with her back to the sideboard in her smart green dress, coat, and hat, high-heeled shoes and silk stockings, with her copper-gold hair prettily groomed, such a change from the unkempt woman of the night before, Roxana regarded him with some amusement, a little smile playing around her shiny scarlet lips. 'I've finished with José for *ever*! Cheers!' She raised her glass defiantly. 'Keir darling, won't you sit down and make yourself comfortable? Or are you as nervous of me now as you were on the night I came to your mother's apartment, alone, in the Avenue de la Paix?'

'Roxana, let's just get one thing straight, shall we? I'm here on official business and haven't time to waste on you if you don't want my help. I want to know the truth about the *Menor* episode, then I will leave. You can either travel with Raven and me back to your husband in Salamanca, or you can stay here and hook for a living. The choice is yours. But Raven and I are still determined to find the whereabouts of Pippa, even if you don't care about your own child.'

'That is *harsh*, Dr Devlin!' She put her glass on the table, came across to him, and prodded him in the shoulder with a blood-red varnished fingernail. 'Pippa is my child, of course I'm concerned as to her whereabouts. Meanwhile, I have to live!'

'Doesn't your husband support you?'

'My husband has *never* supported me.'

'I don't really care about the frills, Roxana, just give me the facts.'

'Very well. I'll give you *facts*, if that's what you want.' She tossed her hat aside, threw off her coat and shoes and settled herself down with her shapely silk legs over the arm of the sofa. She stared up at him, standing in the middle of the room beneath the harsh light-bulb that turned his face into a granite mask in which blue eyes burned angrily. 'Relax Keir! I'm not going to eat you. Just light me a cigarette, darling.'

She had probably spent all evening propping up a bar

with some sailor or other, because she was so pie-eyed. Keir lit her cigarette while wishing to wring her selfish little neck.

Glancing in disdain at the cheap cigarette he had offered her, Roxana removed a fleck of tobacco from the tip of her tongue. 'I thought a sophisticated man like you would at least go for American Virginias, not Government issues.'

'Neither do I often buy a packet. I get them given me by grateful folks.' He pulled out a wooden chair by the table and sat down.

'*Touché*, darling!' Roxana smiled without caring less, then said, 'She wanted to stay with me …'

'Who wanted to stay with you?'

'Vida. The night in the crypt she wanted to die with me …'

'Can we start at the beginning, Roxana, I'm lost already.'

'We were sailing the Cantabrian coast in the Comte's yacht, when we saw the Germans bombing Guernica …'

'You actually saw the Germans bombing Guernica?'

'Yes. We took pictures from the yacht. Is that important to you, darling, or shall I skip the frills?'

He was very interested. 'All reports from the Nationalists claim that Guernica was destroyed by the Republicans, the Anarchists having planted bombs in the sewerage system to blow up the town, and that there was no aerial bombardment by German warplanes, only Russian Chatos.'

'I suppose you read all that in Luis Bolín's Monarchist newspaper *ABC*, as we all did. Well, all those reports were untrue, because Franco had to defend himself somehow, I suppose. We saw for ourselves the Condor Legion's warplanes in action. Louis – Vida's Louis that is – has got pictures of the whole thing. The Germans dive-bombed the town for several hours so it was no mistake, but a deliberate bombardment to destroy the town completely.'

'Who is this Louis?'

'One of Vida's French friends, Louis-Jou. He's a professional fashion photographer who was on holiday with us. He had a *very* expensive camera that could take pictures of anything from any distance or angle.'

'Where is he now?'

'Back in France. He lives in Paris.'

'Go on,' he prompted, as he filed away the name of

Louis-Jou into his mental filing cabinet.

'Well then, the Basques captured us just before the Nationalists arrived. Bilbao was bombed and bombed and I thought we would all die like rats on that stinking prison-ship. Then we were taken off the *Menor* and transferred to the main prison in town where conditions were even worse. Every day cell doors would be opened and the names of the people to be shot would be called out. One night we were taken to the Church of St Zavior and left in the crypt. Then Pippa was taken away from me by an evil-smelling Basque sailor.'

'Why didn't Vida leave Bilbao while it was still in Republican hands?'

'She wouldn't leave me. She said she loved Pippa and me more than Ramiro, and she didn't care what happened to her as long as we could be together. She was – she was crazy! But they didn't kill us. They brought out their guns, those *horrible, fat* militiawomen! Then they began laughing at us when everyone fell down praying. I didn't pray. I don't believe in God or anything. I've never prayed: not when Cassy preached her fire and brimstone gospels, or when Tim and my parents were killed, and not even when Vida was executed. What I want I go out and get for myself, so don't be shocked by this ...' she swept out an expansive, tipsy arm, 'by this lifestyle of mine. It's what I want.'

'Nothing shocks me any more, Roxana. I'm merely curious.'

'Well then, Keir darling, they shot her. Right in front of my eyes. Right there in the crypt of St Zavior where we were left waiting for the Nationalists to take the city. When they found us, they wouldn't listen to me concerning Vida. They said she was a Communist and so they shot her. I can show you the pillar to which they tied her in the crypt of St Zavior before they put a bullet through her head.'

He put his hand to his head. 'I'm confused, Roxana. Who shot Vida, the Basques or the Nationalists?'

'Moors, Dr Devlin, Nationalist offal.'

Roxana smoked her cigarette down to the moment it burnt her fingers and he offered her another. She lit one from the other. 'That is the price of true love, Dr Devlin – a friend who would die for you.'

He cleared his throat, the words sticking. 'Roxana, why did you not return afterwards to Salamanca, to your husband?'

'Because his side shot Vida. I *hate* them and I hate *him*! They ruined the good times for me and for her. I thought at first she was spoiled and selfish, but she was nothing of the sort. She was better than everyone else put together. All of them on board the *Al-gandura*. Axël, Louis, David, Sylvie, *they* were the selfish, spoilt brats, and such sheep! Not Vida. Vida was unique. Vida didn't care a toss what anyone thought about her, she just behaved like – like Vida. She had a heart of gold and was kind to everyone. What's more, she was loyal. Oh, I know she could be a possessive little bitch once she got her claws into someone, but it was only her way of asking for – for affection, I suppose. And she died for Ramiro's politics. I hope he dies too.'

'Where is your daughter?' he repeated.

'Pippa is ...' Her voice, always husky, broke. 'Pippa is – God knows where.' She got up and came to him. Placing herself on his lap, she wrapped her arms around him and sobbed against his shoulder.

'Please don't cry, Roxana.' Taken aback by her misery, he didn't know what to do or say next.

'I never believed – I never believed life could be so ghastly!'

He held her, gingerly at first, and then after a while relaxed and began to smooth her hair. 'Roxana, it's over now. We'll get you back to Salamanca and we'll find Pippa.'

She stiffened in his arms and then raised her tear-stained face to his. Brilliant hair tumbled round her face and over her shoulders, Roxana's sexuality rampant even in a moment like this. 'I don't ever want to see José again, Keir!'

Tactfully he extricated himself from her arms. He heaved himself off the kitchen-chair. 'Pippa, I think, is quite safe. I'm sure she was put aboard a ship from Bilbao sailing for Mexico. If so, we'll get her back in due course. Meanwhile, there is just one other person I have to trace, the nanny, Annuala.'

'Annuala went back to her family. She was from Andalusia.'

'Well, that can be easily verified.'

Things did not altogether tie up. Annuala never went back to her family, he knew that much. Nor had a lot of other women and children from the *Menor* been accounted for. Roxana was lying, and he wanted to know why. But not tonight. Tonight he was far too tired. He said, instead, 'Do you want to see Raven tomorrow?'

'Is she still a nun?'

'For the moment.'

'What does that mean?'

'Let her tell you herself.'

Roxana gave a sly smile. She picked up her unfinished glass of brandy off the table. 'Darling Keir, if you and Raven have secrets between you, that can only mean one thing. Raven, however, will never give up being a nun, she's too much of a martyr. Come back tomorrow by all means. You needn't bring Raven if you don't want to.' She reached up and put her arms around his neck, the glass still in her hand. 'A heart of pure gold, uh? And better than all the men I've ever known put together. You can stay here tonight instead of rushing off in such a hurry, darling. No one will disturb us.'

'I have to get back. I still have a lot of paperwork to get through.'

'Same old Keir! Terrified of women, just like Geneva, uh, you hunky chunk of red tape? Don't you ever take time off to relax and have fun once in a while, darling?'

Through his shirt he could feel her ornate belt buckle digging into his midriff. Again he unfastened her arms from around his neck and this time she took the hint, although her pout was one of disdain and disappointment.

'Oh well, Dr Devlin darling, some other time. To tell the truth I'm a little whacked myself.' At the door Roxana said, 'Keir, as far as I'm concerned my marriage to José de Luchar is at an end. That is trauma enough for me. Every day, all along the streets of Bilbao, even the dockside, I've been searching for Pippa, wondering what became of her on that awful night of Basque resistance. The Comte de Martello blames me for Vida's death. I simply can't face him again should he try to locate me here in Bilbao. Vida's death changed everything. The friends I thought I had have conveniently disappeared. I can't sleep at night because of the terrible nightmares I suffer. I'm taking nerve pills prescribed by the doctor, I can't stomach any food, but throw it all up again. I just want – I just want to feel normal again. All I ask you is please don't think badly of me, and find Pippa for me.'

Everything Roxana did and said reminded him of Francesca. He couldn't wait to get out of that sordid riverside apartment.

Raven refused to see her sister.

'Look, would it help,' Keir asked, 'if I got her to come here?'

'You do as you wish, Keir. You want to extract the truth from her, then you must do it your way.'

'What's the matter, Raven?'

'Nothing.'

'Yes there is. I know you by now.'

'Do you?'

'Hey, hey, come on! Not still thinking that Roxana and I have something going between us, are you? All that Geneva nonsense?'

'No. I just want to get back to Barcelona, that's all.'

'Chickening out again, huh?'

'I don't know what that expression means.'

'It means, I love you. I wish our kisses the other night had been protracted long enough for me to have got you between the sheets before you threw me out. I've come to the conclusion you need a man, my sweet, and soon.'

Raven lowered her head and smiled. She could never feel sour for long in his company. But the reception lounge of a government building with wartime journalists, the Guardia Civil, nurses, doctors and officials everywhere was hardly the place to talk intimately. She put down the magazine she had been browsing through. 'Today I wrote to Dame Superior Olivera to tell her that I cannot be as sincere about continuing as a nun as I once thought I could be. I told her that I wish to renounce my vows as a novice, and I also informed her of Dame Conceptión's death. I had to explain, too, that ...' she took a deep breath and looked at him shyly from under her thick, dark lashes, her smoky eyes beguiling him in that innocent way of hers, 'that you mean more to me than shutting myself away in a convent and denying myself what my heart and body are telling me is right for me.'

He leaned forward in the shiny imitation-leather chair and clasped her hands tightly. 'What are your heart and body telling you?'

'That you're crushing my hands, but that I don't mind a bit, and that I can be a good Catholic *contented* woman by being a wife rather than a discontented nun yearning for something she can't even recognize any more.'

'Oh Raven …' He relaxed his grip and covered her hands beneath his own. 'I can't tell you how glad I am to hear this from you. I love you. You know that. After this war is over things will be so different. We'll be able to start life afresh. Guatemala is a great place. We'll set up a *mestizo* clinic in the wilds on the money Father Silvestre left me, just as he mentioned in his will. You and I and the Indians – and our dozen kids of course – we'll spear for fish in the lakes, barbecue them over a campfire, get frisky on *aguardiente* and frisky without. I just want to spend my whole life with you, sun-up to sundown, lady with the smiling eyes.'

'And your scalpel?'

'I'll keep it as second best.'

'Never second best. You have a wonderful career and – and I just want you to know that I think you're a wonderful person.'

'Don't I know it too.' His eyes twinkled.

'And that Peedee and I are grateful for what you're doing for the family when there are so many other people petitioning you all day long.'

'Perhaps they'll give me a Purple Heart for it.' He stopped being flippant and changed the subject as he glanced around the crowded hotel lobby for Roxana to put in an appearance. 'We're just hanging about this place for Roxana's sake, when really we ought to get to Salamanca as soon as possible and then back to Barcelona.'

'Why do you think Roxana is lying about what happened to her and those other Nationalist women, Keir?'

'A gut feeling. None of those women have so far been traced except Roxana.'

'Why don't you go and talk to her again?'

'I might just do that later on tonight when I've got through my telephone calls and paper work.'

Keir tapped on Roxana's door, glancing at his watch as he did so: eleven o'clock at night and time for his beddy-byes – the door opened.

A powerful man in a navy-blue fisherman's jersey, waterproofs, and gumboots answered the door. His cheeks above the reddish-blond mariner's beard were tanned and weatherbeaten, his head a crowning glory of lustrous curls. The man eyed Keir with fierce green eyes and open hostility as he scowled, '*Ja*?'

Eye-level with him, though not feeling nearly as fit as Roxana's *amorcillo* looked, Keir drew back a pace, 'I have an appointment with Señora Roxana de Luchar.'

Next moment he was sent staggering back from a hefty punch on the chin. The door slammed in his face.

Keir sat down on the top stair and got his breath back.

'I told you he was more crazy than her,' said Fudge Eyes creeping up the dark staircase. 'Does it hurt much, Americano?'

'Not as much as my pride, *niño*,' Keir rubbed his sore chin ruefully. 'I don't think I chose my words very carefully. Why didn't you tell me he was home?'

'I didn't know,' said the boy, seating himself next to Keir. 'Move over, Americano, I have serious business to discuss with you.'

'Why didn't we discuss it sooner?'

'I didn't know you before and liked you less.'

'Thanks, pardner.'

'Why is this *inglesa* so important to you, Americano?'

'Because she's important to the woman I love and want to marry. They're twin sisters, you see.'

'In that case family *is* important. I lost mine at Guernica, so I will try and help you now. But only if you will invite me to stay with you in the United States of America when this war is over. Bernadette and I have seen the movie of King Kong and the Empire State Building and so I would like to stand on top of the tallest building in the world just like

King Kong.'

'That's a promise, Mickey Mouse.'

'Well then, the reason why this Englishwoman is afraid of the big Swede with hair like rusty cotton-wool is because he has a hold over her.'

'How so?'

'He is a mercenary. He only works for money.'

'Don't we all?'

'Sure. But this one is a *canalla*. He buys and sells anything. He sells rebels to the Commies, and Anarchists to the Moors. You get the picture, Americano?'

'I get the picture. He's a real scumbag.'

'He's worse. On the night that the Nationalist women were taken to the Church of St Zavior this man Lars traded them in.'

'Sorry, son, but I've lost you now.'

'Well then, I will explain more clearly since your Spanish is not that good. Some of these women were rich Nationalist women, weren't they?'

'I believe so.'

'One among them was *very* rich – a millionairess?'

Keir nodded. The boy had his attention now.

'The women were traded for ransom money. Ten million French francs minimum. Whew!' The boy whistled between the gap in his eight-year-old front teeth. 'That is a *lot* of money in Spanish pesetas.'

'It's a lot of money in American dollars. Tell me more.'

'Señor Doctor, those women's lives were bartered.'

'Between who and whom?'

'Basque Nationalists and Lars the Mercenary. He had a Swedish boat standing by to take them all off to Mexico to be with their children until the war was over. The Basques had no wish to give back Nationalist women to the other side when so often they could not get back their own Basques. Guernica changed everything, you see. So they wanted the enemy out of the way permanently without actually being involved in their disappearance.'

'So what happened?'

'Once the ransom money was paid up, the women were smuggled onto the Swedish boat on its way to Mexico. The boat with their children aboard had gone on ahead, Bilbao to Havana to Tampico. Lars's boat was to follow the same route.'

'What happened to Lars's boat?'

'It struck a mine and was blown clean out of the water. Everyone aboard the Swedish ship drowned.'

'Where?'

'Off Cap de los Aguillones, where the ocean and the *Mar Cantábrico* – the Bay of Biscay to you English-speaking Americans – both flow together. They are dangerous waters even without mines, which are swept far out into the Atlantic and so ...'

'Yes, I see. Why weren't Lars and Señora de Luchar blown up or drowned like the others?'

'For the simple reason they were not aboard Lars's ship that night.'

'How come?'

The boy shrugged. 'That is the bargain struck between a man and a woman who both want the same thing, sex and money! He fancied her when he first saw her in the crypt of St Zavior and she fancied him. He kept her with him when the boat sailed and she raised no objection. She is an attractive and cultured woman with many rich and influential contacts. His head was turned. It was also turned by the ten million French francs that had been paid for her release as well as for the release of Señora de Martello de Luchar.'

'You know about her?'

'Sure! There is nothing that does not go on in Bilbao that I do not know about.'

'What happened to the Frenchwoman?'

'She was blown up at sea like all the others taken out of the crypt of St Zavior.'

'How do you know all this?'

'Bernadette has told me.'

'Who is this Bernadette?'

'The woman who has become my new mother – you know! The militiawoman who took your money and who takes mine – when I am able to make any. She cries herself to sleep every night because of Guernica. And when she cannot sleep, she drinks and then she talks, just like the Englishwoman who married a Spanish legionnaire and now doesn't love him any more. The Englishwoman also cries because she has a bad feeling for not going with her sister-in-law to Mexico for sake of ten million French francs and the body of a handsome Swedish sailor.'

'Where did those ten million French francs go?'

'I told you. Shared out between certain mercenary parties, Basques and Swedes and all those in between who don't mind selling human cattle on the blackmarket.'

'You're sure?'

'Sure I'm sure. You must remember, Americano, that we Basques are not fighting for anyone except ourselves. The Spanish Socialist Government, the Commies and Anarchists mean nothing to people like Bernadette. We are Basque Separatists who do not want to be joined to a Catalan government or a Madrid government. So this war is very convenient for us. Ten million French francs buy a lot of guns – so does one million come to that. The Basques are short of weapons. Instead of shooting their prisoners and afterwards getting condemned for it by people like yourself, they keep them as bargaining power. They traded well-known rich Nationalist women's lives for weapons: like keeping fat pigs alive for the best price at market. It is as simple as that.'

'You think Señora de Luchar might have told Lars that her sister-in-law's father was a millionaire,' Keir asked the precocious little Spaniard, 'in order, perhaps, to *buy* her way into Lars's favours so that she would be able to remain here in Bilbao instead of being shipped off to Mexico?'

'Who knows, Señor Doctor, the ways of a distracted woman?'

By God! Keir thought to himself, this was not a boy but an old man! 'Hey, hey, Mickey Mouse,' he said, roughing up Gappy-Gob's dark hair, 'I owe you a drink. What's your poison?'

'Coca-Cola, Americano.'

'Glad to hear it. Shall we go?'

Keir checked and rechecked the boy's story, and this time the facts did tie in. A Swedish boat registered in the name of *Junsele Larsvaan* in Stockholm, with refugees on their way to Tampico in Mexico, had run into a mine in the Atlantic Ocean on the night of 24 May, twenty-three days before Bilbao fell to the Nationalists. Vida de Martello de Luchar could not have been shot by Moors in the crypt of St Zavior as Roxana had claimed.

Keir then re-checked his list of the Nationalist women taken from the *Menor* to Bilbao prison, thence to the crypt of St Zavior a month later, against passenger lists of all refugee ships arriving in Tampico between May and June. He was able to trace the surnames of some of the refugee children against the names of the women put aboard the Swedish vessel, also destined for Mexico. The children had arrived safely in Tampico on a French ship that had left Bilbao some days earlier. No survivors had been picked up from the Swedish vessel that had struck disaster. Everyone had perished at sea.

All public records and documentation by the Basques just before the arrival of the Nationalist forces was in such chaos, Keir realized it would take him a lot longer to trace every single fine detail of the *Menor* affair, and to corroborate certain facts, but he was sure he was now on the right track.

Roxana had lied about Vida and Annuala's deaths because she obviously had a very bad conscience about not going to Mexico with them, but had preferred to throw in her lot with the Swede who had bought and sold her friend. After Vida had risked her life for the sake of whatever it was they had going between them, ten million French francs of bad conscience couldn't be easy to live with, although Keir doubted that, even now, Roxana possessed an ounce of guilt over the whole episode.

The following afternoon when they were coming out of the picture-house, Keir presented himself on the pavement to Roxana and her Cupid, Lars.

He slapped an envelope into Roxana's hand. 'From your sister,' then he turned to the Swede. 'I am Dr Keir Devlin. I work for the International Red Cross Organization, and in particular the Central Agency for Prisoners of War. I could get you on an assault charge, but I've got something better. The penalty for smuggling anything in this war, especially human beings, for ten million French francs, minimum, taking into consideration the insurance money you also collected after your boat was blown up, is a firing-squad. To that end, the Spanish Government's Deputy Secretary General of Security in Barcelona, Commissar, Ramiro de Luchar, has issued a warrant for your arrest. His wife, you see, was blown to smithereens along with your boat soon after the ransom money had been paid. Either you stop intimidating this lady with you, Commissar Ramiro de Luchar's sister-in-law, and let her get back to her husband in Salamanca, or the Chief of Police right here in Bilbao gets your curriculum vitae on his desk in one hour from now. The Communists you cheated out of the cache get the same information. Have I made myself clear?'

After that partisan deliverence Keir doubted very much whether Max Huber or Dr Junod would have approved, but, by the look on the cocky Swede's face, he was compensated by an immense inward satisfaction as he got back into the Renault.

Two hours later Roxana presented herself at the Hotel de Ville in a stylish and pricey chinchilla coat and hat, a last-minute parting gift from Lars. She met Keir and Raven in the foyer and dumped a suitcase at their feet. 'All right, you two win. I'll accompany you to Salamanca, but that doesn't mean I'm staying with José. I'm only going there to ask him for a divorce.'

'That's up to you, Roxana,' Raven said. Roxana, it appeared, had not changed her spots in spite of her dreadful wartime experiences.

'Where's stupid Cupid?' asked Keir, the light of battle still in his eyes.

'If you're talking about Lars, he's decided to go back to Sweden.'

'Wise man.'

'You're a bloody Fifth Columnist yourself Keir Devlin! And when I catch that toothless little boot-licker who told you about Lars, I'll fry him alive. His adopted mother, you know, is also a mercenary. Are you going to tell the Chief of Police about her, too?'

'Was sixty thousand pounds really worth it, Roxana? Why don't you stay here with your lovely friends?' he said wearily as he got up from the armchair, and then, because he was desirous of hearing Roxana's full story, the truth this time, sat down again.

'I don't want to stay in Bilbao without Lars. He was very good to me. He protected me from all sorts of ruffians. But I just want to tell you two this, in no way did I realize that ten million French francs had been paid for Vida's life.'

'No! *Five* for Vida, *five* for you, Pippa, and Annuala! And would that really have made you change your mind about accompanying her to Mexico?' Keir put Roxana firmly in the picture.

'Lars told me that if I didn't stay with him, Pippa, Vida, and Annuala would be shot. I had no way of knowing whether or not he was telling the truth at that time. You don't stop to ask questions when you're looking down the barrel of a sub-machine-gun.' Roxana flounced down into a chair. 'God! Can't one even get a drink in this insufferable place? Waiter – *waiter*! Ask him for some champagne, Keir.'

Keir did nothing of the sort, but ordered tea instead.

Roxana had her own cigarettes this time. After offering Keir one, and waiting for him to light hers, she continued, 'When the militiawomen left the crypt, we were suddenly faced with a group of men we thought were Basque sailors. We thought we were then going to be assaulted in some other kind of way. We didn't know they were foreign mercenaries shipping us off to Mexico for monetary gain. Lars split us all up. He told me I wouldn't come to any harm, nor would the others, if I did as I was told. So I did as I was told. Vida and Annuala were then taken away with the other women and put on a boat for Mexico. That's the last I saw of them. I didn't know anything about any ransom money – not then.'

'Why did you lie to me?' Keir demanded.

'Darling, don't get so prickly. I didn't mean to offend you or lie to you. I was afraid of what Lars might do to you if he knew you'd come snooping around the apartment. He has a bad temper. I was unable to think straight. Seeing you out of the blue like that, Keir, was rather a shock to the system – but a pleasant one, Doctor darling.' She flicked ash indolently into the ashtray beside her. 'I knew Pippa was safe because Lars told me she had been sent to a refugee camp in Mexico, and that I would get her back after the war. He said that it was the safest place for her to be at the present time, and I thought so too. As for Vida and Annuala, I'm sorry about what happened to them, but it was something for which I can *not* be blamed. Let's face it, refugee ships are running into mines and being torpedoed all the time.'

Raven tried hard to control her anger and disgust over Roxana's callous attitude. 'The sooner you're back with José the better. Peedee and I will have less of a headache once we know your husband is keeping an eye on you.'

Roxana's smile was condescending and slightly malicious as she glanced from Keir to her sister. 'Raven darling, it's no good pretending you're not still a nun at heart. You haven't changed a bit since Cassy's days, sweetie.'

Raven stood up. 'Oh, I *have* Roxana! I can at last see you for what you really are. Keir, I'm ready if you want to leave for Salamanca right now!'

'Honestly! I don't know why I've bothered to come to Salamanca at all! It's an awful bilious-coloured town full of holy relics with nothing to do day or night. It's so *Franco*-orientated, they lay down the golden flag and kiss his boots every time he steps out of his palace – pinched from the Holy Roman Church, by the way, Raven. José, would you believe, takes him cocoa every night – yuk! I think I might just skip across the border to Portugal.'

'I wish you would,' snapped Raven from behind her toothbrush. She scrubbed her teeth even more fiercely as she stood at the old-fashioned washstand in the tiny lodging-house attic room she was forced to share with her insufferable sister. Why did she always, without exception, Raven asked herself as she rinsed her toothbrush, *always, always, always* manage to lose custody of the senses in Roxana's company?

On the journey from Bilbao to Salamanca, a distance of almost four hundred kilometres, they had had to endure Roxana's incessant carping, which set their nerves on edge. Roxana had been sulky, difficult, and altogether a 'pain in the neck' as Keir afterwards described Roxana and her tantrums.

'I suppose you're going to meet Keir now, that's why you're brushing your teeth so conscientiously?' Roxana taunted. 'To get rid of all Señora Hermanos's horrible garlic smells?'

'Yes!'

'Can I come?'

'No!'

'Are you really giving up the Church for him?'

'No!' Raven fiercely wiped toothpaste from her mouth with the towel. 'I'm giving up convent life, not the Roman Catholic religion.'

'You're fickle. Always changing your mind when something better comes along.'

'And you're – a pain in the neck!'

Roxana, lying on the sagging bed while she filed her nails with an emery board, smiled serenely. 'Human at last! What a man can do for a woman's pent-up libido. What happened at the convent? Did one of the lady Dames try to do a Vida with you, darling, that's why you're now running away from lifelong chastity?'

'Oh, be quiet!'

Raven met Keir at a little café off the Plaza Mayor. In the spring or summer, sitting outside at a Spanish restaurant table might have been the kind of romantic interlude they would have both appreciated. But today there was a war going on and the bitter weather kept them indoors. They had been two days in Salamanca, the hub of Spain these days, with plenty of good food in the smart restaurants and hotels, plenty of night-life, music and dancing. Yet, while Keir had been kept more than ever busy since their arrival, Raven felt her mission was over and there was nothing more for her to do in Salamanca apart from getting under his feet.

'You look very down. What's the matter?' Keir asked over the coffee cups.

'Roxana! You're right, she *is* a pain in the neck! She's doubly put out because José refuses to share his quarters in the Bishop's palace with her. He says the newly-proclaimed

624

'Head of the Government of the State of Spain' wouldn't approve.'

Keir chuckled.

And then, because she, too, could see the funny side of it, Raven shared his mood. She stirred her cup of coffee vigorously while recalling José's military pomposity when he had earlier lunched with her and they had discussed Roxana's and Pippa's futures. 'Anyway,' Raven told Keir, 'Madam has got her wish. José says he's quite willing to give her a divorce – I saw him yesterday, coming out of the cinema with a dark Andalusian señorita clutching his arm, so I think he's not too perturbed about losing a wife. He's making the most of Salamanca's night-life before he's shunted off to the Catalan front, where he tells me General Franco is going. I don't think either of them will shed tears for each other – José and Roxana, I mean. It's Pippa I think about.'

Roxana was safe. She had been given back to her husband, even though neither of them wanted each other. But at least Raven felt her conscience was now clear as far as her twin was concerned. Roxana was no more her responsibility, or Peedee's. Raven herself was only thankful that she had managed in time to escape the faithless philandering clutches of José de Luchar, whom she had once thought she was madly in love with. And how foolish, naïve, and sentimental could a teenage girl be! were her distant thoughts. That left only Pippa, and Keir had promised that he had a good lead as to her whereabouts. Raven felt she might as well get back now to Cabo Alondra and Peedee, rather than hang aroud her sister any longer, or even Keir for that matter, since her presence could only hinder him in his own important work.

'Shall we become her surrogate parents?'

His voice reached her from a distance, cutting across her thoughts. 'Who?'

He put his hand under her chin and made her look up at him. He thought to himself in that moment that he would never grow tired of gazing into her eyes or saying how much he loved her. 'Dreamer. Pippa! We could adopt her as her parents are such wash-outs. So what about it?'

'I'm glad Roxana and José can't hear you.' She smiled almost tearfully, moved by his regard for a child he had never seen, simply because Pippa was her niece. 'You would be willing to do *another* humanitarian deed, Dr Devlin?'

'Sure, why not? Every kid deserves good parents, a good home, a good foundation in life.'

'You have a big heart, Keir Devlin. Now tell me what you've been doing with yourself all day?'

He leaned back in his chair, and though he was smiling, she could see the shadows of tiredness beneath his eyes. 'We had a meeting of the Spanish Red Cross Committee at breakfast. Then we had a meeting with the Minister of Justice, and then a meeting with some foreign journalists. Then Dr Junod and I had a working lunch and discussed the conditions we're finding in the Spanish prisons. Then we talked to prisoners and made notes of their grouses and requests. Then we worked with the Minister of Justice again for the exchange of certain categories of Republican prisoners of war who had been unfairly sentenced to death. And then I had a cup of coffee. After that, I caught up with more paper work and tried to telephone Barcelona again. But the telephone service is mainly in Republican hands and they don't like connecting calls from Franco's capital, so they take their time about it. So I swore a little, though mainly under my breath as I still had my armband on. And then I think I must have had more coffee and more cigarettes until it was time to meet you. Something I've been looking forward to all day.'

'All that saving of souls in one day?' she asked, amazed by his sheer humanitarian fortitude even while she teased him about it.

'And it's not finished yet. Me Tarzan with hairy chest!' He heaved his shoulders up, thumped his chest, and then pulled a very resigned face. 'After I leave you, my darling, I have to attend an official reception with Dr Junod and other delegates. It's at the Episcopal Palace. They always start so blessed late here, ten o'clock, just when I want to go to bed. Everyone, including Franco's Moorish Guard, will sing the National anthem and the 'Cara al sol' and salute the flag, and then they will dislike us even more for interfering in 'their' war and for not joining in their military songs and anthems. Now tell me, what *you've* been doing with yourself all day?'

'Nothing much. I listened to Roxana and then José and then Roxana again. I went for a walk through the town and visited all the places of interest, the House of Shells, and the University, and the place where the Rector of Salamanca, Miguel de Unamuno, had his life saved by Franco's wife, Carmen, and the Convent of Las Duenas and the Convent of Agustinas …'

He was perturbed by the mention of all these convents. 'Do you want me to get you some more Red Cross work? There's always plenty you know, even if it's only stringing food parcels together.'

'Yes, I know. But I think I ought to be getting back to Peedee. You have your own work to do and can't be concerned about where I am and what I'm doing all day long.'

'But I *am* concerned. You're my main concern. Even in the midst of my work I think about you and what we're going to do together *after* this darned war. I can't wait …'

'That's why you must be left alone to your duty. I'll only get in your way, Keir.'

'You're not changing your mind, are you?' he asked in some alarm.

'No, silly! Of course not. But you've got important work to do and it's unfair of me to keep you from it. I've done what I had to, with your help and protection. I'm very grateful for all the time you've given up for me. I don't want to be your crippled limb, Keir, so I'll wait for you at Cabo Alondra.'

'Promise?'

'I promise. I even bought a new dress today, to wear when I give back my novice's wardrobe to dear little Madre Estelle Calmar, who will weep buckets.'

'As long as it's not white or grey you may keep it as a surprise for when I next see you. Having said that, about white, you can have a white dress as long as it's a wedding-dress to marry me and not the Pope.'

She smiled. 'Rest assured. It's kingfisher-blue silk, the latest mode, and it can be worn with or without a little white bolero, Andalusian style.'

'Wow! I can't wait to be dazzled by it, or you,' he said, making eyes. 'So, what's Roxana doing with herself?'

'Going out on a date later on with a former boyfriend. Someone called Lieutenant-Colonel Vittorio Broué, who has a wooden leg and medal for bravery after the battle of Brunete.'

'Same old Roxana! Never away from the honey-jar for too long. When are you thinking of leaving?'

'Tomorrow. If I can get a train to Barcelona.'

'I don't like you travelling across war-torn Spain all by yourself.'

'I'm a grown-up girl now, Keir.'

'That's what I'm worried about. I'll try and arrange some transport for you with the Red Cross. It might mean having to wait a few days, but I'll fix up something.'

She looked down at their clasped hands on the table. 'Your wife couldn't have known what she was losing.'

He held on a bit longer, his grip becoming tighter at the thought of losing *her*, however temporary the separation. Then he said sadly, 'Now I must take you home – and I'm sorry I could only get you and Roxana digs with a *very* noisy Spanish family.'

'Not at all. The Hermanos brood are all perfectly delightful. It's Roxana who's the fly in the ointment.' Raven took Nurse Freya's coat from the back of the chair and Keir held it for her as she put it on. In the cold night air of the main plaza she turned to him, the coat-collar up, her hands deep in the pockets. 'Do you want your Red Cross *mochila* back now that I'm no longer employed by you?'

He touched her cheek, still warm and rosy from the hour they had spent inside the café. 'Keep it as a souvenir.' He held her close, conveying to her in that moment all that she meant to him. Then, his arm around her, they walked back to the Calle San Pablo.

Two days later, Señora Hermanos and her ten children were sorry to see Raven go. Her husband, a draughtsman in peacetime, had been missing in action for more than a year, but had since been traced to a Republican prison by the 'good Red Cross Doctor'. She was so *happy* now that Dr Devlin was going to bring her Ettore back from the dead.

The short, plump, irrepressible Spanish woman mopped her eyes. 'Here he is now, Señorita Quennell. He is a saint! He told me Ettore is with the other side, but they have promised to release him very soon in an exchange of prisoner deal!' She spat on the pavement. '*Red Dogs*! They don't deserve to have back other crucifiers of the Virgin. Do not worry about your sister. I will look after Señora de Luchar as though she were one of my own daughters. Señorita Quennell, if you and your man ever come back to Salamanca, you must not leave again without having *gaspacho* with me and my man, Ettore.'

Keir overheard as he took Raven's holdall and put it in the car. He whispered in English so that Señora Hermanos wouldn't understand, 'Did I hear her say *gaspacho*?'

'You did. Andalusian style. I didn't have the heart to tell her it reminded me too much of Polish *borsch*, but with twice as much garlic.'

'Señor Americano Doctor,' said Señora Hermanos waddling up to him while her children manhandled his car, 'you are my saviour!' She kissed her two plump hands and then wrapped them around his face. '*El Americano*!' she gazed into his blue eyes admiringly. 'You are *really* a man! I kiss you in the name of all Spanish motherhood and wait for you to bring me back my Ettore, who is the father of all my children. Take care of Señorita Quennell on the way to the railway station and don't drive too fast! She is a lovely young woman and you should marry her *como un relámpago* before someone else does.'

'As quick as a flash, huh? I'm doing my best Señora Hermanos.'

He got in beside Raven and they set off towards the Plaza de España and the train station. Raven could see something was very wrong by Keir's face. 'What's the matter, Keir?'

'Ettore Hermanos was shot yesterday morning in Albacete prison. How am I supposed to go back and break that kind of news to her?'

*

629

They found a table for two in the station buffet. The hospital train was delayed. The station-master did not know when it would arrive. It could mean anything up to twenty-four hours or longer, knowing Spanish war timetables.

'Keir,' Raven said anxiously. 'I don't want to delay you. Why don't you go back? I'll be all right.'

'Why don't you stop ordering me about?' he said, and ordered them coffee. 'Do you want anything to eat, Raven?'

'I couldn't stomach a thing ... Poor, poor Señora Hermanos with her ten children – and how awful for you. I don't envy you one bit having to tell her about Ettore. I couldn't do your job for the world.'

'Sometimes, neither can I. Not when one can't rely on the word of government officials, both sides as bad. Let's not talk about it, but pay attention, my sweet. You do have the timetable I've copied down for you, with all the stops the train will be making?'

'Yes.' They were etched on her mind like an epitaph: Plasencia, Talavera de la Reina, Toledo, Cordoba, all Nationalist-held territory. Then into the Republican zone, Albacete to Valencia to Barcelona, following the coastal route.

'I dare say the stations will change according to the whim and politics of the train-driver. It will be a long haul, especially as you'll be taking aboard more and more wounded all the way to Barcelona.'

Raven rechecked everything: 'Timetables, list of Red Cross officers and stations, *salvo conducto*, identity card, ration book, passport, all are safely tucked away in my *mochila* among the bandages and sticking plaster.'

'I hope you can sing both the "Internationale" as well as the "Cara al sol".'

'Both sets of words are etched indelibly in my mind along with your timetables, Señor Doctor.'

'Glad to hear it, my darling. But don't worry, you'll have other Red Cross personnel with you and they know the drill.'

'I'm not worried.'

'Wear your armband at all times. You're neutral

remember. At Cordoba injured Nationalist soldiers will be exchanged for injured Republican soldiers, who will then be taken to either Valencia or Barcelona, got that?'

'Got it. Stop *worrying*, Keir!'

'I can't help worrying about you, you're such an innocent.'

'Thank's a lot, pardner!' she used one of his Wild West idioms to express her feelings. She made a face at him.

'No, I mean it.' He ordered himself yet another coffee, this time, '*café solo – pero con cognac!*' he demanded of the waitress and when Raven raised a surprised eyebrow, he smiled, 'To temper the strain, sweetheart. Got your safe conduct pass?'

'I told you just now, dearest Keir. I even have the *Generalissimo*'s prized signature on it. José got it for me. All is safely tucked away in my *mochila*, so no cause for concern any more!'

'Then for God's sake don't lose your *mochila*.'

After a while he broke the poignant silence. 'Remember that I love you.'

'How can I forget?'

'I shan't be able to wait to see you again.'

'Me neither. How long must you remain in Salamanca?'

'As long as it takes to battle with bureaucracy. As long as it takes to end a war. I don't know.'

'I shouldn't have asked.'

'Yes you should, because I think I've got to go to Tereul next, not Barcelona.' He dropped the bombshell, saving it till last because he did not want to think about it.

After a little pause while she reassured herself that she *would* see him again and that no stray bomb in a second round of fighting in Aragon was about to take him away from her, Raven wanted to know, 'Why Tereul?'

'Because that is where the next big stand is being made between Republicans and Nationalists. The kind of battle-front which always means a lot of bloodshed, heartache, prisoners, refugees, donor-units and hospitals to organize.'

'Like the Ebro offensive?'

'Yep.'

'It's snowy in Tereul this time of year.'

'It's snowy in my heart right now, Irish Eyes.'

'Oh dear ...' she took out her handkerchief, 'I think Christmas for me this year is going to be very miserable indeed.'

He took a deep breath, fumbled around in his pocket, and then passed something across the table.

'What's this?' Raven asked, eyeing the little box tearfully.

'I don't often do this sort of thing, but I feel kind of committed to hanging on to you for dear life now that you're going to be out of my sight for a bit. I don't trust Dame Superior Olivera. The moment you show up again in Barcelona, I've got the feeling she's going to grab you back for her nunnery. Open it.'

Inside was a ring made up of her birthstone.

'Garnets,' he said, 'for constancy. A tryst ring, just in case I'm not back to give you your birthday present on time. It's just the beginning. The next one I hope will be a diamond, and the one after that gold.'

She took the ring from its box, but he insisted in putting it on her engagement finger. 'I would kiss you right now, but if I do that I mightn't stop before the train arrives and then I'll be stuck with you for a lot more days.' Nevertheless he kissed her across the coffee cups.

'Oh Keir – I don't know what to say or do. I just feel like a glow worm who can't light its light.'

'You're just going to love Guatemala, my sweet, so let's both hang on to that for the time being. As soon as the snows of Tereul thaw out, I'll be showing up at Cabo Alondra, so don't you move from there.'

'I won't.'

The hospital train puffed into the station three and a half hours later, which, from the station-master's point of view, was early. Raven, too, had visions of being stuck on the railway platform until the following day. The train was packed with casualties from the northern front. No sooner had Keir taken Raven in his arms to kiss her goodbye, saving and savouring this moment as planned, when someone tapped him on the shoulder. Without releasing Raven, he turned his head to find Roxana over his shoulder.

Surrounded by luggage and porters, Roxana looked like a fashion plate in all her grand furs. 'Hello darlings. Gosh,

Raven, what *would* Dame Superior say if she could see you now! And Keir sweetie, you *must* learn to hold back your desire for my sister. Such passion in public is quite toe-tingling. I had to bribe the officials to get me aboard this train. I've been promised a first-class carriage. Vittorio saw to the details for me. General Franco's name works wonders in this town. I hate leaving him – Vittorio, I mean, but I just can't cope with his vicious little wife *any* longer! Barcelona, I think, will be much more fun than Salamanca now that the tide of war is shifting in that direction. Aren't you coming with us, Keir?'

'No.'

'War and duty call again, I suppose?'

'Something like that.'

'Why is Raven crying?'

'Because you're going to be travelling with her, I suppose.'

'Naughty-naughty, Doctor darling. No need to get saucy with me. Raven, you needn't have anything to do with that stiff-looking hospital bunch back there. You can travel with me up front where we can order champagne and caviar. Do you know who is travelling on this train besides ourselves?' The Minister of War, Señor Indalecio Prieto, no less! He's going to Teruel where they're starting the Catalan offensive, and, I dare say, he'll be wanting to swish back his caviar and champagne before he's frozen to death in the ice-bucket of Aragon's sierras.'

'What happened to your boyfriend?' Raven couldn't help asking.

'I told you, Raven darling, he's decided to give up *other* women. He offended me greatly last night by that remark. I never saw myself as one of his other women, merely as a good friend. I can only assume his ugly little wife has won at last. Vittorio must be growing old. That's when the wives take over. Anyway, I'm bored with him. One-legged men hardly cut romantic figures. Since his war wounds at Brunete, Vittorio has become rather a moaner and has lost his sparkle of former days. José too. My husband is only concerned in creeping his way into Franco's heart. He's become so military-minded it's like talking to a doormat with medals pinned on it. I'm just waiting for my divorce, and then I can start life anew. I wonder how long we'll have to wait on this draughty platform before they sort these injured men out, Keir?'

Keir was unhappy and perturbed because he was saying goodbye to Raven and because he didn't know when he would next see her, and because she would be travelling with Roxana, and he didn't trust the smug sister an inch. Roxana was perfectly capable of starting a mutiny aboard the hospital train or upsetting Raven in other ways.

A large efficient Spanish military nursing sister swept down the platform with her clipboard. She stopped beside Raven displaying her Red Cross armband. 'Nurse Quennell?' She eyed the Red Cross uniform up and down and then said in frosty tones, 'One of your coat buttons is undone, Nurse. Fasten it at once. Your hat is also crooked. Car number seven. There are four men on bunks with stomach wounds. They are your patients until death do you part, or Cordoba, whichever comes first. No water, Nurse, even though they might lynch you for denying them in their hour of need. I hope you have a fully-stocked Red Cross *mochila*, because you're going to need it. Say goodbye to your friends please, and come aboard at once.'

Raven hissed at Keir from the carriage step, 'If this is your doing, I'm going to kill you!'

Keir grinned as he grasped her hand in a last heartfelt farewell, 'With love I hope. Good luck. See you soon.'

Raven watched Keir and Roxana move off to the front of the train reserved for VIPs. She overheard Roxana saying to Keir in the midst of all the bustle and steam, 'I'm *so* looking forward to having champagne and caviar again. I just hope to goodness the Anarchists don't find out that the Minister for War is aboard this train and decide to blow it up.'

PART FIVE

Silk Parachutes and Snowdrifts

'Some, who had gaping wounds already beginning to show infection, were almost crazed with suffering. They begged to be put out of their misery, and writhed with faces distorted in the grip of the death struggle.'

From *A Memory of Solferino* by Henry Dunant, Father of the Red Cross.

CHAPTER EIGHTEEN

Barcelona: March — December 1938

Ramiro de Luchar's role had subtly changed. His powers as a political commissar at the Comintern Headquarters of Soviet Politics in Barcelona were formidable since the Communists had lent their support to SIM, Servicio de Investigacion Militar.

His back to the large bay window before which his desk was placed, he tapped his fingers impatiently on the file in front of him. His frown was deep and sullen. Then he got up and walked to the window with its splendid view of the sea.

This office had once been a classroom: winter and spring, January till March, spent at the castillo right here in Barcelona, the heart of Catalonia. Why did he love Barcelona so much? What a pity José and Jaime had gone over to the other side, that was Papa's influence of course. Poor little Carlos with his passion for aeroplanes. But at least he had chosen the right side to die for: and Vinarosa ... family tradition again. Oh, those tedious hours spent gazing out at the green and blue view beyond the Mas. At harvest time how he had longed to get out there to help in the vineyards, not listen to the voice of his tutor, Señor Peedee, droning away: 'You will not find the Montmorency Heights out there, Ramiro. So now tell me all you have learned about General Wolfe and the battle for Quebec.' And, because he had objected to learning about the battles of other nations rather than his own, he had rebelled in the classroom. Señor Peedee had not liked that, he who had been a real stickler for British discipline and did not hesitate to use the cane if sufficiently provoked.

Ramiro's fine-shaped mouth curved in a little smile of rememberance. But the summers! July and August had been idyllic. Those long hot summers of his boyhood spent rambling carefree across the cliffs in search of gulls' eggs, through the purple vineyards, or swimming in the sea, or just dreaming on the soft, sandy, shell-strewn beach ...

The narrow stony shore below the hill of Montjuic was deserted this morning. The firing-squad must have set to work early.

The sight that usually greeted his eyes each morning were rows of prisoners with their hands tied behind them. They were shot facing the sun as it rose above the sea, just so that they could take their last look of the world and know what they would be missing. It happened all the way along this Mediterranean coastline, from Sitges to Alicante. Afterwards, the sea would wash away the blood.

He bit his thumbnail as he stared across the bay, his reflections morose.

The *limpieza*, the 'cleaning up operation of Spain' had not altered the fact that the war was going badly for the Republic. The Government had had to shift from Valencia to Barcelona. Yesterday, the city had suffered its worse air-raid in an around the clock-bombardment from Italian planes based on the island of Majorca. The battle of Teruel, which at first had seemed like a turning point for the Republicans, ended as a rout and Teruel was taken back by the Nationalists only twelve weeks after the snows of Teruel were made scarlet with the blood of victorious militiamen. The Nationalists hâd launched a fresh offensive in Aragon, while the Republican forces cost four hundred million pesetas a month to run, more than the entire national budget before the war. And, for all that, the soldiers were starving on half a kilo of bread a day. Fascists possessed twice as many competent officers, twice as many disciplined and educated soldiers, twice as much foreign aid and twice as many weapons. What did the Republic have? Three-quarters of the militias could neither read or write nor tell the time of day. Russian officers were only out for personal glorification and battle medals, while causing confusion and rebelliousness in the ranks. Starvation was biting deeply into the whole of

Catalonia, when this part of Spain had been the most prosperous and productive region before the war, and to add to the Republic's troubles, the massive refugee problem had brought cholera, typhoid, and scurvy right into the city of Barcelona itself.

Ramiro scowled, his apprehension making him nervous. Franco as Dictator of Catalonia was an even more sobering thought.

Hitler and Mussolini had only been engaged in a dress-rehearsal on the Spanish stage, made perfectly obvious since Hitler's *Anschluss* implemented a few days ago. That infamous political and economic union between Nazi Germany and Austria was once again *Der Führer*'s iron fist in the velvet glove striking down on the map of Europe. He had tested his weapons on Spain, he was now about to test his military strategy on the Non-Intervention Committees of Europe, and the fools in London and Paris refused to see it!

'*Perdición!*' Ramiro swore aloud and thumped one fist into the palm of the other hand. Let us hope, were his thoughts, that in the event of a major world war, the Republic would be in a position to side with the saner powers of Europe. Even if Spain had to die to save the rest of the world from Fascist domination, Fascism *must* be stopped at all costs, no matter what it took.

And not only was the fate of the Communists on Ramiro's mind should Franco's Fascists take Barcelona, ten million French francs had gone down the Basque drain for nothing. Vida was dead and his father-in-law, the Comte de Martello, devastated by his only child's death, had pulled out of the arms deal he had made with the Spanish Communist Party.

Making up his mind, Ramiro turned back to his desk and picked up the telephone.

An hour later, the contact knocked on his office door. 'Come!' Ramiro barely glanced up at the man to whom he handed a piece of paper on which he had scribbled down a name. 'He is in France at the moment,' he said. 'Pick him up the moment he shows himself at Port Bou.'

*

March, April, May gave way to June, and it was time to sample the sea again, sunbathe on the sands, and soak up the hot sun on the beach at Cabo Alondra after the coldness of winter's war.

But, as she herself was kept busy with war work in Barcelona, Raven left the sunbathing to Roxana, who had turned over a new leaf. Roxana had not budged an inch from Cabo Alondra. The furthest she ever ventured these days was to the cinema in Toril or Vilafranca. Men and the pursuit of pleasure were a thing of the past. Raven couldn't help noticing that Roxana was a changed woman, for she now spent her days peeling onions for Carina, endlessly playing her gramophone records, sunbathing and swimming by herself, and reading as the mood took her: she presented the soul of sweetness and light. She even found time to sit and write to Sonny in Ireland, giving him all the news of the war in Spain.

Raven, herself, while helping the Quakers with one million refugees in Barcelona, six hundred thousand of whom were children, spent her off-duty moments walking the headland or the beach at Cabo Alondra, just waiting for Keir to return. She would take out his letters, read and re-read them, while never having imagined for one moment in her previous half-existence that love between two people could be such a splendid thing. She hugged to herself all the moments they had spent together in their journey across Spain, reliving the hours and the conversations. Even though he was out of sight, he was never out of mind, for the spirit of him was always with her, bringing back his physical presence so that she could almost feel him, touch him, look at him, and answer him face to face when she read his letters out there on the headland or in the privacy of her bedroom.

Since Salamanca they had met only once, and then very briefly. She remembered the day and the hour so clearly, imprinted on her heart along with so *many* things about him. He had just arrived back from the Teruel front, and instead of meeting at the Calle Lauria where it was impossible to talk, they had walked the Rambla together, arm in arm, talking about 'after the war'.

Teruel had been awful, indescribable, he had told her.

In the sub-zero temperatures the dead couldn't be buried because the ground was so rock solid. Soldiers in their mountain dugouts and prisoners in their cells literally froze to death. One would go to them in the morning with medicines, supplies, books, newspapers, and the latest cheery news only to find, a few short hours later, the fellow was a frozen corpse through hypothermia. This was a war, Keir had said, in which everyone was the loser.

Then he had delivered a further blow to their hopes: 'I have to go to France next.'

'When?'

'Three hours' time – when the train leaves.'

'Why?' she had asked, while trying not to let her disappointment become too acute and show on her face. She must leave him free until the war ended, so that he would not have the added burden of her on his shoulders.

'Why?' he had repeated, and then, squeezing her hand tightly, had looked up at the budding plane trees in the Rambla. 'Do you really want to know?'

'Not if you don't want to tell me.'

'Refugees. *Four hundred thousand* of them! France can't cope with them any more.'

'Isn't anyone else doing their bit to relieve the problem?'

'The Red Cross have been given fifty thousand pounds by Britain to do something about the camps, but they don't want any refugees. Nor does America and nor does Russia. Neither does the editor of a certain prestigious New York newspaper want any 'emotional' reports sent to him concerning Spanish or French problems. Belgium has offered to take two and a half to three thousand refugees, but no more. That's what the Red Cross are up against.'

That had been their last romantic interlude together, discussing the problems of the world beyond their control. After that he had had to rush for his train to get him to the border.

Now it was summer: she had not seen Keir for four months.

But he had written to her whenever he had been able. At first he had been at the Refugee Clearing Centre at Le Boulou, before moving on to other camps.

He had described in his letters the appalling conditions

he had found in the sand-dunes of France. *It costs fifteen francs a day to look after one refugee and sixty francs if that refugee is sick or wounded. They are burying them before they're even dead! Sometimes these exiles (wounded soldiers as well as refugees) do not have so much as a roof over their head and make burrows in the sand like gophers. Everywhere barbed-wire assaults the senses. The brutality of the foreign guards in the labour camps has to be seen to be believed. And yet another fresh horror rears its ugly head through this Spanish war, racketeers profiting from a cheap labour-force paid two pesetas a day to do the kind of work that would have killed a Samurai warrior, let alone a sick, starved, and wounded person. I shouldn't be telling you all this, because I don't want to upset you. On the other hand, I know what a stoic lady you are after what you've been through, and I want you to live beside me always, sharing the good and bad experiences of our lives even when we're not together. In this letter (which finds me particularly down) I have made you, in my hour of need, my back-up system. And I will always be yours. Each night I light a candle of my own for you and offer it to the stars – those things, you know, that shine on lovers even when they're miles apart. It is the only thing that sustains me, knowing that when this is all over, we can be together, sun-up to sundown and all through the night. Keir.*

She had written back at once, to a place called Barceres, hoping that her letter would be forwarded to him should he have moved on further down the line. *I wrote to my brother Sonny (Brother Bernard), who is a Benedictine monk at a monastery in Rosscarbery, Ireland, conveying to him the terrible refugee problem here in Spain. I have now received some good news from Sonny. Our old childhood home, Hollyberry House in County Kildare, which passed to Sonny's order, has been put at our disposal. The doughty old Abbot wrote to me, informing me that Sonny had forwarded a request that Hollyberry House should be turned over as a refugee centre for Spanish children for the duration of the Spanish War, and the request has been granted. Sonny is going to attend to all the details for us. I know this offer is only a drop in the ocean of refugees, but at least a few more children can look forward to a roof over their head and food to eat in a country beautiful beyond imagination – and I wax lyrical because I spent my childhood there. I think of Pippa every time. I wish this war would end. I miss you until I am mindless with longing to see you again: R.*

Raven had gone to the Quaker Refugee Organization simply because the Quakers were given the facilities and State recognition which the Catholics were denied. Under a fresh cloak of anonimity, she did the same sort of work Dame Concepción had been doing – feeding, sorting, housing, and comforting the homeless and parentless children crowding the refugee centres in Barcelona.

And the weeks dragged on and on. The world stood still for her even though the seasons did not. The hot winds of the Sahara were replaced by the ravages of the Levanter, and the cold north breath of the Tramontana blew through the feathery branches of the tamarisks on the ledges of the sea, and down the avenue of Monterey pines at Vinarosa.

Until one glorious morning she was walking on the cliff top, and there he was, as wind blown and as storm-tossed as she, running along the road from where the bus had set him down.

He swept her up in his arms and embraced her so tightly she lost whatever little breath remained to her. Without a care in the world he fell with her into the thistles and the cacti and the wind-blown grasses of the headland for the sheer joy of being alive and together again.

'I had to come straight here and tell you the good news.'

'You've found Pippa? She's alive and well?'

'Yes, yes, yes! But that's not the only reason why I feel like a king with a golden crown today.'

'Then what other reason is there?'

'You! You waited for me, right here on the headland where you'd promised. Oh God! I was so afraid you'd forget your promise. I was like a jellybean when I stepped off that bus just now, wondering to myself, will she, won't she be waiting? And here you are, without your awful nun's wings, waiting to marry me.' He kissed her, enthusiastically at first, and then more tenderly. Then he unravelled the scarf that was throttling him. He had been cold, but the fire lit from this kind of body contact, even though they were both bundled in thick winter coats, scarves and gloves, was enough to keep him fuelled all winter.

'Raven, Pippa's not at a refugee camp any more, but with

a Mexican family just outside Tampico. She has been adopted into a real family for the duration of the war, rather than be subjected to the rigours of an orphanage. I'm told she's a very sensitive child. I've had a devil of a job trying to trace her. Apparently, she arrived in Tampico with no identification, nothing. The shock of everything had made her dry up and she *wouldn't* speak a single word. At first, everyone at the camp thought she was a deaf mute, and treated her like one. But the nuns who found her realized that she *could* talk, although she pretended otherwise. They wrote and told me that they've been 'working' on her, and while Pippa still doesn't speak very much, only a word here and there when it suits, her, she's beginning to open up a lot more. They had no idea she was Pauline Inés de Luchar, evacuated from Bilbao in May 1937, until they received my enquiry through the Red Cross.'

'Then how did they discover who she was and where she belonged?'

'In Pippa's pinafore-pocket was an ebony and silver cigarette-holder. The nuns thought she had just found it somewhere, and didn't take much notice of it at first. But it was the only thing Pippa seemed to want to hang on to. After prising it away from her, they found the hallmark to be that of Aspreys, the London jewellers. Engraved on the silver band was the initial 'D', so they sent the cigarette-holder off to them. Aspreys searched through their records and came up with the name immediately. Lady Quennell of Dublin and Kildare, Christian name, Daphne. Your mother apparently liked to have her 'D' scrolled in a certain way, which became her – gimmick, I suppose you'd call it. The nuns still call Pippa, Daphne, how about that?'

Raven smiled. 'My mother's cigarette-holder doubled as a good, shrill whistle, which is why Sonny always wanted it, too. But Roxana hung onto it from the day she pinched it without our mother knowing. Even then, since those early days, Roxana showed signs of a hedonistic future. She must have given it to Pippa to play with on that prison-ship. What good fortune that she did.'

'I should say! So now kiss me.'

She did so. 'You'd make a good detective, Keir Devlin! I can't believe all this is happening to me. All this good news and your being here today. Two Christmas presents, one for me and one for Roxana. What a wonderful man you are.' She held onto him tightly. 'You don't have to go away for a bit, do you?'

'Have you something particular in mind?'

'Yes, some of Carina's soup made from the Prime Minister's little pills. Lentils are all we have to live on these days. After which I shall beg her for a wee dram of de Luchar Imperial brandy from Peedee's prized cellar to warm the cockles of your heart as you must be frozen. And then we can talk and talk and talk.'

'That's all?' he asked, kissing her again. 'The cockles of my heart are doing fine close to you and I don't need soup. I've got some chocolate for you. And plenty of other luxuries from France, including silk stockings to grace your fantastic legs, soaps, and perfume, and, guess what else, my sweet?'

'Fresh croissants?'

'Nope! A sexy French negligée for your bottom drawer – where it can stay.'

'You libertine! Now, will you come back to the villa and have some lunch?'

'I have something better in mind. Not that I'm turning down Carina's wonderful cooking,' he added hastily. 'You come back to Barcelona with me and we can spend the rest of the day wrapped in each other's arms in the back seat of the movies. There's a spendid full-length cartoon-film showing, and we won't have any language problems since it's Walt Disney's *Snow White and the Seven Dwarfs*. Afterwards we can sneak off to a warm soup-kitchen or taverna, and then we'll dance the night away at some cosy little night-club. I'll even look forward to an air-raid so that I'll have an excuse to hold you tighter still.'

She was already well swaddled in her outdoor clothes, and needed only to collect her purse. She told Carina she would not be stopping for lunch, but was catching the next bus back to Barcelona with Dr Devlin. As Roxana was also in the kitchen, Raven told her the good news concerning Pippa. Roxana did not answer, but got up and abruptly left the table where she had been picking out the bad lentils from the good.

Raven caught up with Keir on the cliff road, and slipped her hand into his. He tucked both their hands back into his deep, warm pocket. 'I don't know what's wrong with Roxana sometimes,' Raven said. 'I happened to mention the good news about Pippa, but Roxana didn't utter a word. She left the kitchen to go to her bedroom as though I'd told her she had an incurable disease or something.'

'Well, I suppose she's got to rethink her life now. Roxana's always had things too easy. Without a husband to support her, it isn't going to be a bed of roses for someone who has never been responsible in her life to start facing up to facts at this late stage.'

'That's true.'

'But I'm still willing to care for Pippa if you are,' he said to reassure her, fully aware of how hopeless Roxana was in taking care of herself let alone anyone else. 'We merely have to add Pippa to our own bunch in the pipeline of our Guatemalan *mestizo* paradise, plus the bunch your brother's Benedictines are charitably nurturing at Hollyberry House, and we can found our own kingdom.'

He put his arm around her shoulders and drew her to him as they leisurely paced the coast road in the hope that some sort of transport might come along to take them to Barcelona. 'You and I can do anything since today is the day I am able to wear my crown.' Smiling down into her face, fresh and pink from the sea winds, he added happily. 'Now tell me what you've been doing with yourself from spring to December and I'll tell you why I'm so crazy about you. In fact, I'm so utterly crazy about you, I want to run away with you here and now. Let's not catch the bus at all, but find a haystack where we'll be undisturbed by Anarchists, Communists or *The Seven Dwarfs*.'

He was indeed a *crazy* man; and she loved him for the new dimension he had given her life. War had changed everything, but not as much as love, real and true and unselfish. 'I was looking forward to *The Seven Dwarfs* in the back row,' she confessed, her head smothered laughingly against his chest.

*

So, lucky old her! thought Roxana.

From the kitchen window Roxana had seen Keir get off the bus. She had seen the way Raven and he had greeted one another, as though it were Victory Day, Raven holding out her arms to him as though there were no tomorrow. She had seen the way the two of them in their reunion had huddled together on the cold, bleak headland, oblivious to all, even the weather, as they excluded the rest of the world from their existence. She had heard the echoes of their laughter and watched their clinging arms as they hugged and kissed and no doubt promised each other their undying love for ever and ever, Amen.

And while it was all rather nauseating, she couldn't help feeling envious.

She resented her 'married sister' status proscribing her from the romantic limelight that had always belonged to her. Although she had relinquished her husband, and even her child had been forfeited as a pawn of war so that there was nothing to show for the gold band and marriage certificate José had once given her, she was still regarded as José's *wife*.

Damn Raven for giving up her nunnery! Roxana thought sourly.

Doctor Keiren Hunter Devlin was a free, uncommitted, still wildly attractive man for his age, with an unexpected fortune at his fingertips. She had always found him far more interesting than all those pimply public school youths, those immature playboys, and the insipid fortune-hunters and pleasure-seekers whom she had met on the international scene's social merry-go-round. She had wasted herself on them, men like José, Ramiro, Vittorio, David, Axël and Louis, Lars, and countless others whose names she had since forgotten. She could see them all now, shallow baby-faced, useless creatures, who only wanted to hump a woman without commitment. At least Keir Devlin was a little different. He was intelligent and he did have principles along with his craggy 'lived-in' look and rock-solid dependable shoulders. *Damn Raven!* Roxana repeated to herself: she might have been in with a chance had not her sister stood in the way. Love and money made life agreeable. Now she had neither, whereas

Raven had found both. Why did Raven always get the best, and she second best?

Roxana lay on her bed and chewed over the drab facts and unfairness of her life. She had only stayed on at Cabo Alondra because of *him*! She knew that he would come here as often as he could in order to see Raven, and that's why she had remained docile and obliging in the background, sure as tomorrow's lentils for dinner Raven would again change her mind and go back to her silly Camillus nuns. Now it appeared she was as fickle as ever, switching allegiance whenever it suited her. At one time it had been God, Jesus Christ, and the Virgin Mary. Now it was wanting a man, marriage, and children. She had beguiled Keir with her pristine robes and purer-than-pure demeanour, and he had thought he'd found an up-market basement rarity from Macy's store, just like Mama used to gush about because it was 'so typically American *cute*!'. Miss Ravenna Quennell alias Sister Justina, untouched by human hand, not a flaw to be seen, price one American Red Cross doctor, discounting his Guatemalan fortune and anything as crude as S-E-X for the sake of it: oh no, nothing like that at all! This was real true love! So much love at first sight, it made one want to puke.

But even while she tried reducing Raven in her own mind, Roxana knew that Keir Devlin only had eyes for Raven Quennell, damn them both! She could not help *but* be jealous of Raven's totally undisguised new-found happiness: not the paltry, sordid strangers in the night business that had been so much a part of her own war, but something she recognized as deep and committed and wonderful and as permanent as any woman wanted, as she herself had wanted, but had never found.

Roxana got off her bed. She wasn't beaten yet!

She took something out of her dressing-table drawer and then went downstairs to Peedee's study, where, arrayed on his desk, was an assortment of pens and coloured inks.

Ramiro was livid.

He had only just placed one foot on the threshold of the Comintern building, when the Commandant pounced on him like a rubber stamp on an official document. A nervous tic pulled his handsome mouth to one side and he found difficulty in controlling his temper.

He took off his commissar's flat-peaked hat of the rank of colonel, tucked it under his left arm, and peeled off his leather gloves. He did not go immediately to his office to see what other urgent matters required his attention, but followed the Commandant down many steep steps and through wandering passageways until they came to the lowest reaches of the castillo. Once, long ago, when Catalonian history itself was in the making, these caverns had been dungeons, built into the rocky sides of Montjuic. Now, in more modern times they had become the wine cellars of the Castillo de Luchar, renamed Castillo Palomar. The Commandant opened a door.

SIM was using the castle as one of its many secret prisons.

The man on the plankboard bed was one step away from being a corpse. When the Communist secret police had at last managed to apprehend him, they had put him in a black room, totally black and circular, with no windows, no visible door or ceiling, no light, no air, no escape. The prisoner's feelings of vertigo and claustrophobia had been terrifying as he had tried to claw a way out of that black circular, airless room, a living hell of emptiness.

They had starved him and beaten him, deprived him of sleep and his clothes. Then they had used lighted cigarettes on his body, including the soles of his feet. But even that had not been as bad as their latest method of torture. And though he lay in a pool of his own vomit, his body and mind quiet, they still had not managed to break his spirit; they still had not been able to extract from him the names they required.

Ramiro had difficulty not lashing out at the man to whom he had given the assignment of 'finding out something constructive from such a useful source', his own words when they had at last caught up with their quarry. '*Canailles*!' Ramiro shook with rage, his body trembling with a palsy he was unable to control. He included the Commandant of the prison and his snivelling toadies in his biting attack. 'I said *question* him, not kill him!'

'But he is not yet dead, Commissar de Luchar.'

'*Cojudo!*' Ramiro hauled the fellow up by his lapels. 'Look at him, just look at him! Do you expect him to tell us anything at all after this? Go on, take a good look at him and see what your sophisticated methods of interrogation have reduced him to, you miserable swine.'

'We were only following your orders, Commissar.'

'Pssh! I am surrounded by dogs and fools!' Ramiro let go the lapels of the man he had been holding to ransom and dusted down his own uniform in a hopeless, yet derogatory gesture as he washed his hands of such incompetant vassals. No wonder the Republic was in such a bad way when there was only trash like this fouling things up. 'In future *I'll* interrogate special-category prisoners. Now get him cleaned up and dressed and put him in the back of my car. Let's just hope that a doctor at the Clinic de Rey can patch him up without too many questions being asked. Don't you know he's a neutral who has to be handled gently?'

'We were only following your orders, Commissar de Luchar.'

'Well now, here's another order. If he dies without giving me the information I require, you reptiles will get a taste of your own electrodes for causing this balls-up in the first place. Got that?'

'*Si, Commissar de Luchar.*'

Christmas was a sad affair at the Mas Luchar. Normally the family would have spent Christmas at the Castillo de Luchar in Barcelona. This year it was not possible as the castle was now in the hands of the Communists, thanks to Ramiro. 'Pah! Ramiro will regret what he is doing to us,' spat Doña Maria, her biliouness more than ever apparent today. 'I wish I'd never given him a motor bike, the ungrateful, good-for-nothing slob!'

'That was José', Grandmama,' Nina reminded her.

There were only six of them around the Christmas table, Doña Maria and Nina, Raven and Roxana, Isaba and Carina. Because of their depleted numbers, they ate in the warm kitchen rather than in the formal dining-room with its carved-oak mural of the Last Supper, beneath which, in the past, so many family meals had been enjoyed or suffered accordingly.

Without masculine company, Roxana was tedious, putting Raven herself on edge. 'Where's Keir? I thought he was joining us today?' Roxana said while she assessed the Christmas lunch; she promised herself she would never again in her whole life have lentil soup, even if it was forced down her throat. She would stick to red meat, red wine, and red caviar when this war was over: Isaba could keep her vegetarian recipe-book in which she kept her indigestible secrets.

Isaba had put the wireless on. In the background Dolores Ibarruri was making one of her impassioned speeches: 'Mothers! Women! When the years pass by and the wounds of war are staunched, when the cloudy memory of the sorrowful, bloody days returns in a present of freedom, love, and well-being; when the feelings of rancour are dying away, and when pride in a free country is felt equally by all Spaniards, then speak to your children. Tell them of the International Brigades – they gave up everything; their lives, their country, home, and future, mothers, wives, brothers, sisters, and children, and they came and told us, we are here, Spain's cause is ours. Many of them, thousands of them are staying with the Spanish earth for their shroud ...'

'Switch her off, Isaba!' Doña Maria said irritably. 'La Pasionaria always gets on my nerves with her puffed-up speeches.'

Isaba did so with bad grace and reseated herself at the table amidst a great deal of chair-scraping on the terracotta tiles.

Raven herself was worried about Keir. 'Keir might come later, I know he promised he'd try and get here if he could for Christmas lunch, but he might have had to leave Barcelona at short notice.'

'No one leaves Barcelona these days,' said Doña Maria in her old lady's cantankerous voice, 'unless it is at *very* short notice. Usually in a coffin. The Nationalists have begun to invade Catalonia and all is lost. Even the foreign volunteers have all gone home.' She asked Nina to pass the salt. 'Isaba, you never put enough salt in anything.'

'Salt is bad for you, madam.'

'So is lentil soup. I will be up all night with the wind. What have we to eat for our Christmas dinner?'

'Rabbit in garlic sauce with nasturtium salad, madam.'

'Rabbit and nasturtiums? Dear God,' she raised her eyes to the kitchen ceiling, 'is it not enough to have lentil soup on Christmas day without having *conejo* as well. Whose rabbit was it?'

'It was caught in a trap on the estate, madam.'

'Are you sure it is not a large rat? They are coming up from the sewers these days.'

'There is also what the American doctor brought us from France,' added Carina placatingly.

'Why didn't you say so! What did he bring, truffles, *foie gras*, some *petits fours*?'

'Tinned oxtail soup and champignons, madam.'

'Then he can take them back to France!' said Doña Maria, disappointed with the good doctor.

Nina changed the subject. 'Raven, do you know where your grandfather is?'

'In Barcelona with the Rivales family. Why?'

'He is not there anymore. My uncle is greatly concerned as to Señor Peedee's whereabouts.'

'What do you mean?'

'He has disappeared,' Nina said, looking down at her plate as though she might find Peedee lurking at the bottom of her soup.

'He is always disappearing,' Roxana interrupted dismissively. 'Last time I heard he was off on some sort of fishing jaunt with his friends the longshoremen. He didn't know when he'd be back.'

'Perhaps. But this time he has not returned, and so my uncle is worried. Señor Peedee has been gone for more than a month.'

'Maybe he was after a lot of fish,' Roxana quipped.

Raven frowned. 'I'll go to Barcelona tomorrow and try and find out if anyone has seen him lately.'

'He's too much of a well-known figure down at La Barceloneta with his bicycle-clips and straw hat, so someone is bound to know Peedee's whereabouts.' Then Roxana added brightly, 'Maybe he's found himself a Spanish girlfriend and is spending Christmas with her.'

Later that afternoon Roxana tapped on Raven's bedroom door and entered without waiting for Raven to invite her in. Raven was sitting by the window, ostensibly reading, though her thoughts were more on Keir and why he had not telephoned; if he had been unable to leave Calle Lauria 95 because of the pressure of work, he could have telephoned, so why had he not?

Roxana said, 'This Christmas has been so dull. Would you like to see some snapshots?'

'Lovely!' Raven put aside her book, and Roxana drew up the dressing-table stool. 'Do you remember this one? It was taken outside Hollyberry House – look, Raven, Tim on his new pony, and Sonny and and I on our old nags. Isn't that a hoot!'

'I didn't know you had all these old photographs from Ireland,' Raven said as she turned the pages of the album.

'Sonny sent them to me. He found them in the basement of Quennell House when they were clearing out the rubbish prior to the Benedictines starting their Bible-printing business. Such a shame! All those old Georgian mansions around Merrion Square slowly being turned into characterless offices ... Do you remember La Tart and how Tim always made rude jokes about her? Oops! There I go again, putting my foot in it. I know how you hate being reminded of poor old Tim. Anyway, the cellars didn't get blown up, and so a lot of old junk was found down there. The Benedictine clearance-squad didn't want anything worthless, especially mouldy old photos, so I ended up having them. Now here are some newer ones I took myself – oh, look! This one is all of us on one of the *mouettes genevoises* the day we went to Cologny with Mademoiselle l'Impératrice. Oh gosh, you'd better have this one.' Roxana began taking the snap from its securing-hinges in the photograph album.

'Why?' Raven asked, adding, 'Don't do that, Roxa. I don't want it.'

'It's of Keir, I thought you'd like it.'

'But you and Vida are in the photograph. It's your property, not mine.'

'But Keir might get embarrassed because I have this picture.'

'Keir won't mind.'

'What about you?'

'I don't mind, either. Keir did a lot of living before he met me. I can't be jealous or possessive about things that happened before he knew I existed. And this is just a silly schoolgirl photograph. I expect you were all making thorough nuisances of yourselves in the Parc Mon Repos, and the only way he could get some peace and quiet to read his newspaper was to pose for you all.'

'Oh Raven, you're such a good sport, and so sweet and understanding when I've been so beastly to you in the past. Keir was a good sport, too, letting us take that picture of him with our arms round him. But only after his mother's wedding, when he had got to know us all a lot better! I forget who dared us to do it, but whoever it was must have taken the snap. Oh look, here's another one of us. Vida must have taken this one as only Keir and I are in the picture.' Roxana peered closer at herself and Keir. 'Must have been taken when we were all in Paris together, there's the Eiffel Tower in the background.'

'When were you and Vida in Paris with Keir? He never told me.'

'I don't suppose it was that important to him. He was just about to dash off to London to get interviewed for the Guatemalan job. We collared him one night and carted him off to the Moulin Rouge.'

'Oh I see. But I thought you were in Antibes or San Sebastian, something like that, after our final term?'

'Are you upset, darling, that Keir didn't tell you about being in Paris with me?'

'Not in the least. I was just curious for my own sake, that's all. Keir's got so much on his mind, I don't suppose he even remembers he met you and Vida in Paris.'

'No, I suppose not,' Roxana murmured and took the photograph album from Raven who had finished looking through it. She went to the door and opened it. 'He's probably avoiding me, that's why he didn't show up for Christmas lunch. Mind you, I can't blame him. I haven't exactly been nice to him.' Her arms clasped across it, she held the photograph album to her chest as she turned on the threshold and said, 'I'm just so glad that you and Keir are getting married. I've always known he loved you more than me. Pippa will have a good home with you two. I'm not terribly child-orientated. Children only make me feel more inadequate than ever. If she stayed with me, she'd only be left in the care of nannies and governesses all day, whereas, with you and her father she'll be brought up in a real family.'

'I don't suppose José will have much time for her. Not unless he gives up soldiering. And I can't see that happening just yet. On the other hand, he might prove to be a very good father once he's reunited with Pippa. Fathers usually adore their daughters.' Raven picked up her book again and adjusted the rug around her legs as it was draughty sitting by the window without the room being heated. They were all economizing on fuel, and so she had not put on the electric fire this afternoon.

'I wasn't talking about José, Raven.'

Raven turned around to regard Roxana more carefully. 'Then who are you talking about?'

'Keir.'

'Keir?' Raven hesitated, then her face cleared and she smiled. 'Oh that! Keir told me all about you going to the Avenue de la Paix and giving you a cup of coffee before chucking you out: not a very gentlemanly thing to have done, he said. Don't worry about it, Roxana. It was a misunderstanding, that's all. Now do you mind closing the door because their's a frightful draught from the stairs.'

'Oh well, if you're happy about it, then it's all right. I was worried in case you got angry. It's good to know that he's at last accepting responsibility for Pippa. Finding out the truth about Pippa was a bit of a shock to him. I had to tell him you see, in Bilbao, when he came to that seedy riverside apartment looking for both of us.'

'Look, Roxana, I don't know what you're driving at, but please say what's on your mind. You're making me nervous.'

'I thought you knew: I thought he'd at least told *you* the truth about Pippa, and that was why you were both so eager to have her live with you.'

'I still don't know what you're *talking* about!' said Raven in sheer exaspertion.

'Haven't you wondered to yourself why he has always been so concerned about Pippa, even to the extent of spending every spare moment of his day in Bilbao trying to trace her whereabouts?'

'He was trying to trace a great many other people as well, and to get to the bottom of that *Menor* business. The Basques weren't being very cooperative, so that he had to search out a lot of hidden information for himself. He was also concerned about Pippa because Peedee and I were worried about her. And you, of course. He did it for *us*, the family, and for you in particular.'

'Haven't you wondered to yourself why he was so anxious to adopt her after the war?'

'He'll adopt her *before* the war if you and José want us to! As soon as we're married, if that is your attitude, Roxana.'

'Not my attitude, Raven, your future husband's. Pippa is his child.'

'Don't start that troublemaking business again, otherwise I'll slap you. José is Pippa's father: why else all that kerfuffle when you thought José and I were getting married?'

'I needed a *husband* at the time! And José *was* responsible for that baby that I lost in Tetuan – the one that had me, racing to your side that awful summer of thirty-three. My hasty marriage arranged by Doña Jacqueline on the estate, when she and Don Ruiz discovered they were about to become illegitimate grandparents, was something I had very little say about, what with everyone so anxious to cover up any hint of de Luchar scandal.'

'So how did you explin to José about giving birth to a toddler in a pram?' Raven asked coldly.

'José was away for months on end in the desert. He never knew I lost the child he was responsible for. The first time he saw Pippa was when she was eighteeen months old. Even then José hardly looked at her. He didn't know if she was a child approaching two years or four years. Children are all the same to him. And anyway, Pippa is very small for her age. You and Keir haven't seen her, she's tiny and very fragile. I had a bad time during my confinement in Paris, and it was only Vida who stayed by me.'

'We're talking about July 1933, Roxana!'

'No, we're not! We're talking about Geneva 1931!'

'I don't believe one word of your horrible story. But were it for a moment true, which I very much doubt, why didn't you tell Keir about the child he was supposed to have fathered on you?'

'He was in the wilds of Central America. I had no way of contacting him. I was very ill and had to stay on the flat of my back for weeks. You were at l'École Internationale learning to be a schoolteacher. I wrote and told you and Peedee I was wandering the world with Vida. No one knew about Pippa, except Vida. Pippa was born by a Caesarean section. I stayed in the clinic for three weeks afterwards, and then Vida's old nanny in Paris looked after Pippa. That's why I never had any money. I had to pay to keep Pippa out of sight.'

Roxana paused for effect.

'Go on,' said Raven icily, her face a mask of contempt for her sister. 'There *must* be more to this story.'

'I went sailing with Vida again, met José again, and it all started again. José and I went off to Morocco as husband and wife, and immediately after, he disappeared into the desert on manoeuvres. Only, that time, I lost the baby I was expecting – which was probably on account of my previous Caesarean. I was so lonely in Tetuan suffering as I was from husband-loss and baby-loss, I got Pippa back without anyone suspecting anything. Military wives are all rather a vague bunch, who give birth to their children all over the world, so no one knows who the father might be and who could care less! When one is bored out of one's tiny mind, any scandal is a godsend. I hired Annuala to look after Pippa. Then the Spanish war started, and José didn't give a damn about Pippa or me. When Keir suddenly turned up in Spain as a Red Cross official, it was too late to tell him about Pippa. He had fallen for you and I didn't want to come between you two.'

'So you substituted Keir's baby for José's! You're a *witch*, a *bitch*, and a *liar*, Roxana. Get out of here!' Raven threw the book she had been reading at her sister.

Roxana ducked and the book sailed through the open door, onto the landing. 'All right!' Roxana said, straightening up and setting her shoulders after that unexpected onslaught from Raven. 'You want the truth,

I'll give you the truth. You can't argue with proof, can you?' Roxana fumbled in the back of the photograph album and withdrew a crisp sheet of paper, which she flapped open from its well-defined creases. 'I always keep it in here, along with her baby photographs. It's Pippa's birth certificate, issued in the Clinique de Veille-Ville, Paris and signed by the obstetrician and midwives who attended the birth – with the stamp of the Town Hall, where I registered the birth after my confinement. Go on, take a good look at it!'

Roxana flung the birth certificate at Raven, the names cunningly changed.

Name and Surname, Pauline Inés Devlin. *Sex*, female. *Date of Birth*, 17 April, 1932. *Name of Father*, Keiren Hunter Devlin. *Nationality*, American. *Occupation*, Surgeon. *Registration District*, Faubourg St Germaine, Paris, France.

'Now do you believe me?'

In Raven's nerveless hands the piece of paper fell to the floor.

Roxana picked it up.

'Get out,' said Raven tonelessly. 'I never want to see you again.'

Quietly Roxana shut the door. On the landing, her smile was triumphant.

Raven went to her wardrobe and took out the Red Cross *mochila* that Keir had issued her with. Hugging it to herself, she sat for an hour in the cane chair by the window, staring over the grey sea. The room darkened, and still she clutched the *mochila* as though it was the dead child she had nursed by the bomb-crater in the olive-grove.

Finally she got up, and dressed herself in her smart new Spanish Red Cross uniform issued at the Calle Lauria. She took the *mochila* that contained among the bandages, cotton wool and iodine, his love-letters, her money, passport, and safe conduct pass, as well as Dame Conceptión's bent and broken spectacle-frames. Then she left Cabo Alondra.

Raven sat by the windswept wayside, knees drawn up under her chin, waiting for some sort of transport to come along, while her tears soaked the canvas Red Cross knapsack held tightly to her chest.

*

The day after Christmas Keir went to Cabo Alondra to apologize to Raven for not turning up for Christmas lunch at the Mas Luchar. The Red Cross had been under particular pressure over the Christmas period. Apart from the rigours of normal duty, a special tea for one hundred Spanish orphans had been arranged on Christmas afternoon. He had been conscripted as Santa Claus, a sackful of presents thrust into his hands at the last minute. All this had been arranged behind his back. He would have telephoned to explain, but the lines were down after an air-raid. He felt terrible about not showing up at Vinarosa as promised, but he felt sure that Raven would understand.

Raven would have understood completely, had she been there.

When he walked into the kitchen at Cabo Alondra Roxana was washing up at the kitchen sink. 'Hi, Happy Christmas!' He pecked her on the cheek just to show there were no hard feelings.

'You're too late, darling,' Roxana turned to him with a languid smile and a very innocent air as she dried her hands. 'Raven isn't here.'

'Where is she?'

'She heard that Peedee had gone missing, and so she went bustling back to Barcelona with her knapsack.'

'When?'

'Yesterday afternoon. She was waiting for you to appear for Christmas lunch, darling. When you didn't show up, she flew off all by herself.'

'Where in Barcelona?'

'The Rivales's house. She said she was going to tackle Uncle Salas concerning Peedee's disappearance. As though Salas would say anything, even if he knew! Ramiro keeps his uncle firmly under his Communist thumb.'

'Thanks, I'll go and find her.'

'And Peedee, of course. What a great crusader you are, Dr Devlin. I've no doubt in my mind you'll be able to find Raven and my grandfather as cleverly as you found Pippa.'

'If you've got something to say to me, Roxana, say it!'

'I'm just *so* glad you're joining the family, darling. I'm

ecstatic about having you as a brother-in-law instead of the Pope in Rome.'

'Thanks again – you're a strange girl, Roxana.' He gave her a funny look.

'I'm flattered. I suppose I must seem like a girl to you. No offence, the age gap is quite acceptable. You're wearing well. I've always fancied your hunky baseball body that hasn't as yet turned to saggy flab despite the grizzled locks. And now that you can afford a decent haircut the seasoned look suits you. The salt doesn't show nearly as much as it did during your mad professor era in the Parc Mon Repos. I suppose thirteen years older than us is nothing if not enchanting when weighed against all those years of experience – sexual as well as surgical: as long as you're not intending to use my sister as a young limb – or lamb – for your old age.'

'Go to hell, lady!' He left the sink and her poisonous-aunt presence.

In the kitchen-yard, just as he was getting back into his car, Roxana poked her head in. 'Got a cigarette I can cadge off you, blueberry-pie eyes?'

He tossed her the packet lying on the dashboard. 'Virginias, something you wouldn't know about, honey.'

Her husky laugh was full of tobacco smoke. 'I always knew you had a weak heel somewhere. Hookers to heavenly angels, eh, Keir?'

He grinned. '*Touché*! You smoke too much, you know.'

'See you later, Keir, ta-ta!' She waved him out of the yard.

The same maid that had answered his enquiry once before in the Carrer Sarrià opened the door. 'Can you tell me if a young lady from the Spanish Red Cross, Señorita Quennell, has called here today?' he asked.

'No, Señor Doctor.' She shook her head emphatically.

'You're sure?'

'I am certain, Señor Doctor. I have been answering this door all day to other people, but not once for the Señorita Quennell.'

'Thank you, señorita. Is *anyone* at home?'

'Only Señora Rivales, and she has a sick headache. She has had too many inquisitive visitors today and it has made her ill.'

'May I see her?'

'Wait here one moment, please.'

In a little while the maid took him to the darkened drawing-room where Señora Rivales lay on the sofa with a handkerchief over her eyes. 'It is these air-raids. They upset me terribly. Tomas is dead, you know. He and his cousin Carlos, both. Carlos was killed by Italians, and he an ace pilot just like that Garcia Morato from the other side. In the skies right above Caspe poor Carlos was shot down in flames. Tomas died at Tereul. Silk parachutes and snowdrifts, they are the wreaths of the dead in the valley of the Ebro this winter, Señor Doctor. And, as if the family do not have enough sorrow to bear, Ampro has become nothing but a *puta* for these swanky Assault Guards from Valencia. This is an evil war, Señor Doctor.'

'It is, indeed, Señora Rivales.'

'What can I do for you, Señora Doctor?'

'What has happened to Señor Purnell?'

'I would like you to tell me, Señor Doctor. I have been keeping his dinner warm for over a month.'

'Did he let anyone know where he was going?'

'He was supposed to have been going first to Port Bou, and then on a fishing trip that would take him along the coast and into France. Marseilles, Salas said. But whether that's true or not we have no way of knowing. Salas is worried about the old Englishman. Salas has to be careful now that Ramiro is head of the security section at SIM headquarters. The Communists are suspicious of my husband, I don't know why. So Salas has to watch his step carefully. The Fabrica de Luchar has changed from a collectivized garment-making workshop to ballistics production, just like the Fabrica Hispano Suiza which is also manufacturing high explosives.'

'Yes, I had heard.'

'Salas says that the Communists and workers' cooperatives are ruining the economy of Republican Spain, because of all this change over time and time again. There is no stability any more. Neither do the Communist cooperatives pay up on time. There is never sufficient money to put back into the economy. They're even holding onto mountains of wheat for the best price. Meanwhile, we are all starving. Salas says we Catalonians should be prosperous with all our manufactured goods, and the people of Barcelona should *not* be starving to death. It is the fault of the Communists. They are the ones who are driving the factory workers to produce third-rate weapons and high explosives without realizing that a war is also won through high morale, which can only be fed by bread and meat and milk: the Communists will lose this war for us.'

Keir murmured some sympathetic words while the poor woman continued to pour out her family troubles. 'Poor Salas has so much to think of these days. He has aged twenty years since this war started. Who could have thought that spies and traitors and *putas* would be found in one's own family?'

'Yes, indeed. This war has not been good for families.' Keir desperately searched his mind for a way to change the subject. In the end he came out with it direct: 'Has Señorita Quennell called here in the last twenty-four hours, señora?'

'No, Señor Doctor. I wish she would. She is the only one who knows how to massage my neck properly and relieve me of my terrible headaches.'

He smiled as he took his leave. '*That* I can believe, Señora Rivales.'

Raven was not to be found at the Quaker refugee centre, and she had not called at the Calle Lauria, either.

Puzzled, he went back later that evening to Cabo Alondra. Carina informed him over a cup of cocoa that Roxana had gone to the cinema in Toril.

He decided to wait for Roxana, Carina providing him with endless mugs of watered-down cocoa as he patiently sat out the time, both of them listening to the broadcasts over the wireless in the kitchen.

'Where's Raven?' he tackled Roxana the moment she set foot in the door.

Life for Roxana had become extremely monotonous just sitting around a kitchen-table all day listening to the radio,

662

while sorting lentils and shelling peas. She had almost made up her mind to head for London or Paris on her good, solid British passport. But there was so much talk of a major European war these days, she felt safer staying put at Cabo Alondra for the time being. Neither had she any wish to run into anyone from the international circuit who might start raking up the circumstances of Vida's death. Besides, her so-called avant-garde friends had all melted away like rancid butter. And, she had to face it, she was still tied to José. Until those matrimonial bonds were undone, she felt that if she behaved herself like a good little hard-done-by wife she might just be able to get a worthwhile financial settlement out of it all, especially as there was Pippa to consider. Another reason for staying on was Keir himself. If, as seemed very likely, Raven was contemplating returning to the convent, then Keir was going to want a shoulder to cry on. So she was more than delighted to see him.

'Darling, look here – a telegram that arrived shortly before I went out.' Without removing her coat and hat Roxana rested her handbag on the kitchen table, and fumbled inside it for the telegram. 'Now where is it – she's gone to Paris to be with Jan and Archie Cunningham who are up to their eyes in this Franco-Spanish war and visa business. You do know Archie Cunningham is with the Consular section of our British Embassy in Paris? Oh here, I've found it!' Roxana handed the telegram to Keir. 'Raven sent it from Barcelona, obviously in anticipation of her speedy arrival in France. My sister would never allow a simple thing like Spanish Anarchists blowing up railway trains to stop her in her tasks, hence the hasty holiday! Jan and Archie being her closest friends, by now she's no doubt pouring out her troubles on their stalwart British shoulders – and try saying that when you're sober!' Roxana giggled, her couldn't-care-less attitude where her sister was concerned irritating him.

Keir read the telegram. It was indeed from Raven, advising her grandfather and sister of her intention to spend a few days in Paris with friends.

There was so much confusion in Barcelona, Keir was run

off his feet for the next fortnight so that he hardly had time to think straight. It appeared that the whole of Spain was trying to get to France, including the Spanish Premier, Dr Negrín. The Republican Government had once again shifted, this time to Gerona.

He knew that Raven would contact him from Paris as soon as she was able to 'sort herself out'. He did not imagine this flight and sudden panic of hers was anything to do with her 'dark night of the soul' as before. This was just pre-marriage nerves. His mother, before her second marriage, had suffered from the same. Women were creatures ruled by their hormones: Raven needed a break in the company of her friends. As for him, war work had now to come first, love second, though he wished a thousand times it were not so.

Then, in the middle of one dreadful night, Keir woke up sweating. A horrible dream – no a nightmare – held him momentarily paralyzed with fear. He knew he should have gone after Raven sooner.

His fingers shaky, he got into his clothes as fast as he could and went out into the yard where his car was parked. It wouldn't start. Then the air-raid siren went off. 'Damn and blast!' he cursed, as the first wave of Nationalist war planes began their nightly onslaught. The soft whoosh of air close by was followed by the sound of shattering glass, then the swift torch of fire as a building on the opposite side of the Calle Lauria was hit.

He got out, yanked the cranking-handle, got in, hit the starter-button again, and this time the car spluttered into life as he turned the ignition key. It was sheer suicide to be out on the road, but he couldn't have cared less: he had to find Raven again, or die in the attempt. He didn't even know if the Renault had enough petrol to get him to Vilafranca as he dodged his way through ambulances and fire engines screaming all over the city.

He drove the thirty kilometres to Vilafranca as though the devil were on his tail. Keir then spent fifteen minutes frantically ringing the Mother House bell and generally causing a worse disruption than the air-raids over Catalonia. 'I won't leave these premises until I get to speak to Raven!'

'We don't know what you're talking about, señor!' squeaked Postulant Mother and Novice Mother both, as they peered through the wrought-iron fretwork gates of the Generalate House, before taking another peek at the good Lord above Vilafranca, where tracer-beams rent the night skies, and the anti-aircraft guns jiggered their nerves. 'You should be in an air-raid shelter and so should we, señor! Not out here in the open.'

'*Sister Justina*! You know damn well who I'm talking about!' He rattled the gates. 'Open these goddamn gates,' he said viciously, 'or by God I'll run my car straight through them!'

Shortly after such a show of belligerence, he had been taken to Dame Superior Olivera's office. 'Good morning, Dr Devlin. Once again we have occasion to meet at this extremely early hour of vigils.'

He was in no mood for her, and made it perfectly obvious. 'Cut the pious claptrap, Holy Mother. I'm here to talk to Raven.'

She raised an eyebrow in astonishment. 'Raven?'

'*Yes*, goddammit!'

'Oh – you mean Sister Justina!'

'Yes, Sister Justina! I know she's here, so fetch her to me at once.'

'She is at lauds.'

'She can be playing football for all I care. Just get her here.'

Dame Superior Olivera would not have tolerated such disrespect from anyone else and would have shown them the door without hesitation. But she contained a soft spot in her heart for Dr Devlin, and so she was prepared to forgive him his rudeness. She tried to calm his turbulent spirit. 'What you must understand, Dr Devlin, is that Sister Justina is of a sensitive and emotional nature. Things upset her easily. She hasn't the resilience of other, less intelligent women. She succumbs to her surroundings and to those around her because she lets herself become too emotionally involved. And then she herself suffers. She does not want a transitional earthly love which survives only as long as the mating of cicadas, but spiritual love that will outshine everything, that everlasting joy and inner peace the outside world cannot bring her. Sister Justina has need of the comfort and companionship of her spiritual sisters, Dr Devlin. She belongs in the cloister, that is why she returned to us.'

'*Bring her to me*! I don't believe one word of that holy baloney!'

'Sister Justina is undergoing a period of denial and abstinence. She is under strict vows – with the correct supervision those vows entail. She is unable to see anyone.'

'If you don't bring her to me in five minutes flat, I'll go and look for her myself even if it means invading your sacred cloister.'

'If you try and remove her forcibly from these premises, God will punish you, Dr Devlin. She has asked for sanctuary and I have given it to her. God has chosen Sister Justina to serve him.'

'Serve you, you mean, lady! I know what you are and what you want from Raven. But you're not getting it from her, over my dead body you're not! You *are* corrupt, you and your lesbian Motherhood piously hiding behind your smuggled Bibles containing the word of Franco, not God, while you suppress other Christian religions in Spain and destroy *their* Bibles. Popely power over the people, huh, Holy Mother? Not to mention those poor, frightened, ordinary folk out there, blackmailed into parting with their hard-earned pesetas to the Church in order to purchase salvation for their damned souls in a Catholic purgatory and hell, while *you're* the ones committing the real sins!'

'How *dare* you, Dr Devlin! God will punish you for such blasphemy!'

'And, by God, he'll punish you too, *Dame* Superior, if you don't allow Raven to tell me the truth from her own lips. If she really does want to remain a nun, and tells me so herself, then I shall leave without a word. Now bring her to me please. I want the truth – from her, no one else.'

Dame Superior Olivera took custody of the senses. Serenely, she went over to the bell rope. She asked the extern nun who answered her summons to fetch Sister Justina from her devotions.

*

'Oh God!'

He could not believe his eyes when he saw her dressed once more in her white robes, her white winged head-dress covering her shining dark hair, her hands in her wide sleeves, her eyes downcast to the floor, not looking him in the eye at all while she turned the knife so viciously in the wound of his heart. 'Why, Raven? Please tell me why?'

Dame Superior Olivera, still present in the room, had turned her back upon them. She knelt in front of the huge crucifix on the wall. Her eyes closed, her head high, her hands clasped around her rosary beads, she prayed while the young novice behind her stood like a statue in front of the man who claimed her for love and refused to give her up despite the evidence before him. But God was stronger than the man, and Dame Superior Olivera knew it.

'Raven – don't do this to me. Please, I beg of you – look, if you want me to beg, I'll do it.' He knelt down in front of her and put his face against her as he hugged her tightly round the waist.

'Don't do it, Dr Devlin!' Her voice was sharp, an edge to it he had never heard before.

He held on.

Then, quite unexpectedly, she dropped to her knees before him. 'If you kneel, then I must kneel. I didn't deliberately set out to hurt you. There are some things you don't understand ...'

'No, I'll never understand. Oh, *Raven*.' He put his hands out again, hovering towards her shoulders, and then withdrew them, unsure of what to do, only that if he touched her now he would not let go this time, and he could not humiliate her or himself in the presence of the woman kneeling with her back to them before her crucifix.

Keir searched his mind for all the reasons why Raven should betray him in this fashion. 'Pain I can understand.' He took a deep breath. 'I know about human suffering. I can understand it when it's not of our own choosing. What you've been through, I understand. But what I cannot understand or accept is the pain you're deliberately imposing upon both of us. You don't have to seek a cloister in order to gain salvation for all the sins of the world you're taking upon your shoulders. I *don't* understand what you're doing to yourself – to me, to us. Raven, please think again, that's all I ask of you.'

He got to his feet, sniffing back his feelings for her as he wiped his face with his hand, and she had the grace to stand with him.

'Did you really go to Paris?' he asked as he turned aside and regarded Dame Superior Olivera's grey figure in prayer, the chaperon who had wrecked his life.

'Yes.'

'For how long?'

'Four days.'

'Why?'

'To think things out clearly away from Spain, away from war, and you.'

'I see. What did Roxana say to you about me? Is this something to do with my previous marriage – my divorce? Being the good Catholic girl that you are, are you perhaps having second thoughts about us? Is it something to do with marrying a divorced man so that any children we might have would be called bastards? Is that what it's all about? I thought we'd discussed all this in our private moments in Salamanca.'

'This is nothing to do with my sister, with you, with your previous marriage or divorce. This is my personal choice and my decision entirely.'

'Why do you always protect her? Why do you let her get away with what she does to you?' He turned back to face her. 'Roxana! Christ almighty, Raven, your sister has said something to you about me that has made you flee right back into the arms of Mother Church as though I were the Devil himself. If you turn your back on me now, I promise you I'll spend the rest of my life wringing the truth from your evil little sister's tongue.'

'Please calm down, Dr Devlin. Roxana has nothing to do with this. I can't be your wife. I don't want to be.'

'What do you mean you don't want to be?'

She withdrew something from her pocket. It was the little box he had given her in Salamanca containing his constancy ring of garnets.

'Dr Devlin, I don't love you as much as I thought I did. I love my vocation far more.'

He looked at her in amazement, refusing to believe it. 'Oh, my God! You really are screwed up about everything … Look, my darling, I promise …'

'No more promises. Please, just go!'

He took the ring back. 'Okay lady. Hint taken. I'm not wanted.' He went to the door and opened it.

Dame Superior Olivera got up off her knees and stood with her hands clasped in front of her. Her regality overwhelming as she watched his departure in total silence, Keir held her in his glance for a long, fixed moment and then, retracing his steps, put the jewel-box in her hand. 'Keep it. You were right. Winner takes all. In that little box are all my hopes and dreams. *Salve Regina*!'

He left the Generalate House close to the Iglesia de la Trinitat.

Vilafranca was being bombed as mercilessly as Barcelona. In order to stop Republican troop-movements, the Nationalist Air Force was trying to destroy the strategic Barcelona-Tarragona railway line that passed through Vilafranca.

A bomb fell on the warehouses and bodegas in Commercial Street running on a parallel with the railway line, and Keir had to find an alternative route in order to get out of the town and back on the Barcelona road.

He wished a bomb would land right on top of him and his car; death would be acceptable. It would be God's will, he told himself. His heart and life had been thoroughly screwed around with by Raven Quennell. So much so, that now he didn't give a goddamn one way or another.

After he had gone, Raven went back to her cell in the Mother House.

She couldn't breathe, the pain in her temples and elsewhere was shattering. She closed her eyes and pressed her hands against the place where his head had rested when he had pleaded with her: only then did she come to terms with what she had done to him, and to herself.

CHAPTER NINETEEN

Vinarosa: January 1939

On the morning following the bombing of the railway line at Vilafranca, Ramiro went to the exclusive Clinic del Rey to see his special-category prisoner. The nursing staff informed him that the prisoner had not rallied, and was not expected to live much longer.

Ramiro looked at the sick old man in the hospital bed. He heard the harsh râles from his chest. Pneumonia, he was told, had set in.

Ramiro was sorry.

Now, only the good times with the old man presented themselves: the Englishman might have been an interfering old busybody, but at least he had been an amusing one.

Ramiro wanted so desperately to break the spy-ring that had strangled Barcelona: all those collaborators and traitors who had betrayed Catalonia to the Fascists – but it looked as though he had lost his last chance.

His last chance! Ramiro sucked in his breath, the pain of loss reasserting itself.

There was one person who might just rally the old man!

Ramiro left the clinic and got into his official black Citroën, the car that so often in the past, and without their knowing it, had followed Raven and Dame Conceptión on the occasions of their Bible-smuggling sorties in and out of the city. Ramiro gave instructions to his driver to go to the Plaza Iglesia de la Trinitat in Vilafranca.

Commercial Street was a river of blood: until he realized that one of the wineries had been hit by a bomb. He hoped it was not his father's bodega, for what a waste of all that good, rich red wine flowing as freely as a river.

'The rebel air force, who employ Italian pilots, never were very good at pinpointing their targets,' was Ramiro's salty comment to his driver. 'I wonder whose bodega they hit last night?'

Comrade Ortega, like Don Ruiz's chauffeur, Pedro, came from Vilafranca and knew everything that went on in the small town. 'It is the famous Torres bodega, Commissar.'

'Then I have no cause to worry,' replied Ramiro.

Dame Superior Olivera was getting tired of all these outside demands to see Sister Justina. The moment Sister Justina had presented herself at the Mother House gates, the peace that had prevailed during her absence and period of 'finding herself again' became a thing of the past. It appeared that Sister Justina was the honey-jar to a great many people.

'She is under strict vows, Commissar de Luchar, and she cannot leave these diocesan walls.'

'Dame Superior Olivera, it is still within my power to close down this order,' he said pacing the space in front of her desk, while in his right hand he slapped his leather gloves rhythmically against his thigh.

'You cannot persecute us any more, Commissar de Luchar. Under new laws, the Roman Catholic Church in Spain has been granted amnesty and tolerance.'

'But I am still the law in this part of Spain. The Nationalists are not here yet.' Ramiro smiled at her seductively, before fingering the crucifix on the wall. He examined his finger. 'The patina is superb. Such old wood, polished and dusted with loving care over the years. A pity to see so many precious relics, such as you have here, go up in smoke – as at Toril.' He turned back and faced her, his silvery eyes as placid and as dangerous as a bottomless pool. 'Bring Sister Justina to me, otherwise I will turn this place upside down.'

Dame Superior Olivera swallowed several times, the words sticking in her throat. 'No! She may not leave the cloister.'

'Then I have no choice but to close down this order. I will get my men to take six nuns into the Bishop's garden where they will be shot. Then six more, and six more, until you come to your senses.'

'What possible reason have you to question Sister Justina?'

'Would you rather I arrested and questioned you instead, Dame Superior Olivera? Who is the ringleader of your little Papal spy organization working for the downfall of the Communists in Catalonia?'

'I've no idea what you're talking about, Commissar de Luchar.'

'Oh yes you have. Have you so quickly forgotten about your Bible-smuggling activities?'

'I? *I* never venture beyond my four walls, Señor de Luchar, so do not know what you are implying.'

'Come, come! I'm not here to bandy words with you. *You*, as the Dame Superior over this whole order of Camillus nuns, are as much a part of the downfall of the Jesu María Convent in Barcelona as was the Reverend Dame Infanta herself, hand in glove with the Falangist Franciscan priests living next-door to her in the Puerto del Angel! You Church people may be hoping that the Fascists win the day, but I will tell you one thing, if General Franco grabs power in Catalonia, you will not have the freedom of religion which has been promised you. Franco will make the Church his victims as much as he will make the ordinary people the victims of his Fascist military régime.'

'I do not know what you are talking about, Commissar de Luchar.'

'You will, Dame Superior Olivera, you will. The Holy See of Rome has played a great part in the persecution of the Spanish Church, simply because it has chosen to dabble in politics as well as religion. Behind your convent walls a great deal goes on that is nothing to do with prayer, but everything to do with power-politics and espionage. I believe Sister Justina to be part of this subtle network propped up by Rome and Great Britain: infiltrators, Fifth Columnists, foreign agents, collaborators, all working on behalf of anti-Communist governments. Have I made myself perfectly clear? So now, either you bring Sister

Justina to me, or what was done to the Jesu María will be done to the Convent of the Sacred Heart.'

Dame Superior Olivera licked her dry lips. What was she to do? How could she betray someone who had asked for sanctuary? How could she possibly live with herself should something happen to Sister Justina at the hands of the Communists? Far better Dr Devlin had attained her in marriage than ruffians with ulterior motives. She was at a crossroads, and did not know which turning to take.

The answer presented itself with startling clarity in the very same instant she questioned her own integrity: would you rather have another convent of yours put to the torch? Would you rather another score of nuns die for the sake of one? Raped, humiliated, and violated like those at the Jesu María, for someone this man says is a spy and foreign infiltrator hiding behind her nun's veil?

'Very well, Commissar de Luchar. There has been enough bloodshed. Our order has suffered enough. If I must sacrifice Sister Justina because you say she is a spy and a foreign agent, then you may have her if it means protecting the rest of this order.' She rang the bell, and when the extern nun answered her summons, she said to Sister Jeanne, 'Fetch Sister Justina to me at once.'

Keir was not the only one who presented a guant, red-eyed, and déshabillé appearance that day. He had not gone to his bed at all, but straight to his duties at the Calle Lauria after having left Raven to her nuns in Vilafranca. Most people had been awake all night from the air-raids, and five o'clock in the morning at Red Cross Headquarters was as chaotic as at five in the afternoon.

The weak primrose sunrise of a Catalonian winter's dawn cleansed his spirit. The shrouded mountains surrounding Barcelona were like the shared blanket of a comrade in arms: the city and the camaraderie spirit within it had crept under his skin and he wanted to rid himself of this closed-in feeling that had somehow taken possession of his soul. He was becoming addicted and victimized by his surroundings; Guatemala all over again. This brethren of mankind feeling, all this commitment to a foreign cause on foreign shores engendered by a war that was not his, was going to be another reckoning unless he was careful. He was an American, neutral and constitutional, goddammit, so why get so worked up about all these Europeans!

Keir immersed himself in his routine visits of refugee centres, prisons, orphanages, and hospitals. He knew from bitter experience that only good, solid hard work prevented one from dwelling depressively upon personal problems.

At the end of the day he felt better for it, emotional passion expended in physical and mental labour so that he felt calmer in himself and able to think more clearly. What had Raven said? *Passions can either overcome us, or we can overcome them.* Well, he had taken her advice.

After his tour of duty, he got into his car and drove out to Cabo Alondra.

Through the unshuttered kitchen window he could see Roxana alone at the table, and knew the door would be unlocked. Keir let himself in.

Ready for bed by the look of her, she was a real fashion plate bimbette in her satiny white dressing-gown, her bright curls done up in a big white satin bow. Listening to the wireless while playing a game of patience, a bottle of de Luchar brandy was in front of her along with the cards.

She glanced up as he removed his scarf, her smile feline. 'Hello, darling! You must have known that this is the hour Carina spends up at the Mas Luchar gossiping with Isaba and the rest of the old women. I'm all alone celebrating my twenty-sixth birthday as a grass-widow while Raven remains the wholesome little virgin,. I knew you'd be back sometime … Ouch, Keir!' Startled, she looked up at him, properly this time.

He had taken her wrist in a vice. 'Just what have you said to Raven to make her turn against me?' he asked across the width of the kitchen table.

'What are you talking about, Keir? Please let go, you're hurting me!'

'I'll hurt you a lot more unless you level with me.'

He held his grip a few seconds longer, then let her go.

'Brute!' she said rubbing her wrist. 'What's the matter with you? I didn't know you could behave like this.'

'You don't know a lot about me, lady. Underneath, I'm just like all the guys you've spent your life screwing. I'm reverting to type. My period of rehabilitation is over, *darling*!'

She reached for the bottle of brandy and slopped some into her glass. 'Want some?' She eyed him sullenly.

He went to the draining-board, took a glass from the dish-drainer and slammed it down in front of her. 'Why not? If you can't beat 'em, join 'em. In that way you might learn something, meaning *your*-self! Cheers, honey! Happy birthday!' He took a big swig of the best brandy on the house, and smacking his lips gave Roxana a sadistic little smile. '*Now*, since we both know why I'm here, and what we want, though for very different reasons, do we screw first and talk later, or talk first and then pitch?'

Roxana took a deep breath. 'Raven's gone back to the Camillus?'

'*Damn right*!' His fist crashed down on the table, scattering the cards and making her jump. 'And you put her back there, you scheming little *bitch*!'

'Stop it, Keir! I don't like you in this mood.'

He came to her and took her up by the lapels of her silky dressing-gown, hoisting her out of her chair and her complacency, and aware, as he drew her close, that she wore no nightdress underneath her robe. He said smoothly, 'Don't you? But you planned all this, Roxana honey, didn't you?'

'I did not.'

'Then what did you say to Raven to upset her so badly, she had to go rushing back to her goddamn Mother House after she'd promised to marry me?'

'I've said nothing. Raven's mentally unstable at times. Blame it on the bomb that wrecked our lives in Ireland, not me. Raven's nerves are bad. She's always been the same. Then there was that PSUC and POUM business at the Convent of Jesu María. She was pratically raped by some Anarchists or – or Communists, I don't know. Maybe that turned her off men ...'

'*Plural*, Roxana honey. Not me! She loved me, I know she did.' He released her and went and sat down on a kitchen chair. He put his elbows on the table and covered his face with his hands. His voice broken and muffled, he wrestled with himself. 'She's the world to me. The sun, moon and stars – if you can ever understand that. And she's a bloody sight saner than you are, Roxana. I told her – I told her – no, it doesn't matter what I told her. She's too much of a lady to be discussed with the likes of you.' He took up the glass of brandy, drank it and then poured himself some more.

'Keir, if you want to know everything, I'll tell you. Maybe in that way you can win her back.' Roxana took a deep breath and calmed her own nerves. 'Raven believes Pippa is your child.'

His heard jerked round. He looked at Roxana aghast. 'But that's bloody ludicrous!'

'Of *course* it is! But she's got this fixation, and it won't be shifted. She believed you betrayed her with me: lately, as well as in Paris and Geneva. She thought that in Geneva you and I had an affair.'

'I know. She mentioned it. I told her the truth.'

'So did I. We were looking through a photograph album on Christmas afternoon and she saw some pictures of you, Vida, and me in the Parc Mon Repos, and in Paris. That time you were on your way to London, you remember, when Vida and I came to your hotel and carted you off to the Moulin Rouge to make up a foursome with her papa and ...'

'Yes, I remember,' he said testily. 'But it was a completely innocent interlude. What's this to do with anything?'

'I tried telling her there was nothing between us. Raven wouldn't believe it. She thought we were – were still sleeping together. It was all to do with this Geneva fixation, just because I happened to go to your mother's apartment when she wasn't there but you were – that time you threw me out, much to my chagrin. But we won't go into all that because it isn't important. What is important, Raven believes Pippa is your daughter. Unfortunately, Raven saw a letter from José once, accusing me of having affairs with every Tom, Dick, and Harry, and denying Pippa to be his child – which wasn't really fair. However, the fact remains, Raven thinks your obsession with finding Pippa stems from more personal reasons.'

'It wasn't an obsession, I'd have done it for anybody who had a kid missing.'

'Don't I know that.'

Roxana saw that the brandy-bottle was empty and took another one from Peedee's cubbyhole in his study, where, at his desk, she had perfected her calligraphic skills so convincingly on her daughter's birth certificate. So much so Raven had been duped into believing that the names which had been changed were indeed the real ones! Diligence had its reward, after all, were her smug thoughts in that moment. In school, the only two subjects in which she had shone had been art and calligraphy. Roxana gave a fleeting smile of satisfaction to herself before returning to the kitchen.

She refilled Keir's glass. 'Darling, get that down you. You're overwrought and I can't blame you. I know how much Raven meant to you: she means a lot to all of us. But she's always had this religion thing since childhood. It was all to do with our nurse Cassy being a fanatical old Catholic. For some reason Raven felt secure and loved with that nutty old nurse of ours. Cassy gave us all a sense of permanence in our lives which our parents did not. They were always flitting here, there, and everywhere. There was a lot of hatred against the rich Protestant Anglo-Irish community at that time. I can't help feeling that Raven and Sonny turned to Catholicism because they wanted to belong to the real Ireland into whose bosom they would be accepted by becoming Catholics. Raven always felt that that bomb, which caused the death of our parents, her beloved Cassy, and big brother, Tim, whom she idolized, was some sort of personal judgement on the family, for which she should try and make amends.'

'I can understand that.'

'Then you will understand Raven's need to be with people with whom she feels safe.'

'She was safe with me.'

'But she wasn't! Not as far as she believed.' Roxana came beside him, and wrapped her arms around him. She began smoothing his forehead and tousled hair. Then, her hand under his chin, she looked into his haggard face. 'Poor Keir. I don't think you slept all night, and your chin feels like a boot-scraper.' She poured more brandy and put the glass into his hand. 'Drink this, you'll sleep better for it. Tomorrow, if you like, we'll both go to Vilafranca to talk to Raven. I'll tell her that she's being a fool to herself while hurting you dreadfully. There's still time. She hasn't become a fully-professed yet.'

'You'd do that – for me?' He wrapped the glass to his chest while eyeing her uncertainly.

'Of course, darling. How can I ever forget what you did for me in Bilbao. Rescuing me from that awful Lars fellow and spending so much time on my behalf trying to trace Pippa for me. I have so much to thank you for Keir, this is the least I can do for you.'

He looked down again into his glass. 'Too late,' he mumbled, 'too late – Mother Church has won again. Give me some more of that – stuff, Roxa. It makes me feel good. No wonder Joss liked it – can't blame him, poor old bugger. That O'Reilly was a real bastard … Here, have some yourself, honey.' He missed her glass and sloshed brandy on the table.

Roxana took the bottle from him, not having realized he wasn't used to heavy drinking. 'I think you've had enough for one night. Come on, Keir, bed.' She tried raising him, but he was impossible to move without cooperation.

'Roxahoney, leavemealone – just let me drown – drown in the pisspot of my – my sorrows. I wannabe AWOL with Raven. I wanna screw – no not, screw, wrong word. Youdondothat – do *that*, with a real *trooo* lady like Raven, only hook … hookers, only losers. *Losers!* Love is the goddambest thing … for win-winners, for-for …' He took a deep breath, trying to get a grip on himself and really not caring one way or another, just as he had felt on the road from Vilafranca with Nationalist war planes overhead bombing the living hell out of everyone. 'Ros-Rosy honey, I wanna make love – make love to-to – Rave-Raven. Aw'll friggin' night – as Win – Winnie would've said.'

'Of course you do, sweetie, but it's time for bed, come on. Carina will be returning soon and then there'll be another scandal for me to handle, so let's get you upstairs and out of the way.'

She supported him up the stairs to her bedroom, where he flopped on her bed, out for the count. She undid the laces of his shoes, sighing to herself as she did so, 'So much for your American lover, Raven. In this business, it's called *impotencia*: and the Spanish language being as chauvinistic as the men, they even blame the woman for it by giving it a feminine noun. So long, feller!' His shoes removed, she drew the coverlet up to his chin.

Roxana slept in Raven's room.

At her grandfather's bedside in the Clinic del Rey, Raven had spent the entire day on her knees: *Hail Mary, full of grace, the Lord is with thee: blessed art thou amongst women: blessed is the fruit of thy womb, Jesus* ... Please don't let Peedee die ...'

When she had first seen the state her grandfather was in, Raven was shocked and appalled. The dull red marks all over his body and his feet held an ominous significance. Not for one moment had she believed Ramiro's story about finding Peedee on the waterfront in a state of collapse. Or the doctor's diagnosis of typhus fever. They had tried explaining away the marks on Peedee's body as the 'petechial bloodspots of typhus'.

'And he *has* been away at sea,' Ramiro added after the nervous little Hungarian doctor had spoken with her. 'He has been to Marseilles recently.'

'What has that got to do with it?' Raven demanded as she glared at Ramiro.

'The doctor tells me that typhus can be caused by lice and rat-flea bites, the kind that live on ships and boats. And through bad living. Your grandfather has neglected himself ever since he left Uncle Salas's house and my aunt's good cooking. He has been seen wandering around the waterfront, and so I cannot help feeling that your grandfather has gone a little senile and does not know what he is doing any more.'

'How dare you! My grandfather is *not* senile! He's perfectly sane. Or at least, he was, until – until *you* did this to him!' This was yet another trial for her to bear, sent by the Devil working through other devils: Raven battled with herself even as she turned furiously upon Ramiro. 'These marks on my grandfather are *not* the bloodspots of typhus fever, but the burns from lighted cigarettes held on bare skin, and if I have to Ramiro, I'll bring a Red Cross doctor here to prove it!'

'Dr Keir Devlin, your American accomplice, no doubt, eh, Raven?'

Had she not been what she was, she would have spat on Ramiro. Instead, she had to try and forgive. She turned away from him, her 'dark night of the soul' returning when she thought she had almost conquered her human passions.

Raven picked up her rosary again. 'Go away Ramiro. I don't believe one word of yours, or that doctor you bribed to tell such untruths. I believe your SIM agents had something to do with this.'

'What do you know about SIM, Raven?' Ramiro asked softly.

He stood with his hands clasped behind his back, his feet slightly apart, so close to her kneeling figure, his oppressive shadow over her was unnerving.

'Sister Justina to you.'

'I beg your pardon, Sister Justina.'

'I know what everyone else knows about it. That it's a diabolical instrument of Communist government for the interrogation and torture of innocent people.'

'No one is innocent in this war. Not your grandfather, and certainly not you, my holy little nun who runs illegal errands on behalf of the Roman Catholic Church, and who knows, perhaps the British Government, too?' Ramiro bent over her and hissed in her ear, 'Do you know that I could have you *shot!*'

'Go away, Ramiro. Leave me alone with Peedee. Or I'll fetch someone right now who has everything to do with the Geneva Convention, to see what you've done to my grandfather. How could you when Peedee was your tutor, your friend and – and *comrade!*' She raised her voice in despair, unable to comprehend how any one human being could be so cruel to another.

Obligingly Ramiro turned on his heel and left the private ward. Raven prayed for forgiveness for having lost control, yet again.

Towards the late evening, as she held her rosary beads in her hands, Peedee became a little restless. He appeared to be coming out of his soporific state induced by pain-killing drugs. Quickly Raven reached for the glass of water by Peedee's bed. 'Peedee – dearest Grandpapa, it's me, Raven.'

He licked his cracked, encrusted lips she had swabbed with soothing glycerine. Froth gathered at the corners of his mouth, his chest sounded like a bubbling cauldron. Raven placed the glass to his lips and he sipped once. Then, exhausted, he lay back against the pillows. After a while he squeezed her fingers, gaining strength from her presence. 'Raven?'

'Yes, I'm still here, my dearest Grandpa.'

'Raven – fiv – fiv …'

'Yes, Peedee, five …'

He tried again. 'No – not five, fif-fifth.'

'Fifth?'

He smiled stiffly but courageously despite his sore mouth and the wheezing effort of speech and movement.

She hazarded a guess. 'Fifth Column?'

He hissed between his teeth.

She took it to mean si. 'Who, Grandpapa?'

'Car …' For the moment, he was too breathless to say any more.

Raven tried desperately to understand him. 'Car? What car? Whose car?'

Then he shook his head. 'Rina,' he said quite clearly.

'Car – car – rina. Carina, Grandpapa!'

'Sì!'

'Carina is a Fifth Columnist?'

He shook his head again. His fingers twitching, he lifted them to his face, fingering his cuts and bruises and swellings. Then he reached out to touch her face lovingly. Raven gave him some more water to drink. 'Ahh!' he gasped, the effort too much for him.

'Oh, Peedee, please don't talk any more. Don't, if it's causing you so much distress. It doesn't matter. All that matters is your getting better.'

'Ahn – sk!'

'Ask Carina – ask Carina about the Fifth Column?' Raven stared at him.

He said no more. His breath began to rattle in his throat. Then his grey head sank lower and lower towards his chest until even his breathing quietened and all she had to do was wipe away the yellow phlegm and frothy white spittle from his open mouth.

'Peedee?' Raven whispered. She shook him gently. 'Peedee – oh, no! Oh, don't die … Please, you mustn't die! We need each other – more than ever, Peedee. Dearest Grandpapa!' Her head dropped to his thin speckled hand and she began to cry with a terrible rending inside her, because she remembered who had salvaged Sonny, her, and Roxana from a terrible beginning.

Keir was used to only a few hours' sleep a night. Six hours of undisturbed sleep constituted a whole lifetime. His eyes wide open, it was still dark, and he sensed his strange surroundings rather than saw them. He glanced at the dial of his luminous wristwatch and discovered it to be only four o'clock in the morning.

'Bloody hell!' he groaned to himself, a hammer in his head, remembering the amount of Imperial brandy he had drunk in Roxana's company. He hoped he hadn't done anything else. He felt himself all over but only his shoes appeared to be missing. Cautiously he touched the space beside him, but there was no female body lying naked and close.

He sat up and switched on the bedside-lamp, groaning again as the electric light struck his senses. He quickly switched it off. 'What a turkey you are, Devlin!' he muttered to himself as he got out of bed. He sat on the edge, scrubbing his bristly face with his hands, trying to collect his woolly wits. He wondered if the old man of the house had left a razor in the bathroom. Keir took off his sweaty shirt. Then, quietly, for fear of waking Carina, he crept out onto the landing and to the bathroom. He washed, and used an old razor of Peedee's to shave himself.

Half an hour later, feeling a little more refreshed, his

dull headache receding, he went back into the bedroom and to the window. The dawn was beginning to creep up over the sea. Keir drew aside the frilly net curtains at Roxana's bedroom window, the shutters hooked back as Roxana hated to feel closed in. He opened the window wide, but it was so blowy, he closed it again hurriedly in case it slammed shut and disturbed Carina.

Keir stood by the window, looking-out. Silver-capped waves lapping each other constituted the only background sound. The lilt of the sea, like the repeated strains of a special piece of music one loved and admired, was soothing after the incessant shrill, tooth-cutting whine of the air-raid siren followed by the drone of heavy bombers and the clatter of the anti-aircraft guns dissecting Barcelona's night sky. Here, at Cabo Alondra it was so peaceful, the Spanish War seemed a million miles away. He lit up a cigarette and inhaled the soothing tobacco, while he gathered himself together to face another empty day, his future bleak indeed without Raven. Feeling so dead inside, he thought he might just walk his miseries away along the beach before getting into his car and heading back for Barcelona.

Keir, in the next instant, as though an icy hand had touched him, froze to a macabre alertness, like a dog with hackles raised.

On the headland where he and Raven had been reunited and had embraced each other in such delight, a figure in bridal white walked along the bus route: but there would have been no bus at this time of the pre-dawn morning. White veil blowing in the wind, she was heading straight for the villa. Keir shook his head to clear it: no such thing as ghosts, man, he told himself angrily, so pull yourself together.

It couldn't be Raven, a prisoner in the Generalate House he had visited all but twenty-four hours ago. She had gone back to her convent under a strict oath of confinement and obedience, and this time Dame Superior Olivera would see to it! He was hallucinating, conjuring up her presence because he wanted her to be there, returning to him and to the spot where he had felt like a king, restoring to him his golden crown, giving him back everything they had promised themselves: forgetting about Carina and all else, he flung wide the window, 'Raven! Jesus – *Raven!*'

She stood in the overgrown garden surrounding the villa, looking up at him, her sweet face pale and ephemeral in the dawn light. 'Keir?'

'Oh shit! *Raven – look wait!* Hang on, sweetheart, I'm coming. Let me explain – Roxana and I haven't done a thing, I promise you. That Pippa business is ludicrous – just not true, my love, and Roxana will tell you so. Wait – wait, I'm coming ...' Frantically he groped under the bed for his shoes. Unable to find them, in his urgency he went with bare chest and bare feet, almost falling down the stairs in his bid to clarify himself in Raven's eyes.

He opened the front door, but there was no Raven to be seen, in white or any other colour.

A ghost after all; just a figment of his imagination like his dreams of holding her in his arms and making love to her for the rest of his life. 'Shit, man!' he said aloud, then told himself in pent-up anger and frustration, she's got to you so much, now you're imagining things: Oh, you stupid mutt! Pull yourself together. Raven's never coming back to you, so forget it! Her sister's fault, so face it.

Might as well be hung for a sheep as a lamb. Might as well say goodbye to yesterday: he had lost Raven for good. No good crying over unfulfilled dreams that were only the vain imaginings of yesterday's, today's, and tomorrow's losers, of which he was a prime example; like father, like son, he was a loser – just like Joss ...

Keir went back upstairs and counted the doors: if that was Roxana's room, because he had slept in it surrounded by all her little bits of frippery that only Roxana could cherish, and that was the old man's room, and that was the bathroom, and that Carina's, because Roxana had tried pointing them all out to him in his inebriated state up the stairs last night in case he barged into the wrong one in the middle of the night – then this one must be Raven's. Keir opened the door.

Roxana had not drawn the curtains and the blue shutters were open. Reflected sealight was soft and silvery. The sparse whiteness of the room, the few classy objects of Raven's, the wooden crucifix on the wall above her head, it was all so essentially Raven. Keir closed the door softly. He could even smell her fresh, flowery fragrance in the air.

From all the things that had belonged to her he found the strength and the spirit of her as he wandered around that sacred little room, touching this and that in order to hold onto something that she herself had touched and cared for, until he came to the bed.

Roxana was curled like a shrimp, the feather duvet a snowdrift cradling her sleeping body. Her sateen dressing gown lay like an irridescent puddle on the colourful ceramic floor.

Keir sat down on the edge of the bed. 'Roxana?'

'Hmm-umm?' Sleepily she turned over onto her back, her luxurious hair spread out on the pillow like a fan. She looked pretty. He traced the outline of her mouth with his finger, a mouth that was Raven's. He drew the warm feather light duvet away. Roxana had nothing on. Her breasts were round white shells, like pearl oysters in the cold sealight, the kind of light that never reached one in the city. He was not used to the clear, cool beauty of that seascape aurora transforming everything it touched, or the tranquility of it. It was the magic of Cabo Alondra, magic that Raven had told him about.

Roxana's face was in shadow. One woman, a hundred, they were all the same if you forgot the essentials, the spirit and the smile. 'Honey, wake up ...' He touched one of Roxana's breasts, then he took all of it in his hand. It felt good, exactly what he needed. 'I even cleaned my teeth,' he assured her with a smile, hoping it had been Raven's toothbrush and not Carina's.

'Keir?' Roxana opened her eyes dreamily, laid her hand on top of his, the one that was working her breast while willing her to wake and respond to him. He drew the duvet right away and looked at the sleek beauty of her pale belly and thighs, and the soft down between. She smiled when she saw him looking at her, her body stirring under his hand and his gaze.

Her mouth was so much like Raven's, especially when she smiled and did not pout. Funnily enough, there were other things apart from the curve and the beauty of that special smile that reminded him of Raven, mannerisms he had never noticed before about Roxana: the shy lowering of the eyelids when she was pleased about something, the unconscious seductiveness of the looks she gave a man from under her lashes: hell, they were, after all, two out of the same mould, apart from the hair and eyes. And who cared about hair? Hair felt the same whatever and wherever, while the eyes usually stayed shut. He bent his head and kissed Roxana on a rosy nipple.

She sighed and put her arms around his neck, returning his kisses, her mouth open and hungry and responsive. 'Keir darling – this *is* an unexpected pleasure.' His chest was so masculine, she threaded her fingers in the thick mat of dark hair; his back so broad and muscular was still sensitive enough to respond to her caressing touch. Roxana's hands slipped to his waist. 'Darling, you've still got half your clothes on – oh, look here, let me help you.'

It was as though he did not know what a woman was like; had *never* known what one was like; never held one before, never even *had* one before. It was like the first time and the last time and all the times he had dreamed of this, when desire was too much to bear and had to be expended in passion, and love, uncontainable, spilled over to be shared with she who had become the vessel of his own life. He felt he held Raven in his arms, the same slender, long-legged, exquisite body that he had dreamed about so often.

The dream became the reality.

And then it didn't matter any more, the act itself took over. It *was* Raven he was fucking – over and over again, driving them both to the brink of frenzy and back again because he wanted her to know what it was like, how good it felt, what it was she had given up for sodding Mother Church! Unable to get enough of each other, like animals, coupling for the sake of it because one had been programmed by God Almighty to perform by instinct and not good sense or taste; an act that was devoid of dignity as much as human beings themselves, because doing it was the only thing to do when there was nothing else left in the world only this, the sheer carnal enjoyment, and the satisfaction that came from something so supremely human!

Roxana, hot and breathless pushed him away, bright hair tangled and damp, legs that had been circling him quivering with the dregs of desire. 'No more – for at least five minutes. Just let me recover. Give me a cigarette.'

They shared it.

'More?' he asked, not looking at her.

'More! Always more! Need you ask?' she laughed in delight, welcoming his body against hers.

'You're a nymph – and a fantastic screw – just like Francesca.'

'Am I, darling? And you're the greatest thing that's happened to me for a long time.'

She began to make love to him and nothing else mattered, only this.

'*RA-VEN*!' He couldn't help it, he had to say her name.

When at last they released each other, Roxana's harsh, tearful breathing as she sat up against the carved wooden Castillan bed-head, accused him while she distractedly smoked yet another cigarette.

He sat on the wide windowsill, monitoring the morning sea, and he felt strangely at peace with the world.

Finally, in the great silence that pervaded Raven's room, she said, 'You're a sod, Keir Devlin. It was *her*! My *sister*, you were laying in this bed. *Her* bed!'

'Of course it was her. It will never be anyone, *but* her.' He flicked his ash out of the open window.

A refrain ran through his head, a sad, haunting refrain set to the tune of the 'Red River Valley' song the Lincolns had made their own. The words had been written by an Irishman who had died almost a year ago at the Battle of Jarama. The name of Charles Donnelly might vanish in the mists of time, but the feelings conveyed would always be known to those who had faced the sun.

> 'There's a valley in Spain called Jarama,
> It's a place that we all know too well,
> For 'tis there that we wasted our manhood,
> And most of our old age as well.

Unable to shift the 'Red River Valley' throb from his head, Keir tossed his cigarette-butt out of the window, just as Nina de Luchar appeared around the side of the villa.

Not wishing to be accused of hallucinating a second time, Keir, in his trousers, but having forgotten he'd left his shirt and shoes in Roxana's room, found a baggy V-necked fisherman's jersey in Peedee's bedroom. Struggling into it, at the same time he grabbed up a pair of espadrilles that did not fit properly and rushed down to the kitchen to confront Nina.

Nina was not there.

Keir put a hand to his head. War was finally getting to him! Abyssinia and Spain, it was all getting too much. He was under too much pressure. He would be glad to be relieved of his Red Cross commitments. He was letting himself become too emotionally involved with the people around him: one of the fatal errors of any greenhorn doctor, let alone a veteran of time.

The wireless in the kitchen was tuned in to Radio Valencia, and the smells of the day's meals wafted up from Carina's pots and pans on the stove. Carina was always cooking. Vast quantities of lentils and beans, peas and onions on the table, enough to feed an army of men, which seemed rather odd to him when he considered the fact that there was only Carina and Roxana left at Cabo Alondra. And that was another thing, Roxana, at the kitchen sink, the day after Christmas when only she had been in the house, had been washing up a vast amount of crockery, cutlery, saucepans, and now that he thought about it, none of it made sense.

The kitchen area was at the back of the villa, the dolphin's-tail part of it. In the outhouse beyond the kitchen, winter fuel, provisions, and wine were stored. Here he encountered Carina trying to move a huge wine barrel for no apparent reason. 'Carina – let me do that for you, you'll do yourself an injury.' He went to her assistance.

She appeared nonplussed, her hand on her heart. 'Señor Doctor, you gave me the fright of my life! What are you doing here at this time of the morning?' Then she bit her tongue, noticing whose sweater and *alpargatos* he wore.

She had not noticed his car in the yard last night when she returned from the Mas Luchar, because she had used another entrance to the villa.

Señora de Luchar, it appeared, would take anyone into her bed, including her sister's fiancé: it had happened before and it had happened again. No wonder Sister Justina had gone back to the convent, thought Carina in that moment suspended in time. Her estimation of Dr Devlin sank to the bottom of the well.

'Would you like breakfast, Señor Doctor?' she asked coldly.

'No thanks, I'm not hungry – but I'd love a coffee. Hey, this wine barrel is as light as a feather, a kid could move it. It's empty … What …?'

The villa being so close to the sea, he realized that wintry sand was bound to blow indoors and get everywhere. Keir bent to the floor where recent footprints had not been swept away. They did not correspond to his, or Carina's. The powers of observation, of diagnosis, prognosis, attributes at a good doctor's fingertips, plus the ability to read beyond the ordinary, Raven Quenell's tetra-perception as she had once joked to him about, made him look twice at Carina. 'What's going on here, Carina?'

She put her finger against her lips and turned round fearfully to look over her shoulder. 'Life and death, Señor Doctor. Whose side are you on?'

'No one's *side*! I'm an American Red Cross doctor, I take no sides.'

'Good. But do you love your woman?'

'Raven?'

'*Si*, Raven!'

'More than anyone or anything in the world.'

'Even though you think nothing of betraying her with someone else?'

Keir hesitated, trapped in the guilt he couldn't very well deny. 'Roxana is only a body for sale, Carina. Raven is the soul of my life. More than anything her sister will ever mean to me. But I cannot have the woman I love and want, and I'm not a priest, so what would you have me do?'

And because she was a Spanish woman, conditioned to accept that a man had special privileges a woman was not entitled to, Carina accepted Keir's explanation. 'Then you would not do anything to see your real loved-one harmed in any way, would you, Señor Doctor?'

'No, Carina, I would not.'

'Listen to me ...'

Doña Jacqueline de Luchar and Doña Leah de Luchar, clutching their pathetic bundles of possessions around which their lives had revolved for the past two and a half years, stood in the courtyard of the women's prison. The wardresses of Las Cortes had told them they were free to go.

Go where?

The two women could not understand the word freedom and clutched each other anxiously. Blinking in the wintry sunlight that hurt their eyes when they had been used to only a dark, foetid cell for so long, other women prisoners were doing the same, clutching each other wonderingly. The guardians of Las Cortes having suddenly disappeared, freedom was a word hard to comprehend.

Now that the Nationalists were so close, less then twenty miles away, prisons all over Barcelona were disgorging their pathetic inmates out into broad daylight and freedom. Gaolers vanished like sprites in the night, terrified of what Franco's Moors, or those whom they had guarded, ill-treated, and starved for the past few years, would do to them now that the roles were reversed.

'Home?' whispered Doña Jacqueline to her sister-in-law. She and Tía Leah had spent more hours than it was possible to imagine playing chess, draughts, partnership canasta, and every other board and card-game invented with the other two 'political' women who had shared their cell. Doña Jacqueline felt she would even be able to beat the experts at chess, Jaime and Carlos, if not her husband, Don Ruiz, himself!

'Home,' nodded Tía Leah, determinedly hoisting her bundle of tattered clothing, while the dull boom of big guns could be heard in the distance.

*

Montjuic Fortress, containing so many political prisoners throughout the war, was being bombarded from the sea by Nationalist warships.

A Belgian Red Cross nurse was despatched to Montjuic, where she was taken by the doctor in charge to the prison sick-bay. The nurse raised a white bedsheet on which two strips of red material had been sewn to form a cross, visible to the commanders of the warships. The shelling of the prison stopped at once.

Dr Marcel Junod, who had returned to Barcelona, was asked by Republican officials why the Red Cross of Geneva was being used as bargaining power between the two sides, when Barcelona had not surrendered to the Nationalists and never would.

The neutral flag was removed. Sea bombardment of the city recommenced.

In the end it had been Peedee's heart and not his spirit that had finally given up the struggle against pneumonia, aggravated by what had been done to him at the hands of SIM.

After her grandfather's death, Raven had stayed to pray for his soul.

She had knelt by his bedside for so long, her knees felt riveted to the floor. Her mind was not on the pain in her knees, however, but in her heart and her soul: and on two accounts, Keir's and Peedee's.

After Keir had left the convent, Dame Superior Olivera had given the box containing his tryst ring back to her with the crisp comment, 'I think, Sister Justina, you, I, and Madre Estelle Calmar have a lot of talking to do.' Then, swift upon the heels of Keir had come Ramiro's intrusion into the convent, so that she hadn't been able to think straight at all.

She had wept buckets in the privacy of her cell, seeing Keir's face over and over again when she had handed back that little box to him. She could not tell him then she had had to do it, for his sake, and for the sake of a lot of other people, including the nuns of the Convent of the Sacred Heart. Raven recalled the substance of Archie Cunningham's long conversation with her during her brief stay in Paris. 'You *must* go back – I want you to return to Spain in your previous capacity.'

'No!' had been her vehement retort. 'The reason why I came here was to ask for another assignment. It's all there, in that *mochila* on your desk. Names, dates, places, everything you asked for, so there's no reason for me to go back. I'll do anything, but I cannot use the convent as a shield to my activities any longer. It's not right. Besides, I think Dame Superior Olivera is becoming suspicious. I'll go anywhere, even as a nanny to Berghof if that's what you want. But I cannot go back to Spain.'

'Why not?'

'I can't tell you. My reasons are too personal.' The pain had been too deep concerning Keir and Roxana for Raven to bring herself to even think about them. 'Isn't it enough for you, Archie, to have my grandfather and me doing your dirty work in Spain without demanding *how* we should do it? But I'm telling you this, I'm *not* using the convent any more.'

'Even though they used you. All that Bible-smuggling business?'

'That was different. It was done by the Church for the Church.'

'But you went through it all – even that initiation ceremony in Toril …'

'Reception, I think you mean, Archie.'

'Have you embraced the Roman Catholic faith completely?'

'Of course I have! You know Archie, you have an awful habit – no, not habit, art I think is a better word, of twisting the truth to suit yourself. Sometimes I wish Jan had never met you – but that's her problem. Let's recap, shall we? Do you remember that summer of thirty-three when I was at a loss and idling my time? I spent a little time in England, Westerham in particular, I remember, watching you bowl in endless overs. You and Jan had just become engaged. I was 'unemployed' at the time. You asked me to join the *Civil Service*, and I refused. I told you I wanted to become a nun. I was utterly genuine about it. But you had to come along to my Reception Day and spoil it all for me by dangling a bait in front of my naïve little novice's eyes I could not refuse. A British agent behind Spanish convent walls indeed! You remember, don't you? You'll also recall that I turned you down.'

'But you agreed to be wicket-keeper in the end.'

'In the end I did, simply because you were so persistent. You offered me a far more exciting challenge than just plain and simple chastity, poverty, and obedience. And, once I got roped into all that Bible-smuggling, I felt the Church was making use of me without caring one way or another whether or not I got arrested and had to spend the rest of my life in gaol. After that it was a matter of getting slaughtered for a sheep because lambs were only small fry by now, for I had no idea that Sonny's Bibles were having secret messages coded into them. Oh, not Sonny's doing, of course. The messages were inserted by agents *after* the Bibles had arrived from Ireland. And my final reason for doing this job was because I didn't want Peedee to get into any trouble alone. I wanted to keep an eye on him ...'

Raven brought her mind back from the past to the present: and look where her keeping an eye on her grandfather had ended! He who had been stalwart enough to act as a mediator on her behalf too. *Dios, Patria, Rey* had led to Peedee's death, while her own life and future prospects lay in tatters. She could weep; the price had been far too high, Peedee *and* Keir.

Raven had insisted to the nursing staff at the Clinic del Rey that she alone wanted to undertake those last offices upon her grandfather. She had seen the way the nurses had attended to the dead in the hospitals of this war, the urgency and the disrespect which such a seemingly futile task entailed. After all, she had heard it said so often, only a corpse remained, and there would be a lot more of those to lay out before this day, or this night, was through, so why fuss?

When that dreadful duty had been accomplished, she set out on the first step towards something she never thought she had the courage to do.

SIM, she had learned, was the new counter-espionage organization set up to restrict the activity of uncontrollables, Anarchist or otherwise. All according to Party policy, manifest in the way Ramiro de Luchar had handled her grandfather's case.

Raven felt sure that she would, from now on, be watched and followed by Ramiro's spies. If she went to Uncle Salas's house tonight, she would be jeopardizing not only the lives of the Rivales family, but all that Peedee and she had been working for over the past two years. She couldn't risk that happening.

Ask Carina, Peedee had said. Obviously he had got himself into something deep and sinister and more dangerous than her subterfuge activities inside convent walls, something he hadn't wanted her to know about while he was alive. Now there was no choice in the matter, she had to play this nun-role out to its fullest before there would be any personal life for her.

Archie had been so right; convents and monasteries were archives of valuable information. What a lot she had gleaned! Camillus nuns who went prison visiting came back full of gossip; she had picked up the names of important prisoners, who had interrogated them, who had tortured them, who had put them there in the first place, who had betrayed them. Delivering food parcels, or taking the simple necessities of life to prisoners and wounded soldiers – soap, magazines, books, toothpaste – had the same feedback of information, for a lonely, sick, heartbroken man will talk to anyone, and a nun or a nursing sister more than anyone else. Nuns helped too, by writing letters for the sick and dying, and though the letters were censored afterwards, the first hand information in some of them had been another vital insight into the war in Spain. Then again, through her Red Cross interlude, her 'dark night of the soul' when she had travelled through Spain with Keir and the Red Cross convoys, she had picked up vital information along the way, how the war was going for all parties concerned, anti-Stalinists, Communists, Anarchists, Socialists, Rebels and Republicans. Even within the sphere of her convent life, she had come to know about the Falangists and their infiltration within the Roman Catholic hierarchy, the passing of secret information by coded data contained in religious literature. And, above all, through the trials and tribulations of the de Luchar family themselves, she had been able to burrow into the core of Communist and Monarchist politics. Her people-spotting book, had she still kept one, could not have held more 'blackmailing' information than that which was contained up here now in her very skull!

But now it was time to stop. She wanted to find Keir and tell him everything. She wanted to right the wrong she had done him at the Covent of the Sacred Heart. She wanted him to know that 'going back' had been a matter of necessity. She had a special job to do and to finish, and she could only do it in her present guise. Most of all she wanted him to know that she was not so stupid as to believe Roxana and her vicious lies concerning Pippa.

Her four days in Paris had been spent like a busy little bee, darting all over the city in between arguing her case with Archie Cunningham, and losing it because, in the end, she had agreed to complete her 'assignment' in Barcelona. She had also decided to call Roxana's bluff – although, at that time, she had been uncertain as to whether or not it was a bluff until she remembered Roxana had always been a wonderful little forger of other people's signatures, sick notes, and punishment lines at l'École Internationale.

She had gone to the Registrar of Births in the St Germain district and checked the original records. No child by the name of Pauline Inés Devlin had been born at the Clinic de Veille-Ville, Faubourg St-Germaine, on 17 April 1932: certainly not one with an American father by the name of Dr Keiren Hunter Devlin! She had then got Archie to cable North Africa for her, asking the Spanish garrison's personnel records to be examined. The information had arrived quickly and straightforwardly: Pauline Inés de Luchar had been born in Tetuan, on 17 April *1934*, the daughter of Legionnaire-Captain, José de Luchar and Señora Roxana de Luchar, née Quennell, an Irishwoman by birth. Roxana had changed the names and dates on the birth certificate she had so adroitly produced on Christmas afternoon.

And because she had doubted Keir, even for a brief moment, Raven felt very ashamed, while longing for this

Spanish war to end so that she could shake off the role she had been forced to play through circumstance and not free choice, and start living life as she and Keir had planned for themselves in Guatemala.

Fortunately, Raven found someone who would take her as far as Vilafranca in his car, a doctor out on an emergency call. All the while she prayed that she would reach Cabo Alondra before the Communists. She thought, at least she *hoped*, that she had managed to give them the slip when she had left the Clinic del Rey by a back door.

Archie Cunningham wanted his pound of flesh, he was now about to get it! were Raven's grim thoughts.

From Vilafranca she managed to get a ride on the back of a farm-wagon to the outskirts of the de Luchar estate. The old peasant couple with their donkey and meagre produce for early morning market asked her no questions, only for her blessing.

After that, she had had to make her own way in the dark to Cabo Alondra. The moonlit sea was soothing to her nerves. The wind in the Monterey pines a dirge the closer she got to Cabo Alondra. It was half-past four in the morning before she arrived at the villa.

Raven thought she was imagining things when she saw Keir's Renault outside the villa at that time of the morning. She thought she was hallucinating when she saw Keir's face at Roxana's bedroom window, his chest bare, a cigarette in his fingers in the casual attitude of a man satisfied with himself after having spent the night in the arms of a woman who had given him what he wanted.

'Raven! Jesus – *Raven!*'

After that nothing mattered any more.

After that, after believing that she was imagining it all and that she was going off her head because she missed him so much and had conjured up his presence at Cabo Alondra to suit herself, her heart had turned to stone because she knew she was imagining nothing. Roxana had not completely lied; though Pippa might not be Keir's child, they *were* having an affair, even while he had asked her to marry him …

And the brutal facts hurt like hell.

Oh God – the pain in her chest was so terrible, Raven was amazed by her ability to stand straight and face Carina as though her heart was still beating normally, her life was still intact, and her faith in human nature had not been so rudely shattered one more time, and this time by the man she loved and whom she had thought loved her … *I must take custody – I must, I must …*'

She stumbled into the kitchen to find that Carina was already waiting for her. Raven stared into the bright beam of Carina's torch even while she listened to the urgent footsteps on the cedar staircase. They heard the front-door being opened, and, in that highly charged moment, Carina, who thought it was Roxana clattering about (for it was before she knew of Keir's presence in the house), turned the key to lock the door between kitchen and front hall.

'Peedee – he told me to ask you,' Raven gasped, a stitch in her side because she wanted to be free of the ghost of Dr Keir Devlin, and so many other ghosts haunting her.

'Is he dead?'

'Yes.'

'Was it SIM?'

'Yes.'

Carina crossed herself. Then she slapped a folded paper into Raven's hand. 'This is the underground plan of wine tunnels held by Doña Maria all these years. Just follow this main tunnel marked in red. In the centre of the network, you will find them. But be quick. Just tell them about your grandfather and that he might have given away their whereabouts when tortured by SIM. But you must hurry before the Communists get here.'

Carina thrust Raven down the cellar steps with the underground map and torch in her hand, and then, calming herself, restored everything to order before opening the kitchen door.

Señora Roxana, Carina was thankful to hear, had gone back to bed.

An hour and a half later, Carina had looked up to find the American Red Cross doctor watching her movements. This time it had been Nina de Luchar whom she had been ushering down the cellar steps.

Panic had set in. It was hard to know who to trust in this war.

She regarded Dr Keir Devlin coldly. Carina now knew that it had been he on the stairs and in the front hall, and not Roxana. And because she also realized in whose bed he had spent the night, she looked at him with disdain. Señora Roxana who was supposed to be married to the heir of all that the de Luchar family had left to them from this war was nothing but a red-haired little tramp. Neither was she going to forgive Dr Devlin easily for throwing himself away on a woman of Roxana's sort.

She listened to his explanation about Sister Justina being the soul of his life, accepting it without forgiving him his behaviour. But because there were far more important issues to think about than the gutter morals of two foreigners, Carina hoped she was doing the right thing by trusting him when she said to him, 'Listen to me. If the Communists find you here, they will think you are a spy. You will be interrogated by their own special methods, and you will die slowly and painfully while endangering the lives of a great many others. That is what happened to Señor Peedee.' She thrust a gun into his hand, taken from her apron pocket.

Keir stared at Carina in horror, his thoughts going at once to Raven and how much her grandfather had meant to her. 'I don't want the gun,' he said, fully aware that he would never use it.

'Take it. It is Señor Peedee's. You might have need of it to protect the woman you say you love.' Carina stooped to raise the trap-door, over which she had hoped to replace the wine barrel after Nina's urgent descent underground when Keir had found her.

'What's going on, Carina?'

'Señor Doctor, there's no time to explain. I'm certain that the Communist secret police have followed Sister Justina here. Why else would they have forcibly removed her from her convent? She will die, like many others down there. All of them caught like rats in a trap, unless you can use that gun. Now go.' She shoved him down the cellar steps, then followed it up with a last-minute candle.

The trap-door banged above his head. He found himself

in total darkness, on a flight of steps leading to God knew where. Only the fresh air coming in icy blasts down a long tunnel, and the sound of crashing waves, told him he was closer to the sea than he wanted to be. Keir took his lighter from his pocket. Shielding the flame in the down-draught, with difficulty he managed to light the candle. Then he yelled at the top of his voice. '*RA-VEN!*'

Ven! Ven! Ven! the echoes replied.

Keir followed the echoes.

Ramiro de Luchar parked his black Citroën close to the Red Cross doctor's Renault. Raven and the American Red Cross doctor! His intuition had been right all along. They were both up to no good. He had always suspected them of being anti-Communist agents of their respective governments. The Americans especially were paranoid about the Red menace, as they called anything that came out of Russia.

He went into the kitchen. Carina was peeling onions.

'Where are they?'

'Who, Ramiro?' She refused to kowtow to party politics; she had known him since he was a baby who forever yelled for attention, a baby who could never be pacified without a honeyed dummy.

'Raven and the American doctor.'

'Raven?'

'Sister Justina.'

'How should I know?'

'What are you hiding, Carina?'

'Nothing, Ramiro.'

He looked around the kitchen.

'Give me the plan.'

'What plan, Ramiro?'

'The plan of the underground tunnels radiating off the Caverna Rosa.'

'I don't know what you're talking about.'

'Oh, yes you do, old lady!' He withdrew his revolver from its holster and placed it against her head. 'Where is it? I know it exists. Doña Maria told me.'

'Too late – you've arrived too late! They will be waiting for you, traitor!' She spat at him. '*Kill* me, like you've killed so many others.'

His fingers twitched on the hammer; but he didn't release it. He couldn't blow the head off such a dumb old lady even though he had never liked her in all the years he had grown up with her, she who was the slave of the Englishman. Ramiro struck Carina with the butt of the revolver. She slumped unconscious across the onions she had been peeling at the table.

Ramiro took the stairs two at a time.

He had expected to find Raven and the Red Cross doctor together, never Roxana in her sister's bed. He pointed the gun at her. 'Where's your sister, *puta*?'

'Scram, Ramiro! After all I did for your wife …'

'Where is she?'

'If you're talking about Raven, I haven't a clue. I don't think she's in this bed with me.' Cheekily Roxana peered under Raven's feather duvet. 'Why don't you ask the nuns, Ramiro darling.'

'Get up!' He tossed her her dressing-gown. 'Get dressed.'

Roxana slowly slipped into it, then she played for more time by scrabbling for her slippers under the bed. 'What do you want from me, Ramiro?'

He took two steps towards her, his smile vicious. His gun on the red mark on her throat he said, '*Tch-tch*! A love-bite!' He twitched aside the revers of her dressing-gown, using the revolver as the finger of derision.

'Another one! What a wonderful night you must have spent, Roxana. I wonder what José would say – José, who at this very moment is no doubt preparing to march along the Diagonal and into Barcelona at the head of Franco's victory column. What a *brave* contribution his wife has made to this Spanish war, sexing everything and anything in uniform, Red Cross armbands included. Poor sweet Raven!'

'Go to hell, you Commie bastard!'

He laughed. 'Where can I find a copy of the Caverna Rosa plan that my grandmother has been so windy about lately?'

'I don't know what you're talking about.'

The revolver against her temple, behind her back Ramiro held her tightly around the waist with one strong arm. 'Who else has a copy of the underground tunnels? You've lived here long enough to know what's been going on.' He jerked his arm angrily against her midriff, winding her and making her gasp with pain and fright.

Roxana was suddenly afraid of what Ramiro might do to her in his present unpredictable mood. She didn't prevaricate a second time. 'Isaba.'

'Where?'

'In her cookery book.'

'Thanks, Roxana, *querida*!'

'*Cojón*!'

'*Encantador*! Such Spanish! But then, you know all about ball-games, don't you my little *puta*!' He thrust her out of the bedroom and down the stairs to his car. Shoving her into it, he said with the gun still directed at her head, 'Drive, Irishwoman! Otherwise I blow out your sweet brains.'

'Where do you want me to drive to, you Spanish oaf?'

'To the kitchen at the Mas, where else?'

'Hell, perhaps? You've been watching too many American movies, Ramiro,' she said as she drove erratically down the avenue of Monterey pines leading to the farmhouse.

'And you, *querida*, have spent too much time on the flat of your back. Mind I don't tell my brother what a whore his wife is. Although I expect José already knows what he was forced to marry on account of one moment lost to beauty and not discernment. Still ...' he tucked a stray coppery ringlet behind her pretty ear, again using the gun barrel, 'I might just feel in the mood myself when this is all over, if you're a good girl and do as you're told.'

'Pillow talk is bad for party politics, Al Capone.'

'Roxana, *querida*, of all the women I've met in my life, you are one of the most – entertaining.'

'*Gra-ci-as*, you sod! Now what do you want me to do?' She all but ran into the wall of the farmhouse kitchen, before braking suddenly to send him almost through the windscreen.

'Out! Come on. Get in there ...' He thrust her towards the kitchen door. 'And don't mess about Roxana, because I'll be right behind the door with this gun. Any nonsense and Isaba will be the first to get it. The whole of this area is *full* of *Commie* bastards who'll blow everything apart the moment I give the signal.'

'Hooray! The sheriff has arrived! That's what I've always admired about you, Ramiro, your family loyalty.'

He pushed her into the kitchen. Isaba was asleep on her heavy arms resting on the kitchen table. 'Isaba,' Roxana shook her shoulder. 'Wake up! I need your help.'

'*Qué – qué pasa*?' Isaba snorted into life.

'I need the plan.'

'What plan, Señora Roxana?'

'The plan of the underground tunnels leading from the Caverna Rosa.'

'Why?'

'To warn them – that the Communists are after them.'

'It makes no difference now, the Communists and Anarchists have lost. I heard it just now on the radio.'

'Yes, I know, that's why they're going to kill as many Monarchists as they can before *all* is lost.'

'All *is* lost for those who have crucified the Virgin!' Nevertheless Isaba sleepily went to a shelf and reached down her recipe book. She took out a copy of a plan given to her by Nina de Luchar when all this war nonsense had first started, and handed it over to Roxana. Then she went back to snoring at the kitchen table: the war was won; Isaba dreamed of good, rich Valencian paella once more.

Outside the kitchen door, Roxana handed the plan to Ramiro who smiled when he opened it out. 'To think that all these years not one of us boys knew a thing about such an underground network. My grandfather must have been scared-stiff of the French. Now then, since I have always retained a key to the Caverna Rosa, let's go.'

So *many* familiar faces presented themselves to Raven's startled gaze when Cipi, the cellar master, led her to Don Ruiz. Men like Pedro the chauffeur, Juan the overseer, and numerous others whom she had thought had been shot, deported, or imprisoned after they had mysteriously disappeared one by one at the hands of the *checas* and dawn patrols. Now she saw again those men from

702

Barcelona, Vilafranca, Toril, and Vinarosa whom she had supposed had gone the way of all the others. Not only were they alive and well, they were also extremely active.

Here, in not just one tunnel, but many more deep below the spruce forest, Vinarosa's own 'Fifth Column' had flourished and fought as hard and as fiercely as any legionnaire or International Brigader.

After she had told him what had happened to Peedee at the hands of SIM, Don Ruiz embraced her with tears in his eyes. 'I'm deeply sorry about your grandfather, Raven. Peedee was a wonderful man, the best member of my team, though do not tell that to the others. On his last mission he carried very vital intelligence reports into France, and I'm only sorry he was picked up on his return by the secret police at Port Bou.'

He jerked a fat cigar towards the wall of radio transmitters and receivers, where two men were listening intently to all that was coming through from the various radio stations. 'Here is our nerve centre, a secret wireless station able to monitor everything happening on both sides of the fighting lines and beyond. Even into France and Portugal, and as far away as Majorca. From here we deploy our agents all over Catalonia to fight the "Red" menace, Leninism, Stalinism, Trotskyism, and Bolshevism. Every ism and schism that divides Red from White. Your grandfather was a real Spaniard. I salute him!'

So this then was the heart of Nationalist resistance in Catalonia, Don Ruiz's own ring of espionage. She was glad *El Grandee* had not died as she had believed, she had always been fond of him. But she still had to be careful.

It was up to her now to try and ascertain whether or not Don Ruiz, or any other Fifth Columnist, realized that Peedee's partisan nationalism was also partisan British intelligence fed back to Archie Cunningham at his innocent little visa office in Paris.

Peedee had been 'recruited' by Archie Cunningham at the time that Archie and Jan had attended her Reception Day. Archie had made his reasons for attending the Roman Catholic ceremony perfectly clear in the few moments they had spent chatting together afterwards. But while she herself (at that time) had refused to become involved in anything Archie wanted of her, Peedee had at once taken up the fight. She remembered how excited Peedee had been when that seemingly vague husband of her friend, Janice, had turned out to be not as vague or as doltish as he appeared. Archie was actually recruiting *him*, Percy Dunbar Purnell, to spy out foreign shipping in the Mediterranean and what was happening at Barcelona docks! After that, one thing had led to another until Peedee's final moment of glory had ended at Port Bou.

'We need our own so-called "Fifth Column" in Spain,' Archie had told her on her recent visit to Paris. He had used the term 'Fifth Column' figuratively, for the original Fifth Column was a group of Falangist sympathizers prepared to join the other four columns of insurrectionists marching on Madrid. A Fifth Columnist had thereafter meant anyone who was an 'infiltrator'.

'That's why I approached you and your grandfather in the first place. I knew you could both be trusted to stay 'British-minded' even though you were culturally thoroughbred Spaniards.'

'How could you have been so sure about us?' she had asked Archie.

'Your early upbringing in war-torn Ireland. I also have a nose for people,' he had replied and she had had to smile to herself, for she knew *exactly* what Archie had meant. He had gone on to add, 'I'd like to find out all there is to know about this Spanish war, for I don't believe it's as insignificant as some of us like to think. Hitler's weaponry and everything else about German warfare, including the crack battalion of the Condor Legion, are only part of the picture Spain, and Herr Hitler, are presenting. Spain is the testing ground for something far greater. Churchill, among others of like vision, is sure of it. Therefore, it would be advantageous from Britain's point of view to find out more about Nazi intervention in Spain, so that, if it ever came to a showdown between major European powers, we would know exactly what we were up against. Mussolini, as Hitler's vassal, we are also interested in, though the Italians make more cock-ups than shoolboys and aren't as greatly to be feared as the Germans. You and your grandfather were obvious choices from my point of view, what with his telescope and waterfront friends. And you, of course, amongst the Romans ...'

But Peedee had been fed to the lions, for somehow, frighteningly, Ramiro had discovered what Peedee was doing on behalf of the British Government.

Raven was certain that Ramiro had been the instrument of her grandfather's arrest and death. And, Raven promised herself, to that end, Archie Cunningham, and whoever was behind him at MI6, would now get the full facts of SIM laid well and truly in front of them, plus anything else within her power to glean from the other side.

But, from now on she played the dangerous game *her* way!

All those things passed through her brain in rapid succession while she took in her surroundings deep below the spruce forest. 'What will you do now, Don Ruiz?' Raven found herself saying from a distance of time and space and the death of loved-ones.

'Wait for my wife to come home and then we will have a big celebration.'

'No, I mean about Ramiro and the agents of SIM?'

'Yes, SIM: they have been the hardest to deal with in this war. They infiltrate everywhere, just like lice in the seams of dirty clothing. Don't worry, my dear, we are ready for them. My loyal *rabassaires* are well trained in tunnel and forest warfare. A wonderful guerilla force is at my beck and call, who will make short work of the Communists and Anarchists. The war in Catalonia is by no means over as yet. There will be great resistance to the new régime, and a counter-revolution, as well as a war of contrition, will go on for many more long months. All sorts of bugs will be creeping out of their crevices for a long time to come. Now, my dear child, as long as you remain down here, you yourself are in grave danger, so you must get back to your convent as quickly as possible. Go back the way you came,' Don Ruiz advised her. 'It's the shortest and most direct route back to Cabo Alondra. And please Raven, nothing to anyone, not even your confessor! I have always loved and trusted you like a daughter, you know that.'

'Yes, I know, Don Ruiz. And I'm so glad you're still

around as — as the Grand Grandee of Vinarosa!' Forgetting herself and her role, she kissed him on the cheek as a daughter to her father, and in return he embraced her affectionately, despite the nun's habit.

'Two and a half years is a long time to live like a mole.' he said. 'I shall be glad to see my wife and proper daylight again …'

An alarm sounded, red lights flashing on and off in the tunnel.

'A warning system,' Don Ruiz explained to Raven who appeared concerned. 'It's not a fire alarm, so don't worry. I know you are afraid of fire, and especially down here, it would not be a nice thing to happen. That alarm tells me that the main outside door to the Caverna Rosa has been opened. Any minute now, with the aid of the underground plan he has somehow managed to get hold of, Ramiro will count the number of casks being stored in the caverna until he finds that an odd one has appeared from nowhere. That's if he, like a good cellar master, updates himself by the cellar ledger on the table by the door. Somehow, I think he will look at it, because he is my son, and a perfectionist. He will know what sort of information he can get from that ledger. There is an empty cask, you see, Raven, which gives access through the back of it, into one of these secret tunnels which will eventually lead him to me.'

Wine barrels could be the size of a small room. Jaime had once shown her a cask in which twelve men could sit. Something that size could easily conceal the entrance to other caverns. And that, surely, was how the secrets of the Caverna Rosa had been preserved down the years: until this moment. 'You want Ramiro to come down here and kill you?' she asked in some confusion. 'Why?'

Don Ruiz smiled serenely. 'A family matter. A reunion, shall we say. Ramiro won't kill me, I'm his father.'

Raven wished Don Ruiz wasn't quite so blind to Ramiro's flaws.

What they were unprepared for was the sound of Roxana's voice and disrupting presence. Roxana's dramatic little shrieks were the first intimation they had of Ramiro's cunning. Don Ruiz, who had deliberately allowed his son to gain access without being apprehended by any of his men, turned to Ramiro when he emerged at the entrance to this, the communication tunnel. Ramiro held a revolver to Roxana's head. 'Ramiro *Por dónde*?' Don Ruiz greeted his son, the ball suddenly in Ramiro's court on account of Roxana. 'Please don't be a fool, Ramiro. Don't use your brother's wife as a hostage.'

But even while Don Ruiz asked for Roxana to be spared in all this, Raven knew that Ramiro was not going to pay any attention to Roxana's welfare in a confrontation of this sort.

'*Salud*, Papa. *Salud* Raven! I thought perhaps I might find you down here as well.' Ramiro's arm appeared to be half-throttling Roxana in her thin, slippery dressing-gown vaunting a healthy amount of bosom and thigh. She had lost her slippers and her courage somewhere along one of the tunnels, and Raven could see how terrified Roxana was. Despite Roxana's silliness at times, she was still prepared to defend her sister against Ramiro's brutality.

'Don't hurt her, Ramiro. Let her go and I'll come with you.'

'I thought you'd see sense.' He did not release Roxana. His smile was vindictive as he turned to his father, 'Blood, you see, Papa, is thicker than water.'

'You're either a very brave or a very foolish man, Ramiro my son, to come down here alone when my men have got you covered from all angles,' Don Ruiz, hoping to avert disaster by playing for time, cajoled his son.

'While the rest of them are dying all over the woods, where a bloody battle is even now taking place between Communists and Monarchists.'

'They are fighting for Spain, Ramiro, to the last drop of blood.'

'Fascist blood! Franco will never restore the monarchy that you've been working so desperately for down here in your rabbit warren. He'll crush *all* you Monarchists. You have betrayed Catalonia, Papa, and one day the people of Catalonia will not thank you for it.'

'On the other hand, they might. Why don't you give up, Ramiro? The war is won. Didn't you hear? This morning Great Britain and France were negotiating the official recognition of the Franco régime.'

'The war between Communism and Fascism will never be over. It will go on as a counter-revolution here in Spain, while the rest of the world takes up our fight.'

'That I know only too well, Ramiro. But while there are Communists and Anarchists in this world, sons will put their mothers in prison, hold their brother's wives to ransom, and torture their grandfathers!'

'My mother was held in Las Cortes for political as well as personal reasons. She would have been tortured and killed by other SIM agents while they were searching for you during these past two and a half years. I did her a favour. You and she now at least can be reunited to live out the rest of your lives as an old couple here at Vinarosa!'

'Very noble of you, Ramiro. I would like to believe you, of course, but what about your respected tutor, Señor Peedee?'

Ramiro chose not to answer that question, but looked directly at Raven. 'I want *her* – she is the key figure in all this and I ...'

In that moment a blood-curdling yell, '*RA-VEN*!' put an end to what Ramiro was about to say.

Ven! Ven! Ven! the chilling echoes replied.

Don Ruiz and Ramiro did not move, while Roxana, still held to ransom in Ramiro's unrelenting grip, raised frightened eyes to Raven. Two of Don Ruiz's men brought Keir into view, his arms trussed up behind his back. 'Señor, look what we found in one of the tunnels. He is not one of ours and he says he is not a Communist either.'

'I know who he is,' said Don Ruiz with great composure and assurance. 'It's all right, let him go. He's the American Red Cross doctor who has visited my estate often. *Bon dia y buenos dias*, Dr Devlin,' Don Ruiz greeted him in the two languages of Spain, Catalan and Castillan.

'*Jesus*!' Keir swore as he got the circulation going in his arms. 'Thanks for nothing, you cretins! I told you I was from the Red Cross!' He glared at his assailants.

'Dr Devlin, I'm sorry that you have been so roughly manhandled, but my men are diligent in their duty. For my part, I only wish to thank you for all you have done for my wife and sister and other members of the family. My mother has told me a great deal about you.' He turned

708

back to Raven with a broad smile as he pointed with his cigar to the panel of lights and switches on the wall. 'I knew that Dr Keir, too, was on his way. A light for each entrance, just like the housemaids calling-system in the kitchen at the Mas and my castillo in Barcelona – which will be restored to me now that the Communists are beaten. I know who comes and goes from all the exits and entrances to this place. Carina called me on the internal line between Cabo Alondra and the Mas to say you were on your way, but she never gave your pursuer clearance on my monitoring board. It is a clever system, *si*?'

'Wonderful! said Ramiro impatiently. 'But now, Father, can we get back to business.' He pushed Roxana away from him, towards Keir. 'There he is, *puta*, go back to your lover. Neither of you means anything to me, but this one does.' He turned and pointed the gun at Raven. 'You, my beautiful Irish spy, are the one I really came after. I will pull this trigger, Raven, unless you can tell me more about your anti-Communist friends, your grandfather's double-crossing activities, and who among your holy brethren is behind British interference in Spain. Is it your bitter and twisted brother Sonny – Brother Bernard?' Ramiro sneered. 'Or someone else I have yet to find out about ...?'

Roxana's shrill cry of fear cut across Keir's warning shout. Don Ruiz was held momentarily stunned as the sound of the explosion reverberated through the underground tunnels like hundreds of cannons.

Raven, shattered by that deafening gunshot when all the terror of this war merged into one fleeting second and everything came together in a kaleidoscope of killing, stared with incredulous eyes at the man on the floor.

He crawled towards her, leaving a bright trail of blood as he desperately tried to reach her. 'Why? I – I saved – you so often – from them – from the secret – police – Raven – I – I ...'

All she could do was to shake her head, denying the deed even while she stared at Nina de Luchar who stood over her brother.

'That's for Marcos Martinez, *my lover*, Ramiro! You Red

bastard!' she screamed. The gun trembled in Nina's hand as she pointed it, resolutely, a second time in two hands at her brother's head. 'And this is for the *way* he died, *brother*!'

'*No, Nina, No*!' Don Ruiz leapt towards his daughter and pulled the gun from her in the moment his son lay still. '*Basta – basta* – enough enough! Child, child!' He held her in his arms, and the gun dropped to the floor, beside her brother.

Nina gave herself up to her father, who held her as though she were a baby, pacifying her as though she were a baby, both of them weeping for all the dead lovers, the dead brothers, and the dead sons of this war.

Keir knelt beside Ramiro's body, his fingers on the stilled pulse in Ramiro's neck. Then he looked up at Raven kneeling on the other side of Ramiro, her rosary and crucifix pressed to her lips, and he took a chance even though he knew this was not the right time.

'It's snowy in my heart, Irish Eyes.'

CHAPTER TWENTY

Barcelona: 26 January 1939

Outside her cell window the day was cold and bright.

Raven could see only the blue sky way above her head. Sweet-scented thyme paths, a pretty garden with the Bishop's sundial in the centre, it would have been a view to indulge the senses: as much of an indulgence as eating an ice-cream on a hot day, or wearing comfortable shoes on her treks to and from Montserrat, or even smelling a rose were she ever to have the misfortune of becoming blind like Dame Annunciata.

It's snowy in my heart ...

She stood by the window in her plain linen petticoat, bare feet on the stone floor. She did not feel the intense cold of her nun's cell, her arms wrapped across her breast, hugging against herself: *It's snowy in my heart*, he had said by way of asking her forgiveness.

It was so hard to forgive.

There was so much to think about; to forgive; to forget; to start reliving ...

The spruce forest had gone up in flames after the Communists and Monarchists had battled it out above ground. Even now she could feel the thump thump thump of trees crashing down, hear the rattle of distant machine-guns echoing along the corridors of the Caverna Rosa. She had remained behind with the shrouded body of Ramiro, praying for his soul in the darkness of the cave, while Don Ruiz directed his fighting men against the Communists. Keir had taken Nina and Roxana, who were both suffering from severe shock, back to Cabo Alondra via the tunnel.

When the battle overhead was over, the Communists slinking off into the gathering winter darkness after putting a torch to the spruce forest, the whole of Vinarosa had been lit up like a magnificent tableau. She had stood in one of the vine avenues, watching the blaze on the horizon, fascinated by the sight of all those spars of lighted wood, heavy with resin, bursting into fireballs as they shot through the air. It was like seeing the planets and the stars warring with each other. The air had been heady with the scent of pine amidst all that devastation. It had reminded her of the drugged atmosphere of too much incense at the High Mass.

And then, quietly and alone because no one remembered she was still at Vinarosa, she had returned to the convent.

Now, her greatest worry was what she should wear today.

She hadn't had time to buy a new wardrobe in Paris during those few short days after Christmas. And she did not think she would ever wear the kingfisher-blue dress and white bolero she had bought in Salamanca. It would always remind her of Keir for whom she had chosen the extravagant outfit. She had charged it to her grandfather's bank account at the time as she had no money of her own. She wasn't sure whether or not she even liked the clothes she had purchased on the spur of the moment when love, deep and wild and wondrous, had pervaded every pore of her body.

She wondered if Keir would accompany Roxana to Mexico now that he was no longer required to stay in Spain. Guatemala was just across the border, so all three of them, Roxana, Pippa and Keir, would probably go there after Tampico …

She mustn't think about it.

Madre Estelle Calmar would be here presently with her belongings.

Funny to have a purse again, and money to buy what she wanted. Nice to think she could play Sonny's old mandolin and her guitar once more. She hoped they were still at Cabo Alondra. Terrible to think that Peedee would never be returning to Cabo Alondra, ever again …

She mustn't think about that, either.

Happily, Don Ruiz and Doña Jaqueline would be reunited at Vinarosa along with Tingalinga, so there was

712

something nice happening after all.

Raven wished Madre Estelle Calmar would hurry up and bring her clothes. Perhaps she was having problems in the linen-room trying to track down the Red Cross uniform she, Raven, had arrived in after her Paris interlude. Perhaps it had been thrown out after she had rejoined the novitiate: was it only three weeks ago? It seemed much longer.

Did she have any regrets; no not really. It was just as well Dame Superior Olivera had made up her mind for her, finally, because she would never have been brave enough to do it alone. Now she had no choice in the matter. It had been explained to her that she just wasn't 'temperamentally suited' for convent life and she had disobeyed far too often the rules of poverty, chastity, and obedience, not to mention custody of the senses! She had no idea of what 'blind obedience' meant, for she asked far too many questions.

And so she had been given her marching orders.

In a way it was rather like being cashiered from the army – 'And, therefore, His Holiness's Government has no more wish for your services ...' But it had been rather sad to have to go through that poignant little ceremony last night renouncing her novice's vows and giving back the name of Sister Justina for ever; poverty, chastity, and obedience would hold no special significance for her any more, because she was no longer Sister Justina. And this time it was for real – oh dear. That was one of Keir's Americanisms. She should say, *finis coronat opus*, it is all over.

Her white robe, scapular, guimpe, cincture, head-dress, all were neatly laid out on her nun's cot, ready and waiting for Madre Estelle Calmar to come and collect them. So where *was* she for heaven's sake ...?

Oh, here she was at last! She could hear her bustling about in the passageway. If the extern nun with her was Sister Jeanne, both of them would be fussing and clucking like a couple of old grey biddies, on whether or not Miss Ravenna Quennell's clothes were sufficiently pressed, and is that a faint stain on the blouse or an iron-mark? Are the shoes shined enough? Then they would drop everything on the floor in their trembling agitation: and, if they started to cry, then – then she knew she would burst into tears with them.

But, she was going to be strong and single-minded and save her tears for the moment the convent gates closed behind her one last time.

Raven took a taxi from Vilafranca to Barcelona.

It was good to have her watch back, and she glanced at it many times on the way. She was supposed to be meeting Roxana for lunch at the plush Ritz Hotel: typical Roxana! But she was already very late.

Roxana had told her over the telephone not to be late because all the tables would be taken in view of the victory celebrations. Raven couldn't help thinking that Roxana hadn't changed a bit, still out for a good time wherever she could find it. The streets of Barcelona, amidst the débris and bomb-damage, were awash with red and gold flags, and public buildings displayed General Franco's portrait draped with Nationalist colours. The tanks were already rolling into the city escorted by cheering crowds. The señoritas were out in their colourful numbers, girls in search of handsome uniformed heroes to bring them romance and love and a young man's happy-ever-after promises.

'The Ritz, señorita.' Even though she wore an ordinary utility uniform and carried a Red Cross *mochila* over her shoulder, the taxi-driver had a great deal of respect in his voice as he drew up in his Fiat before Barcelona's oldest and grandest hotel in the Gran Via. Raven tipped him appropriately, and, in the instant she turned around to go into the hotel, she saw Keir walking away from it.

She hesitated; she could easily have caught up with him, but obviously he was avoiding her. Had he been meeting Roxana? Was that why he was now hurrying away from her so guiltily?

Oh, there she went again! Raven drew herself up short. Keeping tabs on people, spying on them, and assigning to them ulterior motives. He probably hadn't seen her. He usually had too much on his mind in any case to pay attention to every person passing by on the street. What did it matter anyway? It was all over between she and Keir Devlin since she had discovered his affair with her sister. She set her chin, walked smartly into the hotel, and asked to be shown to Señora de Luchar's table.

Roxana, in an orange, brown, and russet two-piece costume and hat, and shoulder fox furs, looked wonderful. Raven grudgingly admitted it to herself as she saw herself drab in comparison next to all these smartly-attired people lunching at the Ritz. These were the rich and privileged ones, the ones who could afford to buy themselves out of any war, the ones who hadn't been forced to flee the city like so many thousands of refugees starving to death, or those who knew Falangist mobs would exterminate them if they remained in Barcelona; the killing was not over yet, despite the flags everywhere.

'Darling, it's lovely to see you. I'm so glad you decided to give up all that silly nun business,' Roxana gushed over a new cigarette-holder as the waiter seated Raven and draped the napkin across her lap.

'I didn't decide to give it up, it gave me up.'

'Oh dear, I'm always putting my foot in it, aren't I? Listen sweetie, do you want to order, or shall I?'

'You order. No squid, though.'

'Drink?'

'A glass of milk.'

'You *can't* order *milk* in here, Raven!' Roxana glanced over her shoulder. 'Have a martini! You're not a nun any more.'

'Oh, very well. Now, why did you want to see me?'

'To make a confession.'

'What confession?'

'Let me have my martini first, darling.'

'If it's about you and Keir, I know that Pippa isn't his child and that you made up all those horrible lies as well as changing the names and dates on Pippa's birth certificate in order to unsettle me. *Why?* I should like to know.'

Roxana raised a surprised pencilled eyebrow. 'You know? How?'

'Simple really. I checked the facts. All my life I've been very good at "people-spotting" other people, but where it came to my own sister, I was blind as a bat. *Why* did you tell me Keir was the father of Pippa when it was such a downright lie and a nasty cruel thing to have done?'

Roxana shrugged and then pouted. 'Darling, don't be angry. I didn't *mean* to upset you so much. I never thought you were that serious over him, what with your wanting to be a nun so desperately. And I *was* mad about him. Ever since l'École Internationale when he had eyes only for you and no one else. I was jealous, I admit it. Way back in Ireland, as a child, you were always so *superior*! And Cassy always gave in to you, never me, never! The only one on my side was Mama. But she was always too flighty herself to take me seriously, or somewhere abroad, so that I was unable to go to her with grouses. Cassy indulged you and Sonny. She never cared about me, except to stop me having fun. You grew up to be like her, so *righteous* all the time! Even Peedee thought you were God's gift to the world. That's why I always wanted to bring you down a peg or two. I hated you for coming between me and everyone else for whom I had any regard: all the boyfriends Vida and I secretly met in Geneva on a Saturday evening, you, in your superior capacity, would snitch. Then there was José, Ramiro, even Jaime: and, Monseigneur Paulus who thought the Catholic sun shone out of your Irish eyes! But most of all there was Keir. I thought he was gorgeous after all those namby-pamby boys we grew up with. I still do – think he's gorgeous, I mean. I just wanted to make *you* jealous for a change, that's all.'

'That's all! You wrecked my *life*!'

'How did I know you were intending to leave the convent to go to Guatemala with him? But if it's any consolation to you, he still adores you.'

'It's of no consolation at all to me, Roxana.'

'Darling, if you're worried about that bed business, I tried to trap him. All my fault, I admit it. He saw you – or *thought* he saw you – walking along the headland in your nun's white robe. He thought he was hallucinating, especially when you seemed to disappear into thin air. He started bawling your name from my bedroom window, and I wasn't even in the room. I slept in *your* bed that night.'

'You're lying again!'

'No, I'm not. Ask him yourself. He was absolutely shattered by your walking out on him in such a callous fashion, without any sort of explanation whatsoever. Paris, and then straight back to your convent! You might have let him know what you were intending to do. So he went to Cabo Alondra and ended up blotto on Don Ruiz's brandy, sprawled across Carina's kitchen table. I had the devil of a job to get him up the stairs without Carina hearing us. He flaked out on my bed and stayed there until the early hours. When he woke up and went to the window for a breath of fresh air, he saw *you* coming back to Cabo Alondra and thought he was still under the influence of drink. A man with a bare chest, smoking a cigarette at a girl's bedroom window isn't always guilty of what the onlooker imagines he's done, you know, Raven. It was in your *mind*. You *assumed* Keir had been making love to me.'

Roxana, for once, tactfully refrained from mentioning what happened next.

She put her hand on Raven's arm. 'But he loves *you*, you silly fool. That's what I wanted to tell you before I leave for Mexico with Bennett.'

'Bennett?' By now Raven was so relieved, and so confused by what Roxana was telling her, she found her reasoning once more swamped by her emotions.

'Bennett d'Ildarte, darling! You can't have forgotten him, surely? His mother was an Irish heiress whose family had made their millions in the diamond and gold fields of South Africa, and his father was an Italian count from Tuscany with interests equally as fabulous as those of his wealthy wife, but in Carrara marble. Mother always invited the d'Ildartes to her famous parties.'

'Yes, now I remember liquorice-licking Bennett. But how did you meet him again?'

'Quite by chance. I happened to bump into him right here in the hotel foyer. He's in Spain on some business for Mussolini. Bennett is Italy's Cultural Affairs Attaché, or something like that. He's responsible for their precious Michelangelo heirlooms, Renaissance art and whatnot. He told me that all the paintings in the Prado by famous Spanish artists are being sent to Geneva for safekeeping in case there's a major European war. He's wild about

Picasso's painting depicting Guernica and wants to try and arrange for its exhibition in Italy. You know it's being shown in Paris next, and then the Metropolitan Museum, New York?'

'No, I didn't know.'

'Bennett told me.'

'So you're off to Mexico with him?'

'Yes. He owns a fabulous ocean-cruiser, which he has put at my disposal, and Pippa's of course.'

'And what does *his* wife think of such an arrangement?'

'Funnily enough he never married. He says he was too busy looking out for art treasures to look for a wife.'

'Have you seen José?'

'I saw him earlier. Very briefly at the Castillo de Luchar – the Communists have debunked from there, you know, thank God. Anyway, José was with the first batch of legionnaires to enter Barcelona. He was preparing himself for Franco's victory parade at four o'clock this afternoon, so he couldn't spare me much of his time. But he did promise a settlement on Pippa.'

'Well, I'm glad you managed to get all that sorted out with Pippa's father.' Raven couldn't resist the dig.

But it passed completely over Roxana's head. 'I do think, however, that I'm going to have trouble from Don Ruiz and Doña Jacqueline. Pippa is their first grandchild, and if anything should happen to José before he has a son, then Pippa will inherit everything, their other three sons being dead, as you know. Unless of course, Nina – Marta being dead too – produces a son for them. The Spanish still have this male chauvinist attitude regarding men inheriting everything, just like Sonny and our parents' fortune. All gone to the monks, alas! Perhaps Spanish laws will change for the better under Franco's new régime. However, I shan't be here to find out. Now tell me about yourself, darling. I know you told me over the phone that you were going to Uncle Salas's house later on to sort out Peedee's stuff, but what else are you going to do with yourself now that you're no more a nun?'

'Oh, I don't know. Drift for a little while I suppose, then go back to teaching.' She didn't tell Roxana about Archie Cunningham wanting special agents in France and

Germany. She might even volunteer her services again. After all, she could speak several European languages – Archie's first subtle probe into her suitability as an agent in Spain all those years ago; and oh, how devious could some men be! But those were her thoughts alone. 'Roxa,' Raven glanced at her watch, 'thanks for lunch. The entrecôte was wonderful after all that convent cod and cabbage for so long. But I really can't stay any longer.'

'You're meeting Keir?'

'No, darling. I'm meeting a deadline.'

Before she took the train for Paris, Raven had one more thing left to do in Spain. She went to the Carrer Sarrià.

No one was at home. Not even a maid answered the door. No doubt they had all gone off to the Victory Day celebrations like everyone else: and who could blame them when Barcelona presented the aspect and atmosphere of a national holiday, a holy day, and the second coming all rolled into one glorious victorious Franco flag. Even the streets had been cleaned up for his triumphal procession later on this afternoon.

Raven let herself into Uncle Salas's house with Peedee's key.

Upstairs, on the third floor, she paused outside the door to the room Peedee had occupied when he had been a lodger in this house.

The Morse set and the codes that Peedee had used were what she had come for. Even though Barcelona was now in Nationalist hands, security would be tighter than ever. Partisan Spanish nationalism was not quite the same as British intelligence, so, for the sake of the Rivales family, she had to clear out Peedee's little room. Her grandfather had preferred the telegraph as a means of communication, as he thought it was safer. A short-wave radio transmitter, because of the mountains and the need of a high aerial to receive and send the signals, would have aroused suspicion from someone in the Rivales household, or from one of the occupants of the houses opposite.

Raven caught her breath and held still on the landing outside Peedee's door.

Someone was already in her grandfather's room tapping out a message in Morse on a telegraph coding system Peedee had been using. She turned to ice, from the top of her head to her toes, envisaging the danger firstly to herself and secondly to everyone else involved in the network. She remembered the cigarette-burns on Peedee's body, the way he had been tortured, and SIM were by no means vanquished as yet. If this was one of SIM's agents, because it had been established that Peedee had been using this house as a base from which to pass on secret information to Paris and London, then she, as well as the Rivales family, were in very grave danger.

Her ear pressed to the door, Raven, who had taught herself Morse code among other things in the convent, listened to the blibs that were the dots and dashes being sent out: *A fledgling is only as good as its own beak and wings – the bird in question is fleeing the nest – mission accomplished ...*

Gathering her wits together, Raven, her fingers stiff as goose quills, opened her *mochila*. She wondered who had seen her let herself into the house.

When Nina de Luchar had dropped the gun with which she had shot her brother in the Caverna Rosa, Raven had picked it up. It had been such an unconscious action, she herself hadn't been aware of it at the time. She had just put away the gun in the pocket of her novice's robe because she had not wanted that gun to be used again to kill anyone. Back at the convent in Vilafranca, she had felt so awful, so soiled for having brought a killing weapon into such a holy place. She had not known what to do with Nina's gun, nor how to get rid of it. When Madre Estelle Calmar had brought her her 'worldly' clothes and the Red Cross knapsack Keir had first issued her with, she had thrust the gun right to the bottom of it, hoping to throw it all, gun and *mochila*, into the harbour at the earliest opportunity.

She took that gun from her Red Cross *mochila*, very glad that she hadn't, after all, disposed of it at La Barceloneta.

Raven turned the doorknob carefully, wondering what she would do if the door was locked from the inside. But it wasn't.

The man had his back to her at the table.

He turned around.

'*You*!' Raven was appalled. 'How – how did you get in here?'

'The maid let me in. I told her I had arranged to meet you here. She has since gone off to join the fun and games in the city. I've been waiting over an hour for you to show up.'

'Who told you I'd be coming here?'

'Roxana. I had to give her the name and address of the family Pippa is living with in Tampico. She wanted me to meet her at the Ritz, where she was lunching with you. She told me that you were leaving the convent for good today. I didn't want to miss out on the celebrations, that's why I'm here.'

'How did you know about ...' she jerked the gun at the instrument he had been tampering with, 'about Peedee – and his special Morse codes?'

'I didn't use any of his codes. I transmitted my own message.'

'So! It was *you* all the time. The faceless man behind Archie Cunningham responsible for recruiting British agents in Spain. Very clever! Mind you, using the Red Cross as a cover for *your* 'other' job was hardly ethical either, was it, Dr Devlin?' She remembered his scathing attack upon Dame Concepción and herself when he had discovered they had been using the Red Cross as a shield for their Bible-smuggling activities.

'Wai-wai-wait a minute!' he said, standing up. 'And please put away the gun. I'm not here to molest you.' He moved away from her grandfather's keyboard to take a step nearer, but she held the gun steady.

'Don't come any closer until you tell me more about yourself, Dr Devlin.'

Keir smiled at her tone of voice. But his emotions were still in a very raw state for him to capitulate too readily: Raven Quennell had a mighty lot to make up for, treating him the way she had, without regard for his feelings! However, he was willing to meet her half-way, simply because her uncalled-for jealousy where her sister was concerned, proved to him many things. 'Anything you want to know, I'll be delighted to tell you, sweetheart. You know, for a moment back there, the other day, I remember you standing next to Don Ruiz beside all those wireless sets with *such* a gleam in your eye! I thought to myself then, this is one *hell* of a lady, Doc. And all that toing and froing between your various convents, a disguise to suit the role every time, I couldn't help *but* be impressed. Lady! You should have told me in the beginning you were a spy and I might have forgiven you for being a nun.'

'You're getting carried away, Keir.'

'Damn right I am! So, what do you want to do, shoot me on behalf of Archie Cunningham? Sorry, Raven. I'm just a humble Red Cross doctor guilty of nothing except falling in love with a very complex lady. I'm not Archie Cunningham's boss. I'm not even my own boss.'

'Then how did you know how to transmit that Morse message?'

'It won't go further than the next relay station at Port Bou, I promise. The poor fellow at the other end trying to decipher that rubbish will be very hard-pressed, because it doesn't mean a thing. Certainly nothing sinister. I had to learn to use Morse code, because in Abyssinia, a country so incredibly primitive it was like stepping back a thousand years, we sometimes had to resort to Morse in order to communicate with anyone at all. To get through to Geneva was like trying to send a signal to Mars. Morse code was my standby. So, if you're assigning to me the status of Father Silvestre and his illusions of grandeur concerning FBI secret agents, or whatever else, forget it. I'm *me*, Keir Devlin, Red Cross Doctor, neutral American, nothing more, nothing less.'

She still did not know whether to believe him.

Keir took advantage of her confusion, knowing that it was now or never: and *never* was a travesty of time he wasn't prepared to accept after having almost won her, body, soul, and spirit. 'It's still snowing mighty heavily in my heart, my darling, and the only one to make the sun shine again for me is you. All my life I've been a loser, so this time I reckoned it was about time my luck changed. I came here to take you back to Guatemala with me. Don't make me the loser this time round, because I'll never be able to cope with rejection on that scale.'

Her wrist limp, she slumped against the door-jamb. 'I *hate*

Archie, and I hate you.'

He came to her and took the gun from her hand. Keir tossed it onto her grandfather's bed. Holding her face between his hands he said, 'You love me, and you know it.'

'Yes. I know it.'

'So, if you want to play dangerous games, play them *with* me, not against me. Will you forgive me for hurting you, and for not understanding what you were doing in that goddamn convent?'

'No. I'll never forgive you. But maybe I'll forget about it in time. You see Keir, love is like a poppy growing by the wayside. With its face to the sun its petals are always rosy, vibrant, and alive. Once it's picked and put in a vase, it soon withers and dies. I'm like that *goddamn* poppy! I don't know whether I want to be picked or not.'

He wiped the tears from her eyes and held her close. 'Just face the sun, sweetheart. Just face the sun.'

CONCLUSION

On 27 February 1939, Great Britain formally recognized General Franco's Fascist Military Government. On 2 September, Great Britain declared war on Germany. Spain remained neutral throughout World War II, despite Adolf Hitler's declaration at Hendaye in 1941, to 'bully Spain into the war'.

Under the Franco régime, Catalonian autonomy was dissolved. The national dance of Catalonia, the *Sardana*, was banned. Catalan culture, books, music, and the Catalan language itself were suppressed. The only religious establishment to be allowed to continue celebrating the Mass in Catalan was the Benedictine Monastery of Montserrat.

Pippa de Luchar, groomed for stardom from the age of seven by her overriding mother, continued to have an unsettled childhood between her own father's family in Spain and her stepfather's family in Tuscany. In the early fifties Pippa was a highly paid, highly sought after fashion model. From the famous *haute couture* and perfumerie houses of London, Paris, and Rome, Pippa went to Hollywood. Her face, figure, fortune, and famous love-affairs, two disastrous marriages, first to a Hollywood filmstar, the second to an Italian prince, were *paparazzi* bread and butter. By the time she was twenty-six, she was 'burnt out'. Two notorious divorces and an expensive nervous breakdown behind her, Pippa left the silver screen and her life of glamour to lead her own eccentric, quiet lifestyle raising goats and selling cheese on the tiny Greek island of Pátos, which her multi-millionaire stepfather had given her as a twenty-first birthday present.

Jodi II, educated at Berkeley University, California, was

the eldest son in Keir and Raven's family of seven children. Jodi II became a senator in the House of Representatives. His anti-Vietnam views and 'peace in our time' advocacy were the predominent policy throughout his political life. Patrick became an archaeologist and a well-known establishment figure for his research into ancient Mesoamerican civilizations. Timothea (Timmy-Jo), their eldest daughter, followed in her father's footsteps and studied medicine at Cornell. After her father's retirement, Timmy-Jo became Chief Medical Officer at the Father Silvestre Memorial Hospital. Antigua, founded by Keir. In 1976, according to Father Silvestre's predictions over forty years before, a devastating earthquake in Guatemala destroyed Antigua, including the hospital. Michael was killed in action in Vietnam, his twin sister, Michelle, became one of the 'flower people'. Of the other two children, Stephanie became a famous cellist, playing to packed audiences throughout the world, while the youngest daughter, Lara, kept house at *El Paraíso*, her parents' Guatemalan farm.

Until the Spanish people were liberated from the yoke of dictatorship, Pablo Picasso's famous painting, *Guernica*, was held in New York's Museum of Modern Art. In 1981 the Americans kept their promise to the artist, and returned the painting, which now hangs in the Prado, Madrid.

SAMSARA

Alexandra Jones

An exotic saga of forbidden love and imperial ambition on the grandest scale.

Tibet in the late nineteenth century – an untamed and mysterious land. Lhasa, the residence of its god-king the Dalai Lama, is a forbidden city – and death at the hands of his cruel torturers is the fate of any foreigner who dares set foot inside its sacred walls. But for the mighty British and Russian empires Tibet has become a strategically vital country to be conquered at all costs.

Into this turbulent, dangerous realm come two young people, drawn together by deepest emotions yet torn apart by conflicting loyalties . . .

Lewis Joyden is a handsome Englishman who travels disguised as a Buddhist monk to survey this wild and mountainous land in preparation for a British invasion.

Sonya Vremya is the fiercely independent Russian princess who first bewitched him many years ago at home. Her quest is to find her brother who was sent on a mission by the Tsar, but has vanished with trace . . . And to track down her unloving husband and beg him for a divorce.

Though separated by national conflicts, they are forced up against all the dangers and uncertainties of a strange and magical country, and drawn ever closer by the constant perils which threaten them.

And don't miss

MANDALAY
FIRE PHEASANT

Also in Futura

FUTURA PUBLICATIONS
FICTION
0 7088 4204 6

MANDALAY

Alexandra Jones

Burma, late nineteenth century – land of vast wealth, sumptuous beauty and unthinking savagery. In fabled Mandalay the king lies dying, and his ruthless queen is determined to set her own puppet on the Dragon Throne.

Against this richly exotic backcloth, three unforgettable characters act out a drama of passion and betrayal:

Captain Nathaniel de Veres-Vorne – American remittance man, handsome, reckless and deadly enemy of the vengeful queen.

Minthami – his young and utterly enchanting Burmese mistress, who loves him with a touching dignity and strives to bridge the culture gap that forever divides them.

Angela Featherstone – a rare free spirit in a corsetted world, who endeavours to earn his respect. And, for the sake of Minthami, tries to hold at bay her passionate love for him, which alone could bring her fulfilment.

As Burma seethes around them, these three, locked in a triangle as old as time, struggle with fate and each other to work out their destinies, separate but tragically entwined.

MANDALAY – an epic saga of passion and sacrifice, romance and lust, and history and imperial ambition, a compelling drama told on the grandest scale.

FUTURA PUBLICATIONS
FICTION
0 7088 3680 1

All Futura Books are available at your bookshop or newsagent, or can be ordered from the following address:
Futura Books,
Cash Sales Department,
P.O. Box 11,
Falmouth,
Cornwall TR10 9EN.

Alternatively you may fax your order to the above address. Fax No. 0326 76423.

Payments can be made as follows: Cheque, postal order (payable to Macdonald & Co (Publishers) Ltd) or by credit cards, Visa/Access. Do not send cash or currency. UK customers: please send a cheque or postal order (no currency) and allow 80p for postage and packing for the first book plus 20p for each additional book up to a maximum charge of £2.00.

B.F.P.O. customers please allow 80p for the first book plus 20p for each additional book.

Overseas customers including Ireland, please allow £1.50 for postage and packing for the first book, £1.00 for the second book, and 30p for each additional book.

NAME (Block Letters) ....

ADDRESS ....

....

☐ I enclose my remittance for _____

☐ I wish to pay by Access/Visa Card

Number ☐☐☐☐☐☐☐☐☐☐☐☐☐☐☐☐☐

Card Expiry Date ☐☐☐☐